D1519792

Wollman Library

Barnard College

New York

Felice Rich Bradley Fund

Withdrawn from
Barnard College
Library

Forgeries of Memory and Meaning

Forgeries of Memory and Meaning

Blacks and the Regimes of
Race in American Theater and
Film before World War II

CEDRIC J. ROBINSON

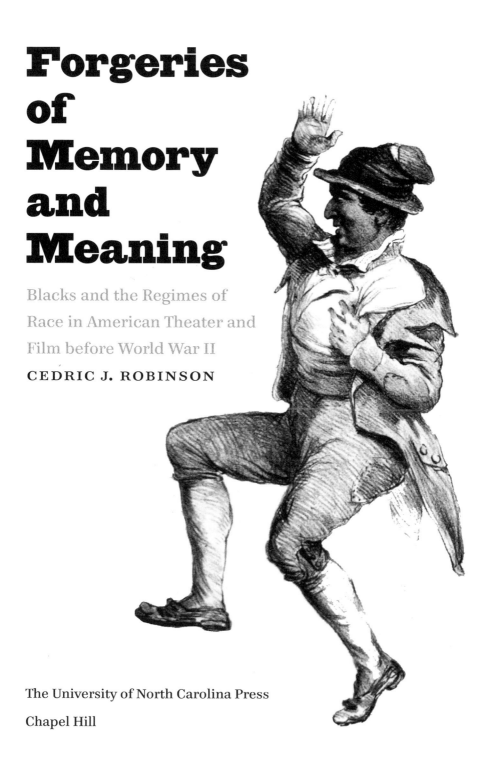

The University of North Carolina Press

Chapel Hill

© 2007 The University of North Carolina Press

All rights reserved

Set in Paperback and Egiziano types

by Tseng Information Systems, Inc.

Manufactured in the United States of America

The paper in this book meets the guidelines for
permanence and durability of the Committee on
Production Guidelines for Book Longevity of
the Council on Library Resources.

Library of Congress Cataloging-in-Publication Data

Robinson, Cedric J.

Forgeries of memory and meaning : Blacks and the
regimes of race in American theater and film before
World War II / by Cedric J. Robinson.

   p. cm.

Includes bibliographical references and index.

ISBN 978-0-8078-3148-9 (cloth : alk. paper)

ISBN 978-0-8078-5841-7 (pbk. : alk. paper)

1. African Americans in motion pictures. 2. African
Americans in the performing arts. 3. Shakespeare,
William, 1564–1616. Othello. I. Title.

PN1995.9.N4R58 2007

791.43′652996073—dc22   2007022091

11 10 09 08 07   5 4 3 2 1

For Jacob

Contents

Illustrations

Preface

Since dominance is always incomplete and monopoly imperfect,
the rule of every ruling class is unstable.
— *Michael Walzer,* Spheres of Justice, *1983*

"Truth" is linked in a circular relation with systems of power
which produce and sustain it, and to effects of power which it
induces and which extend it. A "regime" of truth.
— *Michel Foucault, "Truth and Power," 1980*

Perhaps the most pronounced tendency in American race studies is to mass around explicit or inferred explanatory models which are derivative of Marx or insinuated from Foucault's notion that "power establishes a particular regime of truth." In materialist terms the simplest rendering is that the commercial nexus of the African slave trade and the political apparatus of colonialism, the economies of securing and controlling African bodies, the sinews of patriarchy, and the trade in slave-produced commodities (relations of power) eventuate in the establishment of the Negro and discourses on race (admissible and possible knowledges). And since the historical and cultural African subject has been unimagined, there is no reason to suspect that some of the "imperfections" of domination might originate from the enslaved. Or, alternatively, that the manufacture of the slave might anticipate and absorb the availability of more tractable materials.

In its totality this account of race production is a seductive archaeology, securing revelation, elegance, and precision for the obscurity and chaos which are a constant threat in historical research. However, with it, one is obligated to a kind of unitarianism where *all* the relations of power collaborate in and cohabit a particular discursive or disciplinary regime. The coexistence of alternative, oppositional, or simply different relations of power are left unexamined or instantiated. The possibility of the coincidence of different relations of power colliding, interfering, or even generating resistance remains a fugitive consideration. Edward Said raised the alarm about this last possibility: "The disturbing circularity of Foucault's theory of power is a form of rhetorical overtotalization. In human history there is always something beyond the reach of dominating systems, no matter how deeply they saturate society, and this is obviously what makes change possible, limits power in Foucault's sense, and hobbles that theory of power."[1] Placing resistance to the side for one moment, Said insists that Foucault's "textuality" insulated his inquiry from lived multiplicities, the several histories extant in even the most modestly constructed societies, and the resultant matrices of identity. Racial regimes are subsequently unstable truth systems. Like Ptolemaic astronomy, they may "collapse" under the weight of their own artifices, practices, and apparatuses; they may fragment, desiccated by new realities, which discard some fragments wholly while appropriating others into newer regimes. Indeed, the possibilities are the stuff of history.

Foucault, of course, was not quite the dolt Said makes him out to be.[2] But there is still the impulse in Foucault's thought to elect the dialectic as a privileged site of contestation (even his treatment of subjugated knowledges possesses that tinge: "naïve knowledges, located low down on the hierarchy, beneath the required level of cognition or scientificity").[3] It is as if systems of power never encounter the stranger, or that strangers can be seamlessly abducted into a system of oppression. In our own interrogations this amounts to the presumption that the exposing of the invention of raced subjects is a sufficient method for recognizing and explaining difference. To the contrary, the production of race is chaotic. It is an alchemy of the intentional and the unintended, of known and unimagined fractures of cultural forms, of relations of power and the power of social and cultural relations.

Racial regimes are constructed social systems in which race is proposed as a justification for the relations of power. While necessarily articulated with accruals of power, the covering conceit of a racial regime is a makeshift patchwork masquerading as memory and the immutable. Nevertheless, racial regimes do possess history, that is, discernible origins and mechanisms of assembly. But racial regimes are unrelentingly hostile to their exhibition. This antipathy exists because a discoverable history is incompatible with a racial regime and from the

1. Said, *World, Text, and Critic*, 246–47.
2. See, for example, Foucault on *"the insurrection of subjugated knowledges"* in "Two Lectures," 81–82.
3. Ibid., 82.

realization that, paradoxically, so are its social relations. One threatens the authority and the other saps the vitality of racial regimes. Each undermines the founding myths. The archaeological imprint of human agency radically alienates the histories of racial regimes from their own claims of naturalism. Employing mythic discourses, racial regimes are commonly masqueraded as natural orderings, inevitable creations of collective anxieties prompted by threatening encounters with difference. Yet they are actually contrivances, designed and delegated by interested cultural and social powers with the wherewithal sufficient to commission their imaginings, manufacture, and maintenance. This latter industry is of some singular importance, since racial regimes tend to wear thin over time.

With respect to the social terrain, the degeneration of racial regimes occurs with some frequency for two reasons. First, apparent difference in identity is an attempt to mask shared identities. In the English North American colonies in the seventeenth and eighteenth centuries, for example, white indentured servants and African, Native American, and Creole slaves frequently banded together in violent or passive rebellions against colonial authorities. Nearly two hundred years later, in the midst of the Civil War, insurgent slaves and renegade poor whites conspired against the Confederacy to create the free state of Jones.[4] Like all such antinomies, particularly those of a routine, quotidian frequency, these occurrences sank into the mire of the unknowable. Their long disappearance faithfully represented Sandra Harding's observation that "any body of systematic knowledge is always internally linked to a distinctive body of systematic ignorance."[5] A second source of regime entropy ensues from the fact that because the regimes are cultural artifices, which catalog only fragments of the real, they inevitably generate fugitive, unaccounted-for elements of reality. Abraham Lincoln's insistence that fugitive slaves were "contraband" (in effect, property which had illegally seized itself) did not prepare the president for their role in subverting his war aims. Lincoln believed reuniting the nation did not require the abolition of human property. As fugitives, troops, and sailors, that same property disabused him of his delusional political program. This was an instance of what Hegel termed the nega-

4. For the seventeenth-century example, see Morgan, *American Slavery, American Freedom*, 250ff. For the Civil War episode, see Bynum, *Free State of Jones*.
5. Harding, "Comment," 516.

tion of the negation, flawed or delinquent comprehension colliding with the real.

Regime maintenance, however, takes precedence over wholesale reconstruction. Sometimes, though, the social chaos which is consequent to the failure of racial regimes renders maintenance moot. One early instance of a racial regime evincing evidence of failure is to be found in Aristotle's intervention in *The Politics*. Democracy vied with aristocracy, the former quarreling with slavery, the latter embracing it. Interestingly enough, it was the challenge to the racial justification for slavery which Aristotle chose to address. He conceded that enslavement might on occasion result from accident (that is, defeat in war), but he insisted that far more important was the fact that most slaves were slaves by nature. Inadvertently advertising the absurdities embedded in his proposition, he recommended that in his most perfect *polis*, in order to ensure the long-term exploitation and domination of slaves, slave masters diversify the ethnic mix of their slaves and institute regular manumissions.[6]

The Politics served as a rationale, a maintenance device. And in the service of a racial regime, its author maneuvered history aside, displacing it with the ideological reading of nature. Not unremarkably, the rationale outlasted the slave system for which it had been promulgated. In the modern era it melded with or complemented justifying belief systems spun from subsequent systems of human bondage. But whether slavery was principally rationalized by conquest, ethnic or religious distinctions, cultural differences, dramatic or slight phenotypic distinctions, the powerful classes consistently found their Aristotles, that is, intelligentsias, seduced into or compelled to invent forgeries of memory and meaning.

Moving pictures appear at that juncture when a new racial regime was being stitched together from remnants of its predecessors and new cloth accommodating the disposal of immigrants, colonial subjects, and insurgencies among the native poor. With the first attempts at composing a national identity in disarray, a new whiteness became the basis for the reintegration of American society. And monopolizing

6. It might very well be the case that since poor or impoverished Athenians themselves had been slaves less than two centuries before, Aristotle sensed that public consciousness of that history had not sufficiently dissipated. After all, it was the rebellions of the poor in Athens (and other *poleis*) which had propelled Athens toward the radical regime of democracy. See Ober, *Political Dissent in Democratic Athens*.

the refabrication of a public sphere, with a reach and immediacy not obtained by previous apparatuses (museums, theaters, fairs, the press, etc.), motion pictures insinuated themselves into public life.

In the United States, the technical development of moving pictures in the late nineteenth century was soon enveloped in the formation of an industry, which, in turn, became an agency of power and wealth. Prior to these events, the disintegration of a centuries-long slave system had deposited a racial regime in American culture. Without a hint of irony, that racial regime had achieved its maturity at precisely the moment when its internal contradictions were most marked (the great slave rebellions of the nineteenth century) and domestic and international opposition was amassing. With the collapse of the slave system, a different racial regime was required, one which adopted elements from its predecessor but was now buttressing the domination of free labor.

This work is Black history written through the filters of film and capitalism. Establishing the early movie industry (actually *industries*) as an instrument of American capital, the book interrogates how the needs of finance capital, the dominant center of American commerce in the late nineteenth and early twentieth centuries, determined the construction of successive racial regimes publicized by motion pictures. Racial constructs predate the arrival of moving pictures, and thus the representations of race and ethnicity (as well as gender) were transferred from the stage, literature, and popular culture. This was not an organic transfer, explicable in terms of persistent cultural materials. Racial protocols were contested and subject to deterioration (indeed, this study will examine Shakespeare's *Othello* as the earliest challenge to the emergent concept of the Negro). An alternative explanation rests on the economic, social, and political interests which conspired to arrange, and when necessary, rearrange interpretations of difference. The appearance of moving pictures coincides with Jim Crow and the development of American national identity in the midst of dramatic demographic and economic changes. The silent-film era and the first decade of sound allow us to map the forgeries of memory and representation which served the most powerful interests in the country and their cultural brokers. For instance, I link film minstrelsy with racial segregation, which, in turn, served the labor discipline of emergent industries. I conclude with a treatment of Black imagery in the movies during the Depression decade ended by World War II. Most important, I am concerned with Black resistance to each historical moment of Negrophobic impulses. Thus Black minstrelsy countered blackface minstrelsy; race movies countered the misrepresentation of the Black middle class; and when the capitalization of films all but eliminated an alternative Black cinema, Black comedians produced an oppositional subtext, which they insinuated into "Hollywood" itself.

The present work attempts to alter the terms of interpretation: proposing constant trembles in racial regimes; persistent efforts to repair or alter race as an effective mechanism of social ordering; and a succession of alterations in race discourses (cultural, religious, scientific, etc.). Finally, as film studies becomes a more certain discipline, it is likely that most of the newer scholars will be directed away by specialized research from a consideration of the structural/economic issues raised by Robert Allen and Douglas Gomery (and less satisfactorily by David Puttnam. As a Black studies scholar trained in the social sciences, I am fortunately placed by field (interdisciplinary), historical immediacy (a decade of neominstrelsy in popular culture), and pedagogical mission. From this basis I hope to add some modest contextualization to the considerable efforts of those now dominating the investigation of Black cinematic representation.

In historical terms, the focus of this book extends from the early seventeenth century to World War II. Chapter 1 is concerned with the conditions for the emergence of modern racism in the era before film. Posing Shakespeare's *Othello* as the first contestation of blackness in English culture, I explore the varying constructions of race during the three hundred years which conclude with the appearance of scientific racism. The sheer volume and plurivocality of antiracism resistance set the stage for later oppositions.

The rest of the chapters treat two coincidental and conflicting phenomena: the economic, political, and cultural forces which determined Black representations in early American films; and Black political and artistic resistance to these imaginings. Chapter 2 sets the stage by examining D. W. Griffith's film *The Birth of a Nation* in the context of an emergent American national identity contested by sectional conflict, massive immigration, and dramatic economic arrangements of American capital. In the midst of these societal tremors and uncertainties, film appropriated the conventions of blackface minstrelsy and the racial protocols of American historiography in order to counterfeit whiteness and romanticize a national myth of origins. Chapter 3 proposes that an interrogation of Black minstrelsy, Black musicals, and the revival of Black dramatic theater provides an understanding of the antiracial stratagems evolved from blackface minstrelsy. Challenging the dominant construction of blackness, these artists and intellectuals substantially appropriate blackface minstrelsy only to observe the revival of the form on the ethnic stage and in moving pictures. Chapter 4 reviews the multiplicities of race (Blacks, Latinos, Filipinos, Native Americans) which were insinuated into the movies during the silent era and how these intersected with changes in the control of the movie industry and a contested American imperialism. Inevitably, the Black petite bourgeoisie, forming in the cities, responded to their disfigurement in films as a renegade stratum. Race movies were dominated by "uplift" themes, but Oscar Micheaux pushed race movies into explicit political critiques of the American national myth. Micheaux's extraordinary performance (particularly in silent films) as a subversive was enabled by his adaptation of rhetorical structures gestated in Black music. Chapter 5 reconstructs the contests revolving around race coincident with the appearance of talkies and sound and new controllers of the industry. It proposes that in company with Ed Guerrero's "plantation genre," the jungle films provided the cultural cover required by dominant business interests in their domestic and foreign ventures. And rather than dismissing Black filmmakers of the late 1930s as low-production imitators of big studio productions, the chapter proposes their role as urban archaeologists and their complicity with comedic coons who became the most active and effective agents of Black resistance.

Acknowledgments

With respect to any of my writing, I am obliged to recognize Elizabeth, my wife and companion (and first editor). Without her, and I mean quite literally, this work would never have reached completion. In that same register there is our remarkable daughter, Najda, for whom our efforts are intended. Then, too, there is Clara Whiteside Dyson, my mother. Among my first recollections of motion pictures was the time, some four or five decades ago, when she took her quite young son to see what must have been a revival of Disney's *Bambi* at the Grand Lake Theater in Oakland, California. The more immediate inciting of this project, however, was my teaching of courses on race and Black representation in films in the Black Studies Department here at the University of California, Santa Barbara.

Whether acknowledged or not, research is a collaborative venture. If we are fortunate, there are generous colleagues like Dr. Jacqueline Bobo, Dr. Gerard Pigeon, Dr. Anna Everett, Dr. Avery Gordon, and Sylvia Curtis close at hand. Of equal importance are those like Dr. Hazel Waters in the United Kingdom (Institute of Race Relations), Dr. Abebe Zegeye in South Africa, Dr. William Ellis (University of the District of Columbia), and my former colleague Dr. Faith Berry who encouraged me with their support. I am also in debt to archivists and specialists like Larry Richards (the Free Library of Philadelphia), Erika Piola (The Library Company of Philadelphia), Zoran Sinobad (the Motion Pictures Division of the Library of Congress), the staff at the Schomburg Center for Research in Black Culture in New York, the American Film Institute in Los Angeles, and the ladies in the copy room at Enoch Pratt Free Library in Baltimore. I am also grateful for the generosity and constant attentiveness on my behalf of former students Dr. Helen L. T. Quan, Dr. Tiffany Willoughby Herard, Dr. Francoise Cromer, and Crystal Griffith. They not only contributed to my research but in 2004 also organized with Dr. Marisela Marquez and Dr. Jeanne Scheper a tribute to my work. UC-Santa Barbara's Academic Senate also provided support for my research and funding to support my research assistants Stephen Jones and Donna Lynn.

At the University of North Carolina Press, yeoman awards are extended to Sian Hunter, who guided the manuscript through the review process, and Paul Betz, who gently forced my hand in the editing process. I am also particularly grateful to Charles Musser, initially an anonymous reviewer, who eventually placed the weight of his extraordinary research and scholarship at the service of correcting some of my errors. A second reviewer, Ed Guerrero, made himself known to me quite recently. Of course, the manuscript already relied heavily on their pioneering and courageous work in silent-film history and Black representation in cinema. Those errors which have survived their efforts are, of course, entirely attributable to me.

Forgeries of Memory and Meaning

The Inventions of the Negro

*Doubtless because of the skeletons and bones of
strange animals . . . that came to the Smithsonian
from the early trans-continental surveys the
institution came to be regarded as haunted. This
was especially true in the case with the colored
people, whose superstitious natures made them so
fearful of the innocent building that they could not
be induced to pass the door after sundown.*
— Dr. Marcus Benjamin,
    "Memories of the Smithsonian," May 1917

Counterfeits of History

A pall of sadness becomes almost a constant presence for anyone who
wishes to revisit the corrupt association between American science
and race in the century the nineteenth—which ended with the appearance of moving pictures. In a better world, a world so different
from the one this science helped to create, one might avert one's eyes.
But good manners are a luxury which these scientists forfeited, will-
fully and frequently. They gave little quarter to those whom they regarded as their inferiors, dismissed and hounded those critics whom
they could not summarily dispatch, and thoroughly enjoyed their social standing and each other. Some sense of to what I am referring is
present in the epigraph above, a presumably casual and ultimately un-
important observation really unrelated to the greatness of the Smithsonian. And yet here it is, certainly an unintentionally disturbing, presumably amusing, and insignificant comedic racial gesture smuggled
into Marcus Benjamin's reverential but still cozy remembrance of the
"great and good comrades" who brought the Smithsonian into being
and sustained its realization.

To be sure, Benjamin could be confident of his scientific audience's
shared propensity to be entertained and amused by the superstitions
of colored people. He was the editor of the Smithsonian Institution's
publications, and just two years earlier he had been elected president
of the Washington, D.C., chapter of Sigma Xi, the Scientific Research

Society. Another evidence of Benjamin's confidence is a bit of racial overdetermination. "It is said," he wrote as he sailed into his second anecdote, that a Black man (Benjamin, of course, used the then more courteous "colored man"), upon learning that he was to be employed at the Smithsonian, "became so frightened that he ran away and could not be found for two weeks."[1] He seems untroubled by the paradox that his tale is folkloric yet addressed to a scientific establishment. His demeanor, however, becomes less strange when we more closely inspect the agents who occupied the "innocent building."

Benjamin's "memories" are crowded by the names of the eminent men (all men) who came through the doors of the Smithsonian and frequently stayed on. Of course, he attends the successive administrative heads (the secretary) of the institution up to his own present: Joseph Henry, Spencer F. Baird, Samuel P. Langley, and Charles Walcott. But he reserves a special prominence for two of the myriad of scientists (from chemistry, astronomy, mathematics, geology, paleontology, ornithology, mineralogy, conchology, anthropology, and so on) he recollects: "About the middle of the last century there were two great masters who in this country exerted a tremendous influence upon young men, leading them to the study of natural science. These were Agassiz and Baird."[2] The former was Louis Agassiz, the Swiss-born Harvard zoologist whose championing of polygeny and eugenics had considerably assisted the braiding of these hair-brained notions into scientific doctrine.

In 1981, Stephen Jay Gould exhumed Agassiz from the protective cover draped over him by his widow and later historians of science who had published selectively expurgated versions of his correspondence. In a letter to his mother in December 1846, Agassiz excitedly described his reaction to the Black servants at his Philadelphia hotel:

> In seeing their black faces with their thick lips and grimacing teeth, the wool on their head, their bent knees, their elongated hands, their large curved nails, and especially the livid color of the palms of their hands, I could not take my eyes off their face in order to tell them to stay far away. And when they advanced that hideous hand towards my plate in order to serve me, I wished I were able to depart in order to eat a piece of bread elsewhere, rather than dine with such service.

1. Benjamin, "Memories of the Smithsonian," 469.
2. Ibid., 465–66.

What unhappiness for the white race — to have tied their existence so closely with that of negroes in certain countries![3]

We can only surmise how the senior Mrs. Agassiz responded to this outburst of eroticized images, but in 1895, some twenty years after Louis's death, his widow and her collaborators saw fit to excise these passages from *Louis Agassiz: His Life and Correspondence*. Authenticity was clearly not the rationale for such a cut-and-paste approach to Agassiz's writings, for Louis himself persisted in his racism even when it contradicted the dictums of naturalism. For one instance, notwithstanding the existence of half a million mulattos by the time of the 1860 census, Agassiz persisted in the notion that his own repugnance of Blacks was natural (since he "just 'knew' they were barely higher than apes"), shared widely, and enforceable.[4] He supposed, he wrote to one of the members of Lincoln's Inquiry Commission in 1863, that the threat of miscegenation in the postwar period would be contained, since Blacks could only survive in the isolation of the Southern lowlands.[5] Nevertheless, he seems to have genuinely believed that it was his disinterested inquiry, and not his personal dispositions, which led him to the conclusion that too much learning would swell the Negro brain, bursting the skull wall.[6]

It was thus that race science was staged between performances of burlesque and horror.

The dominant natural scientists in America in the nineteenth and early twentieth centuries had been impaled on Negro slavery and its social and cultural debris. But rather than experiencing anguish at their acute artificiality, they seemed to exist in a perpetual state of conceit. Thinking themselves the heirs to a venerable legacy of philosophy

3. Quoted in Gould, *Mismeasure of Man*, 46.

4. John Trumpbour, "Introducing Harvard," in Trumpbour, *How Harvard Rules*, 20. For the census figures, see Williamson, *New People*, 63. Agassiz had little doubt as to the source of Black-white mulattos: "As soon as the sexual desires are awakening in the young men of the South, they find it easy to gratify themselves by the readiness with which they are met by colored [half-breed] house servants . . . This blunts his better instincts in that direction and leads him gradually to seek more spicy partners, as I have heard the full blacks called by fast young men." Agassiz to S. G. Howe of the Inquiry Commission, Aug. 9, 1863, in Gould, *Mismeasure of Man*, 49.

5. Gould, *Mismeasure of Man*, 50.

6. Jonathan R. Beckwith, "The Science of Racism," in Trumpbour, *How Harvard Rules*, 243.

(love of knowledge) extending back to the ancient Greeks, they almost reflexively appropriated Plato and Aristotle, two of the earlier period's most persuasive defenders of slavery. They were mistaken. To be sure, the race science of the modern African slave era was in truth an American/Atlantic/Western branch of prior racial dogma. But Plato and Aristotle had been inferiorizing very different subjects, such as Scythians, Persians, Thracians, Celts, and so on, who had been contributors to Western civilization. The paradox was lost on the naturalists and anthropologists of the nineteenth century. And so while they parroted the arguments of the ancients as if they had directly telegraphed the methods and protocols of race science, the modernists invented entirely new subjects: indigenous peoples of Africa, the New World, and the Orient.

Race presents all the appearance of stability. History, however, compromises this fixity. Race is mercurial—deadly and slick. And since race is presumably natural, the intrusion of convention shatters race's relationship to the natural world. This is true for the contemptible Black, at one and the same time the most natural of beings and the most intensively manufactured subject. And most relevant to our interest, the imaginings of Blacks in early American films are the reconstitutions of Black which culminated in the spectacle performed within the Smithsonian and exported into the public arena. By the time the moving picture camera arrived on the scene, the Negro was in full costume. But before then, that costume would undergo extraordinary changes in the seventeenth century and then again at the end of the nineteenth century.

A large proportion of, perhaps even most, Western scholars have a great deal of difficulty in assigning the emergence of racial discourses before the advent of the Atlantic or African slave trade. They reason that race is a concomitant to slavery, and as Peter Erickson succinctly puts it, "The systematic racism associated with this structural development cannot be said to exist in the historical stages that preceded, and lead up to, this moment."[7] It would be kinder, perhaps, to leave Erickson and his co-dogmatists to this conceit, but it would not alter actual history. Simply put, the Atlantic slave trade was not the first slave system, nor the first slave system engaged in by Europeans, nor the first slave

7. Erickson, "Representations of Blacks," 500.

system to affect Europeans or their ancestors, and not the only slave system to produce a racialist culture.[8] Europeans enslaved Europeans just as Asians enslaved Asians, Africans enslaved Africans, and Native Americans enslaved Native Americans. And as Orlando Patterson has noted, the designators of inferiorization extend back into what Westerners like to think of as their antiquity. Just as earlier, Greeks had displayed contempt for non-Greeks, by the second century B.C., H. Hill writes, "no Greek could help being distressed by the almost universal contempt shown, at least in public utterances, toward his nation."[9] In the European instance, the frequency with which one nation was victimized at least until the end of the Middle Ages is preserved in most West European languages by the use of the term "Slav" (slave, *esclavo*, *esclave*, etc.) to designate the condition of human property.

> There is scarcely a people in Europe who have not at some time furnished victims to the slave trade. But few furnished them so consistently, for so many centuries, as the Slavic peoples from the Dinaric Alps. Indeed, the word "slave" in most modern European languages is derived from the ethnic term "sclavus" meaning Slav. Furthermore, in Arabic speaking lands, the word "Slav" provides the root for a term meaning eunuch and in Catalan for one meaning "castrated goat." In Castilian, moreover, a word for chain is derived from "Slav."[10]

8. Orlando Patterson declares, "There is nothing notably peculiar about the institution of slavery. It has existed from before the dawn of human history right down to the twentieth century, in the most primitive of human societies and in the most civilized. There is no region on earth that has not at some time harbored the institution. Probably there is no group of people whose ancestors were not at one time slaves or slaveholders." Patterson, *Slavery and Social Death*, vii.

9. Quoted in ibid., 90.

10. Evans, "Slave Coast of Europe," 41. Evans notes, "[the] Arabic word for 'Slav' — 'sakaliba' came to mean ultimately any European slave or a eunuch. Some European derivatives are: German, 'Sklave'; Dutch, 'slaav'; French, 'esclave'; Spanish, 'esclavo'; Catalan, 'sclau'; Italian, 'schiavo'; Sicilian, 'skavu'; Byzantine Greek, 'SKlaboQ' or 'SkleboQ.'" Ibid., 53n3. "[The Vikings'] depredations of the Slavonic world and sale of Slavs at slave markets helped to give the term 'slave' to the Western world." Henry Loyn, "Slavs," in Loyn, *Middle Ages*, 303. "'Slav' meant 'slave' both in the medieval west and in Arabic." Walter Pohl, "Slavs," in Bowersock, Brown, and Grabar, *Late Antiquity*, 701. The older Latin term for slave, *servus*, provides a benchmark for the advent of Slavonic slavery during the late European Dark Ages.

The fact that the phenotypes of the enslaved and the slavers differed insignificantly did not erode the force of the racism which victimized Koreans, Poles, the Irish, and others who experienced the misfortune of long-term slavery or domination. This is confirmed when Theodore Allen writes on English despotism in Ireland: "Irish history presents a case of *racial oppression without reference to alleged skin color or, as the jargon goes, 'phenotype.'*"[11] Only once one evacuates those hundreds of slave systems and the millennia of recorded history which documents them is it remotely possible to consign race consciousness to modernity (that is, the era initiated by the West's encounter with the "New World").

Thus Erickson (and many, many others) trip over several historical fallacies. They stumble when they assume that the Atlantic slave trade was a singular historical event; they falter when they presume that race must incur phenotypic differences as obvious as those between the whitest Europeans and the blackest Africans; and they falter when they seek to periodize the study of race to modernity. Finally, they succumb to the most naïve of beliefs when they insist that Africans and Europeans encountered each other at some determinable date deposed by the Atlantic trade. As Kim Hall observes in her criticism of Kwame Anthony Appiah's embrace of this credo, "His notions of Elizabethan England are a clear articulation of a largely unstated bias against the study of 'pre-slavery' Europe by scholars centrally concerned with race: that studies of race and blackness should primarily be concerned with the construction of black subjectivity (the corollary being that the early modern period cannot be the subject of black studies because there were no blacks to study)."[12]

Hall is right: there is something amiss, something fishy about the

11. Theodore Allen, *Invention of the White Race*, 22. This work is a detailed history of English (and Anglo-Norman) racial oppression in Ireland, beginning in the thirteenth century. Allen agrees with G. H. Orpen (*Ireland under the Normans*, 1913) on the crux of the failure of Anglo-Norman policy in Ireland: "Above all, their lack of sympathy with the Irish, whom they regarded as an inferior race, prevented them from establishing their power on the firm basis of a contented people." Ibid., 54.

12. Kim Hall, "Reading What Isn't There," 23. Elliot Tokson struck a familiar note in the opening line of his first chapter: "Englishmen were first asked to face the question of the humanity of the black man when, in the middle 1550s, English traders brought five black men from Guinea to London." Tokson, *Popular Image of the Black Man*, 1.

putative boundary erected by the notion of a "pre-slavery Europe." But she, too, misses the point when she sutures "race and blackness." They can only be fixed in that way by a sociological imagination which not only miscomprehends Elizabethan England but, as well, much of the history of the cultures and peoples of the world which preceded it. But Elizabethan England will serve sufficiently here as a point of reference. The concern of this work is the representations of blackness which infected the earliest moment of American moving pictures. Much of that American culture which informed film about race "originated" in early modern England, the source of the English colonies so essential to the founding of the American republic. And in the seventeenth century, as Elizabethan England gave way to Great Britain, the cultural manufacture of the Negro from the commercial materialities of slavery trumped the earlier and more diverse significations of blackness. Nonetheless, within the three hundred years separating the English Renaissance from American motion pictures, the subject of blackness deteriorated and had to be repaired on more than one occasion. Change is the nature of historical occurrences, and we must constantly remind ourselves that the Negro is an historical conceit.

English Nationalism and the Negro:
The State and Shakespeare

The invention of the Negro, the inferiorized Black, coincides rather closely with the construction of English national identity. The coincidence, of course, is between the broader context of the formation of the Atlantic slave trade and the local developments of the English state and culture. As is the case with many historical coincidences, the twinned phenomena are not unrelated. John G. Jackson informs us "the word Negro was manufactured during the Atlantic Slave Trade . . . No free Africans were called Negroes; they got that name only after being enslaved."[13] And though at the beginnings of the trade in the fifteenth century, England (that is, its ruling classes) was disadvantaged by location and by economic and technological development and could play only a marginal and parasitical role in the trade, it would acquire the economic and political organization to dominate it by the end of the eighteenth century. What is more, as Jack Forbes has demonstrated, in the seventeenth century (and afterwards) when English agents had barely

13. John G. Jackson, introduction [no page number].

made their entrance into the trade, they appropriated the term "Negro" to signify "Black Africans, the Indians of India, Native Americans, Japanese, and slaves of whatever ancestry."[14] As a dramatic simile, it might be said, in the eighteenth century "the Negro" and England stepped onto the world stage conjointly.

Elizabethan England hosted an emporium of postmedieval cultures embedded with the factors of enslavement. The Romans had taken slaves among the Britons; later the Vikings and Anglo-Saxons had initiated a slave trade of Celts (the Welsh and the Irish).[15] The Vikings had similarly victimized the Anglo-Saxons, and the Danes colonized much of the north and east of Old England, establishing Danelaw.[16] David Douglas insists that "on the eve of the Norman conquest about one in every eleven persons in England was a slave."[17] And then in the mid-eleventh century the Norman ferment (Flemish, Breton, Poitevin, Dane, etc.) did the same. And while slavery declined among the English, the Welsh, and the Scots, it was not eliminated. Not much later, the Irish were colonized and submitted to forced labor by the Anglo-Normans, and so on.[18] And penal slavery in France, Spain, England, and the Netherlands, Patterson reminds us, "was to develop and flourish from the middle of the fifteenth century to well into the nineteenth."[19] The slaves from Africa who appeared in England in the sixteenth century, then, were hardly a phenomenon divorced from the social history of the British Isles. As it were, they were unusual neither in form nor in substance. In substance their slavery was no different from that of all

14. Forbes, *Black Africans and Native Americans*, 2–3. "Several illustrations can be cited to show that not only Africans but also Americans and Asians were called 'black' or 'negro' in Britain itself in the seventeenth and eighteenth centuries. In 1621 a William Bragge claimed compensation from the 'Company of East India and Summer islands' for several expenses, including 'for thirteen Negroes or Indian people, six women, seven men and boys . . . And so much in the name of God as touching that Businesse, and touching the Negroes or Indians' . . . In 1688 the *London Gazette* carried an advertisement for: 'A black boy, an Indian, about thirteen years old, run away the 8th Inst. from Putney, with a collar about his neck with this inscription: "The Lady Bromfield's black."'" Ibid., 84–85.

15. Patterson, *Slavery and Social Death*, 152.

16. R. Allen Brown, *Normans*, 12.

17. Douglas, *William the Conqueror*, 311.

18. Patterson, *Slavery and Social Death*, 152.

19. Ibid., 44.

the others. All of them had been appropriated as labor power, and many of them had been relocated great distances in order to plug labor shortages in the hinterland of the European peninsula or in some colony or other of enterprising merchants or ruling classes. In form, African mercenaries had served with the Roman army at the beginning of the Christian era, and as late as the fifteenth and sixteenth centuries, Black mercenaries were serving in Scotland and England along with African court musicians, entertainers, and domestic servants.[20] And the Moor was familiar enough as a cultural code to inhabit the imaginary and nightmares (and dreams?) of Elizabethan men and women.[21]

One of the Black mercenaries, Peter Negro, had fought with the English against the Scots in the mid-sixteenth century. He distinguished himself at the siege of Haddington in 1547, was knighted at Roxburgh, and received a pension of one hundred pounds for life. I. Habib records that "Negro died in London in 1551, and his burial followed a public funeral procession that, according to one eyewitness, a Tudor London undertaker, had great pomp and ceremony."[22] Culling the *Accounts of the Lord High Treasurer of Scotland*, Habib maintains that it is a "plausible conjecture" that Peter Negro was the same Peter Moryen (Peter the Moor) who was mentioned in 1501, 1503, and 1504 while serving in the court of James IV. The similarity in names, however, does not entirely void the substantial time elapsed between the occasions of Peter Moryen and Peter Negro. Peter Fryer found evidence of Blacks outside of London, in Devon, Plymouth, and Barking, and assesses that "towards the end of the sixteenth century it was beginning to be the smart thing

---

20. Gerzina, *Black London*; Fryer, *Staying Power*.

21. "Reginald Scott in his *Discovery of Witchcraft* (1584) tells us that 'a damned soule may and dooth take the shape of a blacke moore,' and that Bodin 'alloweth the divell the shape of a blacke Moore, and as he saith he used to appear to Mawd Cruse, Kate Darey, and Jone Haarviller.' St. Birgitta (of the fourteenth century) tells us in her *Revelations* that she saw the devil in the form of 'an Ethiope, ferefull in syght and beryng.' St. Margaret had the same experience. In Shakespeare's own day the Enemy was still using this form. Sara Williams, one of the possessed women described in Harsnet's *Popish Impostures* (well known as a source of diabolical names in *King Lear*) was said to have seen 'a blacke man standing at the doore, and beckning at her to come away'; this was a demon, of course. Later, another black figure tempted her to break her neck down the stairs, and (at another time) to cut her throat." Hunter, "Elizabethans and Foreigners," 52.

22. Habib, "*Othello*, Sir Peter Negro," 17.

for titled and propertied families in England to have a black slave or two among the household servants."[23] And Eldred Jones, in his second pathbreaking work, *The Elizabethan Image of Africa*, recovered the long-lost event that "by the end of the century, in fact, Queen Elizabeth had begun to be 'discontented' at the 'great numbers of Negars and Blacka-moors which . . . are crept into this realm,' and issued two edicts, one in 1596 and a stronger one in 1601, in which she complained of the influx and appointed a certain Caspar van Zenden (Zeuden), a merchant of Lubeck, to transport them out of the country."[24] Her first decree, July 11, 1596, concerned merely the ten blackamoors brought into the country by Sir Thomas Baskerville. A week later, she authorized van Zenden to confiscate eighty-nine blackamoors from their owners as an exchange for the same number of English prisoners, who were to be released in Spain and Portugal.[25]

Elizabeth I (b. 1533), whose reign endured from 1558 to 1603, was nevertheless an ambiguous figure in the matter of the Black presence in England. She and her father, Henry VIII (b. 1491, r. 1509–47), had brought Blacks into court for entertainment and service, and as a sup-porter of the English slave trade, she was more directly responsible for the too numerous Blacks "firmly ensconced in Britain's houses, streets and ports and portrayed on its stages" during her reign, as Gretchen Gerzina sardonically puts it.[26] Further evidence of her ambivalence

23. Fryer, *Staying Power*, 9. "In 1570 one Nicholas Wichehalse of Barnstaple in Devon mentioned 'Anthonye my negarre' in his will. The illegitimate daughter of Mary, described as '*a negro of* John Whites', was baptized in Plymouth in 1594 . . . An assessment of 'Strangers' in Barking (All Hallows parish, Tower ward) about the year 1598 shows two 'Negars'—Clare, at Widow Stokes's, and Maria, at Olyver Skyn-nar's—and two 'Negroes,' one called perhaps Jesse or Lewse—at Mr. Miton's; the other called Marea at Mr. Wood's." Ibid. Habib reports that "Kim Hall has furnished pictorial proof of domesticated blacks among the English aristocracy, in the numer-ous portraits of Tudor and Stuart nobility that show blacks as exotic menials." Habib, "*Othello*, Sir Peter Negro," 18. See Kim Hall, *Things of Darkness*.

24. Jones, *Elizabethan Image of Africa*, 20. See also Jones, *Othello's Countrymen*.

25. Fryer, *Staying Power*, 11. One precedent for Elizabeth's actions was the expul-sion of the Jews from England in 1290 by Edward I (r. 1272–1307). See Hillaby, "Beth Miqdash Me'at."

26. Gerzina, *Black London*, 4. Elizabeth sent one of her own ships with the slave trader John Hawkins in 1564 and two others for his third voyage in 1568. Among his other investors were Benjamin Gonson (treasurer of the navy), Sir Thomas Lodge (lord mayor of London), Sir William Winter (master of ordnance of the navy), Sir Lio-

towards the Black presence in her realm is provided by Peter Fryer, who instances a painted panel, *Queen Elizabeth and Her Court at Kenilworth Castle,* by Marcus Gheeraerts in 1575, where the queen "was shown with a group of [seven] black musicians and [three] dancers."[27] And we have seen that the queen and her father were not particularly unusual in such matters, since it was during the reign of her half brother, Edward VI (b. 1537, r. 1547–53), that the actual ruler, Edward Seymour (Duke of Somerset), awarded a knighthood and a pension to Peter Negro.

Before a third of the sixteenth century had passed, Henry VIII had severed ties with the Catholic Church and by an act of Parliament was made pope, or supreme head, of the Church of England. By midcentury, English pirates and merchants had made the first tentative incursions into the slave trade dominated until then by European merchants and bankers, particularly the Italians, Spanish, and Portuguese. That trade and slave production would eventually provide the plantation economy for English colonialism in North America and the West Indies and the margin of surplus for the transition from an agrarian-based mercantilism to capitalist industrial production in England itself."[28] And at the beginning of this process, as Ian Smith observes,

> through the collective and sometimes-collaborative efforts of educated men, English, in the last quarter of the century, finally shed its persistent reputation among Englishmen as a barbarous language. . . .
>
> In the aftermath of Henry VIII's break with Rome, "the project of

---

nell Duckett (another lord mayor), Lords Pembroke, Leicester, and Clinton. Thomas, *Slave Trade,* 155–57.

27. Fryer, *Staying Power,* 9.

28. Elsewhere I have noted that the slave trade's "effects on Britain's economy were varied, ranging from the practical and technical consequences for navigation and the proliferation of capitalist institutions to the acquisition of precious metals and the import of slave-produced commodities. This commerce, intensified by mercantilist monopoly, was a boon to shipping and its ancillary artisans (carpenters, painters, boat-builders) and trades (food provisions, insurance); and provided an impulse for the industrial industries (wool, cotton, sugar, metallurgy) and their related urban centres, Bristol, Liverpool, Manchester, Glasgow, Birmingham and Sheffield." Robinson, "Capitalism, Slavery," 125. See also Pares, "Merchants and Planters," 38, 50. The original author of this thesis is Eric Williams in *Capitalism and Slavery.*

English self-representation" through "writing of England" became the profession of a generation of Elizabethan writers.[29]

And though the evidence is somewhat scattered, most scholars whose attention is on race assert that the Elizabethan period is marked irrefutably by Black inferiorization.[30] The most frequently mentioned purveyors of Blacks as savages and subhuman monstrosities are Sir John Mandeville's *Travels* (c. 1357), which was reprinted, plagiarized, and appropriated for several centuries; Richard Eden's *The History of Travayle in the West and East Indies* (1576); *A Fardle of Facions* (1555); George Best's *True Discourse of the Late Voyages of Discoverie* (1577); Richard Hakluyt's *The Principal Navigations, Voyages, Traffiques and Discoveries of the English Nation* (1589); and John Leo Africanus's *A Geographical Historie of Africa* (translated by John Pory in 1600).[31] How "English" these sources were is debatable, since the *Fardle* was a translation of a European work, much of Hakluyt's work depended on Spanish and Portuguese sources, and Africanus (Al-Hassan Ibn Mohammed Al-Wezaz Al-fasi) was a Christianized Moslem born in Grenada. There is also another problem. Elliot Tokson had to admit,

> although the case against the black man would prove insurmountable in the final balancing of testimony, there were those travelers

29. Ian Smith, "Barbarian Errors," 169.

30. Alden T. Vaughan and Virginia Mason Vaughan are two of the few who evidence some reservation on the quality of the data: "This scattered evidence from the early Elizabethan era suggests that English contempt for dark-skinned people had a long pedigree. When added to the sharp increase in pejorative printed references to Africans in the final two decades of the reign and to the proliferation of Africans in England, mostly as slaves, it bolsters the argument that after centuries of relative ethnic isolation English men and women were jolted by sudden exposure." Vaughan and Vaughan, "Before *Othello*," 29. Of course, as their title suggests, the Vaughans persist in the conceit that "dark-skinned people" never ventured, at least voluntarily, north of the Sahara. This entirely erases much of the history of Islam, particularly the Almoravids who invaded the Iberian peninsula in the twelfth century. See Shillington, *History of Africa*, 90–92. The error is even more egregious, since the Vaughans cite a mid-sixteenth-century work (Andrew Borde, *The Fyrst Boke of the Introduction of Knowledge*) which referred to Barbary where the inhabitants "be Called the Mores, there be whyte mores and black moors." Vaughan and Vaughan, "Before *Othello*," 21n5.

31. See Winthrop Jordan, *White over Black*, 57ff.; Tokson, *Popular Image of the Black Man*, chap. 1; and Vaughan and Vaughan, "Before *Othello*," 22ff.

who could find positive traits among these newly discovered peoples. Most frequently praised were the gentle openness and friendliness of the black people and their physical beauty and hygiene. "We found the people most gentle, loving, and faithful, void of all guil and treason, and such as live after the manner of the golden age," wrote one traveler quoted in Hakluyt. "They are a people of a tractable, free and giving nature, without guile or treachery," wrote another.[32]

In 1578, George Best, one of Hakluyt's informants, testified to both his own color prejudice and the absence of that aversion in at least one Englishwoman: "I my self have seene an Ethiopian as blacke as cole brought into England, who taking a faire English woman to wife, begat a sonne in all respects as blacke as the father was."[33] Moreover, the treatment of the Moor was merely an aspect of an Elizabethan racial kaleidoscope, which, as G. K. Hunter states, was an "England-centred, intellectual pattern of European races." In other words, according to the propagandists of the sixteenth century, English national identity could most effectively be gauged by stereotypic difference—what present-day scholars sometimes refer to as "the Other." The Irish, the Scots, the Welsh, the inhabitants of the Low Countries, the French, and the Italians "were normally seen as absurd deviations from an English norm." And with respect to the Moors, the Turks, and the Jews, drawing on medieval legend and theology which informed a division between Christian, pagan, and satanic, the point of critical differentiation was not generally who was human but who was evil. While the Europeans were "failed Englishmen" to the nationalist scholars of the Henrician and Elizabethan eras, the Moors, the Jews, and the Turks were enemies of Christ.[34]

So the sampling of Elizabethan opinion which suggests "that English

32. Tokson, *Popular Image of the Black Man*, 18. With respect to the inhabitants of the Americas he encountered, Sir Walter Ralegh (Raleigh) displayed a similar sympathy: "Of the wife of one of the chiefs [of Guiana] he writes: 'In all my life I have seldom seen a better favoured woman.' 'Her countenance,' he continues, 'was excellent; her hair almost as long as herself was tied up in pretty knots, while her discourse was very pleasant.' 'I have seen a lady in England,' Ralegh concludes, 'so like to her, as but for the difference of colour, I would have sworn it might have been the same.'" Quoted in Sir Sidney Lee, "Caliban's Visits to England," 339.

33. Winthrop Jordan, *White over Black*, 15.

34. Hunter, "Elizabethans and Foreigners," 43, 45.

contempt for dark-skinned people had a long pedigree" is not entirely English, nor particularly monologic, nor particularly Elizabethan. Just as Elizabeth herself appears conflicted, so were some of her subjects.[35] The sparseness of the evidence in the absence of public opinion surveys bespeaks a problem in historical methodology—after all, we are being asked to accept the notion that the words of "educated men" reflected an English consensus. The fault here is the failure to exact "source criticism," as present-day historians term it.[36] A sixteenth-century text makes the case for singular authenticity but not representative authenticity. A century, two centuries, or three centuries later, a similar sample might simply bring eloquence or ideological reasoning to general opinion confirmed by a host of substantiating evidence. But for the sixteenth century, the issue is still undetermined. Not to put too fine a point on it, "the final balancing of testimony," which Tokson so vaguely reckons, would eventually be imposed from above. In the seventeenth and eighteenth centuries, it was the emergent capitalist bourgeoisies in England and Europe and their cultural and intellectual ancillaries which would weight the scales for racialism.[37]

35. Elliot Tokson devotes a chapter to the "scattered scenes" in Elizabethan and Jacobean theater where Blacks were depicted positively. The premise of the chapter is that these were exceptional and attributable to the needs of dramatic conflict. He dismisses the possibility that "Shakespeare, Dekker, Rowley, and Heywood may have unconsciously harbored ambivalence toward their black subjects." "A more satisfactory explanation for these glimpses of the black man's potential is that their inclusion in the plays frequently heightens the realism of the characters, giving them another dimension and a greater truth, making a stronger impact on the spectator." Tokson, *Popular Image of the Black Man*, 120–21.

36. Sidney Lee provides one example of the notorious unreliability of contemporary accounts. Three Eskimos were first brought to England (Bristol) in 1502 during the reign of Henry VII. Less than a hundred years later, while Elizabeth reigned, a sole Eskimo was enticed to England by Martin Frobisher. A pamphleteer exclaimed: "The like of this strange infidel was never seen, read, nor heard of before. . . . His arrival was a wonder never known to city or realm. Never like great matter happened to man's knowledge." Sir Sidney Lee, "Caliban's Visits to England," 337.

37. Immanuel Wallerstein summarizes the arguments which identified the gentry and yeomanry—the wealthiest and less affluent capitalist farmers—as the critical bases for the rise of a capitalist bourgeoisie in Henrician and Elizabethan England. "The Crown courted the 'bourgeoisie,' that is to say, the conglomerate of landed capitalist proprietors and well-to-do farmers, professional men (lawyers, divines, and medical practitioners), the wealthier merchants." Wallerstein, *Modern World-System*, 258, 228ff.

Shakespeare was, of course, one of those Englishmen who took on the task of the "writing of England." His Henrician works—*Henry VI* (1590), *Richard III* (1592), *Richard II* (1595), *King John* (1596), *Henry IV* (1597), *Henry V* (1599), *Henry VIII* (1613)—are a testament to how diligently and purposefully he assumed that responsibility. The history play, a new form barely off the ground when Shakespeare raised it to classical heights, fructified from the Elizabethan chronicle histories which were riveted on "the story of the state."[38] His principal sources were Edward Hall's *The Union of the Two Noble and Illustrious Families York and Lancaster* (c. 1540), and Raphael Holinshed's *Chronicles of England, Scotland and Ireland* (1587, second edition). A. L. Rowse comments:

> What stands out with his history plays against the numerous ordinary chronicle-plays is that he sees the pattern, the significance of events—in that like Hall, not Holinshed. From the very beginning with the *Henry VI* trilogy he is concerned with the phenomena of social disorder, the awful consequences of the breakdown of authority, a hopeless king like Henry VI or an unreliable one like Richard II, the dire necessity of order and obedience, of competence in the ruler, obedience in the subject.
>
> . . . Shakespeare developed a thoroughly governing-class attitude to these questions (with the corollary in his view of the people). After all, he regarded himself always as a gentleman, which he was through his mother, an Arden; even his father was an alderman, eventually bailiff, i.e. mayor, of Stratford.[39]

And just as he mimicked the civil attitudes of the monarchy and middling bureaucracy, he seems also to have mirrored the changing

38. The phrase in quotation is from Helgerson, *Forms of Nationhood*, 12. Elsewhere, Helgerson maintains that "Shakespeare did not invent the history play. According to most estimates, *The Famous Victories of Henry V* (1586) appeared several years before *The Contention* [i.e., *Henry VI*, part 2]." Ibid., 203.

39. Rowse, *Annotated Shakespeare*, 752. Richard Helgerson is a bit more precise as to Shakespeare's sympathies: "But while achieving his obsessive and compelling focus on the ruler, Shakespeare excluded another object of concern, the ruled. Identifying himself, his plays, his company, and his audience with the problematics of early modern kingship, he left out of consideration the no less pressing problematics of subjecthood." Helgerson adds: "The chief dramatist of the company that became the King's Men achieved his position as England's national poet by what he left out as well as by what he put in." Helgerson, *Forms of Nationhood*, 239, 240.

significations of Blacks. In the English theater of the late sixteenth century, Anthony G. Barthelemy recounts, allegorical morality plays were gradually displaced by secular, mimetic plays. In the same exchange the Vice (representing lust, greed, lasciviousness, etc.) of the prior venue was supplanted by the villain, a human character who embodied the evil designs and deceitful maneuvers and machinations of its predecessor. It appears entirely predictable that alongside the Jew, the "Negro Moor," whose physical blackness reinscribed medieval Manichaean color aesthetics, would occur to some playwrights as a perfect stage villain.[40] Such was George Peele's election in his portrait of Muly Mahamet ("the first Moor of any dramatic significance on the popular stage")[41] in *The Battle of Alcazar* (1589), and Thomas Dekker's Eleazar ("Seeing your face, we thought of hell")[42] in *Lust's Dominion* (1600).[43]

In the xenophobic period of the aging Elizabeth, Shakespeare's constructions of Blacks were unsympathetic. But with the accession of the Stuart monarchy in 1603, Shakespeare created *Othello*, very likely the first, and for a long time afterwards the only, direct challenge to the emergent Negrophobia.

Aaron the Moor, in *Titus Andronicus* (1590–91), was the first of Shakespeare's African characters. As the loyal and amorous consort to Queen Tamora of the Goths, Aaron displays the characteristics which might be taken to have legitimated Elizabeth's eventual distaste for Africans. Emily Bartels detects that

> Aaron is the one character in this play whose malignant differentness is consistently recognized and easily categorized by all, including himself and his allies. His references to his distinctive physical attributes—his "woolly hair" (2.3.34) and his "treacherous hue" (4.2.117)—evoke a stock image of the black man, and his intention to "have his soul black like his face" (3.1.205) reinforces the idea

40. Barthelemy, *Black Face, Maligned Race*, 72–76.

41. Ibid., 76.

42. Ibid., 103.

43. Barthelemy traces the etymological prints of the term "moor" to the ancient Greek word *maurus*, the appellation for residents of Mauretania, centuries before its conflation with Islam. In Latin, at least by the ninth century A.D., the term was synonymous with "black." In the fourteenth century, *Mandeville's Travels* was one source of transfer to England. Ibid., 8–9.

culturally linked to that image, that blackness is not merely skin-deep.[44]

In Shakespeare's dramatic imagination, the blackness of Aaron's and Tamora's child is sufficient to disqualify the infant from the throne of Rome ("Had nature lent thee but thy mother's look, / Villain, thou mightst have been an emperor," 5.1.29). This might very well have been the case in Elizabethan England, but it was not necessarily the case in medieval Rome, or as we shall see, in sixteenth-century Italy. Nonetheless in both *Titus Andronicus* and *The Merchant of Venice* (1596), where the impregnation of an unseen Black female character is unfavorably compared to wedding a Jewess ("I shall answer that better to the common / wealth than you can the getting up of the / negro's belly: the Moor is with child by you, / Launcelot," 3.5.40), Shakespeare represented blackness as repugnant.

Othello (1604) coincides with a very different political and cultural era: in 1603 James VI of Scotland became James I (1603–25), and his wife, Princess Anne of Denmark, reigned as his queen. The old queen's death had occasioned an official ban on stage plays, and the new king, in a concession to the City of London authorities and the onset of the plague, had abolished all troupes of players.[45] The plague had caused a postponement of all public meetings, assemblies, feasts, and even juries—the exception being the coronation spectacle.[46] But, as Ian Wil-

44. Bartels, "Making More of the Moor," 442. As recently as the year 2000, Hollywood was still disseminating this notion of genetically acquired culture. In *Me, Myself and Irene*, starring Jim Carrey and Renée Zellweger, a Black dwarf and a white woman are the parents of dark-skinned triplet boys. Notwithstanding having been raised by a single white parent (Carrey) and having been brought up for eighteen years in an apparently all-white Rhode Island village, the triplets exhibit urban Black speech (salted by "motherfuckers" and "bitches"), body language, and social codes. The genes bequeathed to them by their biological father are the only apparent explanation provided in the film for their cultural disposition.

45. Among the objections to public theater were that "playhouse crowds spread plague and fostered insurrection," and that actors impersonated their betters on stage. Shakespeare himself was criticized by elitist scholar/poets (playwrights who had attended university) for being a player/poet, that is a common actor who had pretensions to becoming a playwright. See Helgerson, *Forms of Nationhood*, 201, 203. For a few of the civil disturbances associated with playgoing, see Dollimore, *Radical Tragedy*, 23.

46. The bubonic plague, a flea-borne epidemic, had reappeared in England in the

son reports, the royal court retained for itself the privilege of theatrical entertainment: James "adroitly reserved to himself the right to maintain one company for his own household, a second for that of his wife, Anne of Denmark, and a third for his nine-year-old son Prince Henry." And on May 17, 1603, the king ordered two warrants for the appointment of Shakespeare's company as the King's Men. "At a stroke," Wilson exclaims, "James had done more for the acting profession and in particular for Shakespeare's company in the first ten days of his taking the reins than Elizabeth had done in all her forty-five years."[47] But notwithstanding James's protection and patronage, at the beginning of the Stuart dynasty it was Anne who was more directly influential in the short-lived salvation of blackness from the accelerating processes of the inferiorization trope.

The evidence is circumstantial but substantial. Princess Anne, married at the age of fourteen, had a "mature moor" as one of her attendants when she arrived in Scotland in 1590. A year earlier, at her wedding in Oslo, James had brought with him as a tribute to his fiancée a retinue of players and dancers, four of whom were Black (after dancing naked in the snow they contracted pneumonia and died). In Scotland, as the newlyweds entered the capital city, among the official greeters were forty-two young men "vizarded like Moors." In 1594, at the baptismal banquet for their first son, Prince Henry, a spectacle was arranged in which Anne's Moor attendant played a central role. Finally, we must recall, Shakespeare had been fascinated by and indirectly involved in the question of accession. Indeed, prior to the transition, in the waning days of Elizabeth I, Shakespeare had explored and exposed the power struggle between Essex (Robert Devereaux) and the Cecils (William, Lord Burghley and his son Robert, Earl of Salisbury) in *Hamlet* (1600–1601). A. L. Rowse informs us that Shakespeare had not made it too difficult for contemporary theater audiences to recognize the English contestants behind the Danish masquerades he devised in the play. Nor did he attempt to conceal his sympathies for the tormented Essex (Hamlet) and his steadfast aide Southampton (Horatio), or his ridicule of the moralizing Burghley (Polonius).[48]

---

sixteenth century but was particularly virulent the next century, in the period 1603–25 and again in 1636. See F. P. Wilson, *Plague in Shakespeare's London*, chaps. 4, 5.

47. Ian Wilson, *Shakespeare*, 296–97.

48. Rowse observes that "there is . . . general agreement that the play has a strong reference to its topical background." Rowse, *Annotated Shakespeare*, 1724. Alison

Topicality is also apparent in *Measure for Measure* (1604), which co-incided with James's authorization of a new English-language Bible as one means of addressing the enervating religious rivalries which emerged not only between Catholics and Protestants but between various competing Protestant sects (Puritans, Presbyterians, Anglicans, etc.) in the sixteenth and seventeenth centuries.[49] That facet of the play does understandably fascinate scholars of literature, but our interest is drawn to the appearance of the English Bible itself. Like the works of Shakespeare, the formulation of this Bible spans the period between the early sixteenth and early seventeenth centuries, which encompasses the invention of the modern English language. And both the plays and the Bible are recalled as critical contributions to that event. William Tyndale, an Oxford-trained cleric, had translated the entirety of the New Testament in the 1520s and at least five of the books of the Old Testament in the early 1530s. But Tyndale lacked the will to match Shakespeare's talent at coddling up to authority. Tyndale's self-appointed mission had been to challenge doctrinal teachings and interpretations which reflected the venal and political interests of the highest clerical class. He believed that by making the Bible accessible to ordinary folk in their own vulgar tongue, the word of God could be better preserved. Among the prelates, Tyndale insisted, "in this they be all agreed, to drive you from the knowledge of the scripture, and that ye shall not have the text thereof in the mother-tongue, and to keep the world still in darkness, to the intent they might sit in the consciences of the people, through vain superstition and false doctrine, to satisfy their

Weir declares that Essex became paranoid after he was convicted of deserting his command in Ireland in 1600 and relieved of his office, title, and lands. On February 8, 1601, he attempted an unsuccessful rebellion against Elizabeth and her advisers and was executed February 24. Weir, *Life of Elizabeth I*, 468ff. Among the chief rebels was the Earl of Southampton (Henry Wriothesley), a patron of Shakespeare who had bestowed upon Shakespeare a considerable amount of money in the mid-1590s. The plotters had requested that Shakespeare's company perform *Richard II* (with its dethronement theme) at the Globe Theatre on February 7. Ian Wilson, *Shakespeare*, 204ff., 272ff.

49. "What, then, are we to make of the play's topicality? Even as we earlier admitted the impossibility of providing proof for this claim, we have been suggesting that the 'cultural situation' being 'mirrored' in *Measure for Measure* is the great royalist project initiated by King James earlier in 1604, a project founded on the notion that the king's own authority was at stake in the public production and reception of biblical texts." Barnaby and Wry, "Authorized Versions," 1250.

filthy lusts, their proud ambition, and unsatiable convetousness, and to exalt their own honour above king and emperor, yea, and above God himself."[50] In 1536, his constant efforts were halted, and he was burned as a heretic. Ironically, an English Bible (largely based on the translations of Tyndale and his colleague, Myles Coverdale) was authorized by Henry VIII three years later.[51] However, in 1543, the Act for the Advancement of True Religion restricted access to the vernacular Bible to aristocratic and propertied classes. Thus it was that the appearance of the King James Bible in 1611, substantially based on the translations by Tyndale and Coverdale, retrieved Tyndale's vision. And the coincidence of Tyndale's translations with the multifaceted elements of Shakespeare's plays greatly influenced the manufacture of English identity.[52]

In 1604, now as Queen of England and Scotland (Great Britain), Anne commissioned and collaborated with Ben Jonson (scriptwriter) and Inigo Jones (set designer) to create a masque (the *Masque of Blacknesse*) in which she and her ladies-in-waiting appeared as actors in blackface. Finally, there is the close coincidence of the performances at court of three works: *Othello* (November 1, 1604), *Measure for Measure* (December 26, 1604), and the *Masque of Blacknesse* (January 6, 1605).[53] Jonson made it clear in his published text that it was the queen's idea to infuse blackness into their collaboration: "Because it was her majesty's will to have them blackamores at first, the invention was derived by me."[54] Jonson might have been somewhat defensive about the work, and for cause. At least one courtier, Sir Dudley Carleton, was outraged:

> Instead of Vizards, their Faces and Arms up to the Elbows, were painted black, which was Disguise sufficient, for they were hard

50. Quoted in Ginsberg, "Ploughboys versus Prelates," 52.

51. See Daniell, introduction.

52. David Ginsberg asserts that "whereas before Tyndale's translation the average man had been incommunicado with Scripture because it was considered classified information, now Scripture opened itself up to the individual's imagination, allowing him to define the text in the image of a socially conscious citizen. Scripture now spoke not only to the individual, but more importantly to the new *society* of individuals who were beginning to be united through their common access to Scripture in the vernacular." Ginsberg, "Ploughboys versus Prelates," 51.

53. This evidence is marshaled by the South African Shakespeare scholar F. G. Butler, in "Fair Queene," <http://www.rhodes.ac.za/affiliates/isea/shake/butler.htm>. (Pagination is cited hereafter from the Internet version.)

54. Quoted in Lewalski, "Anne of Denmark," 344.

to be known; but it became them nothing so well as their red and white, and you cannot image a more ugly Sight than a Troop of lean-cheek'd Moors.

. . . Theyr black faces and hands . . . was a very lothsome sight, and I am sorry that strangers should see our court so strangely disguised.[55]

And Carleton's revulsion to a blackface queen is generally cited as indicative of the scandalousness of the affair. Without much evidence, Barbara Kiefer Lewalski and F. G. Butler imply that there was general disapprobation in the court towards *The Masque of Blacknesse*, but both rely solely on Carleton for that opinion. Carleton's modernist objections to the blackness of the queen and her ladies, Butler suggests, precisely anticipate the "rigid aesthetic convention" Stephen Orgel would employ more than three hundred years later in his own critique of the masque as a paradox ("for blackness is a quality antithetical to the court"). For Butler, the provocation against and subversion of such notions of blackness was the exact purpose of the work: "that the Court itself—in the person of the Queen (who inspired the theme) and who, with her ladies, acted the black parts, is challenging the rigid conventional equation of blackness and ugliness, of light and beauty, and not only by their black disguise, but by certain very cogent arguments advanced in the course of Jonson's fable."[56] In any case, the Venetian ambassador, Nicolo Molin, was thrilled, terming the performance "very beautiful and sumptuous."[57] The only other contemporary references to the masque mentioned differences of opinion on its actual cost and the fact that Anne had thumbed her nose at the king by inviting the Spanish ambassador, thus excluding the French ambassador (an insult she repeated several times).[58]

In *Measure for Measure*, as F. G. Butler notes, Shakespeare seems to

55. Quoted in part in ibid.; and in Butler, "Fair Queene," 12.

56. Butler, "Fair Queene," 10. Butler is referring to Stephen Orgel's interpretation in *Jonsonian Masque*, 120. "But Orgel has misread the symbolism. It is not that black becomes white in the presence of King James, but that in the presence of that Virtue which James is supposed to embody, colour is reduced to an accident . . . James has abandoned Elizabeth's repatriation schemes; blacks are welcome in Britannia. Anne in this masque is complimenting James on his enlightened policy towards blacks." Butler, "Fair Queene," 12.

57. Quoted in Lewalski, "Anne of Denmark," 352n19.

58. Ibid., 344. France and Spain were at war at the time.

have referred to the masque ("When it doth tax itself: as those black masks," 2.4.79).[59] But his own tribute to the royal couple and particularly the queen may well have been *Othello*. What is so striking about *Othello* is the displacement onto Iago, the villain, of the mean-spiritedness towards Blacks of Shakespeare's earlier work. Modern critics and scholars are almost unanimous in praise of the work and its representation of racialism. G. K. Hunter nominates *Othello* "as the most magnificent specimen of the dramatic 'inversion of expected racial values.'"[60] Another Elizabethan specialist, Emily Bartels, insists that in *Othello* Shakespeare anticipates "the conjunction of racism and imperialism" and warns that "racist inscriptions stand as an impediment to imperialist success."[61] And Virginia Vaughan achieves the most succinct articulation of the play's ambition: "I think this play is racist, and I think it is not."[62] Of course, academic opinion is far from unanimous. There are still doubters for whom the whole discussion is either distasteful or ill-formed. Michael Neill, for one, declares that "to talk about race in *Othello* is to fall into anachronism."[63] But Neill is victimized by the presupposition that race must signify the notion of "biological diversity" and that this threshold paradigm requires some clear demarcation of who is Black and who is white.[64]

Shakespeare wove oppositional racial discourses into the fabric of *Othello*. That fact, however, seems to have mattered little to subsequent generations of literary critics and tragedians who more easily found Iago's scheming manipulations, the structural discontinuities between *Othello*, *Hamlet*, and *King Lear*, or the disease of love, and similar moral

59. Butler, "Fair Queene," 6.
60. Hunter, "Elizabethans and Foreigners," 50–51.
61. Bartels, "*Othello* and Africa," 64.
62. Vaughan, *Othello*, 70.
63. Neill, "'Mulattos,' 'Blacks' and 'Indian Moors,'" 361.
64. Neill prefers to interpret pre-seventeenth-century forms of group discrimination as cultural rather than racial: "As with the disdainful attitudes of the English toward the Irish—a people whose physical similarities to the English were conveniently obscured by their cultural differences—categories such as 'civil' and 'barbarous,' 'naked' and 'clothed' were often of far more significance in establishing the boundaries of otherness than the markers of mere biological diversity." Ibid., 366. This is, unfortunately, a weak explanation for the genocide, slavery, and injustices imposed on the Irish by English authorities in the fourteenth as well as the seventeenth century. See Theodore Allen, *Invention of the White Race*, 34, 50.

or ethical conflicts more interesting and compelling.[65] And Shakespeare's subversive placement of these discourses raised questions about the emergent racial conceits of the post-Elizabethan era, questions which were progressively obliterated as the century unfolded. In the order of their appearances in act 1 of the play, it is the second of the racial discourses concerning blackamoors with which we will begin. There are several reasons for this. For one, it is the more alien of the two discourses to modern sensibilities. For another, it boasts the longer historical pedigree and served to justify Othello's appointment as commander of the Venetian forces in Cyprus and his marriage to Desdemona. And, of course, it is the fact of its existence which provides the parameters of the contestation with Iago's racial conceits and lends to that contest a rhetorical context which complements for the English audience the cultural codes of Venice, the geographical dimensions of Venice and Cyprus, and the historical frame of the Battle of Lepanto (1571).[66]

Shakespeare announces and enunciates this discourse at several moments in the play, sometimes as the ironic voice of Iago, elsewhere in the declarative authority of the Duke, as self-description, or the merely descriptive. Iago, in the first instance of its articulation, simply states, "Another of his fathom they have none / To lead their business" (1.1.151–52). Othello, describing his heritage, explains, "I fetch my life and being / From men of royal siege" (1.2.21–22). In the Senate, a highborn member refers to Othello as "valiant Moor" (1.3.47). And the Duke, one line later, echoes the Senator and states his own interest in the Moor: "Valiant Othello, we must straight employ you / Against the general enemy Ottoman" (1.3.48–49).[67] Othello tells us something of his

65. For a taste of such treatments of the play, see Gardner, "'Othello,'" 1–11.

66. The Battle of Lepanto, a naval engagement, took place in October 1571 off the coast of Lepanto (Greece) between ships of the Ottoman Turks and a fleet of Christian allies (Venice, Spain, and Rome). The Christian victory was much celebrated in Europe and England; and James I (while still James VI of Scotland) penned an ode on the subject that contributed to his reputation as a poet. See Hunter, "Elizabethans and Foreigners," 48–49. Also see Butler, "Fair Queene," 7–8.

67. Norman Sanders informs us that "the principal narrative source for the play was the seventh novella in the third decade of Giraldi Cinthio's *Hecatommithi*. This collection of tales within a framework, first published in Venice in 1566, was used by a number of Elizabethan and Jacobean dramatists in their search for plots." Sanders, introduction to *Othello*, 2. J. E. Taylor's translation (1855) of the story begins: "There

service: "For since these arms of mine had seven years' pith / Till now some nine moons wasted, they have used / Their dearest action in the tented field" (1.3.83–85). Dismissing Brabantio's claims that the Moor must have employed some sort of witchcraft or magic to woo his daughter, Desdemona, Othello responds: "She loved me for the dangers I had passed / And I loved her that she did pity them" (1.3.166–67). The Duke rationalizes his selection of Othello to command the Venetian forces with a matter-of-fact observation:

> Othello, the fortitude of the place is
> best known to you, and though we have there a
> substitute of most allowed sufficiency, yet opinion,
> a more sovereign mistress of effects, throws a
> More safer voice on you. (1.3.222–26)

And in his final judgment, the Duke reprimands Brabantio with "Your son-in-law is far more fair than black" (1.3.291). Desdemona herself confirms Othello's account of their romance when she explains to the Senate:

> My heart's subdued
> Even to the very quality of my lord.
> I saw Othello's visage in his mind,
> And to his honours and his valiant parts
> Did I my soul and fortunes consecrate. (1.3.251–55)

We are not surprised, then, to hear the man described as "the warlike Moor Othello" (2.1.27). Nor are we unmoved by the references given him by Montano, the relieved commander at Cyprus. Montano declares Othello "a worthy governor" (2.1.30), "For I have served him, and the man commands / Like a full soldier" (2.1.35–36). Othello, Montano remembers, is "brave" (2.1.38). For Shakespeare and many in his audience, even for the fictive Italians of the play, these attributes were all a possibility.

Assigning to Othello mastery in the art of warfare, courage, eloquence, and ease in courtly intrigue, and a discerning intelligence in

---

once lived in Venice a Moor, who was very valiant and of a handsome person; and having given proofs in war of great skill and prudence, he was highly esteemed by the Signoria of the Republic, who in rewarding deeds of valor advanced the interests of the state." J. E. Taylor, *Moor of Venice*, 1.

the competing demands between the public and the private extended into the past far beyond Giraldi Cinthio's original character (1566) or England's sixteenth-century Peter Negro. Moorish armies, Moorish governors, Moorish scientists, mathematicians, poets, historians, inventors, philosophers, architects, and academics had achieved the most profound impacts on European societies and cultures for nearly a millennium between the European Dark Ages and the Late Middle Ages. The Moors had conquered Spain in the eighth century.[68] And Anwar Chejne, quoting the thirteenth-century Spanish monarch Alfonso X (1252–84), documents the chain of evidence between these Moors and Othello. Describing the invaders, Alfonso asserts, "Los moros de la hueste todos vestidos del sirgo et de os panos de color que ganaran . . . Las caras dellos negras como la pez el mas fremoso dellos era negro como la olla." (All the Moorish soldiers were dressed with silk and black wool that had been forcibly acquired . . . their black faces were like pitch and the most handsome of them was like [black as] a cooking pan.)[69]

José Pimienta-Bey provides another addendum to this second racial discourse in *Othello*, well aware that most historians of the modern period and their readers have had little understanding of its provenance.

68. See Roger Collins, *Arab Conquest of Spain*. Collins, inexplicably, misidentifies the Muslim force which was launched against Spain. He also confusingly identifies Tarik-bin-Ziad as both an Arab and a freedman. Ibid., 28ff. In 1946, W. E. B. Du Bois noted that Tarik-bin-Ziad, a former slave, was the Moorish commander of the conquerors. Du Bois, *World and Africa*, 183–84. Du Bois was relying on Rogers, *Sex and Race*, who received the information in a letter (December 15, 1933) from Mme. Halideh Edib, "Turkey's leading authoress and former Minister of Education" (ibid., 286). And Wayne Chandler, paraphrasing George O. Cox (*African Empires and Civilizations*, 1974) reported: "On April 30, 711 A.D., Tarik crossed the straits of Hercules with his 7,000 men, of which '6,700 [were] native [Moorish] Africans and 300 [were] Arabs.'" Chandler, "Moor," 161.

69. Chejne, *Muslim Spain*, 435n44, 126. See also Pimienta-Bey, "Moorish Spain," 184. Alfonso continued in this passage: "The vile people of Africa, who were not used to kindness and all of whose deeds were accomplished with tricks and deceits and who were not used to protect but to exploit great riches, are now exalted." Chejne, *Muslim Spain*, 126. Alfonso is described as a scholar, a propagandist, a supporter of the early *Reconquista*, and someone familiar with Muslim literature. Ibid., 125. Interestingly enough, Alfonso's description of the invaders differs from that of Chejne, who describes the army as largely Berber but allows Alfonso's characterization to go unchallenged. Ibid., 7.

Few of them have ever heard of the scientific Renaissance in Europe which took place during the "medieval" era, in the 12th and 13th centuries. In my opinion, this is intentional. For behind Europe's "Scientific Enlightenment," we find many African Muslims. In fact, we find that the very foundation and structure of "Western" Science and Academe is built upon the erudition of these people known as Moors. Moorish influence primarily came to the West via the Iberian peninsula, later to be renamed "al-Andalus" by the Moorish and Arab conquerors. But these non-European Islamic peoples would also occupy and control Sicily, parts of the Italian mainland, and Crete.[70]

The *Reconquista* of the late fifteenth century finished off Moorish political dominion in Europe. It did not, however, erase the cultural, intellectual, artistic, and technological achievements which had been contributed to, and had helped to define, Europe.[71] And specific to Othello as the noble Moor, the centuries-long experience in Europe of blackamoors as soldiers, governors, caliphs, sultans, viziers, poets, philosophers, musicians, and artists had not been entirely vanquished even in Elizabethan consciousness.[72]

Iago's manipulations are based on two lies, both of which he knows are false. One is Desdemona's adultery, and the other is Othello's subhumanity. These inventions are necessary for the enraged Iago to pun-

70. Pimienta-Bey, "Moorish Spain," 182.

71. This point is made by Henri Pirenne in *Mohammed and Charlemagne*. By the High Middle Ages, Thomas Goldstein remarks, "Islam had left its traces in streets and gardens and mosques, in the ceramic décor of colorful facades, in walls enlivened by horseshoe arches and delicate filigree on fountains — still splashing even though their Muslim builders were long gone — in the libraries and patios of former Muslim places of learning . . . The effect was an intellectual stimulation without parallel. Virtually every facet of European life, from religion and philosophy to governmental institutions to architecture, personal mores, and romantic poetry, was profoundly affected. For Medieval science, Spain meant the opportunity to advance in one giant step from the abstractions of philosophical thought to the tangible experience." Goldstein, *Dawn of Modern Science*, 94.

72. J. O. Hunwick notes the number of pre-Islamic Black poets in Arabia; identifies Black rulers such as al-Mustansir (r. 1036–94) in Egypt, Mulay Isma'il (r. 1672–1727) in Morocco, and the eunuch Kafur in medieval Egypt. He also details the service of hundreds of thousands of Black soldiers in Muslim armies in India, Morocco, Tunisia, and Egypt. See Hunwick, "Black Africans in the Islamic World."

ish Othello for his two betrayals: his love and marriage to Desdemona (perhaps, but not necessarily, a topical reference to James's homosexuality), and his choice of Cassio for his second-in-command at Cyprus. Iago's plot is all to a single purpose: to "Make the Moor, thank me, love me, and reward me" (2.1.289). To that end, Iago resorts to racial slurs, vulgarity, and crude, provocative imagery when he profanes Othello, and to brute sexual language where he hopes to defame Desdemona. Since his objective is correction rather than destruction, his aim to replace Desdemona and Cassio at the side of Othello, his characterizations of Othello are meant for an external audience. For Iago, race (as well as jealousy) is an agency, not a creed.

In his seemingly hysterical report to Brabantio, Iago attempts to sear into the old man's imagination the base consequences of Desdemona's elopement: "Even now, now, very now, an old black ram / Is tupping your white ewe" (1.1.89–90). And a clearly medieval hatred of the Moors ("the devil will make a grandsire of you," 1.1.92), is quickly followed by another mix of the pornographic and the racial:

You'll have your daughter covered with a Barbary
horse you'll have your nephews neigh to you,
you'll have coursers for cousins, and gennets for
germans. (1.1.111–131)

Once again Brabantio is invited to "see" his daughter furiously mating with a large, powerful, black animal, a "lascivious Moor" (1.1.125). Brabantio is obviously easily infected with a protean Christian prejudice against Othello, since he is soon accusing him ("O such a thing as thou" 1.2.71) of employing satanic potions, charms, drugs, or minerals to weaken Desdemona's judgment or, worse, paralyze her "motion." Again the father is imagining, "seeing" a horrifying rape. And then in anticipation of a political fear which would ravage Reconstruction America, Brabantio vehemently rejects a *marriage* between Othello and Desdemona: "For if such actions may have passage free / Bond-slaves and pagans shall our statesmen be" (1.2.98–99).

In his suit against the marriage before the Duke, Brabantio appropriates Iago's images of bestiaries into a charge that witchcraft has disturbed Desdemona's mind:

To fall in love with what she feared to look on!
It is a judgement maimed and most imperfect

That will confess perfection could so err
Against all rules of nature . . . (1.3.98–101)

But in the second act, Iago reclaims the stage as the chief (and chiefly racial) detractor of the Moor. But now obviously conflicted ("The Moor, howbeit that I endure him not, / Is of a constant, loving, noble nature," 2.1.269–70), he seems incapable of separating the real from anonymous rumors (that Othello committed adultery with Emilia) and from what he himself has invented ("the lusty Moor").

In the final act, Othello now commands the stage, and with the murder of Desdemona the oppositions between the tragedy of sordid jealousy into which he was ensnared, his powerful nature, his extraordinary heritage are fulsomely articulated. When he submits to his arrest, Othello costumes his lack of resistance with a testament to the superior physical power he has chosen to withhold:

I have seen the day
That, with this little arm and this good sword,
I have made my way through more impediments
Than twenty times your stop. (5.2.259–62)

But now, with Othello a self-confessed murderer, even Desdemona's kinsman, Lodovico, still must consent to the magnificence which Othello achieved: "O thou Othello, that wert once so good, / Fall'n in the practice of a damned slave" (5.2.287–88).

The Negro Erasure of the Moor
Lodovico's, or more surely Shakespeare's, verdict quite accurately summarizes the trajectory of racism for the next three centuries, a sort of epitaph to a premodernist, prewhite historical memory. In that odyssey, Shakespeare's *Othello* is the last magnificent public gesture to challenge the transformation of the "good" to that of the "damned slave" in the seventeenth century. As a dramatist, Shakespeare drew his audience into the twisting psychological geometry of racism. Played out in a distant society, *Othello* displayed a pageantry of personal disaster and tragedy which white racial hatred might precipitate. Because it was Venice and not England, and because Shakespeare was circumscribed by history and performance, it would be too much to expect that he might have anticipated the historical consequences of white racism

once it was firmly deposited in English culture. Though the centuries-old racial passions infecting English consciousness were already in place, deposing the Irish, the Scots, and others as savages, their provenance had been confined to tribal and nationalist imaginings. In the centuries which were to follow, white racism would aggregate the global to the domestic, transforming ethnic antagonisms into an economy of difference. All this was far beyond Shakespeare's comprehension and anticipation. Slav, slave, Negro would be inscribed on the canvas of hundreds of millions of lives. Even had it been his intention, he could not have warned us of such consequences. Notwithstanding, the breadth of his intellect and the documentation of his social and political seriousness do license us to read *Othello* with some deliberateness. As *Othello* demonstrates, race could be employed to distort, inflame, and manipulate. And because in an Aristotelian sense it was irrational, that is, without natural limits, it was an uncontrollable causative.

Michael Neill has noted that the *Oxford English Dictionary* "offers no example of the word [European] as a generic term for 'white' people before 1696."[73] And there is something fitting in that peculiar actuality, since it coincides almost exactly with determined critiques of *Othello*. The critic was Thomas Rymer, whose writings of the 1692–93 period (*The Tragedies of the Last Age* and *A Short View of Tragedy*) have been nominated as "among the fundamental critical texts which established neo-Aristotelian theories of art in England."[74]

Rymer disqualified *Othello* from the company of great tragedies because its moral instruction was trivial and because it revolved around several "improbable" or "unnatural" occurrences. For Rymer the most objectionable improbability was the "monstrous" and unnatural marriage between Othello and Desdemona ("the foundation of the Play must be concluded to be Monstrous"). Rymer objected that Shakespeare had provided no preparation, no basis for Desdemona's perversion. In all sincerity (I think), Rymer suggested, "A little preparation and forecast might do well now and then. For his *Desdemona's* Marriage, He might have helped out the probability by feigning how that some way, or other, a Black-amoor Woman had been her Nurse, and suckl'd her; Or that once, upon a time, some *Virtuoso* had transfus'd into her

73. Neill, "'Mulattos,' 'Blacks' and 'Indian Moors,'" 369.
74. Alexander, "Thomas Rymer and 'Othello,'" 67.

Veins the Blood of a black Sheep; after which she might never be at quiet till she is, as the Poet will have it, *Tupt with an old black ram*."[75] That he would have found these possibilities more satisfying than the play's dependence on Desdemona's attraction to the noble Moor might be taken as a testament, perhaps, to the limited nature of both Rymer's imagination and creativity. But what sort of imagination was required? In August 1692, almost exactly the time Rymer was writing his preposterous treatises on tragedy, a Mr. Plummer in the Maryland colony was fined six thousand pounds of tobacco, because his "One Daughter, who unfortunately having too much Familiarity and Commerce with a Certain Negro Man was supposed by him to have a Child."[76] The absence of imagination is not the issue with Rymer; rather, we are peering here into an imagination which has been racialized in accordance with a new cultural regimen. Rymer was proceeding on the basis of a racial arrogance which by the late seventeenth century had become epidemic in English legal, social, and cultural affairs. Infected himself, he would serve as a propagator of further infection:

> The Character of that State is to employ strangers in their Wars; But shall a Poet thence fancy that they will set a Negro to be their General: or trust a *Moor* to defend them against the *Turk*? With us a Blackamoor might rise to be a Trumpeter; but *Shakespear* would not have him less than a Lieutenant-General. With us a *Moor* might marry some little drab, or Small-coal Wench: *Shakespear*, would provide him the Daughter and Heir of some great Lord, or Privy-Councellor: And all the Town should reckon it a very suitable match: Yet the English are not bred up with that hatred and aversion to the *Moors*, as are the Venetians, who suffer by a perpetual Hostility from them.[77]

75. Ibid., 70.

76. Catterall, *Judicial Cases*, 4:28.

77. Quoted in Alexander, "Thomas Rymer and 'Othello,'" 70. Barely two hundred years later, Arthur Bradley, one of the most influential Shakespearean scholars in the twentieth century, acknowledged precisely the very existence of the English aversion to Black but used it in a fashion with which Rymer might have been uncomfortable. Ironically, in a note to a passage where Bradley dismissed as "amusing" American critics who challenged whether Othello was a Negro, he sought to avoid discussing whether Black actors should play the role. Bradley's undiscussed opinion was "I dare say not. We do not like the real Shakespeare . . . Perhaps if we saw Othello coal-black with the bodily eye, the aversion of our blood, an aversion which comes as near to being merely physical as anything human can, would overpower our imagination

Rymer was egregiously mistaken on every one of his historical or cultural premises. We have already seen that on the European peninsula as well as in Britain, there were historical reasons for the association of Moors with military and administrative skills. And even so insular an intelligence as Rymer's might have wondered about the circumstances of the Cinthio tale and its place in Italian affairs. Italy was still centuries from being reunited, but it is no real stretch to assume that a Venetian like Cinthio would have heard of the recent occurrences affecting the nobilities in Florence and Rome. In 1523, thirteen-year-old Alessandro de Medici (also known as Alessandro the Moor) had become the first Duke of Florence. His mother, Anna (after her marriage to a tradesman, she was known as Simonetta da Collavechio), was a black domestic slave in the Medici household, his father was Cardinal Giulio (later Pope Clement VII). In 1562, Alessandro's son, Giulio, was appointed First Admiral of the Knights of San Stephano, an order especially founded to fight the Turks! While they were not Moors in the religious sense (neither is Othello), the portraits of Alessandro and his daughter, Giulia de Medici, clearly display their African as well as their European roots.[78] Finally, there is that extravagant concealment: "the English are not bred up with that hatred and aversion to the Moors." For Rymer to have made such a claim at the end of the seventeenth century, one might surmise that as a child he was suckled by a moron or had transfused into him the blood of a jackal. Rymer's words reek with the odor of the very aversion he denied. And by the time of his writing, British subjects all over the globe were being invited to settle their affairs with the Moor, with prejudice.

For more than a century before Rymer's writings, English monarchs, aristocrats, gentry, merchants, adventurers, and privateers had been engaged in African slavery. And by the first third of the seventeenth century, substantial slave trading and slave exploitation by English factors could be found in the Caribbean at Santa Catarina and Barbados. "By 1653," Robin Blackburn reports, "slaves outnumbered indentured servants by 20,000 to 8,000" in Barbados.[79] While in the Mediterranean,

---

and sink us below not Shakespeare only but the audiences of the seventeenth and eighteenth centuries." A. C. Bradley, *Shakespearean Tragedy*, 173n21.

78. See Rogers, *Sex and Race*, 164, who cites H. B. Cotterill, *Italy from Dante to Tasso*. Most other sources (e.g., the *Encyclopaedia Britannica*) merely recount Alessandro's paternity.

79. Blackburn, *Making of New World Slavery*, 231.

as late as the 1670s, English slavers were indifferent to race and religion, enslaving Muslim Turks, Moors, Native Americans (Wampanoag), and Christian Greeks, the slave system justifiable by whiteness was beginning to congeal.[80] As the agents of capitalist agriculture probed the islands of the Caribbean for the most productive sites secure from the Spanish, tested the marketability of tobacco, indigo, and sugar for the most profitable cash crop, and experimented with labor recruits from Britain, Europe, the Americas, and Africa, the formulations justifying African slavery evolved. And it is difficult to imagine how Rymer had avoided the cultural consequences, the psychological ramifications of the extensive trading of African slaves and dependence on slave production, the political aftereffects, and particularly the metastases of the rationalization of the whole enterprise by Sir Edward Coke in his *Institutes of the Laws of England* published in 1628, quoted here by Blackburn: "'This is assured, that Bondage or Servitude was first inflicted for dishonouring of parents: for Cham the Father of Canaan … seeing the Nakedness of his Father Noah, and shewing it in derision to his Brethren, was therefore punished in his Sonne Canaan with Bondage.' Coke's view chimed in with that of clerics like R. Wilkinson, who added that 'the accursed seed of *Cham* . . . had for a stampe of their fathers sinne, the colour of hell set upon their faces.'"[81] The new English Bible was being put to good use in the pulpits and the instructed readings laid down for the laity.

Moreover, on the secular side, nationalist rhetoric provided another justification for English participation in the slave trade. Fueled by such competition, the French, the Dutch, the Spanish, the Portuguese, the Brandenburgers, the Swedes, and the Danes contrived to export an estimated 370,000 Africans to the Caribbean between 1650 and 1675, and nearly twice that number in the next twenty-five years.[82] Colonialism was another of these nationalist contests, an adventure which not only enriched the English elite (a third of the House of Commons participated in such ventures between 1604 and 1614) but could also siphon off excess population when appropriate (225,000 British emigrants went to the Americas between 1610 and 1660).[83] And not in-

---

80. For English slavers in the Mediterranean, see Aylmer, "Slavery under Charles II."

81. Blackburn, *Making of New World Slavery*, 236.

82. Thomas, *Slave Trade*, 226.

83. Blackburn, *Making of New World Slavery*, 220, 228.

considerable were the manufactured goods destined for African consumption: cloth, metals, weapons, and alcohol.[84] These were some of the pilings that shored up an English system of African slave trading and slave management that neither the agents of Dutch capital, Italian capital, Spanish monarchs, or Portuguese merchants had achieved. As Blackburn observes, "This harsher variant of racial slavery was to be firmly established by the 1660s, and to exercise a direct influence on the English colonies of North America wherever there were significant numbers of slaves. The English sense of private property, sharpened by the rise of capitalist market relationships, was to put the accent on the slave as chattel and almost entirely to eclipse the notion that the slave was a human being."[85]

What, indeed, was Rymer playing at? Not only were the English in the seventeenth century being "bred up with that hatred and aversion to the Moors," but their entire legal codes were being altered to accommodate the new organism, the white race. In the colonies the transfer of human beings to chattel had proven insufficient to that purpose. In the Virginia colony,

> after 1660, a number of laws were passed that provided a window into the colony's troubling relationship with slavery and slaves. In 1662, a law was passed preventing a child from inheriting the father's status if the mother was a "negro woman"; in 1667, another law prevented baptism from freeing "slaves by birth"; in 1680, a law was passed "for preventing Negroes Insurrections"; in 1692, another to aid "the more speedy prosecution of slaves committing Capitall Crimes" established special courts for slave trials. Each of these laws, as well as those passed to regulate the civil rights of free Blacks (in 1668, a new law made free Black women but not other women subject to poll tax; in 1670, another forbid Christian Blacks from purchasing Christian servants; in 1691, another banished from the colony anyone involved in interracial marriage) marked a crossroads.[86]

Anticipating the banishment of mixed-race couples, in 1662 and 1664, the legislatures of Virginia and Maryland warned indentured colonial women that should they marry African slaves ("shamefull Matches"), in

---

84. Thomas, *Slave Trade*, chap. 16.
85. Blackburn, *Making of New World Slavery*, 237.
86. Robinson, *Black Movements in America*, 2.

effect they too would become slaves, and the children of such unions would be slaves "as their fathers were."[87] And I employ the term "colonial women" purposely. For if the Maryland General Assembly's language is attended to carefully, it suggests that "whiteness" was still in abeyance, not yet established in either its rhetorical hegemony or juridical authority:

> And forasmuch as divers freeborn English women, forgetful of their free condition, and to the disgrace of our nation, do intermarry with Negro slaves, by which also divers suits may arise, touching the issue of such women, and a great damage doth befall the master of such Negroes, for preservation wherof for deterring such freeborn women from such shameful matches, be it enacted: That whatsoever freeborn women shall intermarry with any slave, from and after the last day of the present assembly, shall serve the master of such slave during the life of her husband; and that all the issues of such free-born women, so married, shall be slaves as their father were . . . And be it further enacted: That all the issues of English, or other free-born women that have already married Negroes, shall serve the master of their parents, till they be thirty years of age and no longer.[88]

While later scholars would invariably construct these sanctions as applying to white women and Black men, in colonial Maryland, legislatures patrolled the line between English women, freeborn women, and Christian women.[89]

By the end of the seventeenth century, Charles Outwin reports, "Even the names of individual slaves, noted previously as a matter of course, begin to vanish from the [court] dispositions."[90] Quite astonishingly,

87. Catterall, *Judicial Cases*, 4:2. See also Outwin, "Securing the Leg Irons," 17. Lord Baltimore repealed the act in 1681 on behalf of "Irish Nell," one of his servants. Nevertheless, two of her descendants, Mary and William Butler ("first cousins"), were still defined as slaves in 1770. Their daughter, the slave Mary, successfully petitioned for her freedom in 1791, over a century after Baltimore's action. Catterall, *Judicial Cases*, 2–3. Eight years earlier, Eleanor Toogood had gained her freedom despite the fact that her grandmother (Mary Fisher), "a free mulatto woman," had married a slave (her grandfather, Dick), and her mother (Ann Fisher) had been a slave for life under the 1664 act. Ibid., 3.

88. Lubin, *Romance and Rights*, 5.

89. Mumford, "After Hugh," 285.

90. Outwin, "Securing the Leg Irons," 18.

for the sake of inventing the Negro, colonial legislatures were willing to forfeit the English custom of patrilineality, and even more shocking, the salvation imbued in the Christian faith. The Negro marked the boundary beyond which the heritage of English or "white" fathers could not extend. The Negro even dissipated the promise of Christian redemption. No principle, no matter how ancient or sacred, could stand before the gathering onslaught of the industry of inventing the Negro.

The volume of the British African slave trade in the eighteenth century is somewhat inexactly computed. For instance, James Walvin assesses that the British shipped 45,000 Africans each year of the century.[91] Paul Lovejoy comes in with something like half that figure: 2,532,300 for 1701–1800.[92] And Hugh Thomas, only considering numbers from 1721–1800, estimates 1,275,000 for that period.[93] Our concerns here are not with these differences but with the historical context in which the conceits employed by Rymer at the end of the previous century had to give way to more muscular constructions of race in the eighteenth century. The more important consideration is that indisputably a huge transmigration of Africans took place under the most appalling conditions which capitalist agriculture could dictate. And as Oliver C. Cox insisted in *Caste, Class and Race,* some sort of anesthetic was required to desensitize those who observed it from afar or participated in it in the most intimate fashion.

It might be tempting to pursue *Othello* into the eighteenth century if we were writing theater history. To be sure, the work warrants such attention, since from the early seventeenth century and then again after the Restoration of the monarchy in 1660, it remained the most popular of Shakespeare's works and one of the most frequently performed.[94] And the appearances of women on the English stage (the theatrical activities of Queen Anne and her court ladies were a royal prerogative) during the latter period might have contributed something to the racial excitement of critics like Rymer. In the eighteenth century, the play still tempted the best players in England, but now the play was considerably altered in playbooks and on stage by expurgated versions. Marvin

---

91. Walvin, *Fruits of Empire,* 124.

92. Lovejoy, "Volume of the Atlantic Slave Trade," 483, cited in Blackburn, *Making of New World Slavery,* 383.

93. Thomas, *Slave Trade,* 226.

94. Sanders, *Othello,* 17.

Rosenberg declares that "the deepest and cruelest cuts were made to reduce the atmosphere of sexuality into which Othello was betrayed."[95] This more genteel version of the work would explain how, near mid-century, one jealous actor (James Quin) could characterize the performance of a rival (David Garrick) with such asexual cunning: "Othello! . . . Psha! no such thing! There was a little black boy, like Pompey attending with a teakettle, fretting and fuming abut the stage, but I saw no Othello!"[96] Our concern, however, is with events occurring at the end of the eighteenth century, events which further altered the representation of Blacks in English and now American culture.

What is so exceptional about the seventeenth and early eighteenth centuries is not so much the increase of white racism but the opposition to it. That resistance was sufficient to induce a paradigm change for racism from an inferiorization which metastasized physical aesthetics, heresy, and culture to a categorical subhumanity. More directly, as the importance of slave economies expanded, the possibilities of antislavery multiplied exponentially. In the social arena, the conflict matched unequal forces, for the political strength of the slavers was deposited in the state and the propertied classes, while the social power of antislavery was deposited among the much more numerous laboring classes with their diverse antagonisms to actual or putative enslavement, to impoverishment, disenfranchisement, and class humiliations. And as their control over the slave signifiers ineluctably slipped from their grasp, the proslavery propagandists and ideologues were compelled to invest other formal codes and systems of oppression. It was thus, by the end of the eighteenth century, that natural science appropriated the older signifiers deposited in the binaries of white versus Black (or European versus non-European), Christian versus pagan, and civilization versus savagery. If Blacks constituted another species, a not-quite humanity, then civil law was superseded by natural law. Unopposed by contradiction, that belief might be expected to gradually descend upon the English-speaking public. But because they were on the wrong side of domination, the proslavery ideologues were constantly besieged with material contradictions: for example, fugitive

95. Marvin Rosenberg, *Masks of Othello*, 35.

96. Ibid., 42. Quin was referring to the young Moor depicted in *Quarrels with Her Jew Protector*, one of a series of paintings by William Hogarth in 1732 entitled *A Harlot's Progress*. See Webster, *Hogarth*, 50–51.

slaves and marronage. Just as ominous, proslavery was losing its hold over the metropolitan and overseas support it had invented, the white laborers.

Resistance, Abolition, and the Semiotic
Dialectic of the Negro

At this point in history, slavery and the slave trade were essential components of the modern world-system. From the very initiation of the English part of the system (as was the case for the earlier starts to the Portuguese, Spanish, Dutch, etc. systems), there had been those opposed to it. The trials of rebels in the colonies, in the early seventeenth century, provide testimony of one sort of resistance: rebellions by servants, Blacks, and Indian slaves. In 1627, several Caribbean Indians brought to Virginia had been hanged for flight and conspiracy "to kill some of our people." In 1640, the "Negro John Punch" had fled with two others ("a dutchman, the other a Scotchman") and when captured had been sentenced to serve his master for his natural life. That same year, "Negro Emanuel" had conspired with six other servants to flee to a nearby Dutch plantation and upon capture was sentenced to "re ceive thirty stripes and to be burnt in the cheek with the letter R, and to work in shakle one year or more as his master shall see cause."[97] In 1688, for another sort of opposition, the small community of Quakers at Germantown, led by Francis Daniel Pastorius, had sent a petition to the monthly meeting declaring that any effort "to bring men hither, or to rob and sell them against their will, we stand against."[98] Antislavery tracts, sermons, and pamphlets had dotted the colonial landscape for much of the eighteenth century, provided with muscular authority by slave rebellions and the founding of Maroon, that is, fugitive slave, communities.[99]

Suggestions of marronage in the Virginia colony are found in the cases of the Caribbean Indians (1627), Negro Emanuel (1640), Negro Will (1673), and Negro John, whose companions were six English servants (1674).[100] To be sure, Maroons were reported in Spanish Florida in

97. Catterall, *Judicial Cases*, 1:76–77.
98. Robert Wilson, *Philadelphia Quakers*, 88.
99. For more on antislavery social movements, see Robinson, *Black Movements in America*, chap. 1.
100. Catterall, *Judicial Cases*, 1:76–80; and Robinson, *Black Movements in America*, 14–15.

1687 and Virginia in 1691.[101] In South Carolina, the colony was disrupted by significant slave rebellions in 1733 and 1744; and in 1765, a militia was sent against "a numerous collection of outcast mullattoes, mustes, and free negroes."[102] In French-held Louisiana, in 1731, large slave conspiracies, launched from Maroon hideouts, were discovered in June and at Christmas.[103] The colonists of the poorest stratum were also restless, engaging in legal and illegal actions against the colonial governments which facilitated their exploitation by the large landowners. So on the eve of the American Revolution, along with Blacks, Native Americans, and servants, white artisans, workers with lesser skills, small farmers, and farm laborers had as serious grievances against their local aristocrats ("the great and overgrown rich men") as the latter had with the English Parliament and the king. This insured that the American Revolution was actually composed of three distinct revolutionary impulses: the poor colonists against the wealthy, the Blacks against slavery, and the colonial wealthy against the British government. As I have observed elsewhere, "In the politics of their day and later in our historical chronicles, however, the elite had the last word. In 1776, when the Congress met in Philadelphia, it was composed of wealth . . . They disdained popular government . . . and insured that the advantage in pursuing happiness would remain with the plantocrats and their New England business partners."[104] Nevertheless, among the unintended consequences of the hegemonic insurrection was the loosening of social forces which would radically alter the imaging of Blacks in both England and the new republic.

The spur to the British campaign to abolish slavery had several sources. For one, approximately 100,000 slaves were estimated to have found their way behind British lines during the war (1775–83).[105] For those who fought for the British in the Ethiopia Corps or the Black Pioneers, a good part of their motivation was the proclamations of intent by Lord Dunmore (November 1775) and General Henry Clinton (1779) to free slaves who joined the British army.[106] James Walker asserts, "In the confusion of war it must frequently have been easy to desert a master,

101. Aptheker, *American Negro Slave Revolts*, 152; and Landers, "Gracia Real," 13.
102. Robinson, *Black Movements in America*, 15.
103. Ibid., 19.
104. Ibid., 23.
105. James Walker, *Black Loyalists*, 3.
106. Ibid., 1–2.

and thousands of square miles were available to run to, yet the escapes did not simply hide or establish free 'Maroon' communities: they went to the British and offered their services."[107] Of course, Blacks also fought on the side of the Continental Army during the Revolution, but their extraordinary sacrifice would have much less dramatic impact on slavery in the new republic. On the other hand, tens of thousands of Black Loyalists were evacuated (e.g., 5,000 from Savannah in July 1782 and 6,000 from Charleston in November), many with certificates of freedom warranted by their war service, others as slaves attached to white Loyalists with the withdrawing British forces.[108] Most of those freed slaves would leave the republic, moving on to Nova Scotia, to the West Indies, some to Britain, and many eventually to the colony of Sierra Leone in West Africa. They constituted something like a fifth of the slave population of half a million in the colonies in 1780, and their emancipation was the largest emancipation of modern slaves before the Haitian Revolution (1791–1804). They had been emancipated because of their loyalty to the king and England, and the English could now claim a moral superiority to the colonial rebels who deviously sought to protect their slave-owning privileges.

The Black Loyalists who made their way to Britain augmented the extant Black population, particularly the numbers of the Poor Negroes (as the Black London population was officially designated). Their presence thus helped to excite British popular opinion around the issue of the Poor Negroes in particular, and slavery in general.[109] Antislavery forces in Britain (ranging from factory workers to high-ranking bureaucrats) could now rail against the slave economy of the United States without the liability or added political burden of protesting against their own king and Parliament. The United States was now an independent, self-ruled enemy, not a colonial dependency. And the proslavery faction in England, consisting too often of arrogant, conspicuous, greedy, and corrupt plantation owners of the West Indies, was vulnerable to the charge that its insatiable avarice was the centerpiece in the loss of the North

107. Ibid., 4–5.

108. Clifford, *From Slavery to Freetown*, 22. The number of evacuees is approximate, as James Walker notes: "The 'Book of Negroes' listed a total of 3,000, inspected in New York between 27 April and 30 November 1783, bound for Nova Scotia. Others may well have gone the same route either before or after the roll was taken." Walker, *Black Loyalists*, 12.

109. Turner, "Limits of Abolition," 326.

American colonies. Thus abolition joined with parliamentary reform to achieve one of the most startling results in modern English history: a mass popular movement which propelled the British state towards the abolition of slavery and the ending of the slave trade.[110] J. R. Oldfield demonstrates that the rapid growth of a middle class, new industrial towns, expanding consumerism, and better communications contributed to the swell of abolitionism: "But of far greater moment, in retrospect, was the American Revolution. At an ideological level the revolution unleashed a heated debate about political representation, both at home and abroad . . . Almost without exception, radicals likened their own plight to that of slaves . . . In this way, slavery began to take on a more immediate significance, related to the political condition of thousands of native-born Britons."[111]

Whatever the moral, religious, political, or personal motivations which drew thousands to the antislavery party, they launched a propaganda campaign which between the 1780s and 1830s transformed the moral and physical representation of Black people. And the images which they disseminated as visual incitement to the opposition to slavery were so powerful that they leapt the Atlantic Ocean.

The most dramatic political expression of British popular support for the ending of the slave trade was the parliamentary petitions of 1788 and 1792. Oldfield informs us that there were three sorts of petitions: those which emanated from towns and boroughs (35 percent of petitions in 1788, 16 percent in 1792); those which originated in universities, guilds, presbyteries, and provincial synods (20 percent in 1788, 47 percent in 1792), and those which represented counties.[112] And the numbers of the petitioners, Oldfield reports, were "of quite staggering proportions." In Edinburgh, the figure for 1792 reached nearly 11,000; and in Manchester it ranged between 15,000 and 20,000, perhaps representing 50 percent of the male population.[113] Despite a victory in the

110. "To formulate a theory of costly international moral action the best case to study first is Great Britain's effort from 1807 to 1867 to suppress the Atlantic slave trade, because it has the most extreme value on the dependent variable: the most expensive international moral effort in modern history, with most of the cost paid by one country." Kaufmann and Pape, "Explaining Costly Action," 634.

111. Oldfield, *Popular Politics*, 32–33.

112. Ibid., 105–6.

113. Ibid., 114. Women were discouraged from signing petitions, but they did participate as authors, lecturers, and boycotters (the "antisaccharrites"). At its peak,

House of Commons, the campaign eventually foundered on the shoals of planter influence in the House of Lords and then, ironically, on the radical liberationist impulses set off by the French Revolution. A decade or more later, Parliament passed the Abolition Act of 1807, largely due to dramatic changes in the war against France, a new government, and the legislative maneuvers of William Wilberforce.[114] Nonetheless, popular agitation had induced a literary and visual culture in England which subverted the discourse of inferiority.

The "Saints" behind the abolition campaign in England were formally organized as the Committee for the Abolition of the Slave Trade, or simply the London Committee. The founding figures of the London Committee were middle-class: two bankers, four merchants, and two manufacturers. And nine of the twelve founders were Quakers, including Samuel Hoare, George Harrison, William Dillwyn, John Lloyd, and Joseph Woods. Their non-Quaker companions were Philip Sansom, Granville Sharp, and Thomas Clarkson.[115] For our concerns, the most exceptional figure was a subsequent member of the committee, Josiah Wedgwood, master potter, designer, and manufacturer (and Charles Darwin's grandfather). Wedgwood's entrepreneurial and artistic skills proved momentous:

> Wedgwood's knowledge and influence are discernible, above all, in the design of the London Committee's seal, adopted in October 1787, depicting a kneeling slave together with the motto "Am I not a Man and a Brother?" . . . the whole concept was brilliantly conceived, drawing on existing images of kneeling black figures as well as religious and secular belief in the equality of mankind. As Hugh Honour points out: it "neatly encapsulated ideas already widely accepted while giving them a more specific meaning."[116]

The seal was then reproduced, in the hundreds of thousands, in the forms of medallions, pendants, cameos, token pennies, halfpennies, and prints. And the following year, this image was powerfully complemented by a second image

---

some 300,000 families in England supported the boycott of West Indian sugar. Ibid., 139–41, 57.

114. Blackburn, *Overthrow of Colonial Slavery*, chap. 8.
115. Oldfield, *Popular Politics*, 42.
116. Ibid., 156.

in the form of the plan and sections of a slave ship . . . this simple design originated with William Elford and the members of the Plymouth committee in December 1788. Fashioned after the *Brooks* [*sic*] of Liverpool, the print depicted the lower deck of a slave ship, as if viewed from above, "with Slaves stowed on it, in the proportion of not quite one to a ton." The plan was accompanied by a crude representation of the London Committee's seal, together with the motto "Am I not a Man and a Brother?"[117]

These representations of Blacks, either in naturalist or allegorical style, would migrate across the Atlantic and become two of the dominant images of abolitionism in the United States. And in England, as Oldfield recounts, these depictions were augmented by paintings and engravings (for instance, George Morland's *Execrable Human Traffic*, 1788, and *African Hospitality*, 1791) which were reproduced in prints, books, children's literature, and a host of artifacts ranging from ceramics and rally banners to satirical cartoons.

The questions of slavery and the humanity of Africans were not merely contested in the moral, political, and popular arenas. And the certainty that many abolitionists brought into these terrains was most definitely affirmed by the tumultuous spectacles working themselves out in the West Indies. Beginning with the rebellion of the slaves in St. Domingue in 1791, and then the sweep of Caribbean revolts associated with French republicanism after 1796, example after example of Black nobility was paraded before the British public. Though Oldfield makes no mention of it, the subtexts of the French Revolution and the British government's attempt to stave off radical and revolutionary elements in Great Britain and Europe were the military adventures of the British forces in the West Indies. Robin Blackburn tells us that in 1796 "the British Cabinet [dispatched] a veritable armada to the West Indian theatre: nearly 100 ships and 30,000 men were assembled for this purpose . . . one of the largest ever to have crossed the Atlantic."[118] Their mis-

117. Ibid., 163, 165. Seymour Drescher reports, "the slave ship soon hung in homes throughout England . . . Two generations later an aging Birmingham orator movingly recalled how his social conscience had first been awakened when his father unrolled the picture of the slave ship before his gathered family." Drescher, *Capitalism and Antislavery*, 78.

118. Blackburn, *Overthrow of Colonial Slavery*, 231. By 1798, Blackburn adds, "total British losses in the Caribbean theatre were soon to reach 60,000. Disease had taken

sion was to safeguard those interests which over the next decade would accumulate something like 715,000 slaves in the British Caribbean.[119] These enterprises brought the British army, navy, and Westminster into direct conflict with slave insurrectionists in both the Lesser and Greater Antilles. And among the several Black rebels encountered by the tens of thousands of British soldiers and sailors on islands like Guadeloupe, St. Vincent, St. Lucia, and Grenada, there was no more heroic figure than that of St. Domingue's Toussaint L'Ouverture. And even before Toussaint's death in April 1803 as a prisoner of Napoleon in the Jura Mountains, Wordsworth had published a sonnet in the *Morning Post* of London (February 3, 1803) dedicated to him. Finally, in August 1833, following slave rebellions in Barbados (1816), Demerara (1823), and Jamaica (1831), massive petitions, domestic uprisings, and a substantial extension of the franchise, the Reform Parliament passed the Abolition of Slavery Bill. The English people, Lord Holland complained, had reached "a state of madness on the topick"; nonetheless, it was the planters and not the slaves who were awarded compensation.[120]

The icons of British abolitionism were almost immediately appropriated by abolitionists in the American republic. Phillip Lapsansky reports that in 1787 Ben Franklin, as president of the Pennsylvania Society for Promoting the Abolition of Slavery, corresponded with Wedgwood, informing him of the impact of the kneeling slave figure: "I have seen in their [viewers'] countenances such Mark of being affected by contemplating the Figure of the Suppliant . . . that I am persuaded it may have an Effect equal to that of the best written Pamphlet in procuring favour to those oppressed People." And just as quickly the cross-section of the *Brookes* joined other realistic representations of slavery ("depicting whippings and other punishments of slaves, slave auctions, separation

---

a heavy toll and military operations in St. Domingue had yielded very meagre results." Ibid., 239.

119. Ibid., 311. French and Spanish slave owners in the Caribbean possessed in the neighborhood of 175,000 each in 1804, according to Blackburn.

120. Ibid., 456–67. The planters received 20 million pounds compensation (almost full value) for their slaves; the slaves were decreed to serve six years of "apprenticeship" to their former masters. Of course, most planters continued to abuse their former slaves, flogging their "apprentices" and criminalizing their resistance. Ibid., 459ff. For the "Baptist War" in Jamaica, see Mary Reckord, "Jamaica Slave Rebellion of 1831"; for Barbados and Demerara, see Craton, "Proto-Peasant Revolts."

of slave families") in abolitionist propaganda.[121] But the presence (by official counts) of 1,776,562 Blacks in 1820 and 2,328,642 by 1830 substantially broadened the stratagems of American abolitionists. While they did petition and protest like their British counterparts, they could also more directly participate in the subversive activities of the slaves themselves. While moderate abolitionists organized schools for fugitive slaves and free Blacks and supported the Underground Railroad, the most radical of the Black and white abolitionists risked imprisonment and death by organizing "slave stealing" expeditions into the slave states, smuggling insurrectionary tracts like David Walker's 1829 *Appeal to the Coloured Citizens of the World* into slave communities, or as John Brown did in Kansas and at Harpers Ferry, conspiring with slaves in armed rebellions.[122]

Lapsansky assures us that the volume of antislavery propaganda grew to massive proportions in the 1830s: "In 1835, AASS [American Anti-Slavery Society] published over a million pieces of literature, a ninefold increase over previous years." In 1839, Marcus Wood reports, the abolitionists dared even to appropriate one of the most mundane texts from the slave-owners. In *American Slavery as It Is: Testimony of a Thousand Witnesses*, published by the American Anti-Slavery Society, Theodore Dwight Weld and the Grimke sisters extracted hundreds of newspaper advertisements of slave sales, notices for slave fugitives, confessional articles, and so on to produce "an organised literary collage, a catalogue of arbitrary suffering on an enormous scale."[123] A hundred thousand copies of the volume were sold in America. Borrowing, perhaps, from the commercial use of Black icons of the previous century, the graphic representations of Blacks not only multiplied but diversified as well:

> Rolling off the presses primarily in New York, Boston, and Philadelphia were illustrated books and tracts, lithographed prints, and

---

121. Phillip Lapsansky, "Graphic Discord," 203.

122. For a summary of the radical abolitionists' activities, see Robinson, *Black Movements in America*, chap. 3. Of particular interest among the voluminous studies of abolitionists are Quarles, *Black Abolitionists*; Filler, *Crusade against Slavery*; Oates, *To Purge This Land with Blood*; Harrold, "John Brown's Forerunners"; and McKivigan, "James Redpath." Two new works extend the work of Quarles (Goodman, *Of One Blood*, and Jeffrey, *Great Silent Army*).

123. Phillip Lapsansky, "Graphic Discord," 202; Marcus Wood, *Blind Memory*, 84.

broadsheets with woodcuts; monthly periodicals such as the *Anti-Slavery Reporter*, the *Anti-Slavery Record*, and the *Slave's Friend*; annual almanacs; and a wide variety of printed ephemera, including candy wrappers, envelope stickers, song sheets, and stationery. In addition there were the newspapers; best known are the *Emancipator*, the *Anti-Slavery Standard*, the *Friend of Man*, the *Anti-Slavery Bugle*, the *Pennsylvania Freeman*, and William Lloyd Garrison's paper, the *Liberator*.[124]

Coupled with the astounding proliferation of antislavery societies (in 1827, of the 130 slave societies, 106 were in slave states),[125] the sheer audacity and apparently undeterrable stream of antislavery propaganda and the frequent occurrence of actual slave revolts compelled a proslavery counterattack. It was at this moment in the struggle over slavery that many of the caricatures of Blacks which would dominate American film came into existence.

Imagined Blacks: Negro Gentry, Mulattos, Mammies, etc.

One of the first subjects for graphic ridicule was the free Black middle-class residents of Boston and Philadelphia.[126] The historian Emma Jones Lapsansky suggests why Black Philadelphians might have attracted particular attention: "Between 1820 and 1830, the black population of Philadelphia grew by a third, from about 10,000 to about 15,000. And it's in that period that you begin to get tension around race in the city. Philadelphia had at that point the largest, most aggressive, and wealthiest free black population in the western world."[127] Another and related factor was that the principal antiabolitionist lithographers, as far as Phillip Lapsansky is concerned,[128] were Philadelphia natives: James Thackera (1767–1848), Edward W. Clay (1798–1857), and David Claypoole Johnston (1799–1865). And all of them possessed a kind of creative genius. In terms of caricatures, Clay, who was admitted

124. Phillip Lapsansky, "Graphic Discord," 202.

125. Filler, *Crusade against Slavery*, 18.

126. For a more accurate reconstruction of the Black Philadelphia community, see Blockson, *African Americans in Pennsylvania*.

127. Emma Jones Lapsansky speaking on Philadelphia in *Africans in America*, part 3, WGBH-Boston, <http://www.pbs.org/wgbh/aia/part3/3i3116.html>.

128. Phillip Lapsansky is chief of reference for the Library Company of Philadelphia.

Edward W. Clay, "A Dead Cut," 1829. The Library Company of Philadelphia.

to the bar but preferred art as a career, was by far the most vicious and imaginative. Johnston, on the other hand, who took to the stage for some five years to escape from his sometimes powerful critics, was by far the most talented and the best remembered. And, of course, he was the only one of the three to survive long enough to see the fruits of his affection for the planter South. Johnston's physical depictions of Blacks were consistent with his representations of non-Blacks; but his ridicule associated urban Blacks with the same social breaches (drunkenness, petty crimes, mimicry of betters, etc.) that Thackera imagined. Phillip Lapsansky documents that Thackera was employing (or had invented) the dandified coon in etchings by 1819. In his sketchbook, Thackera expounded on how "the Black gentry aping their masters, dress quite as extravagantly, and frequently wear their clothes, long before they are cast off. They not only ape the dress of their masters, but also their cant terms, being well versed in the fashionable vocabulary."[129]

Next came the series of etchings by Clay entitled *Life in Philadelphia* (1828–30). The majority of the surviving plates are Clay's renderings of Black subjects, whose number now reached something like 15,000. Clay's series coincided with the emergence of racial violence in Philadelphia. In 1899, W. E. B. Du Bois reported: "So intense was the race antipathy among the lower classes, and so much countenance did it received from the middle and upper class, that there began, in 1829, a series of riots directed chiefly against Negroes, which recurred frequently until about 1840, and did not wholly cease until after the [Civil] war."[130] Unlike Thackera, whose dandies differed from whites principally in dress and the use of hyperbole in language, Clay employed an invented Black dialect for his subjects, distorted their faces in a manner which anticipates minstrelsy, and etched their bodies to approach simian proportions. Hugh Honour informs us that Clay published his fourteen anti-Black etchings after his return from Europe, probably inspired by Pierce Egan's *Life in London* (1820–21). "Frivolity in dress was of course repugnant to the Quakers of Philadelphia, and dueling still more so. But there is also a strong social element in Clay's images of blacks adopting the finery, the airs, and graces of affluent whites. The barbs of his satire passed through the fancy clothes to hit the bodies inside."[131] Nonetheless, Clay was still attracting influential admirers a hundred years later. In 1933, William Murrell praised *Back to Back* (a dancing Black couple): "It is acute in observation, excellent in drawing, and will stand comparison with anything of its kind done since."[132] It would appear, as Emma Jones Lapsansky has suggested elsewhere, that the very success of this Black middle class was a catalyst for hostility in an earlier and later America.[133] Whatever the case, in the first half of the nineteenth century, far beyond the confines of Philadelphia, imagined Black freemen and even foreign dignitaries (Haitian, Nicaraguan) were assigned pompous dress and an inane dialect by lithographers

129. Phillip Lapsansky, "Graphic Discord," 217–18. For the extraordinary career of Thackera (engraver, politician, prison builder, and a founder of the Columbianum Art Academy), see Crompton, "James Thackera, Engraver."

130. Du Bois, *Philadelphia Negro*, 26–27.

131. Honour, *Image of the Black in Western Art*, vol. 4, pt. 2, 58.

132. Murrell, *History of American Graphic Humor*, 110.

133. Emma Jones Lapsansky, "'Since They Got Churches,'" 75.

parodying Black ambitions for equality and the abolitionists' desire for slavery's end.[134]

Though it is still uncertain when the attribution of this manufactured dialect to Blacks first occurred, scholars commonly claim that Charles Matthews (1776–1835) imported it to England and popularized it in 1822. Matthews, whom Herbert Marshall and Mildred Stock describe as "the most famous of English comedians and monologists," used it to parody the Black tragedian James Hewlett's *Richard III*.[135] Sam Dennison, however, points out that elements of the invention were present as early as 1767 in the colonies (Andrew Barton's ballad opera *The Disappointment; or, The Force of Credulity*) and in England a year later (Charles Dibdin's opera *The Padlock*). In popular culture and performance, the dialect appears then to be at least as old as the last half of the eighteenth century, though using its absence in Thomas Southerne's *Oroonoko* (1695) is not a certain marker, since this work is dramatic rather than comedic.[136]

134. For the Black "emperor" of Nicaragua and the Haitian ambassador, see the two 1839 etchings published by H. R. Robinson (a New York–based printer) in Murrell, *History of American Graphic Humor*, 151. Murrell also draws attention to another antiabolitionist work, *A Dream Caused by the Perusal of Mrs. H. Beecher Stowe's Popular Work Uncle Tom's Cabin* (1855), published by R. Milne of Louisville, Kentucky. Murrell describes it as "quite the most grotesque allegory published in the ante bellum period." Ibid., 196. Allan Nevins and Frank Weitenkampf reprint and when possible identify other antiabolitionist lithographers who used more naturalism in their graphic representations of Blacks while employing the iconic dialect. See the anonymous Boston cartoon "Slavery in America . . . in England" (1850) and Louis Maurer's "The Great Republican Reform Party Calling on Their Candidate" (1856), in Nevins and Weitenkampf, *Century of Political Cartoons*, 68, 76.

135. Marshall and Stock, *Ira Aldridge*, 30. After Aldridge's arrival in London in 1825 and his performance as Oroonoko, Matthews began to insist that it was Aldridge (1807–67) and not Hewlett he was imitating. Since Matthews visited the African Theatre in 1821, this would have been when Aldridge was thirteen or fourteen! Ibid., 40ff.

136. Dennison, *Scandalize My Name*, 4–9. Dennison also effectively criticizes Charles Matthews's claims of authentically impersonating the Black voice; see ibid., appendix 1, 512ff. Southerne's play was adapted from Aphra Benn's novella (1688). To the degree to which the dialect was associated with West African Pidgin English, as Robert McCrum et al. maintain, it was "borrowed from the sailors" who manned the slave ships. Black Pidgin English was also related to Sabir, the commercial and maritime language used in the Mediterranean from around the sixteenth century. See McCrum, Cran, and MacNeil, *Story of English*, chap. 6.

PRACTICAL AMALGAMATION.

Edward W. Clay, "Practical Amalgamation," 1839.
The Library Company of Philadelphia.

Dennison also suggests that Black soldiers fighting on the British side were targets of ridicule in songs and sheet music even earlier than the urban Black middling class. Two such instances are Micah Hawkins's *Backside Albany* (1815) and *Massa Georgee Washington and General La Fayette* (1824):

> The ambivalence in attitude toward the black in popular song began to disappear in the second decade of the nineteenth century, to be replaced by pointed reference to him as an object of humor. Songs reflected the hardening attitudes of whites, contributing to the virtual extinction of reality concerning the institution of slavery. Common stereotypes were established which obliterated the true black image. These stereotypes became so entrenched in the white mind

that no amount of logic could muster the strength required to sup-
plant them.[137]

Dennison is a bit over the top here with his assertion of a "white mind"
being pummeled into a racial submission, but his documentation does
make a less dramatic point: a concerted campaign sympathetic to
slavery appeared to be employing mass forms of culture (sheet music,
songs, operas, graphic illustrations) to produce a new racial consensus.

In the three decades prior to the Civil War, the propaganda wars between the supporters of slavery and the abolitionists produced three
enduring Black signs: the mulatta (and the mulatto), the tom, and the
buck. Paradoxically, despite their later appropriation by the incipient
American film industry as signs of an anti-Negro cinema, their origins
were in the abolitionist camp. From Richard Hildreth's novel *The Slave*
(1836) to Dion Boucicault's *The Octoroon; or, Life in Louisiana* (an 1859
dramatization of Captain Mayne Reid's romance, *The Quadroon; or, A
Lover's Adventures in Louisiana*, 1856), dozens of novels and plays centered on the "mixed-race" figure who served as a fictive chiaroscuro
through which the tragedy of slavery could be sentimentally experienced by white readers and playgoers.[138] The most spectacular and
influential representation of mixed-race slaves was Harriet Beecher
Stowe's *Uncle Tom's Cabin; or, Life among the Lowly*. Originally published serially in the *National Era*, the Free-Soil Party's weekly organ,
Stowe's work ran for forty installments, from June 5, 1851, to April 1,
1852, bolstering the *Era*'s support for abolition and emigration.[139] As
soon as the series finished, *Uncle Tom's Cabin* was published as a book
in March 1852. In that year three hundred thousand copies were sold
and the first of innumerable stage adaptations appeared. Almost rivaling the sales of the Bible, *Uncle Tom's Cabin* was the most popular work

137. Dennison, *Scandalize My Name*, 30.

138. See Roach, "Slave Spectacles"; and Bentley, "White Slaves."

139. "The *National Era* . . . termed the presence of the Negro race an 'inconve-
nience,' supported voluntary black emigration to Africa or to public land in the
United States, and complained that 'the real evil of the Negro race' was that they were
'so fit for slavery'—though the paper was equally capable of criticizing the prejudice
of some former New York Democrats within the Free-Soil party." Eric Lott, *Love and
Theft*, 209.

of American fiction in the nineteenth century.[140] During the silent-film era, beginning in 1903, ten feature film adaptations were produced (and perhaps hundreds of short-feature parodies), and the work was revisited numerous times during the sound era. Nearly all the adaptations on stage and screen downplayed or eliminated Stowe's miscegenation themes.

On the heels of the death of her sixth child (1849) and the Fugitive Slave Law of 1851, Stowe constructed an abolitionist tract which privileged the power of mother-love and Christian stoicism. Stowe was persuaded that her depictions of slave mothers in her melodrama would excite abolitionist activism in sympathy for Black, and particularly whitelike, women condemned to the theft of their children under slave law. Her second ideological device was to construct Christlike characters whose deaths foreground the moral contradictions between slavery and Christianity. While Uncle Tom and Little Eva were the embodiments of Christian forbearance, Eliza and her mother, Cassie, were the dominant figures among the several sacrificing women characters Stowe invented. Eliza, a quadroon, dramatizes the tragedy of slave mothers threatened with separation from their children. Unlike most slave mothers, Eliza successfully escapes to Canada with her son, both relying on their light complexions to occasionally pass for white.[141] Cassie, a mulatta raised by her slave-owning father, suffers a worse fate. Once her father unexpectedly dies, Cassie is hurled into the unforgiving traffic of human property. At first protected by slave-owner lovers, Cassie is eventually abandoned and experiences the sale of her first two children (one of whom is Eliza). Later facing a repetition of that anguish, she poisons her third child. While Uncle Tom is the principal tragic figure of the melodrama (he dies from a severe beating by Simon Legree), the most heroic character in the novel is George Harris, Eliza's husband. A mulatto, George coincidentally makes his escape for Canada, outraged by the degrad-

140. See ibid., 211–12.
141. Eliza flees slavery in Kentucky by crossing the partially frozen Ohio River. With her young son in her arms, she leaps along floating ice cakes which shred her shoes and bloody her feet. D. W. Griffith, not content with appropriating the mulatta as the sexual neurotic who precipitates the Civil War (*The Birth of a Nation*, 1915), borrowed the harrowing flight sequence in Stowe for the ice-hopping scene with Lillian Gish in *Way Down East* (1920).

ing treatment by his slave owner, who resents George for his intelligence, his prideful behavior, and the respect shown him as an artisan by other whites. With his family, George eventually emigrates to Liberia. "The desire and yearning of my soul is for an African *nationality*," he writes. "I want a people that shall have a tangible, separate existence of its own."[142]

An identification with the slave may have been a rhetorical maneuver of particular importance for abolitionist propaganda in the turmoil of the 1830s and afterwards. The American Colonization Society's (ACS) adjuncts had proliferated like cancer across the Northern and Southern states and Western territories: the first ACS had been established in 1816; by 1819, there were 14 in the country; by 1832, there were 251.[143] The support for a program of deporting free Blacks to Canada, the West Indies, or Africa was widespread, but clearly as a support of slavery rather than otherwise. Removing free Blacks from the country would certainly diminish the moral, symbolic, and political resources of the abolitionist movement. The popularity of this new stratagem for the preservation of slavery alarmed abolitionists, exciting them to new levels of activism. In turn, the proslavery forces began resorting to violence. While in the South, Blacks were the principal victims, elsewhere, Leonard Richards recalls, the purge crossed racial lines:

> Northerners dragged the antislavery agitator William Lloyd Garrison through the streets of Boston in 1835; broke up a convention of the New York State Anti-Slavery Society at Utica on the same day; petitioned in 1835 and 1836 for legislation to make the propagation of abolitionist sentiments a criminal offense; supplied the necessary votes to pass the famous gag rule which was renewed at each session of Congress between 1836 and 1844; established the Connecticut gag law in 1836 to bar abolitionist lecturers from Congregational pulpits;

---

142. Stowe, *Uncle Tom's Cabin*, 527. In her 1856 work, *Dred: A Tale of the Great Dismal Swamp*, Stowe portrays the white Christian opposition to slavery as enfeebled and emasculated. She revives the slave rebellion led by Denmark Vessey (1822) by inventing an heir, his son Dred. Dred, whose Christian zeal is messianic, is joined in the Dismal Swamp by Harry Gordon, a mulatto, and together they conspire towards another slave uprising. Stowe appended to this work the court record of Nat Turner's slave rebellion (1831) and other materials substantiating her fictional representations of the torture and murdering of slaves.

143. Adams, *Neglected Period of Anti-Slavery*, 106.

murdered the abolitionist editor Elijah Lovejoy at Alton, Illinois, in 1837; burned down Pennsylvania Hall in Philadelphia in 1836.[144]

Though mob violence focused on other issues (e.g., the Mormons) during the 1830s, more than half of the 105 violent mobs Richards reviewed were antiabolitionist.[145] And as the title of Richards's book suggests, the American Colonization Society and the mobs were organized and led by men of "property and standing" whose defense of slavery and Negrophobia drove them to extreme measures.

According to Edward Reuter in an early study of the question, for the historical period under review in this book mulattos were officially enumerated in the U.S. census in 1850 (11.2 percent of 3,638,808 Blacks), 1860 (13.2 percent of 4,441,830), 1870 (12 percent of 4,880,009), 1890 (15.2 percent of 7,488,676), and 1910 (20.9 percent of 9,827,763).[146] Writing in 1918 (and by that time the mulatto had been appropriated by Negrophobes), Reuter acknowledged that although most mulattos of the slave era had been produced as bastards, it was clear to him that among the relatively few intermarriages between Blacks and whites, there seemed to be "absolutely no evidence of any marriages of a mixed sort in which the white contracting party was not of the lowest and usually of a vicious class."[147] For the males of the slave-owning classes who sexually exploited Black women, Reuter ambiguously conceded the existence of such affairs ("The habit, though not common, was not unusual") but reserved judgment.[148] But he struck repeatedly at the Black women. The use of force had not been an issue, Reuter asserted; indeed, with no evidence he insisted, "to the girl it was, in the great majority of cases, a matter of being honored by a white man."[149] Reuter, of course, was instantiating a contemptuous fiction, and most of those living in the Old South were fully aware of what more recent research has confirmed. As Peter Bardaglio has observed, "This attempt to place the responsibility for race-mixing onto the shoulders of blacks, how-

144. Leonard L. Richards, *"Gentlemen of Property and Standing,"* 3.

145. Leonard Richards recounts that the "three leading anti-slavery newspapers," the *Liberator,* the *Emancipator,* and the *Philanthropist,* reported 209 Northern anti-abolitionist mobs during the 1830s and 1840s. Ibid., 14–15.

146. Reuter, *Mulatto in the United States,* 118.

147. Ibid., 131.

148. Ibid., 176n25.

149. Ibid., 140.

ever, could not disguise the extent to which white men imposed their sexual desires on slave women."[150]

Reuter's evil apology for exploitation (a University of Chicago Department of Sociology dissertation!) gives us a glimpse of what the mulatta/o would become in the hands of the racist at the beginnings of the twentieth century. We will have more to say on the subject when we investigate the influences of antimiscegenationists like Thomas Dixon and D. W. Griffith. But eighty years earlier, when the icon was a piece of the abolitionist insurgency, the mulatto, more specifically the mulatta, had constituted an attempt to signify the humanity of the slave. And through the artifice of the mulatta's resemblance to a white woman, the icon also raised the moral stock of the Black woman. The mulatta displaced the Jezebel, the Black, amoral seductress already present in Southern white consciousness, marketing a mixture of tragedy, white aesthetics, and romance in lieu of the image of Black female depravity, adultery, and social ostracism.[151] Defending this mechanism against "modern pro-Negro commentators," Jules Zanger referred to the propaganda value embedded in the construct of the "tragic octoroon" (or quadroon, or mulatta), which condemned the slaveholders for the prostitution of Black women and the marketing of their own children. "Wendell Phillips, for example," Zanger notes, "called the South 'One great brothel, where half a million women are flogged to prostitution,' and George Bourne spoke of the South as a 'vast harem where menstealers may prowl, corrupt, and destroy.'"[152]

The Civil War and its attendant events precipitated its own spasms

150. Bardaglio, "'Shamefull Matches,'" 117. See also Hodes, *White Women, Black Men*, chaps. 3–4; Clinton, *Plantation Mistress*, 209–10; and Bynum, *Unruly Women*, 41–45.

151. Betty Wood cites a series of articles referring to the Jezebel stereotype which appeared in the *Savannah Republican* in 1817, in "White Women, Black Slaves." For a discussion of the reappearance of the Jezebel, see Manring, *Slave in a Box*, 21ff.

152. Zanger, "'Tragic Octoroon,'" 67. Zanger indicates the commentators to whom he was responding: "[Robert] Bone, for example, writes 'Such novels . . . contain mulatto characters for whom the reader's sympathies are aroused less because they are colored than because they are nearly white.' [Hugh] Gloster describes the antislavery writers as 'sympathetic toward the Negro-white hybrid because of his possession of Caucasian blood, which they often consider a factor that automatically made this character the superior of the darker Negro and therefore a more pitiable individual.' Sterling Brown describes the octoroon as 'a concession, unconscious perhaps, to race snobbishness even among abolitionists.'" Ibid., 64.

of racist propaganda and grotesque Black caricatures. The elections of 1860 and 1864, the initiation of the war itself, Union defeats in 1861 and 1862, the Emancipation Proclamation, the official admission of Black troops into the Union army, and the passage of legislation authorizing the Freedmen's Bureau were some of the most dramatic moments which occasioned anti-Black broadsides. In the Northern and loyal slave states, Copperheads, members of the radical racist wing of the Democratic Party, employed as journalists, lecturers, preachers, songsters, pamphleteers, and publishers (like Bromley and Company, Kimmel and Foster, and A. Zenneck) amused themselves at the expense of the Republican Party, President Lincoln, and Blacks. The Copperhead press—newspapers like the *New York World*, the *New York Daily News*, the *New York Weekly Day Book*, the *Albany Atlas and Argus*, the *Washington Evening Union*, the *Philadelphia Age*, the *Detroit Free Press*, the *Columbus Crisis*, the *Cleveland Plain Dealer*, the *Cincinnati Enquirer*, the *Chicago Times*, the *Indianapolis State Sentinel*—fantasized in print on Lincoln's and the Republicans' "Negrophilia." Their editors feasted on putative Republican conspiracies to emancipate the slaves, promote race equality, mobilize a mass Black migration to the North, and encourage "miscegenation."[153] There was, however, one saving grace. As Forrest Wood observes:

> Although the racist demagogues were a vociferous and prolific group, they did not produce most of the political propaganda of the 1860's. In terms of total wartime literary output, their contribution was relatively small, and they remained a distinct and often hopeless minority. It is doubtful that America has ever witnessed an era of such vast pamphlet production. Led by the Union League movement, war supporters produced an unprecedented quantity of patriotic literature, most of which did not mention the Negro at all.[154]

If war, abolitionists, and Unionists won the day, it was a momentary triumph over Negrophobia. The legacy of the Copperheads would be revived with a vengeance during the final quarter of the century, eventually absorbing state and national institutions well into the twentieth century.

153. See Forrest Wood, *Black Scare*, chap. 2; and Paludan, *"A People's Contest,"* 95–96.

154. Forrest Wood, *Black Scare*, 38.

The secret to the Copperheads' later propaganda victory can in part be attributed to the extraordinarily vivid Black images and icons invented or revived during the Civil War. The "sexually aggressive and dishonest 'Zip Coon' . . . the violent 'Nat the Brute'" would become fixtures in American literature, American historiography, and American newspapers. These were the Black caricatures most essential to the sexual frenzy which dominated Copperhead angst. In late 1863, Forrest Wood reports, David Goodman Croly and George Wakeman of the *New York World* anonymously counterfeited an "abolitionist" pamphlet they entitled *Miscegenation: The Theory of the Blending of the Races, Applied to the American White Man and Negro*. Proposing that "If any fact is well established in history, it is that the miscegenetic or mixed races are much superior mentally, physically, and morally, to those pure or unmixed," Croly and Wakeman coined the term "miscegenation" as a replacement for the milder and simpler term "amalgamation," so frequently employed to designate race-mixing.[155] On the latter score they were wildly successful. John H. Van Evrie (of the *New York Weekly Day Book*) had proposed his own alternative to amalgamation in his pamphlet *Subjenation: The Theory of the Normal Relation of the Races; An Answer to "Miscegenation"* (1864), but like his other literary and journalistic ventures, his objectives were subverted, either by the fanaticism of his version of white supremacy or by his overworked language ("The equality of all who God has created equal [white men], and the inequality of those He has made unequal [Negroes and other inferior races], is the cornerstone of American Democracy and the vital principle of American civilization and human progress").[156]

Ironically, while part of the argument against "miscegenation" was based on the natural repulsion that white women were said to experience in close contact with the Negro male (according to the *Daily News*, in March 1864, a woman would find that "the negro's body is disagreeably unctious, especially in warm weather, and when under the influence of the strong 'emotional' excitement . . . if permitted . . . to lay lascivious hands upon her"), another, but contradictory, fear was the attraction that white women felt for Black men.[157] For this latter hor-

155. Ibid., 55.
156. Ibid., 58. The *Day Book* was originally named *The Caucasian*. For this and Van Evrie's other unfortunate ventures into racist publication, see ibid., 35–36.
157. Ibid., 62–63.

ror, the Copperheads revived Othello. To be sure, for close to fifty years, on the English and American stages, Shakespeare's Othello had been "orientalized." Beginning, probably, with the performances of Edmund Kean in 1814 and continued by Gustavus V. Brooke (1848) and Tommaso Salvini (1875), Othello had been transformed into a "white" Moor, not black but brown.[158] Only Ira Aldridge's dramatizations of the part, from 1826 to the late 1860s, had ruptured the emerging certainty that Shakespeare had never contemplated a Negro.[159] But for the Copperheads, Othello was indeed black. In March 1864, with the Twentieth Regiment of Colored Volunteers' departure from New York, the *World* was not amused by the Union League Club's enthusiastic send-off, according to Forrest Wood: "What a spectacle, the editor exclaimed, to see fair maidens waving white kerchiefs from Union Square and offering their love and honor 'to a regiment of hypothetical Othellos, marching on their way to possible glory in bran-new [*sic*] uniforms, with white gaiters, beneath a spic-and-span silken banner, embroidered by . . . fair white hands!'"[160] The *Philadelphia Age*, two months later, was just as sanguine about the departing of the First Illinois Colored Regiment: "White women were there in attendance to bid farewell to black husbands, around whose necks they clung long and fondly."[161] And the Democratic National Committee, later that year, reminded voters that it was a Republican who had recently referred to "the brave Othellos of the South [who] would come North and claim their fair Desdemonas."[162]

158. Hankey, *Othello*, 57, 73. For the American counterparts to Kean and so on, particularly Edwin Forrest and Edwin Booth as Othello, see Kris Collins, "White-Washing the Black-a-Moor," 90ff. Early in the nineteenth century, Black American thespians had been forbidden to perform Shakespeare. The first Black American theater company, the African Theatre of New York City, was founded by Henry Brown in 1821, following upon popular entertainments organized by Brown, a merchant seaman, in 1816–17. The company was taken into custody by twelve city watchmen. According to the *American* (January 10, 1822), "Finally they plead so hard in blank verses, and promised never to act Shakespeare again, that the Police Magistrates released them at a very late hour." Marshall and Stock, *Ira Aldridge*, 36. The company originally included Anne Johnson, James Hewlett (a talented singer but whose principal acting fare was *Richard III*), and later a very young Ira Aldridge. Ibid., 31ff.

159. Marshall and Stock, *Ira Aldridge*, 52.

160. Forrest Wood, *Black Scare*, 42. For a history of the founding of the regiment, see Lorini, *Rituals of Race*, chap. 1.

161. Forrest Wood, *Black Scare*, 43.

162. Ibid., 65. For the Southern origins of the majority of the more than 200,000

Underlining the sexual hysteria were the grotesque simian caricatures of Black men ("Black Ourang-Outangs" was a frequent jest) which decorated their broadsides and pamphlets. Such brutes could only resort to "spells and medicines," as Brabantio surmised of Othello, or failing in that, committed savage outrages against white women.

The national struggle over slavery did not end with the Civil War or with the subsequent legal abolition of American slavery. In the last third of the nineteenth century, the ideological struggle over the nature and remembrance of the old regime of slavery intersected with forging new fetters for free Black labor. Racial constructs seduced and socialized European immigrants and unprivileged whites, and labor hierarchies insured substantial consent from organized white labor. But Black observance of the new rules of exploitation was patrolled by terror and intimidation: the Black codes, disfranchisement, apartheid, the convict lease system, peonage, and the advent of lynch law later historians associated with the New South. At the time, as we shall see, some Black critics of the post-Reconstruction period more accurately suggested the new oppression should be credited to the conditions of national reconciliation dictated by capital. In 1893, two years before his death, Frederick Douglass, the former slave, wrote:

> It must be admitted that, to outward seeming, the colored people of the United States have lost ground and have met with increased and galling resistance since the war of the rebellion. It is well to understand this phase of the situation. Considering the important services rendered by them in suppressing the late rebellion and the saving of the Union, they were for a time generally regarded with a sentiment of gratitude by their loyal white fellow citizens. This sentiment however, very naturally became weaker as, in the course of events, those services were retired from view and the memory of them became dimmed by time and also by the restoration of friendship between the north and the south. Thus, what the colored people gained by the war they have partly lost by the peace.[163]

There had been a deliberateness among American capitalists in the forfeiture of Reconstruction and the conspiracy in racialism. In 1877, the

---

Blacks who served in the Union army and navy, see Robinson, *Black Movements in America*, 76ff.; and Nalty, *Strength for the Fight*, chap. 3.

163. Douglass, introduction, 13–14.

Commercial and Financial Chronicle of New York had published the announcement: "This year, labor is under control for the first season since the war."[164] In consequence, as Eric Foner reports, "the vast majority of Southerners of both races sank deeper and deeper into poverty."[165] This better explains why so many poor whites (and Asians and Latinos) were placed under or threatened by cultural and social disciplines identical to those facing Blacks.

One of the political penalties of legal emancipation was the unraveling of the abolitionist coalition. This brought progressive and moderate Black elites to the fore in the defense of Black equality. Abandoned by the old white abolitionists, many of whom had been ambivalent towards notions of racial equality, Black political notables and the Black intelligentsia were forced to confront the constantly changing racial terrain of the cultural wars. The supporters of the slave regime had more continuity and more resources. And with their manufacture of the Lost Cause ideological movement, they re-created the Old South in mythic terms, inviting the national culture to indulge in the idea that slavery constituted a racial utopia. In that just order where the races had been deposed by nature to superior and subordinate statuses, certain lessons were to be derived from the chaos concomitant with the unnatural and the tranquility ensuing the natural. Thus the mulatta was appropriated from her origins as an abolitionist figure and transposed into the Jezebel. Complementing the mulatta as an icon of chaos was the "Zip Coon." But even more powerful in the cultural war was the "mammy," the emblem of natural order.

Recent research has confirmed that the mammy was almost entirely invented from whole cloth. She appears, for certain, in the post–Civil War memoirs and novels of writers attempting to reclaim the memory of the Old South; but she is almost entirely absent from the oral histories of former slaves recorded by the Federal Writers' Project in the 1930s. Jessie W. Parkhurst first exposed the fictional sources and equally fictive characteristics attributed to the mammy in her 1938 article, "The Role of the Black Mammy in the Plantation Household."[166] Nearly fifty years later, Catherine Clinton confirmed Parkhurst's find-

164. Quoted in Foner, *Reconstruction*, 596.
165. Ibid.
166. Parkhurst, "Role of the Black Mammy," cited in Thurber, "Development of the Mammy Image," 93.

ings: "The Mammy was created by white Southerners to redeem the relationship between black women and white men within slave society in response to the antislavery attack from the North during the antebellum era, and to embellish it with nostalgia in the post-bellum period. In the primary records from before the Civil War, hard evidence for her existence simply does not appear."[167] And in timing the appearances of the mammy, Cheryl Thurber concludes from her review of the principle sources of white Southern writings, that "references to mammy in the *Confederate Veteran* magazine, American popular songs, memoirs, and fiction confirm that more was written about the mammy at the turn of the century than during the antebellum period, the Civil War, or Reconstruction. The real expansion of the mammy mythology coincided with Progressivism, the New South movement, and the later phases of the Confederate Lost Cause movement."[168] The mammy icon served as a means of retrieval of the Old South, but it also functioned as an oppositional icon to the mulatta as well as a complementary construction to the Southern belle.

The mammy icon functioned as a buttress to the utopian construction of the imagined Old South. The mammy confirmed the notion that in the Old South and the New South, race relations were mediated by nurturing love and kindness. The icon—middle-aged or older, overweight, de-eroticized Black woman—negated the rape of Black women by white men, transferring the responsibility for hundreds of thousands of mixed-race individuals to the Black rapist. Thurber reminds us that Herbert Gutman, in his *The Black Family in Slavery and Freedom, 1750–1925*, had concluded that "most black domestic workers in white households were young single women," and that William Alexander Percy, in his memoir *Lanterns on the Levee* (1941), had described his mammy accordingly: "Nain was sixteen, divinely café-au-lait."[169] In reality, rather than the perverted mythology, this sexually charged circumstance had predictable outcomes. As Darlene Clark Hine has observed, "Virtually every known nineteenth-century female slave narrative contains a reference to, at some juncture, the ever-present threat and reality of rape."[170] But the mammy icon displaced the Harriet

167. Clinton, *Plantation Mistress*, 89.
168. Thurber, "Development of the Mammy Image," 95.
169. Ibid., 90, 106.
170. Darlene Clark Hine, "Rape and the Inner Lives of Southern Black Women," in Bernhard et al., *Southern Women*, 179.

Jacobses, the Elizabeth Keckleys, and the Nains. And in their place was constructed the Southern belle, the beautiful, childlike, white female who incited the lust of Black men. This fantastic crime rationalized the lynching of Black males, transfiguring political violence (intimidation of Black voters, disfranchisement) into acts of moral justice. And as Thurber notes, the popularity of the icons of the mammy and the Southern belle reached their heights simultaneously during the early twentieth century.[171]

It was, of course, Aunt Jemima who would have the greatest import for Black representation in the American public sphere of the nineteenth and twentieth centuries. Originating sometime around 1875 in the lyrics and music of Billy Kersands, a Black minstrel, acrobat, and composer, Jemima would be transferred from Black minstrelsy to blackface minstrelsy and eventually to the mass production of national brands and food processing (Quaker Oats, National Biscuit Company, Proctor and Gamble), retail packaging, household consumption, and mass advertising.[172] As the trade name for a premixed pancake preparation (and, for a time, the brand name of the milling company), Jemima's extraordinary success as a promotional icon in mass consumption became the forerunner for the commercial exploitation of Black imagery. Cream of Wheat's Uncle Rastus, Uncle Remus maple syrup, Uncle Ben's Rice, Gold Dust washing powder's twin pickanninies, and hundreds of other ante- and postbellum Black images adorned cans, boxes, bags, and newspaper advertisements for products as diverse as shoe polish, toothpaste, fruits, tobacco, ice creams, and services.[173] Black servitude or slave labor became the signifiers of class comfort and race privilege.

As we will make clear below when discussing the popularization of race science, it was of singular significance that the actual launching of Aunt Jemima (and the Gold Dust twins) occurred at the Chicago World's Columbian Exposition of 1893. For the fair, the pancake

171. "Although memoirs that mentioned the mammy appeared throughout the period from the 1890s to the end of the 1920s, the number of references to mammy increased from about 1906 to 1912, which was the peak time for the glorification of mammy." Thurber, "Development of the Mammy Image," 96. "The ideal of the Southern belle also flourished, for example in popular songs, between 1905 and 1918." Ibid., 97.

172. See Manring, *Slave in a Box*, chap. 3.

173. Pieterse, *White on Black*, 154ff.

mix's promoters had hired Nancy Green, a slave-born Kentuckian, to impersonate Aunt Jemima. Performing in front of a booth designed to look like a giant flour barrel, Green cooked pancakes, sang songs, told stories, and enthralled her white audiences:

> Aunt Jemima's debut was a smashing success. Crowds jammed the exhibit, waiting for a glimpse of her, and "I'se in town, honey" [the caption for a souvenir button] became a catchphrase. Fair officials awarded the "pancake queen" a medal, and [R. T. Davis of the Davis Milling Company] claimed that merchants who had attended the fair placed more than fifty thousand orders for his pancake mix. But more importantly, the persona of Aunt Jemima had proved to sell a lot of pancakes. Green, whose more pleasant face had replaced the hideous mammy on [the] original logo, began participating in sales promotions across the country.[174]

Though complemented by regional surrogates, Green would dominate the performance of Aunt Jemima until her death in 1923. By then her own biography and the fiction of Jemima had long been merged by the corporate and historical reconstructions of the origins of Jemima. But hers was merely a particle of the fictionalizations of race, blackness, and American history whose appearances would come to dominate American popular culture.

The Best Science Money Could Buy

Contrary to broadly received opinion, scientific thought is not transcendent; it exists within historical and cultural matrices. On this score, science is consistent with all other arenas of knowledge. The historical and cultural embeddedness of science is implicitly consented to when we refer to distinctive discursive scientific practices as medieval science or modern science, Chinese science, Islamic science, or Western science, and the like. These signifiers amount to admissions that the most powerful economic, political, and cultural impulses of a social structure impose themselves as codes and desires on the conduct, organization, and imagination of scientists. In his book *The Structure of Scientific Revolutions* (1962), Thomas Kuhn exposed the intricacies of the sociocultural process from his interrogation of Renaissance astronomy. Kuhn made the case that "normal science" functions as a belief system,

174. Manring, *Slave in a Box*, 75.

resisting "conjecture and refutation" (Karl Popper's phrase) so as to preserve tolerable ideas. Examining a more contemporary example in her *Primate Visions*, Donna Haraway reconstructed how the narratives of twentieth-century biology instanced imperialism, capitalism, white supremacy, and patriarchy. Haraway asserted that "the primate body, as part of the body of nature, may be read as a map of power. Biology, and primatology, are inherently political discourses, whose chief objects of knowledge, such as organisms and ecosystems, are icons (condensations) of the whole of the history and politics of the culture that constructed them for contemplation and manipulation."[175] Thus, the work of scientists can be understood to be both an expression of inquiry and an artifact of powerful interests. As such, the emergence of modern race science, beginning in the eighteenth century, was neither anomalous nor peculiar. And by the nineteenth century, as was the case with much scientific work, it came increasingly under the bureaucratic management of the state and the economic predations of capital. By the middle of the century, the often eccentric academic and medical dabblers in race science, modernism's counterparts to medieval alchomists, had been appropriated into a race science omnibus.

What may have been the first joint venture into race science by the American government and American commerce was the U.S. South Seas Exploring Expedition of 1838–43. Funded and authorized by Congress and conducted by the U.S. Navy, the expedition's four-year itinerary was global: extending across the Atlantic to the Canary Islands, down to Tierra del Fuego, and including visits to Australia, Antarctica, the Oregon Territory, the China Sea, and South Africa. Undertaken to show the flag (gunboat diplomacy to protect American traders, whalers, and sealers) and to chart the vast oceans for future naval adventures (some of its surveys were still being used in World War II), the mission included, among its civilian ("the Scientifics") and military personnel, naturalists, botanists, a mineralogist, a conchologist, and artists.[176] The expedition was a qualified success, at best: one of the original six ships was lost with all of its crew; two officers were killed in an attack on a survey party on Malolo; and two other ships were abandoned. But during its voyages, the expedition collected tens of thousands of botanical and invertebrate and vertebrate animal specimens, and thousands

175. Haraway, *Primate Visions*, 10.
176. Viola, "Story of U.S. Exploring Expedition," 10.

of ethnographic artifacts, including among them one human: Vendovi, a Fijian prisoner.[177] And for much of the next three decades, Charles Wilkes, the controversial commander of the expedition, attended the publication of the nineteen volumes and atlases of the expedition's findings.[178]

Charles Pickering, a Harvard-trained physician, was the lead naturalist on the expedition. And in 1849, he published his own findings, *The Races of Man*. What is particularly stunning is what Pickering's contribution to race science might have been. Culling his observations from the expedition and other travels, Pickering's work boldly challenged the polygenist dogma which had by then come to dominate naturalism in the halls and lecture rooms of his alma mater. His apostasy assumed several forms. From his extensive travels he documented the existence of eleven races (Arabian, Abyssinian, Mongolian, Hottentot, Malay, Papuan, Negrillo, Indian, Ethiopian, Australian, Negro), a much more complex reality than what was being imagined at the core of the new racial dogma. Notwithstanding the extraordinary diversity of humanity, Pickering concluded: "There is, I conceive, no middle ground between the admission of eleven distinct species in the human family and the reduction to one. This latter opinion, from analogy with the rest of the organic world, implies a central point of origin . . . Further zoological considerations . . . seem to favour a centre on the African continent."[179] Illustrating his study with handsome portraits of each race, Pickering carefully detailed how none of the races could be confidently consigned to one level of civilization either historically or in his own time. In Africa, he claimed, he had seen evidence of white slaves on the an-

177. Vendovi, brother of the king of Rewa, was implicated in the 1834 murder of ten crew members of an American ship. He was held prisoner for two years during the expedition, only to die in a naval hospital a few hours after the expedition returned to New York City in 1842. Ibid., 21.

178. Wilkes endured two court-martials: the first, a consequence of his conduct during the expedition; the second, during the American Civil War. In both instances he was found guilty, and the second led to his forced retirement. His five-volume *Narrative of the United States Exploring Expedition* provided him a quite unexpected fame: "[Herman] Melville . . . claimed that he borrowed aspects of Wilkes's personality for his characterizations of Captain Ahab in *Moby-Dick*." Viola, "Wilkes Expedition," 31. Viola references David Jaffe's *Stormy Petrel and the Whale*.

179. Pickering, *Races of Man*, 315. I am indebted to my wife, Elizabeth, for bringing Pickering to my attention. She discovered his work in an antique book store in Ann Arbor.

cient monuments of dynastic Egypt; and on the same evidence Pickering testified to the prominent role of Blacks in both the military and the royal house of the eighteenth dynasty. Further, on the Negro, Pickering was just as blasphemous: "The Negro race seems to occupy about one-half of Africa, and, excluding the northern and southern extremes with the table-land of Abyssinia, it holds all the core temperate and fertile parts of the continent. These limits, to all appearance, would not have been exceeded to this day, aside from foreign interference; but, as one consequence of the events of the last two centuries, the Negro race seems destined to fill hereafter an important place in general history."[180]

In sum, Pickering insisted that the human family constituted a unity whose historical origins were likely in Africa. In the most ancient of civilizations, he observed, the racial hierarchy had been the reverse of that obtained in the last century or two, putting the lie to the conceit that the present racial order was a commandment from God or nature. Further, the African Diaspora had become an auspicious reality in the modern world. Blacks were now situated globally to be a factor in "general history." And to complete his demolition of the justifications for slavery, Pickering pronounced a further apostasy: "I am not aware of any fact contravening the assumption that Negro slavery may have been of modern origin."[181] The London edition of Pickering's work was accompanied by an introduction by John Charles Hall which cited ancient and contemporary scientific opinion and biblical sources for the "unity of mankind." And Hall was quite explicit about the subversive import of Pickering's work, taking to task the influential culprits (notably, Samuel Morton, Josiah Nott, and Agassiz) whose imaginary science supported the notions of separate human origins for each race and the natural superiority of Europeans.[182] Predictably, Pickering's work on race was largely ignored in the United States, his greater fame coming from his last work, *Chronological History of Plants*, which Richard Eyde characterizes as "timeless": "We turn to Pickering today to find a given plant in Homer or Herodotus or writings of Egyptian scribes."[183]

One possible explanation for the shunting of Pickering's work into

180. Ibid.
181. Ibid., 191.
182. Smedley, *Race in North America*, 236.
183. Richard H. Eyde, "Expedition Botany: The Making of a New Profession," in Viola and Margolis, *Magnificent Voyagers*, 41.

obscurity is that it coincided with probably the most muscular phase of American abolitionism. Free Blacks and fugitive slaves had formed an aggressive wing of the leadership of the movement by the 1840s, pushing the opposition to slavery into radical forms like the emigration conventions and providing support and publicity to the Black émigrés to Canada and the West Indies. By the 1850s, Black antislavery leaders were actively exploring sites in West Africa and the West Indies for the establishment of "Negro sovereignty." And among white abolitionists, similar extraconstitutional measures were undertaken: in anticipation of the insurrectionary politics of John Brown, several whites had been imprisoned in Southern states for "slave stealing," that is, participating in the liberation of slaves.[184] As far as I can determine, however, none of the historians of abolitionism or race science make reference to Pickering. Pickering was a creditable and worthy opponent of the racialists, but he could hardly match their extraordinary resources. Agassiz, for instance, was as busy as a beaver during the decades before, during, and after the Civil War. Not only was he training those who would succeed him in the construction of racialized ethnology, naturalism, and anthropology, but he was also proposing new scientific techniques to document race differences and the polygenetic theory. In 1850, for instance, following his featured appearance at the American Association for the Advancement of Science in Charleston, South Carolina, he took a field trip to Columbia (a population of six thousand whites and more than a hundred thousand slaves) to select slave subjects to initiate his collection of ethnographic photographs. His informant was Robert Gibbes, a Carolinian scientist, and the photographer was Joseph Zealy, a local daguerreotypist. Concerning the project, Gibbes would write Samuel Morton: "Agassiz was delighted with his examination of Ebo, Foulah, Gullah, Guinea, Coromantee, Mandrigo and Congo Negroes. He found enough to satisfy him that they have differences from the other races."[185] Something, however, is amiss. The surviving copies of the daguerreotypes document that, according to Agassiz's instructions, the men and women had been stripped naked in Zealy's studio. Their nudity effaced personality, history, memory—everything but their gen-

184. See Robinson, *Black Movements in America*, chap. 3.

185. Wallis, "Black Bodies, White Science," 45. The daguerreotypes were accidentally uncovered in 1975 among the forgotten collections of Harvard's Peabody Museum and first published in Reichlin, "Faces of Slavery." Fifteen of the original daguerreotypes have been recovered.

der, their enslavement, and their blackness. Brian Wallis finds them disturbing:

> It is perhaps not coincidental that by their unprecedented nudity, the slave daguerreotypes intersect with pornography, that other regime of photography so central to the 1850s . . . and so exclusively concerned with the representation of the tactile surface of the human body. While there is no absolute connection between photographs of the nude body and pornography, the vaguely eroticized nature of the slave daguerreotypes derives from the unwavering voyeuristic manner with which they indiscriminately survey the bodies of the Africans, irrespective of the subjects' lives.[186]

When we recall Agassiz's first encounter with the black body four years earlier ("I could not take my eyes off their face in order to tell them to stay far away"), it is striking how revulsion has metamorphosed into perverse fascination, how an acute alienation has been disciplined into an exercise of mastery under the supremacist's gaze. Still, we have only partially captured his kinky ambition: a decade later Agassiz would be assisting the government and interested capitalists in planning the first large-scale anthropometric field study.

The American government, sections of capital, and eminent scientists conspired in race science for a second time during the 1860s. The occasion was the Civil War; the immediate cause being the effectiveness of the Union army. John S. Haller reports that following the First Battle of Bull Run, President Lincoln authorized the establishment of the United States Sanitary Commission in June 1861, charging it with the function of studying the physical and moral condition of Federal troops.[187] Haller indicates that "the life insurance companies of America underwrote a large portion of the Commission's expenses."[188] Because they insured Union recruits, companies like Prudential Life and National Union Life & Limb (later Metropolitan Life) had a vested interest in statistical profiles which might anticipate the relative robustness of British Americans, Germans, the Irish, and Blacks.[189] Mod-

186. Wallis, "Black Bodies, White Science," 54.
187. Haller, "Civil War Anthropometry," 309.
188. Ibid.
189. Haller indicates that both Prudential and Metropolitan Life discontinued life policies on Blacks; and along with the New York Life Insurance Company and Washington Life Insurance Company, organized medical departments pursuing race-

eling its study on the anthropometric work by the Belgian philosopher Lambert Adolphe Jacques Quetelet, the commission began its work in 1863. During the first year of somatological studies, the commission examined 8,004 Union and Confederate soldiers. The next year, with the actual induction of Black troops into the Union military (Congress authorized Black troops in July 1862), under the advice of Louis Agassiz and others, the commission modified its measurements in order to construct and contrast statistical models of the "average" white, Negro, mulatto, and Indian (mostly Iroquois).[190] During the second phase of the study, 10,876 white soldiers, 1,146 white sailors, 68 white marines, 2,020 "full-blooded Negroes," 863 mulattos, and 519 Indian bodies were examined. The quest for the "average" seems more appropriate to the actuarial needs of insurers than scientists, but it also had its uses in the tortured discourse of race science.

The Sanitary Commission's work was nominally under the secretary of war, Edwin Stanton. Stanton's cooperation, however, was desultory, as indicated in the complaints noted by Benjamin A. Gould in his final report of the commission's findings, *Investigations in the Military and Anthropological Statistics of American Soldiers* (1869). Stanton was likely hesitant to give full cooperation to the Sanitary Commission since a parallel study was underway under the authority of the Provost Marshal General's Bureau.[191] A third study was conducted by Sanford B. Hunt, who performed autopsies on 405 soldiers (381 of whom were Black).[192] Hunt submitted his report to the Sanitary Commission and published it under the title of "The Negro as a Soldier" in the *Anthropological Review* of London in 1869.[193] Concerning the three

centered anthropometry well into the nineteenth century. Ibid., 322–24. See also Robert L. Boyd, "Racial Segregation and Insurance Enterprise"; and Pierce, *Negro Business and Business Education*, 12. More recently, Scot Paltrow reported that Metropolitan Life (now MetLife) continued its race-profiling well into the twentieth century. See Paltrow, "Old Memos Lay Bare MetLife's Use of Race to Screen Customers," *Wall Street Journal*, July 24, 2001, A1.

190. Six measurements were added to the original form: "1) distance from tip of middle finger to level of upper margin of patella, 2) height to knee, 3) girth of neck, 4) perinaeum to most prominent part of the pubes, 5) distance between nipples, and 6) circumference around hips." Haller, "Civil War Anthropometry," 313.

191. The results of the bureau's study, J. H. Baxter's *Statistics, Medical and Anthropological, of the Provost-Marshal-General's Bureau*, was published in 1875. Ibid., 314.

192. Ibid., 315–16.

193. Hunt, "Negro as a Soldier."

reports, Haller comments, "nearly all subsequent late-nineteenth-century institutionalized attitudes of racial inferiority focused upon the war anthropometry as the basis for their belief. Ironically, the war which freed the slaves also helped to justify racial attitudes of nineteenth century society. The direction and conclusions of the Civil War anthropometric evidence buttressed the conservative ethos of American social order and stability while, at the same time, encouraged a new 'scientific' attitude."[194]

The Sanitary Commission found that the Black male body was more anthropoid, that is, apelike, than the white body. This was already the generally accepted opinion among these scientists and their colleagues. And, as we have seen, they took pains to add body measurements which emphasized these differences and to characterize these measurements as "the most important physical dimensions." Comparisons of head size, weight, and height permitted the commission to conclude that not only were Blacks inferior to whites but that mulattos were inferior to their "originals." Clearly, race-mixing was a dead-end.[195] On the latter score, the questionnaire of military physicians conducted by the Provost Marshal General's Bureau concurred. Dr. J. H. Mears of Pennsylvania, for example, asserted that "though imitative, the powers of the mulatto were a good deal less than the full black and he exhibited a greater tendency to scrofulous disorders."[196] On the basis of his autopsies, Hunt concurred with the commission and the bureau relative to the physical differences between the races. On the other hand, Hunt recognized the merits of Blacks as soldiers and, paradoxically, warned against inferences respecting intellectual capacities which neglected the fact that most of the volunteers had been "held in ignorance by the southern planters . . . [and] barred from education."[197]

Notwithstanding Hunt's circumspection, the thrust of the two major studies was to blunt the social, political, and cultural impacts of the roles of Blacks in the Civil War. Their courage, heroism, and decisive participation with the Union forces had for a short time earned them

194. Haller, "Civil War Anthropometry," 309.
195. Haller comments: "In its report on the mulatto, the statistics were interpreted as corroboration of earlier racialist assertions that the product of miscegenation was physiologically inferior to the original stocks, and therefore, mixing races was no real remedy to the racial inferiority of the Negro." Ibid., 313.
196. Haller is paraphrasing Mears, ibid., 315.
197. Ibid.

the respect of fellow soldiers, friend and foe, newspaper editors, the radical wing of the government, and their own communities. Their war effort had been a considerable part of Congress's enactments of abolition, citizenship, and voting rights. But over the succeeding decades the memory of their sacrifice would be overwhelmed by unrelenting physical assault and the constant bombardment of racial propaganda. As we noted above, Frederick Douglass would observe on the occasion of the 1893 World's Columbian Exposition that "those services were retired from view and the memory of them became dimmed by time."[198] The fracturing of the antebellum racial consensus was systematically repaired by the activities of social elites, like those who led lynch mobs and corporations, and the intellectual notables who occupied seats of eminence in the most prestigious research institutions and museums in the country.

The new and formidable infrastructure of race science became a collaborator with the nationalist movement for public instruction which achieved its maturity in postbellum America. Just as in the late sixteenth century Shakespeare and his fellow playwrights had driven forward a nationalist agenda with their history plays, from the second half of the nineteenth century the race science establishment became a critical contributor to the deliberate construction of an American public sphere. And frequently the agents of the two missions—race and patriotism—were identical. For instance, Frederick Law Olmstead, the "father" of Central Park, had been secretary general of the Sanitary Commission. And during the year between its formal founding and its undertaking its race study, the commission had focussed on the organization of the antisecessionist Union League Club in New York (the commissioners were almost exclusively from New York). And as part of its effort to oppose the strong secessionist sentiment among New York's most influential trade, banking, and political strata, the Union League Club had funded and sponsored the recruitment for New York's Twentieth Regiment of Colored Volunteers. After the war, Alessandra Lorini reports, "Olmstead went back to his profession of landscape architecture and undertook extensive projects, including Prospect Park in Brooklyn, Riverside and Morningside Parks in Manhattan, the grounds surrounding the Capitol in Washington, D.C., the layout of Boston's ex-

198. Douglass, introduction, 13–14.

tensive system of parks and parkways, and, in California, the campus of Stanford."[199]

In the 1890s, Olmstead was the leading designer of the fairgrounds for the World's Columbian Exposition in Chicago and assisted in the selection for the site of the Pan-American Exposition in Buffalo (1901). Both venues were critical in the dissemination of race science in American public culture. Thus, Olmstead stands as a synecdoche for the convergence of the American public culture: the idea of the museum, public spaces, public health, patriotism, and public morality.

I am employing the notion of the museum both in an historical and a metaphorical sense. As Tony Bennett has shown in *The Birth of the Museum* (1995), the modern museum movement began in the late eighteenth century. Aram Yengoyan maintains that "collecting prior to 1700 or 1750 meant a heterotopia of virtually everything . . . [but the] early eighteenth-century museums were concerned with creating order out of chaos. . . . The grandeur of the nation and the empire were all expressed in and through exhibition and museums, not only as a statement of the present but virtually as a means of creating posterity which could never be defied or dismissed by foreign powers."[200] And as Bennett explains, "That the term *the museum idea* was understood as shorthand for the view that museums and other cultural institutions should serve as instruments of public instruction suggests that this view of museums and their function was seen as belonging to the same class as . . . educational, statistical, and sanitary programmes."[201]

Not to put too fine a point on it, the "museum idea" of radical social reform and public education encompassed public libraries, art galleries, parks, halls, public clocks, and the like. Bennett observes that in England, "In the nineteenth century . . . the most ardent advocates of public museums, free libraries, and the like typically spoke of them in connection with courts, prisons, poorhouses, and, more mundanely, the provision of public sanitation and fresh water."[202]

In England, museums and their associated phenomena were the province of Parliament and local authorities. In the new American republic

199. Lorini, *Rituals of Race*, 36. For the Union League Club, see ibid., 7ff.
200. Yengoyan, "Universalism and Utopianism," 794.
201. Bennett, "Multiplication of Culture's Utility," 863–64.
202. Ibid., 865.

of the nineteenth century, the transfer of the museum movement from Britain and Europe brought these institutions under the command of Congress and its own institutions of knowledge like the Smithsonian, the National Museum (USNM), and the Bureau of American Ethnology (BAE). By the second half of the nineteenth century, these institutions were collaborating in much more audacious projects: the world's fairs of 1876, 1893, and then 1904. Philadelphia was the site for the one hundredth anniversary of the Declaration of Independence. Chicago won the right to stage the event which marked the four hundred years since Columbus's voyage. And the St. Louis exposition would celebrate the century following the Louisiana Purchase. But in each of these, race instruction was embedded into the national curriculum.

In Philadelphia, the Indian display (in the nineteenth century, "native American" referred to Europeans born in the United States) organized by the Smithsonian produced an effect which Robert Rydell characterizes as that of "unassimilable savages." A contemporary reaction, that of William Dean Howells, editor of the *Atlantic Monthly*, was even less charitable: "The red man, as he appears in effigy and in the photograph in this collection, is a hideous demon, whose malign traits can hardly inspire any emotion softer than abhorrence."[203] Fortunately, Blacks were less prominently represented. Nevertheless, the plantation darkies who served as entertainment at one restaurant were sufficient to leave their imprint on Joaquin Miller's "Song of the Centennial": "A new and black brother, half troubador, / A stray piece of midnight comes grinning on deck."[204] Thus, one can surmise, the nearly 10 million visitors to the Philadelphia Centennary came away duly impressed with the new national catechism.

Seventeen years later, at Chicago, the attendance nearly trebled to 27.5 million. And Otis Mason, the lead man from the Smithsonian in the fair's race science, thought it achieved "a vast anthropological revelation." The architects of Department M, where the anthropological exhibits were designed, had come from the Smithsonian, the BAE, the USNM, Harvard, and Chicago universities, many of them trained by Louis Agassiz of Harvard. And along with Boas, Mason, and G. Brown Goode (director of the USNM), they included the most prominent race scientists of the period. Chicago's most prominent businessmen and

203. Rydell, *All the World's a Fair*, 26–27.
204. Ibid., 29.

financiers, men like Philip Armour, Gustavus Swift, and Cyrus McCormick, had raised the $15 million subsidy for the fair (supplemented by $2.5 million from the federal treasury).[205]

The appearance of railroad industrialists, adjunct interests (coal, turpentine, ironworks, etc.), and sectors of finance capital as sponsors of the international and regional fairs marked an extraordinary synergy between commerce and public culture.[206] This convergence was neither new nor circumstantial. As major consumers of the cheapest labor available, these were the interests which had seized control of the postbellum Southern economy by liaisons with the white supremacist "redeemers" who defeated the Radical Reconstruction of the postwar years. Before the Civil War, in Virginia, North Carolina, South Carolina, and Georgia, as Scott Reynolds Nelson observed, the labor for railroad construction had been Black slaves and Irishmen.[207] During the war, when the Confederate government strove to construct a consolidated rail system, its laborers were slaves, and in central Georgia, in one of the Confederacy's largest workshops, it "had relied primarily on the labor of skilled, black workingmen—particularly men trained in railroad works—to staff the armories, arsenals, and powder works."[208] And as the Union army progressively displaced Confederate rule, Herman Haupt, the head of the U.S. Military Railroads, "had detailed freed slaves as construction workers throughout the occupied South."[209] But it was after the war, while Radical Reconstruction was under attack from Klan violence, that Tom Scott of the Pennsylvania Railroad forged an

205. Ibid., 42–3.

206. "Between 1885 and 1907, international expositions spanned the South: the New Orleans World's Industrial and Cotton Exposition (1885); the Atlanta Cotton States and International Exposition (1895); the Tennessee Centennial Exposition (1897); the South Carolina Interstate and West Indian Exposition (1901–2); and the Jamestown Tercentenary Exposition (1907)." Ibid., 73. For examples of this synergy, Rydell documents that at New Orleans, E. A. Burke, director-general of the exposition, was a former railroad official; at Atlanta, William A Hemphill and Samuel M. Inman were bankers with ties to Cyrus P. McCormick; at Tennessee, John W. Thomas, president of the exposition was president of the Nashville, Chattanooga and St. Louis Railway, and the director-general of the exposition was Major Eugene Castner Lewis, chairmen of the board of the NC&SL. Ibid., 77–79. It is also useful to note that the excavation for the Atlanta Exposition was done by chain-gang labor. Ibid., 80.

207. Nelson, *Iron Confederacies*, 12, 16–17.

208. Ibid., 89.

209. Ibid., 172.

alliance with racist conservatives in order to secure the Southern rail system for his Southern Railway Security Company (SRSC) and ready access to Black workers (not infrequently convicts).[210] In the early 1870s the SRSC acquired its ownership of the several state railways, and not long afterwards, "the security company would absorb other state organs, such as penitentiaries and agricultural societies, and use them to reorganize the South into an apparatus for the extraction of cotton, tobacco, and raw materials."[211] And to ensure its immunity from the violence which had terrified Black and white Republicans and had dismantled Radical Reconstruction, the SRSC appropriated Klan leaders and inciters to racial violence like Benjamin Hill (director of the Georgia Central Railroad) and Josiah Turner (president of the North Carolina Railroad) as board directors for its Southern subsidiaries. Simultaneously, through either marketing practices or direct purchase, the SRSC came to control many of the South's most important newspapers: the *Raleigh News*, the *Richmond Enquirer*, the *Memphis Commercial Appeal*, and the *Atlanta Constitution*.[212] And behind this shield of commercial propaganda and race propagandists, the SRSC became identified with Southern Redemption and was the recipient of a grateful international bond market: "Because it was not recorded, we may never know the size of the British market for American railway bonds. It was certainly in the hundreds of millions of dollars, if not in the billions."[213]

The Chicago fair was organized along a simple binary: the White City represented the cultural, technological, and scientific achievements of

210. The SRSC's directors ("many of them the most powerful men on Wall Street") included banking financiers like Morris K. Jesup; Drexel, Morgan and the Brown Brothers; freight carriers like Henry B. Plant and George W. Cass of the Southern Express; and railway investors like B. F. Newcomer, W. T. Walters, and J. D. Cameron, who controlled the "Wilmington & Weldon and the Wilmington & Manchester coast lines." Ibid., 141–42.

211. Ibid., 165. Nelson comments: "Northern capitalists were the chief beneficiaries of the growing prison populations that the new sharecropping and wage systems had created." Ibid., 169. See also 173.

212. Ibid., 153–54. In 1870–71, in Union, York, and Spartanburg Counties in South Carolina, "Klansmen in these three counties may have killed more black southerners than any other group of Klans in the South." Ibid., 116. Tom Scott's first efforts at a railway corridor, the Atlanta & Richmond Air Line, served as a map of Klan attacks. Ibid., 128ff.

213. Ibid., 147.

"modern civilization." Along the Midway Plaisance was displayed "a sliding scale of humanity," as one observer put it. Arranged, it appears, by color, the "living exhibits" consisted of villages of Germans, Hungarians, Chinese, Japanese, Bedouins, Egyptians, American Indians (Dakota Sioux, Apache, Navajos, etc.), South Sea Islanders, and Javanese. And at the site furthest from the White City were the sixty-nine Dahomeans, "in all their barbaric ugliness, blacker than buried midnight and as degraded as the animals which prowl the jungles of their dark land" (as described in *Frank Leslie's Popular Monthly*, in October 1893).

The Midway was a melange of tacky entertainment (the Ferris Wheel, camel drivers, donkey boys, dancing girls, etc.) and anthropology. Frederic Ward Putnam, director of Harvard's Peabody Museum and the central figure in requisitioning and designing Indian exhibits, had promised that his displays would avoid "degrading or derogatory character." But whatever his intentions or his sensibilities, he operated under the mandate of Mason to produce "a chain of human progress along racial lines."[214] A century later, Robert Rydell would conclude that "with Wounded Knee only three years removed, the Indians were regarded as apocalyptic threats to the values embodied in the White City." But the opinion of someone quite close to Department M seems persuasive:

> Emma Sickles, one of Putnam's staff members, raised the only objection to the treatment of Indians that was heard throughout the duration of the exposition, and she was summarily dismissed from her position. In a letter to the *New York Times*, she charged that every effort had been made to use the Indian exhibits to mislead the American people. The display, she wrote, "has been used to work up sentiment against the Indian by showing that he is either savage or can be educated only by Government agencies . . . Every means was used to keep the self-civilized Indians out of the Fair.[215]

A final legacy were the twinned icons of patriotism and race which were inaugurated at the fair. The first was the debut of Nancy Green, a former slave, as the living Aunt Jemima, the pancake queen; and the

214. Rydell, *All the World's a Fair*, 63, 60.
215. Ibid., 63.

second, the Pledge of Allegiance penned by Francis Bellamy as part of the dedication ceremonies for the 1893 fair.[216]

Contrary to the largely unchallenged impression resulting from *The Reason Why the Colored American Is Not in the World's Columbian Exposition*, the work published by Frederick Douglass, Ida B. Wells, and others, there were Black American participants at the fair. Just as with subsequent endeavors undertaken in the name of the nation, there were divisions in Black opinion concerning the racial protocols of the fair's organizers. (Later generations of Black leaders and common folk, for instance, would debate the merits of Black involvement in the "frontier" wars against the Indians, or the military campaigns against Filipino and Cuban resisters to American imperialism, or World War I and World War II.) And in 1892, some of the earliest manifestations of the broad spectrum of postbellum Black social conscience became obvious. Some of the leading Black radical spokespersons, like Douglass and Wells, were conflicted: for them there was sufficient evidence that a post-Reconstruction national consensus was being forged to counterfeit a subhuman Black identity, and they pondered whether a Black boycott of the fair would constitute a resistance or amount to complicity in the drafting of a blueprint for a divided nation. Black liberal integrationists, like Chicago's Fannie Barrier Williams and New York's Joan Imogene Howard, progressive nationalists like Alexander Crummell, conservative nationalists like Booker T. Washington, feminist advocates like Hallie Q. Brown, emigrationists like Bishop Henry McNeal Turner, despite their deep disagreements, were either invited to Chicago or compelled by the momentousness of the event to attend the fair. Young Paul Lawrence Dunbar attended. Sent as a columnist for the *Dayton Herald*, for a short time he worked as a janitor at the fair.[217] And Black students from Wilberforce University and Atlanta University, and Black and Indian students from Hampton Institute, acquired menial but well-paid jobs and sometimes mounted exhibits or gave performances at the fair. Thanks to Christopher Robert Reed, it is now possible to acknowledge the presence of mature and younger Blacks at the fair in contradistinction to the claim made by the title of the pamphlet by Douglass, Wells, Barnett, and their colleagues.

216. For Aunt Jemima, see Manring, *Slave in a Box*; and for Bellamy, see Rydell, Findling, and Pelle, *Fair America*, 37.

217. Reed, *"All the World Is Here!,"* 16, 58.

However, Reed has also claimed that neither the public reception accorded to American Blacks, West Indian Blacks, and the Africans (from Liberia, Dahomey, Algeria, South Africa, and Egypt) nor the intentions of the fair's organizers were entirely negative. He postulates that "the Midway, along with the entirety of the fair itself, offered the observer an opportunity to see the human existence through a prism permitting as much light in and out as was desired. So, no definitive commentary on racism or racial intolerance is possible."[218] As one sort of evidence for the former, Reed has uncovered the impressions of James Weldon Johnson, one of the students at the fair from Atlanta University. One of Johnson's duties was as a "chairboy" wheeling visitors around at the fair. Other chairboys were white college students, lending a certain poignancy to Johnson's impression that "our reception surpassed any expectation we had had. We were treated just as though the question of color had never been brought up."[219] Nonetheless, the fair had precisely the opposite effect. As Reed admits, the popular press swooned over a racist agenda: "Most notable was the spate of bias, misinformation, and falsehood produced by the media of the period—journals, magazines, souvenir books, novels, and newspapers. Most egregious were the souvenir books and photographic collections, numbering over six hundred."[220] The consequence was that the comparatively mild white racism of Chicago was replaced. As one Black old timer would recall in 1930, "before the fair in 1893 there was very little prejudice within or between the races."[221] Chicago, like the nation as a whole, was being transformed by the diffusion of the new racial regime.

The long preparation of the new American public culture, which had begun during the Civil War, was now reaching completion. For thirty years, the artisans of public culture had been industrious, multifaceted, and perversely deceitful. In the Supreme Court, racist justices had struck at equality in *Blyew et al. v. United States* and the *Slaughter House Cases* (1873); *United States v. Cruikshank* and *United States v. Reese* (1876); and eventually *Plessy v. Ferguson* (1896), the latter penned by Justice Henry Billings Brown, a member of the American Social Science Association.[222] Following on the publication of his revolutionary thesis

218. Ibid., xxx.
219. Ibid., 1.
220. Ibid., xxix.
221. Ibid., 14.
222. Klinkner and Smith, *Unsteady March*, 83ff. In *Blyew*, several whites were ac-

On the Origin of Species (1859), Charles Darwin published *The Descent of Man* (1871), where he endorsed the pagan racist notions of Josiah Nott and primitive anthropometry. And while post-Reconstruction, or "redeemed," state legislators of the South created segregation and carceral societies for Blacks, the Congress repudiated the postwar amendments. The presence of federal troops in the South, which in 1868 had numbered 12,000, had all but disappeared as the lynching of Blacks climbed and climbed (49 in 1882, 118 in 1893). On the completion of its study, the Sanitary Commission had donated its instruments to universities and colleges; and now the academies were reciprocating: the "Teutonic" school of history and political science dominated the new graduate schools, fructifying into a new generation of racist academics. And Black disfranchisement proceeded at a breathtaking pace: "As late as 1896, over 130,000 African Americans voted in Louisiana; by 1904, the total was only 1,342. Alabama and North Carolina also saw black voting turnout reduced by over 90 percent during these years, and reductions exceeded two-thirds in Arkansas, Mississippi, and Tennessee."[223] Emancipated Black labor was now subject to the control of Black codes and prison gangs, and the Black voters who had produced the progressive Reconstruction state governments which championed "free public education, land redistribution, public works projects, state-supported colleges and hospitals, and aid for the indigent" had all but vanished.[224]

In 1904, the Anthropology Department of the Louisiana Purchase Exposition staged the next display of racial hierarchy. Nearly 20 million attended the spectacle. Unlike the fairs at Philadelphia and Chicago, no Little Big Horns or Wounded Knees had occurred in sufficiently close proximity to the St. Louis fair to influence the Indian exhibits. However, the United States now occupied the former Spanish colonies in the

---

cused of killing a Black woman, Lucy Armstrong, but Kentucky law did not permit the Black witnesses to the murder to testify. The Supreme Court reversed the lower courts (which had determined there was discrimination) on the grounds that the witnesses were not a party to the litigation and thus the state had not discriminated against them. In *Cruikshank*, a case involving the massacre of hundreds of Blacks following a disputed Louisiana election, the Court reversed the convictions of whites on the grounds that the Fourteenth and Fifteenth Amendments applied only where racism was a motivation, while electoral rights were regulated by the states. Ibid., 87–88.

223. Ibid., 104.
224. Ibid., 92.

The Little Chronicle Natural-Color Series
of Stereoscopic Views.

COPYRIGHT, 1904, BY T. W. INGERSOLL

SOLD ONLY BY SUBSCRIPTION.
The Little Chronicle Publishing Company, Chicago.

533. Negrito Natives Planting Rice, Philippine Village.
St. Louis Fair.

"Negrito Natives Planting Rice, Philippine Village, St. Louis Fair," 1904.
Stereoscope, Little Chronicle Publishing Company.

Pacific and the Caribbean. Accordingly, W. J. McGee, the former head of the BAE, stocked "the most extensive Anthropology Department of any world's fair" with human samples which paraded American power and illustrated his four cultural grades: savagery, barbarism, civilization, and enlightenment.

> Groups of pygmies from Africa, "Patagonian giants" from Argentina, Ainu aborigines from Japan, and Kwakiutl Indians from Vancouver Island, as well as groups of Native Americans gathered around prominent Indian chiefs including Geronimo, Chief Joseph, and Quanah Parker, were formed into living ethnological exhibits. They were supplemented by an adjoining United States government exhibit of nearly one thousand Filipinos and by separate ethnological concessions . . . McGee assembled the nonwhites directly under his charge into a "logical arrangement" [i.e. savagery, barbarism] of living "types" stretched out between the Indian School Building and the Philippines display.[225]

Boas, now of Columbia University, and Ales Hrdlicka, head of the National Museum, assisted in the organization of the anthropometric

225. Rydell, *All the World's a Fair*, 163.

Mobile & Ohio Railroad Card, ca. 1930s.

laboratories which administered tests of endurance and a battery of psychological and other measurements. Frederick Starr, professor of anthropology at Chicago, set up a three-week course on the fair for credit. And the Smithsonian received an added (but expected) bonus: three brains of Filipinos who died while at the fair became part of its collection.

The instigators of this race discourse were drawn from the highest tiers of American commerce, science, and government. And the spectacles that they designed were replicated and multiplied through museums, scientific journals, newspapers, magazines, amusement parks (see present-day Disneyland), circuses, films, popular cartoons, children's toys (puzzles, toy banks, etc.), curios, postcards, and advertisements for cereal, fruit companies, shoe polish, toothpaste, and so on. Under such a cultural and intellectual regime, it became possible to occupy the Philippines, Haiti, Cuba, the Hawaiian Islands, and Puerto Rico while employing the rationale of tutelage. Under such a regime immigration restrictions could be leveled against inferior Europeans and Asians while the Carnegie and Kellogg foundations funded the Eugenics Records Office and Race Betterment Congresses.

Boas began his public recantation of race science in 1906, two years after his involvement in St. Louis. His work over the next thirteen years was marginalized; and he himself was publicly censured in 1919. Boas's crime, according to the American Anthropological Association, was that his opposition to World War I was anti-American and that his refutation of race anthropology was antiscientific.[226] His most prominent critics were based at Harvard, the National Research Council, and the Galton Society. Now bereft of any significant funding support, Boas immersed himself in the study of Black folklore, training many of the cultural anthropologists (Melville Herskovits, Ruth Benedict, Zora Neale Hurston, Irene Diggs, etc.) whose works were rediscovered in the 1970s.

But perhaps Boas's most telling criticism of race science occurred in an exchange of correspondence in 1905. Responding to a request from W. E. B. Du Bois, Franz Boas wrote, "I am sorry to say that I cannot refer you to anything that is particularly good on the physical anthropology of the Negro."[227] This was surely a more accurate description of the ghosts which haunted the Smithsonian. Their purchase on the white American imaginary, however, was now a powerful and certain reality. And with the advent of motion pictures, the ghosts would achieve unprecedented authority. The odyssey of the inventions of the Negro had extended over three centuries, being ruptured and then repaired again and again. But now, at the beginning of the twentieth century, it appeared that finally the noble Moor had been irretrievably erased. It was a foolish supposition and, as we have recounted, there were no historical grounds for the dream that a permanent, stable racial regime could be instituted. Notwithstanding, the new fabulists in the industries of motion pictures gave it their best shot.

226. Baker, *From Savage to Negro*, 148–50.
227. Boas to W. E. B. Du Bois, October 14, 1905, B61, Franz Boas Papers, American Philosophical Society, Philadelphia.

In the Year 1915
D. W. Griffith and the Rewhitening of America

The purpose of racism is to control the behavior of white people, not Black people. For Blacks, guns and tanks are sufficient.
— Otis Madison, "Confronting Racism," January 1997

Patrolling Film Historiography

The conventional narratives of American film history have been launched from different and discrete beginning points. As Robert Allen and Douglas Gomery have detailed, the chronicling of the construction of a movie industry in America has sometimes been recited as exclusively an economic tale, or at other times as a tale of aesthetic accomplishments, or alternatively in terms of technical developments or social history. For historians fascinated by the ironic succession of manufactured artifacts of an industry, movies were determined by a chain of inventions: the nitrate compound of the billiard ball, which foreshadowed the formula for cellulose nitrate; the primitive photographic demonstration of a galloping horse by Eadweard Muybridge; Thomas Alva Edison's Kinetoscope, popularly marketed as a peep show; the projector constructed by Thomas Armat and Francis Jenkins; and so on. We now know that the nitrate pool ball was simply intended to replace the increasingly costly ivory ball; that Muybridge's experiment was to settle a wager on whether horses simultaneously lifted all four legs from the ground during the gallop; that the voraciously commercial impulse of Edison had to exhaust the market for the peep show before the notion of narrative movies could emerge; and that Edison, equally, was drawn reluctantly to the projection of moving images; and so on.[1]

In 1973, contrarily, when the narrative of the imaging of Blacks in film was attempted for perhaps only the second time on a grand scale (the British writer Peter Noble is generally credited as being the pio-

---

1. Allen and Gomery, *Film History*, chap. 1.

neer with his 1948 study, *The Negro in Film*), its author adhered to none of Allen and Gomery's historical genres. Donald Bogle set his sights on iconography, the scaffolding of Black stereotypes, and thus, in his own estimation, justifiably entitled his study *Toms, Coons, Mulattoes, Mammies & Bucks*. Starting from what he assumed was the beginnings of these filmed images, the blackface tom in Edwin S. Porter's 1903 *Uncle Tom's Cabin*, Bogle argued that by the time of the appearance of D. W. Griffith's *The Birth of a Nation* in 1915, "all the major black screen types had been introduced."[2] And though he acknowledged that Noble had identified and denounced some of these same caricatures earlier, Bogle thought that his own work distinguished him from Noble by concentrating on the emergence of an unanticipated art: a "pure art" elevated by what Black "talented actors have done with the stereotype."[3] As the first Black to enter the fray, it is not entirely surprising that the young Bogle ("under twenty-five") sought to emphasize Black *agency*, that is, just what it was Black performers achieved with the "trash" and demeaning roles they were presented.[4]

Following Bogle, essentially a journalist and movie enthusiast, more formally trained scholars (historians, for the most part) entered the field: most notably Gary Null with *Black Hollywood* (1975), Daniel Leab with *From Sambo to Superspade* (1976), Thomas Cripps with *Slow Fade to Black* (1977); and soon after, James Nesteby with *Black Images in American Film, 1896–1954: The Interplay between Civil Rights and Film Culture* (1982). Cripps has distinguished himself from his colleagues by the thoroughness of his research and his realization of a complement to Bogle's study of agency. Though Bogle and the others gave some at-

2. Bogle, *Toms, Coons, Mulattoes*, 17.

3. Ibid., xxiii.

4. Owing to Anna Everett's pioneering research on Black film criticism in the period ending with World War II, it now appears likely that Lawrence Reddick was the first Black analyst to attempt a systematic survey of Black representation in American films. In 1944, Reddick published "Educational Programs for the Improvement of Race Relations." "Compiling a 'checklist' of 175 films, Reddick set out to determine which of these films could be classified as 'pro-Negro,' 'anti-Negro,' or 'neutral' based on their figurations of African Americans. Of the 175, he found 75 to be 'anti-Negro'; 13 were deemed 'neutral,' and only 11 were classified as 'definitely pro-Negro'. . . . His twenty-two page essay (one of the longest film articles of the period) is categorized as follows: (1) 'The Early Years,' (2) '"Birth of a Nation,"' (3) 'The Talkies,' (4) 'The Era of "Gone with the Wind,"' (5) 'Since "Gone with the Wind,"' and (6) 'Pattern of Change.'" Everett, *Returning the Gaze*, 285.

tention to Black filmmakers, it was Cripps who took the appearance and work of Black filmmakers, especially directors, as his principal subject matter. Joined by Nesteby in the latter's too little-known work, Cripps employed the imaging of Blacks by major "Hollywood" production companies as a source of inspiration and opposition for Black film producers. His work has inevitably spawned a generation of Black and non-Black scholars who have undertaken research on the Black-cast film.[5]

Cripps and his academic cohorts largely eschewed Bogle's approach, suggesting that not only was Bogle writing popular rather than formally canonized history, but in method and conceptualization, his theory of an enduring quintuplet of Black representation could only be supported by a kind of primitive historiography. By contextualizing his icons in particular sociohistorical conflicts, they sought to overturn his delimiting analysis. After all, it is in the nature of history to record and explain changes, not the persistence of immutable forms. For certain there was something amiss in Bogle's thesis of constantly repeating forms. Empirically, the problem becomes evident if we ask ourselves whether the performances of, say, Sidney Poitier and Harry Belafonte during the 1950s and 1960s, or more recently, of Denzel Washington, Don Cheadle, Morgan Freeman, Angela Bassett, Halle Berry, or Alfre Woodard fall neatly into the constructions of toms, coons, mulattos, mammies, or bucks? Notwithstanding, we are also compelled to acknowledge that there are the repetitions, the cycles of minstrelsy and neominstrelsy which seem to surface again and again.[6] Can Bogle, then, be both right and wrong?

About a century and a half ago, another historian, Karl Marx, was confronted with an analogous problem. I believe the instance is instructive. In 1857, in his unfinished notes written to himself during the

5. For a sampling of the newer generation of scholars, see Diawara, *Black American Cinema*; and "History of Black Film." More recently, notable contributions have been made by Yearwood, *Black Film*; Jane M. Gaines, *Fire and Desire*; Massood, *Black City Cinema*; Jacqueline Stewart, *Migrating to the Movies*; and the detailed treatments of Oscar Micheaux: Bowser and Spence, *Writing Himself*; Green, *Straight Lick*; and Green, *With a Crooked Stick*.

6. This issue was raised by Mark Reid in *Redefining Black Film*, who argues that only Black female filmmakers have escaped to forge a powerful, liberatory Black cinema. The neominstrels are too numerous to chart, but I have in mind much of the work by Richard Pryor, Eddie Murphy, the Wayans, Chris Rock, and Martin Lawrence.

preparation of his introduction to *A Contribution to the Critique of Political Economy*, Marx struggled with the persistence or recurrence of Classical Greek art and epic poetry as aesthetic norms in nineteenth-century European society; that is, he queried how two societies separated by more than two millennia, by different cultures, by the appearance of a new civilization (Christian), and by untold changes in the forms of production could share criteria of physical beauty and literary artistry. "The difficulty," he wrote, "is that they still give us aesthetic pleasure and in certain respects still hold as a norm and unattainable model." Marx's response was uncharacteristic: "Why shouldn't the historical childhood of humanity, in which it attained its most beautiful development, exert an eternal charm as a stage that will never recur? . . . The charm of [Greek classical] art for us does not contradict the undeveloped stage of society on which it grew. Rather it is its result and is inseparably connected with the fact that the immature social conditions in which it arose and in which alone it could arise can never recur."[7]

The ancient Greeks, Marx claimed, constituted the "historical childhood" of Europe (what he mistook as humanity). But it was also an idealized childhood, a moment, Marx believed, which was marked by humanity's "most beautiful development." The "charm" or authority of an ancient Greek aesthetic rested on the irretrievable loss of that pristine moment when the "true nature" of "humanity" could be made manifest. Charmed, as he was, by this imagined biography, Marx had no need to appeal to his actual cultural history, that is, the deliberate and conscious appropriation of classical Greek culture by the nobilities and bourgeoisies of France, Germany, and England in the late eighteenth century.[8] Overwhelmed by a social phenomenon in which culture superseded historical materialist explication, Marx invented a psychology. And in this less familiar terrain, he approximated the film theory employed by Siegfried Kracauer in *From Caligari to Hitler* in the mid-twentieth century.

As a display, however, Marx does provide us part of a solution. Cultural signifiers are powerful enough to overtake historical time. Transmitted from age to age, even across civilizations, cultural ideals may

7. Marx, preface and introduction, 44–45.

8. For Neoclassicism in Britain, see Ernst, "Frames at Work"; and Donald Dale Jackson, "How Lord Elgin First Won"; for Europe, see Jenkyns, *Victorians and Ancient Greece*; and Mosse, *Toward the Final Solution*, 10–11.

endure, leaping on occasion into the consciousness of men and women far removed from the time or circumstance of their initial development. Marx's affection for classical Greece was learned and absorbed as a signature of the cultivated German or European of his age. But as acutely analytical as he proved to be so often, he was incapable of deconstructing the "charm" in which those aesthetic signifiers held him. In a similar fashion, Cripps found mystifying the speed and power with which Black icons infected early American film. Asserting that from the beginnings of moving pictures and for most of the first decade of the new century, Black imaging was predominantly reportorial, Cripps postulated that as a concomitant with film editing something had gone terribly wrong. Nevertheless he was forced to concede that "it is difficult to attribute causes to the seeming decline in black fortunes after 1910."[9]

For Bogle the mystery would have been the absence of devaluing Black images from an embryonic American film culture. He was persuaded that a natural history served to explain the appearance of these images: "All were merely filmic reproductions of black stereotypes that had existed since the days of slavery and were already popularized in American life and arts. The movies . . . borrowed profusely from all the other popular art forms."[10] This was not the case, according to Cripps. For Cripps there had to be immediate causes which conspired to disrupt an otherwise racially benign form of entertainment. The causes might be, he mused, the racist Southern (white) literati's migration into the fledgling movie industry; the approaching anniversary of the ending of the Civil War; and intersectional reconciliation coupled with a nostalgia among a recently urbanized America for an idealized rural past represented by the Old South.[11]

Bogle, of course, was being intuitive and, unfortunately, historically mistaken. The images he identified have different histories: for example, the buck long antedates the Atlantic slave trade (recall Shakespeare's Othello); and the mulatto, or more precisely, the mulatta would make her appearance in American popular culture in the first quarter of the nineteenth century.[12] But Cripps, too, was intuitive and in error

9. Cripps, *Slow Fade to Black*, 25–26.
10. Bogle, *Toms, Coons, Mulattoes*, 4.
11. Cripps, *Slow Fade to Black*, 26.
12. See Jones, *Othello's Countrymen*; and Roach, "Slave Spectacles," 175ff.

to presume that American motion pictures had some sort of period of innocence and that Southern whites had been the authors of the racialization of film. These are not trivial matters. They are important to our present understanding of American cultural history by what they inadvertently conceal; and we can sense their importance to Cripps by the lengths to which he resorts to defend them.

Cripps maintained that from the 1890s into the early twentieth century, Edison and his contemporary filmmakers produced "relatively benign, vaguely anthropological" shorts when they addressed people of color. While it is true that some of Edison's racial "vignettes" were entitled *A Morning Bath* (1896), *Colored Troops Disembarking* (1898), and *The Ninth Negro Cavalry Watering Horses* (1898), many more bore titles such as *The Pickaninny Dance* (1894), *Buck and Wing Dance* (1895), *Watermelon Contest* (1896), *Chicken Thieves* (1897), *Minstrels Battling in a Room, Sambo and Aunt Jemima: Comedians,* and *Spook Minstrels* (all of the latter series produced between 1897 and 1904).[13] Moreover, none of Edison's films, not even those which were reportorial, appeared to suggest the existence of Black men like Lewis H. Latimer. Latimer, while working with Alexander Graham Bell as a draftsman, had improved the latter's patent design for the telephone. Later, in 1881, he had added the carbon element to Edison's light bulb; and then had worked for Edison (Edison Electric, later General Electric) and Maxim-Weston (Westinghouse) as chief engineer; supervising the installation of electric lighting systems in New York, Philadelphia, Montreal, and London; and authoring the first textbook on lighting systems used by the Edison company.[14] Latimer's apparent intrusion into Edison's commercial world, as inventor, draftsman, patents arbitrator, and engineer, did not alter the transfer of selected Black images to film by his colleagues at Edison. In negating his existence and that of other Black intellectuals,

13. Cripps, *Slow Fade to Black,* 12, 393nn13,15; Musser, *Edison Motion Pictures.* Gerald R. Butters Jr. identifies two films with the title *Buck Dance,* one by Edison in 1898 of Ute Indians (according to Musser), the other by Lubin (1903). Butters maintains that the Library of Congress copy of Edison's film is "indecipherable because of the condition of the film." The Lubin catalog says of its *Buck Dance,* "Here is seen a number of 'Smokes' dancing for their favorite 'watermelon.'" Butters, *Black Manhood,* 22. Butters insists that copies of *Minstrels Battling in a Room* and *The Edison Minstrels* are to be found in the Library of Congress. Ibid., 220n20.

14. Lowe and Clift, *Encyclopedia of Black America,* 505.

their body of work can hardly be taken as a substantiation of Cripps's claims for a period in which film primarily recorded actual Black life.

Biograph, for reasons detailed in chapter 4, was an even worse offender in supplying visual evidence for the superiority of whites. Incorporated in late 1895 as the American Mutoscope Company ("later renamed the American Mutoscope & Biograph Company and frequently called the Biograph Company after its biograph projector"),[15] the company was the dominant film producer between 1897 and 1901. And among its earliest delectable picturizations of blackness were *A Hard Wash* (1896), *Watermelon Feast* (1896), *Dancing Darkies* (1896), *Hallowe'en in Coontown* (1897), *The 'Gator and the Pickaninny* (1900), *Laughing Ben* (1902), *A Nigger in the Woodpile* (1904), *A Misdirected Kiss* (1904), and *Everybody Works but Father* (1905). Henry T. Sampson's exhaustive survey of the period led him to credit Biograph for producing nearly a third (32 percent) of the films which employed black caricatures. Interestingly, Edison came in a distant second at 13 percent, closely followed by Lubin (10 percent).[16] The early resort to imagined blackness by these companies places the existence of Cripps's "reportorial" moment in some doubt, but even more problematic for Cripps is the sheer predominance of grotesque representations over actualities: Sampson insisted that the most persistent characterizations were devoted slaves (27 percent), thieves (25 percent), servants (20 percent), cannibals (14 percent), and Zulus (9 percent), while boxers (4 percent) and preachers (1 percent) brought up the rear (there were no representations of Black professionals).[17] Seven years later, Gerald R. Butters Jr., in his *Black Manhood on the Silent Screen*, largely confirmed Sampson's findings, only differing on distinctions without a difference: "By far, the largest subgenre of early films with black depictions were films that featured African-American men as chicken thieves."[18]

A similar unease adheres to Cripps's other assertions about the silents: that the white racism in them emanated from the "South";[19]

15. Musser, *Emergence of Cinema*, 145.

16. Sampson, *Blacks in Black and White*, 27. For detailed descriptions of these films, see ibid.; Butters, *Black Manhood*; and (for *Nigger in a Woodpile*) Jacqueline Stewart, *Migrating to the Movies*.

17. Ibid., 29.

18. Butters, *Black Manhood*, 24.

19. In common with most American observers, Cripps employs the term "South" and its derivatives in a fashion which evacuates Blacks, all women, poor whites,

and that the proximity of a Civil War observance triggered an imagined transformation of Black filmic representations. For some decades prior to the opening of the twentieth century, Northern as well as Southern and even European racist intellectuals had played an important part in the formation of American national culture, academic life, medicine, art, and popular culture (including high and low theater).[20] Cripps, however, repeatedly constructed white racism as at first a regional impulse which eventually enveloped American society. And it is hard to credit any anniversary related to the Civil War as an inspiration for Woodrow Wilson to publish his Teutonic ode, the five-volume *A History of the American People* in 1903. In its treatment of the Civil War, the Reconstruction, and the Ku Klux Klan, the work was so profoundly negative towards Blacks and solicitous of "white civilization" that Griffith would unabashedly borrow from it to structure *The Birth of a Nation*.[21]

The continuity of the grotesque representations of Blacks between nineteenth-century dramatic and vaudevillian theater, humor magazines, postcards, children's books, the new social sciences, and historical works, on the one hand, and twentieth-century popular culture

---

and Native Americans from the region. For instance he writes: "The dominance of Southern themes in drama was matched by a Southern literary revival in New York. Even though the hothouse plant that was the Southern mystique could not survive in antique purity in Northern cities, its purveyors moved there." Cripps, *Slow Fade to Black*, 10. According to this usage, as a historical or social agent the "South" generally refers to a small fraction of the region's population: white ruling-class males, their activities, ideology, interests, and sympathizers.

20. For the academy, see John Trumpbour, "Binding Them with Science: Scientific Ideologies in the Ruling of the Modern World," in Trumpbour, *How Harvard Rules*; for art and medicine, see Gilman, "Black Bodies, White Bodies"; for theater, see Saxton, *Rise and Fall*, 118ff.

21. Rogin, "'Sword,'" 150–51. Wilson's study was in consort with the "Dunning School." As Eric Foner notes, "This rewriting of Reconstruction's history was accorded scholarly legitimacy—to its everlasting shame—by the nation's fraternity of professional historians. Early in the twentieth century a group of young Southern scholars gathered at Columbia University to study the Reconstruction era under the guidance of Professors John W. Burgess and William A. Dunning." Foner, *Reconstruction*, 609. Foner makes particular note of James Forde Rhodes and Claude G. Bowers, but also notes that by then the former Freedmen's Bureau commissioner O. O. Howard and the Radical Republican Ohio senator John Sherman had publicly ascribed to the notion that Reconstruction was a mistake. In opposition to this calumny, the Black former Mississippi congressman John R. Lynch published *The Facts of Reconstruction* in 1913. Ibid., 610.

and scholarship, on the other, is hard to ignore, but Cripps had largely erased it. He achieved this by presuming that the documentary film, the short, and the vignette sufficed as entertainment during the novelty period of movies and thus had assumed the dominant form; and by audaciously asserting that immigrants, a large proportion of the new entertainment's audience, "not only carried no baggage of racial lore, but were insulated from Southern literary racism by their own illiteracy."[22] But the "vaguely anthropological" documentary shorts were merely an alternative and not the dominant form of the early silents; and the European immigrants were encrusted with racial lore, both intra-European and otherwise, consequent to several centuries of imperial wars, slavery, and colonialism.[23] Cripps thus retrieved a recent past which was as fabulous as the long lost past invented by Marx.

The appearance of Ed Guerrero's *Framing Blackness* in 1993 made transparent the significance of the work in film studies and Black studies during the previous two decades. Drawing on the critiques of the conventions of American sociology and historiography facilitated by the militant rights movements of the 1960s and 1970s, Guerrero marshaled the work of his predecessors like Bogle and Cripps towards a more nuanced and different understanding of American film. Implicitly Guerrero rejected Cripps's assertion that the absence of a "usable past" contributed to the retardation of a Black aesthetic opposition to the perverse representations of Blacks in early American films. Slave resistance and slave rebellions and Black abolitionism, Guerrero asserts, had left persistent ideological materials in Black culture; yet in American films, "the only scenes in the whole plantation genre before the revisionist late 1940s that even come close to admitting that African Americans hated and resisted slavery occur with Griffith's insolent 'renegade negroes' in *Birth*, and in *So Red the Rose* (1935), where Clarence Muse leads a revolt of hundreds of slaves that is fantastically stopped by a slap from the master's adolescent daughter."[24]

22. Cripps, *Slow Fade to Black*, 9.

23. See Robinson, *Black Marxism*, chap. 1.

24. Guerrero, *Framing Blackness*, 34. Cripps commented: "Contributing to the black apathy toward cinema was an apparent lack of a usable past. Even the tradition of minstrelsy gave Negroes no sustenance because white imitators had usurped its forms and cast aside its roots. . . . In the absence of a usable past blacks depended on urban pluralism and the tolerance it produced, along with the sheer primitiveness of movie technique, to preserve them from distortion at the hands of white producers."

The Birth of a Nation, according to Guerrero, was the first fully articulated narrative of the "plantation genre," the depiction of "the benevolence of the plantation and slavery" and the horrifying unnaturalness of racial equality.[25] And since "slavery is the founding historical relationship between blacks and whites in America," the moral character and civility of every Black or white was determined by their ideological positioning to the racial prerogative and natural law of slavery.[26] Citing Antonio Gramsci's apprehension of "cultural hegemony," Louis Althusser's analysis of "overdetermination," and Fredric Jameson's exploration of the "political unconscious," Guerrero submitted his analytical terrain: "Because slavery, and resistance to it, is such a central and formative historical experience deeply rooted in the social imagination of all Americans, cinematic expressions of slavery have become sedimented into a range of contemporary film narratives and genres, and, specifically into the symbolic or latent content of many films depicting African Americans."[27] And mindful of Bogle's static characterology, Guerrero insisted that "because ideology is constantly negotiated, Hollywood cannot construct a permanent, seamless image of white superiority on the screen."[28]

Contrary to Cripps's constructions, neither Edison nor Ellis Island constituted proper historical markings for the defamatory cultural codes employed in early American film. On that score Bogle's observations were the more trenchant: an established racist iconography of Blacks merely acquired new visual techniques in early American film. What Cripps mistook for their supersession was largely reassertion of racial conventions. Thus, as Daniel Bernardi has observed, "racial meanings are a significant, omnipresent part of the birth of cinema."[29] But even this realization masks a more profound emergence: through the intervention of film, a new American social order was naturalized. The new order differed radically from that of the early national period

Cripps, *Slow Fade to Black*, 11. For more on Paramount's *So Red the Rose* (1934), see Cripps, *Making Movies Black*, 5–6; and Paramount's publicity package in the Motion Picture and Television Reading Room, Motion Picture, Broadcasting, and Recorded Sound Division, Library of Congress.

25. Guerrero, *Framing Blackness*, 16.

26. Ibid., 3.

27. Ibid., 43.

28. Ibid., 6.

29. Bernardi, *Birth of Whiteness*, 7.

a century earlier. It required race discourse to function, not to justify the early nineteenth-century ideal of rural republicanism or to forgive its faltering achievement of social justice. At the beginning of the twentieth century, American capital was no longer a middling mercantile player in a global economy commanded by imperial European powers. Now it was a robust industrial society voraciously appropriating a vast but disparate labor force which required cultural discipline, social habituation, and political regulation.

Rewhiting History

If we take 1915 as a particularly auspicious moment in film history, it might be asserted that the number of crucial historical events colluding with the appearance of Griffith's *The Birth of a Nation* suggests that it was a moment during which the mapping of American culture was reinscribed, when the contours of the social practices which came to characterize twentieth-century American society were fixed. Let us consider this possibility for a moment. The year 1915, of course, marked the fiftieth anniversary of the ending of the American Civil War. It was also the second year of World War I, the year that German submarines sank the *Lusitania* and Hugo Junkers developed the first fighter plane. In that same year, and closer to our concerns, Leo Frank was lynched; the second Klan was inaugurated; the United States invaded Haiti; and Jess Willard defeated the Black heavyweight boxing champion, Jack Johnson. And, of course, American nationalism and overseas imperialism were being constantly excited by the social spectacles and patriotic moral catechisms incited by seventeen years of overlordship in the Philippines and the Caribbean. Also implicated in our film history, in response to *The Birth of a Nation*, the six-year-old NAACP launched mass demonstrations, and the Association for the Study of Negro Life and History was initiated.[30] Finally, the phenomenal success of *The Birth of a Nation* (Neal Gabler describes it as "the first block-buster")[31] brought the independents to their definitive triumph over Edison's Trust, thus

30. Cripps, *Slow Fade to Black*, chap. 2; Aptheker, *Afro-American History*, 160.

31. Gabler, *Empire*, 90. In 1916, the *New York Times* estimated that 872,000 New Yorkers had seen the film in the first year: "This is about one-seventh of the population of New York, and computing the admission average at 75 cents, $600,000 was paid by New Yorkers for the privilege. Simultaneously the picture was being shown in the larger cities of the country, and it is estimated 5,000,000 have already seen it." "Written on the Screen," *New York Times*, January 2, 1916, X8.

establishing the governing structure of the movie industry for the next decade.

On the screen, Griffith made several explicit claims for his film. At the beginning of *The Birth of a Nation*, before he introduced his "impersonators" and the roles they undertook, Griffith conflated in one title an alleged sensitivity for social etiquette, his resolve for a broad and clear moral binary, and a claim that his film was art: "We have no wish to offend with improprieties or obscenities, but we do demand, as a right, the liberty to show the dark side of wrong, that we may illuminate the bright side of virtue—the same liberty that is conceded to the art of the written word—the art to which we owe the Bible and works of Shakespeare."[32] A moment later, having privileged Lillian Gish (Elsie Stoneman), Mae Marsh (Flora Cameron), Henry Walthall (Col. Ben Cameron), Miriam Cooper (Margaret Cameron), and Mary Alden (described in the continuity script as "Lydia, Stoneman's mulatto housekeeper"), and then scrolled fourteen other players, Griffith inserted one more claim: "If in this work we have conveyed to the mind the ravages of war to the end that *war may be held in abhorrence*, this effort will not have been in vain."[33] Griffith's film is thus marked by the colliding economic and cultural forces of its time: hegemonic Victorian moral values contended with the meteoric expansion of a culturally diverse working class; insurgent and enterprising businessmen in the new film industry, in order to justify their fragile economic position, became claimants to the status of artists; and movies were proposed as a site of moral instruction.

Huge financial, industrial, and commercial interests had already transformed the American economy from a primarily rural society engaged in agrarian and manufacturing activities into an urban industrial giant capable of superseding the machine production of Great Britain and Germany. And now with its vast industrial plantations ranging from the stark and brutal coalfields in the East and the silver mines of the West to the equally hazardous shipyards and the hard- and soft-goods factories of the Northeast, the slaughterhouses of the Midwest, and the lumbermills of the South and the Far West, in the production of steel, iron, railways, clothing, food, and the horizontal and vertical expansion

32. Lang, *Birth of a Nation*, 43. All quotes from the film titles are taken from the continuity script constructed by Robert Lang, as published in this edited volume.
33. Ibid., 44.

of its cities, the economy appeared to possess an insatiable appetite for workers. They came in the millions: 5.5 million in the 1880s; 4 million in the 1890s; 14 million between 1900 and 1920.[34] Some migrated from the American South, the Caribbean, and Asia, but many more from Eastern and Southern Europe.

In the cities, the immigrants were clustered in squalid ghettos, arranged as they had been recruited: by employment, language, culture, ethnicity, region, and nation of origin. Robert Sklar's assertion that "the old American city, which had been a single community, became the new American city of many communities, separated from each other by social barriers"[35] was not historically true, but the sheer volume of the newcomers might have made it seem so. From colonial times, recruitment for American settlements had been characteristically diverse, homogeneity being the exception. In the countryside, where hundreds of thousands of immigrants were employed in mining and lumbering and were ordered "residentially" by a similar social calculus, they existed in company towns and camps regimented by company enforcers and servers. Numerically dominated by males, these immigrant and migrant assemblages exhibited in their recreational activities what polite society ascribed as the vices of the ignorant poor: alcoholism, drugs (ranging from cigarettes to opium), and rowdy combativeness. And to relieve the sexual frustrations and loneliness which resulted from the separation from their families and native communities, their overt sexual impulses fostered prostitution and the transformation of the cheap burlesque theater into female exhibitionism. The nickelodeons were another matter altogether. Kathy Peiss recounted that when they replaced the arcades, the nickelodeons took on the aspect of "community gathering places." Exhibitors targeted tenement women and families, and by 1910, 40 percent of their audiences were women.[36] In that same year, it was determined that the working class constituted three-quarters of the 26 million who made up the movie audience.[37]

For years, as Griffith implies in his foreword to *The Birth of a Na-*

34. Zinn, *People's History*, 261, 373.
35. Sklar, *Movie-Made America*, 4.
36. Peiss, *Cheap Amusements*, 148–49.
37. Brownlow, *Behind the Mask*, xvi.

tion, the nickelodeons had been the object of elite and middle-class suspicion and revulsion. Tom Gunning has remarked that "the movies represented a working-class pastime that had appeared without the control—or even the knowledge—of the middle-class guardians of culture."[38] The reformers were intent on cleansing the form of its "obscenities and improprieties" in order to transform it into an instrument for moral and cultural education. According to Mary Grey Peck of the Women's Clubs in 1917, "Motion pictures are going to save our civilization from the destruction which has successively overwhelmed every civilization of the past. They provide what every previous civilization has lacked—namely a means of relief, happiness and mental inspiration to the people at the bottom." The *World Today* declared in 1908 that pictures were "the academy of the working man, his pulpit, his newspaper, his club."[39] In his 1915 production, given the enormous financial stake, Griffith had attempted to appropriate the reformers' objectives, but earlier he had been less circumspect. Kevin Brownlow informs us that "D. W. Griffith was particularly contemptuous of them. In 1913, he made an extraordinary film called *The Reformers, or the Lost Art of Minding One's Own Business. . . .* Two of his reformers are obvious homosexuals, and Griffith goes so far as to show prostitutes, dressed as pious churchgoers, continuing to ply their trade."[40]

Brownlow, a filmmaker and historian of the silent-film era, assures us that the period before 1919 was the "richest source of social films," but that many of the directors of the genre, like George Nichols, Barry O'Neill, and Oscar Apfel, were subsequently forgotten (however, more occasional contributors like Raoul Walsh and King Vidor were more fortunate). And probably the most extraordinary of them was Lois Weber. Weber was not cynical about reform, and she devoted her entire career to the cause. A Christian Scientist, in 1913 Weber directed *Suspense, Civilized and Savage,* and *The Jew's Christmas* (concerned with poverty, racism, and anti-Semitism, respectively); in 1914 she produced *The Hypocrites,* exposing the corruption of churches, politicians, and big business; and later she filmed stories concerned with abortion and birth control (*Where Are My Children,* 1916), opium smuggling (*Hop, the*

38. Gunning, *D. W. Griffith,* 89.
39. Both quotes are from Brownlow, *Behind the Mask,* xvii, xviii.
40. Ibid., xviii–xix.

Devil's Brew, 1916), capital punishment (*The People vs. John Doe*, 1916), and alcoholism (*Even as You and I*, 1917).[41]

Griffith's foray into the moral realm in *The Birth of a Nation* was not then singular or unusual. But it did coincide with a profound structural change in the production and exhibition of motion pictures. From 1908 to 1914, motion picture production and exhibition had been dominated by Edison's cartel, the Motion Picture Patents Company ("The Trust," as Carl Laemmle termed it); the combines of Edison and Biograph, which included Vitagraph, Essanay, Kalem, Selig, Lubin, Pathe Freres and Melies, and George Kleine.[42] The members of the near monopoly, based on the patents for cameras, projectors, and so on which were held by Edison's company and American Mutoscope and Biograph, were, as Neal Gabler would have it, "primarily older white Anglo-Saxon Protestants who had entered the film industry in its infancy by inventing, bankrolling, or tinkering with movie hardware." But by 1912, the Trust had been effectively challenged by exhibitors and producers who were "largely ethnic Jews and Catholics."[43] For Gabler these differences were important if not entirely factual. There had been Jewish partners in the Trust and in both of the combines which preceded its formation. Court proceedings, however, provide a clearer measure of the relative power of the partners. On that score Gabler's characterization appears closer to the truth. Tom Gunning's recitation of the punitive and protectionist litigation initiated during the pre-Trust era easily designates Edison and Biograph as the most resourceful, persistent, and powerful interests.[44] Our concern with these matters is more derivative. Early in 1908, at the most critical juncture in its contest with Edison, Biograph converted Griffith from an actor to a director. His prolificacy that year made Biograph competitive. In consequence Biograph's fortunes flourished sufficiently (facilitated by the aggressive pursuit of patents, import and production partners, and marketing strategies) to force a merger with the Edison combine in late 1908.[45] No less important was a secondary conduit, but more recent sensibility, concerning the amusement value of blackface fare: the vibrant Yiddish theater (see chapter 3).

The Trust had signed an exclusive deal with Eastman Kodak, ensur-

41. Ibid., xxi–xxiii.
42. See Gunning, *D. W. Griffith*, 143–44; and Sklar, *Movie-Made America*, 33ff.
43. Gabler, *Empire*, 58.
44. Gunning, *D. W. Griffith*, 61ff.
45. Ibid., 65.

ing that raw film stock would only be available to filmmakers who operated under its licenses. With these several instruments of control, the monopoly had determined that motion pictures would remain one-reel recreations for the poor and had also embedded its own social ethics, including anti-Semitism, in film. According to a 1913 piece in *Moving Picture World*, as Kevin Brownlow tells it, "'Whenever a producer wishes to depict a betrayer of public trust,' ran the report of the Anti-Defamation League, 'a hard-boiled usurious money-lender, a crooked gambler, a grafter, a depraved fire bug, a white slaver or other villains of one kind or another, the actor was directed to represent himself as a Jew.'"[46] The independents like Adolph Zukor, Carl Laemmle with Robert Cochrane, William Fox, and Harry Aitkin successfully challenged the Trust by covertly filming while using Trust-patented equipment, raiding Trust companies for their most recognized screen personalities, bringing lawsuits, introducing feature-length films, and importing films from Europe. And they secured financing primarily from Jewish investment houses like S. W. Strauss; Kuhn, Loeb; and Goldman, Sachs.[47] As a consequence, Brownlow observes, "direct references to Jewish criminals began to disappear from the screen, partly because more Jews were taking control of the picture business."[48] But among their imports were features like the French film *Queen Elizabeth* (with Sarah Bernhardt) and the Italian epics *Quo Vadis?* and *Cabiria*. And when the war disrupted access to Europe, Aitkin's Mutual Company and Kuhn, Loeb (through Felix and Otto Kahn) took up the slack by backing Griffith's project to produce the first American-made epic.[49] It is also instructive to note that Louis B. Mayer, another of the future movie moguls, acquired his first big return in the business (some $500,000) by securing the New England distribution rights to *The Birth of a Nation*.[50] "What is certain is that the period in film history that followed Griffith brought immigrants to Hollywood power."[51]

Returning to the film itself, in the very next moment following Griffith's posturing *Birth* as an antiwar film, he places a marker for white-

46. Brownlow, *Behind the Mask*, 376.

47. Gabler, *Empire*, 117. Fox, the exception, raised capital from the gentile firm of Halsey, Stuart and Company.

48. Brownlow, *Behind the Mask*, 377.

49. Schickel, *D. W. Griffith*, chap. 9.

50. Gabler, *Empire*, 90–91.

51. Rogin, *Blackface, White Noise*, 77.

ness costumed in an Edenic metaphor: "The bringing of the African to America planted the first seed of disunion." He elides the brutality and wrenching pain of the slave trade, the tyranny of the mass appropriation of African life and labor, by following the title with a scene portraying the benediction of a slave auction by a Christian minister. His next subject is the ordinary white abolitionists (thus erasing the Black abolitionists who dominated the movement from the 1840s),[52] sentimentalized by their concern for a Black child; and then he installs the first antagonist of his melodramatic structure: "In 1860 a great parliamentary leader, whom we shall call Austin Stoneman, was rising to power in the National House of representatives." Stoneman's ambitions for power will corrupt abolitionism; but for the moment, the only tension in his otherwise idyllic household is Elsie's discomfort in being excluded from her brothers' plan to visit friends (the Cameron brothers) in the South. Having established Stoneman's household, Griffith immediately herds his audience back to Edenic lore: "Piedmont, South Carolina, the home of the Camerons, where life runs in a quaintly way that is to be no more."

The depiction of the Cameron household differs from Griffith's introduction of the Stonemans in two important markings: exteriors dominate interiors (an extended street scene fronting Cameron Hall visually confirming the easy, leisured, and stylized patriarchy of antebellum life); and the street and the household are decorated with amiable adult domestic slaves (Mammy and the tom role are played by white actors in blackface), the Black children performing amusements for white observers. The Stoneman boys arrive, and the two younger sons bond ("Chums"); Ben Cameron becomes enamored with a miniature portrait of Elsie, while Phil Stoneman is infatuated with Margaret Cameron. The young Camerons and Stonemans visit a slave quarter, and the slaves perform an impromptu dance, stomping their feet, clapping their hands. Griffith has evacuated fugitive slaves from history, vanquishing the Nat Turners and the David Walkers, and with them the very possibility of the hundreds of Maroon communities which struck fear in the hearts of plantation owners, state officials, and their militia has vanished.[53]

Griffith now fuses "the gathering storm" (a Southern newspaper

52. See Quarles, *Black Abolitionists*.
53. See Robinson, *Black Movements in America*.

announces the South's stake in the 1860 presidential election) with scenes depicting Stoneman's dual corruption: his ambition for power and his apparently intimate relationship with his mulatto domestic, Lydia: "The great leader's weakness that is to blight a nation."[54] By associating Stoneman *pere* with mulattos such as Lydia and, later, Silas Lynch, Griffith has evaded another historical truth: grafting the "blight" of miscegenation to a powerful Northern abolitionist! In fact, most of the nearly half a million mulattos in the country resided in the South at midcentury, the issue principally of slave owners and female slaves. Nevertheless, since Griffith will characterize his two mulatto roles with a neurotic sexuality necessitated by plot and ideology, disclosing their relation to the ruling plantocracy would risk an unseemly speculation as to the source of their sexual depravity. Meanwhile the Stoneman boys return North.

The remainder of the first part of the film takes up the Civil War itself. And here Griffith exhibits his extraordinary technical mastery of the medium, establishing the cinematic tropes which will come to dominate depictions of the war for decades: the tragic beauty and ironic elegance of a Confederate ball interrupted by the call to assembly (powerfully imitated in *Santa Fe Trail*, 1940, a film indebted to Griffith cinematically and ideologically); the Confederate troops parading down the streets of Piedmont and led by mounted officers; the mass charges of the armies in battle, cutting to individualized acts of heroism (Ben Cameron leading his troops into a Union barrage; bringing water to a wounded Union soldier; a wounded Ben Cameron rescuing the Confederate flag in the midst of conflagration, etc.); and the torn fraternity ("True to their

54. Thomas Dixon's portrayal of "Austin Stoneman" (bald, clubfoot; mulatta mistress, etc.) made no mistaking that, of course, Stoneman was Thaddeus Stevens, the Great Commoner, and "Lydia Brown" was indeed Lydia Smith. For Stevens's relationship with Lydia Smith, his mulatta "housekeeper," see Brodie, *Thaddeus Stevens*. Wallace, in her treatment of the silent films based on Stowe's *Uncle Tom's Cabin*, asserts that Lydia Brown is based on the characterization of Cassie in the 1914 version produced by World Film Corporation. This completely dehistoricizes Dixon's intentional character assassination of Stevens and Smith; and inadequately deals with the transmutation of a heroic Cassie (in the 1914 film) to a Lydia who is "demonized and horrifically sexualized." See Wallace, "*Uncle Tom's Cabin*," 149. Stevens earned the hostility of the Dunning school of American historians by his involvement in the Underground Railroad and advocacy of fugitive slaves, for championing abolition as the objective of the war, as an architect of Black military service, and for his role in radical Reconstruction.

promise, the chums meet again"), as Tod Stoneman and Duke Cameron expire together. Griffith reenacts the burning of Atlanta (preceded by marvelous shot of Sherman's army in serpentine march) and brings authenticating detail of Robert E. Lee's desperate attempt to break out of a Union encirclement at Petersburg. And true to the promise made to his audience, Griffith provides graphic scenes of the carnage of war.

Meanwhile, in Piedmont, Black irregulars invade ("The first negro regiments of the war were raised in South Carolina"), attempting to put Cameron Hall to the fire, but are frustrated by Confederate rescuers. In the actual war, approximately 189,000 Blacks fought in the Union army, most of them volunteering from the slave states. They fought in some 449 engagements, absorbing 16 percent of the 360,222 killed on the Union side. Confederate troops, at first, murdered captured Union Blacks (at Fort Pillow and Poison Spring, for example); but then when Black units pledged to take no prisoners, Lee and other Confederate officers insisted on and then extended to Blacks the rules of "civilized" warfare.[55] Once again, Griffith bends history to ideology, restricting his reconstruction of the work of Black troops to acts of marauding and victimizing the feeble and the female.

Wade Cameron is killed, and Ben, wounded, ends up in a makeshift Union military hospital (where Elsie, true to the melodrama's use of coincidence, has volunteered), condemned to be hanged as an irregular. Elsie and Ben's mother reunite at Ben's hospital bed; and Mrs. Cameron, learning of her son's plight, travels with Elsie to appeal to Lincoln for her son's life. Lincoln ("the Great Heart") intercedes. Lee surrenders to Grant (Griffith reproduces Horace Porter's painting of Appomattox); and Ben, now recovered, returns to his beloved but ruined Cameron Hall. Five days following the Confederate surrender, Lincoln attends the performance of *Our American Cousin* at Ford's Theater and is assassinated by John Wilkes Booth. In the Stoneman household, Lydia exults at the news, gloating to Stoneman, "You are now the greatest power in America." At Cameron Hall, Cameron *pere* laments: "Our best friend is gone. What is to become of us now?" End of part 1.

Griffith's portrayal of Reconstruction is prefaced by a claim he would recite until the end of his days: "This is an historical presentation of the Civil War and Reconstruction Period, and is not meant to reflect on any

55. See the accounts by the Black Civil War veteran Joseph Wilson, *Black Phalanx*, 330–36; and Cornish, *Sable Arm*, 170ff.

race or people of today." And then, in the sure embrace of language excerpted from Wilson's *A History of the American People*, Griffith assures his audience that the Ku Klux Klan arose to defend "the civilization of the South" from the depredations of Congress and invading "adventurers" who sought "to cozen, beguile, and use the negroes."

In his earlier films, Griffith's racism had assumed a sentimental, paternalistic form. Thus, as Jack Temple Kirby informs us, Griffith's stock Black characterizations in films like *In Old Kentucky* (1909), *Swords and Hearts, His Trust*, and *His Trust Fulfilled* (1911) were Uncle Ben and Mammy, "cheering, weeping, comforting and ever-loyal Negroes" shackled to the plantation aristocracy.[56] Kirby is persuaded that "Griffith's greatest indulgence in the black-as-beast theme was in *The Birth of a Nation*." Thomas Dixon Jr. had collaborated with Griffith in constructing the earlier portions of the film, but now in the second part of *Birth* the brutal virulence of Dixon's race-hating *The Clansman* (1905) became dominant.[57] As Thomas Clark observed in the 1970 reissue of the novel: "There is no comedy . . . in Dixon's characterization of the Negro. He recited every scurrilous thing that had been said about the race. In one passage after another he portrayed the Negro as a sensuous brute whose every physical feature was the mark of the jungle and the untamed animal."[58] And Dixon's Aryan characters, one after another, are nearly overcome by the "African odour" of Black bestiality.

Understandably, Dixon's disaffection with mulattos was even more pronounced. Their mongrel existence is simultaneously alluring and repulsive. He more than once refers to Lydia as a woman of "animal beauty" with the temperament of a "leopardess," unnatural ambition, and the sexual seductiveness to ruin a nation. In the final pages of his

56. Jack Temple Kirby, "D. W. Griffith's Racial Portraiture," 121.

57. Raymond Cook, "Man behind *Birth*." In 1972, Russell Merritt acknowledged that "the second part of *The Birth of a Nation* is, then, an uneasy collaboration between two Southerners who shared similar, but by no means identical, points of view about the South." Merritt, "Dixon, Griffith," 39. But Merritt's own interrogation showed a much broader space of disagreement between Griffith and Dixon. Dixon believed the Civil War was a necessary catharsis from feudalism, not "bitter, useless" (ibid., 41); for Dixon the Klan's formation was a deliberate and corporate revival of the Confederate army inspired by medieval legends and led by General Bedford Forrest, not the spontaneous white populism of Griffith.

58. Thomas Clark, introduction, xvi. The novel actually begins with Elsie's encounter with the wounded nineteen-year-old Ben Cameron, "the baby son," in a military hospital in Washington, D.C.

novel, Dixon has Stoneman confess: "Three forces moved me—party success, a vicious woman, and the quenchless desire for personal vengeance. When I first fell a victim to the wiles of the yellow vampire who kept my house, I dreamed of lifting her to my level." And Dixon described Silas Lynch, Lydia's covert agent, as "a man of charming features for a mulatto, who had evidently inherited the full physical characteristics of the Aryan race, while his dark yellowish eyes beneath his heavy brows glowed with the brightness of the African jungle . . . the primeval forest."[59] As Griffith himself revealed, he managed the difficult task of reconciling the affectionate portrayal of his earlier films with Thomas Dixon Jr.'s unrelievedly vicious construction of Blacks by the interposing of an evil master, the Northern scalawag.

The second part of *The Birth of a Nation* is no more historical than its antecedent; and in its constant manic impersonation of Dixon's race consciousness, it pursues the villainy of Blacks, mulattos, and their abolitionist Rasputin with melodramatic vitality. Under the leadership of Lieutenant Governor Silas Lynch, the Blacks appropriate power, threaten the once safe streets of Piedmont, and begin the destruction of civilization and white women. In their nearly unintelligible imitation of the English language, they demand political and civil rights for which they have not the barest understanding: "Ef I doan' get 'nuf franchise to fill mah bucket, I doan' want it nohow." Their corruption and greed are boundless: the law, the courts, the legislature (scenes of the Black-dominated State House are titled "The riot in the Master's Hall"), the land and real property, social equality, and the most virtuous of white women. Fascinating for its unintended irony, Griffith constructs the indictment of Blacks in a mirror image of the antebellum slave order: fraud and injustice at the polls ("All blacks are given the ballot, while the leading whites are disfranchised"); racial dominion over the law ("The case was tried before a negro magistrate and the verdict rendered against the whites by the negro jury"); the forging of race privileges in legislation ("Passage of a bill, providing for the intermarriage of blacks and whites"); physical terror ("The town given over to crazed negroes brought in by Lynch and Stoneman to overawe the whites"); the routine and public displays of petty racial humiliation and insult, and so on.[60] Like Woodrow Wilson, Griffith repositioned his moral ful-

59. Ibid., 57, 93.
60. In her extensive and near-exhaustive review of the literature on the first Klan,

crum from a support for justice to the preoccupation with race. Both men impersonated history, transferring the crimes of the slave order onto their fantastic myth of Reconstruction.

Meanwhile, as the white tragedies accumulate, Ben has fortuitously imagined ("The Inspiration") the creation of an Invisible Empire: the Klan. This was not Dixon's but Griffith's fabrication of the Klan's origins. Dixon, having dedicated *The Clansman* to his uncle, Colonel Leroy McAtee, "Grand Titan of the Ku Klux Klan," knew better. In the novel, Dixon had paid homage to the Klan leader, Bradford Forrest, and delicately detailed Klan rituals. Woodrow Wilson's version contradicted that aspect of Dixon's verisimilitude, but he shared with Dixon and Griffith the rationale for the secret society: "It threw the negroes into a very ecstasy of panic to see these sheeted 'Ku Klux' move near them in the shrouded night; and their comic fear stimulated the lads who excited it to many an extravagant prank and mummery."[61] One such prank is the castration of Gus, the Black uniformed deviant who, in one of the film's most memorable sequences (the Gus chase), pursues Flora, the youngest Cameron daughter, to her suicide.[62] But it is the specter of just such Black depravity which will reconcile Elsie and Phil Stoneman and Ben and Margaret Cameron in the embrace of the Klan: "The former enemies of the North and South are united again in common defence of their Aryan birthright."

Maddened by an ambition which wreaks havoc on his own congenital instability, Lynch interrupts his partying with depraved mulattas in order to pursue Elsie ("See! My people fill the streets. With them I will build a Black Empire and you as Queen shall sit at my side") and eventually is forced to take both her and her father hostage. Elsewhere, frenzied by Klan raids and open confrontations, Black troops enforce a martial order: arresting whites indiscriminately; taking prisoner innocent white families; intimidating Blacks loyal to their former masters. The Klan routs the Black soldiers holding Piedmont; Ben and his Klansmen

---

Lisa Cardyn cautions, "As a number of contemporary observers readily conceded, klan terror derived its ultimate impetus from its perpetrators' intense resistance to the historical processes by which the former slaves were gaining access to the rights and responsibilities of citizenship." Cardyn, "Sexualized Racism," 777.

61. Woodrow Wilson, *History of the American People*, 60.

62. Manthia Diawara reinterprets the "Gus chase" in some detail in "Black Spectatorship: Problems of Identification and Resistance," in Diawara, *Black American Cinema*, 212ff.

rescue the kidnapped Elsie, the besieged Phil, the Camerons, and their loyal domestics; and the Klan disarms the Blacks. Under the Klan's protection a second election is held, and the natural order is restored. And at the seaside, Phil and Margaret are united; and Ben and Elsie, seated together on a bluff overlooking the sea, contemplate a miraculous vision: "The figure of Christ, projected in the background, is mounted on a horse and with both hands is swinging his sword above his head. On the right, in front of him, lies a huge heap of bodies, and on the left a crowd writhes and pleads with him. The image of the God of War fades out."[63] The concluding images are magnificently costumed and apocalyptic but have also cleverly prepared the audience for Griffith's final nationalist message: "Liberty and union, one and inseparable, now and forever!" The abrupt juxtaposition of these visual constructions fuses whiteness and a race theodicy, patriarchy and filiopiety, historical destiny and Christian civilization on the mass consciousness.

In *The Birth of a Nation*, Griffith invoked structural and discursive oppositions to achieve the representations of good and evil, employing narrative conventions which were thoroughly familiar to the cultural elite and compelling to the popular imagination. As Plato had done in *The Republic* for his immediate audience at the Academy in ancient Athens, Griffith designated the site of his moral contestation as the metaphorical and ideological space occupied by two opposing families, one Northern and one Southern. Unlike Plato, for whom the opposition between Athenian (Plato's brothers and the Sophist Socrates) and non-Athenian (Cephalus, his sons, and their Sophist, Thrasymachus) was immutable,[64] Griffith resolved the contradiction between the real (the South) and the unreal (the North) by transforming the conflict into racial constructions. The Stonemans and the Camerons were white, an Aryan racial fraternity, the imminent "nation." Opposed to this racial utopia was the ubiquitous evil: the Blacks and *their* mongrel mulattos, whose savage, anarchic, sexual desires poisoned the spiritual and biological lifeblood of the good. It was clear that for Griffith as for Dixon, "one of the main reasons for making the film was to help 'prevent the mixing of white and negro blood by intermarriage.'"[65]

63. Robert Lang's description, *The Birth of a Nation*, 155.

64. Robinson, "Slavery and Platonic Origins."

65. Robert Lang, "*The Birth of a Nation*: History, Ideology, Narrative Form," in Lang, *Birth of a Nation*, 17.

Rather than a contest between opposing factions of capital over the domination of millions of Southern laborers (Black and white), Griffith recast the American Civil War as a violent fratricidal confrontation between whites. And in the melodramatic genre he favored, the poignancy of the conflict was crystallized in the romantic and fated liaisons between the elder Stoneman and Cameron children. Griffith then reimagined the Reconstruction as a temporary moment of mulatto political ascendancy and Black triumph, rape, and anarchy. Interposed between the seeing (Southern white plantocrats) and the unseeing (Northern white abolitionists) were what Griffith had dramatically determined to be the "seed of disunion," African slavery. Griffith instructed (or reminded) his audience that Abraham Lincoln ("the Great Heart") had understood the evil in the white American paradise and had made preparations to expel Blacks: "Lincoln's dream" was to return Blacks to Africa, and only his assassination had frustrated his act of cleansing. It was a promise which only the death of the Christlike patriarch had aborted. But Lincoln also had vowed of the white South that "I shall deal with them as though they had never been away." And Wilson, Dixon, and Griffith, each in his own way and now as collaborators, longed to realize that Aryan fraternity.

The film was privately premiered on February 8, 1915, in Los Angeles; and then began a seven-month-long showing at Cline's Auditorium. And from the first, movie reviewers in all the major newspapers and trade papers enthused over the spectacle.[66] "Booth Tarkington, Burns Mantle, and assorted historians agreed that it was eminently worth seeing for its educational value. In New York, secondary school teachers took their advice and brought their classes to special film showings while ministers throughout the country endorsed the movie from the pulpit. In Cambridge, Massachusetts, the rector of the Harvard Street Unitarian Church gave three sermons on The Birth of a Nation. 'The film,' he claimed, 'must be preserved and our histories rewritten.'"[67]

There were some detractors, however, particularly the NAACP's Moorfield Storey, W. E. B. Du Bois, and Oswald Garrison Villard, Rabbi

66. For a host of reviews, see the *New York Times* and the *Christian Science Monitor*; Cripps, *Slow Fade to Black*; Everett, *Returning the Gaze*, chap. 2; and Schickel, *D. W. Griffith*, chap. 10. For the Black press's reaction to the film, see Anna Everett's exhaustive survey in *Returning the Gaze*, particularly chap. 2.

67. Merritt, "Dixon, Griffith," 28.

Stephen Wise of the Jewish reform community, and Monroe Trotter of Boston's National Equal Rights League. Rather than Griffith, the critics observed the mind of Dixon behind the film, and thus Jane Addams of Hull House in Chicago decried Dixon's film as "both unjust and untrue"; Rabbi Wise raged at the presentation of "the Negro of a generation ago as a foul and murderous beast"; and Francis Hackett, in the pages of the new journal *New Republic,* wrote: "Dixon corresponds to the yellow journalist . . . he is a yellow clergyman. He is yellow because he recklessly distorts Negro crimes, gives them a disproportionate place in life and colors them dishonestly to inflame the ignorant and credulous. And he is especially yellow, and quite disgustingly and contemptibly yellow, because his perversions are cunningly calculated to flatter the white man and provoke hatred and contempt for the Negro."[68] And Du Bois, still twenty years from publishing his definitive account of Reconstruction,[69] would add in his editorial in the May 1915 issue of the *Crisis*:

> It is sufficient to add that the main incident in the "Clansman" turns on a thinly veiled charge that Thaddeus Stephens [*sic*], the great abolition statesman, was induced to give the Negroes the right to vote and secretly rejoice in Lincoln's assassination because of his infatuation for a mulatto mistress. Small wonder that a man who can thus brutally falsify history has never been able to do a single piece of literary work that has brought the slightest attention, except when he seeks to capitalize burning race antagonisms.[70]

68. For Addams and Wise, see "Opinions," *Crisis*, May 1915, 19; and for Addams again and Hackett, see Schickel, *D. W. Griffith*, 283–84.

69. Du Bois, *Black Reconstruction.*

70. Originally titled *The Clansman*, Schickel claims, the film was retitled in early March after "Griffith dropped a love scene between Senator Stoneman and his mulatto mistress and a scene in which a black and a white engaged in a fight." Schickel, *D. W. Griffith*, 282. For the more common account of the title, see Merritt: "The famous story about Dixon shouting the title change from *The Clansman* to *The Birth of a Nation* during a New York preview was first printed in [Terry Ramsaye's *A Million and One Nights*, 1926, 641]. The story is at least partially apocryphal; the film was referred to as *The Birth of a Nation* long before the New York City, March 1915 preview. A full-page advertisement in *The Los Angeles Daily Times*, February 9, 1915, reads in part: 'ALL THIS WEEK The Clansman—or—THE BIRTH OF A NATION Produced by D. W. Griffith.'" Merritt, "Dixon, Griffith," 39n32.

The critics sought to ban the film before its release in New York and elsewhere;[71] and short of total censure, they pursued cuts from the film of the most grotesque or frightening scenes, with some success: "They cut out a quote from Lincoln opposing racial equality, though Lincoln had actually spoken the offending words. They censored 'Lincoln's solution' at the end of the film, showing blacks deported to Africa. They eliminated some graphic black sexual assaults on white women. And they cut out Gus's castration."[72] Eventually, the detractors were to be overwhelmed by a most practical collaboration between Wilson, Dixon, and Griffith.[73]

In mid-February, Dixon wrote to President Wilson, requesting an audience with his former classmate at Johns Hopkins. Though Wilson was still in mourning at the death of his first wife, he responded positively. Receiving Dixon in the White House, and upon hearing Dixon's excitement about the potential propagandistic power of films, Wilson agreed to a showing of *Birth* in the East Room. On February 18, the film was displayed before the president, members of his family, and some of his cabinet; the next day, following a visit to another chum, Secretary of the Navy Josephus Daniels, Dixon obtained an interview with Edward D. White, the chief justice of the Supreme Court. White was contemptuous of a "moving picture" ("I never saw one in my life and

71. Ida B. Wells, in Chicago, condemned that city's branch of the NAACP for its failure to prepare properly to resist the exhibition of the film. See Wells, *Crusade for Justice*, 342–44. Wells was a founder of the antilynching campaign in the late nineteenth century, perhaps its most important mobilizer. She was also a founding member of the NAACP in 1909. She left the organization for its lack of radical militancy in opposing lynching, becoming the head of the Negro Fellowship League and a member of Trotter's National Equal Rights League. Both organizations aggressively intervened on the behalf of potential lynch victims.

72. Rogin, "'Sword,'" 174. Lang does not believe that the deportation scenes were shot, but he did discover that "the synopsis submitted to the U.S. Copyright Office on February 8, 1915, includes the comment, 'Lincoln's plan of restoring the negroes to Africa was dreamed of only, never carried out,' which lends credence to the hypothesis that the film once included at least an intertitle to this effect." Lang, *Birth of a Nation*, 11n26. Merritt agrees, citing evidence of the deleted scene "in early notes and outlines of *The Birth of a Nation* kept in the Museum of Modern Art." "Dixon, Griffith," 42.

73. The following tale of Dixon's activities in Washington, D.C., is taken from Rogin, "'Sword,'" 154; Schickel, *D. W. Griffith*, 268ff.; and Raymond Cook, "Man behind *Birth*," 529ff.

I haven't the slightest curiosity to see one"), but when he learned the film championed the Klan, he confided to Dixon that he had been himself a Klansman in New Orleans. That evening, White, other members of the Supreme Court, and guests from the House of Representatives and Senate viewed Dixon's project. Dixon recorded his excitement as he "watched the effects of the picture on the crowd of cultured spectators." Wilson, as we have been assured, proclaimed, "It is like writing history with lightning. And my only regret is that it is all so terribly true."[74] And armed with the president's endorsement and the fact of the film's reception by the most eminent jurists and politicians in the country, Dixon (Griffith may have been at the February 19 screening) returned to New York to face off his critics. He succeeded, and on March 3 the film opened in New York. By the end of its first run, in 1917, Richard Schickel estimates, the film had grossed close to $60 million.[75]

Birthing a New America

What Griffith consciously had served as midwife for was the birth of a new, virile American whiteness, unencumbered by the historical memory of slavery, or being enslaved, undaunted by the spectacle of racial humiliation so suddenly manufactured by the shock of poor white immigrants arriving in the cities, a European war which settled into the slaughter of a generation, and the taunts of the Black giant, Jack Johnson. No force in the world was its equal. No moral claim would dare challenge the sovereignty of race right.

The millions of immigrants, largely from what their "betters" thought of as the "inferior stocks" of Europe, had deserted the Old World. Like wild animals fleeing before some cataclysmic disaster, their infestation of America had anticipated the First World War. From its beginnings in August 1914, the scale of the impending disaster mounted: Howard Zinn observes, "In the first three months of the war, almost the entire original British army was wiped out."[76] And by its end, some 10 million had been lost in battle, and another 20 million—civilians—were dead. If the Old World, the seat of Anglo-Saxon and Western civilization, had such a fragile hold on order and the dignity of life, what could be ex-

74. The three quotes in this paragraph are taken from Raymond Cook, "Man behind Birth," 531, 532, 530. Wilson later disavowed his endorsement of Birth. Schickel, D. W. Griffith, 298–99.

75. Schickel, D. W. Griffith, 281.

76. Zinn, People's History, 351.

pected in America, plagued by Europe's genetic debris of Jews, Catholics, Italians, Slavs, and so, as well as its native-born mongrel races?

One answer was the unsettling specter of Jack Johnson. In 1908, Johnson had defeated Tommy Burns for the heavyweight boxing championship. "[Jack] London depicted the new champion as an 'Ethiopian' 'colossus' . . . In the most influential and widely quoted words of London's career, the writer concluded his account of the fight with a racial call to arms."[77] But over the next seven years, Johnson would substantiate his superior prowess by easily defeating the Great White Hope, Jim Jeffries, in 1910, and a string of lesser white opponents. Even more painful to white Americans, Johnson's mocking performances had been filmed.

In the Burns fight, Randy Roberts asserts that Johnson deliberately extended the bout into later rounds, aware that fight film audiences would hardly pay to see a short contest but also because he hated Burns (whose prowess was restricted to calling Johnson a "big dog," "cur," or "nigger"). Johnson punished Burns, "but punishment was not enough. Johnson wanted also to humiliate Burns. He did this verbally. From the very first round Johnson insulted Burns, speaking with an affected English accent, so that 'Tommy' became 'Tahmy.' Mostly what Johnson said was banal. . . . In almost every taunt Johnson referred to Burns in the diminutive. It was always 'Tommy Boy' or 'little Tommy.' And always a derisive smile accompanied the words."[78] The film of Johnson's fight with Stanley Ketchel in 1909 showed Ketchel's apparent knockdown of the champion. Film audiences stood and cheered, and then "a deliberate Johnson lunged across the ring, smashing Ketchel squarely in the mouth and immediately rendering him unconscious. Johnson leaned casually on the ropes, hand on hip, as the referee counted out his victim."[79]

The films were disturbing to representatives from all sectors of white society, particularly so the film of Johnson's defeat of Jeffries. At the margins there was Al Jolson—always eager for a main chance—who wrote in *Variety* that Jeffries's defeat was "really too sad to write about."[80] In

77. See Gilmore, *Bad Nigger*, chap. 4: "The Suppression of the Johnson Fight Films"; and Streible, "Race and Reception," 173.

78. Roberts, *Papa Jack*, 19, 63.

79. Streible, "Race and Reception," 176.

80. For this I am indebted to Lee Grieveson, who designated the find as "one of those curious surprises of the historical archive." Grieveson, *Policing Cinema*, 126.

San Francisco, Mrs. James Crawford, vice president of the California Women's Clubs, wrote to the *Examiner*: "The negroes are to some extent a childlike race, needing guidance, schooling, and encouragement. We deny them this by encouraging them to believe that they have gained anything by having one of their race as a champion fighter."[81] In Tennessee, "the *Chattanooga Times* editorialized that it would do white men no good to see a motion picture of 'a powerful negro knocking a white man about the ring' and that the films would be a positive injury to blacks as they would 'inspire the ignorant negro with false and pernicious ideas as to the physical prowess of his race.'"[82] And identical sentiments voiced by governors, ministers, and civic leaders were to be heard and read all over the country. At first municipal authorities imposed local bans on their exhibition (there were some exceptions; for example, New York, Philadelphia, and Toledo); and then in 1912, with the encouragement of organizations like the United Society for Christian Endeavor, the Women's Christian Temperance Society, the press, and such notables as Theodore Roosevelt, Congress banned the interstate commerce in fight films in America. Notwithstanding, as Dan Streible recounts, "The 1910 film . . . became as widely discussed as any single production prior to *The Birth of a Nation*."[83]

Worst of all, however, while his films inflamed the imaginations and aspirations of Black audiences, Johnson openly consorted with white women. Indeed, he was to marry four white women in succession. And though Randy Roberts maintains that Johnson's love-hate relations with white women drove him to an association with white prostitutes, it was his romantic relationships which brought him his first grief with the law. Johnson's first white wife, Etta Duryea, committed suicide in 1912; and the mother of his second white wife, Lucille Cameron (ironically, an echo of Dixon's novel), brought charges of abduction against Johnson. Johnson married Lucille in December 1912 and their marriage became fodder for editorials and letters to the editor in Black and white newspapers; the cause for threats of lynching (one by Governor Cole Blease of South Carolina); the instigation for the introduction of an antimiscegenation amendment to the Constitution by Representative Seaborn Roddenberry of Georgia, supported by a score of gover-

81. Gilmore, *Bad Nigger*, 81.
82. Ibid., 83.
83. Streible, "Race and Reception," 193.

nors; and several successful state laws banning such marriages.[84] But a month before the marriage Johnson had been charged by federal authorities with violating the new law, the Mann Act, for allegedly transporting a woman across state lines for immoral purposes. The woman in question was a third white woman, Belle Schreiber, a Chicago prostitute and former mistress of Johnson (in his autobiography, *Jack Johnson Is a Dandy*, he insisted she was his secretary/accountant). The uproar around Johnson now extended to sports pages and escalated to mailed death threats and public calls for Southern white lynching parties to visit Johnson in New York or Chicago.[85] Eventually, to avoid prosecution, Johnson and Lucille fled the United States.

Johnson's display of racial insolence was disturbing because he seemed to be impervious by nature and by his celebrity status to the discipline which controlled more ordinary Black brutes. He also disturbed because, like Frankenstein's monster, he escaped the confines and purposes of the original invention. The national myth of the Black rapist of innocent white women had been employed to patrol Black men for generations and more importantly, of course, to mask the reality of white rapists. Black men accused of white rape or even suspected to be thinking of white rape were lynched or beaten to death. Mobs did the deed, but with the assurance that numbers merely confirmed moral and social approbation.[86] Their members pretended to themselves that Black men were cowards and that the white mass of the lynch crowd signified approbation, not fear. Edison's early documentary silents had done their part in confirming the tribal lore: "The myth of the 'spooked' black fighter, in fact, often appeared in accounts about the first moving pictures."[87] Johnson ruptured whole fragments of the myth, and with a vengeance his fight films documented that terrible truth: he was

84. Gilmore, *Bad Nigger*, 106ff.

85. Ibid., chap. 5: "Jack Johnson and White Women: The National Impact"; Roberts, *Papa Jack*, chap. 5: "White Hopes and White Women."

86. Leon Litwack observes, "Drawn from all classes in southern white society, from the 'rednecks' to the 'best people,' lynchers came together in an impressive show of racial and community solidarity. Neither crazed fiends nor the dregs of white society, the bulk of the lynchers tended to be ordinary and respectable people, few of whom had any difficulty justifying their atrocities in the name of maintaining the social and racial order and the purity of the Anglo-Saxon race." Litwack, "Hellhounds," 19.

87. Streible, "Race and Reception," 170.

not only uncowered but contemptuous of his white opponents. In life, nevertheless, legions of newspaper stories recited that Johnson confirmed the *desire* and *allure* of Black men: his white wife and white mistresses fawned over him.[88]

While Johnson's challenge to white superiority was public, daunting, and counterintuitive in critical ways, other threats from the inferior races were stealthy and assuring. But Griffith would nonetheless merge these dissimilar "Others" in his screenplay. One model for Flora's ("Lil' Sis") suicide in *Birth* was the killing in 1913 of thirteen-year-old Mary Phagan. "The descendant of an established Piedmont farm family that had lost its land and been reduced first to tenancy and then to wage labor," Phagan was murdered at the National Pencil Factory in Atlanta, on the day of the Confederate Memorial Day parade.[89] She died, according to the lead prosecutor, "because she wouldn't yield her virtue to the demands of her superintendent."[90] The accused was Leo Frank, a manager in the factory and a Northern-born Jew.

Originally there had been another suspect: the Black factory janitor, Jim Conley. Conley's role, however, was reduced to an accessory after the fact, because while testifying against Frank, he admitted on the stand that he had helped Frank move Mary's body. But despite a defense strategy which Nancy MacLean characterizes as "a virulent racist offense against the only other suspect . . . Jim Conley," class animosity and anti-Semitism superseded Negrophobia:

> The concern of elites about the Frank case reflected profound fears about the stability of the social order over which they presided. Time and again, they complained about the spread of "anarchy" and "mob rule" as revealed in the case. "Class hatred was played on" by the prosecutors, Frank's attorney complained in court, "They played on the enmity the poor feel against the wealthy" and encouraged "discontent." A prominent Progressive supporter of Frank, the Rev-

88. Randy Roberts asserts that "in cartoons, [Johnson's] shaved head was sometimes pictured as the head of a snake, with all the sexual implications that reptile carried. . . . Sexuality was the essence of Jack Johnson, the driving force behind his success, and this power was perceived by white females and males." Roberts, *Papa Jack*, 74.

89. MacLean, "Leo Frank Case," 921.

90. Ibid., 930.

erend C. B. Wilmer, observed that "class prejudice" "was perfectly obvious" at every stage in the case and warned of the dangers of pandering to it.[91]

And in his summation the prosecutor, Hugh Dorsey, told the jury, "although he had never mentioned the word *Jew*, once it was introduced he would use it. The Jews 'rise to heights sublime,' he asserted, 'but they also sink to the lowest depths of degradation.'"[92] Following a nationally publicized four-month trial, Frank was convicted and sentenced to death. In June 1915, his sentence was commuted to life in prison by Governor Slaton (who then had to declare martial law for self-protection). But on August 16, 1915, Frank was abducted from the Georgia state farm by the "Knights of Mary Phagan," carried to Marietta, Phagan's home town, and lynched.[93]

Many of the cultural signifiers Griffith embedded in *The Birth of a Nation* closely resembled elements from the Phagan-Frank case. In terms of place, Griffith had reconstructed Mary Phagan's Georgia region into the fictive town of Piedmont, and in the process transformed it from a rural redneck region to a center of Southern gentry. More strikingly, in his dramatization of Dixon's *The Clansman*, Griffith replaced the novel's double suicide of Mother Lenoir and her ravished daughter, Marion, with Flora's solitary leap. Yet Griffith's Flora, like Mary Phagan in the scenario imagined by Dorsey, had chosen death when faced with rape. And like Flora (impersonated by the attractive Mae Marsh) whom Griffith had fashioned to serve as an innocent icon for whiteness, Mary Phagan had been refashioned by the press for a similar purpose. As Nancy MacLean informs us, the published photographs of Mary Phagan were altered: Phagan's flat nose was Aryanized; her thick eyebrows thinned glamorously; her hair styled beyond the skill of the hairdressers to whom she had access. In actual life her appearance too closely resembled the notoriously incestuous, poor white Appalachians whom eugenicists had campaigned to eliminate from the American gene pool.[94] But in death Phagan's modified self could serve

91. Ibid., 924, 926.

92. Dinnerstein, "Fate of Leo Frank," 102. The next year Dorsey was elected governor, serving two terms.

93. "Warden Is Overpowered," *New York Times*, August 17, 1915, 1.

94. Gould, *Mismeasure of Man*, chap. 5.

as an emblem of the threat posed by Jews to the white American race, her manufactured innocence and prettiness a proof of race virtue.[95]

To complete his tableaux restaging the Phagan spectacle for a national public saturated in Frank's trial, Griffith used Gus, the Black renegade, to heal the diegetic rupture (Frank being neither Black nor mulatto). In the novel, Gus had been the leader of the "four black brutes" who ravished Marion Lenoir; in the film he was a "bad nigger" from his initial appearance (as a fugitive slave) to his last breath. And with Gus standing in as Frank's substitute, Griffith imported Jim Conley, the murderer of choice for many of Frank's defenders, past and present.[96] As well, the renegade Gus, in his cowering posture and sneaky, simian-like movements, could serve to erase Jack Johnson, the bold, graceful athlete, from the minds of the audience; and Flora's suicidal gesture put the lie to the intolerable ruse that white women would willingly submit to Black men. And since a white actor, Walter Long, impersonated Gus in blackface and with shaved head, Griffith was assured of an interpretive mastery of Jack Johnson not otherwise possible. Thus Long's Gus underscored Griffith's racial contempt. After all, Griffith had explained, "On careful weighing of every detail concerned, the decision was made to have no black blood among the principals." As such, Michael Rogin observes, "Griffith's Negros [sic] were as bad as he painted them because he painted whites black. . . . Griffith allowed a few blacks to act the nigger. But he did not want to let the representation of blackness go."[97] The character of Gus, providing visual reality to the suppositions around Conley, thus debased Johnson and the threatening racial signature Johnson had come to represent.

Life, they say, does imitate art. And so it occurred on Thanksgiving night in 1915 when William Joseph Simmons and a group of friends met on Stone Mountain outside Atlanta, Georgia, and declared a new beginning: the new Knights of the Ku Klux Klan.[98] Over the next ten years, particularly from 1920 to 1925, the second Klan enrolled millions, fre-

95. Griffith had also considerably altered Dixon's feminist rendering of Elsie Stoneman. The Elsie who in an extended debate concerning slavery had declared to Ben, "I don't care to be absorbed by a mere man" (Dixon, *Clansman*, 127), was transformed into a dependent, filiopietistic adolescent by Griffith and Lillian Gish.

96. For attempts to prove Conley's guilt, see Dinnerstein, "Fate of Leo Frank"; Goldfarb, "Framed"; and Frey and Thompson-Frey, *Silent and Damned.*

97. The quotes are from Rogin, "'Sword,'" 181–82.

98. MacLean, *Behind the Mask*, 5.

quently drawing recruits with a showing of *The Birth of a Nation*. To be sure, the second Klan rode to the rescue of abused wives, communities preyed on by corrupt politicians and exploitative employers, impoverished families, and supporters of Prohibition; but its staple was hatred: Blacks, Jews, Catholics, and immigrants.[99]

Aryan-American Expansionism

While Jack Johnson and Leo Frank were signatures of the presence of a troubling domestic enemy, a potentially degrading strain in the otherwise pure, white soul of the country, the nation's commercial, industrial, and political elites were simultaneously pursuing robustly expansive policies which might secure profit, a preferred national identity, and the American share of world power.

The war just begun in 1914 in Europe, of course, provided Griffith the opportunity to manufacture an allegorical counterpoint to the American Civil War. For Griffith, Europe was the place of origin for the mythic white civilization he held sacred, and just as the present war was proving to be catastrophic, the "war between the states," as white Southerners referred to it, had overturned the natural order. And given the substantially European origins of much of his audience, the easy transfer from one war to the other encouraged Griffith to superimpose Negrophobia onto antiwar sentiments. He could empirically, that is, historically, demonstrate the evil of war by giving dramatic realization to its consequences. Moreover, his rhetorical strategy of maintaining that his epic was "not meant to reflect on any race or people of today" was cleverly employed to establish that even with the most delicately contrived fairness, history itself documented Black inferiority.

The Birth of a Nation was conceived, realized, and exhibited two years

99. For an apology of the Klan as typically "a social and civic organization, reinvigorating a sense of unity and cohesiveness in community life with its spectacular social events, civic activities and philanthropic works," see Moore, "Historical Interpretations." MacLean responds to "the trend in recent historical writing about the Klan to de-emphasize the racial hatred of its politics and the violence of its practice," by suggesting that "false polarities" (whether the Klan was primarily rural or urban, concerned with local or national politics, consisted of civic crusaders or vigilantes, was populist or racist) conceal the fact that "it was at once mainstream and extreme, hostile to big business and antagonistic to industrial unions, anti-elitist and hateful of blacks and immigrants, pro-law and order and prone to extralegal violence. If scholars have viewed these attributes as incompatible, Klansmen themselves did not." MacLean, *Behind the Mask*, xiii.

before the American entry into World War I. And though, as Howard Zinn testifies, it is difficult to determine public opinion on involvement in the European war, prior to 1917 "the government had to work hard to create its consensus" for war. "George Creel, a veteran newspaperman, became the government's official propagandist for the war; he set up a Committee on Public Information to persuade Americans the war was right. It sponsored 75,000 speakers, who gave 750,000 four-minute speeches in five thousand American cities and towns. It was a massive effort to excite a reluctant public."[100] Notwithstanding, in need of a million enlistments and faced with a mere 73,000 six weeks after the declaration of war, the Congress enacted a draft. The sale of munitions and other materials to the Allies had transformed the United States — in the form of capital — from a debtor nation to the leading lender nation in the world (a position not relinquished until the war in Vietnam). This was reason enough for American interests to intervene on the side of their new debtors. And as Eric Hobsbawm reports, "Thanks to the flood of American reinforcements and equipment, the Allies recovered, but for a while it looked a close thing."[101]

For a time, Griffith had been on the side of the angels, but by late 1915 or early 1916, he was preparing to exploit his new reputation as "the world's pre-eminent director of military spectacle."[102] Traveling to Britain for the premiere of *Intolerance* (1916), Griffith was charmed by the British prime minister, Lloyd George, into producing a war spectacle, *Hearts of the World* (1918). "Griffith had arrived at the very event that would undo the cultural consensus that had formed his sensibility and informed all his work. But he would emerge from this encounter essentially oblivious to the nature of the war and to the effect it was having on the young generation that bore its brunt."[103] More and more taken up with his own growing legend, Griffith's resolve to exploit "the ravages of war to the end that *war may be held in abhorrence*" evaporated.

Interestingly enough, the first U.S. military intervention on behalf of the Allies was not the declaration of war in 1917, but the invasion of Haiti two years earlier. From 1915 to 1934, American marines would occupy

100. Zinn, *People's History*, 355.
101. Hobsbawm, *Age of Extremes*, 29.
102. Schickel, *D. W. Griffith*, 342.
103. Ibid., 343.

Haiti, providing the repressive force necessary for the conversion of Haiti from a semiautonomous nation to an American colony by American financiers, businessmen, and State Department bureaucrats.[104] The official rationales for the U.S. invasion were the fear of German influence in Haiti, the security of the Panama Canal, and a concern for order and stability in that country (from 1888 to 1915, ten Haitian presidents had been killed or overthrown).[105] On the surface, all of these issues were legitimate, but tarnished: for nearly all of Haiti's existence since 1804, the primary source of its destabilization had been the United States.[106] The Haitian Revolution for independence from France (and Britain) had been the second successful rebellion in the New World, but unlike its predecessor, the American Revolution, it had been achieved by slaves.[107] Thus for the first half of the nineteenth century, Haiti was perceived as a threat to American slavery by the plantocrats and the national government they dominated; and in the second half, pliant Haitian governments headed by American-installed presidents had facilitated the conversion of the country into an American treasury.

Beneath the surface, it was American capital which was the central agent fueling invasion. Roger Farnham was the vice president of the Rockefeller group's National City Bank; Farnham was also vice president of Haiti's central bank, the Banque Nationale, and Haiti's national railway. All these interlocking roles gave Farnham special interests in his additional identity as the principal adviser to the American secretary of state, William Jennings Bryan. Farnham's desire was that Haiti become an American colony, and Bryan's lack of sophistication with respect to Haiti (in 1912 Bryan had commented to John Allen, another American officer in Haiti's Banque Nationale, "Dear me, think of it! Niggers speaking French")[108] forfeited the advantage to Farnham. Farnham was concerned that German (or French) bankers would outmaneuver National City Bank, and he orchestrated American businessmen (United Fruit Company was advised to resist the lure of plantations until an occupation) and the government into actions which would insure total

104. See Hans Schmidt, *United States Occupation*; Plummer, *Haiti and the Great Powers*; and Plummer, *Haiti and the United States*.

105. Hans Schmidt, *United States Occupation*, 42.

106. See Plummer, *Haiti and the Great Powers*.

107. See James, *Black Jacobins*.

108. Schmidt, *United States Occupation*, 48.

American domination of Haiti's economy (the only significant missing element was American control of Haitian custom revenue).

President Wilson, Farnham, and the marines staged a mini-invasion in December 1914, securing $500,000 from the Haitian treasury, which was duly installed in the vaults of National City Bank. And in July of 1915, a full-scale invasion took place. Over the next several years, nationalist resistance ("bandits," the American press assured its public) was extirpated; the Haitian military was reorganized into a colonial force; the country's transportation and communications systems were appropriated; and good government (dictatorships, of course) was established. It was all to the good, as in 1918 Robert Lansing (Bryan's successor) wrote to Rear Admiral J. H. Oliver, another American colonial officer (governor of the Virgin Islands): "The experience of Liberia and Haiti show that the African race are devoid of any capacity for political organization and lack genius for government. Unquestionably there is in them an inherent tendency to revert to savagery and to cast aside the shackles of civilization which are irksome to their physical nature.... It is that which makes the negro problem practically unsolvable."[109]

Lansing's knowledge of Blacks bears an uncanny resemblance to the written and cinematic images which Wilson, Dixon, and Griffith had transmitted into the new American culture in 1915: "The riot in the Master's Hall: ... a representative furtively takes a bottle of liquor from beneath a book and steals a mouthful ... a representative with his feet on his desk takes off a shoe, as another, standing in front of him, eating a joint of meat, turns . . ."[110] Wilson, Dixon, and Griffith had not invented these myths, but they made them accessible to millions, and they made them unforgettable. Wilson, Dixon, and Griffith and their large fraternity of racist intellectuals had supplied a fabulous history, a white history, which portrayed the whites as the forever normal, forever real, the race responsible for the order of the world, the race which was the destiny of the species, the true Subject of world history and its civilizations.

109. Ibid., 62–63.
110. Lang, *Birth of a Nation*, 110–11.

Repressed Consciousness

In the June 1915 issue of *Crisis*, the NAACP organ, it was reported that the *New York Evening Globe* complained that the very title *The Birth of a Nation* constituted an insult to the achievements of George Washington and Abraham Lincoln: Washington had contributed to the beginning of the American nation in the Revolutionary War; Lincoln had fought against "the attempt to denationalize a nation."[111] There was, to be sure, some justification for challenging the peculiar chronology to which race hunger drove Dixon and Griffith. But, as we have seen, this criticism merely skimmed along the surface of the film's racial agenda. Griffith's historical memorial posed and deposed, invented and effaced, to a purpose. His plots, his stagings, his choice of shots, his editing techniques, and his creation of archetypes were complex declaratives intended to flood the consciousness of his audience. He possessed a certain knowledge of what must be remembered, and how, and what was required to make the intolerable past vanish.

Beyond the visual ephemera of the past, that is, settings, costumes, and romanticized dioramas, it is not certain whether Griffith had any firm purchase on social history. Since the stark moral oppositions found in melodrama are generally conceits when framed as historical narrative, many of Griffith's "historical" photoplays were either drafted by marketing strategies (at best, the most generous interpretation) or the product of an inadequately constructed imaginary drifting on sheets of ideology (white superiority) and mythology (the Old South). Even more disturbing, when we review Griffith's portrayal of American Indians, the frantic pace of production conspired with the economies of ideology and myth to imprison the real oppression of these people in the narrative drivel of melodrama and romance. No wonder that Griffith himself referred to his "art" in this period as "grinding out another sausage."[112]

It is still surprising that notwithstanding Biograph's preeminence in exhibiting degrading Black images, before *Birth* Griffith's contribution to these conventions had been modest. Most prominent had been *The*

111. "Opinion," *Crisis*, June 1915, 70. In 1915, contrary to most recent commentary, much if not most of the criticism of the film targeted Dixon, the intellectual and novelist, and not Griffith, who seemed to be considered merely a moviemaker.

112. Quoted from G. W. (Billy) Bitzer's unpublished manuscript in Merritt, "Dixon, Griffith," 30.

Guerrilla (1908), *His Trust* (1911), and *His Trust Fulfilled* (also 1911), all three featuring a blackface servant or slave character who risked life and limb in loyal service to his white mistress or (in the two latter films) to his dead master's family. Instead of Black servants and slaves, Griffith's most frequently racialized juxtapositions were between whites and Indians. And from 1908 to 1914, beginning with *The Redman and the Child* (1908) and concluding with *The Battle of Elderbush Gulch* (1914), Griffith had plied his talents to something like thirty Indian films. This attention to Indian films, though, was not idiosyncratic. According to Eileen Bowser, the dominant genres of the early silent era were comedies, Westerns (then a separate genre), and Indian films.[113] One reason for the popularity of the Indian genre, Bowser surmises, may have been the almost inevitable display of the seminaked Indian male characters in an era still bound by Victorian moral strictures.[114] But at a more profound ideological level, the consumption of the genre may have been more effectively explained by its service to white supremacy doctrine. Gregory Jay comments that "on screen, the silent-era Indian served both as a nostalgic reminder of what was purportedly passing away and a focus for perceiving the superior qualities of the dominant culture." Moreover, there was too the genre's function as a displacement memory: "In terms of its cultural work, the Indian film translated the political struggle between the Indian nations and the United States into a domestic tragedy (or farce) played out among individuals."[115] And unlike the practices conventional to Black representation, actual Indian actors and actresses (like James Young Deer and Miss Redwing) played prominent roles in many of the Indian genre films.[116] In that genre, the

113. Bowser, *Transformation of Cinema*, 173.

114. As Gregory Jay reports, "Estimates are that fifty Indian/western/cowboy one-reelers were released in 1909, and between one hundred and two hundred such films in each year through 1914." "'White Man's Book,'" 6. Jay identifies thirty-one Indian films by Griffith. See appendix in ibid., 23.

115. Ibid., 8, 7.

116. Eileen Bowser recounts that "Young Deer and Miss Redwing [were] both of the Winnebago tribe. James Young Deer, born in Dakota City, Nebraska, was with traveling circuses until he was hired for the movies by Kalem. Young Deer also worked for Lubin, where he wrote, directed, and starred. Biograph hired him to appear in *The Mended Lute*, and Vitagraph for *Red Wing's Gratitude*: he became a director-actor for Pathe American from its beginnings in the east (*A Cheyenne Brave*, *The Red Girl and the Child*) and . . . established Pathe's West Coast studio." Bowser, *Transformation of Cinema*, 174, 175. For Turner, see Cronon, "Revisiting the Vanishing Frontier."

Indian was treated sympathetically, reflecting the "vanishing race" theme popularized by James Fenimore Cooper's *The Last of the Mohicans* (1826) and which appeared, with "a certain irony" (as Roberta E. Pearson comments) in the 1874 memoirs of General George Armstrong Custer. The totality of American colonialism was memorialized as "the frontier thesis" by Frederick Jackson Turner two decades later.[117] But whether framed in a romantic trope of genocide or the territorial imperatives of evolution, Indian films complemented a broad consensus concerning the pathetic savage. They were sentimentalized fodder, the empirical demonstration of the futility of the savage's resistance to white civilization.

In most respects, Jay (and many of his predecessors) finds Griffith's Indian films conformed to the popular culture's sleights of distraction: "In most of Griffith's Biograph Indian films the Indians elicit white melodramatic sympathy and the white miners, pioneers, and soldiers are often depicted as rapacious scoundrels."[118] Filling his films with conflicts engendered by encounters between overwrought savages and demented whites, it is not surprising that when he appropriated Custer's legend for his film *The Massacre* (1912), Griffith would fail to register the general's service as protector of the Northern Pacific Railroad's 1873 survey of routes through Indian land.[119] These, after all, were racial conflicts or cosmic contests between civilizations. In either instance the structural impulses of capitalist accumulation and exploitation were absented or trivialized. But one of the most overt subtexts of these films is Griffith's antipathy to miscegenation. In *The Call of the Wild* (1908), George Redfeather, a football hero and honors student at Carlisle Indian College (a character loosely drawn on Jim Thorpe), resorts to his savage nature after his pursuit of a white girl is repulsed. In a drunken fit of solitary debauchery he strips off his Western clothing,

117. Pearson, "Revenge of Rain-in-the-Face?" 273; and Jay, "'White Man's Book,'" 7. For Cooper's contribution to movie Indians, see Kilpatrick, *Celluloid Indians*, 2–5.

118. Jay, "'White Man's Book,'" 10.

119. Kino Video's version of *The Massacre* does not include what Jay describes as the beginning of the film: "Two southerners ride off to the war after wooing the same lady. The newly wed husband is killed, leaving the rejected suitor, Stephen, to take the news home. Delivery of his message completes the demise of the bedridden wife, whose lively infant daughter is left to Stephen to raise. Years pass." Jay, "'White Man's Book,'" 15. It is at this place that the Kino version begins. See *D. W. Griffith's Biograph Shorts*, Kino Video DVD, New York, 2002.

donning leather, feathers, and blanket. Later, rescuing the same white woman from other "savages," he is redeemed from lust and drunkenness by his recognition of "the superior purity of white womanhood."[120] In *A Romance of the Western Hills* (1910), the evil signature inevitably attached to miscegenation is dramatized by the seduction of an Indian girl (Mary Pickford) by a white rake. Warned by her Indian paramour that "white man's book no good," the young woman is bartered by her father to the whites she adores in exchange for a watch. Eventually disabused of her naïveté, she returns to her people, redeemed by an act of intervention between her white suitor and her original lover.[121] By the time Griffith concluded his Indian "studies" with *The Battle of Elderbush Gulch*, Indians had been reduced to caricatures: the dramatic catalyst for the attack on the whites is the tardy arrival of the chief's son to the drunken orgy of the Dog Feast ("may you eat dog and live long"). As Eileen Bowser observes, miscegenation between Indians and whites was also a persistent concern of Griffith's contemporaries.[122] But with Griffith and his peers, this discourse on miscegenation was decorated by understandable physical attraction. The Indian maidens entrapped in the tragic lures of mixed-race affairs were young and beautiful (particularly so when Lillian Gish or Mary Pickford impersonated them). And the white female characters who fired the erotic desires of Indian males were even more naturally the objects of desire. Such unions, however, were forfeited by the collision of different grades of civilization. Miscegenation in the Indian genre was always positioned on a palette of forbidden beauty. This was not the case when the issue was transferred to the realm of blackness.

As we have seen, Dixon and Griffith had framed race-mixing as a forbidding terrain: the mulatta was the destructive seductress; the mulatto, a compulsive defiler of white women. In the mammy, the dominant characterization of dark-skinned Black women in *Birth*, Griffith erased two or more centuries of what one Black spokesman decried as white "enforced debauchery." Countless slave women (and white indentured women) had, of course, been sexually used by their so-called masters and other males protected by race and class privileges. The

120. Jay, "'White Man's Book,'" 11.

121. Ibid., 12ff.

122. "It was usual for love affairs between Indians and whites to end in tragedy, to avoid miscegenation." Bowser, *Transformation of Cinema*, 176.

documentation of this depravity, Ida B. Wells insisted, could be readily discovered in the large percentage of mulattos, and as she recorded in her autobiography, "I found that this rape of helpless Negro girls and women, which began in slavery days, still continued without let or hindrance, check or reproof from church, state, or press until there had been created this race within a race."[123] Indeed, though Griffith's asexual mammy negated that very possibility, one rationale for the exploitation of Black women had been their lewdness, their own sexual appetites, and their seductiveness.[124] For white males of the plantocracy and its support strata (overseers, militia, etc.), slave society had been a highly charged sexual hothouse: as Catherine Clinton maintained, "Flesh and blood were an explosive mix in the Old South."[125] Griffith's mammy, like her fictional predecessor, displaced the real. And she was already a stock character among similarly grotesque Black domestic servants in American films, as attested to by films like Vitagraph's *Mammy's Ghost, or Between the Lines of Battle* (1911) and Majestic's *Old Mammy's Charge* (1913).[126]

In the stead of his pretentious claims for *The Birth of a Nation*, Griffith had perfected a genre, what Ed Guerrero has termed the "plantation genre," which would dominate Hollywood's representation of the Old South of the antebellum, American slavery and its ending, and Blacks for generations.[127] In this fabulous narrative, the poor whites who had worked and sometimes fought alongside the slaves, and later the free Blacks, disappeared. Their historical complexity and ambiguous race-loyalty could not be contained by the genre. In the plantation genre, only two classes were of any importance: the plantocrats and their childlike charges, the Blacks. Prominent white abolitionists, like the fictional Stoneman, were transfigured, as in *The Santa Fe Trail*, into megalomaniacal fanatics like John Brown (Raymond Massey) or Judases (Van Heflin's role). White Southern aristocratic women were infrequently the responsible adults which Margaret Sullivan constructed in *So Red the Rose* (1935) but more often the irresponsible, childlike, or egotistical materialists so brilliantly portrayed by Bette Davis in *Jezebel*

123. Wells, *Crusade for Justice*, 70.
124. Ervin Jordan, "Sleeping with the Enemy," 56.
125. Clinton, "'Southern Dishonor,'" 52.
126. See Sampson, *Blacks in Black and White*, 83–84, 95–96.
127. See Guerrero, *Framing Blackness*, chap. 1.

(1938), Vivian Leigh in *Gone with the Wind* (1939), and the actual child Shirley Temple.

With rare exceptions, the representation of Blacks in American films degraded even further from Griffith's oppositions between the loyal and the brute. Black actors with professional training as doctors (Rex Ingram) and lawyers (Paul Robeson, Clarence Muse) stood in for modern domestics, slaves, and colonized savages; most training themselves, as Louise Beavers did for her role as Delilah in *Imitation of Life* (1934), to tie their articulate tongues to the cinematic Black pseudo-speech Griffith popularized in *Birth*. During the silent-film era, only the Black independent filmmakers like George and Noble Johnson (Lincoln Motion Pictures) or Oscar Micheaux, and a few non-Blacks producing Black-cast films, like the Norman Film Manufacturing Company, resisted. But their art was largely restricted to the audiences congregated in the all-Black theater circuit—approximately five hundred theaters compared to the twelve thousand or more available to the Negrophobes in the 1920s.[128]

Griffith was fortunate: his maturing as a filmmaker coincided with that moment during which immigrant haberdashers, junk dealers, and garment kings took command of the movie industry. Their historical memory was of the ghettos of Europe and the Pale of Settlement; about America they were largely ignorant. Griffith, whose moral and historical sensibility was borrowed from the rulers of the ancien régime of slavery imagined the American past as the ideologists of slavery had intended it to be remembered: as a race hierarchy. This is precisely what it had not been—a wealthy landed aristocracy had ruled over Black, white, and indigenous labor—but this rule by an oligopoly could only be sustained with the support or indifference of those whose social and political privileges met a bare minimum. Griffith's advantage over his associates in the movie business was that he possessed *some* memory of America, even if it was a fraudulent one.

Griffith was for most of his career a journeyman director. Only

128. See Cripps, *Slow Fade to Black*, chap. 3. See also Pearl Bowser and Jane Gaines, "New Finds/Old Films" (2–5); Alex Albright, "Micheaux, Baudeville and Black Cast Film" (6–9, 36); Gloria Gibson-Hudson, "The Norman Film Manufacturing Company" (16–20); and J. Ronald Green, "The Micheaux Style" (32–34), in "History of Black Film." For the number of movie houses between 1912 and 1921, see Sklar, *Movie-Made America*, 146.

twenty-five of the more than four hundred films he directed were produced after *Birth* and exceeded one or two reels. And only one or two
of the later films (the drenchingly sentimental *Broken Blossoms*, 1919,
and *Way Down East*, 1920) have warranted serious critical discussion
except as the works of the director of *The Birth of a Nation*. Six years
after completing *Birth*, Griffith was creating an omnibus like *Orphans
of the Storm*. In fact, he never matched the narrative creativity, the lyri-
cism and poetic imaging, of the great film directors of the silent era
like Sergei Eisenstein or Jean Renoir.[129] Schickel, his most sympathetic
biographer, could muster only the following defense: "Considering
the pace of innovation from 1914 to the establishment of the first set
of generic conventions for the sound film approximately twenty years
later, it is ridiculous to ask one man, no matter how gifted, to partake
of them all or even approve of them all, let alone take the lead in establishing them all. Griffith obviously had his limitations and if there are
no masterpieces among his last eight films, little innovation and much
imitation, only two or three are out-and-out disgraces."[130] Mechanics
and techniques, as Renoir pointedly remarked about Griffith, are not
the issue.[131] What had distinguished Griffith was that he extended a
fantastic history of America into the most profoundly significant mass
media art form prior to television. His timing was accidental, but no
less determinant, since he offered his vision to an audience largely un-
informed of America with the collaboration of producers, exhibitors,
and financiers equally ignorant of America except as a market.

Together — Griffith (Dixon, Wilson, etc.), his industry cohorts, and
his audience — they constituted the social and cultural platform for
a robust economic and political agenda; an agenda in the process of
seizing domestic and international labor, land, and capital. Under the

129. In assessing Griffith's importance as a filmmaker, more attention should be
given to the contributions of Frank Woods, who wrote one "lost" scenario for *The
Birth of a Nation* and was Griffith's story editor from 1909. Schickel credits (it was
Woods who first brought *The Clansman* to Griffith's attention) and discredits ("not
quite a grey eminence") Woods. Schickel, *D. W. Griffith*, 140, 212, 242. Gunning frequently cites only Woods's earlier columns in the *New York Dramatic Mirror* for
their acute sensibility and impact on Griffith's narrative development. *D. W. Griffith*,
186n66; while Jay maintains that Woods did much of the research for Griffith's Indian
films. "'White Man's Book,'" 10.

130. Schickel, *D. W. Griffith*, 510.

131. Ibid., 597.

imprimatur of race destiny, but irrespective of race, the lives and destinies of men and women all over the globe were dealt with as so many marketable assets, as human capital. White patrimony deceived some of the majority of Americans, patriotism and nationalism others, but the more fugitive reality was the theft they themselves endured and the voracious expropriation of others they facilitated. The scrap which was their reward was the installation of Black inferiority into their shared national culture. It was a paltry dividend, but it still serves.

Blackface Minstrelsy and Black Resistance

We saw that the colored performer would have to get away from the ragtime limitations of the "darky," and we decided to make the break, so as to save ourselves and others.

— *George W. Walker, "The Negro on the American Stage," October 1906*

Minstrelsy and Black Resistance

You might think that blackface minstrelsy could mask a multitude of sins. Costumed as it was in a feigned blackness and staged in a grotesque parody of American life, there were many reasons to suggest it would go on forever. After all, blackface minstrelsy conspired with power.[1] Yet minstrelsy survived its own demise only by an act of migration. At the turn from the nineteenth to the twentieth century, as a performance of the superlatives of whiteness, blackface minstrelsy was momentarily compromised by the economies of public entertainment. Black minstrels became its paradox. While the old blackface minstrelsy waned, racialists energetically plied their trade in the hokum concealed in the natural sciences, in the marketing arts of consumerism, in the designs of children's toys, in the caricatures which infested what passed as home entertainment (for example, stereoviews), and other public amusements. It would prove to be only a temporary setback for blackface. From our perspective a hundred years later, blackface minstrelsy was merely stalled, waiting for the moment it would find its new home, transferring its hideous fruit from the limiting venue of the stage to the expansive flickering reach of celluloid.[2] In its new domicile, the

1. I am referring here to the blackface minstrel show which had become standard during the antebellum era just prior to the Civil War. See Gura, "America's Minstrel Daze."

2. Eric Lott observes, "By 1915 Brander Matthews ["The Rise and Fall of Negro Minstrelsy," *Scribner's Magazine* 57.6 (1915): 754–59] of Columbia University was sadly detailing minstrelsy's decline, which he attributed to the fact that blackface performers were less and less true to life, increasingly 'content to be comic without any effort to catch the special comicality of the darky.'" Eric Lott, *Love and Theft*, 34.

contest between racialists and their opponents would be rather less than equal. Just how unequal is authenticated in the contrast between racialist artists like Griffith, Porter, and their cohorts and those like Micheaux who sought to use film differently.

Undoubtedly, Oscar Micheaux was the most successful and radical Black filmmaker of the silent-movie era. And in his 1920 film *Within Our Gates*, Micheaux achieved a startling subversion of Dixon/Griffith. On that score, a number of Micheaux's silent movies far surpassed the "uplift" gestures of his closest competitors: George P. and Noble Johnson's Lincoln Motion Pictures, Richard Norman's Norman Film Manufacturing Company, and David Starkman's Colored Players Film Corporation. But notwithstanding his energetic and persistent campaign of self-invention, Micheaux was not entirely a creature of his own making. Indeed, he was the heir of a form of Black resistance to the new racial regime which could be traced to late minstrelsy, more particularly Black minstrelsy as it manifested itself in the last decade of the nineteenth century. In the process of spawning Black musical theater from Black minstrelsy, a remarkable cluster of Black performers, choreographers, and writers — Bob Cole, Bert Williams, George Walker, Aida Overton Walker, James Weldon Johnson and his brother J. Rosamond Johnson, Will Marion Cook, and Paul Laurence Dunbar — perfected a host of Black resistance gestures for display before largely white audiences. Acutely race conscious, this group recovered and invented much of the moral and conceptual vocabulary and the sly oppositional stratagems which would sluice Black resistance into public entertainment, preparing an assemblage for Micheaux.

It is apparent that blackface minstrelsy had a considerable impact on early American films. There were some few interludes when minstrelsy was suspended, like in Edison's parodist "actuality" of Black soldiers, *Colored Troops Disembarking* (1898), and in Edwin S. Porter's *What Happened in the Tunnel* (1903) where actual Blacks appeared. But for the most part, the race-patrolling protocols of minstrelsy were maintained. For one — almost inexplicable in a medium so dependent on the visual spectacle — white actors and actresses donning blackface were supposed and allowed to achieve the representations of Blacks in silent films. Even more significantly, it was not merely the impersonation of Blacks which was drawn from minstrelsy but the persistent disfiguring of Black humanity, the reduction to servile, pathetic, caricatured appendices to *real* (white) life. The dominance of the minstrel trope was almost inevitably a consequence of minstrelsy's sovereignty over blackness in the scheme of American race as determined by the new racial regime of the late nineteenth and early twentieth centuries. While Mexicans and Native Americans (Indians) might be easily enveloped by the conquest motifs of the Western as a genre, or Jews, Asians, and Central Europeans might be degraded as lascivious villains in urban melodrama, minstrelsy was its own imperium.[3] Thus in silent movies when melodrama, romance, costume drama, Western, or any of the other genres adapted from the stage or literature drew on blackness, minstrelsy dictated the semiotics. Because for the new racial regime minstrelsy embodied the iconography of blackness, in popular culture minstrelsy held absolute domain over blackness and the imagery of blackness.

The administration of the substitution of filmed blackface minstrelsy for staged minstrelsy was performed with a difference. On the stage, as blackface minstrelsy projected the Negro, the effect, according to James Dormon, was that "the minstrel black was represented as an essentially unthreatening figure. He (or, less frequently, she) was unquestionably ignorant (though not always stupid: the minstrel blacks could be wily and even sage), maladroit, and outlandish in his misuses of the forms and substance of white culture."[4] On the silent screen, this representation transmogrified. We have previously recounted that Gerald Butters Jr., after an exhaustive investigation of surviving films and company production catalogs, maintained that "by far, the largest subgenre of early films with black depictions were films that featured African-American men as chicken thieves."[5] The traditions of Black representation on the minstrel stage were invented during an era in which most Blacks appeared to be permanently confined in slavery a world away. In the urban settings of this minstrelsy, targeting Blacks for caricature was coincident with a lack of concern for any retaliation.[6] In the late nine-

3. In the following, I employ the terms "minstrelsy" for the theatrical genre, "blackface minstrelsy" for the genre as performed by non-Blacks in or out of burnt cork makeup, and "Black minstrelsy" for the performance of Blacks (in or out of black makeup).

4. Dormon, "Shaping the Popular Image," 451.

5. Butters, *Black Manhood*, 24.

6. As was mentioned in chapter 1 (note 145), during the 1820s and 1830s, 209 anti-Black and antiabolitionist mobs were reported by "the three leading anti-slavery newspapers—the *Liberator*, the *Emancipator*, and the *Philanthropist*." Leonard L.

teenth and early twentieth centuries, contrarily, Blacks were loose in American society. They were still grotesque buffoons, but a certain vigilance was appropriate, even a modicum of violence: "Early motion pictures, therefore, supported barbarism toward African-American men because the violence did not really appear to be harmful and because this use of force upheld the moral order."[7] Of course, this "harmless" violence served as an accompaniment to the actual brutality of the new racial regime. The differences between staged and filmed blackface, consequently, were a result of the radically distinct historical eras in which these venues were generated, the audiences for whom they were created, and the cultural shields required by their respective spectators. And, as we shall see, what would complicate this transfer from stage minstrelsy to movies was the now contested terrain of minstrelsy itself. By the late nineteenth century, minstrelsy had come to contain concealed resistances, gestures of opposition smuggled in and hidden by the Black minstrel performers so prominent in the form.[8] Their impact was to be reflected in a second cinema: the independent Black film or all-Black-cast film.

Richards, *"Gentlemen of Property and Standing,"* 14. And Richards estimated that "in nine instances out of ten, whites were the aggressors, and blacks the victims" (ibid., 33). For instance, in Providence, Rhode Island (1824), one Black neighborhood was razed; and in Cincinnati (1829), following the destruction of "bucktown," "about half of the Negro population [approximately 4,000 in total] had left the city" (ibid., 35). Antislavery activists provoked white Cincinnati mobs in 1836, 1841, and 1843. Emma Jones Lapsansky maintains that in Philadelphia in 1834, Black affluence and white/black labor competition precipitated attacks on the largest free Black community in the North (some 15,000 in 1830). The Black community experienced four more major race riots between 1835 and 1849. See Emma Jones Lapsansky, "'Since They Got Churches.'" Richards insists that fear of amalgamation ("promiscuous intermarriage between the two races") precipitated the race riot of 1834 in New York. Richards, *"Gentlemen of Property and Standing,"* 115. In the Fifth, Sixth, and Eighth wards, where Blacks constituted 10-11 percent of the population, the three days of rioting were concentrated: "In the midst of large numbers of middle and lower-middle class whites, some 6,500 blacks huddled together in poverty and desperation. . . . If the dread of amalgamation—rather than the fear of cheap Negro labor—was the central issue . . . then these [white] men were ripe for anti-Negro and anti-abolitionist violence." Ibid., 154-55.

7. Butters, *Black Manhood*, 28-29.

8. Allen Woll recounts that "by 1890, most of the 1,490 black actors enumerated by the census were employed in touring minstrel companies." Woll, *Black Musical Theatre*, 2.

Blackface minstrelsy, the counterfeit of black culture, as Frederick Douglass characterized it in 1848, is routinely assigned by its historians to the nineteenth century.[9] Indeed, minstrelsy is frequently nominated as the dominant venue of popular entertainment in America in that century. As far as it goes, such constructions are instructive, but at least in one or two important aspects they display a failure of the imagination. For one, with very little effort, it becomes quite obvious that minstrelsy persisted into the twentieth century and beyond. It most certainly survived on the stages of burlesque and musical comedy in the earliest decades of the last century and acquired its most robust impact on American popular culture as a persistent trope in American silent films. The presound films featuring racist figures were complemented by radio. In the 1920s, Freeman Gosden and Charles Correll had created the characters *Sam 'n' Henry* (January 12, 1926) and *Amos 'n' Andy* (March 19, 1928) as radio serials.[10] In the 1930s, the talkies, of course, retrieved the fuller presentation of the original form, employing blackface "plantation" mockeries ranging from movies which employed real actors to animations like Van Beuren Studio's *Pickaninny Blues* (1932) and *Rasslin' Match* (an *Amos 'n' Andy* cartoon, 1934), Leon Schlesinger Studio's *Hittin' the Trail to Hallelujah Land* (1931), and Fleischer Studio's *I'll Be Glad When You Dead You Rascal You* (1932, with Louis Armstrong), and so on.[11] As a testament to its cultural vigor, minstrelsy eventually trolled through post–World War II American television. And in the late twentieth century, inasmuch as a persistent form may be so described, it was revived in television and films, thus acquiring the privilege of being the most recognized form of Black performance.[12] But while the overtext

9. Eric Lott informs us that Frederick Douglass had written that blackface performers were "the filthy scum of white society, who have stolen from us a complexion denied to them by nature, in which to make money, and pander to the corrupt taste of their white fellow citizens." Eric Lott, *Love and Theft*, 15. Douglass's comments were published in *North Star*, October 27, 1848.

10. Both Gosden and Correll had worked in blackface minstrelsy. See Ely, *Adventures of Amos 'n' Andy*, chaps. 3 and 4.

11. See *History of Racist Animation*. Amdee J. Van Beuren's company, a subsidiary of RKO Radio, was incorporated in Delaware in 1928. In addition to its animation, four jungle adventure/documentaries are credited to Van Beuren: *Bring 'Em Back Alive* (Frank Buck adventure in Malay, 1932), *Adventure Girl* (1934), *Wild Cargo* (1934), and *Fang and Claw* (1935). For Van Beuren, see Maltin, *Of Mice and Magic*, 195ff.

12. Philip Gura notes, "I recently was made aware of the pervasiveness of this institution. One of my graduate students reported (with some embarrassment) that she

of counterfeiture was retained, minstrelsy constantly changed in fascinating and unexpected ways, evoking from Eric Lott a brilliant caution: "Cultural critics have recently become more aware of the uneven and contradictory character of popular life and culture, the ambiguities or contradictions that may characterize the pleasures of the masses."[13]

If the consensus on the death of minstrelsy is premature, a similar foreshortening has been accepted as its beginning. At the earlier end of the periodization, something beyond a failure of imagination accounts for the error. For one, since as proposed minstrelsy is a copy, a counterfeit, it might be more precise to point out that what was being appropriated was not Black culture but Black performance. That will draw us back into the eighteenth century, at least some six or seven decades before the usual dating of blackface minstrelsy. The dating of minstrelsy has served as an archaeological marker for the earliest evidence of the appearance of a white working class. This interpretation posits that minstrelsy was the invention of, and the inventor of, a white identity which was bonding foreign (principally Irish and German) and "native" urban workers. Eventually it becomes clear that the convention of minstrelsy's dating is an act of misdirection. For many scholars the actual subject is not the phenomenon of minstrelsy but the emergence and consolidation of a white American working class in the early national period.[14]

Prior to the Civil War, blackface minstrelsy was predominantly (but not exclusively) an entertainment for young male workers, many of them Irish and German immigrants. And while Irish minstrel performers and composers—Lott identifies Stephen Foster, Dan Emmett, Dan Bryant, Joel Walker Sweeney, and George Christy among them—may have muted some of the anti-Irish materials of blackface minstrelsy, David Roediger notes that "Irish drinking and 'thickness' drew mockery from the minstrels as did German speech."[15] The coincidence of Irish artists and Irish spectators with the blanket of blackness draped over the African and European poor in the new nationalist culture facilitated the trope of "the plantation" as a public display of blackness with a differ-

herself had seen a blackface show in her hometown in Tennessee in the 1980s." Gura, "America's Minstrel Daze," 603n2.

13. Eric Lott, *Love and Theft*, 4.

14. For a recent instance of the emphasis on minstrelsy as a white working-class culture, see Cockrell, *Demons of Disorder*, chap. 2.

15. Ibid., 95; Roediger, *Wages of Whiteness*, 118.

ence. The differences marked by the comic shenanigans of the black-white Irish could now be subsumed within a white kinship when played out against the slave and the (semi-) free Black. Blackface, as a masquerade for public revelries, ribald stage antics, or even city mobs, appropriated the class, racial, and ethnic ambiguities of blackness. Again, we need to be reminded that "such words as *coon*, *buck* and *Mose* had more than ambiguous or multiple meanings: they had trajectories that led from white to black . . . each of them went from describing particular kinds of whites who had not internalized capitalist work disciplines and whose places in the new world of wage labor were problematic to stereotyping Blacks."[16]

It is not mere hindsight which makes Irish entertainers the most likely candidates for the lures of blackface minstrelsy. In the new American republic, many of their contemporaries would have thought that Irishmen masquerading as Blacks was redundant. Roediger reports that in the early decades of the nineteenth century, "it was by no means clear that the Irish were white."[17] For most Irish Americans this remained the case well into the twentieth century, since as Noel Ignatiev observed, "no one gave a damn for the poor Irish."[18] In the early republic, "nativist folk wisdom held that an Irishman was a 'nigger', inside out. . . . The Census Bureau regularly collected statistics on the nation's 'native' and 'foreign' populations, but kept the Irish distinct from even the latter group."[19] Between 1815 and 1845, nearly one million Irish immigrants had come to America; and in the decade following the Great Famine, in the years 1845–55, that number doubled.[20] In Southern and Northern cities, "the Irish were thrown together with black people on jobs and in neighborhoods."[21] Consequently in New York and Boston, Irish women accounted for the majority of "mixed-race" matings with Blacks.[22] In the South, in many cases where slaves were deemed more valuable, Irish laborers were used as substitutes: "Gangs of Irish immigrants worked ditching and draining plantations, building levees and sometimes clearing land because of the danger of death to valuable slave

16. Roediger, *Wages of Whiteness*, 100.
17. Ibid., 134.
18. Ignatiev, *How the Irish Became White*, 178.
19. Roediger, *Wages of Whiteness*, 133.
20. Ignatiev, *How the Irish Became White*, 38, 39.
21. Ibid., 40.
22. Ibid., 41.

property (and, as one account put it, to mules) in such pursuits."[23] In the North, domestic service and prostitution became the preserves of Irish women; and young Irish men and women filled the ranks of the waning institution of indentured servitude.[24]

W. T. Lhamon makes the case that the earliest impromptu expressions of blackface minstrelsy emerged from the labor camps of slaves, free Blacks, and Irish immigrants associated with canal building in the North:

> The early canals in North America, including the Erie (1817–1825), were dug largely by unfree labor. Slaves built southern canals. Slaves working alongside indentured laborers bought from European boats docking in Philadelphia, Baltimore, and other eastern ports, shoveled canals in the mid-Atlantic and northern states. In the early days of canal work, free workers also contracted to work alongside the slaves and the indentured workers. But that changed during the years of the Erie's construction.[25]

Since waterways were the most important means of the long-distance transportation of goods in the new republic, the building of canals (largely dependent on slave labor) was initiated in the South in the 1780s. By the early nineteenth century, canal construction had become the nation's most significant examples of capital-intensive public works. Built in the middle of the canal construction boom, the Erie Canal extended along some 363 miles, nearly a third of the 3,326 miles of canals which had been dug in the United States by the 1840s.[26] By then the Irish immigrants were the predominant labor force among the 35,000 canallers.[27] But from the late eighteenth century and throughout the most intensive period of canal construction, immigrants and slaves were connected. "The Chesapeake and Delaware [canal directors] reported in 1826 that whites and blacks no longer worked in separate gangs 'but labour together, promiscuously'"; and at another canal site, "Slaves worked and lived together with little turnover for one

23. Roediger, *Wages of Whiteness*, 146.
24. Ibid.
25. Lhamon, *Raising Cain*, 62.
26. Way, "Evil Humors," 1405.
27. Way cites Segal, "Cycles of Canal Construction," 206, for the estimate that canal workers constituted 5.5 percent of the total nonagricultural work force in ten northern canal-building states in 1840.

James River Canal contractor in the 1840s and 1850s, whereas his hired white hands quickly came and went."[28] Thus it was in the work culture generated in their shanty towns, tribal villages, grog shops, family huts, and work camps, the Irish drank, sang, danced, fought, and rioted (immigrants from County Cork against Fardowners from the west coast: Corkonians versus Connaughtmen), engaged in all sorts of vices, and staged their imitations of Blacks for entertainment. Generally illiterate, their *métier* was recital and impersonation.

By the 1830s, blackface minstrel performances were an integral part of this immigrant culture:

> What too often has seemed like sentimental rhyming is also a way of declaring within the surveillance of the minstrel theatre the terrible exhaustion, loneliness, and privation forced on the lowest workers of the Atlantic.
>
> It makes a gnarled sense that the cultural song and dance representing back-stooping labor of shoveling and carting dirt, of building locks and being uprooted from family and home for long periods of time, should appear at the same moment on Lake Erie and along the Atlantic coast. What looks like polygenesis, simultaneous generation of the same form in more than one place, is really the appearance of that form at about the same time at both ends of the waterway whose making matured the symbolism of the labor.[29]

By the time of its appearance in commercial settings like music halls, blackface minstrelsy was predominantly a "white" male working-class entertainment—riotous, raucous, and participatory and performed by solo entertainers. Describing an 1833 engraving of T. D. Rice's "fifty seventh night" at the Bowery Theatre (New York), Eric Lott comments: "It is a crowd of some variety, except for the almost total absence of women: workers in smocks and straw hats rub elbows with militiamen; clerks ape the betters they hope one day to become; a few respectable men intervene in scuffles that have broken out in two places on the stage. . . . Much of the crowd is interested in the brawl at stage left, or in conversation among themselves; some of those conversations seem concerned with the brawl, not Rice."[30] Principally famous for their

28. Way, "Evil Humors," 1422, 1419.
29. Lhamon, *Raising Cain*, 66.
30. Eric Lott, *Love and Theft*, 124, 126.

"nigger dancing" and dialect singing of often ribald lyrics, the earliest blackface performers had advertised their appropriation of Black performances they had encountered on plantations and in frontier towns of the canal regions (e.g., Cincinnati, Pittsburgh, Louisville). This form acquired its theatrical structure and unambiguously racist character with the appearance of the blackface minstrel bands the Virginia Minstrels (New York City) and E. P. Christy's Christy's Minstrels (Buffalo, New York) in 1843. By the 1850s, Lhamon insists, with the appearance of the blackface minstrel bands and the intervention of theater entrepreneurs who preferred middle- and upper-class audiences, blackface performances tended to suppress class antagonisms by stressing degrading representations of Blacks: "Thus as black gestures are taken up by white workers at first, then attended to, or policed, by more powerful whites, the uses of the tokens will alter in the transfer."[31]

By the end of the nineteenth century, the draft of a new, that is, scientific, racial regime had been presented to the public through world's fairs, museums, popular science magazines, and other forms of public instruction and amusement. Older forms of racial construal, like the blackface minstrel show, still survived, but they were sovereign over an earlier and more vulgar representation of the racialized other. Located on this same stream of culture were the new industry of postcards and the older conduits like dime museums, amusement parks, children's toys, books, illustrated magazines, and the like. On the other hand, race science could command the resources of the state and its auxiliaries, which, in turn, collaborated with the dominant sectors of American capital.

The racial conspiracy seemed to be proceeding swimmingly. As Robert Rydell reconstructs the moment, whiteness appeared unassailable: "The fairs between 1876 and 1897 all shared a number of commonalities. They were organized by the wealthy, white business-oriented elite of their host cities; they showed off the latest in American (and, to a lesser extent foreign) technological achievement, and they emphasized anthropological exhibits that attempted to persuade the white middle- and upper-class visitors of Anglo-Saxon heritage that they were indeed members of the superior race."[32]

31. Lhamon, *Raising Cain*, 76.

32. Rydell, Findling, and Pelle, *Fair America*, 44. The fairs referred to were the Philadelphia Centennial International Exhibition (1876), the International Cotton Ex-

I come from America a long time ago,
Since which I larn to wheel about & jump *Jim Crow*.
Him used to study Blackstone ebry morn & arter noon,
Me charm de House where Chatham died & dance inde saloon,
Wheel about & turn about & do jis so.
   Ebry time I wheel about I jump *Jim Crow*.

JIM CROW, the American Mountebank
performing at the Grand Theatre.

London, Published by S.W. Fores, 41 Piccadilly

"*Jim Crow, the American Mountebank,*" S. W. Fores, London, 1836.
The Library Company of Philadelphia.

"Distinguished Ethiopian Artists: Burgess, Prendergast, and La Rue's Minstrels," program, ca. 1865.

"Chopped Up Niggers," children's puzzle.
McLoughlin Bros. Publications, New York, 1874.

The Chicago World's Columbian Exposition in 1893 had incited an amateur blackface minstrel movement in the country which was drilled and amused by skits and suggestions for costumes and makeup by guides such as Mrs. Silsbee and Mrs. Horne's *Jolly Joe's Lady Minstrels* (1893), Frank Dumont's *The Witmark Amateur Minstrel Guide and Burnt Cork Encyclopedia* (1899), and the anonymous *Boys of New York End Men's Joke Book* (1902).[33] The protests by Blacks of their exclusion from the Chicago fair, the exhibiting of the Fon from Dahomey, and the installation of a "Colored People's Day" (August 25) occasioned a volume of minstrel-inspired cartoons and caricatures in newspapers, magazines like *Harper's Weekly* and *World's Fair Puck*, souvenir booklets, postcards, and the like ridiculing Blacks.[34]

The "coon song" fad paralleled the amateur blackface minstrelsy movement. Beginning in the mid-1880s, according to Dormon, in the course of a decade over 600 coon songs were published, "and the more successful efforts sold in the millions of copies."[35] Though the participants in the coon song craze and the amateur minstrel movement probably overlapped, there were significant differences in the two phenomena. For one, several Black composers were central to the creation and popularity of the coon songs. Sam Lucas authored the offensive (Blacks as watermelon and chicken thieves) "Coon's Salvation Army" in 1884; and the most widely acclaimed and influential early coon song, "All Coons Look Alike to Me" (1890), was the creation of Ernest Hogan, another talented Black minstrel.[36] Not too surprisingly, the song's title became a popular catchphrase, completely eviscerating the love song's lyrics; and the sales and royalties of "All Coons Look Alike to Me" reportedly set Hogan up for life. And though Hogan went on to many achievements in entertainment, as a performer and composer, accord-

position in Atlanta (1881), Louisville's Southern Exposition (1883), the World's Industrial and Cotton Centennial Exposition in New Orleans (1884–85), Chicago's World's Columbian Exposition (1893), the California Midwinter International Exposition in San Francisco (1894), the Cotton States and International Exposition in Atlanta (1895), and Nashville's Tennessee Centennial Exposition (1897). It was at Atlanta's Cotton States and International Exposition that Booker T. Washington delivered his (in)famous "Atlanta Compromise" speech.

33. Bean, "Black Minstrelsy," 188nn1,4.

34. See Rydell, *All the World's a Fair*, 53ff.; and Reed, *"All the World Is Here!,"* 149ff.

35. Dormon, "Shaping the Popular Image," 453.

36. Ibid., 452; and Woll, *Black Musical Theatre*, 2.

ing to James Weldon Johnson, he never forgave himself for his part in the coon song fad ("a song which he, later in life, expressed regret at ever having written").[37] His self-reproach is understandable when we turn our attention to the second distinction between the coon songs and the amateur minstrel movement.

Dormon, who investigated the lyrics of one hundred of these songs, details the difference:

> In the songs, for example, blacks began to appear as not only ignorant and indolent, but also devoid of honesty or personal honor, given to drunkenness and gambling, utterly without ambition, sensuous, libidinous, even lascivious. "Coons" were, in addition to all of these things, razor-wielding savages, routinely attacking one another at the slightest provocation as a normal function of their uninhibited social lives. The razor—the flashing steel straight razor—became in the songs the dominant symbol of black violence, while the "coon" himself became that which was signified by this terrible weapon.[38]

Thus, an extraordinary montage of conflicted and complementary images of blackness was being consumed by Americans in the last decade of the nineteenth century. Race science and anthropological displays documented the natural antipathy between Blacks and civilization. The coon songs stripped from the urbanized Blacks the pretense of civility, suggesting the utter futility of philanthropy and the limits of Christian charity. The amateur blackface minstrel movement embraced a more domesticated, sentimental, and benign construction of the Black slave past, images consistent with national reconciliation and an expanding affection for the antebellum South. And all of these conspired, as it were, to craft a more solid and confident white identity.

But now the predominantly male and immigrant wage laborers identified with antebellum minstrelsy were supplanted by a largely middle-class presence. In small part, the property of blackface minstrelsy might be believed to have been transferred from the lower classes to their "white" middle-class descendants two generations later. But given the prominent and unprecedented participation of white women in the amateur blackface minstrel movement (and as consumers of fairs and coon songs), the late nineteenth-century middle class probably was

37. James Weldon Johnson, *Black Manhattan*, 114.
38. Dormon, "Shaping the Popular Image," 455.

autochthonous. The class which a half century earlier condescended to the view that all the social strata below were somehow "black" now appropriated the masquerade as an amusing signature of its own unassailable whiteness. In the midst of Black lynchings, peonage, battalions of chain gangs, spiraling segregation, disfranchisement, and judicial injustices like *Plessy v. Ferguson* (1896), the artifice of race invited repetition, a near-hysterical collective rush towards the bonding comfort of the fad, the fashionable. But since it was all built on the sands of lies, scientific frauds, and the perquisites of power, something was bound to go wrong. There were, however, some suggestions that a rupture in the minstrelsy form was building from another corner of the society.

The faults in minstrelsy as an agency of white supremacy and Black degradation were embedded from the very inception of the form. Eric Lott, W. T. Lhamon, and Dale Cockrell have chased the origins of minstrelsy to Black public performances documented as long ago as the mid-eighteenth century. Culture, of course, is a "pluriverse" of influences. Thus, while Lhamon had elected the shared worksites of Black laborers and Irish immigrants, Lott selects a complementary space of performative exchange. Dismissing the self-serving fiction of white minstrels visiting plantations to research their impersonations, Lott insists that white mimicry evolved from the more routine encounters characteristic of presegregationist colonial and early national times: "Minstrel men visited not plantations but racially integrated theaters, taverns, neighborhoods, and waterfronts—and then attempted to recreate plantation scenes."[39] As early as 1750, in cities like New York, Albany, Boston, Philadelphia, Pittsburgh, Cincinnati, and Louisville, Black annual street festivals like Pinkster, Election Day, and John Canoe brought the spectacle of Blacks performing ribald stories, dancing, and making music to the cultural agora of late colonial and early national North America.[40] And like the great festivals of fifth- and fourth-century BCE

39. Eric Lott, quoting Eileen Southern (*The Music of Black Americans* [New York: Oxford University Press, 1938], 91–92), in *Love and Theft*, 41.

40. Election Day, or Negro Election Day, according to David R. Roediger, "began in the mid eighteenth century as an offshoot of more staid white New England election celebrations, initially took shape when slaves came to towns with voting whites and began to choose Black 'governors' and other officials amidst great African-influenced festivity.... No fewer than twenty-one New England cities left records of having celebrated the day [actually four to six days]." Pinkster, a festival of three or four days,

Athens, the Lanaia and City Dionysia, some of the policing rules of the political and social order were temporarily suspended. And with the "extensive elbow-rubbing among [Black and white] apprentices, servants, slaves, journeymen, sailors, and laborers," Black performance was insinuated into the democratic tapestry of working-class social entertainment. Shane White asks us to

> consider, for example, the minstrel show's stump speech, one of the genre's central attractions and distinguishing characteristics, in which the star performer gave a disquisition, loaded with malapropisms and ludicrous verbosity, often on some contemporary issue. This recalls the *parmateering*, or parliamenteering, that preceded Election Day outside of Boston, as, sometimes for weeks, candidates for king or governor solicited votes . . . these goings-on were not entirely serious; they were tinged with burlesque, as blacks lampooned whites. Minstrelsy's stump speech may have been a white parody of blacks who were already parodying whites.[41]

Appalled, local authorities began to suppress these Black practices in the early national era, inscribing the class conflicts of the previous two generations onto the public sphere. As one proper critic declared, the Pinkster "partook so largely of savage license that it gradually came to be shunned by respectable whites."[42]

---

was a Black adaptation of a Dutch celebration of spring. "The same amusements that characterized Negro Election Day prevailed at Pinkster, along with spectacular African dancing, the building of beautiful arbors and the crowning of a Black king." Roediger, *Wages of Whiteness*, 101, 102. John Canoe (or Jonkonnu) was a Southern Christmas festival imported from the West Indies. It was also the most provocative of the three festivals. Dale Cockrell has characterized Pinkster, Election Day, and John Canoe as "Lord of Misrule" rituals, and John Canoe was extremely provocative since it involved Canoe, a slave, masquerading as the British governor. It also appears to be most directly traced to West African traditions, since *john ki-nu* is the Ewe title for a shaman, and Ewe-speaking captives were numerous in Jamaica. Cockrell, *Demons of Disorder*, 38ff. See also White "'It Was a Proud Day.'" White adds another New England holiday to the list: General Training, associated with the drilling of Black militias. Ibid., 18.

41. White, "'It Was a Proud Day,'" 26–27.

42. Eric Lott, *Love and Theft*, 47, 46. Roediger cites another contemporary informant: "Excesses of the negroes gave rise to the vile manner in which [Negro Election Day] was observed by some of the lower class of our own complexion." Roediger, *Wages of Whiteness*, 102–3.

The American Revolution, appropriated by that one-third of the colonists who were propertied and middle class, had been institutionalized as an aristocratic state aggressively institutionalizing a political, moral, and cultural divide between "respectability" and the "blackness" of the more numerous, unpropertied lower classes. Thus the new national identity, confined to an oligopoly, submerged the frequently seditious practices of the American-born poor, the recognizably subversive impulses of free Blacks and slaves, and the incendiary potential of new immigrants to a rough, untutored (i.e., democratic) mob.[43] Early blackface minstrelsy became thus a substantiation of this class identity and a spectacle where white pleasure gradually overtook class antagonisms. "But for a brief time in the nineteenth century," Lott recognizes, "it seemed that the blackface impulse, based so firmly on the association of 'blackness' with the white working class, was backfiring."[44]

Black Blackface Minstrels

Black street performers, actors, and musicians were the cultural and theatrical props of blackface minstrelsy. T. D. Rice plagiarized an old Black stableman's songs and dances; Dan Emmett was taught his first musical "chops" by a Black man named Juba; Stephen Foster frequented the wharves of his native Pittsburgh and attended Black churches in search of Black secular and worship music; E. P. Christy befriended a Black church singer, One-Legged Harrison, who became a source of Christy's act; Charles Matthews attended the Black performances of the African Grove Theatre and mongrelized the work of James Hewett and Ira Aldridge.[45] But within a decade or two, Black performers themselves began to reclaim minstrelsy. P. T. Barnum opened the door in a typical but inadvertently significant act of fakery. In 1841, having lost the services of his white "negro dancer," John Diamond, Barnum employed the black performer William Henry Lane (Master Juba) as a substitute. Lane danced in burnt cork makeup and a wig in order to impersonate a white man impersonating a Black man.[46] That same year, as a reflection of the expanding economy of public amusements, blackface minstrel

43. The two other revolutions concealed in the national myth of the American Revolution—the class struggle of the poor and the rebellion of the slaves and free Blacks—are discussed in Robinson, *Black Movements in America*, chap. 2.

44. Eric Lott, *Love and Theft*, 87–88.

45. Ibid., 51–52, 44.

46. Ibid., 112ff.

troupes were organized for the first time. And in 1855, a few short years before the Civil War, Lisa Anderson maintains, the first black minstrel band, the Mocking Bird Minstrels, performed in Philadelphia.[47]

The accessibility of minstrelsy to Black talent mutated the form into a breathtakingly diverse location for the public performance of race. Denied the alternative sites of show business, music, and performance, Black actors, musicians, composers, dancers, choreographers, playwrights, set designers, and painters, even operatic singers, acrobats, and athletes, migrated to Black minstrelsy to exhibit their talents, trades, and training. They brought new talents, new demands, new disciplines, and new creativity to minstrelsy, eventually employing Black minstrelsy as the space for emergent forms, such as the Black musical comedy. But in the intervening years, Black minstrelsy was obliged to serve as the entertainment headquarters for tributaries of Black religion, social criticism, popular history, contemporary legends of resistance, and the more particular offenses of slavery, racial oppression, and blackface minstrelsy itself.

In his classic and still provocative study of minstrelsy, *Blacking Up*, Robert Toll argued that it was slave religion, specifically Black religious songs, which centered the place of Black performers in minstrelsy. Minstrelsy, as a predominantly Northern form of entertainment, was commercially sensitive to the cultural tastes and curiosities of its audience. And in the midst of the Civil War, "Northerners began to report on the slaves' curious music. In 1867 the first book of *Slave Songs of the United States* appeared, followed two years later by the reprinting of Thomas Wentworth Higginson's collection of slave songs in his *Army Life in a Black Regiment*. Then, in 1871, a group of Negro students from Fisk University . . . first traveled to the North singing the religious music of the plantation. By mid-1875 they had toured widely, including Europe, and had created a public sensation."[48] Consequently, in the postbellum period, the "jubilee" songs were incorporated into minstrelsy. Not surprisingly, blackface minstrels could only muster a trifling counterfeit of the cultural and emotional sources of this powerful music, a wholly insufficient authority from which to transform it into the familiar farce of their form. Black minstrels, on the other hand, acquired privilege from both their own cultural familiarity with "the sorrow songs" and

47. Lisa Anderson, "From Blackface to 'Genuine Negroes.'"
48. Toll, *Blacking Up*, 235–36.

AT LIBERTY HALL.

Tuesday & Wednesday, March 13 & 14.

BROOKER & CLAYTON'S
GREAT ORIGINAL AND ONLY

GEORGIA

MINSTRELS
AND BRASS BAND!

THE CELEBRATED

SLAVE TROUPE!

The only "Simon Pure" Negro Troupe in the World, composed of men, who, previous to April 15th, 1865, were Slaves in Macon, Georgia,—consisting of the following:

J. WILSON,
E flat Cornet, Flutist and Leader of Brass Band.

W. SMITH,
Violinist and B flat Cornet.

A. MALLORY,
Baritone Balladist.

J. E. JOHNSON,
Dancer and Comedian.

LEWIS SLATTER,
Tamborinist and Female Impersonator.

JOHN MOORE,
Bass Drum and Alto.

MASTER NEIL,
The Wonder of Eastern Dancer.

J. A. BROOKER,
Violinist and Bari one.

JOE CLAYTON,
2d E flat Cornet and B flat.

L. LAMAR,
Alto Horn and Tenor Soprano.

A. JACOBS,
Bass and Tenor Horn.

H. FIELDS,
The Excelsior "Shoulder Bones."

J. KEISER,
Violoncello and Interlocutor.

C. B. HICKS,
Eccentric Comedian.

PROGRAMME:

Part First:—Parlor Opera

GRAND INTRODUCTORY OVERTURE, (New.) . . . . ORCHESTRA
OPENING CHORUS,—To Night, the Moon is Beaming . . . . . GEORGIA MINSTRELS
BALLAD—I'm Lonely since my Mother Died . . . . A. MALLORY
COMIC DITTY,—"Tapioca,"—(new version) . . . . H. FIELDS
SENTIMENTAL—Sleeping for the Flag . . . . J. A. BROOKER
REFRAIN—Ring the Bang . . . . L. SLATTER
BALLAD . . . . A MALLORY
FINALE,—Quickstep . . . . BRASS BAND

PART SECOND---OLIO.

PLANTATION JIG AND JUBA DANCE, - - By the Georgia Champion. - **J. E. JOHNSON**

THE SLAVE'S DREAM, - - - C. B. HICKS.

POLKA MILITAIRE---Southern,
SLATTER and FIELDS.

BANJO SOLO . . . . **J. E. JOHNSON**

THE AFRICAN RECRUITS
SLATTER, FIELDS and MALLORY.

ESSENCE OF GEORGIA—Original, - - - - - **MASTER NEIL.**

BOSS. VERSUS & CO.,
SQUISTUM . . . . KISER; SLIM JIM . . . . . . SLATTER; PETE . . . . FIELDS

Song and Dance, by the Little Picaninny, **Master Charlie**

BALLAD, - - - - - - - - - - - **J. CROSS.**

Concluding with an Original

PLANTATION KITCHEN DANCE
As Performed only by this Company,

Brass Band Serenade through principal Streets and in front of Hall each Evening

Tickets 35 Cents;   **Reserved Seats 50 Cents;**

Doors open at 6 1-2 o'clock.   Commencing at 7 3-4 o'clock.

PIKE & HATCH, Managers.

Printed by Providence Press Company, 16 Weybosset Street, Providence, R. I.

"Brooker & Clayton's Great Original and Only Georgia Minstrels," Black blackface minstrels program, ca. 1865.

their liberationist counterparts and their audiences' identification of slave culture with blackness.

Toll asserted that "with the introduction of Afro-American religious songs, black culture revitalized minstrelsy."[49] Paradoxically, he also provides substantial evidence that the same transfer subverted minstrelsy. In contrast to the formal traditions of blackface minstrelsy, Black minstrels represented the anguish, the privations, and the pain of plantation life and the singular achievement of Black religion in providing an escape:

> Both black slaves and black minstrels sang of heaven as a paradise of freedom and plenty. It was where "de white folks must let de darkeys be," where they would not be "bought and sold," where everyone would have three meals a day and occasional feasts of milk and honey, even if they "ain't got any money." Again like the black folk, black minstrels felt themselves on intimate terms with God. They asked Him to "open dem doors" so they could get a glimpse inside, reminded Him that "nobody knows what trouble we've seen," and implored Him to give them the means of escape.[50]

As Toll has demonstrated, during the Civil War and before, minstrelsy had become a rather remarkable mirror of the emergent public sphere in the North. In the beginnings of the war, blackface minstrels had been nationalists and pro-Unionists. When the Northern war effort required a draft, blackface minstrels had ridiculed those exempted by wealth or affluent enough to purchase draft substitutes. And when as a maneuver to encourage Black volunteers, the war objectives of the North became an appropriation of the abolitionists' agenda, blackface minstrels had railed against this new project. As such, by the time Black performers had made considerable inroads into minstrelsy, the form had already displayed its power to reflect public sentiments and its capacity to influence that same opinion. The result was that a new minstrelsy, in the hands of Black performers, acquired the capacity and the occasion to transport its audiences towards a more profound comprehension of slavery and racism. In Black minstrelsy performance, Blacks became more than caricatures, displaying the broader human register which had heretofore been reserved for the men and women whom they

49. Ibid., 238.
50. Ibid., 239–40.

entertained. In addition, Black performers infused the form with their talent.

Minstrel lyricist Billy Kersands, who created a comedic act based on his large mouth, composed "Old Aunt Jemima."[51] James A. Bland, one of Howard University's early students, was portrayed without black makeup on the sheet music of his compositions "Carry Me Back to Old Virginny," "Oh, Dem Golden Slippers," and "In the Evening by the Moonlight."[52] In the late nineteenth century the concert circuit in America, and particularly Europe, celebrated the voices of Madame Selika, the mezzo-soprano Flora Batson Bergen, and the soprano Sissieretta Jones, but it was as the "Black Patti" of Black minstrelsy that Jones achieved her greatest and most enduring public acclaim. Dubbed "Black Patti" in recognition of the comparability of her voice to the Italian diva Adelina Patti, Jones was featured in a minstrel show, *Black Patti Troubadours*, by Bob Cole (she sang arias in the second act), which toured from the 1890s to well into the twentieth century.[53]

Among the most enduring and versatile of the early Black minstrels was Sam Lucas. Born a free Black in Ohio in 1850, Lucas became a musician, composer ("My Dear Old Southern Home," "Carve Dat Possum"), singer, actor, and minstrel comedian. Lucas took up minstrelsy in 1869 and quickly became one of the first Black celebrities of that form. In 1875, he redirected his talent to musical drama, joining Emma Louise and Anna Madah Hyers's Negro Operatic and Dramatic Company to perform in renditions of *Uncle Tom's Cabin* and *Out of Bondage* (and later, *The Underground Railroad*).[54] Black musical drama was not as commercially successful as minstrelsy, so Lucas shuttled between the venues. In 1878, Charles and Gustave Frohman hired Lucas for their production of *Uncle Tom's Cabin*, earning Lucas an historic marker: the first Black actor to play Tom in a non-Black production in America. In 1890, Lucas performed in Sam T. Jack's pathbreaking musical, *The Creole Show*, and in 1898, he appeared in Bob Cole's *A Trip to Coontown*.

51. Manring, *Slave in a Box*, 68.

52. Lisa Anderson, "From Blackface to 'Genuine Negroes,'" 20, 22. "Carry Me Back to Old Virginny" became the state song for Virginia.

53. For Madame Selika and Flora Batson Bergen, see Richings, *Evidences of Progress*, 420–21; and Tanner, *Dusky Maidens*, 28–29, 29–30. For Jones, see ibid., 56–60; and Dodson, Moore, and Yancy, *Black New Yorkers*, 109–10, 114.

54. See Toll, *Blacking Up*, 217–19; and for the Hyers Sisters, see Tanner, *Dusky Maidens*, passim.

Next, his prominent appearances were in *Shoo Fly Regiment* and *Red Moon*, both works collaborations of Bob Cole and J. Rosamond Johnson. And at the very end of his career, Lucas earned another historic entry. In 1914, World Film Corporation hired Lucas to play Tom in its version of *Uncle Tom's Cabin*.[55] In an era when Black characters of any critical dimension in silent film were impersonated by whites in black-face, Lucas became the first Black to portray a serious role. Fittingly, as Toll reminds us, James Weldon Johnson determined that Lucas had been "The Grand Old Man of the Negro Stage."[56]

The successes of the earlier generations both accommodated and concealed the even more subversive significance of the next generation of Black minstrels. By the latter part of the nineteenth century, as a consequence of the national betrayal of equal rights, Jim Crow segregation, and the vigorous diffusion of cultural racism, a critical proportion of the Black middle class and the Black intelligentsia embraced Black nationalism. One element of this resuscitation of a consciousness which had been robust in the antebellum period was the re-imagining of the satellite and sometimes semiautonomous institutions which had been evolving among Blacks for some decades.[57] The former slaves and their descendants were characteristically settled in separate Black communities and sometimes all-Black settlements created in the wake of Reconstruction's abandonment. V. P. Franklin reports that "all-black towns began to spring up in the 1880s and 1890s: Mound Bayou, Mississippi, Nicodemus, Kansas. As part of the 'great black march westward' in Oklahoma in the 1890s, over twenty all-black communities were founded. The origins of these settlements can be traced directly to the chaos and upheaval associated with southern redemption and the removal of blacks from the political arena." And in the same work, Franklin observed, "in nineteenth- and early twentieth-century America, the Afro-American masses opted for self-determination, and this value manifested itself in the thousands of black-controlled churches, schools, social organizations, and cultural institutions."[58] Notwithstanding the reality that these were generally poor communities, with extraordinary frequency Black schools and adult literacy pro-

55. Wallace, *"Uncle Tom's Cabin,"* 148.

56. Toll, *Blacking Up,* 219.

57. For Black nationalism in the antebellum period, see Moses, *Golden Age of Black Nationalism*, chap. 2.

58. Franklin, *Black Self-Determination*, 143, 196.

grams, churches, towns, farmers' cooperatives (the Colored Farmers' Alliance, for instance), benevolent societies, emigration societies, mutual aid and burial associations, and even missionary projects had appeared. And in accord with its class ambitions, a substantial portion of the Black petite bourgeoisie had colonized this infrastructure, facilitating the transformation of separate churches into regional and national denominations, burial societies into funeral companies, benevolent societies into banks and insurance companies (e.g., the Southern Aid Society, 1893), and the like.[59] The radical stratum of the Black petite bourgeoisie, however, reimagined these institutions as aspects of a proto-nation, a Black country parallel to America with the immediate mission of its own development, its own defense, its own aesthetic and moral destiny.

Minstrelsy functioned as a Trojan horse for this militant segment of the Black petite bourgeoisie. And though the determinant narrative of their insurgency into American popular culture was provided in 1930 by James Weldon Johnson in his *Black Manhattan*, he muted their radicalism and employed frequent misdirection.[60] In that sense, Johnson's historical reconstruction of the subversion of minstrelsy mirrored some of the deceptive techniques of his Black minstrel collaborators. Johnson was a master dissembler, constantly on his guard, gauging just how far the cultural insecurities of his non-Black readers might allow him to brave. As a lyricist in the Black minstrel/musical campaign against the racial protocols of blackface minstrelsy, Johnson had firsthand experiences of the limits of the spoken (or sung), whatever the enabling masquerade. And when the master narrative, the framing device, was particularly bold (for example, an African kingdom or a self-loathing nouveau riche), strands of Black dependence or buffoon caricature

59. For the Colored Farmers Alliance and the Southern Aid Society, see Low and Clift, *Encyclopedia of Black America*, 294–95, 206–7.

60. James Weldon Johnson (1871–1938) was a lawyer, poet, lyricist, and novelist (*The Autobiography of an Ex-Coloured Man*). From 1901–6, with his brother, J. Rosamond Johnson, he composed "Since You Went Away," "Congo Love Song," and "Lift Every Voice and Sing" (often referred to as the Black national anthem) as well as numerous other songs for a number of Black musical comedies. Johnson served as U.S. consul in Venezuela (1906–9) and Nicaragua (1909–13), returning to the states to edit the *New York Age*. For a time he served as the field secretary for the National Association for the Advancement of Colored People (Walter White was his deputy), investigating crimes against Blacks as far afield as lynchings and the U.S. occupation of Haiti. He was the NAACP's first Black executive secretary.

were an often necessary disguise. The sting of Black assertiveness, the prick of genuinely human Black existence, could be done and then immediately undone by a bit of tomfoolery. Nearly two decades earlier than *Black Manhattan*, Johnson had employed the trickster stratagem in his treatment of passing and mixed-race relations. He had anonymously published *The Autobiography of an Ex-Coloured Man* (1912), assuming the identity of a Black man light enough to pass for white.[61] It behooves us then to be cautious readers, particularly when Johnson wished to preserve and at the same time give sanctuary to the audacious Black minstrels who created the Black musical.

Johnson's misdirection often took the form of casting the Black minstrels as passive participants in the transformation of minstrelsy. In one instance, for example, when he was commenting on the induction of Blacks into minstrelsy, Johnson constructed minstrelsy as the master and the Black minstrels as the apprentices: "[Minstrel] companies did provide stage training and theatrical experience for a large number of coloured men. They provided an essential training and theatrical experience which, at the time, could not have been acquired from any other source." And in another instance, Johnson recited the now familiar tale of how the first erotically attractive Black women came to appear on the minstrel stage in the *Creole Show* (1890): "Sam T. Jack, a prominent burlesque theatre owner and manager, conceived the idea of putting out a Negro show different from anything yet thought of, a show that would glorify the colored girl." In his first account, Johnson muted the vicious racial caricatures and demeaning roles into which Black performers were being inaugurated and minimized the musical, compositional, and dancing skills which Black performers brought to minstrelsy.[62] In the second, Johnson took pains to avoid pointing out how subversive the exhibition of these Black women was to the desperate racist construction of Black women as unattractive. This, of course, undermined a major ideological support for the antimiscegenation rationale for the lynching of Black men. And on the symbolic level, the collision between these beautiful Black bodies and the signifiers of the

61. In a letter to his college chum George A. Towns, Johnson had written, "When the author is known, and known to be one who could not be the main character of the story, the book will fall flat." Kawash, *"Autobiography,"* 59.

62. James Weldon Johnson, *Black Manhattan*, 93, 95. Johnson, of course, was well aware of these achievements, but in this particular moment of his narrative he chose to construct the Black performers as untutored, inexperienced subordinates.

sexless, de-eroticized Black woman was its own spectacle. Indeed, in 1893 during the Chicago world's fair, Jack brought the *Creole Show* to that city, providing a dramatic (but probably inadvertent) refutation to the fair's display of Aunt Jemima as an icon of Black women and the sentimentalized Old South.[63] In her study of Florenz Ziegfeld Jr. (who was also at the Chicago fair), Linda Mizejewski eloquently asserts what Johnson dared not articulate:

> The circulated images of white women were dependent for their value on the presence and performance of other racial and ethnic identities. Beginning in the 1890s, the desirable African American female body "on show" in a parallel theatrical venue heightened the stakes of the upscale chorus girl's whiteness and in one sense necessitated the rhetoric of the Glorified American Girl. Overall, the two chorus girl categories illustrate how blacks and whites "invented one another," to use Henry Louis Gates Jr.'s elegant phrasing, how we "derived our identities from the ghostly projections of our alter egos."[64]

In reality, the Black chorus girls who first appeared to white audiences on the burlesque stage and eventually graduated to Broadway tended by their light complexions to implode the binaries to which Gates referred.[65] To Johnson, however, their singular importance was that they were "attractive" and "pretty"; just as the singular attributes of the performers with backgrounds in the Black petite bourgeoisie were that they were "educated" or "trained."

63. *The Creole Show* contained not only Black chorus girls but also featured the first Black female interlocutor (Florence Brisco) and replaced the end men, Tambo and Mr. Bones, with two other females, Florence Hines and Marie Lucas (Sam Lucas's wife). Sampson, *Blacks in Blackface*, 6ff. It was still being performed in 1897.

64. Mizejewski, *Ziegfeld Girl*, 199, 122. Mizejewski is quoting from Gates, "Welcoming Table," 152.

65. Referring to a 1903 review, Mizejewski writes: "The fascination of these young women for white audiences is evident in remarks by the *New York Times* reviewer of *In Dahomey* who was compelled to make a 'minute inspection' of black bodies onstage: 'The actors were dark, medium, and light,' he reports. 'Some of them were so light that they may have passed for white, except that the flare of a nostril, the weight of an eyelid, or the delicate fullness of a lip betrayed them to minute inspection. One of the chorus girls clearly had blonde hair that was not peroxide. She had a smile like the smile of Sarah the divine.'" Mizejewski, *Ziegfeld Girl*, 123.

Black minstrelsy, however, had reclaimed the mulatta as an anti-racist agent. Drawing on her desirability, Black minstrelsy employed the mulatta as a means of exhibiting and marketing Black musical and theatrical talent spawned from the still new Black colleges and the older conservatories. They maneuvered, however, in rather dangerous waters, for the lure of these women was fixed in the sexual economy of the slave era. As Walter Johnson has observed:

> It is well known that slaveholders favored light-skinned women . . . to serve in their houses and that those light-skinned women sold at a price premium. . . . The words the buyers used—*griffe, mulatto, quadroon*—preserved a constantly shifting tension between the "blackness" favored by those who bought slaves to till their fields, harvest their crops, and renew their labor forces and the "whiteness" desired by those who went to the slave market in search of people to serve their meals, mend their clothes, and embody their fantasies.[66]

This prior claim was upheld. After all, the consumers of Black minstrelsy and Black musicals believed themselves the natural heirs to the racial privileges once claimed by slaveholders. And thus the reprieve was short-lived, as we have seen, for by the end of the decade, Thomas Dixon and his racist collaborators were to weave the mulatta into the anti-miscegenation fantasies of the "unnatural." Just how imperative it was for white supremacists to assign the mark of the beast to these women might be suggested by the contemporary evidence. For example, up until the U.S. Navy revoked its legal protectorate in 1917, New Orleans's Storyville had boasted the country's most infamous brothels. And among the most famed were those stocked with octoroon females and operated by octoroon madams, such as Lulu White and Countess Willie Piazza.[67] As a consequence of the increasingly hostile public attitudes towards light-complexioned female entertainers, many of the most accomplished and ambitious of the mulatta stars, women like Dora Dean,

66. Walter Johnson, "Slave Trader." Johnson's study is about the attempts by Alexina Morrison, a fifteen-year-old slave, to have herself declared white and thus illegally enslaved.

67. Rose, *Storyville, New Orleans*, 8off. Between 1898 and 1917 Storyville was the only district in New Orleans where prostitution was neither legal nor illegal. In the 1860s, one of the prominent predecessors of White and Piazza was the mulatta Minnie Ha Ha. Ibid., 12.

Inez Clough, and Laura Bowman, abandoned their careers in America, taking up long-term engagements in England and Europe.[68]

James Weldon Johnson was just as studiously circumspect as he continued his recounting of the rupture of the minstrel formula by the evolving appearances of the Black musical. The *Creole Show* was followed by *The Octoroons* (1895), which, of course, made even more audacious use of the Black chorus girls ("a half-dozen of them were used as principals") while adding the cakewalk and other Black popular dances. The next year, *Oriental America* augmented the chorus girls and the cakewalk with operatic selections (*Faust, Martha, Rigoletto, Carmen, Il Trovatore*), "some of the best-trained Negro singers available" (Sidney Woodward, J. Rosamond Johnson, Maggie Scott, William Elkins), and a dramatic actress, Inez Clough. And then in 1898–99, Johnson mentions three shows, Bob Cole's *A Trip to Coontown*, Will Marion Cook and Paul Laurence Dunbar's *Clorindy — The Origin of the Cakewalk*, and Cook's *Jes Lak White Folk*, which constituted significant "departures" from minstrelsy. To be precise, Johnson actually attributes real importance only to the first two: Cole's *A Trip to Coontown* is characterized as "the first Negro show to make a complete break from the minstrel pattern, the first that was not a mere potpourri, the first to be written with continuity and to have a cast of characters working out a story of a plot from the beginning to end; and therefore, the first Negro musical comedy";[69] and Cook and Dunbar's *Clorindy* "was the first demonstration of the possibilities of syncopated Negro music."[70] Johnson's treatment of *Jes Lak White Folk* is so truncated that the play seems to have been included more for historical accuracy than for any inherent importance of the show itself. Closer inspection of the three shows, however, as well as the more recent work of scholars, assist immeasurably in our understanding of why these shows were of importance to Johnson and his colleagues.

Unquestionably, one of the first indicators of the deliberate racial mischief of their creators are the actual titles of several of these shows. "Creole," "Octoroons," and "Oriental America" are not simply marketing markers advertising the light-complexioned chorus girls. The terms

68. See Tanner, *Dusky Maidens*, passim.
69. James Weldon Johnson, *Black Manhattan*, 102.
70. Ibid., 103.

also draw attention to a challenge from the Black minstrels to the racial construct of white supremacy. Exposing the myths of racial purity hidden by the icons of Aunt Jemima and the mammy and enforced by lynching and Jim Crow segregation, the Black minstrels paraded the actual ambiguities of race. Moreover, one can confidently assume that Johnson must have been acutely aware that the radical gestures in *A Trip to Coontown* went far beyond plot and continuity, for in the show Cole performed in whiteface the role of Willie Wayside, a white tramp. David Krasner suggests that "Cole's performance in whiteface make-up was a revolutionary act because it emerged without preconceived signifiers; nothing in the cultural system of racial signs in America at that time prepared white audiences to 'gaze' at Cole's newly devised racial construct. *A Trip to Coontown*'s carnivalesque atmosphere, moreover, obscured Cole's whiteface performance; too much was happening on stage for anyone to really notice Cole's radical play on racial signs."[71] Helen Armstead-Johnson provides evidence that Cole's artistic collaboration in *A Trip to Coontown* was consciously political and deliberately aesthetic. For in the same year that he staged the show, Cole had written his "Colored Actor's Declaration of Independence of 1898," wherein he declared, "We are going to have our own shows."[72] And in his "own show," Krasner declares, "Cole reversed the meaning of racial representation by turning the tables on the process of mimicry. His reversal of the racial mask was, to borrow Eric Sundquist's expression, 'imitation with a vengeance.'"[73]

While Cole was committed to challenging the dominant culture on its own terrain, Cook enmeshed himself in Black cultural materials. Trained in music and the violin at Oberlin Conservatory and then in Berlin, Cook was convinced that the Black artist should "eschew white patterns."[74] And following his triumph with *Clorindy* at the Casino Theatre Roof Garden in 1898, Cook proceeded to challenge the racist pretensions of both the dominant culture and the Black bourgeoisie. Kras-

71. Krasner, *Resistance, Parody*, 32. In his article version of this chapter, Krasner reproduced a drawing of Cole as Willie Wayside. See Krasner, "'Mirror up to Nature,'" fig. 3.

72. Armstead-Johnson, "Themes and Values," 134. Cited in Krasner, *Resistance, Parody*, 30, 169n45.

73. Krasner, *Resistance, Parody*, 32.

74. Woll, *Black Musical Theatre*, 6.

ner has conducted an extensive study of the lyrics of three of Cook's plays: *Jes Lak White Folk* (1899), *The Cannibal King* (1902, coauthored with James Weldon Johnson), and *In Dahomey* (1902). Krasner demonstrates that the latter two plays were revisions of *Jes Lak White Folk*, each designed to mute the bold social critiques of their parent in order to mollify white audiences.

> The three plays can be seen as portraying degrees of black representation: *Jes Lak White F'lks* satirizes black pretensions as well as white consumerism; *The Cannibal King* also uses satire, humor, and folk culture, but in a benign way—it offends neither blacks or whites; *In Dahomey* is a show for whites to enjoy, though it includes subtle innuendoes designed for the benefit of African Americans. By viewing the three plays as a continuum, we may be able to account for the appearance of some middle ground between outright parody of whites in *Jes Lak White F'lks*, to a combination of parody, self-satire, and general amusement in the other plays.[75]

Here, again, Johnson's misdirection in his account of the failure of *Jes Lak White Folk* is both audacious (for those in the know) and sufficient (for those who neither created the play nor understood it). Johnson assures his readers that the play's failure was due to Cook's being "less fortunate in his sketch material and in his cast." But as Krasner demonstrates, Cook had attempted a rather bold provocation, employing dialect to masquerade his social criticisms of American racism:[76]

> Day am near when Zion
> Gwine to tif' it han
> In de brook 'am written
> Ob ol' Zion's lan
> White fol'ks no use tryin
> Fu to do us ha'm

75. Krasner, *Resistance, Parody*, 66.

76. James Weldon Johnson, *Black Manhattan*, 103. Will Marion Cook recounted in his own memoir of the gestation of this work an episode which underlines his acute consciousness of his provocation. Hearing the libretto for the first time, his mother tearfully exclaimed, "Oh, Will! Will! I've sent you all over the world to study and become a great musician, and you return such a nigger!" Will Marion Cook, "Clorindy," 63.

BERT WILLIAMS   GEORGE   WALKER

Bert Williams and George Walker (probably from In Dahomey*), 1902. Photographs and Prints Division, Schomburg Center for Research in Black Culture, New York Public Library, Astor, Lenox and Tilden Foundations.*

Lord's gwine raise his people
High up in his ahm
Lord's gwine raise his people
High up in his ahm.[77]

Moreover, Cook's principal character, Pompous Johnson, had sought desperately to be "jes lak white folks." And in the final stage directions, Cook had written that Pompous Johnson "decides to quit acting jes lak white folks."

Like Cook and Cole, Aida Overton Walker, George Walker (her husband), and Bert Williams shared a deep resentment towards the dominant representation of blackness in American popular culture and entertainment. Another similarity between these artists was that they all possessed the inventiveness and resolve to appropriate minstrelsy for their own ends. On this score it might be argued that Aida (formerly Ada) Overton Walker far surpassed her husband and Bert Williams. This may account, paradoxically, for the two males' greater celebrity. But it must be remembered that what Aida Overton Walker achieved was in the context of her collaboration with Will Marion Cook, George Walker, and Bert Williams and the extraordinary popular reception of the close-to-minstrelsy act perfected by George Walker and Bert Williams. Within the setting of the substantial commercial alterations and racial accommodations which set off *In Dahomey* from its predecessors, Walker and Williams's act concealed the two maneuvers for which their collaborators might have been most proud.

In Dahomey (Cook, Dunbar, and Jesse A. Shipp) and its successor, *Abyssinia* (1906; with Cook, Shipp, and Alex Rogers), were both largely located in African settings. This was not the Africa represented in the world's fairs of Chicago and St. Louis which had constituted that continent as a locus of primitiveness and savagery. Instead, Walker and Williams presented on the American stage an Africa of empires and state structures, while reminding their audience of recent military victories even over European powers. But ironically, it was the Chicago fair which had provided George Walker and Bert Williams the personal experience and cultural materials with which they rehabilitated the image of Africa. In 1906, at the very pinnacle of his popularity, George Walker told the story:

77. Krasner, *Resistance, Parody*, 56.

In 1893, natives from Dahomey, Africa, were imported to San Francisco to be exhibited at the Midwinter Fair. They were late in arriving in time for the opening of the Fair and Afro-Americans were employed to be exhibited for native Dahomians. Williams and Walker were among the sham native Dahomians. After the arrival of the native Africans, the Afro Americans were dismissed. Having had free access to the Fair grounds, we were permitted to visit the natives from Africa. It was there, for the first time, that we were brought into close touch with native Africans, and the study of those natives interested us very much. We were not long in deciding that if we ever reach the point of having a show of our own, we would delineate and feature native African characters as far as we could, and still remain American, and make our acting interesting and entertaining to American audiences.[78]

For educated as well as uneducated Blacks, the evocation of Ethiopia in *Abyssinia* carried its own powerful significations. One of the characters in the play was Menellk, the actual ruler of the country who had unified that land and who in 1898 had led an Ethiopian army into victory over an Italian force. And for almost forty more years, the existence of this independent African country was to prove to be a provocation to the West's imperial powers. As an almost intolerable contradiction to white supremacy and imperialism, it was not surprising that not even Ethiopia's membership in the League of Nations was sufficient to save its independence following the Italian invasion of 1935. But even more significantly, embedded in Black American culture was the notion that Ethiopia represented the African homeland. As that symbol of home and liberation, Ethiopia had been invoked in Black spirituals from the slave period and afterwards in the independent Black church movement, giving rise to the term "Ethiopianism." As such, Williams, the Walkers, Cook, and the writers, Jesse Shipp and Alex Rogers, had conspired to antagonize the imperial and racist forces in America and inspire Blacks. Allen Woll comments: "The Africans of Abyssinia were depicted as representatives of an ancient and praiseworthy culture, and Americans were the targets of humor."[79]

The second provocation of these collaborators was the showcasing

78. George Walker, "Negro on the American Stage," 247–48.
79. Woll, *Black Musical Theatre*, 42.

of Aida Overton Walker (1880–1914). Unlike the Black chorus girls of previous productions and, indeed, these plays themselves, unlike her costar in *Abyssinia*, Lottie Williams (Mrs. Bert Williams), Aida Overton Walker was dark-skinned.[80] And over the span of her career, she would broaden from the timid implications of Black romance in *Jes Lak White Folk*, *In Dahomey*, and *Abyssinia* to a full-blown eroticism. Performance, racial caricature, and minstrelsy are implicated in what is known of the earliest years of Ada Overton. She was born and raised in an area of Greenwich Village known as Coontown; and by the age of fifteen or sixteen she was performing as a singer in *Black Patti's Troubadours*. She met George Walker when she and the "Two Real Coons" (the title assumed by George Walker and Bert Williams) were invited to pose as dancing the cakewalk for an American Tobacco Company trade-card photograph. She and George were married in 1899. She joined the Williams and Walker company when it took over the Eastern tour of *Clorindy* in 1898; and choreographed the dances for the company's first all-Black musical, *The Policy Players*, in 1899. She received program credit for both this show and the company's next production, *Sons of Ham*, which according to Richard Newman, "made her one of the first recognized black women choreographers."[81]

Ada Walker not only performed and choreographed the cakewalk but she taught the dance to English aristocrats and the cream of white American society.[82] She was, indeed, a central agent in the first national

80. Two of the most celebrated of the very light-complexioned stars of the Black musical were Dora Dean (the "Black Venus") and Abbie Mitchell. The attractions and talents of Dora Dean (Mrs. Charles Johnson of the first Cole-Johnson team—J. Rosamond Johnson collaborated with Cole later) were sufficient to inspire Williams and Walker to write a song, "Dora Dean." Dean's first professional stage appearance was in *The Creole Show*. On tour in Europe and England in the early twentieth century, Dean's portrait was painted by Ernest von Heilmann; and in England her photograph card ("The Sweet Caporal Girl") was enclosed in packs of cigarettes. Abbie Mitchell (Mrs. Will Marion Cook), whose father was a German Jew, made her debut (at fourteen) in the Chicago run of *Clorindy*. She was also a favorite of Edward VII during *In Dahomey*'s London tour; and later became a classical singer and a dramatic actress. See Tanner, *Dusky Maidens*, 53–58 for Dean, and 128–32 for Mitchell.

81. The biographical materials are reported in Newman, "'Brightest Star.'"

82. On the authority of other scholars (e.g., Lawrence Levine), Newman and Krasner both attribute the origins of the cakewalk to "Africa," or "West Africa." It does not seem to have occurred to any of these commentators that geography lacks any precision as a cultural reference. In any case, the origin of the term is traced

Aida Overton Walker, ca. 1900. Photographs and Prints Division, Schomburg Center for Research in Black Culture, New York Public Library, Astor, Lenox and Tilden Foundations.

dance craze, which involved the transfer of Black dance and ragtime into American popular culture. Having become a recognized authority on the cakewalk, she was interviewed by and written about in the mainstream press. "By promoting cakewalking's grace and 'grandiloquence,' Walker used her choreography as a *letter of entry* into the social elite. . . . Walker exploited this even further, refashioning the dance to suit the necessities of a new American elite based on acquired wealth rather than birth."[83] And by the time she was appearing in *In Dahomey*, Ada Walker "was now second in popularity and importance only to the two principals." Newman's report of a royal invitation while the show was on tour in England provides some evidence of the fascination which

———

to American plantations, where competition for a prize cake was staged for whites among slave strutters, singers, and dancers. See Krasner, *Resistance, Parody*, 77–79; Newman, "Brightest Star," 467ff.; and Levine, *Black Culture and Black Consciousness*, 16 (cited in Krasner, *Resistance, Parody*).

83. Krasner, *Resistance, Parody*, 88.

*Aida Overton Walker
and George Walker, 1905.
Photographs and Prints
Division, Schomburg Center
for Research in Black Culture,
New York Public Library, Astor,
Lenox and Tilden Foundations.*

the woman inspired: "While the royal family watched approvingly from lawn chairs, Ada sang and performed a solo dance on the parquette floor that had been laid on the grass. She met and was complimented by the king and queen, and Edward VII, who had an eye for attractive women, gave her a diamond brooch."[84]

An English reviewer (for the *Star*) found her "black but comely," and it was precisely the implied contradiction of her complexion and her sensuality which would provoke such consternation when Aida Walker performed in *Bandanna Land* (1907), the last revue staged by Williams and Walker. Newman recounts:

> Somehow a Salome dance found its way in the third act, and Walker was apparently the first black woman to perform this "modern" dance. There was public anxiety, especially in Boston, about the display of John the Baptist's head and Aida Overton Walker's body. The *Sunday Herald* assured concerned readers, however, that there was nothing offensive about the Baptist's head, and another paper explained that although Aida appeared to be scantily clad, she was

84. Newman, "Brightest Star," 470.

in fact actually wearing bronze trunks over what the paper delicately referred to as "her frame."[85]

Infected with syphilis, George Walker retired from the stage in 1909 and passed away in early 1911. For the next three years, Aida Walker performed in reviews (*The Red Moon* in 1909, *His Honor the Barber* in 1910) before she reprised her role of Salome in William Hammerstein's production of the same name in 1912. In late 1914, at the age of thirty-four, Aida Overton Walker died of a kidney ailment.

The Rise of Black Dramatic Theater

From his own vantage point in Manhattan, James Weldon Johnson termed the period between 1910 and 1921 an "intermediate period" for Black theater. He argued that the deaths of Bob Cole (1909) and George Walker (1911) and "the defection of Bert Williams" (to Ziegfeld) "put a sudden stop to what had been a steady development and climb of the Negro in the theatre." And fifty years later, Henry Sampson substantially concurred, at least with Johnson's juxtapositions and interpretations: "After the deaths of Bob Cole, Ernest Hogan and George Walker, black shows were usually absent from Broadway between 1911 and 1920."[86] We have suggested above that Johnson is not as artless a chronicler as he might first appear. Always mindful of the sometimes submerged racial sensitivities of his non-Black readers, he was careful to center on the dominant culture while expressing an appreciation for those gestures of generosity which granted small privileges to Black artists. But here Johnson seems to have been not so much deliberately dissembling as exposing a surprising provincialism (for one so widely traveled), an imagination hedged by integrationism, as well as a tendency to exaggerate the importance of his own professional circle. There are spurious presumptions here, decidedly ahistorical and unflattering. The most obvious is, of course, that the quantity of talented Black writers, performers, and choreographers was so limited that the subtraction of three or four men would grievously injure the enterprise. The second is that Black women could be entirely evacuated from the field of agency. The third is that the cultural vitality in the nation was limited to the race-patrolled and capital-intensive stages of New York City. Curiously,

85. Ibid., 472.
86. James Weldon Johnson, *Black Manhattan*, 109; Sampson, *Blacks in Blackface*, 10.

neither Johnson nor Sampson actually believed that the interval constituted a hiatus for Black theater, and for sound reasons. Black theater, indeed, thrived in this period. And ironically, among our most authoritative sources for this declaration are Johnson and Sampson.

Notwithstanding Johnson's delinquency, the second decade of the century was one of intensive social volatility. This should not be surprising, since so many economic, political, and cultural contradictions in place for generations were propelling international confrontations and historical struggles. The United States was one magnet for many of them. North American industrialists and capitalists pursuing the convenience of combining imperialism, colonialism, and monopolies pushed the state into far-flung colonialism in the Pacific, the Caribbean, and Central America. And in order to supply the newly acquired markets and to assure their possession, cheap labor was drawn from the fractured and more marginal economies of Southern and Central Europe and Mexico. It would not do to have any of these ambitions exposed as expressions of greed, so counterfeit rationales were constructed for the unsuspecting respectable citizenry. Manifest Destiny was one of them: the Old Europe, its regimes exhausted and decadent, was transferring its historical mission and its excess populations to America. Another was that the new immigrants were "sub-whites." They were intellectually and morally limited, fit for and accustomed to the hardest and most grueling labor, and incapable of the strenuous cultural task of assimilation. They would be socially tolerable only if segregated in the cities and industrial suburbs and robustly patrolled. Racial protocols of inferiorization were extended to blanket them, legitimating the quarantines of location and language. But a third cultural subtext, forfeiting and anesthetizing these necessary cruelties, served to obscure any objective social consciousness. The reception, exploitation, brutalization, and humiliation of millions of lesser Europeans (like their racial equals) were all a gesture of beneficent generosity: "Give me your tired . . ."

None of these myths could mask the real for long. And so disruptions of the social, cultural, and ideological texts were the rule. In retrospect, the tear and repair of the racialized and national texts should have been transparent. During the first half of the period which Johnson nominated as an "interval," the reign of Jack Johnson as the heavyweight champion began. We have seen its destabilizing effects, but there were other cultural injuries, some superficial, some profound. The fiftieth anniversary of Lincoln's abolition was acclaimed by some, only to be countered by the onset of the Wilson presidency and the spate of Jim Crow laws (including the segregation of Washington, D.C., and the Mann Act) which were its concomitants. As its preamble the decade was costumed by a series of violent racial confrontations (Atlanta and Brownsville in 1906, and Springfield, Illinois, in 1908); and dwarfing domestic conflict, 1914 marked the beginning of World War I. The second part of the interval was distinguished by America's entry into that war. An assuaging cultural intervention was attempted by the release of *The Birth of a Nation* and a moralizing reconstruction of the fiftieth anniversary of the Civil War's ending. These initiatives spurred the reconstitution of the second Klan, the reigniting of urban anti-Black violence in the postwar period (Chicago in 1917–19; twenty-five cities and towns in 1919; Ocoee and Orlando, Florida, in 1920; Tulsa in 1921), and the rise of lynchings. With respect to public or mass entertainment, the period was also distinguished by the first maturity of the motion picture industry. And beneath the surface of these "historical" occurrences, and because of some of them, ordinary Black people were enacting a remarkable demographic movement which would permanently alter the American city. But a rather different conjunction of history makes nonsense of the "unflattering" presumption in Johnson and then Sampson that the further development of Black performance required access to Broadway.

During the "interval," Black theater had taken two decisive turnings which influenced the representation of Blacks in the emerging industries of mainstream and independent Black film. While the Black musical form continued (Sampson, for instance, lists three pages of shows produced in the period 1911–15 by prominent entertainers like Flournoy E. Miller, his brother Irvin, Will Marion Cook, Salem Tutt Whitney, Sissieretta Jones, and Billy King), its venue was radically transformed.[87] Predicated on the Black urban migrations of the early twentieth century, Black theater circuits had been organized which crisscrossed the South, the Midwest, and the Northeast. Sampson recognized the phenomenon: "The year 1910 was one of the most memorable in the history of black theatres as many big cities harkened to the demand for exclusive theatres for blacks."[88] Since the migration was simultaneously local and long-distance, significant Black settlement

87. Ibid., appendix B.
88. Ibid., 124.

was now characteristic of many of the towns and cities of these regions. In the South, for instance, despite the extraordinary emigration from the region, between 1900 and 1920 the Black urban population steadily increased from 1,364,000 (19.2 percent of the region's Blacks) to 2,251,000 (25.3 percent).[89] Carole Marks reports that the U.S. Census Department estimated that some 724,000 Blacks out-migrated from the South in this period, and between 1920 and 1930 (generally referred to as the Great Migration period) another 749,000 joined them.[90]

The imperious structure of American theater, dominated by the Theater Syndicate (the "Trust") comprised by the three partnerships of Charles Frohman and Al Hayman, Abe Erlanger and Marc Klaw, and Samuel Nixon and J. Frederick Zimmerman was hardly in the position either to make note of or challenge the Black theater circuit.[91] The Trust's extensive facilities were generally segregated or managed in racially inhospitable fashion. And by the end of the second decade of the twentieth century, the cartel had lost one of its most influential agents (Frohman died on the *Titanic* in 1915) and was deeply embroiled in a struggle against Actors' Equity.[92] Nonetheless its organization and power served as both model and spur. By a curious contrivance of circumstances, men like Ziegfeld, Marcus Lowe, and Adolph Zukor provided sanctuary for blackface minstrelsy as well as the transit point from stage to screen. The short version is that Jewish theater owners and producers began to dominate Broadway in the early 1900s.[93] With them came the attractions which they had first developed for their Yiddish-speaking audiences: performers ensconced in comedy, burlesque, and musicals derived from Yiddish popular culture. The most celebrated of them, entertainers like Sophie Tucker, Eddie Cantor, and Al Jolson, included blackface in their routines. The overt incentive was commercial, but no one seemed particularly distressed that the predominant mood was exploitative. Sophie Tucker could be bawdier in blackface, and "Ziegfeld Girls in café au lait makeup [were] perhaps the apotheosis of the circular logic of blackface: representing 'bad' sexuality, they also remarkably imitated the light-skinned black chorus

89. Marks, *Farewell*, 41–42.
90. Ibid., 2.
91. McArthur, *Actors and American Culture*, 214.
92. Ibid., 218–33.
93. Howe, *World of Our Fathers*, 557; Most, *Making Americans*, 33.

girl from the competing theatrical tradition, who was in turn the 'bad' version of the white chorus girl."[94]

Neither Cantor nor Al Jolson nor George Jessel evoked any true identification with Blacks, so it is reasonable to import a kind of mean ridicule to their performances.[95] The same might be said of Ziegfeld's commentary on the popularity of Black revues on Broadway in the 1910s and 1920s. In 1922

> the *Ziegfeld Follies* included a song about the growing visibility of black entertainment, "It's Getting Dark on Old Broadway," conceding that the Great White Way was no longer so, given all the "pretty choc'late babies" dancing on Broadway's stages and streets. . . .
>
> A lighting effect caused the chorus girls and their white costumes to take on a brown tint as they danced, so they were instantly transformed into dusky belles. As the song ended, the lighting picked out their white dresses and made their bodies "recede into undistinguishable black," according to reviewer [George] Seldes. . . . The image sums up the ghostly projection of beautiful, black, "primitive" bodies, used to fetishize the blondness and fashionability of the Ziegfeld enterprise.[96]

Following the stunning successes of the Black musicals, Ziegfeld bought coon songs, hired Black songwriters, and engaged Black performers to train his dancers. Simultaneously, producers like Lowe and Zukor were transferring blackface to the movies.

The first attempt to organize the Black theaters into regional chains

---

94. Mizejewski, *Ziegfeld Girl*, 131. "As Jeffrey Melnick [*Right to Sing the Blues*, 109] has observed, the 'holy trinity' of blackface entertainers of the 1920s were all Jews: Al Jolson, Sophie Tucker, and Eddie Cantor." Most, *Making Americans*, 32.

95. One irony is the contrast between the approaches taken by these performers in their appropriation of blackness and the earlier interpretations of the Jew by Ira Aldridge. In 1858, in St. Petersburg, Aldridge played Shylock from Shakespeare's *The Merchant of Venice*. One Russian reviewer commented, "He presented to us Shylock as tight-fisted and greedy, but at the same time proud and firm in his convictions, filled with revenge, hatred and anger towards the Christians, enemies of his people and race. . . . In Shylock he does not see particularly a Jew, but a human being in general, oppressed by the age-old hatred shown towards people like him, and expressing this feeling with wonderful power and truth." Quoted in Marshall and Stock, *Ira Aldridge*, 234. See also Lindfors, "'Mislike Me Not.'"

96. Mizejewski, *Ziegfeld Girl*, 128–29.

occurred in 1909 when the Barrasso brothers and Sam Zerilla combined their Memphis theaters to form the hub of the Theatre Owners Booking Association (TOBA). Three years later, Sherman H. Dudley, the Black veteran of minstrelsy, musicals, and vaudeville and now a theater owner in Washington, D.C., and Virginia, formed the Southern Consolidated Circuit, the first Black chain. By 1916, Dudley controlled the booking of Black performers in twenty-eight theaters stretching from Washington, D.C., to Chicago.[97] And Dudley could boast to his retinue of acrobats, magicians, minstrels, musicians, high-wire walkers, athletes, circuses, and vaudevillians that Consolidated could guarantee them bookings for eight months of the year. Finally, Consolidated competed effectively with TOBA (a "lily-white syndicate," according to the *Chicago Star* in 1921) by inaugurating benefits for its Black clientele, like shorter traveling distances between engagements and fewer bookings in all-white venues. Consolidated and TOBA merged their operations in 1921; and the next year, the new TOBA came to an arrangement with the Managers' and Performers' Circuit (M&P), a spin-off from Consolidated.[98] Their orbit now combined about one hundred theaters. On the foundation of Black-owned theaters and Black-managed circuits emerged a second profound event: the reappearance of the Black dramatic stock company.

Black dramatists had appeared on the American stage as early as the 1820s. Though popular with some audiences, the African Grove players were frustrated by police harassment and an increasing public intolerance for anything other than Black caricatures. It would take another ninety years before Black performers undertook a second major initiative in "serious" theater. The organizational setting which facilitated Black dramatic acting was the Black stock companies. The first, according to Sampson, was the All-Star Stock Company organized by Cole and Johnson and housed at E. M. Worth's museum in New York in the late 1890s.[99] In Chicago, the Pekin Players Stock Company was formed in

---

97. Hill, *Pages from the Harlem Renaissance*, 67ff. Leigh Whipper, who would give such an extraordinary performance in *The Ox-Bow Incident* (1943), managed Dudley's Theater in Newport News, Virginia.

98. Among the officers of the M&P Circuit was John T. Gibson, owner of the Strand and Dunbar theaters in Philadelphia. Sampson, *Blacks in Blackface*, 38ff. Hill describes Gibson as "the wealthiest black man in the amusement world." Hill, *Pages from the Harlem Renaissance*, 79.

99. Sampson, *Blacks in Blackface*, 68. E. M. Worth's Model Museum and Family

1906. Producing Black musicals and popular comedies, the performers at Robert Motts's Pekin Theater comprised a number of notable personalities. Among these were William Foster, the acting manager, who is generally credited as the first Black filmmaker (*The Railroad Porter*, 1912); Lottie Grady (who starred in that film); Charles Gilpin (the first "Emperor Jones" in 1920); Abbie Mitchell (whose film career started with *Uncle Remus' First Visit to New York*, 1914; but also included the drama *The Scapegoat*, 1917); and Arthur "Dooley" Wilson ("Sam" of *Casablanca* fame).[100]

Although Elizabeth Williams began the teaching of dramatic acting to women in the Cole and Johnson show the *Red Moon* in 1909, Susan Curtis argues that "stock companies like the Pekin did not form in New York until 1913, when Henry Creamer, Alex Rogers, and Will Marion Cook formed the New York Players. The purpose of the company, clearly articulated by Cook, was 'to aid in the development and perfection' of black musical and dramatic talent . . . to produce plays that provided 'real pictures of Negro life both of city and plantation,' an aim that encouraged the development of black playwrights as well as black actors."[101] Anita Bush, a performer who had done her apprenticeship under Aida Walker, Bert Williams, and George Walker (she started with the company in 1903 in the chorus of *In Dahomey*), founded the Anita Bush Stock Company in 1915. Consisting of five performers — Anita herself (who would star in Norman Film's *The Crimson Skull*, 1921, and *The Bull-Dogger*, 1923), Charles Gilpin, Arthur "Dooley" Wilson, Carlotta Freeman (the prima donna of Ernest Hogan's company and the Pekin Players Stock Company), and Andrew Bishop (star of Micheaux's *A Son of Satan*, 1924; *The Ghost of Tolston's Manor*, 1934; *Murder in Harlem*, 1935; and *Temptation*, 1936) — the company gave its first performance in April 1915 at the New Lincoln Theater in New York.[102] Initially, the com-

---

Theater, at Sixth Avenue and Thirtieth Street, was opened in 1891 as a venue for "freak" shows. See Dennett, *Weird and Wonderful*, 58.

100. Sampson, *Blacks in Blackface*, 115ff. For film credits, see Larry Richards, *African American Films*, passim.

101. Curtis, *First Black Actors*, 42.

102. For Gilpin and Freeman, see Sampson, *Blacks in Blackface*, 120; for Wilson, see Bogle, *Toms, Coons, Mulattoes*, 140. For film credits, see Larry Richards, *African American Films*, passim. Charles Musser and his colleagues maintain that *The Ghost of Tolston's Manor* was the working title for *A Son of Satan* and date the former as 1923; see Musser et al., appendix B, in Bowser, Gaines, and Musser, *Oscar Micheaux*, 229.

pany was made up almost entirely of light-complexioned performers (the notable exception was Wilson) and staged plays adapted from Broadway which featured "white" characters. Responding to criticism that the company had ignored the social reality of "Negro life" in its productions, the company offered a prize for Black playwrights in 1916. That same year the company, now renamed the Lafayette Players in deference to their new home, hired Clarence Muse, a dark-complexioned actor/composer, who would later become one of the top Black actors in both Black independent and mainstream films. In a 1969 interview with Sister M. Francesca Thompson (the daughter of Evelyn Preer of Micheaux's *Within Our Gates*), Muse admitted "he felt out of place as an 'Ethiopian' among all of the other 'high-yellow Negroes . . . and decided to change his appearance on stage by skillful use of white make-up and a blonde wig."[103] On the other hand, Inez Clough (in 1921 alone, she would appear in Micheaux's *The Gunsaulus Mystery* and Reol Picture's *Easy Money, The Simp, Ties of Blood,* and *Secret Sorrow*), another light-skinned actress, who also would join the company in 1916, faced no such difficulty. Drawn, like Bush, Wilson, Muse, and Freeman, from the Black musical form in earlier years, Clough would assist the Lafayette Players in their presentations of plays like *Sherlock Holmes in Sign of the Four* and *Charlie's Aunt.*[104] Without a hint of irony, and in the total absence of parody, innocent or mean-spirited, Black performers were now re-creating European or Euro-American culture on the stage.

The impact of the Lafayette Players was immediate. James Weldon Johnson, for one, was ecstatic: "With the establishment of the Negro theatre in Harlem, coloured performers in New York experienced for the first time release from the restraining fears of what a white audience would stand for; for the first time they felt free to do on the stage

---

Larry Richards identifies *Ghost* as a 1934 release. Larry Richards, *African American Films*, 68.

103. Thompson, "Lafayette Players," 21. Dooley Wilson, also dark, had already appeared in whiteface with Chicago's Pekin Stock Company. Specializing in Irish parts (with a brogue), Wilson sang a song entitled "Mr. Dooley," from whence originated his stage name. Sampson, *Blacks in Blackface*, 451.

104. For Clough's film career, see Larry Richards, *African American Films*, passim. For a list of the Lafayette Players' performances in 1916, see Tanner, *Dusky Maidens*, 70, 80. Clough ended her film work with one more appearance, in Paragon's *The Crimson Fog*, 1932.

whatever they were able to do."[105] Johnson reports that Black audiences were thrilled by this "entirely new experience"; and the downtown audiences, still comfortable with the mixed-race residential and commercial clusters of Harlem, witnessed performances which challenged their received notions of race. Their success was such that in 1916 Bush was brought to Chicago in order to organize a satellite company, and by the end of the year there were Lafayette Players companies based in Black theaters in Washington, D.C., Philadelphia, and Baltimore as well.

Less than one year later, the Lafayette Players company and its predecessors formed the core of a defining event. Johnson described it thus:

> April 5, 1917 is the date of the most important single event in the entire history of the Negro in the American theatre; for it marks the beginning of a new era. On that date a performance of three dramatic plays was given by the Coloured Players at the Garden Theatre in Madison Square Garden, New York, and the stereotyped traditions regarding the Negro's histrionic limitations were smashed. It was the first time anywhere in the United States for Negro actors in the dramatic theatre to command the serious attention of the critics and of the general press and public.[106]

The production was *Three Plays for a Negro Theater*, a work by Ridgely Torrence, staged by Robert Edmond Jones, and produced by Emilie Hapgood. Ironically, as Susan Curtis has evidenced in her remarkable study of the performance (*The First Black Actors on the Great White Way*), neither Torrence, Jones, or Hapgood had the slightest knowledge of Black theater or Black performers. Between 1914 and 1917, Torrence had written three plays, the tragedy *Granny Maumee*, the passion play *Simon, the Cyrenian*, and a comedy, *The Rider of Dreams*, based on a sketchy and frequently exaggerated experience of Black life in his native Xenia, Ohio. But in his search for an archetypal "American" play, he had intuited that Blacks were at the center of America's folkloric tradition. Jones was already recognized by the theater's elite as a creative genius in set design and costuming, so his directorial debut with the

105. James Weldon Johnon, *Black Manhattan*, 173.
106. Ibid., 175.

Three Plays guaranteed an illustrious and important audience. Finally Emilie Hapgood, the former wife of a powerful theater critic (Norman Hapgood of the *New York Commercial-Advertiser*), and an increasingly important theater producer in her own right, brought an emphatic importance to the event.[107] Like most of the non-Blacks in attendance at the Garden Theater, these three had begun the project for their own reasons, erroneously convinced, as Torrence would write, "There had been no serious racial drama; there were no actors with experience of it. The men and women who had professional training had only been in minstrel or 'pick' (pickaninny) shows or they had 'Tommed' (been with an *Uncle Tom's Cabin* troupe)."[108]

Like most of the later accounts of the event, James Weldon Johnson's tells us little, aside from their titles and casts, about the plays. Indeed, even some of the contemporary reviews gave most attention to the singing orchestra conducted by J. Rosamond Johnson which performed between the staging of the three plays. Curtis has corrected that "oversight" by detailing the startling issues addressed by Torrence. Blanche Deas, Joseph Burt, Opal Cooper, and Alexander Rogers comprised the cast of *The Rider of Dreams*, a comedy remarkably like Lorraine Hansberry's much later drama, *Raisin in the Sun*. The play pitted a frugal laundry woman, saving her money to purchase their home, against her husband, a jovial and irresponsible musician who has just spent her savings to invest in a fraudulent business venture. Torrence injected race into the comedy by making the villain of the piece a white man and the hero an educated Black landlord who retrieves the money, grants the wife the deed, and exacts from her husband the promise to conduct himself more responsibly.

Granny Maumee, a play which originally had been performed in 1914 with a non-Black cast, tackled the much more provocative themes of miscegenation and interracial marriage. Now performed by Marie Jackson-Stuart, Fannie Tarkington, and Deas, the play had as its central

---

107. At the premiere, Curtis notes, among those in the audience were celebrities like William Faversham and Billie Burke; wealthy arts patrons like Otto Kahn, Mrs. George Gould, and Miss Constance Collier; critics such as Alexander Woollcott (*New York Times*), Louis De Foe (the *World*), George Jean Nathan (*Smart Set*), Heywood Broun (*New York Tribune*), James Metcalfe (*Life*), and Charles Darnton (*Evening World*); and Black notables like W. E. B. Du Bois, James Weldon Johnson, and Lester A. Walton. Curtis, *First Black Actors*, 1–2.

108. Ibid., 25.

character a blind, scarred old woman who is anxiously awaiting the return of one of her two great-granddaughters. Granny had been blinded and burned while attempting to rescue her innocent son from a lynch mob. Adept in the beliefs of voodoo and devoted to her family, Granny is now excited by the news that her great-granddaughter has given birth to a son, the first man-child in her "royal black line" since the death of her son. In the excitement of the moment her sight is partially restored, but when she learns that the infant's father is white and a descendant of a member of her son's lynch mob, she plots the killing of her granddaughter, the child, and the white husband. At the last moment, Granny invokes her Christian beliefs, renders a monologue contrasting Black forbearance with white brutality, and then suddenly dies.

The final play, *Simon, the Cyrenian*, characterized Simon, who is recruited by a Centurion to carry the Cross, as a Black Libyan rebel. The large cast included Inez Clough, Andrew Bishop, Lottie Grady, John T. Butler, Alexander Rogers, Jesse Shipp, and Theodore Roosevelt Bolin. Staged as a spectacle of design and costume by Jones, it was featured in most of the publicity for the *Three Plays*.[109] The critic for the *New York Evening Post* thought of the play as "an object lesson of the cruelties suffered in the past, by the negro at the hands of the white race."[110]

Susan Curtis provides a masterful display of the conflicting aesthetic and ideological currents which framed the critics' responses to the performances. Most were enthusiastic and laudatory (Francis Hackett of the *New Republic* wrote, "It is, all things considered, as fine an enterprise as the American theatre has seen for years"), but they were silhouetted by racial discourse.[111] One particularly exemplary instance was Metcalfe's review in *Life*. Marred by a printer's calligraphy, the *U* in "Under," the first word in his article, "became an enormous, curved piece of watermelon whose center had been gobbled away by a thick-lipped, bucktoothed African American who grasped the piece with both hands and appeared to be about to take another big bite."[112] And on a different plane of the same sensibility, Arthur Hornblower in *Theatre Magazine* found the presence of light-complexioned actors confusing: "Whites were used in the minor numerous parts," he concluded.[113] However,

109. Ibid., chap. 5.
110. Ibid., 159.
111. Hackett, "After the Play."
112. Curtis, *First Black Actors*, 158.
113. Ibid., 159.

what troubles Curtis most and provides the central problematic for her study is the fact that after a few weeks of intense excitement and expectation, the *Three Plays* were almost entirely ignored. Indeed by the end of the year, the "historic night on Broadway," which so many critics had recognized, had evaporated from the critics' annual awards and as a consequence was unrecorded in subsequent histories of the American stage. James Weldon Johnson inaugurated the explanation that the American entry into the war (April 6, 1917, one day after opening night) was the downfall of the Colored Players. Curtis is more circumspect:

> The critical response to the Negro Players' performances and the three race dramas—especially those that appeared in the first few days after the initial showing—demonstrate the preconceptions, ignorance, and partial sight that many in the critical community brought to the race plays. . . . The war, however, generated its own kind of cultural skirmishes—over who qualified to bear arms in defense of the nation, what constituted a genuine American culture, and how to construct a narrative of America's victorious campaign after the war came to an end. These cultural conflicts in an age of anxiety left little space for American citizens of color. . . . American culture absorbed very little of the *Three Plays for a Negro Theater*—on the grounds of race and politics.[114]

Since Blacks were not thought of as truly American citizens, Curtis proposes that their deaths and triumphs in Europe, just like their anguish and tragedies in America, had to be erased for the good of the nation. Policing the boundary of race inspired a startlingly quick mobilization.

The relatively short duration of American participation in World War I (April 1917 to November 1918) provided one more occasion for the presentment, repair, and actualization of scientific racism. And just as before and later, it was a multidimensional offensive. One maneuver intended to preserve the fiction that Black troops were only competent or courageous enough for service or menial labor required deputizing the majority of the 42,000 Black combat troops to the French military.[115] As Colonel William Hayward would put it, "Our great American general [John J. Pershing] put the black orphan

114. Ibid., 201–2.
115. Nalty, *Strength for the Fight*, chap. 8. Something like 380,000 Blacks served in

in a basket, set it on the doorstep of the French, pulled the bell, and went away."[116] Mindful that this necessary but still problematic device might expose their French allies to the fabled seductions infesting American racial lore, the U.S. high command issued an instruction manual. Granting the protocols of military courtesy, still "we must prevent any pronounced degree of intimacy between French officers and black officers," the mission advised; and in the local cantonments where Black troops might be housed, "any public expressions of intimacy" by white women towards Black men was to be discouraged.[117] The American army, of course, was segregated, for all intents and purposes, into two armies: one white, the other Black. A second and far more long-term stratagem was the technical augmentation of military psychology. Under the direction of Colonel Robert M. Yerkes (a Harvard faculty member), Lewis Terman (Stanford) and H. H. Goddard participated in the design of the Army Mental Tests which were employed on some 1,750,000 American recruits in 1917–18.[118] Rather than the body which had so concerned the anthropometrists of the previous century, the new measure would be the cultural information consigned to middle-class whiteness. Social segregation, labor segregation, and inadequate public resources for the education of the poor would conceal and conserve for generations this invalid correlation between information and intelligence. On the home front, even the most minimal efficiencies of military training required the infrequent occurrence of some negroes with guns garrisoned in military camps.

---

the wartime army, 200,000 of them in France. The combat troops were organized into the 369th, 371st, and 372nd Infantries. Ibid., 112ff.

116. Ibid., 117. In May 1918, Sergeant Henry Johnson and Private Needham Roberts became the first Blacks awarded the *Croix de Guerre* by the French authorities. The Black units fighting with their French hosts were notable in the final months of the war, suffering 2,500 casualties in the Meuse-Argonne in September and October, and 665 casualties (for the 370th alone) in the Oise-Aisne offensive. Ibid., 120.

117. Ibid., 114. "The Secret Information concerning Black American Troops" was published in the *Crisis*, May 1919, 16–17. It was still a source of enormous indignation on James Weldon Johnson's part nearly a decade later. See *Black Manhattan*, 245.

118. Gould, *Mismeasure of Man*, 192ff. Goddard was director of research at the Vineland Training School for Feeble-Minded Girls and Boys (New Jersey) where he pioneered the inferiorization of Appalachians and Central and Eastern European immigrants before World War I. Terman was a professor at Stanford University who popularized the Stanford-Binet examination protocol into a national psychometric industry in the postwar period. Ibid., 158–92.

When these units resisted racial violence, as occurred in Houston in August 1917, an unambiguous display of official white supremacy was warranted: nineteen Black troops were hanged for the race "riot" precipitated by police brutality.[119]

In the National Archives, Curtis pursued and uncovered a treasury of official military correspondence concerning cultural initiatives. She was interested in detailing the rejection of Black dramatic materials as acceptable entertainment for either Black or white troops and discovered that many of the illustrious civilians and ranking commissioned officers responsible for the decision were unmitigated racists. Her irrefutable evidence was the numerous memoranda which were frequently peppered by the term "nigger" and what the correspondents presumed were humorous imitations of Black dialect.[120] Despite the considerable efforts of Lester A. Walton (a former co-owner of the Lafayette Theater and the longtime drama critic of the *New York Age*) to promote the war effort and deracialize the recreational and training venues for American soldiers, the army insisted on organizing minstrel shows.[121] And its collaborator, the Commission on Training Camp Activities, led by Marc Klaw and dominated by Broadway notables (David Belasco, Lee Shubert, A. L. Erlanger, Edward F. Albee, George M. Cohan, Irving Berlin, Arthur Hammerstein), insisted that white troops demanded minstrel shows, musical farces, comedies, and concerts by coon quartets.[122] Given the extent of official involvement in promoting racism, the dogged persistence of the cultural gatekeepers during World War I in countering the real-world potential for disrupting the fragile racial order, it would appear to be somewhat excessive to credit *The Birth of a Nation* for nurturing the Klan into a national race police after the war.

119. The incident began when a Black soldier interrupted a white policeman's beating of a Black woman. Nalty, *Strength for the Fight*, 102–6.

120. Curtis, *First Black Actors*, 182–85, 194.

121. Walton (1882–1965) and his partner C. W. Morganstern purchased the Lafayette Theater in 1914 and sold it in 1916. In 1919, Walton returned to the Lafayette as manager. Earlier, from his home base in St. Louis, Walton had worked as a reporter for the *St. Louis Globe-Democrat*, the *St. Louis Post-Dispatch*, and the *St. Louis Star Sayings*. Upon his transfer to New York in 1906, Walton collaborated with Ernest Hogan, the Black minstrel performer and composer, on the lyrics for Hogan's musical comedy *Rastus Rufus*. See ibid., 43ff. From 1935 to 1946, Walton served as U.S. ambassador to Liberia.

122. Ibid., 187–88.

But notwithstanding the vigor and apparent finality of the conceits of white supremacy, and the terrible disappointment of having come so close to the jealous and frightened gatekeepers of American culture, Black artistry continued.

In 1928, the original Lafayette Players Company, having changed hands several times, was transferred to the Lincoln Theater in Los Angeles.[123] Meanwhile, in 1922, a second important dramatic company, the Ethiopian Art Theatre, was inaugurated in Chicago. Premiering in January 1923 under the direction of Raymond O'Neil, an Irish American, the Ethiopian Art Theatre largely depended on the professional talents of former Lafayette Players like Evelyn Preer, Laura Bowman, Sidney Kirkpatrick, and Edna Thomas. Within two months of its first public performances, the Ethiopian Art Theatre (under the encouragement of W. E. B. Du Bois) was presenting the works of a Black playwright, Willis Richardson. Traveling a circuit between Washington, D.C. (the Howard Theater), New York (the Lafayette and Frazee), and Chicago, the short-lived company showcased a varied fare, including Richardson's *The Chip Woman's Fortune*, Oscar Wilde's *Salome*, a jazz version of Shakespeare's *The Comedy of Errors*, and Flournoy Miller's *Going White*, during seasons in 1923 and 1924.[124]

And far beyond the confines of New York and Chicago, "serious" Black theater persisted in a variety of forms. Before launching his career as a first-rank researcher in zoology and biology, Ernest Just (Dartmouth; University of Chicago) had taught English at Howard University and in 1909 had developed the College Dramatic Club. In 1919, Montgomery Gregory (a Harvard graduate who replaced Just in 1910) founded Howard University's Dramatic Art and Public Speaking Department. And based on his recruitment of talented professionals like Marie Moore Forrest (acting coach) and Cleon Throckmorton (design), Gregory established the Howard Players that same year. Declaring that "If art is self-expression, it is necessarily race expression," Gregory guided the Howard Players towards acclaimed productions of such works as Eugene O'Neill's *Emperor Jones* (as supporting cast to Charles Gilpin) and Torrence's *Simon, the Cyrenian*. But more importantly the Howard Players staged the works of emerging Black playwrights

123. Thompson, "Lafayette Players," 23.
124. Addell Austin Anderson, "Ethiopian Art Theatre."

like Richardson (*Mortgaged*), May Miller (*Within the Shadow*), Lottie Beatrice Graham (*The King's Carpenters* and *Holiday*), and others.[125]

In his 1940 survey of Black dramatists, Frederick W. Bond identified other Black playwrights with the Black Little Theater movement: for instance, Langston Hughes (*Mulatto* and *Don't You Want to Be Free?*); Randolph Edmonds (*Six Plays for a Negro Theatre*); George Norford (*Joy Exceeding Glory*); Wilson Williams (*Le Bourgeois Gentilhomme*); John Matheus (*Ti Yette*); Dennis Donoghue (*Legal Murder*); and Wallace Thurman (*Harlem*).[126] Denied access to the dominant venues of American theater, these playwrights circulated their works where Blacks served as the predominant audience. In Cleveland in 1923, a Black little theater group called the Gilpin Players was established and was still performing as Bond went to press. In 1930, Edmonds founded the Morgan College Players, providing the basis for the formation of the Negro Intercollegiate Dramatic Association (Morgan College; Howard University; Virginia State; Virginia Union University; Shaw University; Lincoln University; and the Agricultural and Technical College of Greensboro) that same year. After leaving Howard in 1924, Gregory went on to direct the Neighborhood Players (founded by Mario Bedio) in Atlantic City; and Edmonds transferred his interest in dramatic theater from Morgan College to Dillard University. In sum, while Broadway producers ultimately returned to the Black musical comedy in the 1920s (Flournoy Miller, Aubrey Lyles, Eubie Blake, and Noble Sissle's *Shuffle Along*, 1921, is credited with this revival), the small stages of Black colleges, universities, and amateurs moved forward, cultivating performers and writers and audiences. But Broadway, with the likes of non-Blacks like O'Neill (*Emperor Jones, All God's Chillun Got Wings*), Paul Green (*White Dresses, In Abraham's Bosom*), Leon Gordon (*White Cargo*), Edward Sheldon (*Lulu Belle*), James Tully and Frank Dazey (*Black Boy*), and DuBose and Dorothy Heyward (*Porgy*), had no interest in Black playwrights who might exceed the strictures of melodrama by replacing personal demons with themes of racial oppression.

James Weldon Johnson, of course, had been naïve to believe that what was happening on the American stage before the war or even afterwards would profoundly alter the manipulations of race in American popu-

125. See Bond, *Negro and the Drama*, 122ff.; and "The Black Renaissance in Washington, D.C.," <http://www.dclibrary.org/blkren/bios/gregorytm.html.>.

126. Bond, *Negro and the Drama*, chaps. 7 and 8.

lar culture. Moreover, writing at the onset of the Great Depression, he could not have understood how devastating the economic and political impact of that event would be on Black performers and the Black theater circuits. Nevertheless, by the year *Black Manhattan* was published (1930), the Black theater circuits had all but vanished. In their stead, inundating the rupture, the "stereotyped traditions" were reinstalled through the mediums of film and stage. Urbane and literate, Johnson was also ill prepared to reckon on the consequences of the cinema on public or mass entertainment. For certain, a Black independent film movement, drawing on the talent encased in the melodramatic genre of Black dramatic theater, had sought to counter Black representations in the dominant movie picture industry. The contest, however, was hardly a fair match. The "downtown" audiences of America's cities and towns would seldom see these films. The film-producing industries were segregated; film distribution was segregated; film exhibitions were segregated; and film audiences were segregated. The notion of separate but equal was never applicable to the motion picture business; no more relevant in this instance than anywhere else in American society.

Resistance and Imitation in Early Black Cinema

Before we expect to see ourselves featured on the silver screen as we live, hope, act and think today, men and women must write original stories of Negro life, and as the cost of producing high class photo-plays is high, money must be risked in Negro corporations for this purpose— some, many will perhaps fail before they have got to going right, but from their ashes will spring other and better men, some of whom in time will master the art in completeness, and detail and when so, we will have plays in which our young men and women will appear to our credit as finished silent drama artists.

— Oscar Micheaux, "The Negro and the Photo-Play," Half-Century Magazine, *May 1919*

Jim Crow, American Capitalism, and the Motion Picture Industry

The commercial exploitation of motion pictures, beginning in the last decade of the nineteenth century, coincided exactly with the onset of Jim Crow—the judicial and legislative regimes of racial segregation. This coincidence of the manufacture of an embryonic mass culture and a profound restructuring of race relations serves as one critical rationale for the transfer of blackface minstrelsy and other icons of Black inferiorization to the emerging filmic culture. Most histories of the early American film industry adhere to the notion that the anarchy of production, distribution, exhibition, and content of films which characterized the industry until 1908 or so was brought to order by the logic of economics.[1] But there is also compelling evidence that cohesion and con-

1. The literature on this question is voluminous. Two examples, drawn from sources a decade apart, must suffice. In 1985, Robert C. Allen and Douglas Gomery maintained that "in 1908, ten leading producers and equipment makers combined to form the Motion Picture Patents Company (MPPC). Why? Because as a cartel . . . the MPPC could set prices and quantity, and create additional profits by virtue of its economic size and position." Allen and Gomery, *Film History*, 145. In 1997, David Puttnam asserted that "the principal rationale behind the creation of the MPPC was to allow

trol of American motion pictures was spurred by the powerful interests implicated in the formulation of the new racial regime. There was much at stake; it is no exaggeration to suggest that from the 1890s to World War I the country had no national political consensus, no hegemonic cultural core, no dominant historical identity, no definitive social solidarity. And while our attention will be principally attached to the treatment of the "Negro problem," it would be well to remember that it was merely one source of threat to wealth and power. It gains primacy, however, not from the accident of historical perspective but from necessity. The new racial regime would coalesce with American nationalism as the two master narratives instituted to reassert political control over an American order frayed by domestic rebellion and social diversity.

In the world economy towards the end of the nineteenth century, American finance capital had begun to shoulder aside more senior centers of hegemony. For instance, the financial capital which supported Southern agriculture in the late nineteenth century no longer "originated" in London but flowed from banks and investment houses in New York and Boston.[2] For another, in world trade Germany's predominance in machine production was now being challenged by American firms following the example of McCormick-Deering (International Harvester) based in Chicago and producing farm implements.[3] Despite massive unemployment among American workers, and perhaps because of long-term declines in wholesale prices, finance capital surveyed the globe for even more desperate and cheaper labor. The largest surplus of unemployed workers was in the South. The Southern economic colony, however, barred outside labor recruitment because the labor intensive production of the dominant plantation economy required a surplus pool of Black and white day laborers to maintain the complementary institutions of gang labor, sharecropping, tenant farming, and convict lease. Maintaining political order among this mix

---

Edison and AM&B [American Mutoscope and Biograph Company] to reassert what they saw as their rightful dominance of their home market, regardless of whether the competition was American or foreign." Puttnam, *Movies and Money*, 41.

2. "Before the Civil War . . . the planter was typically in debt to the factor, who was in debt to an English merchant house, which in turn was financed by a London bank. Now the farmer was in hock to the furnishing merchant, who was under obligation to local or New York bankers." Cell, *Highest Stage*, 108. See also Beaud, *History of Capitalism*, 122–27.

3. Bryant and Dethloff, *History of American Business*, 83–84.

of an impoverished majority had become a principal function of white racism. But even this protocol was showing wear and tear where local or historical conditions allowed. For example, on the docks of New Orleans, Black and white riverfront unions avoided the superexploitative conditions of their Galveston counterparts by inventing a share system ("half-and-half"). These alliances persisted well beyond World War I.[4] Among firemen and brakemen on Southern railroads, Blacks retained their dominance inherited from the antebellum period. While Northern railroad brotherhoods of conductors, engineers, firemen, and brakemen barred Blacks from these occupations, as late as 1900 an observer noted, "It is an every-day occurrence in the South to see white locomotive engineers and colored firemen seated in the same cab."[5] Employers, already made uneasy by the formation of national labor unions like the American Federation of Labor (AFL), were further distressed by the antiracist strategy of the Knights of Labor and the United Mine Workers.[6] And in the New South, those whom John Cell characterizes as Black and white peasants (but usually referred to as farmers in the parlance of other American historians) were edging towards class solidarity in the Farmers' Alliances movement and some sectors of Populism.[7] All these processes were taking place during the fits and starts of the depressions (1873–95) which beset the capitalist

4. See Daniel Rosenberg, *New Orleans Dockworkers*, chap. 3; and Hirsch, "On the Waterfront," 511–17.

5. Arnesen, "'Like Banquo's Ghost,'" 1609.

6. See McLaurin, *Knights of Labor*; Gutman, "Negro and United Mine Workers," 121–208.

7. "Everywhere in the world except England and America, sharecroppers and small independent farmers are called peasants." Cell, *Highest Stage*, 111. "In the 1870s and more aggressively in the 1880s, organizations of white farmers and artisanal laborers amassed to challenge the nation's merchants, bankers, railroad corporations, and the like. . . . Spawned from local circumstances rather than from national headquarters, they nevertheless achieved a formidable unity of purpose: the establishment of cooperative stores, purchasing initiatives, and cooperative markets for buying and selling of cotton and other produce." In 1888, the Colored Farmers' National Alliance and Cooperative Union was formed, and "by 1890–91, its membership was considerable, including 40,000 Black alliance members in South Carolina and 20,000 in Virginia." The rapprochement between the two movements was fitful. And while the white alliance was co-opted by Populism and racism, the Black alliance collapsed in 1893. Robinson, *Black Movements in America*, 102, 103–4. For Populism and race, see Cantrell and Barton, "Texas Populists."

world economy.[8] And immigrant alien labor made matters worse. In the manufacturing, industrial, and extractive sectors of the economy, the recruitment of skilled, semi-skilled, and unskilled labor from mainly Central, Eastern, and Southern Europe had unhinged the platform of (white) American cultural and historical homogeneity.

The appearance of Populist parties in the early 1890s and the Populists' resort to the "fusion" maneuver (with Republicans in the South and Democrats in the North) in the elections of 1894 and 1896 threw the final scare into the planters and the politicians, merchants, lawyers, and publishers who formed their political infrastructure. Populism was a rebellion of the rural poor which clearly articulated a collective contempt for the class rule of wealth. On that score its political impulse was towards extreme democracy, that is, the rule of the poor (not to be confused with the then-ruling Democratic Party). The planter class responded with disfranchisement and segregation. Disfranchisement, Edward L. Ayers asserts, "removed the great majority of black voters from the rolls and a large portion of poor and illiterate white men."[9] As John Cell suggests, while many of the South's poor whites might have supported *Black* disfranchisement, it is unlikely they would have sacrificed themselves to that cause. In either case, "they lacked the power" to protect themselves, much less choreograph attacks on Black voters.[10] It was the planters who pursued and directed disfranchisement.[11] Under the camouflage of the "Negro threat" economically to poor whites and sexually to white women, Southern patricians and their minions denuded the polls by secret ballots, new franchise requirements, fraud, intimidation, deception, and routinely, violence. Voter participation plummeted and with it the dangers of electoral democracy.

The patricians, however, had inadvertently incited a new and virulent phase of the race war. And in opposition to the racial demagogues (Ben Tillman of South Carolina, James Vardaman and Theodore Bilbo of Mississippi, Furnifold Simmons of North Carolina, Tom Watson of Georgia) who appropriated the rhetoric of Populism or emerged from its ruins, that same powerful class was compelled to impose Jim Crow as a "moderate" compromise. Where the logic of the demagogues led

8. Beaud, *History of Capitalism*, 117–22.
9. Ayers, *Promise of the New South*, 409.
10. Cell, *Highest Stage*, 153.
11. Kousser, *Shaping of Southern Politics*.

to genocidal consequences — "from the contention that no negro shall vote, to the contention that no negro shall learn, that no negro shall labor, and (by implication) that no negro shall live," as Edgar Garner Murphy described it in 1910 — the planters substituted segregation.[12] As Cell insists, "segregation was related to the formation of the Southern capitalist power elite. . . . Racial segregation was thus closely related to the New South's strategy of capitalist development."[13] And alongside the native elite, Northern capital stood, subsidizing the railroads, extracting the coal, denuding the timber fields.[14]

The railroads are of particular interest in the formulation of the emerging racial regime of the late nineteenth century with which Jim Crow was associated. In Florida as early as the 1870s, convict labor laid the track for the St. Johns, Lake Eustis and Gulf Railroad Company in the infested marshes and jungles. In Tennessee, convict labor put in sixteen-hour days for track construction for the Cincinnati Southern Railroad. Labor regimes akin to death marches were the norm for the convict laborers of the Western North Carolina Railroad, for the Greenville and Augusta Railroad in South Carolina, and the Great Northern Railroad and the Gulf, Colorado, and Santa Fe Railroad in Texas.[15] The prisoners were overwhelmingly Black (for instance, in South Carolina in 1880, of the 431 state prisoners, only 25 were white), some as young as twelve years old, and their mortality rates were astronomical. In Arkansas, state authorities did not even bother to record deaths. In South Carolina in 1877–79, the 285 convicts leased to the Greenville and Augusta Railroad had a mortality rate of 45 percent. In the coal mines of Alabama, county prisoners (97 percent Black) toiled for the Tennessee Coal and Iron Company, dying of lung disease, dysentery, and sometimes in catastrophes (128 convicts killed in the Banner Mine explosion in 1911). The extraction of turpentine and resin in Florida, the timber fields and the sawmills from the Carolinas to Texas, all added to the death litany of hard labor. "The 'Accident Record Book' of a small Southern line in a single year gives a clear sense of the peril to life and limb: 'hand crushed, collision'; 'killed, collision'; 'struck by bridge and killed'; 'fall from train . . . death'; 'son of Rev. J. W. Miller killed'; 'skull

12. Cell, *Highest Stage*, 179.
13. Ibid., 170.
14. Ayers, *Promise of the New South*, chap. 5.
15. Oshinsky, *"Worse than Slavery,"* chap. 3.

fractured, death resulted'; 'negro boy run over and head cut off'; 'leg run over necessitating amputation'; 'wreck caused by broken wheel, killed.'"[16] Finding them superfluous, the state of Florida did not even construct state prisons, relieving taxpayers of that burden by leasing and working convicts to death. In sum, David Oshinsky remarks, this was Jim Crow justice. And while some have argued that the institutionalization of Jim Crow coincided with a decrease in lynching and other forms of mob violence in the New South, they have neglected to take into account other solutions to the Negro Question, not the least of which was the emergence of an extensive carceral system operated by the states.[17]

It is not surprising, then, that railroad corporations and their complements in lumber and coal played such a pivotal role in sponsoring the world's fairs and regional fairs of the late nineteenth and early twentieth centuries where the new race order was exhibited.[18] With so much invested in the Black representations mounted by anthropologists (African savages) and hawkers (Aunt Jemima) at the 1893 Chicago world's fair (and elsewhere), what was there not to like when American Mutoscope Company (Biograph) weighed in with, among its first ventures in the amusement field, *Oh! That Watermelon, Watermelon Feast, Dancing Darkies*, and *Hard Wash* (a Black woman frustrated since

16. Ibid., 58–59.

17. Clarke, "Without Fear or Shame."

18. Among the most important sponsors of the Centennial Exposition in Philadelphia in 1876 were the Philadelphia and Pennsylvania Railroad, the Lehigh Valley Railroad, and the A. P. Railroad. Rydell, *All the World's a Fair*, 18. (Hereafter, page references in Rydell are cited parenthetically.) The lead for staging the 1893 Columbian Exposition in New York was undertaken by Chauncey Depew, president of the New York Central Railroad, and his friend Cornelius Vanderbilt; among their rivals in Chicago were George Pullman, manufacturer of railroad cars (42). Pullman was also a major sponsor of the Tennessee Centennial Exposition in 1897, and the president of the exposition, John W. Thomas, was also president of the Nashville, Chattanooga and St. Louis Railway (78–79). At the Atlanta Cotton States and International Exposition in 1895, railroad companies were the major stockholders, and the attractions for the Midway Amusements were organized by Edmund A. Felder, "secretary for various railroad companies" (94). The Trans-Mississippi and International Exposition at Omaha in 1898 was substantially subsidized by five railroad companies (108). The Vanderbilt Lines contributed substantially to the 1901 Pan-American Exposition in Buffalo. Charles W. Goodyear, lumberman and railroad magnate, was one of its directors, along with John M. Brinker, of coaling and railroad interests (129).

no matter how hard she scrubbed her child it never was clean—i.e., white) in 1896. And it seems this was no coincidence. Incorporated at the end of 1895, American Mutoscope was bonded for $200,000 by the New York Security and Trust Company. The company's president was George R. Blanchard, "one of the most prominent railroad executives in the country"; its first vice president was a national bank examiner; on its board was F. J. Berwind, part owner of the Berwind & White Coal Mining Company; and one investor was Abner McKinley, the brother of a future American president.[19] Smarting from the competition of this new upstart and suffering from declining profits, Edison Manufacturing Company turned to filming sex (*The May Irwin Kiss*, 1896), train wrecks, and, of course, racist comedies like *Watermelon Contest* (1896 and 1900) and *Chicken Thieves* (1896).[20] Another caricature was presented in the film *A Morning Bath* (1896), which apparently complemented a "Negro Babes on Exhibition," a sort of competition of which the *New York Herald Tribune* observed: "As there are no standard comparisons of colored beauty, the voting was carried on with no little mirth" (August 12, 1896).[21] Finally, another noncoincidence should be noted.

By the end of the nineteenth century, for the most part the railroads themselves were no longer independent entities. Greed, mismanagement, credit scandals, deplorable treatment of workers, and the like had taken their toll. Corrupt service rates also played havoc with long-distance trade. The public outcry over the misdeeds of railroad owners provoked the passage of the Interstate Commerce Act in 1887 and the forming of the Interstate Commerce Commission (ICC) to rationalize

19. Musser, *Emergence of Cinema*, 148.

20. Ibid., chap. 2; and Cripps, *Slow Fade to Black*, 393n12. To give some sense of these films, consider the reaction of one exhibitor, C. O. Richardson of Skowhegan, Maine, who wrote to Vitascope, the distributor, that *Watermelon Contest* needed to be replaced because it was "nasty and vulgar because of the spitting and slobbering." Musser, *Emergence of Cinema*, 130. An interesting contrast is the respectful treatment accorded to the Chinese former viceroy in a series which included *Li Hung Chang at Grant's Tomb* (1896). See "Earl Li at Grant's Tomb," *New York Times*, August 31, 1896, 1. As a "modernizer" of the Chinese military, Li had become a favorite of European and American armament manufacturers, war departments, and financiers. "Li Hung Chang," *New York Times*, August 23, 1896, 4. Native Americans, on the other hand, were represented by *Indian Scalping Scene* and *Rescue of Capt. John Smith by Pocahontas*. Musser, *Edison Motion Pictures*, 233, 194.

21. Musser, *Edison Motion Pictures*, 250.

the rail system. The ICC's attempts at the regulation of rates, rebates, and so on, however, were almost entirely savaged by the Supreme Court, which sided with the railroads in fifteen of sixteen cases between 1887 and 1905. Their creditors, though, were less forgiving. Consequently, in the final years of the century, institutions of finance capital intruded into the management and reorganization of the railroad operations. By that time, Keith Bryant and Henry Dethloff report, seven financial investment groups had gained control over two-thirds of the rail mileage in the country. Among the most influential of the investment houses were J. P. Morgan and Company, the Kuhn, Loeb firm, and J. and W. Seligman. These same companies would prove to be critical to the future finance and incorporation of the emerging film industry.[22]

With the advent of salesmen and traders into the industry, the practices of the retail market were smuggled almost immediately into the prepubescent film industry. Smaller producing companies, like those of William Selig (Selig Polyscope Company) and Sigmund Lubin seized upon the successes of Biograph and Edison. Both Selig and Lubin knew from experience that sex, sensationalism, and racism made for attractive film fare. According to Mel Watkins, about a third of the films made before 1912 were comedies, a genre replete with barely concealed sexual titillation and blatant racial and ethnic caricatures.[23] Additionally, quasi-documentaries or melodramatic "sex-problem photoplays," particularly those capitalizing on the white slavery hysteria of the early years of the century, were a staple of the Motion Picture Patents Company's (MPPC) producing companies as well as their smaller enterprising competitors.[24]

22. Bryant and Dethloff, *History of American Business*, 124.

23. Watkins, *On the Real Side*, 183.

24. Perhaps the most sensationalized issue was that of "white slavery," that is, white female prostitution. Kay Sloan's own contribution is to document the production of sexploitation photoplays from the earliest cinema. See *Loud Silents*, chap. 4. John D. Rockefeller Jr. had been the foreman of a special grand jury which reported on white slave traffic in New York in 1910. The grand jury findings led to the creation of a Bureau of Social Hygiene, which established a Laboratory of Social Hygiene in Bedford Hills to conduct clinical studies of prostitutes housed in the adjacent reformatory and to conduct a citywide survey, directed by George J. Kneeland, of houses of ill-repute and 2,000 prostitutes. See "Rockefeller Way to Deal with Vice," *New York Times*, January 27, 1913, 1, 2; and Keire, "Vice Trust." Francis G. Couvares asserts that conflicts around "sex-problem photoplays," coupled with race, contributed to the demise of the National Board of Censorship before the beginning of World War I.

Selig, a former manager of minstrel shows and now based in Chicago, produced *Shooting Craps* (1900), *Who Said Watermelon?* (1900), *A Night in Blackville* (1900), a coon version of the *May Irwin Kiss*, entitled *Something Good—Negro Kiss* (1900), *Prizefight in Coontown* (1902), *Wooing and Wedding a Coon* (1907) and *The Masher* (1907). Lubin, a former exhibition factor for Edison, unabashedly rationalized his larceny of Selig's title by announcing that his own *Who Said Watermelon?* (1902) was a result of "the demand for a new watermelon picture."[25] Lubin's catalogue was, as they say, on the money. For as admirably summarized by Thomas Cripps, one film company after another rushed into the business of producing Black caricatures:

> Catalogue writers who described the hundreds of films in release described their products as though they had learned nothing and forgotten nothing since the first "darkey" stories. The pages were thick with chicken thieves and crapshooters, and their appeal was to the "proverbial" and the old fashioned, one catalogue urging its wares because "these darkies are of the 'Old Virginny' type." Compared with the days of movie infancy, the films were a deluge. . . . Another catalogue entry pleaded authenticity because "all coons like chicken." Worse still, one catalogue listed a movie depicting "the catching, taring [*sic*] and feathering and burning of a negro for the assault of a white woman."[26]

For the most part these were minstrel movies, non-Black actors and actresses corked up to represent Blacks. Though survey data on the impact of films on audiences was still decades in the future, it is a reasonable assumption that the volume and persistence of such images reinforced the myriad of other degraded Black significations available for urban and rural audiences.

There were ambiguities, of course, questions which may have arisen

---

Couvares, "Good Censor," 240ff. An unexpected spin-off of the Rockefeller grand jury was that Samuel H. London, one of its investigators (and a former special agent of the U.S. government) sought to capitalize on the movie market by making his own white slavery film, *The Inside of the White Slave Traffic* (1913). See "Police Confiscate White Slave Films," *New York Times*, December 21, 1913, 5; and Couvares, "Good Censor," 241–42.

25. Musser, *Emergence of Cinema*, 331; and for Selig, see ibid., 292, 478.
26. Cripps, *Slow Fade to Black*, 13–14.

from the very fact of the staging of a Black presence, or from the ruptures occasioned by actual Black performance. Despite the possibly apocryphal tales of early film audiences ducking to avoid onrushing trains or returning the fire of on-screen gunmen, is it credible that some seventy years into the American minstrel phenomenon that even newcomers weren't aware that these performers were not actually Black? That the outrageous dilemmas besetting these characters bore only the barest traces of the brutal realities of Black life? That these amusing parodies of an existence carried a whiff of the horror they were meant to conceal or to distance? Is it possible that the absence of burnt cork makeup from the interiors and exteriors of the ordinary experiences of the audiences was not a determinative clue that the whole contrivance was unreal? While more sophisticated audience members (and Blacks) might have discerned that these figures were imitations, that is, European Americans performing in the guise of Blacks, there is a possibility that these depictions were received as having no more purchase on the real than the anthropomorphized animals of animation cartoons. But it is more probable that the constancy of the disguise, its repetition in film after film, and its reinforcement in other sites of the public sphere may have exhausted that reservation. On the other hand, since filmmakers found it necessary to cast non-Blacks as Blacks, that might appear as substantiation of Black inferiority: Blacks, it would seem, were not even competent enough to portray themselves! Another source of ambiguity is Cripps's notice that there were a "handful" of releases—he calls them "modest breaches"—like the boxing films of Jack Johnson and some treatments of *Uncle Tom's Cabin*, which depicted a different Black presence. But he demurs from any evaluation of their significance because he finds it impossible to reckon the frequency of their exhibition.[27] But what would it matter when set against the mass culture products of cereal boxes, household ceramics, children's literature, games and toys, humor magazines, popular science and serious science, postcards, newspaper comics, playing cards, and history books; in natural museums, history museums, and dime museums; in circuses, state fairs, county fairs, and world's fairs; and in classrooms ranging from elementary education to university, where the vicious view of Black people was reproduced in a million different ways?

27. Ibid., 18–19.

As one might suppose, the synergy between American capital and the racial representations displayed in American silent movies extended beyond the domestic sphere. Mexicans (and Mexican Americans), too, were signified by chromatic categories determined by the binary set of black and white. As the second largest national minority of color, Mexican Americans had both a social presence and some significance in film consumption.[28] For instance, of particular interest here, Mexican laborers comprised some 70 percent of the rail workers in Texas and the Western railroads and were being recruited as mineworkers in Arizona.[29] But of far greater significance for William Randolph Hearst, John D. Rockefeller, and the Guggenheims, Mexico itself was a potentially lucrative site for investment, exploitation, and further territorial appropriation (Texas and California had been seized in the mid-nineteenth century).[30] Hearst, for example, owned "the huge hacienda of Babicora in Chihuahua" and in 1912 had urged the Taft administration to support the counterrevolution led by Pascual Orozco Jr. against Francisco Madero's government.[31] Frustrated on that score, during the Wilson administration, Hearst chose different tactics. Carl Mora reports, "in 1915 William Randolph Hearst helped to finance a fifteen-part serial entitled *Patria.* . . . The film depicted a Japanese-Mexican invasion of the United States and clearly was designed to capitalize on the nervousness many Americans felt over revolution in Mexico."[32] Concerned with U.S. relations with the Japanese, but not with Mexico, Wilson requested that the popular serial be withdrawn from distribution. In the meanwhile Hearst papers and others continued to link revolutionary

28. The U.S. census did not officially enumerate "Mexicans" until 1930; previously they were included among Indians and whites. The 1930 census put the "Mexican" population of the United States at 1.3 million. This number was comprised of the bulk of the 890,000 Mexican legal immigrants fleeing the 1910 revolution who arrived between 1910 and 1920 and the roughly 750,000 Mexican Americans deduced from the 1920 census.

29. Mellinger, "'Men Have Become Organizers.'"

30. See Gonzales, "United States Copper Companies," and "U.S. Copper Companies."

31. Katz, *Life and Times of Pancho Villa*, 157.

32. Mora, *Mexican Cinema*, 24. Katz reports that Harry Aitken and the Mutual Film Company gave Villa a sympathetic treatment in *The Life of General Villa* (1914); however by 1916, *Villa Dead or Alive* (Eagle Films Manufacturing and Producing Company) and *Following the Flag in Mexico* (Feinberg Amusement Corporation) were more in accord with American capital. Katz, *Life and Times of Pancho Villa*, 324–26.

Mexico with German, Russian, and Japanese plans to invade the United States.[33]

The social base of the peasant-dominated 1910 revolution was the largest threat to American capital, consequently it is understandable if the film industry distinguished between a white, virtuous Mexican aristocracy and a darker, villainous peasantry. In short, the "greaser," the mestizo peasant, became a nigger. For certain, revolutionary upheavals in Mexico invited color-coding. In the 1810 independence movement, Afro-Mexicans working the hot lowlands south of Mexico City had proven to be a critical, and the most persistent, social base of the revolutionaries. Mulatto leaders like Vicente Guerrero and José Maria Morelos y Pavón had been spawned in that struggle.[34] In 1910, dark-skinned mestizos and Indians in the northern states (e.g., Chihuahua) joined with similarly dark-skinned southern peasants (e.g., Emilio Zapata in Morelos) to overthrow the dictatorial state headed by *don* Porfirio Díaz. In American films, light-skinned Mexicans like Antonio Moreno (Antonio Garrido Monteagudo y Moreno), Ramón Novarro (José Ramón Samaniegos), Gilbert Roland (Luis Antonio Dámaso de Alonso), Dolores Del Rio (Lolita Dolores Martínez Asúnsolo y López Negrete), and Lupe Vélez (Maria Guadalupe Vélez de Villalobos) were accorded honorary white identities: "In 1978, Del Rio informed the author [George Hadley-Garcia], 'Skin tone was very important then, and Spanish-speaking actors in Hollywood fell into two categories. If light-skinned, they could play any nationality, including American. Dark-skinned actors were fated to play servants or appear as villains.'"[35] On the other end of the spectrum from white, Mexican and Mexican American players displaying Indian, mestizo, or even Black features remained largely unrecognized,[36] sunk into the anonymity of the nigger-greaser: "Even when less than vile, the greaser image subjected Hispanics to ridicule. Almost invariably he was an idiotic incompetent, on

33. Mora, *Mexican Cinema*, 243n96.

34. Vincent, "Blacks Who Freed Mexico." Guerrero was the second president of Mexico (1829) and had abolished slavery, a crucial demand of the independence movement. Afro-Mexicans tended to be concentrated in what are the present states of Veracruz, Morelos, Michoacán, Guerrero, and Sinaloa. As Vincent notes, two of these states were named after Afro-Mexican heroes.

35. Hadley-Garcia, *Hispanic Hollywood*, 29.

36. For a treatment of Afro-Mexicans as early as the seventeenth century, see Cope, *Limits of Racial Domination*; and Robinson, *Black Marxism*, 129–32.

top of being a ruthless villain whose vices outstripped those of paler movie villains. . . . The depressing greaser phenomenon was abetted by such hits as *The Greaser's Gauntlet* (1908), *The Girl and the Greaser* (1913), *The Greaser's Revenge* (1914), *Bronco Billy and the Greaser* (1914), and *The Greaser* (1914)."[37]

World War I ruptured this habit. Germans and then Russians became the foreign villains of choice. And after the conflict, the new Mexican government initiated a boycott against American films at a time when foreign revenues were becoming increasingly important to the industry. The boycott softened the treatment of Mexicans as characters, but the Mexican Revolution still needed containment, both actually and symbolically. The socialist, syndicalist, and anarchist currents emanating from the Mexican Revolution were intolerable to American capital. The American government, of course, intervened on several occasions to attempt to protect American "interests."[38] Not surprisingly, Hadley-Garcia appears to be disappointed that Hollywood's treatment of the Mexican Revolution "squandered its dramatic potential."[39] The studios, for certain, had no interest in pursuing Mexicans or Blacks attempting to secure social justice. Just what kind of revolution would be realized by idiots and buffoons? Carl Mora concludes, "The sporadic official hostility between Washington and Mexico throughout the 1910s–1930s did little to uplift the Mexican image in American films."[40]

There was nothing inadvertent or accidental about these images. This is perhaps confirmed by the history of social, moral, and political surveillance of the film industry while blackness was being defiled and ridiculed. Given the censorial energies and attention movies attracted, the disfigurement of Black existence could hardly have been missed. Even if the obvious didn't register, there were Black critics and observers who had made a quite early appearance, pleading for relief, for some small gesture of recognition of a true Black identity. For example, Anna Everett has uncovered Lester Walton's plaintive attempt, "The Degeneracy of the Moving Picture Theatre." Published in the *New York Age* on August 5, 1909, Walton commented in his column:

37. Hadley-Garcia, *Hispanic Hollywood*, 36–37.

38. See Vanderwood, "Picture Postcard"; and Meyer, Sherman, and Deeds, *Course of Mexican History*, chap. 8.

39. Hadley-Garcia, *Hispanic Hollywood*, 40.

40. Mora, *Mexican Cinema*, 24.

While passing a moving picture theatre on Sixth avenue several days ago, the writer was surprised to see a sign prominently displayed in front of the place bearing the following large print: JOHN SMITH OF PARIS, TEXAS, BURNED AT THE STAKE. HEAR HIS MOANS AND GROANS. PRICE ONE CENT! A crudely-painted picture of a colored man being burned at the stake completed the makeup of the offensive as well as repulsive-appearing sign. Judge the surprise of the writer when two days later while walking down the Bowery a similar sign met his gaze, the same earnest appeal being made by the proprietor of the moving picture theatre to the public to walk in and enjoy the sight of a human being meeting death by burning, with the moans and groans thrown in for a penny. . . . The promoters of moving picture theatres make the assertion that their pictures are of an educational nature. . . . We would like to know where do the elements of education come in so far as the picture in question is concerned?[41]

But the business of films and social management proceeded as if such appeals had never been voiced. The acknowledged clamor for moral standards in films intruded into the public arena with full confidence that white racism was one of its core principles. With that premise, an explicit ban on race-mixing was the only race-sensitive imperative. And to lend support for the construction of miscegenation as an intolerable, unnatural deviance, the industry's representations of nonwhites consistently illustrated their ill-formed natures.

Films had been under some sort of official patrol since as early as 1897 when a New York judge deemed one film "an outrage against public decency."[42] Incited by films exposing a railroad magnate, in 1907 the Chicago City Council enacted what seems to be the first public ordinance censoring movies.[43] Two years later in New York, the People's

41. Quoted in Everett, *Returning the Gaze*, 19–20.

42. Jowett, "'Capacity for Evil,'" 21.

43. Kevin Brownlow asserts that among the offending films was Lubin's *Unwritten Law*, a treatment of Harry Thaw's shooting of Stanford White in 1906. Thaw was the unstable and paranoid heir to William Thaw's mining and (Pennsylvania) railroad fortune. White, America's most famous architect, was the designer of Madison Square Garden, ironically the site of his death. Thaw's abused wife, the actress Evelyn Nesbit, had been White's abused mistress before her marriage. Thaw's trial was deemed "the trial of the century." He was acquitted by reason of insanity. Brownlow, *Behind the Mask*, 4. See also Grieveson, *Policing Cinema*, chap. 2.

Institute, a civic organization, formed the National Board of Censorship (renamed in 1916 the National Board of Review) and proceeded to an agreement with the MPPC to advise its producers on the moral and social content of their films during production. In actuality the brainchild of the MPPC, the function of the board was to protect the industry from censorship, or "from any ill-advised efforts to hamper its growth or smother it, before it could confer its benefits on the American people."[44] For the next several years, Garth Jowett maintains, the board reviewed something like 85 percent of the films released in the United States.[45] As the 1916 change of name suggests, the board had only limited powers and a relatively short life as an effective public relations vehicle. Within only a few years of its coming into existence it had already come under fire as an in-house agency, concealing the failure to impose the sorts of moral standards social reformers demanded of the industry.[46] In 1915, its existence was prolonged inadvertently by a Supreme Court decision on *The Birth of a Nation* (*Mutual Film Corporation v. Ohio Industrial Commission*), which determined that motion pictures were not speech and thus not protected under the First Amendment.[47] The following year the U.S. Congress considered the establishment of a Federal Motion Picture Commission under a bill authored by Dudley Hughes of Georgia. The move was supported by the testimony of several reformers who for years had promoted the creation of such an entity. One of them, Reverend Wilbur Crafts, played the race card. Recalling his earlier role in 1912 in the suppression of boxing films from interstate commerce following Jack Johnson's defeat of Jim Jeffries, Crafts was euphoric: "The initiatory work on this law was my first work in re-

44. Brownlow, *Behind the Mask*, 5.

45. Jowett, "'Capacity for Evil,'" 24. Brownlow puts the figure at 95 percent. Brownlow, *Behind the Mask*, 6.

46. In 1911, Mrs. Gilbert H. Montague, chairperson of the Woman's Municipal League, authored a critical report on the National Board of Censorship which documented its funding by the Motion-Picture Patents Company and their attempt to conceal this relationship. Mrs. Montague's husband was counsel to the league and had obtained a letter from Charles Sprague Smith (the former secretary for the People's Institute) to J. J. Kennedy (treasurer of the MPPC) in which Smith advised that the contribution to the board should be kept secret. Mrs. Montague advised the league to withdraw from the board on the grounds that the MPPC's subsidy had undermined the board's independence. See "Say Motion-Picture Censorship Is Lax," *New York Times*, November 8, 1911, 8.

47. Brownlow, *Behind the Mask*, passim.

straining motion-picture films. . . . It would have been worth while to have lived if only to save the country from being flooded with pictures of a negro indicted for white slavery and a white man voluntarily standing on the same brutal level, which, but for that law, would have been shown all over the country as a brace of heroes."[48]

The bill failed, but the reprieve of the board's shield for the movie industry was almost moot. Pennsylvania (1911), Ohio (1913), and Kansas (1914) had already created state censorship commissions. Maryland was added in 1916. And then a series of public relations disasters struck the movie business: in 1920, Mary Pickford, the highest salaried actor in the industry, was alleged to have committed bigamy with her new marriage to Douglas Fairbanks; in 1921, Roscoe "Fatty" Arbuckle was charged with manslaughter (in the press, the charges were rape and murder) in the death of starlet Virginia Rappe; and in 1922, director William Desmond Taylor was shot and killed at home, with rumors of sex (with actresses Mabel Normand and Mary Miles Minter) and drugs splashed across the nation's newspapers.[49] Confronted with declining box office receipts and even more intense activity from film reformers, the industry's collective response to these setbacks was the creation of a new, formal self-regulatory agency, the Motion Picture Producers and Distributors of America (MPPDA). To head the MPPDA, it recruited Will Hays, President Hoover's postmaster general. And Hays's first official act was the banishment of "Fatty" Arbuckle from films for life.

The organizational foundations of the Production Code, Ruth Vasey reports, can be traced to the other significant gesture Hays made in 1922. He established the Committee on Public Relations as a consulting group on motion picture standards. And among the sixty organizations recruited to the committee, Hays included the expected interested parties. By avoiding the more aggressively hostile associations like Crafts's International Reform Bureau or collaborators of Christ Church (Brooklyn), Canon William Sheafe Chase's New York Society for the Prevention of Crime, Hays proceeded to institutionalize self-regulation.[50] Hays's recruits included prominent Catholic and Jewish organizations; moral education agencies like the National Congress of

48. Ibid., 33.
49. Koszarski, *Evening's Entertainment*, 206.
50. Kevin Brownlow insists that Chase was "a supporter of the Ku Klux Klan." Brownlow, *Behind the Mask*, 7.

Mothers and Parent-Teachers Associations, the Boy Scouts, the YMCA and YWCA, and the General Federation of Women's Clubs; business associations like the U.S. Chamber of Commerce; and Anglo-patriots like the Daughters of the American Revolution. But among Hays's consultants were interest groups which had contributed to the new architecture of scientific racism and Jim Crow: the Academy of Political Science, the American Federation of Labor, the American Museum of Natural History, the Cooper Union for the Advancement of Science and Art, and the War Department. Over the succeeding years this committee metamorphosed into the Department of Public Relations (1925), the Studio Relations Committee (1927), and eventually into the Production Code Administration (PCA) in 1934. And culled from the processes of MPPDA negotiations and consultations and from the eliminations required by state censorship boards emerged first the "Don'ts and Be Careful" guidelines of 1927 and then, the Production Code.[51]

Vasey is most concerned with the "industry policy" which almost invisibly shadowed the more public and publicized Production Code controversies over sex and crime. Outside the Code's jurisdiction, the PCA prosecuted its industry policy, a far weightier solicitation of the film business's friends and sponsors. Filmmakers were admonished for considering ill-advised but sometimes realistic representations of railroads (a train wreck in *Imitation of Life*, 1935), oil companies (Standard Oil in *Oil for the Lamps of China*, 1935), the coal-mining industry (a mine workers' strike in *Black Fury*, 1934), and unflattering portrayals of clergymen, social workers, charity workers, women's clubs, philanthropic organizations, newspaper publishers, and radio broadcasters.[52] Though the process of review was meant to minimize the costs and waste of censoring films at the point of exhibition—one of the arguments of the PCA advocates was that in 1928 such eliminations had cost more than $3.5 million—the more clever and evasive filmmakers ran just that risk.[53] For the PCA, in the end, money costs were secondary to political costs. As Vasey understands these policies, they all were deemed special interest groups which could prove (or had proven) meddlesome to the industry. But Vasey recognizes that on some occasions the restrictions were fueled by political as well as economic forces.

51. Vasey, "Beyond Sex and Violence," 102–4.
52. Ibid., 105–7.
53. Ibid., 120.

"The Production Code itself stipulated that 'the history, institutions, prominent people and citizenry of other nations shall be represented fairly,'" and filmmakers were compelled to halt or alter projects which contained unflattering representations of substantial import markets such as Mexico, France, Italy, and (after World War I) Germany.[54] Even "the Irish represented a powerful combination of interests, the least influential of which was the Irish state."[55] Less consistently, however, were the protections extended to Asian peoples.[56]

Conspicuously absent from all this close monitoring of the industry was any concern for the degrading representations of American Blacks

54. Ibid., 123ff.

55. Ibid., 119.

56. Despite anti-immigration sentiments against Asians (Congress effectively barred Chinese immigrants in 1880, and agitation against Japanese was intense in the early twentieth century), Asians in America had powerful supporters (like Leland Stanford). Donald Kirihara recounts Sessue Hayakawa's amazing career in the silent era: "Hayakawa's early feature roles at Lasky from 1915 to 1918 encompassed a range of characterizations, from the sadistically brutal authority (*The Cheat, The Jaguar's Claws* [1917]), to the accommodating immigrant (*The Honorable Friend* [1916], *Forbidden Paths* [1917], *The Bravest Way* [1918]), to the temporary foreign student or worker who intends to return home (*Hashimura Togo* [1917], *The City of Dim Faces* [1918]), to the native defending Western encroachments upon his homeland (*The Call of the East* [1917], *The White Man's Law* [1918], *Hidden Pearls* [1918]). Hayakawa also portrayed a variety of ethnic and racial types: Japanese, Chinese, Mexican, Asian Indian, and Arab." Kirihara, "Accepted Idea Displaced," 91–92. See also Yu, "Mixing Bodies and Cultures," 444–63. Gina Marchetti captures Hollywood's ambivalence when she describes the Chinese warlord General Yen (Nils Asther in *The Bitter Tea of General Yen*, 1933): "At times, Yen seems quite Western, the very picture of the knight-errant who platonically places a woman on a pedestal to worship her from afar. At other times, however, he takes on the guise of a sex-crazed demon, with only one thought on his mind—violating Megan [Barbara Stanwyck] as expeditiously as possible. As the polished mandarin, Yen hovers between the equally polished but diabolical Fu Manchu and the cultivated and benevolent Charlie Chan, both popular at about the same time in Hollywood." Marchetti, *Romance and the "Yellow Peril,"* 52–53. Both Asian male and female characters were often encased in sexual and erotic frames. Of Anna May Wong's character in *Shanghai Express* (1932), Marchetti writes: "Although Hui Fei is marginalized within the film, she remains part of that ideologically disturbing 'excess' in *Shanghai Express* that can too easily be dismissed as part of a brilliant, but empty visual façade. Hui Fei functions as part of the exotic promise of Shanghai; she embodies its sensuality, beauty, and freedom to indulge any desire." Ibid., 66. See also Robert G. Lee's treatment of Cecil B. DeMille's *The Cheat* (1915) and D. W. Griffith's *Broken Blossoms* (1919), in *Orientals*.

and the lesser races (e.g., Africans, Slavs, Filipinos, Native Americans) who had been exhibited at the 1893 and 1904 world's fairs. No Black or even multiracial organizations participated with the committee, and the PCA's principal concerns with race were the enforcing of Jim Crow: "The Code banned miscegenation in movies, but industry policy had more to say about the treatment of race relations on the screen. Southern states objected to social mingling of blacks and whites, and in order to preserve their trade such scenes were consistently altered during production."[57] Here Vasey's analysis falters. In both language and causality there is a regrettable lack of precision. By "social mingling," for example, she actually means "on equal terms." We can discern no objections to Black servants and buffoons. More importantly, she attributes the Code's race discipline to some vaguely referenced regional sensitivities, an oft-made misattribution which consigns Negrophobia to "the South." It was not "the South," not all "the South," or most of "the South" which championed Jim Crow but actually the planter class and its political apparatus, and more importantly, the capitalist sectors in London, New York, Boston, Philadelphia, and Chicago which provided the necessary support for the planter class aristocracy. Villainizing "the South" thusly ruptures the historical relationships between white racism and mercantile, agrarian, industrial, financial, and presently global capital.[58] Vasey has certainly staked out a powerful and laudable position when she critiques those film historians who have dwelled almost exclusively on the Code's interventions in matters pertaining to sex and crime. Her exposition of "industry policy" constitutes a significant correction to that seduction. But her evoking of "industry policy" does more than extend the horizontal boundaries and significations of the Code. Embedded in "industry policy" which patrolled the political

57. Vasey, "Beyond Sex and Violence," 111.

58. Cripps makes the same leap. For the earliest Black representations, Cripps maintains, "Most early Negro appearances in film followed the Southern stereotypes of the wretched freeman, the comic Negro, the black brute, the tragic mulatto, in keeping with literary and theatrical tradition." For the Code period, he asserts, "The most liberal Jews who managed the studios had no way of knowing how to render black life honestly . . . Negroes . . . had as friends at court only white Southerners." Cripps, *Slow Fade to Black*, 10, 119. As rejoinders to Cripps's characterization of the Jews who headed the principal studios, see Sklar, *Movie-Made America*; and Gabler, *Empire*. Both assert that notwithstanding an ignorance of American life, the Jewish studio bosses managed to invent an imagined America ruled by benevolent patricians and patriarchs and inhabited by Andy Hardy and his neighbors.

order and civil society were protocols which reflected the ideological designs of those interests which were dominant in the film industry's management and financing. They were instrumental in the codification of Jim Crow, and they were in place as the dominant sources of capital and management in the film industry when Jim Crow was embedded into the Code.

The one charge that the studio bosses couldn't shake was that they were Jews pursuing a Jewish agenda antithetical to white America. In one form anti-Semitism took the guise of the accusation of greed; almost as frequently, the issue was one of hegemony ("The thinly veiled fear of a Jewish plutocracy destroying a Protestant democracy").[59] Consequently, as Steven Carr documents, many of the film industry's critics insisted that the true purpose of the Production Code and its immediate predecessors was to disrupt or at least deflect the engulfing of movie reformism by anti-Semitism. "In 1926, as Representative W. B. Upshaw from Georgia introduced his bill for federal censorship of motion pictures, he quoted from the New Testament. His high expectations for Hays dashed, Upshaw drew a biblical comparison. Just as the disciples had hoped Jesus 'would deliver Israel at this time,' or disappointed Americans 'had fondly hoped that Will Hays . . . would strike the shackles that bound the motion picture business to so much that was unclean."[60] Upshaw's admonishments were among the more temperate ones which made up the chorus of anti-Semitism on the platform of reformism. And Carr extensively records both the diversity and vehemence of the voices raised against the role of Jews in the movie industry. But there are one or two concerns about how Carr approaches his subject. For one, he never responds to the apparent paradox that while studio agents and their PCA collaborators forcefully employed the Code to the benefit of white ethnics, they did not extend it to the steady presentation of Black stereotypes. On occasion their purblind attentions seem to have stretched the limits of credibility. In sharp contrast to the progressive Jews so critical to the American Left and Socialism for several generations, the studio managers facilitated rather than challenged racial domination.

For instance, Carr relates the negotiations between Warner Bros. and the PCA over *Black Legion* (1936), a film whose original script cen-

---

59. Carr, *Hollywood and Anti-Semitism*, 107.
60. Ibid., 66.

tered on the Ku Klux Klan.[61] The script presented "a KKK-like group recruiting a disgruntled factory worker after he loses a promotion to a Jewish coworker." The head of the PCA, Joseph Breen, a Catholic, found the script "basically satisfactory," except for one troubling element. "In censoring this treatment, Breen cited Code policy as forbidding 'stories which raise and deal with the provocative and inflammatory subjects of racial and religious prejudice.'"[62] Neither Carr nor his protagonists seem the least concerned that for nearly seventy decades the principal targets of white supremacists had been Blacks! Jews were victims too (as Warner Bros. argued), but when had Hollywood raised issue with the terror campaigns of the "black legions" against Blacks?[63] Like his subjects, Carr is enveloped by the problem of anti-Semitism. It is such a compelling discourse that Carr and these earlier filmmakers are entirely shielded from the industry's opportunistic and ultimately habitual Negrophobia.[64]

Secondly, since Carr never distinguishes between reasonable and hysterical criticisms of studio cinematic practices (nor analyzes films objectionable to Catholic, Protestant, and even Jewish organizations), his readers are confronted with apparently inexplicable examples of extreme anti-Semitic emotions. *The Irish World and Independent Liberator* suggested that Hollywood should confine itself to ridiculing 'the

61. An actual secret organization named the Black Legion was uncovered in Michigan and Ohio in the mid-1930s. Its targets were Blacks, Jews, and Catholics, among others. Trials of Black Legion members were news in 1936 when several were indicted for the murders of Silas Coleman, a Black, and Charles A. Poole, a white Catholic. See "Officers of Black Legion Hunted by the Police in Michigan Deaths," *New York Times*, May 25, 1936, 1, 3; "Black Legion's Spread Surprising to Midwest," *New York Times*, May 31, 1936, E6; "5 of Black Legion Guilty of Murder," *New York Times*, November 29, 1936, 15; and "Helped to Wound Negro, Says Dean," *New York Times*, July 26, 1936, 2.

62. Carr, *Hollywood and Anti-Semitism*, 157.

63. Cripps maintains that *Black Legion* was in imitation of MGM's *Fury*, nearly a year earlier. *They Won't Forget* (1937) completes the short burst of KKK films. Cripps terms them "waffling failures," since they all displaced Black victims with whites. Cripps, *Slow Fade to Black*, 295.

64. Carr's one reference to Blacks in his study is in the context of his treatment of Neal Gabler's rejoinder to the charges of Black anti-Semitism (see "Jews, Blacks and Trouble in Hollywood," *New York Times*, September 2, 1990, H7). Gabler's moral about the excesses of assimilation is trivialized by Carr as "a compelling, bittersweet story of Jewish success in America." As "an old story, expertly refurbished by Gabler," it is never available, then, for Carr to use as one explanation for the collaboration with the Negrophobia in films. Carr, *Hollywood and Anti-Semitism*, 2–3.

Rebeccas and Marthas of their own families. If they want filth and stupidity and indecency, they needn't go out of the Ghetto to find it. If they want grotesque figures, Hester Street is full of them.' The paper then promised that moviemakers were never 'going to put their filthy hands on Irish women any more.'"[65] Whatever the Irish American press was objecting to in *Irish Hearts* and *The Callahans and the Murphys* (both 1927) is entirely submerged by Carr into the filth-strewn pit of anti-Semitism. And finally, Carr does not seem to even dimly perceive that by the 1930s—the principal site of his interrogation—whoever and whatever the studio moguls were, they were all in thrall to the major centers of capital in America.

It would appear, then, that white supremacy in early American films was a privileged domain, a protected discourse. The burlesque and grotesque Black, the savage, primitive Indian, the sinister, erotic Oriental, the brutally stupid Mexican were not oversights of casually contrived art. And their mixed-race "others" were suspended in the attendant, inevitable tragedy of the unnatural. Films were a thoroughly policed product. Little was left to chance. Regulations emanating from corporate boardrooms in New York, official state and municipal censors all over the country, the Production Code Administration, and studio headquarters provided the formal rules of industry policy and for decency while religious organizations and other moral reform groups steadily drummed complementary themes in the background. At the onset of mass movie production, apartheid was the structural instrument of American capital, and American filmmakers supplied a galaxy of imagery and story lines which naturalized and popularized white hegemony. The persistent, enduring character of these constructions in movies is owed not to popular culture but to mass, that is, manufactured culture. In the actual world of social experience they were constantly being altered or subject to deterioration. Neither who was white (the Irish, the Italians, the Poles, the Jews?) nor who was Black (octoroons, quadroons, Filipinos?) was fixed. Nor was it always clear what those identities meant. And it did not help matters that Congress had officially recognized thirty-six different races of whites.[66] But in the

65. Ibid., 78.

66. In 1911, the Dillingham Commission's fifth volume of its forty-two-volume report identified thirty-six separate European races among the recent immigrants to the United States. See U.S. Congress, *Dictionary of Races*, 2–3. The commission was appointed by the Senate in 1907 and headed by Senator William P. Dillingham (Ver-

fictive, imagined world of the silent films these were visible demarcations. Class and gender were contrived to privilege whiteness and demote the Others to the margins of human destiny.

The Black Middle Class and the Mulatto Genre

> *The door of hope might have remained closed so far as the progress which the negro was to make for himself was concerned. He has never risen above the government of the club. He has never written a language. His achievements in architecture are limited to the thatched-roof hut or a hole in the ground. No monuments have been builded by him to body forth and perpetuate in the memory of posterity the virtues of his ancestors. . . . And it is lamentable that his civilization lasts only so long as he is in the hands of the white man who inculcates it. When left to himself he has universally gone back to the barbarism of the jungle.*
>
> —*Senator James Vardaman (D-Mississippi), February 6, 1914*

In his fourth chapter of *Slow Fade to Black,* Thomas Cripps achieved an almost poetic construction of 1920s Hollywood where, as he puts it, racism had become "simply normal intellectual baggage."[67] Cripps's dense display of the mundane discourtesies and institutionalized discriminations occasioned by blackness grazed across the boundary separating studio matters from the complex tapestry of everyday existence. Racial jokes on the lot merely pantomimed casting practices; and Black film roles stood in as doubles for the victims of the county's agencies of realtors, the police, employers, and public services. Suturing the Los Angeles conclave's locational, social, discursive, economic, and industrial systems of racism, Cripps eloquently reassembled the racial matrices that were mirrored in the representations of Blacks on screen:

---

mont). Matthew Frye Jacobson comments: "Europe's linguistic groups are irretrievably cast as racial groups throughout the *Dictionary,* so that even within the unifying construction of a grand 'Caucasian' race, among European peoples difference itself is consistently defined as both biological in nature and extreme in degree. (Indeed, even the *Dictionary*'s definition of 'Caucasian' is begrudging: it includes 'all races, which, although dark in color or aberrant in other directions, are, when considered from all points of view, felt to be more like the white race than like any of the other four races')." Jacobson, *Whiteness of a Different Color,* 79. See also Lund, "Boundaries of Restriction," <http://www.uvm.edu/~hag/histreview/vol6/lund.html>.

67. Cripps, *Slow Fade to Black,* 96.

Underlying the whole Hollywood organism was the supportive fabric of hierarchical race relations with blacks in conflict with the quiet deep-seated racial prejudices of the workers in the studios. Job, status, residence, social circles were defined, as in the rest of America, by race. The important difference was that in Hollywood such arrangements became the premise upon which moviegoing Americans reinforced their racial attitudes. Powerless darker races lived far down in the Los Angeles basin away from the centers of studio vitality and power.[68]

In this last decade of silent films, Black talents were reduced to playing servants and jungle dwellers; studio bootblacks like Oscar Smith at Paramount "cadged more roles than many trained performers"; like other Black actresses, Julia Hudlin struggled to get by, working as a personal maid to Dolores Del Rio; others, like Evelyn Preer, worked in saloons; and on the set, electricians referred to black lights as "niggers." Playing Rastas and Mandys or tribal "Gibboneys" and "Joconeys" in *Trader Horn* (1931), they were in a sense the lucky few, for most Negro roles went to non-Blacks in burnt cork makeup.[69]

Cripps provides two, rather contradictory "causal stories" for the complementarity between the racism of the Los Angeles area and the racial imaginary reproduced by Hollywood studios. Of course, there is his notion of "a Southern mystique" ("Many blacks and whites had drifted from the South to California and found work in the studios, and their beliefs colored life in the movie colony").[70] And while he spins and elaborates on this theme, identifying nine or so "white" executives and directors with Southern origins, this is a flawed interpretation with excessive tributaries.[71] His second but more interesting ascription of movieland's practices is confined to two lines: "Like the old *intendants* of the king, the Eastern bankers sent supervisors to the studios to over-

---

68. Ibid., 95.

69. Ibid., 100ff. Cripps observes: "The studio research department even forgot the names of the tribes, eventually labeling them 'Gibboneys' and 'Joconeys' after Cedric Gibbons and J. J. Cohn, two studio executives." Ibid., 99.

70. Ibid., 98.

71. Cripps goes so far as to credit the "Southern mystique" for the racial prejudices of Europeans in Hollywood, like the German actor Emil Jannings and unnamed Englishmen (the anecdote is attributed to Errol Flynn, who was not English). Cripps is suggesting that neither the Germans nor the English had their own histories of racism. Ibid., 98–99.

see their investments and to insure that they made 'entertainment the public wants.' The directors gradually lost control over the content."[72] Notwithstanding Cripps's succinct attention to the subject, this is the more robust thesis, since it not only engages the issue of who controlled American filmmaking but also draws us to the arenas of capitalist intervention beyond the studios. The segregation of Los Angeles laborers in auto production, aircraft manufacturing, steel plants, public service, and public education; the development of white suburbs and Latino and Black ghettos; the planning of public transportation to decentralize the region, like the street cars operated by the Pacific Electric; the establishment of race-based and racist municipal and county public safety (police and firemen) organizations; the design of electoral districts and voting systems hostile to the poor and minority communities; racially restrictive access to loans and investment capital—these initiatives spanned far beyond the reach of the studio moguls.

In 1920 the U.S. Census enumerated slightly over 900,000 residents in Los Angeles County; in 1930, the figure had grown to something over 2.2 million. The phenomenal growth and development of Los Angeles County was owed to developers like Harry H. Culver (Culver City), W. P. Whitsett (Van Nuys), and Leslie C. Brand (Glendale), and regional boosterism was orchestrated by magnates like Harrison Gray Otis and Harry Chandler (the *Los Angeles Times*'s owners) of the Merchants and Manufacturers Association and the All-Year Club, and Frank Wiggins, president of the Chamber of Commerce.[73] They were of equal importance on the racial front. For example, one of the selling points of the Glendale brochures was that "there are not a half dozen other than Caucasian [in the schools]." And Los Angeles City police chief James E. "Two Gun" Davis added his own unique contribution, setting up auto blockades at the state border in early 1936 to turn back the white poor and the darker races. Chandler's *Los Angeles Times*, of course, endorsed the chief's initiative.[74] Hollywood, to be sure, was a creature of big capital, and it was the Bank of Italy's (later to become the Bank of America) Attilio and then Amadeo Giannini who first began subsidizing the fledgling film industry months before investment houses like Kuhn,

72. Ibid., 94.

73. See Henstell, *Sunshine and Wealth*, chaps. 1 and 2; and Halberstam, *Powers That Be*, chap. 3.

74. Henstell, *Sunshine and Wealth*, 17, 21–22. See also Domanick, *To Protect and to Serve*, 61–63.

Loeb provided a $10 million line of credit to Famous Players (the future Paramount Pictures).[75]

In the pre–World War I period, before the arrival of Wall Street bankers and investment houses, it was high rollers like Felix Kahn who provided the capital for the future giants of the movie industry. Kahn was the leading financier behind the Mutual-Majestic-Reliance-Epoch entanglement which ultimately brought *The Birth of a Nation* to the screen. And in tandem with all its other achievements, it was the Griffith-Dixon collaboration which most singularly launched the campaign to deface the Black middle class. It was not however the advent of the independents which determined the sorts of representations of the Black middle class which dominated American films in this period. *The Birth of a Nation* deserves the extraordinary attention paid to it by film scholars and cultural historians not because it invented the iconography of the "mulatto genre" but because of the efficiency and artfulness by which it sutured the genre into a fabulist national narrative. The commercial impact of *Birth* accounts, in part, for its ability to evacuate competing signifiers of the Black middle class. Relying solely on explanations encased by film commerce or aesthetics, however, is mistaken. The emergence of the "mulatto genre" coincided with challenges to American capitalism and the dominant racial regime by the very existence of the Black middle class, and particularly by a militant faction of that class.

One of the primary concerns which agitated political and economic elites was the increasingly visible links between Socialism and Black militancy. The founding of the NAACP, for instance, had resulted largely from the efforts of Black and white socialists.[76] If elements of the Black petite bourgeoisie continued to move towards the political Left, they might well draw Black workers into a political terrain which could be more resistant to the lures of white supremacy. To some gatekeepers it

75. Felice A. Banadio writes: "[Amadeo] Giannini depended on these movie moguls and screen celebrities to serve as Bank of Italy 'boosters' in attracting the payroll accounts from Hollywood's major studios and the savings accounts of the industry's tens of thousands of employees . . . [and in 1922, Cecil B.] DeMille became president of Bank of Italy's Culver City branch . . . the bank's advisory board included Louis B. Mayer . . . Joseph and Nicholas Schenck . . . Harry Cohn, Howard Hughes, Sol Lesser, Jack Warner and Darryl Zanuck." Banadio, *A. P. Giannini*, 113. For Kuhn, Loeb, see Gomery, *Hollywood Studio System*, 28.

76. See David Levering Lewis, *W. E. B. Du Bois*, 386ff.

appeared that no sooner had a rural collectivist movement of Black and white farmers been disposed of than a similar political force would be assembling in the cities. An aggressive and ofttimes brutal program of white supremacy had effectively constrained farmer cooperatives. And though it had fueled certain tendencies towards Black genocide, it had paid dividends in rutting the farmer and then the Populist movements away from anticapitalism.[77] Now, however, Socialist parties were being revived in the country, growing in direct proportion with the pace at which Central, Eastern and Southern Europeans were becoming the primary source of immigrant labor.

Many of the social reform movements of the late nineteenth and early twentieth centuries were infused with Socialist principles and Socialist parties. According to Wilson Record:

> During the period from 1901 to 1920 the Socialist Party of the United States was the foremost advocate of a radical reorganization of the American economic structure. It enrolled thousands of members. It established an elaborate organizational apparatus, with local and state branches scattered throughout the country. It supported an influential press that turned out newspapers, magazines, books, pamphlets and other propaganda on a large scale. It entered politics and was able frequently to elect its candidates to local and state offices. Its nominees for president and vice-president rolled up an impressive number of votes in several elections.[78]

Pointedly, and as a consequence of several factors, Socialism housed a progressive faction opposed to racism. For one, many of the immigrant socialists came from societies in which they were the despised ethnic or racial Other. Moreover, for many of these immigrants their new American experience was more of the same. And the time required for them to officially qualify as whites might be considerable. Socialism also trumped the impulse of bourgeois anthropology to construct racial hierarchies disposed along the division of labor exploited by the world-system. "Nigger work" sounded too close to "Wop jobs" and so on to many immigrants. Thus at its founding convention in 1901, the new party passed a resolution on the Negro Question which read in part:

77. The 1917 Draft action would revive militant anticapitalist movements in the rural South. See Keith, *Rich Man's War*.

78. Record, *Negro and Communist Party*, 16.

"The capitalist class seeks . . . to foster and increase color prejudice and race hatred between the white worker and the black, so as to make their social and economic interests to appear to be separate and antagonistic."[79] The party's program resolved to enlist Black workers into the mobilization of labor in general, thus creating a race-blind radical movement. And though the party had minimal results with ordinary Black workers, such declarations did attract Black radical intellectuals such as Chandler Owen, A. Phillip Randolph, and Du Bois. In the 1912 presidential election, Socialist candidate Eugene Debs attracted nearly a million votes, and "over a thousand Socialists [won] state and local office." Woodrow Wilson won that election, but among Teddy Roosevelt's "third-party" supporters were wealthy men "well aware that it might take Progressivism to head off socialism."[80] Given the increasing threat from the Left, other powerful facets of American capitalism resolved that the Black middle class was a necessary target.

The Black elite middle class was the bane of those who subsidized the Black caricatures which naturalized Jim Crow and white supremacy. Handsome, affluent, sophisticated, and educated Blacks contradicted the closed texts of racism. It is understandable, then, that from the vantage point of American movies, the Black middle class simply had never existed. In the movies Black simpletons and servants were all "negroes" belonging to the one class, the lower class. In films, the infrequently encountered well-dressed Blacks were domestic servants, their clothes subtly mirroring their parasitism on the affluence of their white employers. More frequently the burnt cork figures in films were costumed as if they had just dropped from the plantation in the sky or simply exhibited the bad taste of buffoons. In actuality, by the turn of the century and even earlier, a rather severely Victorian and soberly fashioned Black middle class had made "its" appearance.

The Black middle class of the late nineteenth and early twentieth centuries constituted a remarkable transcendence. Ensconced in professions, public service positions, education, and frequently upperworking-class jobs, they had become increasingly visible in American society.[81] In 1901, Du Bois had provided some measure of this conspicu-

79. Ibid., 18.
80. Phillips, *Wealth and Democracy*, 52.
81. Willard Gatewood reports: "Male members of the black upper class were virtually all 'working aristocrats,' who provided the principal source of income for their

ousness when he published a partial profile of his class in the *New York Times*.[82] Of course their social functions (debutante parties, receptions for visiting notables, musical and dramatic recitals, etc.) were reported in the Black newspapers which were published from Boston to San Francisco (Washington's *Colored American, People's Advocate*, and the *Washington Bee*, Baltimore's *Afro-American Ledger*, the *New York Age*, Detroit's *Plaindealer*, the *Indianapolis World*, or *Recorder* or *Freeman*, Xenia's *Ohio Standard* and Cleveland's *Journal* or *Gazette*, the Kansas *Weekly Blade*, Chicago's *Broad Ax*, Denver's *Colorado Statesmen*, San Francisco's *Pacific Coast Appeal*).[83] But on occasion their presence was noted in non-Black papers like the *Detroit News-Tribune* ("Detroit's Most Exclusive Social Clique: The Cultural Colored '40'," April 27, 1902). They organized exclusive private social clubs like Trenton's Eclectic Club, or they met as the multistate New York and Newport Ugly Fishing Club and the Society of the Sons of New York; in Boston they were the Descendants of Early New England Negroes; in Washington, D.C. they grouped as the Pen and Pencil Club, the Treble Clef Club, Mu-So-lit Club, the Monocan (formerly the Cosmos Club), the Lotus Club, and Monday Night Literary Club. In Philadelphia there was the Sigma Pi Phi (better known as the Boule); in Chicago elite congeries were the Old Settlers Club or the Fellowship Club or the Lotus Social Club; in Cleveland the elite met in the Social Circle; in Baltimore there was the Baltimore Assembly or the Banneker Social Club; in upstate New York there was the Home Social Club of Albany. Atlanta had the Young Men's West Side Social Club; Charleston, the Brown Fellowship or Friendly Moralist

------

family. Most were employed in white-collar and managerial occupations. Many of the older members of the aristocracy of color were likely to be found in service trades—such as catering, barbering, and tailoring—or in government positions and small businesses. While some were attorneys, physicians, and teachers, a greater number of their children were more likely to be found in these professions." Gatewood, *Aristocrats of Color*, 191. Much of the following is drawn from ibid., chaps. 7 and 8.

82. "The older families of well-to-do free negroes who count an unspotted family life for two centuries gather at St. Phillip's Episcopal Church, on Twenty-fifth Street. This church is an offshoot of Trinity and the lineal descendant of Nean's Negro School early in the eighteenth century." W. E. B. Du Bois, "The Black North: A Social Study," *New York Times*, November 24, 1901, Sunday Magazine, 11.

83. Gatewood employs the term "upper class" in deference, I suppose to their own self-description and their tendency to act as an exclusive caste. On the other hand, the most wealthy of them were by income standards upper class, but the largest proportion of the group fell into the upper-middle or middle class.

Society; and in New Orleans there were the Société d'Économie or Société des Jeunes Amis de Bienfaisance et d'Assistance Mutuelle.[84] These were principally men's clubs devoted to class consolidation and occasionally fund-raising for charities, settlement houses, and the like.

As a national and aggressively civic phenomenon, the club movement was more indebted to Black middle-class women than their male counterparts. In the mid-1890s, Black women organized the National Association of Colored Women (NACW), an amalgamation of Washington's Colored Women's League and the Federation of Afro-American Women (prompted by Boston's New Era Club). Led by such figures as Josephine Saint Pierre Ruffin of Boston, Mary Church Terrell of Washington, and Fannie Barrier Williams of Chicago (and earlier Boston), organizations like the NACW gave shape to civil rights and feminism in the early twentieth century. Paralleling the efforts of Black women of more modest incomes who provided much of the organizational muscle for the independent Black church movement (e.g., the National Baptist Convention), these elite middle-class Black women pursued their own interpretation of race solidarity. "The club movement among colored women," Fannie Barrier Williams wrote in 1904, "means something deeper than a mere imitation of . . . white women, because it has grown out of the organized anxiety of women who have only recently become intelligent enough to recognize their own social condition and strong enough to initiate and apply the forces of reform. It is a movement that reaches down into the sub-social condition of an entire race and has become the responsibility and effort of a few competent in behalf of the many incompetent."[85] From the "uplift" of the race and the protection of Black women's virtue and comportment, it was only a short step for these women to begin laying the groundwork for the most important Black political initiative of the late nineteenth and early twentieth centuries: the antilynching movement. This transition, however, was not without cost: the condescending founders of the club movement like Terrell and Ruffin were shunted to the sidelines by more aggressive,

84. For the clubs, see Gatewood, *Aristocrats of Color*, chap. 8. Some of the clubs were athletic associations. For instance, in 1914, William M. Franklin of the Smart Set Athletic Club (Brooklyn) was defeated by Dr. R. S. Fleming of New Haven, in what was reported to be "the first indoor tennis match played in New York before a colored audience." "Dr. Fleming Defeats Mr. Franklin at Tennis," *New York Age*, March 26, 1914, 1.

85. Gatewood, *Aristocrats of Color*, 243.

militant, and darker-complexioned women like Ida Wells Barnett and Madam C. J. Walker (Sarah Breedlove), members of the working middle class.[86]

To minimize the humiliations of Jim Crow, the Black middle class entertained at home, in comfortable, richly furnished buildings with salons sufficiently large to accommodate select social gatherings. Frequently they lived anywhere they could afford, startling otherwise non-Black neighbors into new realizations or relocation. In Chicago, for instance, Dempsey Travis reported, "there were blacks living throughout the North Side and elsewhere. Though we were small in numbers, we were represented in every census tract."[87] In Washington, D.C., Mary Church Terrell and her husband, Judge Robert Terrell, lived in the then otherwise exclusively white LeDroit Park as early as the 1890s.[88] And in 1917, in exclusive Westchester County, Madam C. J. Walker—not an elite but nearly a millionaire—built her mansion, Villa Lewaro, at Irvington-on-Hudson.[89] The Black elites were not consciously ostentatious, but their pursuit of the good life inevitably drew public attention to them. In the summers they escaped the city heat by training or driving to their farms or resorts (Saratoga Springs, Newport, Atlantic City, Cape May, Highland Beach, Sea Isle, Benton Harbor, Idlewild) on the coast, in the forests, or in lake districts conveniently near enough to Washington, New York, Boston, Philadelphia, or Detroit.[90] But sometimes their summer resorts beckoned as relief from urban boredom and a chance to mingle together their offspring or momentarily suspend their responsibilities to the "dirtier" classes. Since many of these retreats (like Oak Bluffs on Martha's Vineyard) were deliberately close to the summer resorts of the nation's white aristocrats, they became visible as irritations and contradictions to the official racial creed.

Notwithstanding the elite's accommodationist maneuvers and the conscious patrolling of their private social sphere, they inevitably collided with Jim Crow. Lawrence Otis Graham recounts that one of his relatives, "Uncle Telford," a successful businessman in Chicago, had

86. Ibid., 245–46.
87. Graham, *Our Kind of People*, 189.
88. Ibid., 234.
89. Bundles, *On Her Own Ground*, 215–16.
90. Graham details the history of East Coast and Midwest Black elites in resort towns like Oak Bluffs (Martha's Vineyard), Sag Harbor, Highland Beach, and Idlewild, in *Our Kind of People*, chap. 8.

preserved a copy of a 1920 Hyde Park neighborhood newspaper that declared, "Every colored man who moves into the Hyde Park neighborhood knows that he is damaging his white neighbor's property. Consequently . . . he forfeits his right to be employed by the whiteman. . . . Employers should adopt a rule of refusing to employ Negroes who persist in residing in Hyde Park." Graham relates that "soon after that time, restrictive covenants making it illegal to sell homes to blacks, regardless of their wealth, were strictly enforced."[91] Attaching themselves to Booker T. Washington's strategy of self-development and social segregation, most of the elite shrugged off these debasements. Some did not.

This elite Black middle class was educated and justly proud that many of its members had graduated from some of the most prestigious universities and colleges in the country (and beyond). A goodly proportion of them also were light-complexioned, some the descendants of the most eminent of patriarchs of eighteenth- and nineteenth-century America. Frederick Douglass and Booker T. Washington, for example, were the sons of white slave owners. The succeeding generations were often as arrogant as Douglass and strident where Washington had feigned humility. So when they entered the political arena, their existence jarred white supremacists on several levels. In the late nineteenth and early twentieth centuries, representatives of this elite—most prominently W. E. B. Du Bois, Mary Church Terrell, and William Monroe Trotter—banded with other Blacks in the creation of a succession of militant organizations like the NACW, the Niagara Movement (1905), the National Equal Rights League (NERL, 1907), and the National Association for the Advancement of Colored People (NAACP, 1909). All were concerned with race violence, segregation, and the lack of educational resources for Blacks. They had no reticence in bringing such issues to public attention. In one such highly publicized instance, their boldness interfered with the White House. Late in 1914, Trotter had led a delegation of what was now called the National Independence Equal Rights League to a meeting with President Wilson. The subject of the meeting was the Wilson administration's imposition of segregation among government employees. Obviously outraged by Wilson's patronizing and condescending comments defending his policies as a charitable gesture towards Blacks, Trotter had contradicted Wilson, speaking over

91. Ibid., 190.

the president's attempts to interrupt him. Wilson was insulted, claiming no one had dared speak to him in that manner since he assumed office. In the future, Wilson demanded, any further discussions with the organization would require Trotter's absence.[92] And in 1915, Terrell and other aristocrats lobbied against antimiscegenation legislation being considered by Congress.[93]

Just so long as the Black middle class kept to themselves and their private comforts and accommodations, the far-flung apparatus of the new racial regime tolerated them as a necessary evil—a broker stratum between capital and the superexploited Black workers. Prematurely retired from the national political arena by the crushing of Reconstruction, the majority of the Black middle class seemed to have learned its place. But Jim Crow savagely eviscerated this social contract, producing a significant cohort of renegades from within the Black elite. Behind the banner of antilynching, all the obliging compromises embraced by Booker T. Washington in Atlanta in 1895 were rescinded. In the political sphere, Black male suffrage was championed once again and its political and moral force immeasurably deepened by the demand that Black (and non-Black) women be accorded the same right. On the ideological plane, Washington and those Black newspapers he controlled were targeted for their dependence on "charitable" American capitalists and their adherence to "that part [of the truth] which certain powerful interests in America wish to appear as the whole truth."[94] And these young Black (and often mulatto) rebels were particularly effective in attaching their social agenda as codicils to the new social sciences. They disrupted the white supremacist manifesto of the new nationalist history and the racial conceits embedded at birth in anthropology and sociology.

Du Bois was the most singular architect of this renegade catechism. His principal social and cultural instrument was the *Crisis*, the NAACP's monthly magazine which he inaugurated in November 1910. Together

92. "Wilson behind Segregation," *New York Age*, November 19, 1914, 1. The delegation had asserted that the architects of the Wilson policy were Treasury Secretary William G. McAdoo, a former president of the Hudson and Manhattan Railway, Postmaster General Albert S. Burleson, a former Texas congressman, and John Skelton Williams, controller of the currency and former head of the Georgia and Florida Railroad.

93. Gatewood, *Aristocrats of Color*, 179.

94. David Lewis, *W. E. B. Du Bois*, 414.

with his colleagues and collaborators, Du Bois created a journal of phenomenal importance. In the first two years of its publication, Du Bois reported that the *Crisis* sold 350,000 copies.[95] Earlier, he had conducted and published *The Philadelphia Negro* (1899), his investigation of Black employment which Alice O'Connor characterized recently "as the most impressive of the Progressive-era social surveys."[96] In 1915, he published *The Negro*, his most audacious challenge to the racist canons of modernist historiography. On the surface, *The Negro* was a study of the history of Africa and the African Diaspora. And years afterwards, later readers would attempt to pinion its significance. In 1970, George Shepperson declared *The Negro*'s originality was that here Du Bois "tried to pull together into one succinct but comprehensive whole the different elements of African history, at home and abroad, as they were known by the first decade of the twentieth century."[97] Twenty-eight years later, while in substantial accord with Shepperson's estimation of the volume, Joseph C. Miller sought to broaden the vista. In "History and Africa/Africa and History," his presidential address to the American Historical Association in 1998, Miller observed, "The scholarly W. E. B. Du Bois led several African-American colleagues at the beginning of this century in creating a professional history for Africa against the backdrop of American racism."[98] But as Shepperson had pointed out, Du Bois's objective in writing *The Negro* had more to do with the unchecked contempt for Black people that men like Senator Vardaman could openly express on the Senate floor by 1914.[99] Respond-

95. Ibid., 416. Some incidental evidence of Du Bois's political visibility is the 1924 memo describing a briefing of William R. Castle (the State Department's lead official on Liberian affairs) by Sidney De la Rue (the General Receiver of Customs in Liberia). De la Rue advised Castle that Black support for Firestone's acquisition of a rubber plantation in Liberia could be increased if Firestone hired Black graduates from Black technical schools: "Then, he ventured, 'we should have all the radical press controlled by Du Bois also on our side.'" Chalk, "Anatomy of an Investment," 20.

96. O'Connor, *Poverty Knowledge*, 33.

97. Shepperson, introduction, xiv.

98. Joseph C. Miller, "History and Africa," 5.

99. Fishel and Quarles, *Black American*, 238. Leslie H. Fishel Jr. and Benjamin Quarles appended the following in their foreword to Vardaman's declaration: "Vardaman's speeches drew heavily from many of the scientific theories which were widely accepted during the 1910's. Northern publishers and readers applauded *The Negro, A Menace to American Civilization* (1907), written by Robert W. Shufeldt, a popular biologist associated with the Smithsonian Institution, and *The Color Life: A Brief in*

ing to Vardaman and his pseudoscientific brethren, Du Bois proposed that ancient Blacks indeed had made history in Africa and elsewhere, and that they had created civilizations at which the world still marveled. But Du Bois's treatment of prehistory endures as the most startling of his interventions. The "Negroid stock" of primitive man, original man, Du Bois asserted, had been mulatto, surviving in the modern world as the "reddish dwarfs" of central Africa and the Bushmen of South Africa.[100] "From prehistoric times down to to-day Africa is, in this sense, primarily the land of the mulatto. So, too, was earlier Europe and Asia."[101] If this, then, was the origins of the human species and its civilizations, the North American abhorrence of race-mixing and interracial marriage was an absurd anachronism.

A federal law against interracial marriages might appear to have been redundant in 1915 given the fact, as Peggy Pascoe reports, that forty-one colonies and states had enacted antimiscegenation laws, and that by the early twentieth century, the frequency of such laws "formed a virtual road map to American legal conceptions of race."[102] And Mary Church Terrell might be excused for opposing the passage of a law which reflected badly on her own mixed-race heritage. But the broader context was incited by the release of *The Birth of a Nation* earlier in 1915, a film which Clyde Taylor eloquently characterized as centered on "the unification of national sentiment around the theme of miscegenation as a threat to 'civilization.'"[103] Following Thomas Dixon, as we have seen, D. W. Griffith had employed mulattos to score how near America had come to civil annihilation. As an amoral, hypersexualized interbreed whose "unnatural" appetites precipitated first the Civil War and then the horror of Black-dominated Reconstruction rule, it was evident to

---

Behalf of the Unborn (1905), authored by William B. Smith, a philosophy and mathematics professor at Tulane University." Ibid.

100. Du Bois, *Negro*, 11–12.

101. Ibid., 13.

102. Peggy Pascoe observes: "Laws that had originally prohibited marriages between whites and African Americans (and, very occasionally, American Indians) were extended to cover a much wider range of groups. Eventually, twelve states targeted American Indians, fourteen Asian Americans (Chinese, Japanese, and Koreans), and nine 'Malays' (or Filipinos)." Pascoe, "Miscegenation Law, Court Cases, and Ideologies of 'Race' in Twentieth-Century America," in Hodes, *Sex, Love, Race*, 467–68 (originally published in *Journal of American History*, June 1996, 44–69).

103. Clyde Taylor, "Re-Birth of the Aesthetic," 22.

white supremacists like Dixon, mulattos embodied chaos. And while most whites living in America in 1915 were too far removed from those earlier "tragedies" to have memorialized those implicated mulatta "Jezebels" like Lydia Hamilton Smith and Rachel Knight, their equally culpable kin were easily sighted.[104] The Black elite, obviously a mulatto caste, posed the present danger. Their vocal opposition to lynching threatened an effective protection to the virtue of white women; their physical being threw into confusion the natural markings of racial difference; their professional achievements and education contradicted the lore of white supremacy and the authority of the white upper class; and now their civil activism disrupted governance and the rules of social etiquette. Eschewing the terms of the debate favored by the mass of the Black elite ("uplift," education, moral propriety, proper conduct), the film industry addressed the breach in the most primitive language: the mulatto genre. The Black elite became signified by the lustful, unstable mulatto.

Birth premiered in February 1915. But in April of that year, William Fox's studio responded, releasing *The Nigger*. Despite its provocative title, *The Nigger* muted some of the racial conceits of *Birth* while drawing its audience into the more topical subject of prohibition. But unlike *Birth*, *The Nigger* did not shy away from the historical origins of mixed-race Americans. Yet it shared with the earlier film the conviction that the very presence of the African in America was the source of a national tragedy.

According to a two-page advertisement which appeared in the March 13, 1915, edition of the *Motion Picture News*, *The Nigger* first had been successfully presented on the stage of the New York Century Theatre.[105] The film, written by Edward Sheldon, a Southerner, and directed by Edgar Lewis, starred William Farnum ("The Hundred Thousand Dollar Face"). Four elements of the advertisement provide some

104. Lydia Smith was the mulatta housekeeper of Radical Republican leader Thaddeus Stevens. Dixon and Griffith portrayed her as Stevens's mistress and the catalyst for the Civil War. Rachel Knight, another "cunning, seductive" mulatta slave, was credited with inspiring the slave and poor white anti-Confederacy rebellion in Jones County, Mississippi, during the Civil War. See Victoria E. Bynum, "Misshapen Identity: Memory, Folklore, and the Legend of Rachel Knight," in Hodes, *Sex, Love, Race*, 240ff.

105. See Sheldon, *Nigger*. A playbill published with the play indicates the play opened at The New Theatre, December 4, 1909.

clue to the marketing strategy for the film. First, the largest and boldest lettering was devoted to "William Farnum," and only slightly smaller, "The Nigger" and "Fox Film Corporation." Second, Farnum's portrait photo is inset in the upper-right corner. Third, in the background are two drawn figures: on the left, a white male clothed in a classical Athenian cliton (robe), holding a sword and standing on a white globe; on the right, a half-naked Black male, his wrists in chains, standing on a black globe. Finally, the advertisement included dialogue presumably from the film:

> Phil [Morrow] — "Are you trying to tell me with a straight face, Cliff, that my granmothah was a nigra?"
> [Cliff] Noyes — "What I'm telling you is not only that yo granmothah was a niggah but that yo a niggah too. Now you've got it square between the eyes."

The advertisement is an amazing collage of manipulation and the imaginary. There is, most obviously, the product-recognition strategy represented by the emphasis given to the producing studio, the star, and the term "nigger." The dialogue centers the reader's attention on the dramatic and conflict-ridden themes of race mixture, racial misdirection ("passing"), and exposure/discovery. But in the background, the two illustrated male figures confront each other from the perspective of different worlds: while the white figure impassively stares at the Black man from the vantage of an ancient and noble civilization, the Black man, costumed in the ragged trousers and chains of modern slavery, beseeches his superior for recognition. In this historical imposture (the confrontation of two eras separated by two thousand years), the advertisement for *The Nigger* reproduces the conceits of *Birth*: whites signify the world's civilizations; Blacks, chained to a dark world of perpetual enslavement, are reduced to supplicants. There is no direct relationship, however, between the plot of *The Nigger* and this illustration.

Alan Gevinson has recapitulated the film as a drama concerning a Southern governor (Morrow) who is extorted by a whiskey-distilling political boss (Noyes) to oppose prohibition.[106] The boss has discov-

---

106. In the play, Phil (the grandson) and Cliff are cousins and share contempt for Blacks. Phil owns a cotton plantation which employs six hundred Black workers. At one point Phil declares, "And while I'm good to my niggahs — I reckon that's a well-

ered that the governor is Black and threatens public exposure; the governor signs the prohibition legislation, then resigns, and moves to the North in order to champion his newly assigned race. Other sources contemporary to the release of the film alter this reconstruction in several ways. The synopsis of the film copyrighted on April 5, 1915, in the Library of Congress begins with another, significantly different, narrative:

> Ol Marse Phil Morrow and Hank Noyes were rivals for the affection of Belle, the quadroon slave at Morrow's Rest. Morrow discovers Noyes trying to win the affections of the girl from him and the personal encounter between the 2 old southern planters starts a feud that continues for generations.
>
> The death of Mrs. Morrow and her infant suggests to the old southern gentlemen, that he might take the child of Belle, his slave girl and of whom he is the father, and substitute it for his own still borne babe. Fearing that the girl may talk he decides to send her to the Auction Block and she is taken away to New Orleans and sold as a slave, but not before she writes a letter appealing to him not to forget his quadroon baby. Morrow never gets the letter, which is placed in his tobacco box to be discovered sixty years later, as incriminating proof against succeeding generations, and Morrow himself is killed in battle in the Mexican War.[107]

Like so many other films of this era, *The Nigger* is a lost film. But if the actual film reflected the synopsis, then the publicity department at Fox mischievously deceived the public by linking *The Nigger* with *The Birth of a Nation*. The central mulatto figures of the former differ radically from Griffith's mulattos, Lydia and Silas. The quadroon Belle is not merely an innocent victim (recall she is referred to as a "girl," suggesting a gulf between her and the maturity of "Ol Marse"); she is twice abused: leaving aside the circumstances of her impregnation, she is separated from her infant and put up for sale. Further she enlists the audience's sympathy by the plaintive letter which contains only an appeal for her child's welfare and no recriminations concern-

---

known fact, too! — I don't think they ought to have the franchise and I won't treat 'em as equals." Ibid., 43.

107. William Fox, "Synopsis of *The Nigger*," by Edgar Lewis, LP 5235, Library of Congress.

ing her own abandonment. Nobility also characterizes the quadroon Phil Morrow:

> Shocked at the thought of the sins of his fathers, Phil determines to do his duty as he sees it, and then struggles with his conscience as to his fiance [*sic*] Georgie, and then decides to tell her so that she may be spared such a marriage. At his confession, Georgie recoils with the thought that she has barely escaped marrying a man with negro blood in his veins. Phil shows ... his passion for the girl[,] embraces her and tries to force his love upon her, and then recovering his control tells her that his negro grandmother was superior to her because she gave up her life for the man she loved. Later apologizing he decides that he must renounce Georgie, complete his work, force the liquor interests out of business and then resign as Governor.[108]

Sheldon's, or perhaps Lewis's, characterization is a far distance from the lust-driven Silas Lynch of the Dixon/Griffith collaboration. Morrow has power and refuses to misuse it, eventually renouncing his office. Morrow also displays control over his emotions and appetites, first angrily injuring his fiancée by the unflattering comparison with the courage shown by his quadroon grandmother and then voluntarily separating. (The synopsis reads: "Phil shows his respect for the girl, bows, kisses her hand and turns to door . . . and taking his hat exits with Georgie holding out her arm to him as he goes.")[109] Again, in *The Nigger* the romance between Georgie and Phil is honored. (The last intertitle has Georgie declaring to Phil, "I'm wrong and you're right. You've got to tell the nation what you are and all through your life you'll feel me beside you helping and loving you. Goodbye, and God Bless.")[110] And because their love is honored, it contradicts the opinions of Dixon and Griffith that such a relationship is unnatural.

Paradoxically, Edward Sheldon admitted to having no inkling of the sympathy his play suggested. In an article published in *Motion Picture News* in March of 1915, he discussed his long exposure to the "negro

108. Ibid.
109. Ibid.
110. Phil was one of the few "good" octoroons who survived. In Kalem's *The Octoroon* (1911), Zoe commits suicide before her freedom papers arrive; and in Republic's *The Octoroon's Sacrifice* (1912), the heroic octoroon dies after confessing that she is responsible for killing the villain. See Sampson, *Blacks in Black and White*, 94–95.

problem" growing up as a child in the South. "From my earliest days, the negro problem was a familiar subject to me. I heard it discussed as a child from a hundred different angles and by all grades of men and women. All appeared to agree that there was no solution to it."[111] Sheldon, however, disagreed, asserting that *The Nigger* was intended as both an analysis and a corrective of the originating vice which culminated in the "negro problem": "As I have pointed out in the play the negro problem is in my belief due largely to bad whiskey. There is hardly one of the 'usual crimes' of the Southern negro, for which the penalty is usually lynching, that has not alcohol as an underlying cause. Take liquor out of the South and the race problem would cease to be one. The negro is naturally primitive. Alcohol brings the worst in him to the surface. It makes him worse than the brutes."[112]

Sheldon's retelling of *Othello* founders on the unflattering conflation of his racism and his temperance. It is almost as if Brabantio had rewritten Shakespeare for his own ends. Desdemona (Georgie) is redeemed from a "judgement maimed" marriage, Othello is disgraced by his blackness and overthrown. Sheldon's "Othello," however, intrudes into the poetic magnificence of the original because he has a compulsion to display Black primitiveness. The first act of *The Nigger* ends with the lynching of Joe White, a "niggah" guilty of the "usual crime."[113] Drunk, Joe has raped and killed Mamie Willis, a young white girl. Sheldon's description of Joe is licentiously racist: "He is a huge, very black young African, his lips gray with terror, the whites of his eyes rolling . . . a horrible picture of bestial fear" (79). The author appears to have no more emotional discipline than his lynch mob. Sheldon has subverted his preachment on prohibition by inventing a creature who has no need for whiskey as an explanation for his deed. Only because the debasement of Blacks is unquestioned is it possible for Sheldon to maintain that Noyes is the villain, one of those distillers "who fatten their pockets at the expense of the negro's soul."[114] Sheldon seems to have no understanding that the theodicean dictates of the melodramatic form had

111. "Author of Fox Play."
112. Ibid.
113. Sheldon, *Nigger*, 60. (Hereafter, page references in Sheldon are cited parenthetically.)
114. "Author of Fox Play."

McVicker's Theatre

CHICAGO ∴ ILLINOIS

LITT & DINGWALL, Lessees and Directors   SOL LITT, Manager

The Safest Theatre in the World—40 Exits.
Established in 1857, and now in its 54th year.

"As regards protection to life, McVicker's is unsurpassed."—Chicago Tribune Editorial, Jan. 9, '04.

"Entitled to advertise itself as one of the safest amusement temples in the world."—Chicago Evening Post, Sept. 5, '04.

"If there is a safer playhouse extant than this new-old theatre its exit plat has never been made public."—Chicago Inter-Ocean, Sept. 5, '04.

"The most modern, handsome and safest playhouse in the city."—Chicago Chronicle, Sept. 8, '04.

Red lights, operated on an entirely independent gas system, are kept constantly burning over every exit in this theatre.

The management urgently requests the audience to use the different exits at the end of each performance; thus patrons will thoroughly familiarize themselves with the various means of egress.

COMMENCING SUNDAY NIGHT, DECEMBER 4th, 1910

Wm. A. Brady, Ltd., Present (By arrangement with the New Theatre, N. Y.)

"THE NIGGER"

A Play in Three Acts, by Edward Sheldon.
With GUY BATES POST.

THE CAST.
(In the order in which they appear.)

SIMMS, Morrow's Butler..........................WM. CULLINGTON
JINNY, Morrow's "Mammy".........................MAUD DURAND
CLIFTON NOYES....................................J. M. COLVILLE
    President of the Noyes' Distilling Works.
GEORGIANA BYRD...............................FLORENCE ROCKWELL
PHILIP MORROW.................................GUY BATES POST
    Of Morrow's Rest and Sheriff of Westbury County.
PURDY, Deputy Sheriff of Westbury County..........T. C. HAMILTON
MRS. BYRD.......................................JULIA HANCHETT
JOE WHITE..HENRY HULL
JAKE WILLIS......................................R. C. FORREST
BARRINGTON, the Governor's Private Secretary.........JACK BARNES
CHIEF OF POLICE TILTON.............................D. W. HAYNES
COLONEL KNAPP, of the 5th Militia..................J. W. GREGORY
THE GOVERNOR'S DOORKEEPER.....................SAMUEL JOHNSON
SENATOR THOMAS R. LONG..........................FRANK PETERS
    Members of the Governor's Staff, Reporters, Etc.

SYNOPSIS OF SCENES.
ACT I—June 3rd, Evening at "Morrow's Rest."
ACT II—April 23rd, the Governor's Study in his City House. About 10 o'clock in the Morning.

Edward Sheldon's The Nigger, *McVicker's Theatre, Chicago, 1910.*

ACT III—April 26th, the Governor's Private Office at the Capitol. Evening.

PLACE—The South.   TIME—Now.

EXECUTIVE STAFF FOR WM. A. BRADY, LTD.

Harry Elmer...Manager
Wm. Cullington..Stage Manager
Wm. Allen..Carpenter
John Taylor,..Properties
Jos. R. Powell..Electrician

McVICKER'S MUSIC PROGRAM.

1. Overture—Concert ....Kalliwoda
2. Selection—Sunny South..............................Isenman
3. Cornet Solo—Oh, Believe Me..........................Moore
4. Suite...Kate Vannah
   1. Dawn. 2. Sleepy Baby. 3. For Thee.
5. March—Insurgent ....Walker

compelled him into a contradiction. His whites, "Ol Marse" and Clifton Noyes, were the unprincipled characters; the Blacks (quadroons) the virtuous. Unfortunately hardly any of Sheldon's peers fell into the same trap, for until Micheaux's intervention, *The Nigger* would be one of the last heroic characterizations of the mulatto in Hollywood films.

In 1916, Selig Polyscope released *At Piney Ridge*, in which another race-mistaken mulatto marauds through white society.[115] He impregnates one woman, embezzles bank funds, shifts the blame for both deeds to a rival, adding the final insult that his rival is of mixed blood. The mulatto is eventually killed by a distraught father, and while dying is told that his mother was Black. In *Pudd'nhead Wilson*, the same year, Lasky Features presented an adaptation of the play by Frank Mayo (1894). Here a quadroon baby is switched by his mulatto mother with a white child having the same patrician father. Later the quadroon murders his uncle and tries to blame his half brother for the deed. His original identity is revealed by fingerprint evidence, and he is sent to prison.[116] In *Bar Sinister* (1917), Edgar Lewis Productions exhibited its first film. Lewis, the director of *The Nigger,* now tells the story of a mulatta who kidnaps the child of a man whose cruelty had caused the death of her husband. She raises the child as her own daughter but eventually confesses the truth. This is the only other film which departed from stock characterizations of the mulatto. "Ben Swift" is a mulatto character who falls in love with Belle, the kidnapped white woman, and vies with Page Warren, a white man, with whom Belle has become "tragically" involved. Swift is described as "a noble character" in the *Moving Picture World*, which provided a succinct summary of the film's denouement:

> The attacking of Page by a gang of bad blacks, following his fight with one of their leaders, his rescue by Ben Swift, who has learned of Belle's love for the white man, the discovery by Page that Belle is a mulatto, the sensational disclosure of the fact that she is the last daughter of a prominent Southern family, the death of Ben Swift while defending Page and Belle from an enraged mob and the beau-

115. All the following summaries of the "mulatto genre" are augmentations of the descriptions in Gevinson, *Within Our Gates*.

116. The theme of octoroon mothers substituting a mixed-race child for a white baby was taken up by the Rex Company in *In Slavery Days* (1913) and *The Slave* (1916). See Sampson, *Blacks in Black and White*, 75, 108–9.

tiful handling of the subject of the spiritual equality of men makes "The Bar Sinister" an intensely interesting drama with a powerful appeal to all classes.[117]

In *The Renaissance at Charleroi* (Broadway Star Features), also in 1917, a wealthy aristocrat destroys the romantic liaison between an octoroon and a white man. Again that year, in *Sold at Auction* (Balboa Amusement Producing Company), a white child condemned to servitude is mischievously identified by her custodian as a mulatta in order to halt a marriage to a young reporter. She is then surrendered to a prostitution ring, paradoxically auctioned to the father who had abandoned her years before, and only saved from incest by the intervention of her fiancé.

The following year, 1918, the depiction of mulattos took another turn for the worse. In *Broken Ties* (World Film), a mulatta kills her white foster father because he opposes her marriage to a white man. Her fiancé is accused of the murder, but she confesses and then stabs herself to death.[118] In *Free and Equal* (Thomas H. Ince), a mulatto betrays his race by succumbing to his congenital character. Trained at Tuskegee Institute, the mulatto is employed by a white philanthropist who has created a Society for the Uplift of the Negro. In gratitude the mulatto frequents brothels, seduces and secretly marries his benefactor's daughter, and later rapes and kills a maid. At his trial, he is revealed as a bigamist and imprisoned. The philanthropist understandably renounces race equality. Gevinson notes that the film was released despite Ince's objection that "it was not complimentary to blacks."[119] There was more of the same in *A Woman of Impulse* (Famous Players–Lasky) that same year. Here a mulatta stabs to death her wealthy paramour while he is assaulting another woman. The mulatta finally confesses at the trial of

117. Abrams and Werner review of *The Bar Sinister*, *Moving Picture World*, May 5, 1917, 751.

118. In this instance, race-mixing is divorced from the plantation legacy: "The heroine has negro blood in her veins, her father having been shipwrecked on an island inhabited by blacks and became the husband of the chief's daughter." Weitzel, "Broken Ties."

119. Gevinson, *Within Our Gates*, 356. Ince's role was described in *Photoplay*, April 1919, 104. After a brief exhibition in 1918 the film was re-released in 1925 with an epilogue and prologue which transformed the original film into a nightmare experienced by the mulatto, which substantiated the Tuskegee creed that "the Negro should stay in his place." Gevinson, *Within Our Gates*, 356.

the other woman, thus erasing any suggestion that her action was motivated by anything other than jealousy.

Summarizing the era, Peter Noble, the earliest historian of Blacks in film, observed: "From 'The Birth of a Nation' to 'Jazz Singer' there were dozens of films produced in which coloured actors were seen, and some thirty or so productions with Negro themes, none, however, with any particular significance."[120] For Noble "significance" meant an impulse towards racial fairness, a cinema in opposition to an appeal to Negrophobia. In its stead the execrable mulatto genre complemented the minstrel conventions by adding contemptuous disavowals of the Black petite bourgeoisie and miscegenation. And not content at merely detailing the anarchic misbehavior of what was believed to be an inherently unstable racial cohort, the most powerful studios also provided models of appropriate "negro" behavior.

The coincidence between the emergence of organizations embodying Black middle-class resistance and the "faithful slave" genre is striking, indeed too close to dismiss as accidental. Like gangster films of the 1930s, or the horror movies of the Cold War era (*The Thing*, 1951; *Invasion of the Body Snatchers*, 1956; *Forbidden Planet*, 1956), or the antifeminist films of the late 1980s and early 1990s (e.g., *Fatal Attraction*, 1987; *Pretty Woman*, 1989), earlier American filmmakers displayed no reluctance to leap at the opportunity to produce films which undermined progressive social change.[121] Consequently, just as the Niagara Movement, the NERL, and the NAACP were beginning to draw attention to the resolve of activists from the "respectable" Negro classes to rupture the new racial regime, a spate of "faithful slave" films was released. At Biograph, Griffith produced a succession of proper Black catechisms: *The Guerrilla* (1908), *In Old Kentucky* (1909), *The Honor of His Family* (1910), *His Trust* (1911), and *His Trust Fulfilled* (1911). In each film white actors in burnt cork impersonated slaves who either forfeited their lives or their

120. Noble, *Negro in Films*, 47. Noble amended his remarks: "Possible exceptions included such movies as 'Free and Equal,' a direct appeal to intolerance, which attempted to capitalise on the eternal theme of Negro inferiority; and an adaptation of Edward Sheldon's 'The Nigger,' starring William Farnum. The latter film was a puerile attempt to foster even more racial hatred than already existed in American social life. 'Broken Chains' [*sic*] followed in the traditions of 'The Birth of a Nation' and showed the Negro as a murderous and scoundrelly agitator." Ibid.

121. Hoberman, "Paranoia and the Pods"; Shapiro, "Universal Truths"; Greenberg, "Rescrewed"; Steinbrunner and Goldblatt, *Cinema of the Fantastic*.

well-being to secure the virginity, happiness, or safety of slave-owning patricians or their families, and even in some instances the Confederate cause! In *The Confederate Spy* (1910), the Kalem studio provided its own version of the darkies who preferred slavery to the uncertainties of freedom. And in Pathe's *For Massa's Sake* (1911), a freed slave voluntarily sold himself in order to rescue his master from debt.[122] There is no trustworthy tally of the number of such films displayed before the nation's audiences in this period, nor any certainty as to how often some semblance of this message of the decorum of Negro loyalty was rehearsed in other silent-era melodramas, jungle films, and the like. What does seem incontrovertible is that these films helped to insinuate into the popular culture the principle that the loyalty of the Black subordinate to the white upper classes trumped any claims or demands that the Black middle-class militants might infuse into the national discourse. No ambition attached to the Black masses or articulated on their behalves could possibly compete with the "legitimate" needs of the white upper classes, and by extension, all whites. In stunning contrast, these films depicting "faithful" slaves demonstrated that, as Gerald Butters Jr. observes, "faithful African American compatriots seemed not to exist in the modern era."[123] Coupled with the casual violence meted out to Black "chicken thieves" in the minstrel comedies which dominated Black cinematic representations, the corollary was obvious. Given the self-serving stridency of leaders drawn from the damaged stock of race mixing, no American (immigrant or native) should wonder about or object to the necessity of lynchings or occasional anti-Black pogroms to put things right.

Race Films and Resistance

The present state of research indicates that race films made their first appearance somewhere around 1910 with William Foster's *The Pullman Porter*. Back then they were called "race films" because they were targeted for a Black movie-going market, frequently arranged in separate or segregated theaters. These audiences quickly recognized and adapted to the emergence of race films since they were already familiar with the terms "race men" and "race women." For at least one generation before the decade 1910–20, race men and women were famil-

122. For plot summaries of these films, see Butters, *Black Manhood*, 58–61.
123. Ibid., 62.

iar figures, usually educated or affluent Blacks who publicly, or at least noticeably, championed causes for the "uplift" of the race.[124] Among Blacks, accustomed to the seminationalist solidarity and identifications of these designators, race films were easily distinguishable from racist films which, too, pursued a collectivist vision, but one driven by white racism. Still, within the genre of race films there were important differences between the many which appropriated "Hollywood's" caricatures of Black representation and the few which directly attacked them.

This puts the matter rather too simply, since conflicting claims have been made about these films. Michelle Wallace, for one, has asserted that race films were produced "usually for the specific purpose of rescuing the image of blacks from the deleterious impression made by the caricature films."[125] Jane Gaines has gone even further, maintaining that "ironically, although the race film pioneers started from the assumption that they knew who they were and who the race audience would be, they were, as they produced, directed, and exhibited their product, actually *constituting* that race community."[126] Granted, we are all somewhat disadvantaged by the near-total loss of these films; however, such claims are really unsupported by the surviving evidence. While in the year immediately following the release of *The Birth of a Nation* (1915), Lincoln Motion Picture Company was producing "uplift" romances and melodramas like *The Colored American Winning His Suit, Trooper of Troop K,* and *The Realization of a Negro's Ambition,* the following year Ebony Film Company released a litany of parodies and slapstick comedies: *A Black Sherlock Holmes, A Busted Romance, Dat Blackhand Waitah Man, Devil for a Day, Ghosts, The Hypocrites, Mercy, the Mummy Mumbled, Shine Johnson and His Rabbit Foot, Some Baby, Spooks, Spying the Spy,* and *Wrong All Around.*[127] The balance challenges Wallace's presumption that race films generally countered race caricatures. And on its face, Gaines's notion that race community was "invented" by race films appears as an ahistorical inflation. In either case, a seminal question goes begging: on what terms were race films Black?

More than a decade ago, Tommy Lott provided a standard by which

124. Kevin K. Gaines, *Uplifting the Race.*
125. Wallace, *"Uncle Tom's Cabin,"* 139.
126. Jane M. Gaines, *Fire and Desire,* 16.
127. See Larry Richards, *African American Films.*

to distinguish "Black cinema" from the plethora of "race films" which appeared during the silent-film era. Though Lott's immediate subject was the films nominated as Blaxploitation (1968–75) and post-Blaxploitation (after 1975), his strictures, I will argue, are relevant to the earlier period. Responding to what he determined was the "essentialism" employed by Thomas Cripps to define black film ("theater films about the black experience that are produced, written, directed, and performed by black people for a primarily black audience"), Lott countered: "The white cultural nationalism of Hollywood's Eurocentric empire requires something like a Third Cinema movement to help nonwhite people survive the oppressive and self-destructive consciousness that empire seeks to perpetuate." In short, Lott's construction of Black cinema was defined by "black film-making practices . . . fundamentally concerned with the issues that currently define the political struggle of black people."[128]

As far as can be determined, many of the hundreds of race films were produced in their own silent-film period (between 1910 and 1931) and later approximated the description that Cripps supplied; that is, the films were produced by Blacks, with Blacks, and for Blacks. Yet few directly addressed the issues around which political struggles were being waged during the first half of the twentieth century: peonage, sharecropping, lynching, segregation, inferior public education, the sexual exploitation of Black women, and child labor. As C. L. R. James put it in a critique of *Gone with the Wind* published in 1939–40, "the essentials of Negro slavery still remain over large parts of the South."[129] Using Lott's criteria, then, these films would not qualify as Black Cinema. To the contrary, drawing on Michelle Wallace's categorization, many of them exploited Black caricatures for the amusement of their largely Black audiences. This raises issues with the overt evaluations of Cripps or the partially concealed essentialism in hooks.

Butters's characterization of the companies which produced race films offers some relief at first glance: "I distinguish between three predominant artistic forms of black cinematic imagery. The first category includes films produced by companies owned and controlled by

128. Tommy L. Lott, "No-Theory Theory," 139, 151 (originally published in *Black American Literature Forum*, 1991). Lott was summarizing Cripps's argument in *Black Film as Genre*, 3–12.

129. James, "On *Gone with the Wind*," 51.

African Americans. The second category includes all-black films produced by independent companies owned by Euro-Americans but with African-American creative participation. These companies were outside the Hollywood studio system. The third category includes films produced by major (white) motion picture studios."[130] Butters insists that at least between 1913 and 1929 the majority of Black independent features, his first category, were "dramatic," in contrast to the comedic form favored by "Hollywood" studios.[131] Leaping beyond this construction, it would be comforting to learn that the Black-owned production companies more frequently rose to the challenge of defending the race from its detractors. But film historians have had difficulty in characterizing the cultural, moral, or aesthetic import of the race film. This should not be completely surprising, since race films had in common mostly the superficialities of being produced with Black casts for predominantly Black audiences. Splitting this simplistic formulation, on the other hand, was a myriad of intervening variables between the idea and the realization of race films.

Many of the Black independent companies survived only long enough to produce one film, sometimes two. This lack of longevity, however, was not necessarily a measure of the importance of their films. For instance, in 1920 Royal Gardens Film Company of Chicago produced *In the Depths of Our Hearts*, a six-reel film. The film was an exposé of colorism in which a rebellious son rejects his light-skinned mother's color-caste prejudices. In 1915, a Birmingham-based company, Southern Motion Picture Company, produced *When True Love Wins* (a screenplay by Isaac Fisher of the Tuskegee Institute) which interrogated class prejudices among Blacks.[132] Some of these producing cohorts were headed by small businessmen; others were inspired and organized by community organizations like churches, colleges, and volunteer organizations.[133] The more successful companies were distinguished by such

130. Butters, *Black Manhood*, 94.

131. Ibid., 108.

132. These two films are discussed in Larry Richards, *African American Films*, 89, 184; Bowser and Spence, *Writing Himself*, 89–90; and Butters, *Black Manhood*, 105–6, 186–87.

133. Pearl Bowser and Louise Spence provide some examples: George Broome's Broome Exhibition Company of Boston, which in 1910 sought to support the Tuskegee Institute's fund-raising; the Afro-American Film Company of New York (1913), which started by documenting meetings of the National Negro Business League; Peter P.

factors as social geography and the cultural sophistication of their original locales. For instance, Chicago could generate studios like those organized by William Foster, Peter P. Jones, and Oscar Micheaux; Los Angeles could support the Lincoln Motion Picture Company; New York could host the Afro-American Film Company (1913), Hunter Haynes Photoplay Company (1914), Robert Levy's Roel Company, and the Frederick Douglass Film Company (in New Jersey actually); and the Norman Film Manufacturing Company was based in Florida.[134] In Philadelphia, David Starkman's Colored Players Film Corporation could rely on the old networks of exhibition sites that his Black partner, S. H. Dudley, had developed as head of the Black vaudevillian agency Southern Consolidated Circuit. In the 1920s Dudley's circuit had eventually merged with the Theatre Owners Booking Association (TOBA) and Managers' and Performers' circuit (M. & P.), the dominant handlers of Black vaudevillian talent and venues.[135] Sometimes these circuits brought talented Black artists in close enough proximity to prospective filmmakers to produce a film based on a routine or theatrical performance. Just as often, amateur actors and actresses were recruited. Raising capital for independent productions was equally capricious. As Charlene Regester has demonstrated, the most successful and therefore the most inventive Black filmmaker was Oscar Micheaux. Like many of his cohorts, Micheaux was frequently forced to accompany the single print of his film on tour, collecting rentals from exhibitions and inveigling small investors to support his next film. And he was an infamous cost-cutter. In Roanoke, Virginia, during his 1921 filming of *The House behind the*

Jones Film Company of Chicago (1914), which was the brainchild of Jones, a still photographer whose earliest concerns were documenting the heroism of Black soldiers; the Heart of America Film Corporation of Kansas City, Missouri (1916), which collapsed before its first project was completed; Charles Allmon's Allmon-Hudlin Film Company of St. Louis (1916), which produced documentaries of local churches, schools, "the St. Louis Colored Orphan Home; the St. Louis Old Folks' Home; the annual public schools' field day . . . the Masonic parade; and a baseball game between the St. Louis Giants and the Nashville Giants." Bowser and Spence, *Writing Himself*, 102–6. For a more complete listing, see Sampson, *Blacks in Black and White*, chap. 5; and Butters, *Black Manhood*, chap. 8.

134. For a review of Haynes's *Uncle Remus' Visit to New York*, see "New Photo Play," *New York Age*, August 13, 1914, 7. For Norman Film Manufacturing, see Bernstein and White, "'Scratching Around.'"

135. For Dudley, see Butters, *Black Manhood*, 195; and Hill, *Pages from the Harlem Renaissance*, 65ff.

Cedars, Micheaux persuaded prominent local Black businessmen to invest in the project, obtained housing for his crew and talent in the private homes of these Black notables, and successfully appealed for the use of their homes for his interior shots. Finally, he further ingratiated himself in the community by casting several of Roanoke's Black residents in the film.[136] All the while, Micheaux was bean-counting, keeping at bay the author Charles Chesnutt's attempts at collecting his fee for the use of his novel.

While Bowser and Spence maintain that it was "more usual [that these] were self-congratulatory movies testifying to racial progress," there was also the temptation of broader exhibition.[137] Butters suggests that one avenue open to Black independents with access to white entrepreneurs impacted the choice of Black comedies over Black melodrama. "Black comedies were accepted in white theaters but all-black dramas were not."[138] On that score, American distributors have remained fairly consistent for the past one hundred years. Black comedies were also less likely to attract the attention of the numerous censor agencies. Anesthetized from sensing omnipresent images which degraded Blacks, local boards were more concerned with suggestions of race-mixing in dramas, and so on. In sum, race movies were a variable lot. The outcome of the contest between genres, between "Negro comedies" and melodramas, was largely determined by exhibitors rather than producers or distributors. And the genre competition fluctuated back and forth from a situation of total dominance of comedies at Black box offices to one where melodramas held their own as prestige presentations. As best as can be determined, the Great Migration and World War I fueled a growth in the ranks of Black exhibitors, adding new movie houses to the core of vaudevillian theaters organized by Dudley and his peers in the earlier portion of the century. This increase in Black audiences supported a challenge by Black filmmakers to the dominion of films burlesquing Blacks. According to Larry Richards, the first spike in the production of Black silent films came in 1918 (something like thirty-six films); a second in 1921 (fifty-two films); and a third in 1929 (fifty-six films).[139] The first two spurts coincided with the ap-

136. See Regester, "Oscar Micheaux"; and Bowser and Spence, *Writing Himself,* 33ff.

137. Bowser and Spence, *Writing Himself,* 106.

138. Butters, *Black Manhood,* 184.

139. Larry Richards, *African American Films,* 273–76.

pearances of the Lincoln, Micheaux, and Norman companies. By the third spurt all but Micheaux had discontinued production. Partly this was the result of one important change during the interval. As Sampson observes, "White businessmen seeking the financial success of black theaters began to buy out black-owned theaters and build new ones in black neighborhoods."[140] Unlike their predecessors, these new owners did not charge higher admission prices for Black-produced prints. Production values degraded, and the Black press became increasingly critical of these films, withdrawing another resource supporting race films.[141] But then again, exhibition was so chaotic it is impossible to determine with exactness what films were seen in a particular year, which of the edited versions were seen, or how often films reappeared with new titles.

Race film thus constituted an anarchic cottage industry rather than a genre. And since the only regulatory enforcement was the market (and the censors), race films acquired few conventions in narration, cinematography, aesthetics, finance, production, and the like. In order to probe resistance in the race film, superficialities must be set aside so as to distinguish between the majority of race films and those few which evidenced an opposition to the racial regime. While some of these movies pursued the regime through a contesting iconography, others delved deeper into the very construction of knowledge which collaborated with racism.

Employing the standard suggested by Lott, then, there were only a few Black films among the legion of race films. Rather than a profound challenge or radical critique of racial capitalism, the most daring of the race film producers seemed to have been contented with displays of bourgeois respectability and modest uplift themes. On occasion, however, some of their films achieved a kind of aesthetic poetry. Among those which have survived, probably the most stunning of them is David Starkman's *Scar of Shame* (1929), produced by his Colored Players Film Corporation of Philadelphia. This film rises to unfamiliar heights with its evocation of the beautiful and tragic figure Louise Howard (Lucia Lynne Moses). *Scar of Shame* transcends melodrama by its portrayal of

140. Sampson, *Blacks in Black and White*, 9; and Bobo, "'Subject Is Money.'"

141. For the Black press, see Regester, "African-American Press"; and for deteriorating production values, Clyde Taylor, "Black Silence." It was not uncommon to find newspaper entertainment columnists also hired by film companies to assist in distribution and publicity.

Louise as a young Black working-class woman fatally enmeshed in a vice of class prejudices and masculine privilege. Like tragic figures in the ancient dramas of Aeschylus, Louise is propelled ineluctably towards her own destruction. In the end, driven by jealousy and fear, Louise renounces her claim to her feckless husband, eventually committing suicide to restore the now matured hero to his own social class.[142] Like the discarded black doll seen earlier in the film, Louise's grace and beauty (Charles Musser maintained that "soft-focus cinematography and attentive lighting . . . makes her the most glamorous of black actresses on the silent screen") suffer in the unequal competition between class and the imaginary.[143] But Black actresses sufficiently experienced like Moses to carry off such performances were rarely engaged outside the orbit of Micheaux or Starkman.[144] The same was true for trained Black actors, dramatists, and writers. Some instances substantiate this reconstruction. Anita Bush's dramatic authority was effectively negated by her roles in a Norman Western pot-boiler, *The Crimson Skull* (also

142. As a serving girl in a boarding house, Louise is subjected to unwanted advances from a slick boarder and then physically abused by her stepfather (played by William E. Pettus). She is rescued on both occasions by Alvin Hillyard (Harry Henderson), a young upper-middle-class Black man who is striving to become a composer. Struck by her vulnerability and attractiveness, Alvin impetuously marries Louise. However, he conceals the marriage from his mother, who intends him for "one of our set." This deception infects his marriage and eventually estranges Louise. While preparing to leave Alvin, Louise and her stepfather are confronted by him, and in the ensuing struggle over a pistol, Louise is wounded in the neck, resulting in the metaphorical scar of shame. A complete synopsis is developed in Jane Gaines, "*Scar of Shame.*"

143. Musser, "Colored Players Film Corporation," 187.

144. Bowser and Spence report that "besides [Evelyn] Preer," Micheaux employed "members of the Lafayette Players, including Ida Anderson, Andrew Bishop, Laura Bowman, Lawrence Chenault, Inez Clough, A. B. De Comathiere, Cleo Desmond, Alice Gorgas, Iris Hall, Lionel Monagas, Susie Sutton, and Edward Thompson." He also employed veteran vaudevillians like E. G. Tatum, Salem Tutt Whitney, J. Homer Tutt, and S. T. Jacks. Bowser and Spence, *Writing Himself*, 43–44. The only other company to take advantage of such talent was Robert Levy's Reol Productions, which in 1921 and 1922 appropriated the themes of the fading Lincoln Motion Picture Company, which no longer had the services of its founder, Noble Johnson. Levy was what Cripps terms "the white angel" of the Lafayette Players and employed them in such uplift melodramas as *The Burden of Race* (1921), *The Call of His People* (1921), *The Leader of His Race* (1922), and *The Sport of the Gods* (1921). See Cripps, *Slow Fade to Black*, 82; and Larry Richards, *African American Films*, 255.

exhibited as *The Scarlet Claw,* 1921) and then *The Bull-Dogger,* which featured the audacious horsemanship of Bill Pickett. Clarence Muse, another Lafayette Player alumnus, may have broken the race film mold in *Toussaint L'Ouverture* (Blue Ribbon Pictures, 1921), but we may never know. Muse directed and produced the film, but Larry Richards is of the opinion that it was never released.[145] Charles Gilpin, perhaps the most frequently acknowledged dramatic talent of the era, was embedded in the Afro-American Film Company's comedies *Mandy's Choice* (1914) and *One Large Evening* (1914).[146] In his one remaining silent-film appearance, he starred in Starkman's *Ten Nights in a Bar-Room* (1926), a movie whose pedigree and casting alone suggest it was of excellent quality. Harry Henderson and Lawrence Chenault, both of *Scar of Shame,* appeared in the film with Ethel Smith, whose frequent work with Starkman and Micheaux lends her credibility. Certainly the dramatic death of the child Mary, the accidental victim of a barroom fight, and her father's (Gilpin) grief-stricken cradling of her body constitute one of the most powerful sequences in race film.

Henry Sampson asserts that the standard for the race film melodramas was Lincoln Motion Picture's *Realization of a Negro's Ambition* (1916), "the first successful classy Negro feature film produced without burlesque comedy."[147] Lincoln's *Trooper of Troop K* (1916) followed within months; and then *The Law of Nature* (1917), *A Man's Duty* (1919), and *By Right of Birth* (1921).[148] Because no surviving print of *Realization* has yet been discovered, no thick analysis of the film is possible. The reconstruction of the bare narrative of the film, however, has been attempted. From Sampson we learn that James Burton (Noble Johnson), a Tuskegee-trained civil engineer, leaves his father's farm for work in his profession. Bidding good-bye to his parents and sweetheart Mary

145. Larry Richards, *African American Films,* 174.

146. The reviewer of the *New York Amsterdam News* commented on *One Large Evening:* "There are many scenes of excruciatingly funny complications. . . . The picture caused great laughter among the previewers, the actors seemed to catch the spirit of the situation and succeeded in bringing out all the laughable points artistically." Richards, *African American Films,* 129.

147. Sampson, *Blacks in Black and White,* 130.

148. The company also produced documentaries or actualities: for example, *Lincoln Pictorial* (1918), which featured "views of the black community of Los Angeles," according to Larry Richards, *African American Films,* 102; and *A Day with the Tenth Cavalry at Fort Huachuca* (1922).

Lawrence Chenault and Anita Bush, The Crimson Skull, *1921, Norman Film Manufacturing Company. Photographs and Prints Division, Schomburg Center for Research in Black Culture, New York Public Library, Astor, Lenox and Tilden Foundations.*

Hayden (Beulah Hall), he leaves for California's oilfields. Seeking employment in his profession, Burton suffers job discrimination when an oil field owner rejects his application. Leaving the field, Burton observes a frightened young woman in a runaway two-horse rig and rescues her in a daring display of horsemanship. She is the daughter of the oil field owner, who promptly engages Burton, hiring him to head an exploratory team. In his surveys, Burton encounters oil-rich geological formations which resemble those on his father's farm, and with financing from his boss, Burton returns home. Related to his homecoming, Mary has been socially ostracized by a rival, the wealthy Doris Babbit (Lottie Boles) who, desiring Burton for herself, conspires with her brother George (Clarence Brooks) to sully Mary's reputation. Burton, in the meanwhile, finds oil and becomes independently wealthy. He eventually exposes the unjust accusation against Mary. Burton and Mary encounter one another once again when Burton purchases a city home from her realtor boss (Mary is a stenographer in the office). He proposes, they marry, and the film ends happily: "James in later years, with ambition realized, home and family, a nice country to live in and nice people to live and enjoy it with."[149]

Compared to *Realization, Trooper of Troop K* was a production extravaganza, employing hundreds of uniformed extras to play the roles of the Mexican army and the all-Black Troop K of the Tenth U.S. Cavalry. The film's battle segment was based on an actual skirmish—the Carrizal Incident—which had taken place earlier in 1916.[150] Noble Johnson played "Shiftless" Joe, an indolent bumbler who in naïve desperation at his failures in civilian life takes Clara Holens's (Beulah Hall) advice and joins the army. In the cavalry Joe's love for animals and genial disposition earn him respect. At Carrizal, Troop K is nearly annihilated,

149. Butters, *Black Manhood*, 112. Butters, expectedly, ignores the subplot of Mary's social ostracism. The fuller synopsis is in Sampson, *Blacks in Black and White*, 267–68.

150. In March 1916, spurred by border incursions by Franciso "Pancho" Villa, the American government launched the Mexican Punitive Expedition to pursue and destroy Villa's forces. The Mexican government objected to the invasion, and the United States found itself confronted by both Villistas and Mexican soldiers. On June 19, 1916, under the command of Captain Charles Boyd and Captain Lewis Morey, Troops K and C of the 10th Cavalry attempted to advance against a Mexican garrison at Carrizal. In the resulting fighting, Boyd and twelve other Black troopers were killed, an equal number wounded, and twice that number taken prisoner. After several months of negotiations between President Wilson and Venustiano Carranza, the provisional Mexican president, the American prisoners were returned and the expedition recalled. Nalty, *Strength for the Fight*, 98ff. Two years earlier, in a series of articles based on interviews with Black veterans of the Tenth Cavalry, the *New York Age* had asserted that Villa was actually George Goldsby, an American Black and a former member of the Tenth Cavalry. See "General Villa, Head of Rebel Army, Said to Be an American Negro," *New York Age*, February 26, 1914, 1; "Says He Talked with Gen. Villa," *New York Age*, March 19, 1914, 1; and "'Villa a Negro' Says Explorer," *New York Age*, March 26, 1914, 1 (in this instance, the informant was Frederick Inman Monsen, a Norwegian explorer); the paper also insisted that "in the ranks of the Mexican rebels are several hundred American Negroes [including] J. W. Day, Jr., Arthur Harvey, C. N. Thompson, Jas. Blackshear, Ralph Carouthers, and Kid Jonathan." "Chicago Negro Is Colonel under Villa," *New York Age*, April 23, 1914, 1. The colonel was Thomas J. Francis, originally of Chicago, who now claimed to own a ranch in Texas.

but Joe heroically rescues his captain and they escape. Newspaper accounts of Joe's deeds reach Clara. She rejects his rival. And when the decorated trooper returns home on leave, Clara's embrace implies a romance fulfilled.[151] The central character in Lincoln's next production, *The Law of Nature*, was played by Albertine Pickens. Employed as a governess, a young woman of Eastern society ventures West and eventually marries her employer. She induces him to return with her to the East with its more sophisticated and busy social life. His lack of social graces embarrasses her, and the husband and children return home. Her gay social existence begins to degrade and she becomes dissipated. She returns to the West to reconcile with her husband and children. Somewhat enigmatically, Sampson's synopsis ends: "The regeneration complete, she succumbs to the will of God."[152]

Under pressure from his Universal Pictures bosses, Johnson resigned from the company after the completion of these three films. In the post-Johnson era, the final two productions of Lincoln Motion Pictures, *A Man's Duty* and *By Right of Birth*, appear to be much thicker melodramas than their predecessors. In *A Man's Duty* false accusations, mistaken identities, coincidences, and regretful relationships abound, buried in a moral tale which exposes the evils of drink, prostitution, and mendacity. Like the classic melodrama, all ends well for the reformed and virtuous, and villainy receives its just proportion. *By Right of Birth* employs similar devices, but in lieu of the narrative of male dissolution and redemption in its predecessor, the last feature film by Lincoln disposed concentrated sympathy on three female characters: an "orphaned" daughter, her secretly attentive mother, and a resourceful grandmother. By the conclusion of the film they are extricated from a web of deceit woven by a dissolute foster mother and an unscrupulous stockbroker. The plot revolves around an oil-rich Freedman allotment in Oklahoma (Sampson avers, "Freedmen were slaves or their descendants, who, when freed, received allotments of land from the government, much of which land was proven to be immensely valuable oil land").[153] At the film's conclusion, the three virtuous women are reunited, and their wealth is secured against the machinations of the villains.

151. Sampson, *Blacks in Black and White*, 273-74.
152. Ibid., 258.
153. Ibid., 290.

The era which paralleled the race melodramas was quite a troubled one for Black Americans, filled with excitement and (almost) unprecedented violence. A major contributing factor was that factions of capital and, on the other hand, the state, had conflicting racial agendas. These oppositions crystallized with the onset of World War I. The war constituted a powerful influence on American manufacturing, on the country's industrial production, and on American international trade and finance. For one, almost immediately, the nation emerged from the war as the dominant political entity in the West. American institutions of finance capital had led the country into the war largely as the most convenient means of protecting the massive loans forwarded to the Allies as well as its large investments in war production. Howard Zinn recalls:

> With World War I, England became more and more a market for American goods and for loans at interest. J. P. Morgan and Company acted as agents for the Allies, and when, in 1915, Wilson lifted the ban on private bank loans to the Allies, Morgan could now begin lending money in such great amounts as to both make great profit and tie American finance closely to the interest of a British victory in the war against Germany. . . . When the United States entered the war, it was the rich who took even more direct charge of the economy.[154]

For the first time in its history the United States had become a creditor nation, American finance capitalists plunging their tentacles into the public and private centers of finance in Western Europe. Even before the country's belated entry into the war as a combatant, the European powers had demanded larger deliveries of American-made war materials. The resultant expansion of production precipitated an increase in labor requirements, and this excited new waves of Southern migrants to centers devoted to production and shipping of war goods. The inevitable partial relaxation of segregated labor incited race conflict. For one, striking and unionized white workers, habituated to the protections of Jim Crow, were suddenly exposed to a lowered racial barrier. Employers, responding to the lure of windfall profits, had introduced work speed-ups. Consequently, white workers were frequently faced with Black strikebreakers. Not surprisingly, in 1917 and 1918 race riots and lynchings occurred with some regularity. "That summer of 1917 a

154. Zinn, *People's History*, 353–54.

rash of racial clashes spread through major cities, North and South; Chicago, New York, Newark, Danville (Va.), Lexington (Ky.), Waco (Tex.), and Chester (Pa.). But the worst of all took place in Illinois, in the tough industrial town of East St. Louis."[155] But Blacks in uniform, or at least in the armed services, fared even worse.

As an appendage of the state under the Wilson administration, the American military too had grown even more complacent about its accustomed institutional segregation. As such, the American military mobilization initiated in 1917 had exasperated the army. And the draft and general mobilization required for the war effort had affected millions of Americans. Nearly twenty-four million men were registered in 1917 alone. And now the American General Staff which had jealously guarded its privilege to administer race policies in the services was confronted with a vast sea of Black troops. As Arthur Barbeau and Florette Henri observed, "blacks, who were 10.19 percent of registrants during the entire war, provided 12.6 percent of those actually taken." And the Southern draft boards were no help.

> In the South, blacks provided grossly more than their share. By the end of the war, figures for Alabama, Florida, and Virginia showed that blacks made up more than 30 percent of their total registrants; for South Carolina, Georgia, and Louisiana, more than 40 percent; for Mississippi, 50.42 percent. Five states, all in the South, inducted more blacks than whites; Florida (+900), Georgia (+1,800), Louisiana (+1,200), Mississippi (+4,700), and South Carolina (+7,500). In Clarke County, Georgia, blacks formed 45 percent of those registered, but 58 percent of those mustered into service.[156]

As a consequence of these exercises in racial dominion, nearly 270,000 of the Black troops serving in the U.S. forces would come from the Southern states.[157]

The General Staff was openly hostile to Blacks. Consequently, when forced by public opinion, activists (Du Bois among them), and politi-

155. Barbeau and Henri, *Unknown Soldiers*, 23.

156. Ibid., 36.

157. Nalty maintains that "the number of men assigned to combat units totaled some 42,000, but this represented a bucketful drawn from the vast reservoir of black manpower created by the draft. The total in these organizations amounted to just 11 percent of the 380,000 blacks serving in the wartime Army." Nalty, *Strength for the Fight*, 112.

cians to train some of the Blacks as combat troops (nearly 90 percent of the Black soldiers were in service and labor companies), General John J. Pershing made the decision to attach the Black infantry units (the 369th, 370th, 371st, and 372nd Infantry Divisions) to the depleted French army. Not entirely satisfied that the French would comprehend their new responsibilities, Pershing had Colonel Linard prepare a "read before opening" instruction, "Secret Information concerning Black American Troops." The document prompted French military authorities to manage these Black troops in accordance with official America's wishes and customs: "The approximately 15 million Negroes in the United States presented a threat of race mongrelization unless blacks and whites were kept strictly separated."[158] In July 1919, the French National Assembly ridiculed the document and the Chamber of Deputies passed a resolution reaffirming "loyalty to the immortal principles of the rights of man; condemning prejudice based on religion, class, or race."[159] In combat these Black soldiers performed heroically, receiving individual and divisional awards from the French government. Even the uniformed Black laborers displayed honorable service, providing support for a military establishment little concerned for them. At stateside before being shipped to Europe, Black troops were segregated from the rest of the army; training was minimal, food often inedible, and in some camps there were no tents for quarters and often no uniforms or winter gear. The danger of attack by white civilians or white soldiers was constant; and attempts to secure better treatment were often met with court-martials. And when they returned home, the Black veterans were subject to ongoing investigations by military intelligence, each instance fueled by the presumption that any Black activism for civil rights or fair treatment was the invention of a "secret organization."[160] The return of

158. Barbeau and Henri, *Unknown Soldiers*, 114.

159. Ibid., 115.

160. Nancy MacLean reports: "A 1918 military intelligence report described as 'a potential danger,' not white vigilantes, but the black soldier 'strutting around in his uniform,' particularly if he was 'inclined to impudence or arrogance.' If these men tried to act on 'the new ideas and social aspirations' they had acquired in France, the author declared (in allusion to rumors of romantic liaisons with white women), 'an era of bloodshed will follow as compared with which the history of reconstruction will be a mild reading, indeed.' So alarmed was the Division of Military Intelligence over 'Negro subversion'—defined as black veterans' fighting 'any white effort, especially in the South, to reestablish white ascendancy'—that it undertook a secret

Black veterans was one of the raisons d'être for the increase in lynchings and race riots in 1918 and 1919. In 1918, fifty-eight of the sixty-two lynching victims were Black; in 1919, seventy-seven of the eighty-three were Black (at least ten of whom were in uniform).[161] And in the riots in Washington, D.C., and Chicago in June and July of 1919, when Blacks organized defensive positions against white marauders, the *New York Times* disinterred rumors of the "secret organization."[162]

What is so striking is how few of the racial melodramas broached the subject of the mistreatment of Black troops and Black civilians in this horrendous era. Among the still-lost race melodramas are William Foster's *Mother* (1917) and Peter P. Jones's *The Slacker* (1917). While both films chose Black troops as their protagonists, what dramatic conflict they may have embodied seems forfeited to the melodramatic style and patriotism. Larry Richards describes *The Slacker* as "the inspirational World War I film [which used the] ghost of war past and a sweetheart to convince a young man to join in the war effort"; and he describes *Mother* as a six-reel war drama with "some fifty scenes, 4000 people. Presenting the race of this great World's War."[163]

Adhering to Edwardian social conventions and the Hollywood style, Lincoln's films privileged the rites of passage of young Black middle-class men and women, each constituting the other's reward for initiative and feats of heroism or regained virtue. The only challenge to the existing ruling order was the complaint that some Blacks were deserving of equality of treatment and entry into the approved human family. As Jane Gaines observed, "What was problematic about the black bourgeois uplift philosophy was that the better society it proposed was not significantly different from the one that held all blacks down."[164] The blanket racial characterization of white supremacy was rejected in favor of meritocratic social instruments. Butters, however, fends off criticism of such a social philosophy as exhibiting a species of present-

---

investigation to find out whether they had a collective organization to promote their goals." MacLean, *Behind the Mask*, 29.

161. Barbeau and Henri, *Unknown Soldiers*, 176–77.

162. Ibid., 179, 183. The *New York Times* articles inferring Black conspirators were, for Washington, D.C., "Capital Clashes Increase," July 22, 1919, 1, and for Chicago, "Street Battles at Night," July 29, 1919, 1.

163. Larry Richards, *African American Films*, 155, 117.

164. Jane Gaines, "*Scar of Shame*," 6.

ism.[165] The hegemonic call of the race film melodramas was for complete assimilation into Anglo-Saxon identity and culture. Black Saxonism was imagined and cinematically realized as the ideal status in American society. In both private and public spheres, race melodramas presented characters entirely fluent with the social conventions governing the white middle class, whether it be in professions, lifestyles, family, or intimate relations. A class-based combination of white and Black was Black Saxonism's most covetous ambition. The imagined universe of whiteness invested in these films was, of course, largely an artifice. It normalized the middle class by obliterating all other classes of Blacks (or trivializing them in caricatures or representations of villainy). But it could seem to be authentic because it assumed knowledge of the moral and civil society which reiterated the first order of the racial binary. Like the natural order of race which distinguished whiteness and white-likeness from blackness and Black-likeness, Black Saxonism distinguished and marked the good and the bad in the divisions of labor, social recreation, power relations in the family, and intimacy. The contest between good and evil was easily discerned and evaluated.

But in the end, no matter how compelling their exposition of interpersonal conflicts or how appealing their characters, the best of the race films fell short of Lott's call for a cinema which confronted "the oppressive and self-destructive consciousness the empire seeks to perpetuate." While the Black comedies dared to transgress beyond the boundaries of an imaginary all-Black world, melodramatic race films quarantined their Black subjects from even the suggestion that, outside the movie frame, Blacks were in a struggle for their very lives. Notwithstanding their liberal conceits, race films most likely secured a magic window for their Black consumers, inviting them into a world where racial antagonisms were somehow held in abeyance and ordinary Blacks functioned without constraints in the achievement of their class and material ambitions. Whether in the form of comedy or melodrama, the fabulist world of race films dissolved race by exclusion. Much like the imaginary in the mainstream cinema, they projected a

165. "In my analysis, this should not be a criticism of the Lincoln team, who were operating under enormous pressures both economically and artistically and who were using the medium of film as a tool of empowerment." Butters, *Black Manhood*, 112.

homogeneous society which was consequently untroubled by racial conflict. Such a social construct had no need for Black cinema.

Micheaux's Black Film

Black cinema, an authentically oppositional cinema, required a center, a central, culturally rich terrain at which converged sufficiently vital sources of Black social and political energy and the historical, expressive, and intellectual textures of Black life. It should not be entirely surprising that it was in Chicago that a genuinely Black cinema appeared. While New York hosted its share of Black and faux Black independent film companies, there is some evidence that Chicago boasted a Black audience which expected a more militant cinema. Given the absence of more direct measures of Black public opinion in Chicago, it is still possible to glean something of the maturity of Black Chicagoans in the writings of Black filmmakers based in that city and attuned to that community. In 1915, William Foster (writing under his stage name of Juli Jones Jr.) published these comments in the *Chicago Defender* in response to the release of *The Birth of a Nation*: "In a moving picture the Negro would off-set so many insults to the race—could tell their side of the birth of this great race . . . the things that will never be told only by the Negroes themselves. . . . It is the Negro business man's only international chance to make money and put his race right with the world."[166] Two years later Luther J. Pollard, the Black front for Ebony Film Corporation, maintained that in his company's comedies, "we proved to the public that colored players can put over good comedy without any of that crap shooting, chicken stealing, razor display, watermelon eating stuff that colored people generally have been a little disgusted at seeing."[167] Just like Foster before him, Pollard's comic productions tended to mimic the degrading stereotypes of his white counterparts.

166. Quoted in Bowser and Spence, *Writing Himself*, 97. Cripps provided the following about Foster: "A clever hustler from Chicago, he had been a press agent for the Williams and Walker revues and Cole and Johnson's *A Trip to Coontown*, a sportswriter for the *Defender*, an occasional actor under the name of Juli Jones, and finally a purveyor of sheet music and Haitian coffee. He may have made the first black movie, *The Railroad Porter*, an imitation of Keystone comic chases completed perhaps three years before *Birth of a Nation*." Cripps, *Slow Fade to Black*, 79–80.

167. Quoted in Shipton, *New History of Jazz*, 565. According to Larry Richards, Ebony Film Corporation produced about twenty-seven of these comedies in 1917 and 1918, the only two years of its active film production. *African American Films*, 248.

This seems to be substantiated by *Moving Picture World*'s review of *The Bully* (1918) as "exaggerated slapstick. . . . It is about on the average with the previous issues of this brand and contains some laughs."[168] Nonetheless both Pollard and Foster were sufficiently savvy to comprehend that marketing to Black audiences required the pretense of some racial integrity.

At first impression, Micheaux might appear to have been cut from the same cloth as Foster and Pollard. Since they all can be facilely categorized as Black independent filmmakers, the temptation to which many film historians have succumbed is to cluster them, ignoring their differences. On closer inspection, Micheaux is easily distanced from his peers. Of course Micheaux advertised himself as a race man. And Bowser and Spence, Gaines, Cripps, and others enumerate the multiple instances where Micheaux publicized himself as a filmmaker intent on exhibiting the prodigious promise and achievements of Black people. There was, however, a distinction in Micheaux's sense of his mission which profoundly altered the relationship he sought with this audience. Micheaux insisted on the obligation to display the truth: "I have always tried to make my photoplays represent the truth, to lay before the race a cross section of its own life, to view the colored heart from close range. My result might have been narrow at times, due perhaps to certain limited situations which I endeavored to portray, but in those limited situations, the truth was the predominant characteristic."[169] This ambition pushed Micheaux beyond the puerile huckstering of Foster and Pollard, beyond the "genteel" uplift themes of George and Noble Johnson, beyond the formulaic heroism of Norman's Hollywood imitations, and beyond the alluring melodramas of Starkman. In Micheaux's hands the race film became almost unrecognizable. Of *Within Our Gates*, his second film, Bowser and Spence proposed that

> although Micheaux wrote in 1924 of film as a "miniature replica of life," it is best to think of his works as complex sign systems with both real and imaginary referents, different cultural matrices inter-

168. Larry Richards, *African American Films*, 30.

169. Here Micheaux was responding to critics of his 1924 adaptation of T. S. Stribling's novel *Birthright*. Micheaux's letter was published in the *Pittsburgh Courier* as "Oscar Micheaux Writes on Growth of Race in Movie Field," December 13, 1924; and in the *Baltimore Afro-American* as "Micheaux Answers His Philly Critics," December 27, 1924. See Bowser and Spence, *Writing Himself*, 182ff.

acting, a heterogeneous ensemble. The lavish details are used to tell a story that is not unique but representative of people's broader experiences, familiar landscapes. Not that his story is a singular truth, but rather it speaks to people in a knowing way. Because the multiple lynchings and spontaneous acts of violence . . . were an essential reality for many and a significant part of the Grand Narrative, the horrors of the film were intensified.[170]

Of course, public narratives for many of these social spectacles already existed. In the hegemonic popular culture, Micheaux's subjects—lynching, peonage, rape, Black outlawry, even the mixing of races—had been accommodated to discourses of Negro inferiority, Negro degeneracy, and Negrophobia. So, rather than the fictive and fantastic veils employed by Norman, Levy, and the Johnson brothers, Micheaux plumbed the resistance cultures of common Blacks, the lower classes.

By the time Micheaux resolved to make moving pictures toward the end of the second decade, Black settlements in Chicago were harvesting the creative impulses of many of both the longer term residents and the migrants now streaming into the city. Coincident with the working-class migration which swelled the Black presence (14,000 in 1890, 28,000 in 1900, 44,000 in 1910, and nearly 110,000 in 1920),[171] the Black elite of Chicago strove even more vigorously for a bourgeois identity which frequently mimicked the manners, exclusions, and tastes of a white upper middle class. If Edward E. Wilson is any measure, the elite response to the increase of Blacks in Chicago was a tendency towards even greater exclusion. In 1907, Wilson, a lawyer and politician, published a critique of his community distinguishing between Black "society proper" and a more ostentatious nouveau riche group and complaining that "an excess of democracy existed among Negroes which, though beneficial in some respects, has a fatal policy of dragging everything down to its level."[172] However, more politicized and democratic race agents in the growing Black community encouraged the formation of a coherent and self-conscious Black public sphere.[173] This endeavor acquired

170. Bowser and Spence, *Writing Himself*, 131–32.

171. Gatewood, *Aristocrats of Color*, 122.

172. Ibid., 123.

173. Black elite tastes frequently pertained to Black vernacular music (gospel), ragtime, and jazz: "The black elite encouraged the migrants to admire, play, and listen to genteel white art music and to pursue formal music instruction. . . . Lucien

both monitoring and promotional aspects: it was deemed necessary to tutor the Black working class, ballooned by Southern immigrants, into urban life while simultaneously constructing public festivals and public spaces for the formation of a robust Black civil culture. The pages of the *Chicago Defender* in the early twentieth century provide ample evidence of both impulses. On the one hand, the *Defender* editors and writers constantly took up surveillance of Black public behavior, employing morality tales in the form of editorials, cartoons, letters to the editor, and sermonizing articles.[174] On the other, as early as 1912, the *Defender* publicized and helped organize public events attended by thousands, like the State Street Carnival ("a creative amalgam of Barnum, the Chicago World's Fair, the minstrel show, the county fair, and other commercialized entertainments"), bathing beauty contests, fashion advice, and the like.[175] Such interventions were proffered as templates of Black civic life. They had to compete, however, with more mundane forms of recreation and entertainment generated by the working class. More frequent and exhibiting a seemingly unquenchable vitality, the cabarets, the nightclubs, bars, brothels, and sporting houses (and further south the riverboats) displayed another face of early twentieth-century Black urbanity.

The essence of Black Chicago entertainment was music. At the turn of the century, New Orleans had been the great exporter of blues and ragtime to New York, Chicago, and Los Angeles. In Chicago, by 1900, according to Thomas J. Hennessey, 256 Black musicians (one-fifth of them women) were earning their livelihoods as artists; and in 1902, they provided the membership for the Black Local 208 of the American Federation of Musicians: "A black American could make a living as a musician in Chicago—something that was still rare then even in New Orleans."[176]

White, of the *New York Age*, attacked jazz in 1921 as a symbol of 'unthinking' musicality. In his opinion, the jazz musician did not appreciate 'serious application and hard work. He failed to realize the connection between mentality and musicianship.'" Peretti, *Creation of Jazz*, 61.

174. In 1914, the *Defender* was printing articles critical of Black behavior on the Stroll; in the 1920s, it criticized the frequency of parades in the community, for example; and in the early 1930s, it began printing a series entitled "Folks We Can Get Along Without," which lampooned layabouts in spite of the Depression-racked economy. See White and White, *Stylin'*, chaps. 7 and 8.

175. White and White, *Stylin'*, 181.

176. Hennessey, *From Jazz to Swing*, 23. According to Hennessey, among the most

These were some of the principally migrant musicians who evolved jazz from blues and ragtime by the middle of the second decade of the century. And they were coming to the North at an increasingly rapid pace. John Chilton determined that among 427 Southern Black jazz musicians, "270 (63.2 percent) left the South (the old Confederacy and Missouri) for permanent or long-term residence in the North, Midwest, or West between 1917 and 1930. Another twenty-eight (6.6 percent) had migrated before the general exodus between about 1900 and 1916, and seventy-six (17.8 percent) followed the major group between 1931 and 1941."[177] And they brought their work into the emergent movie industry. Louis Armstrong and Count Basie, for example, played in pit bands in Chicago, providing accompaniment to silent films. In Los Angeles some film companies even brought Black musicians to the studio to play mood music for filming.[178] The Pekin Inn—cabaret, beer garden, theater, and host of the Pekin Players Stock Company (1906)—had opened in 1905, securing for its proprietor, Robert Motts, the reputation of running one of the country's first Black-owned theaters. In February 1918, Manuel Perez's Creole Orchestra was playing at the Pekin Dancing Pavilion. The *Defender*'s report of that event brings delight to jazz historians since it marks one of the first uses of the term "jazz" in print and documents the arrival of the new New Orleans sound.[179] Armstrong played with Joe "King" Oliver's Creole Jazz Band in cabarets and on Okeh recording dates, and soon afterwards with Professor Erskine Tate's Symphony Orchestra at the Vendome Theater. "Tate's strongest competitor was Sammy Stewart's classically-oriented twelve-piece group from Ohio at the Metropolitan Theater. When the Regal Theater opened in February 1928, it featured a twenty-piece orchestra put together by Dave Peyton including men raided from Tate. Smaller theater bands included the septets of Jimmy Bell and Clarence Jones, Wal-

---

successful Black musicians coming to Chicago from New Orleans or the proximate Southern "territories" were pit band leaders Charles Elgar and Dave Peyton; pianists/ composers Jelly Roll Morton and Tony Jackson, and blues singers Lucille Hegamin, Ada "Brick-top" Smith, and Mattie Hite; and on cornet, Louis Armstrong and Joe "King" Oliver (ibid., 23, 24, 30, 34).

177. The data from Chilton's *Who's Who of Jazz* are summarized in Peretti, *Creation of Jazz*, 43–45.

178. Peretti, *Creation of Jazz*, 115.

179. Ibid., 37.

ter Dyett's quartet, and Lovie Austin's duo."[180] But keep the Vendome in mind, for it had already played a significant role in the coincidence of jazz and Black silent films. Some six years before Armstrong joined Tate at the Vendome, Oscar Micheaux had debuted *Within Our Gates* there on January 12, 1920.

The purpose of these recitations is to document the appearance of this extraordinary form in Chicago where Micheaux was formulating his vision of an appropriate refutation of the Dixon-Griffith film. For certain, and for a multiplicity of reasons, he sought to skewer the mimetic social impulses of the Black petite bourgeoisie and its hegemonic model of acceptable ambition. This would be achieved in his contestation with the uplift contraptions of the race film. More substantive and radical was the means by which he shredded the melodrama genre — the favored storytelling device of both the dominant racial narrative and its imitators — by appropriating the melodic and rhythmic constructs of jazz. Here he was employing the expressive voice of a collective Black stratagem of hidden transcripts asserted against narratives of oppression. The convergent negations of race and antiracism, of bourgeois-class arrogance and working-class subjectivity, of "white" conceit and historical realities, of the litany of racial insults exposed to Black nobility, transformed *Within Our Gates* into perhaps the only Black film of the silent-film era.

The historical and technical provenance of jazz determined its form, function, and structure. As composer and ethnomusicologist Earl Stewart maintains, blues, gospel, and jazz retained the basic *call-and-response* binary characteristic of spirituals. The spirituals were the slaves' "sorrow songs," which achieved public notification with the publishing of Frederick Douglass's autobiography in 1845.[181] The blues emerged during the final four decades of the nineteenth century, the secular expression of Black men and women nominally free.[182] The stories unfolding in the blues form concerned the exploitation of labor, racial oppression, and the tragic experiences of love and sex, but the musical structure of the blues retained the binary.[183] The same form

180. Ibid., 70. For the Vendome, see Jacqueline Stewart, *Migrating to the Movies*, 180, 226.

181. Cruz, *Culture on the Margins*, 3.

182. Davis, *Blues Legacies and Black Feminism*, 4.

183. Earl Stewart, *African American Music*, 39ff.

was passed on to ragtime and then to gospel, the religious construct of principally urbanized Blacks in the early twentieth century.[184] In each succeeding form, however, the mechanics of call-and-response became increasingly complex and nuanced. By the time of the appearance of jazz, the "conversational" (improvisational) element of call-and-response had imploded. Each instrument, whether artifact or voice/body, became part of the interactive and signifying praxis. And in his review of Ingrid Monson's *Saying Something: Jazz Improvisation and Interaction* (1995), Guthrie P. Ramsey Jr. captured the totality inherited from the previous forms:

> Monson begins with the notions that musical gestures signify and that African American music in general can be explicated by recognition of its structural, aesthetic, political, and ideological relationship to the dominant culture . . . she provides a close analysis to reveal transformation, irony, and humor as signifying tropes, which, depending on one's "cultural literacy," could be understood as commentary on other works, styles, performances, or on the larger issue of African-American culture itself.[185]

By the time of Micheaux's creative work in films, "the classic-jazz harmonies were basically diatonic, embellished sporadically by secondary structures and occasionally by upper extensions (sevenths, ninths, elevenths, and thirteenths) occurring in or against the underlying harmonies, and especially in extemporized renderings of the melody."[186] In *Within Our Gates* Micheaux would employ counterpart and fragments and scales of counterthemes (i.e., flashbacks within flashbacks) to mark ruptures or interceptions of the melodramatic style, to signify irony and paradox, and to construct alternative narratives, in effect an hermeneutic of the oppressed.

In the spirituals, the slaves had responded to the Christian "call" for Black humility and submission by appropriating biblical narratives of exodus. This resisted the demand of slave discipline with evocations of God's condemnation of regimes of tribal (or racial) oppression and ex-

---

184. "The first key popularizer of gospel music was Charles Albert Tindley (1859–1933). Tindley sponsored concerts beginning in 1902 that spread the gospel style and is also credited as the first person to publish gospel songs that included both text and music." Ibid., 66.

185. Ramsey, "Who Matters?," 213.

186. Earl Stewart, *African American Music*, 106.

ploitation, with tales of organizing armies of liberation and long journeys to freedom. The two voices occupied a Manichaean world where
the good confronted an omnipresent evil which required oppositional
discursive tactics of misdirection and subterfuge. Consequently, the
transparently contrived call of the Christian rationale for slavery was
responded to by the thematic completion of ultimate resolve ("Before
I be a slave, I be buried in my grave"). In the blues, the counterfeiture
of freedom evolved new tales reciting the disappointment, betrayal,
grief, and triumph of everyday life during Reconstruction and the
Nadir. The experiences of the freedmen and their descendants proliferated as the divisions of labor became more complex. While slavery
had been the common denominator of Black artisans, field hands, and
domestic workers, now the blues reflected experiences associated with
laying rails, picking cotton (or cultivating rice, tobacco, etc.), independent farming, domestic service, the intimate sphere of emotional,
gender, and sexual abuse, alcoholism and drugs, rape and abandonment, chain gangs, Jim Crow, and the Black Codes.[187] Notwithstanding
this extraordinary diversity and the burden of accommodating so many
different stories, Stewart declares the blues form preserved the call-
and-response binary and "remained essentially intact since its crystallization during the first quarter of the twentieth century."[188] Established in these two formative languages, the spirituals and the blues,
the Black perception of a world operated and policed by power, hypoc-
risy, and self-deceit persisted.

By the 1920s, American silent films had begun the crystallization of
narrative structure and technique which would later become known as
the classic Hollywood narrative. As Robert Allen and Douglas Gomery

187. The one forbidden subject until the 1960s, according to Adam Gussow, was
lynching: "Unspecified 'hard times' and 'bad luck' are bewailed, after all, in countless blues recordings (such as Bessie Smith's 'poor Man Blues' [1928]) that contest
economic inequality; chain gangs, high sheriffs, big cruel bossmen, and mean old
railroad engineers are apostrophized in ways that can clearly be construed as racial
protest. 'I'm tired of being Jim Crowed, gonna leave this Jim Crow town,' proclaims
Alabama bluesman Cow Cow Davenport in 'Jim Crow Blues' (1929), and to his sectional plaint might be added dozens of other titles, among then Lightnin' Hopkins's
'Jail House Blues' (1949), Kokomo Arnold's 'Chain Gang Blues' (1935), Texas Alexander's 'Section Gang Blues' (1927), Bukka White's 'Parchman Farm Blues' (1940),
Victoria Spivey's 'Bloodhound Blues' (1929), Blue Boy's 'Dyin' in the Electric Chair'
(1929)." Gussow, *Seems like Murder Here*, 18–19.

188. Earl Stewart, *African American Music*, 40.

argue, "The story the Hollywood film relates involves a continuous cause-effect chain, motivated by the desires or needs of individual characters and usually resolved by the fulfillment of those desires or needs."[189] This linear organization of the story-film with its interior explanatory conceits was adapted from nineteenth-century literature and the theater.[190] And the novel, the play, and the film were expressions of the emergent bourgeois culture which required a singular protagonist whose consciousness gave order and meaning to whatever events were encountered or relationships realized. Capitalism sacralized the metaphorical wolf as the most efficient agent in the market, and bourgeois culture costumed the model in an extravagance of materialist rewards and crowned its subject with a Darwinian nobility. Under the discursive reign of the world-system, the American (or "Western") story-film's narrative structure would dominate world cinema for decades. Nonetheless, the style was contrived and not an inevitable construction determined by cinema's capacities. And in the Soviet Union, for one, alternative cinematic styles were being introduced barely a decade later.[191] Even before the emergence of a Soviet film culture, when indeed the total of annual production of race films exceeded the number of Soviet films, Micheaux had transferred to the screen the polyvocal practices of Black musical aesthetics (and speech).

In *Within Our Gates*, from the opening sequences an audience might

189. Allen and Gomery, *Film History*, 81.

190. The genealogy of the narrative was a theoretical formulation drawn from Eisenstein's linkage of Griffith with Charles Dickens in an essay entitled "Dickens, Griffith, and the Film Today," published in Jay Leyda's *Film Form*, 1949. Rick Altman challenged the canonical interpretation which dismissed theater as a seminal source of American cinema: "What Eisenstein claimed in a limited context, others have raised to the level of general pronouncement: a fundamental continuity connects the narrative technique of the nineteenth-century realist novel and the dominant style of Hollywood cinema," and Altman persuasively demonstrates the intervention of stage adaptations as precedents for Griffith and other early filmmakers. See Rick Altman, "Dickens, Griffith, and Film Theory Today," in Jane Gaines, *Classical Hollywood Narrative*, 11ff.

191. James Goodwin asserts that Sergei Eisenstein was not only a major Marxist film artist but also the first film theorist to analyze the relationship between ideology and filmic forms. Eisenstein opposed positive realism (cause and effect) as a proper filmic narrative, employing in his silent films, for instance, montage and representations of collective heroism as alternative (materialist) styles and subjects to the classic Hollywood narrative. See Goodwin, *Eisenstein, Cinema, and History*.

get the impression that Micheaux's theme is Sylvia Landry's (Evelyn Preer) noble renunciation of personal romantic fulfillment for a resolute dedication to her race's uplift. This seems to be almost entirely unrelated to the harsh tones of the opening intertitle: "At the opening of our drama, we find our characters in the North, where the prejudices and hatreds of the South do not exist—though this does not prevent the occasional lynching of a Negro" (explain that if you can!). And from the film's first ten minutes or so, the audience might reassuringly surmise that the provocative advertisements for the film were merely hyperbole. The deliberate lure of the form is unmistakable, inviting us to forgive any momentary transgressions. The melodramatic frame for Sylvia's sacrifice is immediately supplied by stock characters: Alma Prichard (Flo Clements), a scheming, jealous female relative; handsome suitors like Conrad (James D. Ruffin); and incidental male villains. Micheaux further stipulates a privileging of the melodramatic genre by careful casting consistent with previous race films (handsome, light-skinned protagonists), portraits of genteel, costumed Black middle-class characters, sequencing of race-neutral scenes, and filmic cues. Habituated to the genre, the audience (then and now) would have likely succumbed to the familiar structure of the tale in the early scenes: the protagonists (heroine and her distractors), the problem, the quest, the inevitable crisis, and the presumed resolution.

In the first fourteen scenes Micheaux introduces his principal characters: Sylvia, Alma, Conrad, Alma's thoroughly rotten step brother, Larry "the Leech" Prichard (Jack Chenault),[192] and Black police detective Philip Gentry (William Smith). Alma plots to scuttle Sylvia's engagement to Conrad; the Leech hopes to seduce Sylvia while pursuing his nefarious activities and eluding the law; and Gentry pursues the Leech. Scene 15, then, is a startling rupture of the foregoing: Conrad, having returned from his work in Canada, discovers Sylvia having an intimate conversation with a white man. (Alma's machinations have worked to perfection.) Declaring that he will listen to no explanation, Conrad confronts Sylvia and begins to violently throttle the heroine, who is so shocked by his behavior that she is incapable of defending herself. Alma intercedes, saving Sylvia from a certain death; Conrad is devastated at Sylvia's "betrayal" and his own nasty behavior and leaves the city (this

192. In his recording of the cast of *Within Our Gates*, Cripps mistook Jack for his brother Lawrence Chenault. Cripps, *Slow Fade to Black*, 186.

scene is missing from the surviving print). Conrad's sudden physical attack on Sylvia probably alienated the audience from him. Micheaux has exposed the suppressed anger as well as the privileges invested in Black patriarchy which are concealed behind the mannered gentility of the Black middle class. The audience is chastened by the discovery of its self-deception: like the Black middle class itself, where outward appearance has primacy, the audience had taken Conrad's handsome, professional exterior as a signifier for romantic suitability. In actuality he is a patriarchal monster.

Conrad's display of rage partially salvages Sylvia (as a victim of physical violence) but leaves unexplained the apparent compromise of her virtue. Surprisingly, no critics have explored this rupture. Yet it is the first fragment of a crucial countertheme to the melodrama. The white man is Sylvia's biological father, and the only other occasion he is on screen is in the last third of the film, when he attempts to rape her. So as Micheaux's opening intertitle promised, race is ambiguously intruded into the story-film. Yet until the final third of the film Micheaux proceeds as if to restore the film's melodramatic structure. He achieves this by introducing "The Problem": recovered from Conrad's assault, Sylvia begins teaching in a Southern rural school for poor Black children; she discovers the appalling lack of funding for Black children in the South; she travels to Boston in search of support; she is befriended by a Black city thief who then snatches her purse; her purse is restored to her by the heroic Dr. Vivian (Charles D. Lucas); and she and Vivian seem destined for each other.

Sylvia's priority, however, is the plight of the race as manifested in the oft-repeated theme of the need for Black education. This is "The Evil" which fashions Sylvia as a melodramatic heroine representing "The Good." At this point in the film, Alma and the Leech are momentarily set aside as her antagonists. Instead, we are introduced to Mrs. Catherine Stratton (Bernice Ladd),[193] a rich white Southerner who is opposed to suffrage "because it appalls her to think that Negro women might vote." Micheaux now intercedes with coincidence, a convention of the melodrama. Discouraged by her failure to meet possible contributors, Sylvia is sitting on a public bench when she sees a white

193. J. Ronald Green has already noted Ladd's physical resemblance to Lillian Gish, Griffith's principal heroine in *The Birth of a Nation*. See Green, *Straight Lick*, 9–10.

child about to be hit by an automobile. She rushes into the street and pushes the child to safety, only to be struck herself by the automobile. The chauffeur-driven car belongs to Mrs. Elena Warwick (Mrs. Evelyn), philanthropist, who is the passenger, and she then makes certain that Sylvia receives hospital care. In recovery, Sylvia relates her problem to Mrs. Warwick, who resolves to aid Sylvia and her quest for $5,000 for Piney Woods.[194] Sylvia is elated and relates her good fortune to Dr. Vivian, who is obviously ambivalent about Sylvia's return to Piney Woods. But before Mrs. Warwick acts, she seeks advice from Mrs. Stratton who is visiting Boston. Mrs. Stratton assures Warwick that support for Black education is unnecessarily wasteful ("Their ambition is to belong to a dozen lodges, consume religion without restraint, and, when they die, go straight up to Heaven"). As an alternative, Mrs. Stratton suggests that $100 should be donated to Old Ned ("the best colored preacher in the world who will do more to keep Negroes in their place than all your schools put together"). Here, once again, Micheaux ruptures the parent genre to display "Old Ned, as he is."

Leigh Whipper portrayed Old Ned, a character surprising in the texture presented by Micheaux and Whipper. Whipper had attended Howard University and St. Paul's (England) and as a veteran of the Black theater had gone on to many successful years in Hollywood as a character actor. Old Ned was one of his classic performances, rivaling in nuance the role he would later play in the 1943 antilynching film *The Ox-bow Incident*.[195] We see Old Ned teaching his Black congregation the racial virtues, imploring them to forsake schooling and wealth in order to qualify for Heaven. Part of the congregation is ecstatic, others slumber. In their description of Ned's final scene Bowser and Spence are emphatic:

> Ned becomes more complicated at the end of this scene. After he is "playfully" kicked in the butt by his "benefactors" (one of the gestures that clustered around the "Tom" character in minstrelsy), he leaves the office, drops his mask for a moment, and we see in the closer shot of his facial expression, the shame and anger beneath

194. Bowser and Spence note that "the Piney Woods School, where Sylvia teaches, was an actual school, founded in 1909 in Braxton, Mississippi, to provide industrial education for rural Blacks." Bowser and Spence, *Writing Himself*, 137.

195. For Whipper's education and early career, see Curtis, *First Black Actors*, 39–40; and Cripps, *Slow Fade to Black*, 359, 366.

his submissive grin. . . . Micheaux forces Ned out of his "acceptable role" and shows us that in allowing himself to be demeaned, he has betrayed himself and his Race, selling his "birthright" for a miserable "mess of pottage." The character performs the stereotype *and* comments on it.[196]

Actually, Ned could well have been commenting on the majority of roles that Whipper had performed on the stage and would reprise in Hollywood. More pointedly, Ned's self-contempt might well have been a constant current among the larger fraction of Black filmmakers and performers who animated Black representation on the minstrel stage and on celluloid after the demise of George Walker in 1909. On the subject of racial humiliation, their record was quite inferior to that of their contemporaries, the Southern Black preachers who had assisted in the construction of Black communities, schools, mutual aid societies, and the accumulation of real property.[197] The confession, then, might be credited to Whipper himself. On the other hand, Micheaux had balanced his critique of the Black preacher by portraying Reverend Jacobs. Though Jacobs possesses no congregation, with his sister he does constitute one of the noble pillars of Piney Woods. For the racist Mrs. Stratton, however, it is Old Ned who comes to mind as an agent of Black suppression.

The Old Ned sequence is a parable of race betrayal. It not only interrupts the natural flow of the melodrama but constructs a self-standing moral declaration. While the preceding rupture (Sylvia and her father)

196. Bowser and Spence, *Writing Himself*, 152.

197. E. Franklin Frazier reported: "As DuBois pointed out more than fifty years ago, 'a study of economic co-operation among Negroes must begin with the Church group.' It was in order to establish their own churches that Negroes began to pool their meagre economic resources and buy buildings and the land on which they stood." Frazier, *Negro Church in America*, 34. A few pages later, Frazier comments, "The work of the Negro preacher in establishing schools was especially important since the southern States provided only a pittance of public funds for the education of Negro children." Ibid., 40. But like many of the scholars who had earlier drawn highly negative portraits of Black preachers (for example, Frazier cites Benjamin E. Mays and Joseph W. Nicholson, *The Negro's Church*, 1933), Frazier was also highly critical of the "Jack-leg" preachers found among "demonstrative" or "semi-demonstrative" congregations: "The masses of Negroes were still impressed by the ignorant and illiterate minister who often boasted that he had not been corrupted by wicked secular learning." Ibid., 41.

was brief and bereft of explication, Old Ned "performs" and "comments." By the ironic maneuver of introducing conscience into Old Ned, the scene clearly appropriates Mrs. Stratton's apprehension of the Black preacher, transposing her tale of natural Black simplemindedness into a scathing critique of the conceits of white Southern paternalism.[198] It is not, then, what Stratton is telling Warwick but what Micheaux tells his audience which justifies Warwick's determination to contribute not $5,000 but $50,000 to Piney Woods. In his treatment of Old Ned, Micheaux chooses to address his audience directly, momentarily forsaking the filmic illusion of the closed text. In that instance of the sequence, the filmmaker cancels the wall of the screen which separates the spectator from filmed reality. Micheaux will use this device repeatedly in the final third of the film in order to differentiate Black-experienced reality from racial illusion and racist deceptions. Quite obviously these truths are too important to Micheaux to be arrested by obligatory adherence to formal filmic protocols. But at this earlier moment in *Within Our Gates*, Micheaux is content to ignore the break, continuing his tale as if Warwick's resolve requires no justification interior to the plot.

Warwick's charity allows Sylvia to complete her quest, returning to Piney Woods and resuming her role as teacher to her Black charges. This kind of happiness, however, is an insufficient finality to the genre's formula. Either she must end tragically or live happily ever after. And this latter, more acceptable ending is achieved through the intervention of the Leech. Now operating in the environs of Piney Woods, the Leech intercepts Sylvia and threatens to destroy her life by exposing something about her past (presumably the content of the threat is one of the missing segments from the film). Sylvia rebuffs him, but she can no longer remain at Piney Woods, and in the midst of a rain storm (fittingly), she flees to Boston. The Leech has also returned north, and true to his nature, during the commission of a burglary is fatally wounded by Gentry. *Coincidentally*, the wounded Leech is treated by Dr. Vivian. This establishes the rationale for a meeting between Alma and Vivian.

198. "One of the most novel aspects of *Within Our Gates* is its use of stereotypes for sentiments other than simply comic — to demonstrate that stereotypes can be serious and eloquent. Reclaiming the stereotypes in the service of revising the narratives fashioned by members of the dominant group, Micheaux gives these characters back their humanity." Bowser and Spence, *Writing Himself*, 154.

And Alma, confessing her selfishness and jealousy of Sylvia, proceeds to enlighten Vivian about the hidden past of his beloved: "Sylvia's Story," as the intertitle announces.

The presumptive master narrative of *Within Our Gates* concerned the trials of Sylvia Landry, a virtuous young mulatta school teacher. It is startling to an audience, then, that with "Sylvia's Story" Micheaux abandons the melodramatic form entirely. In its stead, Micheaux switches to the social drama, the more appropriate form for his new subject, white racism. Micheaux will pursue this subject matter through a vigorous and directly subversive refutation of Griffith, Dixon, and their racially bigoted confederates in film, stage, and literature. So, while under the regime of the melodrama Sylvia's romantic impulses contradicted the bestial mulatta favored by Griffith and Dixon, Micheaux was engaged in a muted and implicit opposition to Griffith. Now, employing the aesthetics and practices of the social drama, the previously episodic fractures of the melodrama (Sylvia and her father, Old Ned) are merged into the alternative subject. New significations are introduced.[199] But all the elements of the photoplay conspire to exhibit Micheaux's negation of *Birth*'s identification of whiteness with nobility.

Employing the flashback device, Micheaux constructs Sylvia's hitherto hidden past: the legitimate child of a marriage between a Black woman and a white man, as a young woman Sylvia had experienced the lynching of her foster parents (and the attempted killing of her foster brother) and the near rape by her own father, Armand Gridlestone (Grant Gorman)! In this sequence, Micheaux portrayed the bloodlust of a white lynch mob made up of Southern patricians and farmers, women and children. And collapsing two of Griffith's most powerful depictions of Black rapists (the "Gus chase" of Mae Marsh as Flora Cameron, and Silas Lynch's assault on Elsie Stoneman, the abolitionist senator's daughter, played by Lillian Gish), Micheaux begins the preying on Sylvia by Armand as an exterior, and then moving to an interior has Evelyn Preer reenact the trapped Elsie's horror by almost exactly duplicating the histrionic gestures of Lillian Gish in *Birth*. Tear-

199. For instance, in the social drama, education is less an engine of uplift than a political tool. Sylvia employs her education to calculate Jasper Landry's (her foster father) actual earnings as a sharecropper to Philip Gridlestone. Jasper's new knowledge precipitates the crisis with Gridlestone, who continues to insist on his racial and financial prerogatives.

ing at her clothes, it is only at the last moment that Armand, seeing a scar on her breast, recognizes her as his own child and, distraught, halts his attack. Micheaux had sought to rupture Griffith's black bestiary by displaying the cruelty of whites as lynchers and rapists.

Micheaux crosscuts between the assault on Sylvia and the capture and lynching of her foster family. Her foster father, Jasper (William Stark), had been accused of killing the white patrician Philip Gridlestone (Ralph Johnson) by the Black tattletale, Efrem (E. G. Tatum). The audience knows that Efrem is mistaken (Efrem had not seen Gridlestone shot by a disgruntled white sharecropper). And the audience is mollified by the spectacle of the bemused Efrem tumbling down to his twice-erred fate: Efrem first race-betrays the Landrys; and then he fails to register the danger a white lynch mob poses to his own life. At both these junctures, Micheaux directly addresses his audience. Utilizing framed newspaper articles, Micheaux displays one article which totally exonerates Gridlestone from the brutal greed which precipitates his demise; and another article which refers to the lynched Efrem as "the recent victim of accidental death at unknown hands." As a "first draft of history," journalism makes claims for objectivity and truth. Historical truth was the currency traded on by Griffith, Dixon, and Woodrow Wilson while they concocted white fantasies. And Micheaux is dramatizing the discrepancy between the reality of racial experience and a journalism immersed in reproducing relations of power. In the vortex of a racial regime, history, like journalism, must consistently invert reality, making, as Protagoras reputedly practiced, the weaker argument (the lie) appear to be the stronger (the truth).[200] But the Efrem character also doubles Old Ned, asserting Micheaux's disgust of the "loyal" Black servants so beloved by Griffith and Dixon. Efrem wallows in his supposedly privileged status among his white masters ("T'ain' no doubt 'bout it—da whi'fo'ks love me") and is unceremoniously murdered by them, his loyalty rewarded by the white mob in a senseless, unsentimental outrage of his body. But there is one other loyal servant to be dealt with, and in his treatment of the "mammy," Micheaux took his renunciation of Griffith into the realm of sublime cinematography.

In Griffith's sexual economy of slavery and the postbellum, the onus

200. Cynthia Farrar reminds us that "Protagoras was infamous in antiquity for his ability to argue both sides of any question, and to 'make the weaker argument (*logos*) the stronger.'" Farrar, *Origins of Democratic Thinking*, 63.

for miscegenation in the South was entirely identified with the Black rapist. Slavery had generated a white knowledge of blackness which documented its subhuman nature and marshaled the policing of Black desire and savage licentiousness. And with his adoption of the Mammy in films like *His Trust* (1911) and *Birth*, Griffith presented a physical, visual proof that slavery had provided no social context for the suspension of the natural racial laws. He thus obliterated from the historical record what some Southern whites had openly rationalized two generations earlier: that the sexual exploitation of Black women by white men was practical, moral, and a patriarchal obligation. The Mammy exorcised this admission and effaced the historical record: "George Fitzhugh of Caroline County [Virginia] defended the sexual pursuit of Black women as necessary to avoid infecting White womanhood with erotic degeneracy. He praised slavery for allowing slave owners to 'vent their lust harmlessly upon slave women' and contended that slavery protected Black women from abuse by Black men."[201] In the slaveholders' households, domestic service was usually performed by young Black women. The compelling attractiveness of these Black women was memorialized by nineteenth-century American (and European) painters. Eastman Johnson documented the comeliness of the young domestic slaves when he recorded his father's slaves in Washington, D.C. (*Negro Life at the South*, 1859, later entitled *Old Kentucky Home*); and during the Civil War, when he witnessed the arrival of a "contraband" family at an army camp (*A Ride for Liberty — The Fugitive Slaves*, 1862). Richard Ansdell captured the haunting beauty of one Black woman in *Hunted Slaves* (1861). And Winslow Homer's *At the Cabin Door* (1865–66) depicted a handsome young Black woman forlornly watching the forced march of captured Union soldiers.[202] No matter. Griffith's "Mammy," like her fictional predecessor, displaced the real. She became a stock character among similarly grotesque Black domestic servants in American films (and later on television, with characters like Beulah).[203] And her im-

201. Ibid.; Ervin Jordan, "Sleeping with the Enemy," 56.

202. Honour, *Image of the Black*, vol. 4, pt. 1, chap. 3. In the first year or so of the war, Lincoln ordered his officers to treat fugitive Blacks as contraband and to return them to their masters when possible. See Berlin et al., "Destruction of Slavery."

203. As Donald Bogle recalls, "Beulah had been around for years. The character had first appeared on the NBC Radio program *Homeward Unincorporated* in 1939. A few years later, Beulah drifted onto other programs: NBC's *That's Life* in 1943 and then *Fibber McGee and Molly*. Audiences liked the giggly, nurturing maid so much

portant actuality in this mutilated historical memory was eventually confirmed when Hattie McDaniel received the first Oscar awarded to a Black for her Mammy in *Gone with the Wind* (1939).

In *Birth*, Griffith's Mammy (Jennie Lee in blackface) had defended her domestic space and the household of her patrician master, Dr. Cameron. Responding to intrusions of the Cameron domicile by Northern and renegade Black Union troops, Mammy had employed insults. Later, when the Camerons themselves are at risk, Mammy would eventually resort to physical assaults (she wrestles three Black soldiers to the ground). Micheaux, however, effaced Griffith's creature by both the display of white debauchery in the rapacious attack on Sylvia and the extraordinary sequence which was its antecedent: the white mob's week-long hunt of the Landrys; and eventually, *on a Sunday*, the lynching and burning of Mother Landry (Mattie Edwards) and her husband.[204]

Sylvia's family life is shattered by Efrem's false accusation. The Landrys (Sylvia, Jaspar, Mother Landry, and their son, Emil, played by Edward Grant) hide in the swamp, establishing a camp. And at this juncture, Micheaux begins his privileging of the Mammy. Accompanying a close-up of a serene Mother Landry, Micheaux displays an intertitle: "Meanwhile, in the depth of the forest, a woman, though a Negro, was a HUMAN BEING." Here Micheaux is mounting a visual and graphic frontal breach of mammy iconography. He has used the camera to capture a portrait of a beautiful dark-skinned Black woman which colonizes the techniques of lighting, filters, and angles used to idealize many white actresses like Gish, or in the race movies, young, light-

---

that finally in 1945 Beulah was spun off onto a show of her own on CBS Radio." From 1950 to 1953, *Beulah* (starring first Ethel Waters and then Louise Beavers) appeared on ABC television (thus completing the circuit of major networks). Bogle observes: "Beulah, of course, was a type long present in American popular culture: the large, often dowdy, usually darker, all-knowing, all-seeing, all-hearing, all-understanding mammy figure, whose life is built around nurturing and nourishing those in the Big House. Lest she appear as a threat or rival to the white women she works for, the mammy, of course, has to be desexed; thus her large size and darker color. Her asexuality also makes her an ideal mother surrogate." Bogle, *Prime Time Blues*, 19, 22.

204. Mattie Edwards, according to Henry Sampson, had begun her film career with Lubin "between 1913 and 1915. . . . The Lubin 'colored' stock company was headed by John (Junk) and Mattie Edwards, both veteran vaudeville and road-show performers who had been featured with P. G. Lowery's minstrel company." Sampson, *Blacks in Black and White*, 28.

complexioned women. His motion picture camera mimics the portrait style of his contemporary, the Harlem still photographer Van derZee.[205] He thus extracts the Mammy from the lore of plantocratic apologetics, establishing her as not some fictional creature, serving the ideological functions of a fabulous Southern narrative of sexual and racial deceit, but as a mother capable of familial love and anguish. Around her is the evidence of her history: her children, her husband, and their forlorn condition. She is no longer an asexual figment of plantocratic conceit, no longer the ever-jovial and conscienceless faithful servant. Indeed, as the next intertitle establishes, her faith and her loyalty are attached to a vision which far exceeds the mundane tribulations rained down on her family by racial conceits. Thumbing her small Bible, Mother Landry implores, "Justice! Where are You? Answer Me. How Long? Great God Almighty, HOW LONG?" And Micheaux supplies an unequivocal reply. When we next see Mother and Jaspar Landry, they are being prepared for hanging by a lynch mob. Her outer garments torn from her body, Mother Landry stands next to her husband and son. Micheaux has partially exposed Mother Landry's breasts, affirming her sexuality and reminding his audience that Black women were routinely raped in the wake of lynch mobs.[206] The mother and father are not resigned, however. Struggling with their tormentors, the parents manage to distract the mob long enough for young Emil to escape.[207] Then their nooses are drawn taut. They are hung by white justice administered at the hands of women as well as men.

Sylvia's Story ends with Armand Gridlestone's shocked reaction to the realization that he has assaulted and nearly raped his own daughter. The entire sequence has taken up something like twenty minutes. It has been like an extended jazz improvisation, amplifying, to be sure, some of the structures of the prior narrative, but at base effectively subverting and trivializing the melodrama. Because the closed text has been ruptured, we now apprehend that the principal forces acting on our characters are not love, or romance, or jealousy, or even coincidence. Their lives are actually hedged in by a racial conspiracy enforced by

205. Julie Dash pays homage to Van derZee in *Daughters of the Dust* (1991). See Bobo, *Black Women as Cultural Readers*, 133ff.

206. See Royster, introduction, 30; and MacLean, *Behind the Mask*, 144, 146.

207. In the surviving print, Emil's fate is undetermined. Bowser and Spence have published a still of Emil pleading with law officers after his escape, but the scene was not preserved. See Bowser and Spence, *Writing Himself*, 145.

spontaneous acts of violence. In the final two minutes or so remaining to the film following Sylvia's Story, Micheaux halfheartedly strives to re-install the melodrama. Vivian recovers the lost Sylvia and declares his love while spouting racial-uplift non sequiturs.[208] It is a thin evocation of Griffith's conclusion in *Birth*, with Christ on a throne surrounded by celestial beings, all consecrating the white romantic pairing. Micheaux could never hope to reproduce the grandeur of Griffith's production values, but he has achieved his challenge: the association of blackness with American destiny. The sovereignty of the melodrama has been dissolved, however. Neither Griffith's ending or Micheaux's ending can trump the enduring impact of the images of violence and hatred which preceded them. Happy endings, bourgeois couplings, are fake resolutions, an escapist fantasy lacking even the imaginative power to will away the horrific sights and sounds emanating from a society engaged in racial conflict.

In his silent films Micheaux persisted in his employment of elements of Black film. In his two other surviving films, *Symbol of the Unconquered* (1920) and *Body and Soul* (1925), racial conflicts contended with narratives of greed and social parasitism. And in some instances he exercised the grammatical structure found in *Within Our Gates*. Glad-

208. Vivian earnestly declares, "Be proud of our country, Sylvia. We should never forget what our people did in Cuba under Roosevelt's command. And at Carrizal in Mexico. And later in France, from Bruges to Chateau-Thierry, from Saint-Mihiel to the Alps! We were never immigrants. Be proud of our country, always. And you, Sylvia, have been thinking deeply about this, I know—but unfortunately your thoughts have been warped. In spite of your misfortunes, you will always be a patriot—and a tender wife. I love you!" Unless one subscribes to the notion that Micheaux was an incompetent, Vivian's declaration suggests that a portion of the film in which Sylvia's "warped" race politics were made explicit has been excised. If that is the case, then one surmise is that Sylvia had raised troubling questions about justice in America for Blacks. This would accord with the present interpretation of the film. Ruth Vasey has made clear that all silent films were routinely censored, and that the point of censorship varied from intervention by the MPPDA, local authorities, distributors, and exhibitors. Often censors cut scenes offensive to local tastes or even to international sensitivities. Films were even shortened by exhibitors in order to accommodate two-hour program formats. See Vasey, *World according to Hollywood*, chap. 3. Micheaux's experience with censors is recounted in some detail by Bowser and Spence, *Writing Himself*, 15–18; and Green, *Straight Lick*, 208ff. And in this instance, it might well be that Micheaux himself cut Sylvia's criticisms of America from the film in consideration of domestic or international distribution (recall that the surviving print of *Within Our Gates* was discovered in Spain).

stone Yearwood, for instance, recently commented on the filmic style which Oscar Micheaux employed in *Body and Soul*: "Micheaux's cinematic style focused on developing a black visual iconography. . . . The narration begins with a loose plot and conceals a lot of plot information, which is exposed later."[209] While Yearwood proposed this instance as a singular construction of Micheaux, it would appear to encompass several of Micheaux's earlier films. Building on Yearwood's contrast between one Black filmmaker's approach and the "Hollywood classical narrative," it seems that on closer inspection this formulation might serve a paradigmatic function as one of the principles underlying the signifying practices and aesthetics of Black cinema and all liberationist filmmaking.

Yearwood's impression of "looseness" and his discernment of concealment and exposition are, at first blush, incompatible categories, mixing the descriptive with the analytical. Yearwood has juxtaposed the sensory, his sensing of a presentation of a multitude of spatial and narrative elements, with his eventual slide to a conceptual recognition of the filmmaker's intentionality, that is, concealment and exposition. But readings of later films—for example, Julie Dash's *Daughters of the Dust* (1990) and M. Night Shyamalan's *The Sixth Sense* (1999) and *Unbreakable* (2000)—provide evidence of similar stratagems in a later and more highly sophisticated alternative cinema. These later films also suggest the enduring subversiveness of such narrative maneuvers, as well as Micheaux's inventiveness in the earliest era of filmmaking. Whether Micheaux's work operates as a direct, indirect, or entirely unrelated practice for this alternative grammar is less important than the appearance and reappearance of these techniques as markers of departure from dominant cinema.

Like Micheaux, Dash initiates the audience's spectatorship with a series of seemingly scattered and unrelated bits of the film's representations which do not immediately cohere into a narrative whole. As such, Micheaux anticipated, and Dash appropriated, Dziga Vertov's critical reaction to "bourgeois" narrative structure which proposes that the filmmaker place the responsibility for the construction of meaning onto the viewer.[210] Both filmmakers address their audiences with iden-

209. Yearwood, *Black Film*, 34.

210. In May 1919, Micheaux published his manifesto on Black filmmaking, "Negro and the Photo-Play," in *Half-Century Magazine*. Anna Everett commented on

tical propositions: Here are some of the fragments of everyday life as we routinely experience them; what do you make of them? The sovereignty of understanding, the imposition of meaning, devolves onto the audience just as that responsibility is regularly exercised in ordinary experience. But in Micheaux's *Body and Soul* and *Within Our Gates*, and Dash's *Daughters of the Dust*, the centers of these films mat the initiatory bits into recognizable structural meanings which then are finally subverted by inversion.

In Micheaux's *Within Our Gates*, Sylvia's betrothal, her cousin Alma's subterfuge, Sylvia's fiancé's forested seclusion surveying in a foreign country constitute distinct and presumably self-contained moral imaginaries: the romance of wedding and marriage; the melodramatic insertion of an amoral character; the Black professional of racial uplift. Micheaux continually plies us with a profusion of unrelated social markers: a gambler, a detective, a surreptitious interracial embrace, and so on. All of these compete for the sovereignty of meaning until Micheaux weaves them into a still-smattered displeasurable whole: Sylvia is deservedly exposed to her heartbroken fiancé as a cruel flirt by her envious cousin Alma. Little of this survives in the film's penultimate revelations: Sylvia is and has always been virtuous; Alma is redeemed; and the discovered embrace was between an estranged white father and his mulatto daughter.

Dash collages the opening of her film *Daughters of the Dust* with disparate images of what we later apprehend as a similarly challenging narrative of a single Black family's experience of reconciliation and dispersal. Toni Cade Bambara informs us of Dash's deliberate and oppositional appropriation of colonial/imperialist representations of whiteness in the display of a sloop filled with several elegantly dressed passengers gliding serenely along a beautiful river.[211] The passengers,

---

Micheaux's philosophy: "To the extent that he wishes to enlist art in a revolutionary program of sociopolitical transformation, his remarks foreshadow, in some ways, the volatile debates about the best approach to efficacious agitprop films for social reorganization that polarized Sergei Eisenstein and Dziga Vertov in revolutionary Russia nearly a decade later." Everett, *Returning the Gaze*, 134. For Vertov, see Petric, "Vertov, Lenin, and Perestroika"; and Zimmermann, "Reconstructing Vertov."

211. "Following the credits, a boat glides down a thick, green river. Standing near the front of the boat is a woman in a long white dress and a large veiled hat. The image is familiar from dominant cinema's colonialism-as-entertainment genre. But we notice that this woman stands hipshot, chin cocked, one arm akimbo. These ebon-

however, are Black, not white; two of the three women are lesbian lovers; the third is a Christian zealot; and modernity is counterposed to race in the figure of a Black photographer declaring his knowledge of Greek as he amuses his fellow passengers with a kaleidoscope. On the shore we are introduced to a young Black married couple in some distress; an elderly Black woman obsessed with her roots and talisman; another young married couple enthralled with each other; and other numerous fragments of island life. Which is the master tale? How are these vignettes related in time, in space, in social and narrative significance?

The Sixth Sense appears to be an elaborate ghost story. In the film, a child psychologist Dr. Crowe (played by Bruce Willis) is brutally attacked by a former patient. Recovered, two years later Crowe takes on a young patient who is disturbed by sightings of dead people. The dead visit the child, Cole, because they are troubled (for example, a young girl murdered by her mother), and they are beseeching him to use his special gift. Crowe assists the child in reconciling to his visitors, teaching Cole not to be afraid because the dead have come to him for help. As the film ends, Crowe discovers that he is himself one of Cole's ghostly visitors. With Cole's help he has found a way of communicating with his widowed wife. In *Unbreakable*, Shyamalan invites us into the narratives of another horror film (the broken body of a Black infant: child abuse or medical incompetence?) and suddenly propels us into a catastrophe movie (a train which is about to derail), seasoning that seduction by introducing us to a philandering middle-aged man. These, too, constitute a multiplicity of misdirection. The film is actually an interrogation of a pre-Christian, non-Manichaean metaphysics which proposes that the moral universe is a symbiosis of nonbeing (the good) and being (evil). Though raised in Philadelphia, Shyamalan was born in eastern India, in Pondicherry, a place associated with the Vedic Revelations. The plot is Vedic, fueled by a tale of origins which proposed that man's first experience is solitude: "Real anxiety is only fear of fear and thus a dread of utter nothingness. Our own image is frightening when it reflects its hollowness."[212] In his existential solitude, one man (Samuel L.

---

ics signify that filmmaker Dash has appropriated the image from reactionary cinema for an emancipatory purpose. She intends to heal our imperialized eyes." Bambara, preface, xii.

212. See Heehs, *Indian Religions*, 39ff. The quotation is on 40.

Jackson) finds it necessary to discover and then bring to consciousness another (Bruce Willis). As acts of creation, catastrophes pile on catastrophes until the alternative man achieves self-recognition. Like Shyamalan, Dash invites her audience beyond the conventions of Hollywood narrative by alternating the narrative voice of Nana Peazant with that of the Unborn Child. Dash thus evokes a West African Black metaphysics, as Shyamalan had returned to an ancient Indian one.

All three films inaugurate the audience into a cinematic space which is inhabited with alternative significations. The signs deployed by the directors/writers are appropriately fragmentary because the filmmakers are conscious that as such, most members of the audience will recognize the prescriptions and assemble them into appropriate narratives. In the compelling need for meaning and the habituation of the film experience, audiences will grasp at each narrative fragment in a succession of meaning-rewards, as if this were surely what the filmmaker wants privileged. Bambara has asserted that this maneuver constitutes a foundation for "democratic" cinema. As Vertov theorized and Micheaux, Dash, and Shyamalan realize, the Hollywood classical narrative functions as a form of tyranny. It lulls active intelligence into the forfeiture of critical or independent thought by costuming all lived reality into the boundaries of closed narratives. These clusters of meaning are the genres so familiar to film scholars, analysts, reviewers, and spectators: that is, the romantic comedy, drama, melodrama, the Western, the gangster, and so on. Simultaneously, then, the Hollywood classical narrative habituates audiences to the forfeiture of meaning production and transports them to an imagined terrain of social activity. The dominant narrative trope is reductionist: social, structural, or political conflict is dehistoricized and psychologized; collective agency is obviated by individual performance; moral dilemmas are defined from the surveillance point of the heroic will which singularly possesses the capacity for the preservation of the good.

While progressively succumbing to the commercial and aesthetic seductions of the Hollywood classical narrative, Micheaux formalized elements of a resistance cinema. Both his individual films and the long trajectory of his work, each in its own fashion, attest to the conflictual agendas of his sensibilities. On the one hand, Micheaux was fully immersed in the racial uplift movement of the early twentieth century. Yearwood characterizes this aspect as Micheaux's commitment to Black modernism: the forging of a new knowledge of society grounded on the forms of Black "cultural and personal folk expression that had long been repressed."[213] The experience of centuries of domination and exploitation had been countered by the production of diverse liberationist stratagems in Black communities. But whether assimilationist, emigrationist, or separationist, they all shared in the premise that American society was profoundly flawed, that the society as advertised and promoted was in fact a delusion. On that basis Micheaux appropriated the several voices contained in the Black folk traditions (colorism and race consciousness, religious skepticism, racial chauvinism, social uplift, the vigorous prosecution of Black female exploitation, for some examples) eliding their contradictions to produce films which were self-consciously didactic. His silent films were more complex than his later films precisely because their production costs were sufficiently modest to permit his dependence on the Black community. The higher production cost demands of sound films, and the subsequent enlistment of non-Black capital by Micheaux, led to his abandoning his political films.[214] From the early 1930s on, Micheaux would seek to emulate, that is, transfer to his Black audiences, the genre and narrative formulas prescribed in the Hollywood studio system.

Micheaux devoted much of the melodrama in *Within Our Gates* to the explicit publicizing and rehabilitation of the mulatto. This mission, of course, he had already undertaken in his earlier films. It could be almost plausibly argued that Micheaux's casting of light-skinned players was an accident of his recruitment of actors from the professional ensembles like the Lafayette Players, the Ethiopian Art Company, the Dunbar Players, and so on. But while many players in these troupes were light-complexioned, just as often prominent thespians were not.[215] Alternatively, with more plausibility, his casting decisions might

213. Yearwood, *Black Film*, 33.

214. Green disagrees: "Race movies did not 'place white cupidity off-limits' [Cripps's assertion in *Slow Fade to Black*, 260–61]; white cupidity was placed off-limits by white boards of censorship. Micheaux fought such censor boards for years and still managed to treat white oppression both directly and indirectly in films such as *Within Our Gates*, *Symbol of the Unconquered*, *The Girl from Chicago*, *Birthright*, and others." Green, *Straight Lick*, 45. Green has indeed achieved a powerful reclamation of Micheaux's sound films as acts of "cultural autonomy," but it is still apparent that Micheaux's most pointed and *direct* representations of political opposition to white supremacy occurred in his earlier work, in striking contrast to the *indirect* allusions he employed once he was no longer an independent.

215. See Hill, *Pages from the Harlem Renaissance*.

be attributed to marketing considerations; that is, simply employing known names from the theater and vaudeville, or deferring to assumed standards of beauty and attractiveness (for instance, the hiring of untrained Shingzie Howard).[216] Nevertheless, neither accidents of recruitment nor market strategies completely explain the fact that in *The Homesteader* (1919), *The Brute*, and *The Symbol of the Unconquered* (both in 1920), the characters his principal light-skinned players portrayed were virtuous and sympathetic while there seemed to be sufficient numbers of dark-skinned actors and actresses to play his villains and morally ambiguous roles.

More credible is the likelihood that Micheaux had been taken in by the castelike definitions and social patrols established by elements of the Black middle class in the nineteenth century. The most prominent of that stratum, self-identifying as a social elite superior to both Blacks and most whites, had given inordinate value to their mixed-race ancestry, taking particular pride in possessing, as Senator Blanche Bruce's bride was described in 1878, "no visible 'trace of her African ancestry.'"[217] As Henry McFarland observed of this stratum in the *Philadelphia Record* in 1894,

> they have very little to do with the mass of colored citizens except in a business way or by making speeches or addresses to them. With their families and friends these leaders of their race form a society as exclusive as the most fashionable white society, and socially have almost as little to do with their brethren as if they were white, instead of almost so, as most of them are. The colored people do not feel identified with them, and although they are in a way proud of their prominence, they are not fond of them personally.[218]

Micheaux's debt to this creed of the Brown upper class was displayed in both his films and his novels. Janis Hebert commented in an analysis of *The Conquest* (1913) and *The Homesteader* (1917) that Micheaux "on the one hand views himself as being different from or 'better' than other blacks, while on the other hand he castigates the whites for impeding the progress of all African Americans."[219] Ironically, while Micheaux

216. Howard volunteered this information in the 1994 PBS documentary *Midnight Ramble*, Pamela Thomas, producer.

217. Yearwood, *Black Film*, 3.

218. Ibid., 9.

219. The paraphrase of Hebert ("Oscar Micheaux: The Melting Post on the Plains,"

would advertise the social values of this upper class, he was forever disqualified from entry into their ranks by color, ancestry, wealth, or education. Nonetheless, *Within Our Gates* followed the color codes of his earlier and later films: virtue, social responsibility, race loyalty, duty, education, and professional status were reserved for his light-skinned players; while darker actors portrayed the urban working class, rural sharecroppers, and social parasites (storefront preachers, gamblers, muggers, and thieves).

The End of the Beginning

To see Micheaux and the other independent filmmakers of race movies as arrayed against "Hollywood" is an understandable error. It is an erroneous claim, since it begs the question of its premise: what does one signify by the term "Hollywood"? Something called "Hollywood" has existed in the imaginaries of film historians for several decades, consequently haunting cultural authorities. A self-standing, self-sufficient enterprise, Hollywood has seldom been analyzed outside the boundaries of the industrial topography invented to sustain the illusion. Unlike other corporate apparatuses or commercial complexes, early (and later) Hollywood has most often been treated as if it stood in magnificent isolation from the humdrum practices or interests of American capitalism.[220] Like Willy Wonka's chocolate factory, Hollywood's commerce is supposedly transparent: capital accumulation and risk capital (M) → movie production (C) → box office profits (M →), and so on. And inside the box (that is, the studios), where commodities (movies) are produced, according to this model, bosses manage capital and mold artists and technicians into formidable combinations of cultural pro-

---

South Dakota Review 11.4 [Winter 1973–74]: 68) is from Regester, "Misreading and Rereading," 430; and Green's critique of Joseph A. Young's treatment of Micheaux's novels (*Black Novelist as White Racist*) is in *Straight Lick*, chap. 13.

220. Notable exceptions are Stanley, *Celluloid Empire*; Gomery, *Hollywood Studio System*; and Puttnam, *Movies and Money*. Gomery observed in 1986 that "before the coming of television to the US in the 1950s, no industry received more publicity. Newspapers, magazines, and radio alike continually spilled forth gossip, reviews, and advertisements. Specialized fan magazines lined news-stands. . . . But despite this presence, precious little was actually known about the handful of companies which created and marketed nearly all available feature films, newsreels, and short-subjects. Even today, with libraries brimming with surveys of film history and specialized film journals, our accumulated knowledge of these giant corporations hardly fills one bookshelf." Gomery, *Hollywood Studio System*, 1.

duction. This fabulous (imaginary) process strips capital of every competence and every motivation except that of greed (capital accumulation). It also entirely misconstrues the film industry. Douglas Gomery observes that in the 1930s and 1940s, at the height of the "studio system," production (5 percent) and distribution (1 percent) accounted for 6 percent of the total assets of the studios; exhibition (the ownership of movie houses) accounted for the rest. "The amount of capital required for production paled when compared with the cost of financing a chain of several hundred theaters."[221] In short, real estate was the predominant form of capital in the Golden Age of the movie industry. Few film historians, however, find it appropriate to interrogate the implications for movie production beyond the organizational structures of the studios, the eccentricities of studio heads, the prominence and success of certain genres, and the contributions of creative artists.

Film scholars can live with this conceit as long as their herd remains in step. But few inside the production process can afford such naïveté. From the very onset of motion picture exhibition, there has been the persistent need to reckon just what it is that capital requires of the industry and how to deliver it. Some of this sophistication was reflected in the self-congratulatory stories the film industry produced touching backstage theater: in so many of these films a bankrupt company was saved by an "angel" investor who in exchange set a condition. And with respect to the silent-film industry itself, the "angel" (investment houses, banks, financiers) made their conditions apparent as early as the 1910s. As we shall discuss in the next chapter, by the time of the conversion to sound, only from a far distance or the intimacy of a co-conspirator could the Hollywood film industry be seen as a "studio system."

As we have documented in the present chapter, sectors of American capital either transferred to, or enforced, certain social regulations on the early film industry. These concerned protocols of race, class, gender, and authority. Economic and cultural historians have termed the previous era (1870s–90s) the Gilded Age, emphasizing the extraordinary wealth and conspicuous consumption which had been led by magnates like Rockefeller, Carnegie, Vanderbilt, and the like. Black historians, however, named the same period the Nadir, characterizing the dramatic degradation of Black lives during and following Recon-

221. Gomery, *Hollywood Studio System*, 8.

struction. The diametrically different perceptions of the same historical moment provide some clue about the conditions under which these
immense fortunes were acquired. The transfer of wealth from the many
poor to the few rich, oligopoly, did not only involve Black impoverishment. The rural poor were predominantly white laborers and farmers,
and between the late nineteenth and early twentieth centuries, European immigrants and the Asians and Mexicans who served as a rural
labor reserve augmented their miserable legions. Since the political
system was still largely immune from the supplications of democratic
politics, those imperiled, abused, and offended by the Gilded Age were
radicalized. Consequently, by the first decade of the twentieth century,
American capitalists were under siege, floundering between the alter-
natives of violent repression and masquerades of reform. While pallia-
tives like the popular election of senators, the introduction of the personal income tax, and industry regulation were useful to the defenders
of wealth, it occurred to some representatives of capital that a longer-
term solution might be messaging popular culture to achieve the rejection of radical politics and radicals.

As we documented in an earlier chapter, in the last quarter of the
nineteenth century the then-hegemon of American capitalism, the railroad industry and its financiers, was the first to craft a public sphere to
deposit a national identity in the postbellum period. Race, that is, the
white race, served as the explanator for the nation's contributions to
civilization and its achievements in commerce, manufacturing genius,
and the social and industrial sciences. Museums of knowledge, national histories, parades, and public rituals of all sorts signified a destiny made transparent by domestic and then international wars of conquest. World's fairs and regional fairs culled this public sphere for the
first mass spectacles of the new racial regime. With the advent of motion pictures, the whole complex of representations was mimicked on
the screen. And blackface minstrelsy was among them. An even earlier
form of Black representation which, ironically, had gestated within an
immigrant working-class culture of the early nineteenth century, minstrelsy was now appropriated to serve as a race pedagogy for the newer
immigrants.

With the exception of comedies, race movies were seldom exhibited to non-Black audiences. Jim Crow effectively quarantined Black
subversions of screened minstrelsy and was complemented by the
commercial exigencies of mass entertainment. And on the other side

of race segregation, the accommodationists among the Black middle class patrolled the Black "lower classes" and race movies for signs of rebelliousness. When Black nationalism, Black radicalism, Black resistance, or Black insurgencies did erupt, they were either absent or caricatured in race movies. Black melodramas might employ referents to the social ideology of Booker T. Washington, but with respect to the Niagara Movement, the NAACP, Black Socialism, the Universal Negro Improvement Association, or Black resistance to lynching, there was almost a total silence. The one anomaly was Oscar Micheaux. He boldly deployed Black discursive materials to rupture the Hollywood classical narrative. His template for editing his photoplays was jazz. In that maneuver he replicated the subversive acts of his predecessors in Black minstrelsy who had merged earlier forms of Black music to stage critiques of racism. Micheaux's filmmaking, however, could not surmount the powerful forces mobbing against Black film or the extraordinary changes in movie-making. As spokespersons for an "uplift" social program, Black newspapers were fitful in their support of his silent films.[222] And then came the "talkies" and the Great Depression. With respect to these two occurrences, they were evidence of profound changes in the American economy and the capitalist world-system. And the impact they were to have on the representation of Blacks in American movies might make even the most accommodating of the Black middle class nostalgic for Micheaux's infractions.

222. For instance, see Lester Walton's comments on Micheaux's *The Brute* in 1920: "So far as the story which 'The Brute' unfolds, it is neither original nor any too pleasing to those of us who desire to see the better of Negro life portrayed." Quoted in Everett, *Returning the Gaze*, 161.

The Racial Regimes
of the "Golden Age"

If there's one thing I wouldn't want to be twice,
zombies is both of them.
— *Mantan Moreland, in*
      The King of the Zombies, *1941*

The Sounds of Racism

Fourteen years into the sound era, Mantan Moreland's shrouded decla-
mation constituted an astoundingly bold critique of the caricatures
which passed as Black representation in the movies produced and released by the major studios. We shall return to Moreland in due time,
teasing out the subtlety of his resistance. Suffice it to say for the present
that Moreland was publicly rejecting movieland's insulting Black tropes
of the happy slave and the dumb darky. The zombie — dead-brain Black
labor — was as perfect a slave as could be conjured up by a racialized
imaginary.[1] Moreland declared that living as a dead man was not an
option. No fool, he had resorted to an elaborate and imaginative subterfuge — the language of the Negro jester — cleverly costuming his resistance to these dehumanizing Black icons in a comedic trope. After
all, it was 1941. It must have seemed to Moreland and many other Blacks
that nothing in their experience would crack a racial regime which had
received the most emphatic cultural endorsement with the reception
accorded to *Gone with the Wind* two years earlier. A generation later,
following a world war and a postwar social revolution, it was no longer
necessary for film observers to be quite so circumspect.

In the late 1920s sound had opened the studio gates to Black talent. Musicals, the new genre, had made it obvious that few white
actors could convincingly impersonate Blacks and that Black artistry
and Black music were money-makers. Unhappily, this was hardly what
one might consider as even a mixed blessing. Much later, in the 1970s,

1. As early as 1932, in a review of *White Zombies* (United Artists, 1932), "L. N.," of
the *New York Times*, put the matter of zombies rather boldly: "They make good servants. They can carry off blondes without getting ideas in their heads, which helps in
these mad days. When they have served their fell purposes, moreover, they can walk
off high cliffs and out of the picture." "The Screen," *New York Times*, July 29, 1932, 18.

Donald Bogle, at his most generous, could only lament at what was ushered in by the first decade of sound movies. He dubbed the period "the Age of the Negro Servant." Looking back at the 1930s Bogle seems dumbfounded by a genuine wonderment at "all those strange, neurotically engrossing personalities who were thought of fondly despite the fact that they tommed or jermimaed their way through scores of bad movies."[2] That, however, was merely on the surface. A more sinister and persistent current was closer to reality. Inspecting the identical age, Ed Guerrero reported that the imagining of blackness had been dominated by the "plantation genre," a film form which romanticized the antebellum South and rehabilitated slavery: "The film industry began to conceptualize and produce the 'Old South' as an escapist vehicle, a panacea for depression-era anxieties."[3] And even Thomas Cripps, who gave the era's movie industry its thickest analysis, was hard-pressed to extricate virtues from the racist mud. Noting that the beginning of Blacks in sound films was Fox's 1929 *Hearts in Dixie* ("among the best feature-film treatments of Afro-Americans"), Cripps admitted to some disappointment at its reception: "Nevertheless neither black nor white viewers took notice of the missing ingredient in the dramatic conflict — the oppressive system that had put the blacks on the bottom rail. But that would have been asking too much."[4]

Cripps was mistaken. It would not have been asking too much in 1929 when something like 80 percent of American Blacks still lived in the South. As Moreland might have cautioned, there was something deliberately evasive in the film and its reception. The "oppressive system" was peonage, and its existence was well known to Blacks and others. Micheaux knew enough about peonage to expose and critique it in *Within Our Gates* in 1919-20. Given his well-documented marketing instincts, it is hardly imaginable that Micheaux had not relied on his Black audience's familiarity with and hatred of this form

2. Bogle, *Toms, Coons, Mulattoes*, 35, 36.

3. Guerrero, *Framing Blackness*, 20. Guerrero added: "Plantation life was reproduced in romantic, nostalgic scenes of splendorous wealth, cliches such as white-columned porticos, mint juleps, and white ladies in lavish formal gowns. The plantation class in these films spends its time gossiping and flirting at endless parties, balls, and dinners. Nowhere do these slave masters give much attention to what must have been a very demanding business — the punishment, torture, and exploitation involved in the day-to-day affairs of running a slave system." Ibid., 21.

4. Cripps, *Slow Fade to Black*, 241.

of exploitation. However, Blacks were not the only ones in the know. One Justice Department investigator, A. J. Hoyt, concluded in 1907 that "in Georgia, Alabama, and Mississippi 'investigations will prove that 33 ⅓ per cent of the planters operating from five to one-hundred plows, are holding their negro employees to a condition of peonage, and arresting and returning those that leave before alleged indebtedness is paid.'"[5] Pete Daniel documents that the Justice Department had been receiving complaints about peonage for more than twenty years. And Daniel documented how, in the 1920s, notwithstanding the Justice Department's designed indifference, Hooper Alexander, a U.S. Attorney in Georgia, had thought the situation was so desperate that he brought charges of peonage against white planters.[6] Furthermore, cases of peonage had been reported occasionally in the mainstream press. In 1922, for instance, the *New York Times*, the *Florida Times-Union*, and the *Washington Post* published stories of peonage, some of which implicated Florida's governor, Sidney J. Catts.[7] In 1927, on the occasion of the devastation caused by the flooding of the Mississippi River, published reports and formal complaints from the NAACP had forced Herbert Hoover, then Secretary of Commerce, to institute a formal investigation into charges of peonage in Mississippi. In short, peonage was in the public domain.[8] It is not entirely beyond the realm of possibility, then, that in neglecting the subject of peonage in *Hearts in Dixie* the studio and some film audiences were acting out of vested interests rather than ignorance.

5. Daniel, *Shadow of Slavery*, 22. Daniel asserted: "Peonage that existed throughout the American South was most obvious in three patterns. First, the cotton belt from the Carolinas to Texas and including the Mississippi Delta supplied most peonage complaints, a testimony to the enduring plantation system. Second, the turpentine areas of northern Florida, southern Georgia, Alabama, and Mississippi furnished numerous peonage complaints. Third, for a relatively brief time railroad construction camps became the scene of peonage." Ibid., 21. See also Benno Schmidt Jr., "Principle and Prejudice."

6. Daniel, *Shadow of Slavery*, chap. 7.

7. Ibid., 140–48.

8. Daniel observes that the evidence of peonage marshaled by the Colored Advisory Commission was suppressed by Hoover. Walter White reported on peonage in the *Nation* ("The Negro and the Flood," June 22, 1927, 689); and W. E. B. Du Bois did publish much of this material in three parts in the *Crisis* ("The Flood, the Red Cross, and the National Guard," January, February, and March 1928). See Daniel, *Shadow of Slavery*, 163–69.

Hearts in Dixie was the first full-length Black musical produced by a major studio. Released in February 1929, it made it to American screens just a few months before *Hallelujah*, MGM's all-Black musical, debuted in August. Whether because as "audible pictures" they were still unique or because of their "unconventional" casting (the majority of Black characters in big studio films were still non-Black players in blackface), both films attracted comment in unusual places. And thanks to the uncharacteristically close attention of the *New York Times*, we have sufficient details to recognize how these films intersected with the cultural-economic landscape and with each other. Clearly the films shared commonalities, but the significant differences between them concerning their creative inspirations, production origins, and their subsequent realizations served to establish alternative strategies as studio models for Black representation during the sound era. To suggest one difference, the Black rurality, which vested the visual and musical cues of *Hearts in Dixie* with authenticity, would seamlessly ease the transfer of its principal performers (Clarence Muse and Lincoln Perry, a.k.a. Stepin Fetchit) and a faux Black culture to the "plantation genre." On the other hand, *Hallelujah* introduced specific ornaments and conventions of representation of Black urbanity which would reappear in musical features in the 1940s (*Cabin in the Sky*, *Stormy Weather*) and the 1950s (*Carmen Jones*) and in the musical shorts of those decades.

At an historical juncture in America marked by substantial Black migration to the North and to urban areas, the plots of the two films were insinuated into racial conceits necessitated by King Cotton and Southern agriculture. Subscribing to the public belief that cotton production was owed to Black laborers, the films adhered to the protocol of the emergent "plantation genre" in the movie industry by erasing poor white workers. The film industry, having already deemed poor whites superfluous in national memory, proved instrumental in concealing the present capitalist agenda for them. During the 1920s, as Jack Kirby relates:

> In notable advertisements southern companies, trade associations, and governments vied with one another in portraying white laborers (children of the Populist masses) as degraded and docile. The Atlanta Chamber of Commerce, for example, promised prospective industrialists that "in the South, the worker is your friend . . . efficient, willing, Anglo-Saxon." The Carolina Power and Light Company an-

nounced: "you can make it for less in the Central Carolinas," and the Duke Power Company celebrated "willing labor, unhampered by any artificial restrictions output; native born of old pioneer stock and not imbued by un-American [read 'union'] ideas or ideals."[9]

In retrospect, taking pains to conceal the white poor appears a futile instance of "wretched excess." Even while these films were in production, the economy of greed and social anarchy was only moments away from generating the spectacle of mass white poverty captured in the iconic photographs of the Depression. But conventions of racial representation which had persisted for three decades in the imaginaries of filmmakers are not casually disposed of or easily replaced. Cotton cultivation was administered by racial protocols which preserved the subordination of a class while distinguishing nicely between the races on matters of access to violence and other important social rituals. In Georgia, for instance, where cotton amounted to 75 percent of agricultural income, Black sharecroppers and white tenant farmers were the primary producers. And like the Black families depicted in *Hearts in Dixie* and *Hallelujah*, white cotton tenant farmers were mired in economic exploitation and domestic ruin. Tenancy, for example, was more common among whites in 1920 (67 percent) than was the case forty years earlier (in 1880 it was 45 percent); and in 1920, two-thirds of the white tenants were working someone else's land.[10] And the domestic squalor framed by blackness in the two films was just as familiar to rural whites. As Nancy MacLean reported, "As late as 1930, fewer than one in ten Clarke County farm households enjoyed electricity, telephones, or running water. Like their grandparents, most rural people still lived in unpainted houses on dirt roads, drew their water by hand, and travelled by wagon or buggy when need arose."[11] But before the Depression hit the urban working classes, the only contemporary cinematic evidence of the multiraciality of poverty was the prison reform pictures begun in 1930 with *The Last Mile*.[12]

9. Jack Temple Kirby, *Media-Made Dixie*, 45.

10. MacLean, *Behind the Mask*, 37.

11. Ibid., 34.

12. Cripps reported in *Slow Fade to Black* that "among the first, *The Last Mile* (1930), with a bit by Daniel Haynes, and *The Big House* (1930) established a pattern of Negro convicts among the white, and the prototypic crooning black whose plaintive song served as an editorial" (281). Another notable "reformatory melodrama" was *Hold Your Man* (MGM, 1933), which starred Clark Gable and Jean Harlow. In the original,

In each of the Black musicals, the pathetic condition of Black laborers was represented through the narrative convention of privileging the plight of one Black family. The films inferred a rural Black society wasted not by the crushing exploitation of peonage but by a fateful, "natural" poverty. Audiences were assured that cotton production generated no actual riches. From the vantage point of those deposited on the level of the soil and the plant, poverty was as much an aspect of nature as cotton itself. And since slavery, peonage, racial oppression, and segregation were entirely absent from the film, no recognizable history, no specific economic system, no identifiable social order had relegated Blacks to the bottom rung of Southern agriculture. *Hearts in Dixie* and *Hallelujah* were ethnography seasoned with melodrama, minstrelsy performed with interludes of pathos.

In February of 1929, an anonymous reporter at the *New York Times* explained that *Hearts in Dixie* had been originally scheduled by the Fox studio as a two-reel musical short, "merely as a vehicle for offering the singing of spirituals."

> After seeing its first prints [Winfield R. Sheehan, vice president and general production manager of Fox Films] requested J. J. McCarthy to find a story which would fit it. Mr. McCarthy thereupon assigned Walter Weems to write one. Mr. Weems, a Southerner, had had no previous experience with motion-picture production worth mentioning. He had been a vaudeville entertainer, a "blackface" tuba player, who had gone to Hollywood to study the writing of scenarios. The story and dialogue which he turned in for "hearts in Dixie" convinced Mr. Sheehan that the film might go beyond two reels.[13]

In choosing Paul Sloane (essentially a scenarist) to direct the picture, Sheehan persisted in his stratagem of delegating production responsibilities to second-raters, conceding to experience only in his choice of

the Black actor George Reed played a minister whose daughter (played by Theresa Harris) was confined in a multiracial ménage of female inmates (among them at least one Asian woman) including Harlow. In one scene a tearful, hysterical Gable pleads with Reed to perform a marriage ceremony. After drawing the attention of censorship advocates like the National Conference of Catholic Charities, the film was reshot, replacing the Black minister with a white one. See Philip K. Scheuer, "'Hold Your Man' Clicks," *Los Angeles Times*, July 21, 1933, A7; and Scheuer, "Bishops to Consider Cinema 'Black List,'" *Los Angeles Times*, October 8, 1933, A1, A6.

13. "Screen Negro Melodies," *New York Times*, February 24, 1929, 120.

A. H. Van Buren as stage director to handle the coaching and rehearsal of the performers. It must have come as something of a surprise to Sheehan that the critics and reviewers (as well as audiences) received what was effectively an afterthought with enthusiasm.

The film's setting was within a year or two following the Civil War. The central characters in a small, rural, Black settlement of cotton workers are Nappus (played by Clarence Muse), his older daughter, Chloe (Bernice Pilot), and young grandson, Chinquapin (Eugene Jackson). Chloe is married to Gummy (Perry, billed as Stepin Fetchit),[14] whose whimsical aversion to work (or even walking) provides the film both comedy and the starkest reprisal of blackface minstrelsy. Chloe and her baby fall ill with a fatal fever. Gummy's efforts at intervention through the incantations of a "voodoo woman" prove ineffective; and Nappus, who finally secures the service of a white doctor (Richard Carlysle, the only non-Black actor in the film) acts too late. Chloe and the baby die. Bereft of a breadwinner, Gummy remarries. The grief-stricken Nappus, however, resolves that Chinquapin represents the future of his community and will be educated in the North. The film ends with "Nappus on the primitive quayside, tears rolling down his smiling face as he waves farewell to his son aboard the North-bound boat."[15]

Reviewers on both sides of the Atlantic were ecstatic. Almost in unison, they lamented the "slender" plot but insisted that the sheer vibrancy of the performances—whether dramatic, musical, or comedic—launched the film into an unanticipated ascendancy into artistry. In London, *Bioscope* opined that *Hearts* "is surely one of the best films we have yet heard and seen" and observed that "the whole cast just fits into the story with perfect naturalness. There appears to be very little acting."[16] A month earlier, *Billboard* was certain that *Hearts*'s success

14. In 1929, Mordaunt Hall asserted that Lincoln Perry (Hall claimed "Joe Perry") adopted his stage/screen name from a horse. See Mordaunt Hall, "Art in Negro Picture," *New York Times*, March 10, 1929, 131. According to Charlene Regester, Perry's full name was Lincoln Theodore Monroe Andrew Perry, and his father was Joe Perry, his mother Dora Monroe. Regester also reports that Perry himself in 1926 (in his column, "Lincoln Perry's Letter," *Chicago Defender*, December 18, 1926, 7) revealed that his future screen name originated from his stage act (first with Buck Abel and then with Ed Lee), which was known as "Step and Fetch It." Regester, "Stepin Fetchit," 504.

15. Review in *Bioscope* (London), April 3, 1929; reprinted in Sampson, *Blacks in Black and White*, 319.

16. Ibid. By early 1929, American, British, and European critics had been exposed

would be "sure to start a cycle of all-colored pictures" and praised "Slone" and "Van Beuren" for their presentation of "Negro life in the raw, so to speak, showing the happier and more sorrowful moments in the quaint existence that is theirs."[17] In the *New York Times*, Mordaunt Hall also commented on the film's authenticity: "truthful in its reflection of the black men of those days down yonder in the cornfields."[18] Though Hall discerned that the film said something about "the education of the negro," for his own part he was best pleased by its use of spirituals: "Going to see it, after hearing the spiked melodies of modern times [he meant jazz] is an hour of peace."[19] Robert Benchley, writing in the April 1929 issue of *Opportunity*, went furthest of all: "Many people will remember *Hearts in Dixie* as the first talking-picture in which the characters seemed really to talk, and will remember its Negro cast as the first real actors they ever saw in talking-pictures."[20]

The issue of ethnographic authenticity, so frequently asserted in these reviews, is interesting here because it implied historical accuracy. None of the critics appeared distressed or even mindful of the fact that the film depicted a postbellum era at odds with D. W. Griffith's megahit *The Birth of a Nation*—barely fourteen years earlier. Here there were Blacks apparently at peace with their station. In the place of the grotesque, marauding brutes which preoccupied Dixon and Grif-

---

to a spate of musicals. Warner Bros. studio had released Al Jolson's *The Jazz Singer* in October 1927. In October 1928, Universal released *Melody of Love*; Warner Bros. had waded in with another Jolson vehicle, *The Singing Fool* (September 1928) and Fanny Brice's *My Man* (October 1928). In February 1929, MGM released *The Broadway Melody*; Tiffany-Stahl had premiered *Lucky Boy* that same month. Warner Bros. studio's third musical, *Queen of the Night Clubs*, and Paramount's *Close Harmony* were released in March 1929. In January 1929, *Variety* had reported that eighteen musicals were scheduled by American filmmakers in 1929. And Edwin Bradley reports that of the twenty-two musicals exhibited by American studios in the first seven months of 1929, seventeen were based on "backstage" (i.e., entertainment) settings. Bradley, *First Hollywood Musicals*, 25.

17. Sampson, *Blacks in Black and White*, 316–17, taken from *Billboard*, March 9, 1929.

18. Mordaunt Hall, "The Screen," *New York Times*, February 28, 1929, 22.

19. Ibid. For still obscure reasons, Hall took another turn at reviewing *Hearts in Dixie*, praising it as "an outstanding achievement in dialogue and singing." Mordaunt Hall, "Art in Negro Picture," *New York Times*, March 10, 1929, 131. An anonymous report in the paper stated there were thirty-two spirituals performed in the film. "Filming Musical Comedy," *New York Times*, March 24, 1929, 136.

20. Bogle, introduction, xx.

fith, *Hearts in Dixie* proposed that there had been no postwar onslaught against the old system. Now free, the ex-slaves solemnly rededicated themselves to servility even in the absence of masters ("Massa's in the Cold, Cold Ground"), seeking their accustomed and natural level. For American critics, reviewers, and audiences, alike, the power of film to counterfeit the past, to dismember and dis-remember even the most precious historical events is manifestly apparent. While the incongruity between Griffith's Reconstruction and Weems's Reconstruction might have been excused or occluded by an aesthetic sophistication towards film as mere illusion, there still remains the displacement of both films from the remembered experience of still-living survivors. Griffith and his collaborators, at least, had acknowledged the turbulent chaos of those times, only insisting on their own perverse interpretation of the troubles. Weems, however, had totally flushed the horrors away, "screening" his audience from the filth of memory of the racial pogroms coincident with the Civil War and its aftermath. Even Black cultural pundits like Alain Locke and Sterling Brown evacuated historical ground, praising the film as "the truest picturization of Negro life to date" and terming Stepin Fetchit's "Gummy" "as true as instinct itself, a vital projection of the folk manner, a real child of the folk spirit."[21] But not everyone agreed.

Zora Neale Hurston, for one, was appalled at the petitions addressed to the public by Black and non-Black reviewers which asserted the film was culturally authentic and the actors merely playing themselves. Trained as an ethnographer under Franz Boas, in 1926 and 1927 she had conducted field research (funded by Carter G. Woodson's Association for the Study of Negro Life and History and by Elsie Clews Parsons at the American Folklore Society) as part of the Negro Folklore project overseen by Boas. Her mission was to record "the stories, superstitions, songs, dances, jokes, customs, and mannerisms of the black South." And in Florida, Alabama, and Georgia, Hurston documented a vibrant culture far removed from the "quaint existence" impersonated by Muse and Perry.[22] Now in an act of resistance, she took to task the more senior Black literati who participated in the spectacle. She publicly re-

---

21. Alain L. Locke and Sterling Brown, "Folk Values in a New Medium" (1930), quoted in Everett, *Returning the Gaze*, 190–91. According to Hyatt (*Afro-American Cinematic Experience*, 99), the essay was originally published in Botkin, *Folk-Say*.

22. Valerie Boyd, *Wrapped in Rainbows*, 142; see especially chap. 16.

jected their certifications of approval for *Hearts in Dixie* (and *Hallelu-jah*) as displays of disingenuous conceits and ignorance: "The truth is . . . the Negro leaders who champion the Negro's cause at so much per champ, don't know the Negro themselves . . . so flattered [by white attention] that they actually believed that they were authorities on Negro religion."[23] Hurston, on the other hand, was just such an unimpeachable authority.

Hurston's wrath roiled over *Hearts in Dixie* and *Hallelujah* as well as the Black intelligentsia she charged with an obsequious betrayal of real, existing Black culture. She had, it appears, made no effort to distinguish between the two films. Yet there is some evidence that her conflation of *Hearts in Dixie* with *Hallelujah* was not as circumspect, nor in the end, as persuasive as her rebuke of the "collaborators" like Locke, Brown, and James Weldon Johnson. One piece of that evidence is the homage paid to King Vidor by Spencer Williams, and later, Julie Dash. Jacqueline Bobo points out that the baptismal scene of *Hallelujah* is reproduced in Williams's *The Blood of Jesus* (1941) and Dash's *Daughters of the Dust* (1991).[24] Williams, of course, had displayed a serious attention to Black religious devotion in *The Blood of Jesus*, *Brother Martin* (1942), and *Go Down Death* (1944).[25] Dash was equally deliberate, having devoted ten years of research to the achievement of her screenplay.[26] But even in 1929, film reviewers employed very different standards to *Hallelujah* than to its predecessor.

The separation of *Hallelujah* from *Hearts in Dixie* commenced with their radically different inceptions. To put it bluntly, *Hallelujah* was not, like *Hearts in Dixie*, an afterthought by some studio head of how to wring larger profits from a musical short. On the contrary, as King Vidor recalled, his project had been realized despite persistent studio indifference and some overt hostility. *Hearts in Dixie* was a bricolage of

23. "Too Much Pampering of White Writers by Negro Leaders: Zora Neal Hurston Raps Harlem's Literati Who Praise All Nordic Creations on Negroes," *Baltimore Afro-American*, September 27, 1930, 8, quoted in Everett, *Returning the Gaze*, 184.

24. Bobo, *Black Women as Cultural Readers*, 139ff.

25. See Arthur LeMont Terry's doctoral dissertation, "Genre and Divine Causality." Terry also points out that in both *Dirty Gertie from Harlem, U.S.A.* (1946) and *Juke Joint* (1947), Williams addressed "issues of faith and religion in a secularized context." Ibid., 135.

26. Patricia Smith, "A Daughter's Tale: Julie Dash Finally Gets to Tell Her Story of Gullah Life," *Boston Globe*, March 15, 1992, B35.

commodified Black performance (spiritual singers), an imaginary inscribed with blackface minstrelsy (Weems) and exchange-value marketing (Sheehan). The slave past of the spirituals, consequently, was detached and disconnected by being framed by a sham Black universe in which Stepin Fetchit was present as a natural being. The sense that Muse's melodramatic sentimentality was meant to be the center of the film constituted a trick, a mirage produced by the mixing of the forms of melodrama and minstrelsy. Just such a reading of *Hearts in Dixie* might prosper years later, but it was at odds with the film's promotion in 1929: the Fox studio and the exhibitors represented their own construction by advertising that Stepin Fetchit's performance was the principal attraction. Was it really possible that his one previous appearance in a film (*The Ghost Talks*, 1929) had made Fetchit so commercial? More plausibly, *Hearts in Dixie* was concerned with and being sold as blackface minstrelsy. The deliberateness of this star-making, as Cripps noted, could be gauged by the fact that "except for Stepin Fetchit in his shuffling stock character, no black star with a continuing following emerged."[27]

The confluence of historical, cultural, and biographical materials, which provided the grounds for *Hallelujah*, differed on several particulars. From childhood, King Vidor had encountered actual Black people rather than the grotesque misrepresentations which had populated Weems's earlier career. And in lieu of the comedic monotony of caricature, Vidor recalled a broad spectrum of Black cultural practices created to resolve competing and sometimes conflicted interests and intentions. Sixty years after the event, Vidor confided to Nancy Dowd and David Shepard his motivation and long association with the idea for *Hallelujah*:

> In Texas and Arkansas I was constantly with the Negro people and had a very large appreciation of them. Our family employed one Negro woman, and my father had mostly black men working in his sawmills. I saw very much of them as a group. I was very impressed with their music, their feelings, their attitude toward life, their feelings about religion, and their feelings about sex and humor. As long as I can remember I wanted to make a film about them.
>
> This one Negro woman was in our family for years. When she died I had a big desire to dedicate a picture to her. I didn't put the title

27. Cripps, *Slow Fade to Black*, 105.

down anywhere, but it was always in my mind. I listed all of these things that I remembered, things that were marvelous to photograph and make into a film.[28]

Of course, given the long period of its germination, the project had been initially conceived as a silent film. But despite the importance of the project to Vidor, for three years "the studio kept turning the idea down."[29] His studio bosses dismissed Vidor, notwithstanding his already formidable commercial and artistic reputation as the creator of *The Big Parade* (1925)—an antiwar film they mistakenly believed would not prove a box office hit—and *The Crowd* (1928), even then recognized as a critical success. Finally in 1928, while in Europe, Vidor had been informed of the successful advent of "audible pictures." Cutting short his tour with *The Crowd*, he returned to New York to pitch the idea of a sound film to Nicholas Schenck, president of MGM. On the second day of discussions, after Vidor had forfeited his salary and committed some of his own money to the project, Schenck relented, telling Vidor, "Well, if you think like that, I'll let you make a picture about *whores*."[30] To Schenck, Vidor's memorial to one Black woman's faith—framed as a struggle between physical obsession and a moral creed—was simply about Negroes and their sexual depravity.[31]

Hallelujah was filmed on location in Memphis and Arkansas and at the MGM studios in Southern California. Almost in a documentarian style, the location shots in Arkansas (using silent cameras) included

28. Dowd and Shepard, *King Vidor*, 98.

29. Ibid.

30. Ibid., 99. In his 1929 account, Vidor recalled that it was Albert Kaufman who informed him that "the silent picture was finished." He also indicated that it took three weeks to persuade his bosses; a more credible account, since "They consulted newspaper men, exhibitors, anybody, and then decided that 'Hallelujah' wasn't box office and never would be." Philip K. Scheuer, "King Vidor in Fresh Venture," *Los Angeles Times*, October 13, 1929, 15.

31. It is possible that Vidor was less candid in 1929 in his interview with Philip K. Scheuer of the *Los Angeles Times* than he was in 1988. Scheuer reported: "The business superiors were, as the saying goes, leery. Vidor was all right—good fellow, and don't forget 'The Big Parade'—but you had to watch him. His ideas were doubtless artistic enough, but the real gauge was the box office. What about his last big idea, the one that reached the public as 'The Crowd'—beautiful stuff, and exquisitely directed, maybe, but did it knock 'em for a loop? It did not. And now a negro picture? Come, come, King—here's a good lively farce that will suit you right down to the ground; forget the other, and get busy." Scheuer, "King Vidor in Fresh Venture."

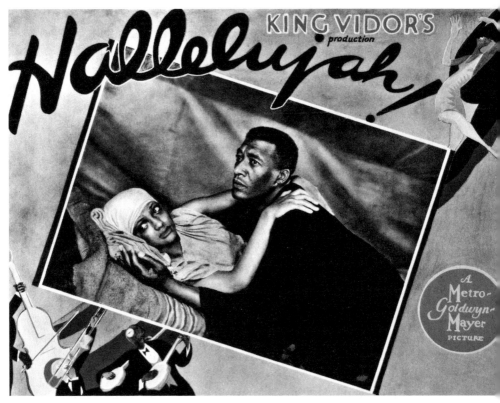

King Vidor's Hallelujah *(with Nina Mae McKinney and Daniel L. Haynes), 1929, MGM.*

scenes of cotton pickers and Black workers operating the huge machinery that bundled raw cotton into bales which then were loaded onto riverboats for shipment to processing mills.[32] At the center of the plot was the Johnson family of eight: an aging mother and father, their five children (three quite young and two older brothers), and an adopted daughter.[33] Mammy Johnson has clearly intended that Zeke (Daniel L.

32. Vidor evidently changed his mind about his location shots, since the *Los Angeles Times* had reported earlier that "cotton . . . is to at last be immortalized in film. King Vidor is filming the entire process of harvesting and ginning cotton on Mississippi plantations as a background for 'Hallelujah,' his new Metro-Goldwyn-Mayer picture, and first all-negro film play in history." "Bosworth Recalls Early Barrymore Associations," *Los Angles Times*, November 18, 1928, C22.

33. Mammy Johnson was played by Fanny Belle DeKnight. Pappy (Parson) Johnson was played by Harry Gray. Reportedly, Gray, a former slave, was eighty-six years

Haynes), the oldest son, will soon be married to the adopted daughter, Missy Rose (Victoria Spivey); and Zeke and Missy Rose seem quite pleased with the prospect.[34] At the end of the picking season, Zeke and the next oldest son, Spunk (Everett McGarrity), transport the family's crop to market. With the family's cash in his pocket, Zeke visits a honky-tonk and is lured by Chick (Nina Mae McKinney), the beautiful young singer/dancer, into a crooked card game with Hot Shot (William Fountaine).[35] Realizing that he has been cheated, Zeke confronts Hot Shot,

old. He was described by Grace Kingsley as a "picturesque character." "A former revivalist preacher, and at present associate editor of the *Amsterdam News*, a negro newspaper published in Harlem, New York, he will enact on the screen a role he long occupied in life." Grace Kingsley, "Warner Arrives Tomorrow," *Los Angeles Times*, October 30, 1928, A8. *Variety* (August 28, 1929) thought Gray was employed as a porter at the Black newspaper. Sampson, *Blacks in Black and White*, 314. Cripps also contradicted Kingsley: "But to the blacks on the *Tatler* he was a fool who 'struts around Harlem in a plug hat and cutaway coat reminiscent of the days when minstrelsy was in flower.'" Cripps, *Slow Fade to Black*, 245.

34. The role of Zeke was originally intended for Paul Robeson. He had a schedule conflict, and Haynes, an understudy in *Showboat*, replaced him. J. Ronald Green observes that "Haynes, who plays the country hick who becomes an urban rube, not only went to the elite black college, Atlanta University, but also the elite white college, the University of Chicago, as well as to Turner Theological Seminary, and the City College of New York." Green, *With a Crooked Stick*, 100–101. Victoria Spivey, according to Grace Kingsley, was an "18-year-old Harlem singer and maker of phonograph records." Kingsley, "Warner Arrives Tomorrow." Another casting change apparently involved Harold Allen "Slickum" Garrison, now a bootblack at MGM studios, whose previous career was in vaudeville. Garrison was originally cast as the film's "heavy," according to Kingsley. It was announced that Slickum would also serve as second assistant director to Vidor: "Vidor chose Slickum for his post because of his familiarity with studio detail and the fact that many of the colored actors never before have been in front of a camera." Kingsley, "Pathe Chooses First Talker," *Los Angeles Times*, October 19, 1928, 10.

35. Nina Mae McKinney, then a chorus girl in *Blackbirds*, replaced Honey Brown, who either became ill or simply lost out in competition with McKinney. (For an early publicity still of Honey Brown and Daniel Haynes, see the *Philadelphia Tribune*, October 18, 1928, 9.) Philip K. Scheuer reported: "The decision as to who, Honey or Nina Mae, would win the part hung fire until the day of the making of the big baptism scene on location near Hollywood. Vidor favored Honey, but he took along Nina Mae anyway. A last-minute phone call to the studio convinced him of the wisdom of this. Nina Mae had been chosen by the powers-that-be." Scheuer, "Fame Calls on Colored Chorus Girl," *Los Angeles Times*, January 20, 1929, C13. It appears that McKinney, reportedly raised on the Edgar Elliot White plantation in South Carolina, was sixteen when she was cast by Vidor and still had not reached her majority when *Hallelujah*

and struggling over Hot Shot's pistol, accidentally shoots Spunk, who, searching for Zeke, has just entered the joint. Filled with remorse, Zeke must now carry his dead brother's body back to their family; and while he declares his contrition to the night sky, he discovers he possesses a power to preach the word.

The family rallies around Zeke, and they begin their sojourn as an evangelist troupe, traveling by train from community to community. During one such stop, fate steps in again, and Chick reappears. Initially contemptuous of Zeke's calling, Chick attends an outdoor meeting and responds to Zeke's message of salvation. Soon after, Zeke performs river baptisms of hundreds, one of whom is Chick. His passion for the woman, however, leads to a second fall, and they run away together, leaving behind Zeke's family and the heartbroken Missy Rose. Zeke becomes a laborer in the lumber mills; Chick becomes bored and re-unites with Hot Shot. Zeke discovers that he has once again been be-trayed and chases the two into a swamp forest. The horse-driven buggy in which they are fleeing overturns, killing Chick. Zeke murders Hot Shot and is imprisoned. With his prison term completed, Zeke returns home, making the long journey perched on the roof of a freight train car. Zeke surprises his family on the road from the cotton fields and is joyously welcomed by his parents, his young siblings, and the ever-faithful Missy Rose.

The film premiered in New York in late August, simultaneously being exhibited at the Embassy Theater on Broadway and at the Lafayette Theater in Harlem. The *New York Times*'s Mordaunt Hall, whose glow-ing review of *Hearts in Dixie* seemed largely attributable to his perverse pleasures in Stepin Fetchit's antics and Hall's distaste for jazz, generally praised *Hallelujah*. Nonetheless, somewhat in character, Hall gener-

---

was making a sensation. During an interview with a reporter, "A telephone call re-minded the little actress that once again she had forgotten to go to the M.-G.-M. school, compulsory for players under 18 years of age." "Religious Ecstasy Genuine," *Los Angeles Times*, October 20, 1929, 26. William Fountaine was a veteran of Black vaudeville, having joined the Smart Set Company in 1913. He remained with Smart Set for five years, later participating in dramatic and musical comedy productions. He had as well recorded with the Black Swan Record Company, either with the Expo-sition Four or as lead tenor of Strutt Payne's Quartet. In 1922 Fountaine had played an important part in Black independent films as a member of Oscar Micheaux's stable of actors, starring in *The Dungeon*, *Fool's Errand*, *Uncle Jasper's Will* (also exhibited as *Jasper Landry's Will*), and *Virgin of the Seminole*, that year. Sampson, *Blacks in Black and White*, 299, 312ff., 344ff., and 512.

ously peppered his review with racist conceits, referring, for example, to "the peculiarly typical religious hysteria of the darkies and their gullibility"; and elsewhere, assuring his readers that "the humor that issues from 'Hallelujah' is natural unto the negro, whether it deals with a hankering after salvation, the dread of water in baptism, the lure of the 'come seven, come 'leven' or the belated marital ceremonies." Forswearing the apparent limitations of black-and-white film stock, Hall points to Hot Shot as a "loudly dressed person" and invents his own colorism as he describes Zeke's having "jilt[ed] a girl, as black as coal, for the chocolate-colored Chick."[36] On the other hand, Norbert Lusk of the *Los Angeles Times* was more respectful of *Hallelujah*, observing that "virtually every critic confessed himself unable to do it justice in the short time at his disposal." Without the slightest sympathetic gesture towards Hall, Lusk characterized the film as "a marvelous portrayal of negro psychology, neither sublimating nor ridiculing the superstitions, religion, sensuality, music and optimism inherent [oops] in all members of the race."[37] Hall subsequently recanted his racist priorities, but only by switching his attention from the "clever negro cast" to Vidor's excellence as a filmmaker. Even then Hall's recurring discomfort with Blacks was apparent. Praising Vidor's detailed documentation of the processing of cotton and lumber and the recording of a prisoner labor camp, Hall lamented, "it is a pity that more footage was not devoted to these incidents instead of using up film in other sentimental bits."[38] Whatever his misgivings, it is interesting that Hall eventually conceded that *Hallelujah* was one of the ten best films of 1929.[39]

By its mid-October opening in Los Angeles, it was obvious that *Hallelujah*'s reception was overwhelmingly positive. James Warnack, a second film critic for the *Los Angeles Times*, shed every shackle of restraint. He began his review, "If art is the expression and interpretation of thought and feeling, then 'Hallelujah,' the M.-G.-M. negro life production at the Palace, is a masterpiece." Warnack insisted that *Hallelu-*

36. Mordaunt Hall, "The Screen," *New York Times*, August 21, 1929, 33.

37. Norbert Lusk, "'Hallelujah' Rings to Sky," *Los Angeles Times*, August 25, 1929, B11.

38. Mordaunt Hall, "Vidor's Negro Film," *New York Times*, August 25, 1929, X4.

39. Mordaunt Hall, "The Best Ten Films," *New York Times*, January 5, 1930, X6. In Germany, the novelist Ernest Toller was to write: "Of the dozens of American sound films I saw, one stood out as a really great work—the Negro film 'Hallelujah.'" "Foreign Notes of the Screen," *New York Times*, June 15, 1930, X4.

jah transcended race: "It introduces the spectator not so much to the colored people of the old South as it reveals him to himself." And chiding "scientists, philosophers, and modern psychologists" for having neglected what is recognizably a Platonic notion, Warnack viewed *Hallelujah* as a reminder of "the foundation of all philosophy and religion": "This fundamental quality of the human soul, this desire for 'life more abundant,' is fully recognized and manifested in 'Hallelujah' and constitutes the grace, power and calm beauty of a production which, without that saving element, would be merely another representation of the sickening human tragedy to which there would be no answer and for which there would be no consolation."[40] Edwin Schallert, also in the *Los Angeles Times*, was similarly impressed. Schallert began his review, "Barbaric, weird, fantastic—an orgy of sight and sound—King Vidor's impression of negro life, 'Hallelujah,' unfolded itself as a strange new experience of the sound-film screen last night at the Fox Palace Theater." But Schallert was not insensitive to the consequence of (white) spectators being subjected to such a raw, unmediated experience of Black sexuality: "Either [*Hallelujah*] will be considered as the maximum of art; or treated as an abhorrent nightmare."[41] While white critics successfully naturalized the peonage depicted in *Hearts in Dixie* and *Hallelujah*, they had not failed to register that Vidor's film was somehow disturbing. Part of the reason was that the dominant constructs of Black identity "picturized" in the two films were so mutually contradictory. *Hearts in Dixie* would propel "zombies" like Stepin Fetchit and Muse into prominence. Contrarily, Nina Mae McKinney was the principal social imprint of *Hallelujah*. This was evident from the media attention devoted to her.

McKinney's stardom was short-lived, of course, because it constituted a paradox to the racial regime in place before the Depression. Her fame was intentional, the consequences unintended. As Reinhart Koselleck observed: "There always occurs in history more or less than is contained in the given conditions. Behind this 'more or less' are to be

40. James Warnack, "Negro Drama Strikes Deep," *Los Angeles Times*, November 3, 1929, B13.

41. Edwin Schallert, "Vidor Picture Unique Event," *Los Angeles Times*, October 18, 1929, A11. Schallert concluded, "This picture, I believe, will not escape offense to many who see it, because of its obviousness in dealing with certain of the sex elements, but for all that it may be almost unpleasant at times; it is strangely powerful in many phases of its appeal."

found men."[42] Reportedly, Vidor's authority over his project was compromised on two occasions, both related to market considerations. In the second instance, Irving Thalberg, head of production at MGM, had inserted Irving Berlin's "End of the Road" into *Hallelujah*. (Vidor confided to Dowd and Shepard: "Even today, if I watch *Hallelujah* and see the Irving Berlin song in it . . . I feel like getting down on the floor and hiding my face because it didn't belong in the picture.")[43] The first intervention, however, concerned McKinney, when "the powers-that-be" overrode Vidor's casting, substituting McKinney for Honey Brown.[44] In succumbing to the dictates of the star system, the bosses at MGM had inserted a profoundly subversive and astonishingly public element into the film. (*Variety* put it candidly: "Perhaps the best way of describing Nina Mae is that she comes closest to being the Clara Bow of her race, so far seen on the screen.")[45] McKinney's Chick, unlike all the mulattas of the silent era who were impersonated by white females (for example, Mary Alden's Lydia Brown in *The Birth of a Nation*), was an unmediated sign. As such, McKinney was a magnet to the critics who variously described her as "yellow" (Hall), "chocolate-brown" (Scheuer), "octoroon" (Schallert), and so on. None of these descriptors could be empirically read from the whites, grays, and blacks on the flickering screen, so they were residues of a racialized coloration. Griffith and Dixon had adjudicated miscegenation as unnatural; Vidor's bosses and Vidor's realization of his homage had instigated miscegenation. McKinney was the critical apparition in what Schallert anticipated would be for some "an abhorrent nightmare."

McKinney's Chick would prove to be an anomaly in American films. For the next decade or more, McKinney's performances, for example, would consist of characters relegated to the Caribbean (*Safe in Hell*, First National, 1931), or Africa (*Sanders of the River*, London Films, 1935), and even minstrelsy (*Minstrel Days*, Universal, 1930; *Pie Pie Blackbirds*, Warner Bros., 1932) by major studios (whether American or British).[46]

42. Koselleck, *Futures Past*, 211–12.

43. Dowd and Shepard, *King Vidor*, 281 (and for Thalberg, 103ff.). All the sound, including dialogue, was dubbed in postproduction. *Variety* reported that "Swanee Shuffle," sung by McKinney, was a second Berlin song. Sampson, *Blacks in Black and White*, 315.

44. On McKinney and Brown, see note 35.

45. Sampson, *Blacks in Black and White*, 314.

46. In his capsule review of *Safe in Hell*, one reviewer (A. D. S.) still remembered

She was accorded some range only in the Black-cast films (like *Black Network*, Vitaphone, 1936) produced by Poverty Row studios in the 1930s and destined for Black audiences. For the major studios there was simply no place for the historical and social complexities signified by an actress like McKinney in their constructions of race and their representations of American life during the Great Depression. The onset of the Depression was not marked by a cycle of enlightened treatments of race, as occurred after World War II. Indeed, the lords of the world-system were in quite a different frame of mind.

As Anna Everett has documented, the Black press was constitutionally incapable of intervening on behalf of the more subversive impulses contained in Vidor's moral inclinations or McKinney's cinematic orthography. The Great Depression had already devastated the few surviving independent Black filmmakers who had been wily enough to compete for Black audiences against the majors. Now struggling for their own survival, the publishers of Black newspapers became more and more accustomed to advertising revenues from the major studios and exhibitors. Consequently, the entertainment pages and columns of the Black press mimicked the performances and reiterated the star-based discourse of the mainstream fan magazines. And once it became apparent that Stepin Fetchit was Hollywood's HNIC (head negro in cinema), the Black press followed suit. Striking an essentially integrationist posture, the entertainment news and copy of Black newspapers were shunted into a movie culture in which the few glimpses of Black talent and creativity were relegated to shorts.[47] Not coincidentally, the overwhelming majority of Black representations were employed in genres implicated in imperialism, colonialism, or white supremacy.

The Counterfeiture of the Golden Age
The advent of sound completed the conversion of the major studios from "independents" to subsidiaries of the dominant capitalist conglomerates in the United States.[48] The change was rather quick and

---

her: "Nina Mae McKinney, the too seldom seen temptress of 'Hallelujah,' as a dark-skinned barmaid, is about the most entertaining item in the film." A. D. S., "In a Crook's Retreat," *New York Times*, December 19, 1931, 16.

47. See Cripps, *Slow Fade to Black*, 219.

48. For an early attempt to document the large capital appropriation of the movie industry, see Stanley, *Celluloid Empire*. More recently, see Puttnam, *Movies and Money*.

quite public, so it is rather startling that so few film historians have registered it. On the contrary, most American film histories concerned with this era are premised on the imaginary "Golden Age" of American movie-making when dictatorial studio heads and their key minions drew up production schedules, imposed managerial agendas, inscribed moral standards, and tyrannized "talent" (writers, directors, actors, actresses, etc.). This myth was the official story. In one form or another, in variants at times imaginative and at others uninspired, this account was repeated in newspapers and fan magazines, in trade papers and studio gossip, and in film hagiographies. It was not true. But it did serve: it shielded the real rulers of American motion pictures from discovery, publicity, and criticism. In their place were the Zukors, the Mayers, the Goldwyns, the Warners, the Laemmles, and so on; that is, prominent (and for the most part) foreign-born Jews, vulnerable to anti-Semitic campaigns and thus eminently compliant to whatever the cultural and ideological needs of their overlords might be.

Spurred by the financial and organizational opportunities presented by World War I, American capitalists had aggressively expanded into the controlling heights in the world market. During the first two decades of the twentieth century, military adventures had brought areas of the Pacific (the Philippines) and the Caribbean (Cuba, Puerto Rico, and Haiti) into the fledgling empire, and the logic of imperialism would inspire similar expeditions to Central America (Panama, Nicaragua, and Mexico), and Asia (China). The war had also instigated the technical development of broadcast equipment and simultaneously brought the control of that technology into the hands of a few corporations: Westinghouse, General Electric, AT&T, and the United Fruit Company. In the postwar era, these interests had incorporated as the Radio Corporation of America (RCA).[49] Of course, their financial and technical resources dwarfed the movie industry. Consequently, when the production of sound film required access to their patents and equipment, and when the industry's theater conversions required massive infusions of capital, the giants consumed the dwarfs, transforming the American film industry into an adjunct, a subsidiary of the multinationals. For years to come, the major decisions about American films would be made in the corporate boardrooms of New York–based investment houses and banks. Just as importantly, it should be understood that a few years be-

49. Barnouw, *Tube of Plenty*, chap. 1.

fore this conversion, the movie industry had itself invented the instrument through which its close supervision and regulation would operate.

In the earliest decades of the twentieth century, the outside attempts to regulate film content were generated from local civic organizations or particularly energetic individuals. These initial protests concentrated on exhibitors rather than producers and spurred actual and attempted censorship by local authorities. One exception, of course, concerned race. In 1912, under the impression that Jack Johnson's defeats of white boxers constituted a threat to white supremacy, Congress enacted a law prohibiting the interstate exhibition of boxing films. Subsequently, civic organizations and local authorities could expend much of their regulatory energies on films exploiting sex. The development of the film industry, however, provided new opportunities for censorship in the post-Trust era. As film production and exhibition became more concentrated, the large studios more visible in the public arena, and the star system an important marketing strategy, producer studios became targeted. The studios were vulnerable. Feature films were more costly to produce than the earlier two-reelers, and the prominence of individual stars opened the industry to the specter of private scandals. In this circumstance, and in response to mounting public attention and calls for federal regulation, in 1922 the studios combined to form a central public relations agency, the Motion Picture Producers and Distributors of America, Inc. (MPPDA).

To head the MPPDA, the bosses of the big studios chose William Harrison Hays. Hays was now postmaster general of the new Republican administration under President Warren Harding. Hays and Harding were from Indiana (coincidentally the state with the most active Ku Klux Klan organization), and though Harding was president, Hays was probably the more powerful of the two. Hays had been in charge of the political machinery requisite for Harding's political emergence and his eventual election as president. As the leader of the Indiana Republican Party and eventually chairman of the Republican National Committee, Hays had groomed his candidate. And now once again in the private sector, Hays chose his aides carefully from among Washington's wise guys. His second in command (the Committee on Public Relations) was Colonel Jason S. Joy, more recently executive secretary of the American Red Cross, but previously a military procurer in the War Department. To head the MPPDA's International Office, Hays selected Lt. Colonel Frederick L. Herron. Herron had been in the diplomatic service before the war, an army officer (13th Engineers and 1st Division) during the war, and served in Army Special Services in Europe in the postwar years. Herron remained in the post from 1922 to 1941, training the New York–based foreign departments of the big studios and facilitating their sales and marketing personnel in Europe and elsewhere. Colonel Edward G. Lowry was the MPPDA's representative in Europe. Lowry was a former military aide to the White House, administered German property in London during the war, and was a journalist and former managing editor of Philadelphia's *Public Ledger*.[50] Together, Joy and Herron drew on their contacts at the State Department and the Commerce Department to support the movie industry, the "selling agency" for American business and products. Multinational corporations and their state adjuncts poised to envelop the movie industry.

The original charge of Hays was to defend the industry from regulation already imposed by several states and municipalities and beat down the crescendo of demands for federal regulation of the movie industry. Hays's strategy was to embrace a legion of civil organizations whose representatives under the authority of the MPPDA would review completed films and provide certificates of good moral standing. Those films found wanting would be returned to the studios for revisions and then MPPDA certification would be granted. It was, however, the ambiguous nature of the MPPDA's function, the increasing interest of big capital in the movie industry, and the energies and ambitions of Hays, Joy, Herron, and others which would fashion the agency into a central administration of American movie-making. The MPPDA had begun as a public relations adjunct of the studios. But shortly afterward the studios themselves lost their autonomy, trading away their independence for infusions of capital (presumably an advantage in their mutual competition) or finally bargaining for access to sound technology and equipment. Since self-deception can be boundless, it is a bit tragic that many of the studio bosses counted themselves fortunate that they were permitted the illusion of autonomy.

Within two years of its inception the MPPDA was beginning to intervene in the actual production of motion pictures. The initial impulse grew from foreign distribution, the purview of Herron and Lowry, and

50. For Hays, Joy, and Herron, see Moley, *Hays Office*, 32–33, 135–36, and 171–72. For Lowry, see Vasey, *World according to Hollywood*, 40.

a market of increasing importance to American filmmakers. By 1927, receipts for foreign distribution accounted for some 30 percent of the American industry's revenues. This alone was an impressive achievement, but in many of the foreign markets the volume of American film exhibition simply swamped national production.[51] Not only were British, French, and German filmmakers upset by their inability to compete with the American product but their complaints were now joined by that of national politicians concerned that the dominance of American films might undermine political institutions, morality, and national culture. Moreover, first in Mexico and then Germany, France, and even Great Britain, concerns were being raised about the characterizations of their nationals in American films. Foreign governments were now considering the banning of American films, or at least the use of quotas to limit the import of them. In 1922, the MPPDA intervened in Mexico. The caricature of Mexicans was a frequent "Hollywood" strategy, and after the Mexican government officially banned American films Hays sent a representative to Mexico City to resolve the controversy.

The most egregiously hateful stereotypes of foreigners were reserved for Germans. Targeted by propaganda efforts of the Allies during the war, Germans were the most frequent foreign villains in Hollywood melodramas and comedies. Despite the fact that the German market for American films was comparatively modest (the United Kingdom accounted for 30.5 percent of Hollywood's foreign revenues; Australasia, 15.2 percent; France 8.5 percent; Germany 5.25 percent),[52] Hollywood responded to Germany's concerns. Not too surprisingly, in the aftermath of the Russian Revolution, Russian villains were substituted for German villains. Notwithstanding the fact that a disproportionate number of studio bosses were from families with roots in Eastern and Central Europe, there was very little sympathy among them for the Russian Revolution.[53] International labor championed communism; consequently, the Russian Revolution was perceived as a threat to Ameri-

51. Ruth Vasey reports, for instance, that in 1925 in the United Kingdom, Australia, New Zealand, Canada, and Brazil, American films constituted 95 percent of films shown in these countries; and in Mexico, Spain, Portugal, and Argentina, the proportion was 90 percent. Vasey, *World according to Hollywood*, 70.

52. Ibid., 85.

53. Adolph Zukor (Paramount) was born in Hungary; Carl Laemmle (Universal), in Germany; William Fox, in Hungary; Louis B. Mayer (MGM), in Russia; Harry Cohn (Columbia) was the child of a German father and a Russian mother; Harry Warner

can capitalism, now the most powerful center of the world-system. On the other hand, Italian fascism had few detractors in Hollywood. Fascism was capital's response to communism, and some powerful Americans even conspired to orchestrate a fascist revolution against Franklin Roosevelt's administration.[54]

In the earlier days of American capital's affection for fascism, Hays was quite pleased that his personal intervention had facilitated the filming in Italy of Samuel Goldwyn's homage to Italian fascism, *The Eternal City* (1925): "We made a picture that pleased Italy, pleased Mussolini himself; and we told the story of Italy as Italy would have it told, that all other nations might understand it."[55] In 1927, Moses Koenigsberg, president of Hearst's International News Service and Universal Service, met with Mussolini and enthused, "I think that Mussolini is the busiest man in Europe and told him so."[56] Koenigsberg was echoing the admiration his boss had displayed for Mussolini since 1922. It was a sentiment also shared by Millicent Hearst, the boss's wife, who published flattering articles on Mussolini in 1930. From 1927 until well into the 1930s, Mussolini was a regular paid feature writer for the Hearst newspapers. Mussolini had admirers like the Hearsts sprinkled throughout the American film industry. Otto Kahn (Zukor of Paramount's banker) was another. So was Joseph Kennedy, who capitalized Gloria Swanson's film company, Amedeo Giannini, whose Bank of America was an early backer of Hearst and MGM, and Nicholas Schenck and Louis B. Mayer of MGM.[57] Neal Gabler notes that Harry Cohn of Columbia Pictures felt a deep identification with the dictator and "had his own office redecorated to look like Mussolini's, right down to the blond, semicircular desk that surrounded him like some massive appendage."[58] Irrespective of their personal attraction to Mussolini, Hearst and his colleagues were not entirely motivated by Mussolini's fascist policies. Mussolini had assumed direct control over the Italian film industry, and Hearst pursued

---

(Warner Bros.), the oldest of the brothers, was born in Poland. See Gabler, *Empire*, passim.

54. Archer, *Plot to Seize the White House*; and Robinson, "Fascism and Intersections."

55. Vasey, *World according to Hollywood*, 50.

56. Pizzitola, *Hearst over Hollywood*, 264.

57. Ibid., 260, 266.

58. Gabler, *Empire*, 152. For more on the affections of Cohn, Hal Roach, Walt Disney, and others for Mussolini, see Horne, *Class Struggle in Hollywood*, 123.

a deal with the dictator to ensure access to the Italian market.[59] In 1927, Hearst's newsreel service (as part of a consortium including MGM and Gaumont) signed an exchange agreement with LUCE, Italy's largest film organization. Thus while MPPDA censors closely monitored films to ensure that no communist messages might leach into scripts, the big studios routinely produced films like Columbia's *Mussolini Speaks* (1933) or *Man of Courage* (1934) celebrating fascism.

When the war propelled American capitalists to dominance at the core of the world-system, the rule of capital was at a critical political juncture. The Russian Revolution had profoundly altered international relations in the West and wherever European powers claimed primacy. Never before in its history had the capitalist world-system encountered a state dedicated to the abolition of private property and the championing of workers. In the Soviet Union, the Bolshevik Party seized on these socialist ideals as its raison d'être, promoting revolutionary movements far beyond the old Russian Empire. In Europe, capitalist interests surmised that workers who had already been exposed to the miracle of capitalism could be politically immunized by fascism masquerading as a workers' movement. However, elsewhere, in Asia, Africa, the West Indies, and Latin America, communist parties inspired by Leninism probed local realities of power in order to overthrow elite classes co-opted by Western imperialism or colonialism. In the peripheral societies of the world-system, where predominantly unskilled workers could produce raw materials, brutal systems of forced labor were camouflaged for the metropole as a civilizing mission of empire. And the inevitable native insurrections in China or Syria or India or Haiti or the Congo or Nicaragua were suppressed by a violence whose savagery was muted by distance from imperial homelands and propaganda. These affairs, conveniently, took place in some exotic jungle far from the citizens of New York, London, or Paris. Those who were targeted were "bandits" or "religious fanatics" recruited from among the darkies or jungle bunnies inhabiting the outlands of the empire. The sanctity of private property, that is plantations and mines, had to be respected. The process of the transfer of civilization to these unfortunates

59. Until his death in 1932, Stefano Pittaluga, the founder of L'Unione Cinematografica Educativa (LUCE), was Mussolini's surrogate in controlling the Italian film industry. Peter Bondanella reports: "After the disappearance of Pittaluga, governmental interventions increased dramatically." Bondanella, *Italian Cinema*, 13.

was inevitably painful but hopefully of short duration. And of course, the darker peoples all over the globe had to learn through experience of the majesty of the white man. Conjoined with the inviolability of the white woman, these were the principles which constituted the "regime of truth" of the white man's burden for much of the twentieth century.

American Imperialism and the Jungle Film Genre

Understandably, some film historians (I have in mind Thomas Cripps and Donald Bogle) when concentrating on the representation of Blacks during the 1930s have drawn attention to the all-Black cast or Black-theme films, *Emperor Jones* (1933), *Imitation of Life* (1934), and *The Green Pastures* (1936). These films were, of course, the exceptions, unique instances in which "Black" themes (respectively, Black self-governance, passing, and Negro religious devotion) were accorded serious or at least considerable attention by major studios (or distributors), providing the occasion for a host of Black actresses and actors to record extraordinary and historic performances. Only for a very brief moment did they stall the relentless juggernaut of Black interiorization. In reference to this onslaught of racial degradation, at least one influential historian (Ed Guerrero) has nominated "the plantation genre" as the modal genre of the 1930s. The first decade of sound films, however, could no more be characterized by such enterprises than *Hearts in Dixie* or *Hallelujah* typified the movies of the 1920s. Indeed, in this previous decade, when the legendary "Hollywood" actually existed, the predominant filmic representations of Blacks for future generations had already been crystallized in a largely neglected genre. One contemporary informant, Floyd Covington, put the matter quite succinctly.

Writing in 1929, and concentrating on the use of the thousands of Black "extras" working in Hollywood, Covington had reported that most were employed "to create atmosphere in jungle, South Sea Island and African scenes as natives, warriors, and the like."[60] Covington was not ungenerous, so he did acknowledge that "others are employed to do individual roles or 'parts' such as mammy types . . . and their names

60. Covington, "Negro Invades Hollywood." In January 1926, fourteen of the largest studios created the Central Casting Corporation to centralize the casting of extras. Covington's assessments were based on data supplied by Central Casting. "The approximate number of Negroes employed through Central Casting is available for the years 1924 (3,464), 1925 (3,559), 1926 (6,816), and 1927 (3,754)." For 1928, the figure was almost three times as large, at 10,916. Ibid., 112, 113, 131.

are included with the other principals in the respective pictures."[61] Covington was reporting something which is now more apparent: that the plantation genre was an "also-ran," for in sheer numbers, savages ("natives, warriors") predominated. Covington's subject was, of course, what is now referred to as the jungle genre. The two genres, however, should not be seen as having been in competition. It was more like each required its own space to enact its report on Black nullity. The jungle film fashioned the present and the quite distant past into a racial pageant. The plantation genre policed the civic body and domestic labor; the jungle film patrolled the frontier. And like distinct organs of state violence, the genres collaborated in general and differed in particulars. The counterfeit of Black speech in the plantation genre, for an example, provided evidence of the small-brained Negro. The cinema's Black dialect had to resemble an organized language so that it could capture fugitive Negro works like the blues and spirituals as the play of children. In the jungle film there was no Black language: the savage speech inhabited a proto-linguistic realm somewhat approximating rudimentary semaphores of insect colonies. The savage of the jungle film was simply a part of the fauna. Jungle films constituted a genre spawned from a specific subtext in the political, economic, and cultural habitat of American movies.

A colonial ambition had been a part of the origins of the United States in the late eighteenth century. The nation's founders had christened their assembly the "Continental Congress," thus announcing their intention to colonize the lands west of the Appalachian mountains—a land of savages. That vast remainder of the continent had been denied the republicans *qua* settlers by the British Crown, which had relinquished (by the Proclamation of 1763) such claims to the original inhabitants, Native Americans.[62] During the nineteenth century, the political and ideological heirs of the new American republic proceeded to abrogate every legal and political impediment standing in the way of the Continental Congress's foundational appetites.[63] In the wake of the near-total expropriation of Native American territory—90 percent, according to Ward Churchill[64]—Manifest Destiny became the

61. Ibid., 111.
62. Zinn, *People's History*, 71.
63. McDonnell, *Dispossession of the American Indian*.
64. Churchill, *Fantasies of the Master Race*, x.

omnibus discourse rationalizing American imperialism. While domestic colonization settled down to a mundane protocol of exploitation, foreign shores excited visions of a Greater America. Within three decades of one another, Hawaii, the Philippines, Puerto Rico, Cuba, Santo Domingo, Haiti, Nicaragua, Colombia, and other lands were subjected to American military or economic domination. Inevitably, certain sectors of American corporate and financial interests were reconfigured to exploit the broadened vistas of American power. One exemplar of this movement of capital was the American-Hawaiian Steamship Company, and by imagining it as one instance among hundreds, we might obtain a sense of the accelerating economic mass of a country where "as late as 1896, except for some railroads, there were probably fewer than a dozen American corporations capitalized at more than $10 million. By 1903, again excepting railroads, there were more than three hundred corporations capitalized at $10 million or more, approximately fifty at $50 million or more, and seventeen at $100 million or more."[65] In such an era, the predatory instincts and appetitive rationales of the American-Hawaiian Steamship Company could be arguably attached to the natural history of the Continental Congress.

The American-Hawaiian Steamship (a corporate entity of Flint and Company; Williams, Dimond and Company; National Sugar Refining Company; and eventually H. G. Lapham and Company) was founded in 1899. And by the onset of World War I, the company owned something like 25 percent of the deadweight tonnage under U.S. registration.[66] Based on the then-novel idea of using ships powered by steam to transport freight between Hawaii and the states and between the

65. William Miller, "American Historians and the Business Elite," 188. Among the largest railroads in 1903, Miller listed the Pennsylvania Railroad ($873 million), the Rock Island Company ($490 million), the Southern Pacific ($460 million), the Atchison, Topeka & Santa Fe Railway ($458 million), the Union Pacific Railroad ($451 million), the Reading Company ($394 million), the Baltimore & Ohio Railroad ($392 million), the New York Central & Hudson River Railroad ($382 million), the Erie Railroad ($372 million), the Southern Railway ($365 million), the Chicago & Northwestern Railroad ($303 million), the Atlantic Coast Line ($297 million), the Northern Pacific Railway ($286 million), the Missouri Pacific Railroad ($233 million), the Chicago, Milwaukee & St. Paul Railroad ($230 million), the Illinois Central Railroad ($226 million), the Great Northern Railway ($205 million), and seven others which topped $100 million. Ibid., 193–94.

66. Cochran and Ginger, "American-Hawaiian Steamship Company," 343. The following description of the company is drawn from this article.

East and West Coasts, the company was capitalized by powerful banking interests: National City Bank, Hanover National, and National Park Bank in New York; Old Colony Trust in Boston; and Bank of California in San Francisco. Among manufacturers employed by American-Hawaiian were Union Iron (San Francisco), Roach Shipyard (Chester, Pennsylvania), and Maryland Steel. Among its partners were the U.S. government's Panama Railroad; Sir Weetman Pearson's London-headquartered Tehuantepec National Railway; and Mexico's own national Ferrocarril. American-Hawaiian subsidized technological developments (the oil burner; flush-decked ships; twin screws); promoted commercial infrastructure (the rebuilding of the San Francisco waterfront after the 1906 earthquake; the Wilmington harbor pier); and even spawned important corporations (Texaco). With powerful friends in Washington, D.C. (President Taft's brother, Henry, and his former attorney general, Wickersham),[67] American-Hawaiian was able to seize on the commercial consequences of the annexation of Hawaii, the development of the Tehuantepec Isthmus railroad, and the Panama Canal to provide substantial reductions in transportation time and freight rates. As was the case in continental America, all these extraterritorial acquisitions required a national resolve to use military muscle to pacify and bring civilization to savages. Consequently, many of the maritime interests of the company coalesced with America's most powerful military service: the U.S. Navy—the most critical agency of early twentieth-century American imperialism.

The jungles of Asia and the forested mountain refuges of the Caribbean and Central America were becoming familiar landscapes to the American public. Lurking in these dark, forbidding places were brooding savages, inhabitants with no recognizable claims to sovereignty or human rights. The unknown was known, however, since language, literature, and mass culture served to merge the savages of preceding eras (Native American, African) with their twentieth-century cousins (Filipinos, Cubans, Haitians, Hawaiians, etc.). It is not difficult to substantiate the broad cultural reach of this new racial catechism. A couple of instances will suffice. At the world's fair in St. Louis in 1904, U.S. marines attacked Filipinos, calling them "niggers"; and in the Philippines, with the American war still unconcluded, white Americans reverted to type:

67. Henry Taft, for a time, was also a director of the Ferrocarril; see Parlee, "Impact of United States Railroad Unions," 470.

as one Black soldier reported to his Milwaukee paper, "They talked with impunity of 'niggers' to our soldiers, never once thinking that they were talking to home 'niggers.'"[68] No wonder, in sympathy with the Filipino cause, "an unusually large number of black troops deserted during the Philippine campaign." One of them, David Fagan, "accepted a commission in the insurgent army and for two years wreaked havoc upon the American forces."[69] The rise of social Darwinism as the master narrative of human history provided the necessary cautionary tales. Savages were peoples arrested in an earlier stage of human evolution. Held back by some critical absence in their own makeup, their fate, at best, was to become wards of the civilized; at worst, to be exterminated. On their own they could make no intelligible demands on (Western) civilization. What would become of them could only be determined case by case, by the extent or degree or obduracy of their savagery, that is, their resistance to benevolence. "Sir Richard Burton felt that the natives of East Africa belonged 'to one of those childish races'; Lionell Phillips wrote of the 'childlike simplicity' of southern Africans; and John Speke declared the average native in the northern part of the continent to be 'a grown child, in short.' Even David Livingstone, perhaps the most sympathetic of the Victorian travellers, regarded his charges in similar terms. 'They are merely children,' he said, 'as easily pleased as babies.'"[70]

The American spokesperson who most perfectly articulated this imperialist discourse was Teddy Roosevelt, the president of the United States from 1901 to 1909. Undeterred by the succession of debilitating shocks experienced by Britain at the beginning of the century (e.g., the Boer War, Queen Victoria's death, World War I), Roosevelt seemed entirely prepared to underwrite (on behalf of the United States) the faltering European responsibility to those occupying the "world's waste spaces." Composing an imperialism from the paternalism entirely familiar to his Victorian predecessors, Roosevelt declared in 1901: "It is our duty toward the people living in barbarism to see that they are freed from their chains, and we can free them only by destroying barbarism itself. . . . [I]t is the duty of a civilized power . . . to put down savagery and barbarism."[71] During his administration it was nigh im-

68. For the fair, see Rydell, *All the World's a Fair*, 177; and for the Black soldier, see Gatewood, *"Smoked Yankees,"* 280.
69. Gatewood, *"Smoked Yankees,"* 15.
70. Dunae, "Boys' Literature," 84.
71. Beale, *Theodore Roosevelt*, 34.

possible to disentangle the ambitions of commerce, finance, and the state. In one small but exemplary instance, Teddy's muscular paternalism towards colored peoples molded American policy in the Dominican Republic. In a tiny, half-of-an-island nation politically deranged by cultural colorism, apparently inexhaustible conflicts between elite families, and competition between American and European businessmen for command of the economy, Roosevelt's public posturings fueled expansionism. The chorus led by American sugar planters and rail interests for the annexation of the Dominican Republic was joined by civilian proponents of American imperialism sending letters to the administration, naval officers dispatching memoranda to the War Department, and government diplomats maneuvering.[72] By 1906, American financial institutions (like National City Bank) legally controlled the republic's budget through the Customs Receivership, while American warships and marines protected sugar production and export from the inevitable deprivations of "banditry." Eventually, from 1916 to 1924, during the administrations of Woodrow Wilson and Warren Harding, an American military occupation followed, precisely what the chorus had demanded.

Rubber replaced sugar in the American scheme to exploit native labor in Liberia. The conduit, however, was finance capital. In 1912, collaborating with British, French, and German institutions, J. P. Morgan, the Kuhn, Loeb firm, and National City Bank had provided a loan of $1,700,000 to the Liberian government. Borrowing a page from the Dominican Republic adventure, a Customs Receivership had been negotiated whereby Liberian revenues were administered by a troika of British, French, and German receivers under an American general receiver. In the earliest years, the Customs Receivership controlled as much as 91 percent of Liberia's revenues.[73] The project borrowed something else from the Dominican Republic. Sidney De la Rue, the American general receiver in Liberia from 1922 to 1928, had been the American military government's auditor, purchasing agent, accountant, and so on in the Dominican Republic from 1918 to 1920. Recruited into government service by the spectacularly racist administration of Woodrow Wilson and now working for National City Bank of New York

72. Rippy, "Initiation of the Customs."
73. Chalk, "Anatomy of an Investment," 19.

"Billiken & Bobby," cartoon, San Francisco Chronicle, *1909.*

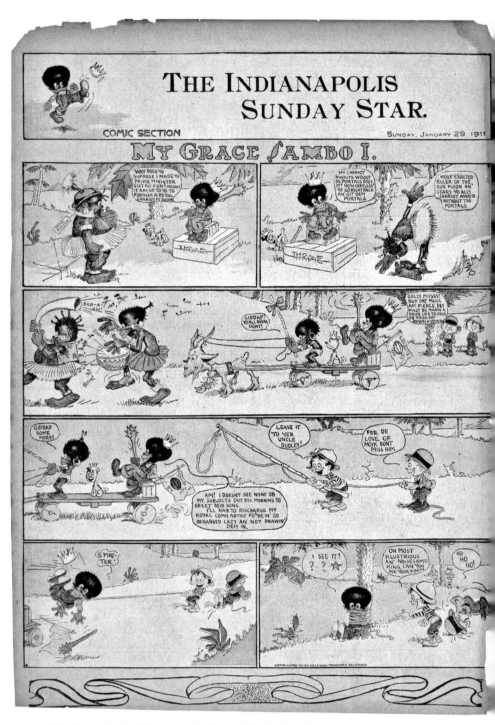

"My Grace Sambo I," cartoon, Indianapolis Sunday Star, *1911*.

as receiver, De la Rue reveled in his dominance over the "idiot" natives in the Dominican Republic, Liberia (and later Haiti), and indulged his own anti-Negro impulses (commenting on Solomon Porter Hood, the Black American who was U.S. consul to Liberia, in an official letter, "You never really know where you are with a Negro. . . . It took him nearly a year to forget he was black the time he first came out").[74] And when the rubber import crisis of the post–World War II years occasioned Firestone Tire and Rubber to attempt to obtain massive fields for rubber plantations in Liberia, De la Rue exercised his natural privilege.

The "Big Four" American producers of rubber products were U.S. Rubber, B. F. Goodrich, Goodyear Tire and Rubber, and Firestone. Between them they produced 55 percent of the rubber products sold in the United States, a market estimated by the Department of Commerce as worth $1,138,200,000 in 1919. Over two-thirds of the rubber imports for the industry came from British colonies in Asia (like Sumatra). When in 1922 the British government acted to limit rubber exports, Harvey Firestone first sought to control his own sources of rubber by investing in the Philippines, and after being frustrated in that effort, turned to Liberia. De la Rue and the Firestone interests, each for their own, and sometimes conflicting, purposes packaged the Firestone concession (a million acres of Liberian land for ninety-nine years) with a $5,000,000 loan which would serve to refund the 1912 loan (and give Firestone or the General Receivership almost total control over Liberian revenues).[75] In late 1926, the deal was signed. And apparently in order to secure the needed labor force for the rubber fields (some 150,000 workers), Firestone induced the League of Nations to expose and halt Liberia's export of native workers to Fernando Po.[76] American financiers, industrialists, and manufacturers, sometimes collaborating with their European counterparts, sometimes not, recruited native workers in Asia, Africa, Central America, and the Caribbean. These laborers frequently worked under murderous conditions. But the exploiters and their cultural propagandists insisted that for savages dehumanizing work was freedom, forced labor the passage to civilization.

The savage, however, also contained a danger, a temptation to de-

74. The letter was to William Castle Jr., Chief, Division of Western European Affairs, Department of State, December 21, 1924. Ibid., 24.
75. Chalk, "Anatomy of an Investment," passim.
76. Sundiata, "Prelude to Scandal," 109.

scend to anarchy, hedonism, and licentiousness. Sympathy for them, consequently, should not be allowed to interfere with generosity. The jungle film husbanded these historical and racial certainties and their accompanying cultural and psychological insecurities.

Kenneth Cameron suggests that, on strictly technical rather than generic terms, the first American-made jungle film was D. W. Griffith's *The Zulu's Heart* (1908).[77] Griffith's film was timely, since South Africa was once again in the news in America in 1908. Both the death of Sir Redvers Buller and the treason trial of Dinizulu were reported in the American press; and both figures were reminders of the Anglo-Zulu (or Kaffir) war of 1878–79.[78] Descended from nobility on his mother's side, Buller had fought for the empire in China, west Africa, and in South Africa (against first the Zulu and then the Boers). On the receiving end of empire, Dinizulu ka Cetshwayo had an even stronger claim to nobility. The son of Cetshwayo, the last king of the Zulu nation, Dinizulu had been at the center of Zulu resistance since the death of his father and his own designation as king (1884). Exiled by the British to St. Helena for several years, he had returned to his native land in 1898 and was now on trial for leading the "rebellion" of 1906.[79] Though South Africa was the setting for *The Zulu's Heart*, Griffith was constitutionally incapable of producing a film which bore any resemblance to South African realities or to the dramatic dynamics of the lives of Dinizulu or Buller. Griffith counterfeited the conflict of invasion, war, resistance, and expropriation by casting white actors in blackface and smuggling in his then-recurrent theme of the loyal slave: "[He] used a white actor in blackface and made his action the saving of a white child and her mother."[80] African agency bedeviled British policy everywhere on that continent, but for Griffith Blacks were merely a passive canvas on which white sensibilities were illustrated. Blacks lacked the imagination or intelligence to portray even themselves. As Franz Boas declared in another context, "unlike causes produce like effects."[81] In the American racial regime, Griffith was a contributor to the erasure or mythologizing (e.g., rape) of Black militancy; in the empire, hatred of the "kaffir" was served

77. Cameron, *Africa on Film*, 97.

78. "Sir Redvers Buller Dies," *New York Times*, June 3, 1908, 7; "Dinizulu's Defense," *New York Times*, August 16, 1908, C8.

79. See Nicholls, "Zululand, 1887–1889."

80. Cameron, *Africa on Film*, 182.

81. Hegeman, "Franz Boas," 461.

by memorializing the Black horde (the war, the "troubles"). Griffith's Negrophobic imaginary was framed by historical particularities (most notably American slavery and postbellum Jim Crow) which concealed from him a discourse (savagery) emanating from the political economy of imperialism. For that reason, *The Zulu's Heart* was not a jungle film, for the jungle film proper co-opted setting, deposing the jungle into a zone for a racial regime fitting to imperialist narratives and appetites.

The literary forefathers of the jungle film genre were H. Rider Haggard (*King Solomon's Mines, She, Allan Quatermain*), Edgar Wallace (*Sanders of the River*), and Edgar Rice Burroughs (*Tarzan of the Apes*).[82] The immediate precursor of the jungle film genre in popular culture was British imperial literature. And Haggard and Wallace were creatures of the "juvenile" or boys' magazines, which after 1880 came to dominate imperial literature: "The adventure novels sold in their thousands; the penny weeklies in their millions."[83] Haggard was an important contributor to these publications (along with G. A. Henty, Gordon Staples, etc.); and Wallace quite obviously imbibed the heady brew.[84] In the sedate pages of *The Boy's Own Paper* (1879–1967), *Chums* (1892–1934), *Boys of Our Empire* (1900–1903), *The Captain* (1899–1924), and their stentorian "penny-dreadful" counterparts (e.g., *The Boys' Friend*),

82. Born in Britain (1856), Haggard first went to Natal in 1875. He published *King Solomon's Mines* in 1885; and *She* and *Allan Quatermain* in 1887. Haggard's African novels were influenced by the European encounter with the ruins of Great Zimbabwe (1871), the first European excavations of diamonds in South Africa (1870), and the older legends of the Queen of Sheba. Martin Hall, "Legend of the Lost City," 186ff.; and Cameron, *Africa on Film*, 24. Wallace, also born in Britain (1875), was serving in the British army when he was sent to South Africa in 1896. Later, he was the editor of the *Rand Daily Mail*. He eventually returned to Britain, working as a journalist. In 1909, he began publishing a series of colonial stories, "Sanders of the River." This led to the publication of *Sanders of the River* in 1911. See Adrian, *Edgar Wallace*. Burroughs was born in Chicago in 1875. But unlike Haggard and Wallace, he never visited Africa (despite "research" on Africa in the Chicago Library, he initially included tigers in his African jungle). After several desultory careers, he began publishing serials in boys' magazines in 1911. In 1912, "Tarzan of the Apes" was accepted for publication in *All-Story* magazine; and it was published as a book in 1914. See Porges, *Edgar Rice Burroughs*, 1:213ff.

83. Dunae, "Boys' Literature," 106.

84. MacDonald, "Reproducing the Middle-Class Boy." Complementing the propaganda literature were the formations of paramilitary youth movements like the Cadet forces, the Boys' Brigade, the Boy Scouts, the Church Lads, the Empire Day Movement, and the like. Ibid., 526.

the male children of the middle and working classes were instructed in what constituted the differences between British character and the denizens of the empire.[85] Haggard and Wallace were profoundly immersed, culturally and psychologically, in colonial South Africa and the production of racial oppression. Their reactions to these influences were related but different. While Haggard pursued a radical vein of racial invention, Wallace adhered rather more closely to the racial conceits which assembled and lubricated the British machinery of indirect rule. Nevertheless, the cultural impact of the ritualization of their tales exposed many in England and America to the presumption that Africa belonged to the whites. We might surmise that one such convert was the young Hugh Trevor-Roper. Later, as an eminent British historian (inevitably advanced to Lord Calvert), Trevor-Roper declared:

> Perhaps, in the future, there will be some African history to teach. But at present there is none: there is only the history of the Europeans in Africa. The rest is darkness, like the history of pre-European, pre-Columbian America. And darkness is not a subject of history. Please do not misunderstand me. I do not deny that men existed even in dark countries and dark centuries, nor that they had political life and culture, interesting to sociologists and anthropologists; but history, I believe is essentially a form of movement, and purposive movement too.[86]

Given that his principal narrative was "the rise of Christian Europe," it was almost axiomatic that a tale concerning the origins of one civilization (the West) would require the total negation of modernity's Other. Trevor-Roper's remarks were merely emblematic of generations of Western scribes who ferreted around the human past like burglars. Consequently, for generations African history had no place in the modern European or American academies, because it would constitute a countertext to colonialism and imperialism. It was the same in popular culture. Accordingly, in both arenas, African history was concealed behind a liturgical wall of racial fantasies. African history was displaced by the myth of an alternative (white) past. Contemporaneously, while European antiquarians were "Aryanizing" ancient African history,[87]

85. Dunae, "Boys' Literature."
86. Trevor-Roper, "Rise of Christian Europe."
87. Bernal, *Black Athena*.

writides like Haggard were imagining audacious reinventions of the past.

In the most remote mountains and valleys of pre-Africa, Haggard imagined the existence of an ancient white civilization of prodigious learning, powerful spiritual mysteries, and fabulous wealth. Such a mythical space was the compelling subtext of *King Solomon's Mines*, *She*, and *Allan Quatermain*. In *She*, Haggard deposited the Kor civilization. In his racialized imagination, the mythical civilization of Kor had existed for nearly five thousand years before its people were totally ravaged by a plague: "One with another," a long-deceased Kor priest recorded, "they turned black and died."[88] For more than two thousand years, the ruins of Kor had been inhabited by Ayesha—"*She*-Who-Must-Be-Obeyed," who despotically rules over the savage Amahagger (for Haggard, a degenerate race of hybrids of the Kor and Blacks). Ayesha, an ancient Arab, has only a faulty understanding of the Kor's astounding achievements in science, art, and culture. But guiding a small group of strangers through the ancient caves, temples, and crumbling public works of the walled city of Kor, *She* provides tantalizing glimpses of "the white memories of a forgotten human history."[89] Given the consistent misogyny of much imperial literature, a great deal of attention has been given to Haggard's invention of a powerful white queen of unsurpassed beauty and intelligence: the Eternal Woman's appearance in an unrelentingly masculine terrain, and so on. There is much that is fascinating about this specter, but here we are more interested in the liminality of the figure: Ayesha's appointment as an alluring conduit between the imaginable (the quest of white men) and the unreal (Kor), and her substantiation of the natural order (white rules brown and black savages). Ayesha is Haggard's faithful repository of Victorian neo-Platonism ("'Ah,' she said, 'a democracy—then surely there is a tyrant, for I have long since seen that democracies, having no clear will of their own, in the end set up a tyrant, and worship him'")[90] and prejudice ("'My people! Speak not to me of my people,' she answered, hastily; 'these slaves are no people of mine, they are but dogs to do my bidding till the day of my deliverance comes'").[91] Even more importantly, she is

88. Haggard, *She*, 182.
89. Ibid., 186.
90. Ibid., 254.
91. Ibid., 156.

the source and inspiration for the reader's awe of the fictitious wonders of Kor. Thanks to Haggard, with the filming of *She* in 1908 as the first jungle film, lost cities, lost treasures, lost white civilizations, and white queens became staples of the genre. And beginning in 1908, at least six screen versions of *She* were made in the United States and Britain during the silent era.[92] British filmmakers returned to the novel in 1935, their American counterparts in 1965; and the British again in 1967 (*The Vengeance of She*).[93]

According to Kenneth Cameron's study, approximately twenty-eight jungle films were produced in the United States alone between the first appearance of *She* and the arrival of the first cinematic version of Burroughs's *Tarzan of the Apes* in 1918.[94] There was no question then that a genre had emerged. The thematic reiterations of Black savages, dangerous jungles, intrepid white hunter/trapper/explorer, abandoned or endangered white women, and wild beasts became formulaic:

> The steady beating of the war-drums grows stronger. An exotically painted black face peers out behind a bush. The African porters drop their packs and cower in fear, but the tall, courageous white hunter forces them on. Suddenly a spear flies out of the bush and hits a porter in the chest. The rest of the porters, screaming, disperse into the jungle, only to be cut down by the savages. With his trusty gun, the white man fends off the brutes and retreats to a nearby cliff. As the tension mounts, the audience sits spellbound.[95]

Woven among the escarpment were clusters of representational subtleties, each determined by its own economy of appropriation. Colonialism required that the savages should be divided into two: the good (colonized, domesticated, civilized, loyal) savages, and the bad (raw,

92. Kenneth Cameron asserts that "male fear of female sexuality is at the heart of *She*." Cameron, *Africa on Film*, 22. Given this interpretation, Cameron pays little attention to Haggard's insertions of ancient white civilizations in his African fantasies (*She*, *Allan Quatermain*, and *King Solomon's Mines*).

93. Ibid., passim; Dunn, "Lights . . . Camera."

94. Cameron's filmography for the period 1908–18 records a dozen or more British-made jungle "documentaries" as well as two versions of *She*; in South Africa, filmmakers produced at least six jungle films in the period, including *The Symbol of Sacrifice* (1918), and added a version of *King Solomon's Mines* in 1918 and *Allan Quatermain* in 1919. See Cameron, *Africa on Film*, 211–29.

95. Dunn, "Lights . . . Camera," 149.

wild, prehistoric, aggressive) savages. Imperialism required that no semblance of a native economy—other than hunting—or civilization would be attached to the savages. They did not farm, they did not cook, or clean, or read, or make (and wear) clothing, play music, or teach their children. They possessed no religion, only superstition. And they had achieved only the barest rudiments of art or language. The world-system determined that untold (and untolled) wealth was to be found (discovered) in Africa, India, or the jungles of the Americas.

In the public imagination, Africa became more and more a propitious site for revealing the natural orders of race, gender, and class. And since there were no compelling claims of African domain, any agency authorized in the West—commercial, moral, political, and so forth—was licensed to exploit, cajole, or rule the continent as it deemed fit. Sampling the American press coincident with the first jungle films, the impression is that it was slavishly publishing numerous uncorroborated accounts of self-promoting missionaries, amateur travelers, and the ever-persistent but influential racial bigots which confirmed white conceits. Augmenting the popular impact of the jungle films, reports on primitive beliefs and savage practices were interspersed with eye-witness tales of the exotic, uncivilized, unnatural practices of Africa's natives. On those rare occasions when, say, a solemn Franz Boas disputed demeaning and ill-informed opinions of Africa pronounced by demagogues like Hoke Smith (a governor and then senator of Georgia), it might be reasonably inferred that it was of little consequence.[96] The volume of racialist dicta and white supremacy propaganda was deafening, naturalizing Black inferiorization and exploitation.

In the United States, however, certain elements of the earliest jungle films would prove to be expendable. Ayesha, the fabled white queen, was one such archetype. Kenneth Cameron, somewhat cavalierly, suggests that it was more a question of displacement by casting directors than any profound cultural differences between the United States and Britain: "By comparison with Ayesha, the American White Queen spin-offs—jungle princesses, jungle goddesses, white priestesses, et al.—were most rosy-cheeked and scrubbed. Some were jungle girls; some were magicians; a few were bad; but most were good and sweet and as American as Chase Manhattan. And, sexily though they were dressed,

96. "Scientists Answer Hoke Smith's Attack on Negroes," *New York Times*, September 24, 1911, Sunday Magazine, 10.

they were chaste, waiting for Mister Right."[97] Rhona Berenstein believes the issue was more complex. Beginning her analysis with *Trader Horn* (1931), Berenstein supposed that in the 1930s jungle films, for filmmakers and their audiences alike, the white women in the jungle instantiated Black subhumanity, white male uncertainties about white female sexuality, and racial loyalties:

> While the rapport between the white goddess and black beast takes form in the jungle films, the particular form assumed is inflected by more than a heritage of white (good) vs. black (bad) archetypes. For the oppression of blacks within United States history lends a particular dimension to the mythology in question. . . .
>
> As the relationship between black men and white women in the US historical and mythological discourses suggest, the role of white heroines in jungle films is coded in racial terms—they represent the civilizing "superiority" of their race, and their interactions with male natives and gorillas invoke the white fantasy of an uncontrollable black man ravishing a helpless white woman. . . . [H]er presence also re-casts historical realities. In the history of American race relations, especially during slavery, black women were victims of white rapes. . . . As indicated by jungle movies, white women fall prey to black creatures in the wilds of the third world, far from the racial tensions of their homeland.[98]

So this absence of the Black woman in the jungle genre functions on several terrains. Concealing or diminishing the existence of Black women serves as a suppression of an unacceptable sexual history (for both slavery and colonialism); as a complementing fragment to the substitution of the Black male rapist for the white male rapist; as a negation of the suggestion of Black/African family or that Africa might serve as anyone's *home*; and as a species blank which allowed for the identification of Black men with apes. Woman is a white female, thus she is the natural object of desire for an indeterminate variety of sexual males. Berenstein's psychodrama, unfortunately, fails to disconnect the intentions and compulsions of the filmmakers from their audience. And given the evidence (the films themselves), it is much more certain that sexual and racial fantasies haunted the scriptwriters, directors,

97. Cameron, *Africa on Film*, 190.
98. Berenstein, "White Heroines," 318.

and producers of the jungle films and other genres. It is more difficult to infer what audiences made of the constant recitation of this social instruction and titillation. Clearly, however, the absence of older white women in the genre (effectively negating their abduction by gorillas or savages) can be taken as an indicator that filmmakers thought they were targeting an audience which shared their adolescent sexual desires and anxieties and racial conceits. It can be surmised, in any case, that complex reasons lay behind the quite sudden subordination of the Ayesha figure by king Tarzan, the most important American contribution to the jungle movie.[99]

Unlike Haggard or Wallace, Edgar Rice Burroughs was entirely unfamiliar with Africa, or the English aristocracy, for that matter. Unfortunately, there were substitutes for ignorance. Amy Kaplan informs us that "historical romances, in fact, were the major best-sellers on the earliest published lists from 1895–1902."[100] And Henry Seidel Canby, Burroughs's contemporary, like Burroughs himself, greedily consumed the rituals and creeds of American imperialism: "I cannot separate in my own memory the bands and cheering of '98, Hobson, Dewey, and manifest destiny in an expectant world, from the extravagant romanticism of the shallow, unphilosophical, un-psychological novels we had all been reading. One carried over into the other, and the same color was infused through both."[101] Anglo-Saxonism dominated the hundreds of American historical romances. And merging the identities of English and American, Old World aristocracy and the New World's wealthiest classes, these novels indiscriminately plugged American heroes into European history ("from Rome to 19th-century Italy"), or frequently "insert[ed] overt American heroes into the revision of a popular British genre set in mythical kingdoms."[102] It was relatively easy, then, for

99. One exception is Selig Studio's animal-training series filmed between 1911 and 1914. Kathlyn Williams starred as what Cameron terms "the Strong Woman" in *Captain Kate* (1911), *Capturing Circus Animals in the African Wilds* (1911), *Lost in the Jungle* (1911), *Back to the Primitive* (1911), *The Leopard's Foundling* (1914), and *In Tune with the Wild* (1914). Notwithstanding their titles and the publicity which accompanied them, all the films were made in the zoos Selig organized first in Chicago and then Los Angeles. Cameron, *Africa on Film*, 127–28. Tom Mix, the emerging star of Selig's silent Westerns, played supporting roles in several of these films. Birchard, "Earliest Days," 38.

100. Kaplan, "Romancing the Empire," 660.

101. Ibid.

102. Ibid., 667.

Burroughs to appropriate from these fables the crucial props for his fantasy jungle "romances" published in the American equivalent of the juvenile literature so successful in Britain. Burroughs's birth place was Chicago (1875); and his family was upper middle class (his father, George Burroughs, was vice president of a successful firm, the American Battery Company). As a young man he had been an indifferent student (at mostly private schools); by 1911, now married and the father of three children, Burroughs had failed at every sort of job, career, or venture imaginable. Then, the long-elusive muse appeared: in February 1911, *All-Story* magazine published "Under the Moons of Mars," a science-fiction yarn, and then in late 1912 (October), *All-Story* published "Tarzan of the Apes."[103] The reader response to Burroughs's Martian tales, and to Tarzan, was outstanding.[104] Over the next two years, Burroughs estimated that something like a million readers joined the Tarzan congregation; and he rather promptly began work on a sequel. "The Return of Tarzan" was published in *All-Story* in August 1913. And though the science-fiction stories written by Burroughs were quite well received, it was Tarzan which had the larger popular appeal, resulting in newspaper syndication and a book form by 1914.

As far as the literary realm is concerned, Burroughs would credit the legend of Romulus and Remus and Rudyard Kipling's *Jungle Book* as his most immediate inspirations for Tarzan.[105] This, of course, was only part of the story, since there were plenty of influences closer to home. Irwin Porges, the author of a two-volume authorized biography of Burroughs, observes, "The philosophic themes that were generally associated with *Tarzan of the Apes* may be listed as follows: the conflict of heredity and environment; the lone man pitted against the forces of nature; the search for individual freedom; escapism—flight from the boring routines of daily life; a destructive civilization, with man, its

103. With the exception of Tarzan, Burroughs is best known for his science-fiction works. However, between these first two publications, Burroughs was encouraged to write *The Outlaw of Torn*, a medieval romance.

104. At least one reader pointed out, however, that Sabor the Tiger was on the wrong continent. For the subsequent book, Burroughs promptly changed Sabor into a lioness. See the authorized biography by Irwin Porges, *Edgar Rice Burroughs*, 1:227.

105. From Kipling's autobiography, *Something of Myself*, Porges quotes Kipling's reference to Burroughs as an imitator: "'If it be in your power, bear serenely with imitators. *My Jungle Book* begot Zoos of them. But the genius of all genii was the one who wrote a series called *Tarzan of the Apes*.'" Porges, *Edgar Rice Burroughs*, 1:217.

representative, displaying all its vices, as opposed to the simple virtues of nature's creatures."[106] Some of these issues might be credited to the fact that Burroughs was nearing his fortieth birthday and that he was the product of a fantasy-filled boyhood disciplined by a turn in a military academy. A midlife crisis of a self-described flop could easily be the source of this psychological soup of escapism and Promethean delusions. Less problematically, Burroughs's hereditarian beliefs could have been direct reflections of the dominant creeds of contemporary American biologists. H. H. Goddard had appropriated Alfred Binet's work to construct his theory of intelligence and IQ; Lewis Terman was constructing the Stanford-Binet scale for measuring intelligence; and Goddard and Robert Yerkes were preparing to conduct their famous "testing" of nearly two million U.S. Army recruits.[107] Goddard's evaluations of immigrant arrivals at Ellis Island in 1912 and 1913 had resulted in preposterous statistics: "83 percent of the Jews, 80 percent of the Hungarians, 79 percent of the Italians, and 87 percent of the Russians were feeble-minded." (Stephen Jay Gould reports that "Goddard himself was flabbergasted: could anyone be made to believe that four-fifths of any nation were morons?") Goddard had altered his photographs of the "Kallikaks" in order to demonstrate their deficiencies to amateur observers; and Yerkes had uncovered the astounding fact that the "average mental age of white American adults stood just above the edge of moronity."[108] Despite the charlatans, people like Burroughs— privileged underachievers—felt comfortably superior to the masses. After all, Goddard was to pronounce that "the people who are doing the drudgery, are, as a rule, in their proper places." And summarizing Goddard's remarks to Princeton undergraduates in 1919, Gould supplied the complement: "At the upper end, intelligent men rule in comfort and by right."[109] On the basis of this creed, Tarzan, the heir to Lord Greystoke, would naturally become "the king of the jungle." For Burroughs, clearly heredity (Tarzan's English aristocracy) trumped environment (the African jungle).

Burroughs was native to an intellectual culture which racialized class and naturalized exploitation and domination. On matters of

106. Porges, *Edgar Rice Burroughs*, 1:219.

107. See Gould, *Mismeasure of Man*, chap. 5.

108. Ibid., 196, 201, 226.

109. Ibid., 191.

blackness, however, biographer Porges seems to have been at pains to make certain that Burroughs's private papers reflected racial benevolence. For instance, Burroughs had attended the world's fair in Chicago in 1893. Indeed, as part of a promotional scheme for his father's firm, Burroughs had driven an electric car all around the fairgrounds.[110] Given Burroughs's subsequent involvement in one of the most influential (mis)constructions of Africa, one would expect Porges to document Burroughs's impressions of the African village at the fair. Porges declined, implying that either the village was nonexistent or Burroughs never visited it. On the other hand, Porges does recount that during Burroughs's short army career in the Arizona Territory in 1896 (his father secured an early discharge for Edgar from the Secretary of the Army), he served under a Black sergeant: "Without exception they [Black officers] were excellent men who took no advantage of their authority over us and on the whole were better to work under than our own white sergeants."[111] Porges also noted that two or three years later, while managing his own bookstore in Pocatello, Idaho, Burroughs quite likely wrote "The Black Man's Burden," a parody which appeared in the *Pocatello Tribune* of Kipling's "The White Man's Burden."[112] Yet, in *Tarzan of the Apes*, Burroughs displayed no such sensitivity. His only Black American character, Esmeralda, was directly drawn from minstrelsy. Expectedly pedestrian, Burroughs's introduction of Esmeralda was far from flattering: "After these came a huge Negress clothed like Solomon as to colors. Her great eyes rolled in evident terror, first toward the jungle and then toward the cursing band of sailors."[113] As maid to Jane Porter, Esmeralda was the mammy, who served the dual purpose of ornamenting Jane's young white beauty and Jane's courage and levelheadedness when skeletons were uncovered or a lion attacked. The only Black among the small group of castaways, Esmeralda was the least generous towards Africa, the least forgiving for the absence of modernity's amenities, the least curious about the world of Africa. And, of course, the African savages were superstitious cannibals.

The National Film Corporation, the company which brought the novel to realization in 1918, seems largely to have been a creature of William

110. Ibid., 76. Although there are references to Blacks and Africa in the text of Porges's biography of Burroughs, no citations to either are listed in the index.

111. Porges, *Edgar Rice Burroughs*, 1:112–13.

112. Ibid., 1:130.

113. Burroughs, *Tarzan of the Apes*, 115.

Parsons, credited as producer of *Tarzan of the Apes*.[114] And in the quirky odyssey of raising capital for the relatively expensive project, Parsons had touched up a broad array of funders which included Burroughs himself; Robert Lay (National Life Insurance Company, Chicago); J. M. Rumsey and Robert Middlewood (both officers in Stock Growers National Bank in Rawlins, Wyoming); and unnamed others. The high production costs of the film were the result of two production strategies. The first was to ensure the film's realism through location shooting. Crews were sent to the interior of Brazil (where Afro-Brazilians were cast as African natives) to build sets of native villages. Cast and crews also spent time in Louisiana's forest and a jungle habitat in Los Angeles. The second important but costly choice was to hire proven talent for many of the principal roles in front of and behind the camera. Elmo Lincoln, who played the blacksmith in *The Birth of a Nation*, was eventually assigned the role of the adult Tarzan (Gordon Griffith appeared in the early scenes of Tarzan as a child), and he was supported by Enid Markey (Jane Porter), True Boardman (Lord Greystoke), Kathleen Kirkman (Lady Greystoke), George B. French (the good sailor, Binns), Colin Kenny (Cecil Clayton), Thomas Jefferson (Professor Porter), and Bessie Toner (Esmeralda).[115] The screenplay went through several drafts, the first by William E. Wing, and the final form produced by Lois Weber and Fred Miller.[116] Weber was a crusading director (the controversial birth control films *Where Are My Children?*, 1916, and *The Hand That Rocks the Cradle*, 1917; and *The People vs. John Doe*, 1916, opposing capital punishment) and screenwriter (*John Barleycorn*, a temperance yarn) whose importance in the early American movie industry was retrieved by Kevin Brownlow.[117]

The Weber-Miller script differed with Burroughs's original on several important points. For one, there were those changes in the plot most likely attributable to the world war. In the novel, Lord Greystoke had been commissioned by the Colonial Office to undertake a delicate

114. David Fury's partial listing of the crew included Scott Sidney, director; Parsons, producer; Lois Weber and Fred Miller, adapters. Fury, *Kings of the Jungle*, 13.

115. Ibid. Elmo Lincoln was born Otto Elmo Linkenhelt and had participated in several of D. W. Griffith's films (including *The Battle of Elderbush Gulch*, *The Kaiser*, and *Intolerance*). Linkenhelt was awarded his screen name by Griffith. Porges, *Edgar Rice Burroughs*, 1:432.

116. Porges, *Edgar Rice Burroughs*, 1:427; Fury, *Kings of the Jungle*, 13.

117. Brownlow, *Behind the Mask*, 50ff., 125ff., 259.

investigation of "another European power" which, under the guise of recruiting for its army, had enslaved African men "solely for the forcible collection of rubber and ivory."[118] In the film, Greystoke's charge was changed into one of exposing Arab slave traders. Apparently, Weber or Miller or Parsons had come to the realization that to implicate a "European power" might jeopardize American public sympathy for an Entente nation like France or German-occupied Belgium, both desperate and both guilty of despicable colonial practices in Africa. The Arabs, on the other hand, were centuries-old enemies of Christianity and were for the most part enlisted as soldiers by Germany and the Ottomans. Constructing Arab slave trading as a major subtext of *Tarzan of the Apes* thus elided the slave histories of Britain and America and provided an occasion to display Arabs as brutal (several scenes depicted slave traders driving yoked African and European captives) and certainly undeserving of any postwar consideration. The film also considerably diminished Tarzan's hereditary instincts. In the novel Tarzan had taught himself to read and write English fluently; in the film, he is taught a rudimentary mastery of English by Binns. In the novel, an African tribe is driven into Tarzan's vicinity in flight from white slave traders, providing at first a tragic dimension to their migration. In the film, the savages have no history; they exist merely as unthinking predators. In the novel, Jane and her party return to Baltimore, and Tarzan gives chase while undergoing a tutored transformation into a European gentleman (his first spoken language is French). The novel appropriates a Romeo-and-Juliet-like sequence of misapprehensions: Jane believes Tarzan is dead and does not realize that the half-naked white savage who rescued her is the same Tarzan who has written her of his love for her. When they are reunited in America, Tarzan, now aware of his lofty title, refuses to divulge his true inheritance, thus seemingly forfeiting Jane and his lands to his cousin, Cecil. In the film, following his rescue of Jane from the clutches of a leering Black savage, the final scene is Tarzan and Jane embracing in a clearing just beyond the jungle.

Though *Tarzan of the Apes* was a counterfeit of British colonialism, the casual racial meanness of the film seemed calculated to profit from the hatred broadly disseminated among white Americans. Watching the bulky Black savage loping back into the Louisiana ("African") woods, carrying the dead weight of Jane Porter, it was as if D. W. Grif-

118. Burroughs, *Tarzan of the Apes*, 2.

fith's imagined predator, Gus, had now captured Lil' Sis. This time, however, the menace was more real, for the distancing gimmick of Griffith's illusion, a blackface white Gus, had been dissolved. *Tarzan of the Apes* employed real Black actors to play the savages and Esmeralda, and this second Gus had at last gotten his hands on the white woman. In Burroughs's novel, it had been an ape that had taken Jane; in the film it was a half-naked savage. Thus was signified the vast historical space which spanned the deceptively short markers between 1912 and 1918, and 1915 and 1918; between Burroughs's and Griffith's imagined threat and the real menace of the war years. To ordinary Black Americans, the release of *Tarzan of the Apes* in early 1918 was barely a blip on the cultural and political onslaught of white racism which coincided with the war in Europe, Asia, and Africa. The shock of *The Birth of a Nation*'s reception was still reverberating in their communities, and from its new location in Hollywood, the movie industry seemed to delight in representing the most conflicted forms of racial amelioration like social assimilation and miscegenation as unacceptable. The Klan had been revived. Segregation was intensifying. And in the midst of a public debate concerning the inclusion of Blacks in a national conscription, East St. Louis had erupted into race massacre (thirty-nine Blacks killed; nine whites) and race cleansing in July; and then in August, in Houston, after months of harassment, Black troops had retaliated against their tormentors, killing seventeen whites. Mississippi's Senator Vardaman objected to the possibility that any Blacks might be drafted, while other Southern white politicians, conceding that point, objected to the training of armed Blacks in army camps in the South.[119]

Looking back at that era, James Mennell observes, "Indeed, the race problem may have posed more danger to American unity than did the better known fear of suspect loyalty among recent European immigrants [from countries allied with Germany]."[120] Even in Europe, race seemed to trump the war effort. Tyler Stovall reports that "the spring of 1917, a time of crises and the low point of the French war effort, ushered in a series of racial incidents, ranging from brawls between individuals to riots involving hundreds of people."[121] In this country, in the mean-

119. "Fear Negro Troops in Spartanburg," *New York Times*, August 31, 1917, 4; "Protest in Behalf of Negro Troops," *New York Times*, September 1, 1917, 5.

120. Mennell, "African-Americans and the Selective Service Act," 276.

121. Stovall, "Color Line," 750. Nearly 137,000 of the 300,000 colonial workers in France during World War I came from Africa; another 86,000 came from China and

while, President Wilson rejected pleas from Black leaders to publicly condemn lynching and racial violence. Wilson and Secretary of War Newton Baker refused to address the steadily increasing military segregation of the past two decades. And when the Black academic John Milton Waldron requested that the president rescind the government's policy of race discrimination, the president rebuked him with sophistry: "Your letter was the first notice I had that many of the members of the colored race were not enthusiastic in their support of the Government in this crisis."[122] Nevertheless, in the spring of 1917 Wilson and Baker ordered the establishment of Camp Des Moines (Iowa) for the training of Black officers (470 Black men had volunteered by May). And in October 1917 (the timing, one contemporary argued, was dictated by the end of the cotton harvest), the conscription of Blacks began.[123]

There is one other moment in *Tarzan of the Apes* which appears fugitive to the race regime being fabricated for early twentieth-century America. The scene is so jarring that one surmises that it, too, may have been a residue of the war. Confronted by Tarzan, the savage who has abducted Jane stands his ground. The anonymous Black actor is as powerfully built as Elmo Lincoln, and their ensuing struggle is prolonged and, at points, the outcome uncertain. Jane's fearful reactions, displayed as crosscuts to the action, are allowed to reflect a curious combination of feminine revulsion to violence and the possibility that her rescuer will not succeed. Unlike the death of a savage at the hands of Tarzan earlier in the film, this is a fight between equals. Then, finally, Tarzan kills, but the killing of this savage is cinematically unconvincing, the close-up of the native's prone body eerily reminiscent of Jack Johnson lying in that Havana ring in 1915, putting the lie to Jess Willard's victory by casually shading his eyes from the sun. Cripps, too, recognized the audacious rupture, commenting, "at that, awkward problems of racial ambiguity emerged because black men fought with a white for power—no mat-

---

Indochina. Some 330,000 immigrant workers came from Europe (principally Spain and Italy). While immigrant workers had been targeted by French civilians before the war, racial violence and killings by French civilians and French soldiers were restricted to colonial workers during the war. The violence was not directed against colonial soldiers or the 200,000 Black American troops stationed in France. Ibid., passim.

122. Mennell, "African-Americans and the Selective Service Act," 277.

123. Heywood, *Negro Combat Troops*, 3. By the end of 1918, 367,410 Blacks had been drafted. Mennell, "African-Americans and the Selective Service Act," 284.

ter how faltering—and moved dangerously close to being 'bad niggers.' As a result Tarzan's cinema locale in time gradually shifted away from Africa."[124]

The film's preparation and shooting had coincided with two of the first four years that the war persisted. During those years, and as the principal powers wasted their armies through a combination of questionable strategies by incompetent leaders and a reckless willingness to employ increasingly lethal technologies (tanks, poison gas, rapid-fire machine guns), manpower shortages were evident from almost the very beginning. Having already employed natives as security forces in the colonial context, the warring states were forced to suspend the Pax Britannica, or whatever they called it. Their gift to the savages, civil order, had been based on a patent deception shockingly exposed as an obvious lie: that civilized nations did not war. Now standing under the banner of future equal rights for the colonized, the big powers rallied (and frequently kidnapped) Black and Brown bodies for the conflict. Colonial African troops, taking their place among other colonial subjects from India, Indochina, the West Indies, and elsewhere, had been recruited by the tens and hundreds of thousands on both sides of the conflict: the French, the British, the Ottomans, and the Germans impressed colonial subjects into combat and service roles. The American public had been inundated, consequently, by comforting tales of colonial troops fighting to the death for their colonial masters, each instance challenging the racial myths that the military and the apologists for colonialism had taken pains to manufacture and distribute: that Africans (or Asians, or . . .) were too intellectually deficient, too backward, too frightened, too superstitious, too lazy to acquire the discipline needed for soldiering. The ancient myths which had rationalized the monopolization of violence by a propertied class long before Plato, Xenophon, and Aristotle had found it necessary to defend them had now been insinuated into modern racism. But the conduct of modern warfare suspended these truisms. Now in desperate straits, the leaders of the warring nations, most times reluctantly but nevertheless ineluctably, drifted towards the decisive policy of the war: the recruitment of colonial combatants. And many of these Black and Brown recruits served with distinction, fighting the white powers' war not through loyalty to the metropole but in the hope of reforming if not

124. Cripps, *Slow Fade to Black*, 125.

entirely eradicating colonialism in the postwar period. Their spokespersons lauded this sacrifice, imagining that it could be transferred into national autonomy or political equality.[125] Mimicking the colonial soldier, the native confronting Tarzan displays resolute determination and fearlessness. It can be said that his like (much different from the gun-bearer who dies in order to save the white hunter), for all practical purposes, will disappear from American screens for the next several decades.

The success of *Tarzan of the Apes* inspired the construction of a franchise. And over the next fourteen years, that is, before the period which catapulted Johnny Weissmuller into the role, Tarzan features and serials set in Africa monopolized the representation of the white hero in jungle pictures. Among the thirty or so silent jungle films and serials after 1918, Tarzan's name appeared in the titles of eight of them. Lincoln reprised his role in *The Romance of Tarzan* (1918) and the 1921 serial, *The Adventures of Tarzan* (Weiss Brothers–Numa Pictures). Lincoln's immediate successors were Gene Pollar (*The Revenge of Tarzan*, Numa Pictures, 1920); P. Dempsey Tabler (the 1920 serial *The Son of Tarzan*, National Film, which was edited and released in 1923 as a feature, *Jungle Trail of the Son of Tarzan*); James Pierce (*Tarzan and the Golden Lion*, RC Pictures/FBO Gold Bond); and Frank Merrill (the Universal serials *Tarzan the Mighty*, 1928, and *Tarzan the Tiger*, 1929). Minstrel representation of Blacks continued their popularity in the form of plantation tales and slapstick comedies. Only the Black independent filmmakers like Lincoln Pictures (*Trooper of Troop K*, 1916) and Micheaux (*A Daughter of the Congo*, 1930) attempted to memorialize the impact of Blacks on the war.[126] So notwithstanding the sacrifices of Black American, West

125. This was very close to Du Bois's position when he wrote his "Close Ranks" editorial in *Crisis* in the summer of 1918.

126. Cripps suggested two exceptions: "Goldwyn's *Too Fat to Fight* (1919) with its black soldier, and Griffith's war film *The Greatest Thing in Life* [1918], in which a black soldier gives his last drop of water so that his white buddy may live." Cripps, *Slow Fade to Black*, 137–38. The latter film is lost. Lillian Gish, one of Griffith's enduring collaborators (and defenders), told Richard Schickel that she lamented its loss, since it would correct the impression that Griffith was a racist. In any case, Schickel's reconstruction differs radically from Cripps's: "The crucial scene occurs when Livingston, wounded in battle, is rescued by a black soldier, who is himself wounded in the effort. They tumble into a shell hole together. When the Negro feels his life beginning to fade, he calls out for his 'Mammy,' asking for a kiss, which Livingston, cradling him in his arms, bestows upon him in his final moment." Schickel, *D. W. Griffith*, 384. It is

Indian, and African troops in the war, the savage, the slave, the docile servant, and a menagerie of Black fools continued to thrill audiences, complementing the lynchings whose narratives transmuted Black valor into Black vice. As Cripps laments: "Black soldiers, labor organizers, Pan-Africanists, Zionists, cool cats, intellectuals, all the blacks who broke the molds in Northern ghettos, were unseen on the nation's screens. In spite of the montage of new Negroes a sense of order and the rightness of things demanded that only the old stereotypes be trotted out across the screen."[127]

Yelling at the Screaming Savages

The events which propelled jungle films into the first tier of American movies in the sound era are fascinating in and of themselves, since they contradict and alter the conventions of colonialism and colonial discourse. Considering the historical nexus between the genre and colonial literature, the setting was familiar: South Africa. After that locator, things get really interesting. More than occasionally, the most immediate, urgent, and contradictory intelligence of empire forms at the periphery of that realm. There, at the border between global accumulation and local commodity production, where the latter may or may not be transferred to the sphere of the former, the tendrils of appropriation are barely dressed. *Trader Horn* presents one such instance. Rather than the spun-out boys' adventure stories invented by a failed farmer (Haggard) or a frustrated colonial civil servant (Wallace), in this instance our principal was a woman with decidedly feminist ambitions and ambiguous attitudes towards imperialism and colonialism.

When Ethelreda Lewis collaborated in the realization of *Trader Horn*

---

a measure of Gish's immersion in the racist brew that she would consider as an act of redemption Griffith's composition of his stock loyal Negro with the sentimentality of a white man's kiss. Gish claimed that audiences were touched by the scene, and as Schickel documents, "Many reviewers mentioned the sequence favorably ('possibly one of the finest things ever presented on the silver sheet' said one trade paper), but again the querulous note that Griffith seemed to be doing no more than repeating himself crept in." Ibid. In any case, the importance of the Black presence in the war seems not to have been addressed by this small gesture. Griffith's most enduring construction of Blacks in uniform was the negation encapsulated in *The Birth of a Nation*; and in his prior films, like *His Trust* and *His Trust Fulfilled* (both 1911), the theme of the loyal slave had completely displaced the brutality of slavery and the centrality of slavery as an issue in the Civil War.

127. Cripps, *Slow Fade to Black*, 115–16.

(Jonathan Cape, 1927), she was already in her early fifties and had already displayed a talent for historical novels.[128] Yet at the onset of the appearance of *Trader Horn* as a publishing and literary phenomenon, Lewis took a back seat to "Alfred Aloysius Horn," a former white trader and her coauthor. And though early on some reviewers questioned the authenticity of the tales spun by Horn, for eight decades attention has primarily converged on Horn rather than Lewis.[129] Lewis, the colorless white wife in the Johannesburg suburb of Parktown, could never compete with Horn, but then she never intended any such contest.

Ethelreda Lewis invented "Trader Horn" from the whole cloth of Aloysius Smith. She (re)named him (dubbing him Alfred Aloysius Horn), transposed his rambling, repetitive reminiscences from their oral and jotted forms into constructed narratives, and arranged his final years as a world-traveling celebrity. She concealed her inventiveness behind a masquerade provided ready-at-hand by the patriarchy and paternalism of colonial culture. While effectively invisible, she deposed into biography a relationship between a mature female adjudicator and an aging adventurer (Smith was actually sixty-five in 1926 but generally added five or ten years to his age). On those terms Lewis suborned Smith-Horn, who had never come to terms with the ravages of European imperialism on either himself or Africa, into her own project of settling scores with a tyranny of race and gender. As Lewis would have her readers believe, "'Trader Horn' was written by candle light on scraps of paper, billheads and envelopes in a Johannesburg lounginghouse. During the day Alfred Aloysius Horn hawked aluminum ware. He sold Mrs. Ethelreda Lewis, South African novelist, a gridiron she didn't need, lingered to give her a recipe for oat cakes, and thus began a series of weekly editorial conferences, unlocking his treasure-chest of memories of the Ivory Coast when he was a youth of 18."[130]

But Ethelreda was no ordinary confessor, no ordinary white woman in colonial South Africa. The same year she was coaxing Smith-Horn into recalling his youthful adventures in the Ivory Coast (present-day Gabon), she was also playing an important role in Black trade union politics. H. J. and R. E. Simons credit Lewis as being one of a small

128. See Ethelreda Lewis, *Harp*. The novel is based on a legend associated with fifteenth-century Portuguese explorations in East Africa.

129. For some early doubters, see Couzens, *Tramp Royal*, 18–19.

130. "America Greets Trader Horn," *Los Angeles Times*, April 8, 1928, C24.

group of "European women" who helped to persuade Clements Kadalie to expel Communist Party members from the Industrial and Commercial Union and to affiliate with the moderate International Federation of Trade Unions.[131] Even more unlike the majority of white women in Britain's colonial domain of South Africa, Lewis did not participate in the "suppression of perception" which depersonalized Blacks. As Simon Dugat observes of her peers: "Middle and upper class settler women who had been born in South Africa, or who had spent decades there, came by their social distance from Africans very easily. It was among established settlers that the suppression of perception was most well-developed."[132] To the contrary, Lewis advertised an affection for Blacks and "Coloureds" in her domestic sphere. Writing in her introduction to *The Ivory Coast in the Earlies* (published as *Trader Horn* in America) about Ruth, Lewis referred to "my coloured housekeeper and friend."[133] And in her 1931 novel *Four Handsome Negresses* (now out of print), Lewis was even more provocative.

Wendy Woodward is one of the few scholars to have seriously analyzed *Four Handsome Negresses*, or to situate it as an important instance of an anti-imperialist novel. Among Woodward's achievements is her interrogation of the sources of the work:

> Joao de Barros reports that Bartolomeo Dias took "four negresses" from the coast of Guinea on the orders of King John of Portugal. The monarch's plan was to treat the women well, furnish them with samples of trade, and then have them returned to the coast of Guinea in the hope that they would reach the natives of the area and spread

131. "The decision to affiliate followed a resolution of the ICU's annual conference in April 1926 to join the British Trade Union Congress (TUC) as a means of bringing the case of the African workers before the League of Nations and public opinion throughout Europe. The TUC suggested as an alternative that the union should apply for affiliation to the International Federation of Trade Unions, the so-called Amsterdam International. Kadalie agreed, the more readily because he was advised to do so by a group of socialists and liberals in Britain and South Africa. A 'factor behind the scenes,' which led him to adopt 'a middle course, was the advice and help given him by certain European women.' Among them were the novelist Mrs. Ethelreda Lewis, Miss Margaret Hodgson (later Mrs. Ballinger), Miss Mabel Palmer of Durban, and his chief sponsor, Miss Winifred Holtby, then lecturing in South Africa." Simons and Simons, *Class and Colour*, 360–68.

132. Dugat, "Gender, Colonial 'Women's History,'" 569.

133. Horn, *Trader Horn*, 10.

information about "the grandeur of his kingdom and the many things to be found there" . . . To these ends, three of the women (the fourth having died) were abandoned along the coast. E. G. Ravenstein is more sedulous in geographical and historical detail in his description of Dias's voyage of 1487 and 1488 and seems a likelier source for *Four Handsome Negresses*, given his description of the women who were to be "handsomely dressed" on their forced landings.[134]

The four African women, then, were enveloped in an imperialist gambit typical of Portuguese mercantilism. And as "factors" they seemed to fare no better in the esteem of scholars than they had in that of their fifteenth-century captors. In Lewis's hands, the vagueness of the historians concerning the fortunes of the women is replaced with horrifying specificity:

> The various fates of these women function as metonymies of other colonized women's lives under imperialism. At the Santa Maria's first putative trading stop on Africa's shore, the deerlike, young Azize is abandoned. Diseased after repeated rapes by the crew, she dies of shock at the sight of an ape "shambling lustfully to the painful embrace that had destroyed a maiden child" (p. 164). Sapi, now an alcoholic and impregnated by the Governor, drowns after falling from the deck. A "dark figure lost in the fever of primitive obscenities" in her drunken frenzy, she is pursued by the "inflamed" crew (p. 174). Arigacho, under the merchant's surveillance, has been made an unwilling prostitute, her body commodified and diseased. Her landing on the coast offers primitive closure; she is seen as a "goddess" by the Bushmen who offer her to their Gulliver, a castaway because of his leprosied hand. But the "race" (p. 205) they are destined to perpetuate will surely suffer from leprosy and venereal disease. Only Regeunda, the mother, desired by the impotent Brother Secundus and subsequently by the Governor, remains unviolated, but she commits suicide, bereft of her friends, her son, and her home.[135]

This, then, was an unadulterated Lewis, boldly parading her revulsion of the predator sexuality with which imperialism licensed white males. In *Trader Horn*, Lewis had successfully submerged her feminist identity under the putative authorship of Alfred Horn and disguised her liberal

134. Woodward, "Metonymies of Colonialism," 65.
135. Ibid., 66.

anti-imperialism by proposing "adventure" in the boastful arrogance of Horn's accounts of an exploitative "trade" with natives and "gentle Africa." Lewis, in fact, was too successful. For when the American film-makers seized on her project, they centered *Trader Horn* on the one total fiction Lewis had allowed Smith-Horn. In his tales, Smith-Horn had invented Nina T. (in the South African and British editions, she was known as Lola D.), the daughter of a white trader and octoroon, who had become a priestess among the savages. Tim Couzens doubted the story, and Albert Schweitzer, who established his hospital at the same trading post where Smith-Horn worked as a youth, had demurred: "There never has been anything of the nature of a vestal virgin in this country."[136] For MGM's Irving Thalberg and W. S. Van Dyke, such concerns were like water off a duck's back.

In South Africa, Britain, and America, the publication of *Trader Horn* was a phenomenal success. Sales were jump-started by reader sub-scriptions from the Literary Guild and by a promotion which included literary critics like Carl Van Doren (who compared Horn to Joseph Conrad). John Galworthy lent his prestige, having written a foreword to the book, objecting only to its reference to the Black wives of David Livingston and Cecil Rhodes (Smith-Horn had mused, "Rhodes was nought but a man").[137] In 1928, the "traveler's tale" was fourth on the best-sellers list for that year.[138] The book's success was sufficient to interest Thalberg into adapting it to a film project.[139] Originally envisioned as a silent film, the box office success of musicals in general and *Hallelujah* in particular persuaded MGM's bosses to proceed with the filming of *Trader Horn* with sound. Eventually, the cost of production reached some $1,322,000, almost three times the budget of the average sound film in 1929–30.[140]

Even now, some seventy years after the fact, *Trader Horn* remains a

136. Couzens, *Tramp Royal*, 184.

137. See ibid., 13–15. For the reference to Rhodes, see Horn, *Trader Horn*, 183. The offending remarks were struck from the British edition but remained in the first American publication.

138. For some early indication of its success, see "America Greets Trader Horn"; and Couzens, *Tramp Royal*, 16.

139. Originally conceived as a silent film, the concept for the project remained muddled even after filming had begun. See "Radical Picturization Due in New Film Tales," *Los Angeles Times*, July 8, 1928, C33.

140. Behlmer, "Tarzan, Hollywood's Greatest," 39.

remarkable viewing experience. Part melodrama, part documentary, it fascinates with its bricolage of colonial myths and Hollywood sexploitation. Probably the shock of authenticity is owed to the effect of the deluge of increasingly artificial jungle films which followed it. As a sound film, *Trader Horn* surpassed the jungle silents which preceded it, augmenting somewhat familiar visuals of a remote world with the languages and music seldom encountered by outsiders. Forests, too, thickened with their own concatenation and the solitude of river travel in immense spaces were punctuated by the occasional grunts of disturbed hippopotamuses, the menacing roar of crocodiles, and the distant thunder of elephant herds seemingly indifferent to the river's unusual passengers. And unlike the jungle films of the 1930s which it inspired, *Trader Horn* recorded normal village life, perhaps inadvertently, given the filmmakers' compulsion to melodramatics. Sadly, the films which followed it seemed premised on the notions that the only sustaining African entertainment was chasing whites and the only certain occupations were carrying supplies for whites on safari or plunging into an abyss.

Over a span of ten months, *Trader Horn* was shot in British East Africa (Tanganyika and Uganda) and the Belgian Congo by W. S. Van Dyke, the director, and Clyde de Vinna, his cinematographer. The team had previously collaborated successfully on two Polynesian romances, *White Shadows in the South Seas* and *The Pagan*, and their efficiency on those location shoots had encouraged Thalberg to schedule their African assignment.[141] Eschewing mere location shooting, this time the studio had sent cast and crew to Africa. The veteran Western actor Harry Carey was to play Horn, and relative newcomers Duncan Renaldo and Edwina Booth would play, respectively, Horn's trading apprentice Peru and Nina.[142] After some missteps, Olive Golden (Carey's wife) was assigned

141. At first Van Dyke had assisted Robert Flaherty on *White Shadows in the South Seas*. Flaherty's *Nanook of the North* (1922) and *Moana: A Romance of the Golden Age* (1926) had inspired the first use of the term "documentary" by John Grierson (*New York Sun*, February 8, 1926), but Flaherty had become increasingly frustrated with the studio script for *White Shadows* and resigned after several weeks in Tahiti. Couzens, *Tramp Royal*, 515–16; and Stull, "In Africa with Trader Horn."

142. Renaldo was actually a Rumanian, Basil Coyanos (Couzens insisted his real name was Vasile Cughiearas). The fact of Renaldo's illegal entry into the United States was exposed when his wife, Suzette, filed for divorce in September 1930, alleging that Booth had stolen Renaldo's affections. Renaldo was arrested in January 1931 and de-

the role of Nina's missionary mother; and Mutia Omoolu (Mutia wa Mula), a native Kenyan, was appointed to the role of Renchoro, Horn's native assistant. The film crew's safari in East Africa seems to have been much better planned than the film itself. For Hollywood, putting up the money (William Randolph Hearst was one contributor) with only a vague notion of the final project was not unusual. There was, of course, the additional obstacle of a location thousands of miles from New York and California, but since a shared conception of Africa was already in place, the film's structure simply assembled itself from familiar materials. With "thirty-five whites and 180 blacks . . . ninety-two tons of paraphernalia, including a nine-ton generator truck and two sound wagons each weighing seven tons,"[143] this was reportedly the largest Western safari ever staged in Africa. Yet ten months later, upon his return to Hollywood, Van Dyke still had only the disparate rudiments of a completed film. Shooting more "interiors" in Hollywood and jungle terrors in Mexico, Van Dyke and his studio bosses needed several more months to cobble together their interpretation of *Trader Horn*. The film was finally released in early 1931.

Behind the opening credits, an untenanted map of Africa assured those who had read the book that the film's setting was West Africa. Since the topography, fauna, cultures, and peoples portrayed in the film were not West African (Horn identifies Kikuyu and Masai, Kenyan nations), one takes this as an early signal of the filmmakers' indifference to African realities. But even more important was an explicitly racist conceit. The vast, vacant expanse of the film's map recalled those premedieval and medieval representations of *terra incognita* which documented a truer ignorance of the continent. But in the 1930s representing Africa in this fashion was more likely the consequence of a more deliberate denial of African histories; the disappearance of civilizations, nations, cities, towns, villages was calculated. The map informed its audiences that Africans had no past which the West was obliged to acknowledge.

Peru's apprenticeship was the movie's device for instructing its audi-

---

ported. He was subsequently pardoned by Franklin Delano Roosevelt and appeared on television as the Cisco Kid. See "Movie 'Trader Horn' Held," *New York Times*, January 17, 1931, 24; and Couzens, *Tramp Royal*, 539–40, 548. Edwina Booth was actually Constance Woodruff, born in Utah. Muriel Babcock, "Safari Scenes Grip Memory," *Los Angeles Times*, December 15, 1929, B13, 20.

143. Philip K. Scheuer, "Trek Yields Jungle Film," *Los Angeles Times*, January 20, 1931, A9.

Trader Horn *poster, 1931, MGM.*

Trader Horn *poster, 1931, MGM.*

ence, while the wizened sophistication of the Horn character served to undermine misdirected innocence. Coming upon their first village, Horn alerts Peru that the natives are cannibals. Peru, alternatively, sees only "happy children." Though Peru's reductionism smacks of paternalism, certainly Van Dyke's montage of the village erases the menace in Horn's assertion. Images of iron-working, women grooming hair, women carrying water jars and firewood, smiling infants, young men playing games, women thrashing and winnowing grain, young girls prideful of their jewelry, all suggest the ordinariness of a day in lives devoted to subsistence agriculture. Then the drums announce the beginning of "ju ju," a "magic" which disfigures Blacks into "homicidal maniacs," Horn testifies. Suddenly all normality becomes sinister, and the leisurely trek of the narrative erupts. Insistent that he still intends to trade, Horn steers his small party upriver, encountering Edith Trent's safari. Despite his solicitous protests, she informs Horn and Peru that she will not desist because of "ju ju," continuing the search for the daughter she lost twenty years earlier. Aware of the danger, she implores Horn to continue her quest should she be killed. Days later, Horn, Peru, and Renchoro spy her body at the foot of the thunderous Murchison Falls (almost defeating the sound equipment). Horn's bearers bury the body under rocks, and the party, true to Horn's promise, ascend the falls into "Isorgi" country. After the film documents the extraordinary array of beasts on the high plain (wildebeests, giraffes, impi, hyenas, wild dogs, lions, etc.), they are captured by the Isorgis. In the midst of a "ju ju" orgiastic rite for which all the tribes of the region have gathered, Horn's bearers are sacrificed (on inverted crosses!), Horn, Peru, and Renchoro being saved for last. Facing death, first Horn and Peru reconsecrate themselves to a display of white courage; then Horn, placing his hand on Renchoro's shoulder, announces, "I guess the white race won't be disgraced by any one of the three of us."

At that moment, the "ju ju" appears, and it is Nina, the White Goddess, costumed in immodest bits of fur adorned with a small animal skull. Unlike She, this is a White Goddess who represents no ancient lost civilization. Edwina Booth's performance is riveting. Neither octoroon nor mulatta (as one supposes would be the case for Nina T.), she is blonde. She is a very white, luminous savage who is captured in the center of successive cinematic frames (long-shot: in front of her grass Joss hut; medium-shot: confronting the prisoners; close-up: whipping her minions; in the midst of their captors, etc.). Her hair and her skin radiate whiteness (possibly an effect of the "little diffusion" de Vinna remarked upon).[144] Her jerky physical movements, which distinguish her from her jungle film sisters — She's aristocracy or Jane's urbanity — are ornamented by her speaking Swahili at a frenetic, aggressive pace.[145] Nina appears entirely immersed in the homicidal mania of her holiday, so she fairly screeches her words. In a state of the moment's hysteria, and for no obvious reason, she suddenly strikes her Black followers, reducing one to a cowering mass. She stares at the prisoners as if they were vermin. And when Peru touches her without permission, pleading with her, "Don't you understand? White people must help each other," Nina (who understands no English) lashes him too. But unlike the Blacks, Peru unflinchingly endures Nina's whip, his eyes locked on hers. Apparently intrigued by Peru's handsome stoicism, Nina returns to her people, intent on the final three sacrifices. Only when the three men are slashed to the crucifixes does Nina relent. With her eyes riveted on Peru, she halts the ceremony, and then boldly leads the men through the armed assembled throng to the lake and to freedom. Their flight is predictable: with the Isorgi in pursuit, the four endure the dangers of the jungle; Nina chooses Peru over Horn; Renchoro sacrifices himself to save Horn; on his own, Horn uses his knowledge of the terrain to reach safety; aided by Pygmies, Nina and Peru wend their way back to the trading post. During the pursuit, Nina's authority has entirely dissipated, reducing her to the helpless damsel rescued by white male courage.[146] As the river steamer takes Nina and Peru to the coast and civilization, Horn looks bemusedly at the African gun-bearer who has replaced Renchoro. He then turns and gazes out at the river

144. "You see most of our work was done on the plains, high above sea-level, where the air is so much thinner that although the sunlight beats down plenty hard from above, there is little diffusion, and the shadows are just so many big ink-spots." Stull, "In Africa with Trader Horn," 9.

145. Commenting on her dialogue, Booth remarked: "Swahili . . . contains no words any American ever heard of. In speaking it as Nina T, I had to watch my characterization every minute. My emotional reactions had to be exact and accurate, for the words I was speaking did not help." "Actress Emotional under Difficulties," *Los Angeles Times*, February 2, 1931, A7.

146. Rhona J. Berenstein maintains there is a symbiosis between the changes in Peru and Nina: "Peru's renunciation of cowardice and homosexual proclivities corresponds to Nina's loss of jungle life. Peru's heroism depends not only on rescuing a white woman . . . but also on the woman's transformation from the cruelest woman in Africa to the prototypical heroine-in-distress." Berenstein, "White Heroines," 324.

and the horizon (on which a portrait of Renchoro has been superimposed) and ruminates on the death of his friend, Renchoro. Horn's face reflects his devotion to Africa, which unlike a woman (Nina) will never "grow old."

At the film's ending, though Horn has seemingly regained command of the film, his triumph is hollow. The studio-produced trailers, display advertisements, and publicity confirm this in their privileging of Nina (Booth) and her relationship with a primitive Africa. One trailer clamors, "the cruelest woman in all Africa rules Pagan Tribes." And all of this revolves around the spectacle of Booth's body. Even before filming, Booth had promised filmgoers that she would wear little clothing in *Trader Horn* ("Miss Booth's costume weighs exactly one pound and three ounces"),[147] and the trailer and display advertisements confirmed her young body would be on exhibition. And in one display ad announcing the opening of the film at Grauman's Chinese, her partially clad form appears six times in one guise or another.[148] From the moment of her appearance Nina dominates the picture's action. Horn, Peru, and Renchoro remain under her sway throughout, either as her captives or her protectors: they cajole her, carry her, fight over her, kiss her, dash to her rescue, and strategize her transition to "civilization." She seems to have even more importance for the Isorgi. She is their goddess, their fetish, their ruler. And once she has chosen to renounce her magisterial role, the Isorgis are willing to risk death in their relentless resolve to reclaim her. Notwithstanding all the attractive and virtually nude Black women displayed in the film, Nina is irreplaceable to these savages. And filmgoers are lured to theaters by the spectacle of Booth's white body and the vicarious heroism experienced in salvaging that whiteness from darkness.

But what explains the Isogis' frenzy? The film circumspectively portrays one explanation. But is it purely white fantasy? Nothing in the multiple reports from location documents or even hints that what is implied in the film has any basis in the factual experience of the safari.[149]

147. "Actress Departs for African Film," *Los Angeles Times*, March 22, 1929, A8.

148. *Los Angeles Times*, February 9, 1931, A7.

149. Van Dyke reeled off a steady stream of dispatches to newspapers and in 1931 published an autobiographical account of the safari, *Horning in Africa*. In addition, John McClain, a reporter for the *New York Sun*, spent six months on leave with the expedition and recounted his experiences; see "Picturing Jungle Scenes for 'Trader Horn,'" *New York Times*, February 22, 1931, 99.

MGM's publicity department was more forthcoming, complementing the racial and gender signifiers embedded in the movie. In a display advertisement printed in the *Los Angeles Times* (January 18, 1931, B13), an artist has depicted Booth menaced by a "lion." She is perched in a tree and stares fearfully down at the growling beast only bare inches away. The musculature of the arms and torso of the lion, however, is that of a Black man. As Rhona Berenstein has observed of African males and gorillas, in such films as *Ingagi* (Congo Pictures, 1930), "Black Africans are conflated with a dark animal."[150] Nina's presence plunges Black savages into a festival of killings, ripping away the façade which lured Peru into mistaking them for happy children. Though Nina may well be the governor of these rituals, her whiteness renders her innocent of their inhumanity. Her immersion in this blackness is conditional, an effect reversible by her transfer to white civilization in which sexual desire is legislated by bourgeois manners. In the film she is never threatened by Black sexual abuse; it is sufficiently degenerate that she has been denied her racial legacy. In marketing the film, however, her displayed body rather than her mind becomes the object of racial fears. The savage has become the representation of the Black rapist who is subject only to animal lust.

In the hands of corporate MGM, the colonial matrix of the original has been appropriated and reconfigured on behalf of an American racial regime.[151] In Smith's (Horn's) experience (or his imagination), Nina's existence had been a result of the sexual privileges claimed by white adventurers in the African hinterland. In the film, Nina's octoroon mother is replaced by a white Victorian lady missionary (in a stylized performance by Olive Golden), and no vestige of white agency in miscegenation is preserved. Nina, consequently, becomes a fittingly white prize for the contest between Black desire and white patriarchy. The film thus instantiates a double erasure. It rejects Smith's contention that the heroes (Livingston, Rhodes) of Western expansion into Africa desired and often exploited Black women. And with the same gesture the movie adjudicates against the actual history of slave (and

150. Berenstein, "White Heroines," 316.

151. One confirmation of this is Couzens's report of one objection by British colonial authorities: "In Singapore the film was cut down to four reels by the censor because 'a white man simply does not suffer at the hands of a native, and the native never is permitted to have the advantage of a white man.'" Couzens, *Tramp Royal*, 546.

subsequent) miscegenation in America. The historical past, of course, is inimical to white supremacist mythology. Consequently, in the textual venue of early American film it is possible to discern a protocol which vigilantly patrols for outlawed fragments of the actual past and whereby the ensuing vacancies are consciously covered by invention or are rendered invisible by the ritual repetitions of white myths. Black savages displace white savagery; Africa had no civilizations or history; white patriarchy is the natural and inevitably superior social order.

In the summer of 1932, when John Scott in the *Los Angeles Times* surveyed the impact *Trader Horn* was having on the movie industry, his attitude was almost conversational. Like most insiders, Scott felt under no obligation to document the phenomenal success of the film. At this juncture he was more interested in detailing how flattery had metamorphosed into imitation. Summarized by the headline, "Loin Cloth, Leopard Skin, Hot Weather Film Vogue," Scott recited the parade of studio productions trailing after *Trader Horn*. MGM, of course had been the first out of the gate with what would prove to be the first of the Johnny Weissmuller Tarzans. Columbia was filming *Fury of the Jungle*; Paramount was starting *The Isle of Lost Souls* and *Bird of Paradise*; RKO had scheduled *King Kong* and *The Most Dangerous Game*; Universal was producing *Pagan River* and a jungle serial starring Carl Buck Mundy; and Douglas Fairbanks was developing *Robinson Crusoe of the South Seas*.[152] Unremarked upon were the numerous rip-offs, like Monarch Pictures's *Savage Girl*.[153]

A close inspection of Scott's list reveals that he supposed an interconnection between jungle films and the horror film genre (*The Isle of Lost Souls*, *King Kong*, and *The Most Dangerous Game*). For Scott the interconnections might have seemed almost natural. They were no such things, but as he was immersed in this cultural landscape he functioned as an ideologue. The mood of the industry was captured in one prerelease thought up by the publicity department at RKO: "King Kong,

152. John Scott, "Loin Cloth, Leopard Skin, Hot Weather Film Vogue," *Los Angeles Times*, June 26, 1932, B11, B16. One interesting note: Noble Johnson, the Black actor and cofounder of Lincoln Pictures, convincingly plied with white makeup, played a Slavic henchman in *The Most Dangerous Game*.

153. Tino Balio estimates that the eight majors made around thirty horror films between 1931 and 1936. There is no estimate from the Poverty Row studios, which generally accounted for a quarter of the films released each year. See Balio, *Grand Design*, 298.

of a former world, comes to destroy our world—all but the soft, white female thing he holds like a fluttering bird!"[154] The complex coding entangled in these imaginings is simply astounding. The slave trade is recoded as a monstrous (Black) invasion; the invaders originate from a place which is alien by virtue of distance and time; a degraded, unnatural representation of sexual desire is conjured; and implicitly the fate of civilized society converges with the duty to protect white women. One must entertain the possibility that certain cultural materials migrated between the two genres and when reassembled outside specific sites might signify thematic conventions. The genres are robustly, rigorously Manichaean, easily exhausting the discursive confines imposed by privileging the triumph of good over evil. Patriarchy vanquishes anarchy; science triumphs over superstition; Christianity trumps paganism; rationality defeats instinct; modernity supersedes the premodern; and so on. Concluding her inspection of film texts, publicity and exhibition materials, Production Code Administration memoranda, and the like of the early 1930s, Rhona Berenstein discerned another link: "The genres also share a focus on (white) women as the vehicles through which borders are crossed, such as the assumed divisions between human and nonhuman, male and female, attacker and victim, heterosexual and homosexual, black and white, masculine and feminine, and sexual and asexual."[155] To make these conflicts compelling popular entertainment fare, they are conscripted into the more seductively emotional dialectics of race and gender. The horror and jungle film genres become heuristic devices for truth telling. And their resistance to political and dramatic variance substantiates their identification with the verities of the moment.

Trader Horn's production costs went well over a million dollars; *Tarzan, the Ape Man*'s costs more than six hundred thousand before its release date. These were costly features and the decisions to make such films were being made at a time of increasing crisis in the American movie industry. The Depression was reaching its lowest point: for the three years following 1929, an average of 100,000 workers were becoming unemployed each week; by the end of 1932, 28 percent of the country's population was without any income at all; the national income had dropped from $81 billion in 1929 to $41 billion in 1932. The-

154. Lasky, RKO, 94.
155. Berenstein, *Attack of the Leading Ladies*, 203.

ater attendance continued to plummet: in 1931, 70 million customers visited movie houses per week; in 1932, that was down to 55 million. Not surprisingly, by 1932, four thousand of 1930's twenty thousand theaters were closed, placing over 40,000 staff in unemployment; and annual payrolls of studio staff fell off from $156 million in 1931 to $50 million in 1932.[156] As noted in a previous chapter, the industry had already been bankrolled by investment houses and banks like Kuhn, Loeb; Goldman, Sachs; and then Halsey, Stuart; and with the coming of sound, the Morgan and Rockefeller banking groups. Tino Balio reports, "When motion-picture firms went under during the Depression, these same bankers installed themselves in the top management positions and took charge of the distressed companies."[157] And though they proved incompetent at the job and soon returned studio administration to experienced entertainment managers, it is fair to say that the bankers were the most influential decision-makers during the heyday of the jungle film and horror film genres from 1931 to 1936. And yet, for instance, in Rudy Behlmer's "Tarzan, Hollywood's Greatest Jungle Hero," one of the most detailed reconstructions of the production process, there is not one mention of the capitalization of MGM during the Depression. Over the next ten years, MGM would release *Tarzan, the Ape Man* (1932), *Tarzan and His Mate* (1934), *Tarzan Escapes* (1936), *Tarzan Finds a Son!* (1939), *Tarzan's Secret Treasure* (1941), and *Tarzan's New York Adventure* (1942).[158]

The suffocating fears and anxieties which erupted from the Depression composed MGM's *Tarzan* into a ferment of ideological and cultural seductions.[159] Certainly it was escapist fare, but the constant rehearsal and recitation of thematic representations amounted to social pedagogy. While the plantation genre drew audiences into an idyllic, mythical past quietly proportioned between aristocratic privilege and the natural racial order, *Tarzan* proposed that even in a near-primeval

156. Balio, *Grand Design*, 13–15.

157. Ibid., 23. RKO, Paramount, and Universal sued for bankruptcy; Fox's takeover was financed by AT&T and Chase National Bank. Ibid., 16–17.

158. For production history, see Behlmer, "Tarzan, Hollywood's Greatest"; and Behlmer, "Tarzan and MGM." An unreleased version of *Tarzan Escapes*, directed by James McKay, was completed in 1935, but the released version (and all the subsequent MGM Tarzans) was directed by Richard Thorpe.

159. For a review of the Depression-era studies of the social and psychological traumas of the economic times, see Sternsher, "Victims of the Great Depression."

chaos an untutored white masculine subject might construct an outpost of civility. For millions in America, economic crisis had overturned the social contract and smashed the conceits of individualism. It also raised questions about the transcendence of race over class, threatening to overturn the successively subsidized orthodoxies of race which helped to fracture America's working class. The indicators of contestation to a race-determined interpretation of American society were numerous. The Black radical Du Bois had revised a class interpretation of race, rewriting the history of the Civil War, Reconstruction, and American imperialism in his 1935 classic, *Black Reconstruction in America*. Other Black radical militants like Ralph Bunche critiqued race-based organizations like the NAACP, proposing an alliance with the white working class.[160] The Communist Party itself gained enormous publicity in its defense of the Scottsboro Boys.[161] And when Bunche faltered, others like Richard Wright and the Trinidadian C. L. R. James reinvigorated a Marxist agenda.[162] Among the most active of labor organizations, the Congress of Industrial Organizations began its renunciation of the American Federation of Labor's apartheid structure.[163]

Race, mediated through several discursive maneuvers, stands as the centering locator of *Tarzan, the Ape Man*. On the other hand, it is almost as if Ivor Novello and Cyril Hume, the writers of the film, W. S. Van Dyke, the director, and Harold Rosson and Clyde de Vinna, the cinematographers, were entirely oblivious to the assault on race being taken up beyond the confines of their film world. Simpler still, this film was originally conceived as a sequel to *Trader Horn* (in the earliest script Horn and Tarzan were partnered against savages), and what better continuity could be achieved than that the racial imaginings of the first would be endorsed in the second? Hume had collaborated with Van Dyke in the revised dialogue for *Trader Horn*,[164] and their shared privi-

160. John B. Kirby, "Ralph J. Bunche."

161. See Carter, *Scottsboro*.

162. See Robinson, *Black Marxism*, passim.

163. One useful example of the massive literature on this event is Marshall, "Negro and Organized Labor."

164. Behlmer, "Tarzan, Hollywood's Greatest," 40. Among the other continuities between *Trader Horn* and *Tarzan, the Ape Man*: C. Aubrey Smith played Horn's trader friend and then plays Jane's trader father; Tarzan's domain, the Mutia Escarpment, was named after Mutia Omoolu; and in *Tarzan Finds a Son!*, Uriah Banks played the African lead, Mooloo.

leging of whiteness persists in *Tarzan, the Ape Man*: "Responding to her father's objections about this ape man, [Jane] says, 'I thought he was a savage, but he wasn't. . . . *He was happy*.' (To which her father says, sensibly, 'He's not like us,' and she replies, 'He's white.'")[165] Just as feared (imagined), like other white goddesses, Jane's sexual appetites betray civilization. In this instance, the weakness may be forgiven since she has chosen a white rather than a Black savage. (And we should never forget that whatever Maureen O'Sullivan contributed to the role, Jane was a shared invention of the collaboration of white males: Burroughs, Van Dyke, Novello, etc.)

In other aspects, however, the Depression times did rupture the text. Tarzan was no longer Burroughs's fictional peer, born to the manor, but now (as Kenneth Cameron characterized him) a "monosyllabic lowbrow." Gone were Tarzan's inherited, aristocratic intelligence and his eventual legacy of wealth. There was a mood in the original which didn't travel well. As Eric Cheyfitz charged Burroughs's work, "In this imperial romance the lower class is as much a foreign country to the upper class as Africa is to Europe."[166] In accordance with studio-driven marketing practices, the principal audience for *Tarzan* in such horrific times was not those Americans particularly admiring of the upper classes. While, as Ed Guerrero maintains, the plantation film genre's slave aristocracy could still be entrusted to entice the sympathies of working class and poor white audiences, Burroughs's creature could not make the same claims. Tarzan had not been the genteel architect of an idyllic antebellum order "memorialized" by countless films, plays, and novels; Tarzan had not led a noble family and caste into the lost cause; Tarzan lacked the disciplined intelligence to tame the Black savages into a submissive work force for a sophisticated economy. Moreover, as Kenneth Cameron maintains, the staple of the Weissmuller-O'Sullivan films seemed explicitly charged with a message for the bleak times: "Tarzan and Jane became a Depression-era fantasy: a stable couple in which the husband was stronger than the chaotic forces of life, able to provide a home and food and security. . . . The lions and leopards were now Tarzan's 'job'—a form of day at the office. The intrusive whites and the hostile blacks were the irrational and unpredictable agents of the outer

165. Cameron, *Africa on Film*, 42.
166. Cheyfitz, "Tarzan of the Apes," 347.

chaos, and it was in dealing with them that Tarzan rose from the worka-day to the heroic."[167]

There were, of course, deeper symbolic materials in these films than Cameron's evocation of a Depression-proof suburbia. And Jane is implicated in one way or another in many of them. Jane incited whiteness; she incited sexual desire; she incited murder and brutality; she incited greed, plunder, and possessiveness. For Jane whiteness demarcated real existence from nullity. Not only does Tarzan's whiteness distinguish him from the rest of "his" world's inhabitants, but in successive films Jane must be with whiteness or at least see whiteness (*Tarzan Escapes*: "But *White* people? Where?"). In *Tarzan and His Mate*, she dresses and undresses in order to entice sexual desire in and competition between Tarzan and his two rivals. And she constantly acts as a lure or herself lures her white companions into quests which violate Africa's hidden treasures (ivory, gold, etc.). Because she is language-laden, immersed in a symbolic universe in which class distinctions, racial hierarchies, gender differences, and materialism are encrusted, she can never truly be in Tarzan's world. She is the ambivalent, often duplicitous Eve in the "Lost Eden" which Tarzan has wondrously secured.[168]

The Africa of Van Dyke and his successor, Richard Thorpe, constantly oscillates between paradise and nightmare. Since none of MGM's Tarzans were filmed in Africa, the paradisiacal Africa was most often represented by stock footage from the *Trader Horn* safari. In contrast, the terrors of Africa were enacted by the "Zambeli" (named after Sam Zimbalist), the "Gibonis" (Cedric Gibbons), the "Hymandis" (Bernard Hyman), and the "Jaconi" (J. J. Cohen), tribes manufactured from Black extras more at home on Los Angeles's Central Avenue.[169] The directors carefully edited out the filmic record of Africans as people: "There are never images of Africans involved in 'normal' acts such as cooking, working, eating or sleeping."[170] For *Trader Horn*'s ethnography, they substituted spear-chucking dark Angelenos and bizarre spectacles like the blackface maniacal dwarves of *Tarzan, the Ape Man*. The two Africas almost exactly matched the real and the made-up. This doubling is important, Kevin Dunn insists, because the Tarzan movies "are ar-

167. Cameron, *Africa on Film*, 43.
168. McGhee, "'There's Something Sad.'"
169. Behlmer, "Tarzan and MGM," 37.
170. Dunn, "Lights . . . Camera," 159.

guably the largest shaper of the West's perception of Africa."[171] Topicalities of the 1930s are present in the films (for examples, designer clothing, the reference that one treasure-hunter is destitute because of the 1929 crash, etc.), but they are rarely African topicalities. Ironically, though the films are a direct endorsement of colonialism with overtones of fascism (Tarzan as a superman), neither of the Tarzan films coincident with one of the most publicized colonial adventures of the decade, the 1935 Italian invasion of Abyssinia, makes mention of the event. Perhaps because Tarzan must go it alone, he is "always violent toward Africans, because they are always presented as attacking him." "Tarzan's domain," Cameron notes, "is in the air; the African earth, to which he sometimes descends, is a lower world inhabited by hostile animals and plants and black Africans."[172] To negotiate in this nether world, he can rely on nothing more than his predator cunning and "umgawa, which originally meant get down, but as time went on it became a multi-purpose expression incorporating raise up, let's go, get up, go away, go for help, etc."[173]

To its studio instigators, Tarzan's eugenic violence was always a part of his charm. From accounts regaled in every recess of the popular press and mass media, the natives were unreasonably hostile (apparently to their lands being appropriated and themselves converted into property). No actual harm to them is intended, however, since the whole enterprise is merely entertainment, not serious commentary. Seventy years later these beliefs and their accompanying apologetic complements endure. In 2004, Turner Entertainment and Warner Bros.' Entertainment released *The Tarzan Collection*, a DVD collection of the MGM Tarzan films. The fourth disc is devoted to Tarzan's evolution from book to film; casting the roles of Tarzan and Jane; the Tarzan yell; the Production Code Administration's censoring of the nudity in *Tarzan and His Mate*; the insertion of Cheetah as a comic device; and so on. No one

171. Ibid., 155.

172. Cameron, *Africa on Film*, 42, 44. Weissmuller had been an Olympic swimming champion in 1924 and 1928, so water was his métier; on the other hand, he and O'Sullivan were doubled by the Flying Codonas for the aerial swinging sequences; O'Sullivan was doubled by 1932 Olympic swimming champion Josephine McKim for the nude underwater sequences in *Tarzan and His Mate*, segments which reappeared in later films. Behlmer, "Tarzan, Hollywood's Greatest," passim.

173. Behlmer, "Tarzan and MGM," 35. The Africanist scholar Joel Samoff informs me that *umgawa* is closest to the Swahili for "although."

bothers themselves about Africa, colonialism, or racism. Obviously, for its market audience, an exploration of these elements in the collected films would merely be disruptive.

RKO's *King Kong* (1933) was the discursive bridge between the jungle film and its influential complements, the plantation genre and minstrelsy. The tale of a monstrous gorilla forcibly transferred from its native domain to America might appear too literal a displacement of the African slave trade to work as fantasy. But the detailed reenactment of African slavery—the kidnapping, transfer, and commodification of African labor—became romantic fare because of the manipulation of the white goddess myth and special effects. Kong and his prehistoric companions were activated through stop-motion animation, a technique perfected by Willis O'Brien for his *Creation*, a scientific vision of life on earth before anthropoids, but the originator and director of the project was Merian C. Cooper ("I believe that it is right that black, brown and yellow men should be dominated by the white").[174] Now the same tedious, painstaking process was employed to portray a fabulous counterscience: the naturalization of race. Yet the most revealing stratagem of the filmmakers was their treatment of the white goddess: on screen, the exhibitionists of the goddess figure expose in filming-within-the-film the manufacturing of a rather ordinary white female into a white goddess. Like that of her immediate predecessor, Edwina Booth, Fay Wray's body becomes a double lure: for Kong and movie-goers. In the film, Kong develops a totally unrealistic (and, of course, unnatural) sexual attraction for Wray (she is small enough to fit in his palm). This marks him as "the bad nigger." Consequently, once he is transferred to America, his desire frustrates any effort to domesticate him, and he is killed.

RKO's Radio Pictures was the most naked outpost in finance capital's colonization of the movie industry. Hobbled together in 1927–28, RKO remained a creature of the bankers, investors, manufacturers, and media moguls who ruled over General Electric, Westinghouse, RCA, NBC, Marconi Wireless and Telegraph, and so on. Considering its pedigree, not unexpectedly RKO produced more than its share of the worst pictures released during the early years of the Depression. But given

---

174. Vaz, *Living Dangerously*, 82. The quotation is from Cooper's memoir (penned under the name "C"), *Things Men Die for* (New York: Putnam's, 1927), 147. For O'Brien, see Vaz, *Living Dangerously*, 205ff.

its ready access to capital, it might be surmised that the studio possessed a degree of immunity from its profit losses and even the most dire fall out to bankruptcy. With the extraordinary political latitude afforded the studio, its films could range from treatments of the movie industry's corrupt and sexist practices (*What Price Hollywood*, 1932) to scathing critiques of arrogant renegades like William Randolph Hearst (*Citizen Kane*, 1941).

Race was another subject on which RKO could display a bald directness. In 1930, seizing on Warner Bros.' success with Al Jolson, the studio had produced *Check and Double Check*, a blackface minstrel film starring Charles Correl and Freeman Gosden, who played *Amos 'n' Andy* on NBC. Because of the almost unprecedented popularity of the duo on its radio affiliate, RKO's controllers could suppose that they had organizational synergy and mythological energy working for them. "Yet after the first splash," Cripps reports, "grosses slumped and only the familial ties of RKO with radio assured a second film."[175] Another explanation was that like Death Row Records sixty years later, the message was more important than the money.[176] Even in previews, *King Kong* worked. And two days before David Selznick officially left for MGM, Merian Cooper was appointed RKO's studio production head. Coinciding with FDR's inauguration, Betty Lasky exclaimed, "[in New York] more than 150,000 movie-goers took their pocket money out of their sugar bowls and plunked down more than $100,000 at the box office to see *King Kong* in the first week's run."[177] Finally, in 1935, in as near a mockery of cultural reflex as one might encounter, Cooper, "having descended from a long line of Southern plantation owners,"[178] filmed Haggard's *She*.[179]

Putative Alternatives

Paul Robeson's performance in *Emperor Jones* in 1933 provided an almost seamless complement to *King Kong*. Robeson brought a physical

175. Cripps, *Slow Fade to Black*, 269.

176. See Alix M. Freedman and Laurie P. Cohen, "'Gangsta' Life: In Rap Music Saga, Was Elite Accountant Victim or Perpetrator?" *Wall Street Journal*, March 20, 1997, A1.

177. Lasky, *RKO*, 95.

178. Ibid., 93.

179. This *She* was transplanted from Africa to the Manchurian arctic and starred Helen Gahagan (Douglas). Kor was now the proto-civilization which had parented the civilizations of China, Manchuria, and Korea.

graphicness to the railroad porter, Brutus Jones, authenticating Eugene O'Neill's portrait of a Black sociopath indifferent to his community and his race. Jones is a predator and parasite. In the first half of the film, Jones abuses the trust of the girl to whom he is betrothed; extorts money from a white businessman; casually uses and discards a Black vamp (Fredi Washington in brownface); kills a brother porter (Frank Wilson) in a club fight; is imprisoned on a chain gang; and escapes after killing a white guard. Stoking coal on a cargo ship, in the second part of the film, the fugitive Jones maroons himself on a Caribbean island populated by poor Blacks; he befriends a white trader (Dudley Digges) and connives in the cheating of the natives; tricks the threadbare court into dethroning the reigning monarch; and replaces him as "de Emperor Jones." For two and a half years Jones plunders and brutalizes his followers, reducing an already destitute population until they rise up in desperate rebellion. The rebels, utilizing their own black magic, drive Jones into the jungle and madness and eventually murder him.

O'Neill had written the play in 1920, the fifth year of the American occupation of Haiti, and *Emperor Jones* had been transferred to film in 1933, the last year of direct rule under U.S. marines. O'Neill claimed that the political elements of the second half of the film were based on an account of the rule of Guillaume Sam (president of Haiti from February to July 1915); while the character of Brutus was a composite of two Blacks he had encountered during his travels, one a powerfully built bartender and deacon, the other, a "colorful Negro, Joe Smith, one of whose sayings—'Dey's some tings I ain't got to be tole, I kin see 'em in folks' eyes'—appears intact in the play."[180] O'Neill's fantastic reconstruction of the short, nasty rule of President Sam bore only a superficial resemblance to reality. The peasant-based rebellions which shortened the administrations of several Haitian presidents in the late nineteenth and early twentieth centuries were largely precipitated by factors originating outside Haitian society. Haiti's social turmoil resulted from a foreign-dominated economy organized to impoverish most of its one and a half million citizens. Brenda Gayle Plummer recounts that by near the time of Sam's presidency in Port-au-Prince, 93 percent of the merchant bankers were foreigners; 56 percent of the importers and exporters were foreigners; 78 percent of coffee exporters were foreigners; and so on. As Plummer reports, "Foreigners dominated six out of the

180. Raleigh, "Eugene O'Neill," 372.

seven categories of importation."[181] Simultaneously, an imperialist foreign policy establishment in Washington, residing in the White House, the Congress, and the War Department, citing the Monroe Doctrine, conspired with American bankers and financiers to wrest control of Haiti's government and resources from European competitors. Governance of Haiti had become a thin veneer for plundering the small booty left and collecting bribes supplied by foreign interests in exchange for "legal" concessions (treaties, contracts, loans, etc.). By the time that Sam's rebellion had secured for him the presidency it was effectively worthless.[182] In 1920, James Weldon Johnson concluded from his investigation of the American occupation that the American invasion had been precipitated by American banking interests:

> More powerful though less obvious, and more sinister, because of its deep and varied radications, is the force exercised by the National City Bank of New York. . . . Behind the Occupation, working conjointly with the Department of State, stands this great banking institution of New York and elsewhere. . . . The United States Marine Corps and the various office-holding "deserving Democrats," who help maintain the status quo there, are in reality working for great financial interests in this country, although Uncle Sam and Haiti pay their salaries.[183]

And the economic havoc which fueled the political turmoil in that country and legitimated the American invasion continued under an occupation administered by what Johnson termed "deserving Democrats" largely drawn from Louisiana (the head of customs; the superintendent of Public Instruction; and Haiti's financial adviser); and Mississippi (the deputy collector of customs).[184] With their marine counterparts, they superintended the reintroduction of forced labor, the massacre of resistance fighters, the rape of Haitian women, and the installation of a series of supine dictators.

DuBose Heyward was brought in to add a backstory for Jones, complementing the Haitian counterfeiture which dominated O'Neill's play. The merging of these two authors produced a characterization of

181. Plummer, "Metropolitan Connection," 129.

182. See Plummer, "Afro-American Response"; and Pamphile, "NAACP and the American Occupation."

183. James Weldon Johnson, "Self-Determining Haiti," 295.

184. Logan, "James Weldon Johnson and Haiti," 399.

Brutus Jones which seems closer to "The Exotic Primitive" stereotype which Sterling Brown attributed to non-Black writers who scoured the dives of Harlem in search of the "Negro, *au naturel*": "The figure who emerges from their pages is a Negro synchronized to a savage rhythm, living a life of ecstasy, superinduced by jazz (repetition of the tom-tom, awakening vestigial memories of Africa) and gin, that lifted him over antebellum slavery, and contemporary economic slavery, and placed him in the comforting fastnesses of the 'mother-land.'"[185] The import of *Emperor Jones* was to confirm that Black sovereignty was doomed and chimerical. From his Black cultural nationalist perspective, the playwright Loften Mitchell issued a caustic judgment of the play: "O'Neill implicitly suggests there is really no need to look toward the freeing of black people because, once freed, they will do the same thing as whites."[186] Thus in the fifth year of the occupation, when the NAACP was finally launching its long campaign of opposition to American rule in Haiti, the play provided one more reiteration of the official American position that only white people could bring order to that society. And in 1933, in concert with the imagery of *King Kong*, the release of *Emperor Jones* as a film might be seen as substantiating the message while reversing the plot trajectory. Neither Kong nor Jones could come to terms with civilization. Their dysfunction was not a consequence of where they were but what they were.

The moods of the film ranged from tabloid sensationalism (Heyward's contribution) to paternal, colonial disapprobation. Hays's office had toned down some of the sensationalism, cutting out one or two of Heyward's murders and insisting that Fredi Washington wear brown makeup so she wouldn't be mistaken for a white woman in sexual congress with a Black man. Still, the nightclub scenes were electric with Black lasciviousness, jealousy, and a catfight; Washington's Undine was sensually seductive and corrupt; and the gambling joint reeked of a Black underworld indifferent to violence and death. Consistent with the monitoring of miscegenation, the race patrol found nothing problematic about the opening of the film where the director, Dudley Murphy, dissolved African or "Haitian" tribal dancers to Black circle dancers in a backwoods church. This cinematic device made the point that Blacks were immune to history and civilization: you could certainly take Afri-

185. Sterling Brown, "Negro Character," 198.
186. Mitchell, *Black Drama*, 76.

cans out of the jungle, but even after the passage of hundreds of years, you could not extract the jungle out of Blacks.

Cripps has described the closeness of the collaboration between O'Neill, Heyward, and the others involved in the film's production ("All of the principals worked easily together. After meeting with them at his southern estate, O'Neill allowed Murphy and Heyward to adapt his materials").[187] Consequently it does not seem untoward to suggest that the filmmakers employed elements in Brutus Jones's backstory which registered strongly with the experience of Black laborers in the early twentieth century. For one, the film's construction of Pullman porters is less than flattering, displaying a then-elite Black occupation as inducing debauchery, womanizing, and selfish aggrandizement. It was precisely the sort of demeaning characterization which might bring ill-repute to the union movement begun by the Brotherhood of Sleeping Car Porters (and Maids) in the late 1920s. George Pullman had first hired freed slaves to serve on his traveling "hotels" in the 1860s. For decades, as far as the Pullman Company and its non-Black passengers cared to know, the men were all named "George," a designation which for most of these Black men was emblematic of slavery's practice of naming laborers on the basis of ownership.[188] In 1927, they hired the socialist labor organizer A. Philip Randolph to head their union organizing movement. The Pullman Company, still immersed in a slave-owner's mentality and intent on destroying any such effort, responded with firings, beatings, jobbing punishments, and eventually, a company union, "The Employee Representation Plan." In 1928, the Brotherhood joined the American Federation of Labor; in 1933, the promise of a strike compelled the Roosevelt administration to champion legislation banning company unions under the National Industrial Recovery Act; and on "July 25, 1937, twelve years to the day of the union's founding, the Pullman Company recognized the Brotherhood of Sleeping Car Porters as the sole legal organization representing the porters employed by the Pullman Company. Never before had a major industrial giant signed an agreement with a labor organization of black men; never before had black men successfully organized."[189] This struggle was entirely effaced by the representation of porters in *Emperor Jones*. Brutus Jones and his

187. Cripps, *Slow Fade to Black*, 216.
188. Santino, "Miles of Smiles," 403.
189. Ibid., 406.

sidekick Jeff (Frank Wilson) were entirely devoid of social conscious-ness or moral authority, characterizations which would certainly lend sympathy to the Pullman Company's position that subservience and company loyalty were the most fitting postures for porters.

A second instance of the film's intertextuality with postbellum Black labor is Brutus Jones's consignment to a chain gang. It was the identi-cal form of convict labor which had been meted out to Zeke in *Hallelu-jah*, in both instances the punishment for murder. Blacks convicted of murder, however, would hardly have provided a sufficient base for the chain gang's purposes.[190] In the late nineteenth century, convict labor was a fact of life in many states but was particularly concentrated and persistent in the former Confederate states, where the vast majority of prisoners were Black.[191] As David Oshinsky has documented, leasing convicts to private parties operating coal mines, brickyards, turpentine farms, and sawmills had enmeshed thousands of Black and poor white men, women, and children. However, at the beginning of the twentieth century, led by public officials in North Carolina, the leasing system was abolished and replaced with the chain gang. After 1908 the most aggressive transmutation of leasing into chain gangs was undertaken by Georgia. Ostensibly this constituted a "progressive" reform, publi-cized for humanitarian reasons, but as Alex Lichtenstein argues, it was largely propelled by a growing momentum for economic moderniza-tion. In Georgia (and elsewhere), the chain gang wrested convict labor from private hands so that the penal system might provide state and local authorities with labor for "Good Roads." It also extended to these states a patina of racial moderation: "Thus disfranchisement, segrega-tion, and prohibition were all promoted as reforms to check the cha-otic tendencies of southern race relations and to protect against the 'moral and physical reversion' of what nearly all whites believed was the inferior race."[192] In 1908 Georgia had five thousand felony and mis-demeanor convicts (about 10 percent of them white), almost all of them assigned to road work. The impact of these convicts and their succes-sors on road improvement is demonstrable. In 1909, only 7.25 percent

190. "Many of the short-term convicts in these camps were sent to the chain gang for between thirty days and one year for petty crimes such as gambling, carrying a concealed weapon, drunkenness, fighting, disorderly conduct, loitering, and va-grancy." Lichtenstein, "Good Roads and Chain Gangs," 94.

191. Mancini, *One Dies, Get Another*.

192. Lichtenstein, "Good Roads and Chain Gangs," 91.

of Georgia's 82,000 miles of road was surfaced; by 1915, "Georgia had 13,000 miles of surfaced rural roads, more than any other southern state, and the fifth largest number of miles of surfaced rural roads in the United States."[193] In *Hallelujah* and *Emperor Jones*, the chain gang melded into the natural landscape, a fitting deposit for Black men who lacked the talent or disposition for right behavior.

Emperor Jones was independently produced by John Krimsky and Gifford Cochran. It was distributed by United Artists. As Sterling Brown has argued, the play and the movie borrowed from the palette of racist stereotypes, sometimes sympathetic but more often hostile, which were exhibited in American literature and embedded in white popular culture.

While *Emperor Jones* percolated from the racist boilerplate of O'Neill and Heyward, *Imitation of Life* exposed the equally durable racial conceits enmeshed in an imaginary ostensibly sympathetic to the plight of Blacks. Fannie Hurst had been raised in St. Louis, Missouri, by her Jewish parents. By the time of her death in 1968 she had published eighteen novels, over ninety short stories, and numerous articles, and her fiction had been culled for twenty-nine moving pictures. In an article devoted to the first *Imitation of Life*, Andre Sennwald, the *New York Times* reviewer, had described Hurst as "America's favorite philosopher."[194] Politically a liberal, Hurst quite publicly had taken on issues like the exploitation of domestic workers, the misery of mining communities, and racial equality. During the Roosevelt administration, Hurst had been befriended by Eleanor Roosevelt, officially served as a consultant to the WPA, and raised funds for Roosevelt's election campaigns.[195]

In 1933, Hurst published her best-selling novel, *Imitation of Life*, and in 1934, Carl Laemmle produced the picturization of the book adapted by William Hurlbut and directed by John Stahl. The central character of Hurst's novel was Bea Pullman, a young white girl who, following an arranged marriage, almost immediately finds herself widowed and pregnant. Taking over her late husband's maple syrup distribution to Atlantic City hotels, Bea hires Delilah, a Black woman, as a live-in servant. Accompanying Delilah is Peola, her own "white nigger baby" (Delilah's description). As Bea's business skills mature, she discovers the com-

193. Ibid., 102.
194. Andre Sennwald, "Screen," *New York Times*, November 24, 1934, 19.
195. Brandimarte, "Fannie Hurst," passim.

modity value of Delilah. Critically augmented by Delilah's mastery with waffles and maple syrup candies, Bea builds a million-dollar chain of restaurants. In the meanwhile, through neglect Bea has alienated her own daughter, Jessie, and Delilah has continually frustrated Peola's compulsion to pass for white. Bea pursues Frank Flake, a man eight years younger than she is, only to lose him to Jessie, who is twelve years younger than Flake. Mirroring Bea's loss and desolation, Delilah loses Peola, whose hatred of her mother stems from Delilah's smothering opposition to her racial ambitions ("Gawd don't want His rivers to mix. . . . Black wimmin who pass, pass into damnation").[196] Peola has herself sterilized, marries a white man, and passes over to whiteness in Bolivia, removing both her mother and her history from her life. Delilah, incapable of recovering from her daughter's betrayal, dies.

Ironically, for many Hurst enthusiasts and detractors, it became a shared notion that the novel actually exploited Hurst's relationship with Zora Neale Hurston. The two had first met in 1925 when "Hurst, a contest judge for the National Urban League's *Opportunity* awards, met Hurston, a prize winner. Hurst hired Hurston as her personal secretary, but within a year the job had switched to chauffeur and general companion and the two women shared a home and traveled together for over a year. Fannie Hurst, among others, was an important connection for Zora Neale Hurston, providing her with an introduction to white literary society as well as to publishers and sponsors."[197] That relationship and her constant public defense of Hurst would bemuse Hurston scholars, particularly in the light of Hurston's uncompromising criticism of the claims by Black intellectuals of authenticity for *Hearts of Dixie* and *Hallelujah*.

For the film Universal assigned the role of Bea to its current box-office draw, Claudette Colbert. And according to the same logic, the studio cast Warren William as her romantic costar.[198] Since William was older than Colbert, this required a major revision of the Flake character, so William became the much older Stephen Archer. Louise Beaver played Delilah, but the casting for Peola was more difficult. Noble Johnson was the best known of the light-complexioned Black actors and had played

196. Hurst, *Imitation of Life*, 299.
197. Caputi, "'Specifying' Fannie Hurst," 704.
198. The same year, Colbert played the title role in *Cleopatra* with William as Marc Antony.

a variety of "ethnic" characters. But Hollywood had generally shunned physical types like the "White Negro" that Stahl was convinced would lend credibility to his film. According to Fredi Washington's account, during the 1934 publicity campaign, despite the testing of hundreds of aspiring "white Negro women," Stahl had quite early settled on her.[199] Washington was signed on as the adult Peola.[200] The rewriting of the Flake character was not the only change. The studio added comic turns by Ned Sparks and Henry Armetta (the latter as a bumbling Italian ethnic). Delilah's genius was transferred from maple syrup candies to pancakes (a conscious allusion by the studio to the popularity of Aunt Jemima pancakes); and Peola's sterilization, marriage, and emigration were excised, producing an ending which allowed her, with complete remorse, to attend her mother's funeral. Afterwards Peola resumes her Black identity. Paradoxically, in their real lives, it was Fredi Washington who was the Black militant, while Louise Beaver traded racial identity for employment as a Black caricature in the movies.

Both the novel and the film retained one signification of the Depression: two single-parent females, one white and one Black, had combined to construct an economically self-sufficient household. In an era marked by unusual numbers of males deserting their families, either permanently or in the search for employment, millions of abandoned women were thrown onto their own resources.[201] However, Hurst had employed the mammy character to overshadow the codependency of the two women. And Hurlbut's adaptation gave an even greater play to Hurst's strategy of tamping down the exposed failings of patriarchy. The film mediates the emotional and social crisis caused by the Depression by emphasizing the themes of racial difference and white hierarchy. For

199. Bogle, *Bright Boulevards*, 134ff.

200. Beavers played opposite three Peolas. While Washington garnered the most attention, Sebie Hendricks played Peola at four, and Dorothy Black played Peola at nine. I presume it was Miss Black who, on the set, objected to Beavers as too dark to play her mother (see Bogle, *Toms, Coons, Mulattoes*, 63–64). In any case, when the *Detroit Monitor* interviewed Black in 1979, it was apparent that her film work had ended with *Imitation of Life*. Bob Calverley, "Film Group Finds a Missing Star Here in Detroit," *Detroit Monitor*, March 17, 1979, 3A.

201. Helmbold found in her study of families during the Depression that in South Bend, Chicago, Philadelphia, and Cleveland the number of female-headed households increased 20.9–25.9 percent in the years 1930–40; and for the same period, married women's proportion of female employment increased 28 percent. See Helmbold, "Beyond the Family Economy," 650–51n17, 636.

RRING PACES PRISON YARD

ED TO KILL,
E CALMLY
YS PENALTY

By WADE H. LUCAS

N C., Sept. 21—A common ordinary house-
.t on the naked knee of Johnnie Lee Friday
und-sized 21-year-old mulatto from Dunn
h in the electric chair at State's prison for
Negro for $75.

matttered not to the little fly that the body

rol pump out of
aft that mar
cells of eier-
th mulatto's
hurled Lee
ed no effort
which was

kept but $25
tering, former
twn demon-
him to kill
Negro barber
Herring Lst
Lee said no
Hdones and Joe
Negroes who
the part they
Herring want-
te hope of g l-
he never got it
red Negro and
s 30 years in
were been any
p to the chair
the law he would
et already, but
l stand in the
the this little
the chair Lee
n n s to die in
cerar

generally se
time Ander-
et of eight
the switch at
$75 for it—
Lee sald he
14-11 But Mr
the sovereign

Appeal

A Oxley,
dorr made a
democracy to
Friday morn-
add not see
ne ns to the
t Thursday, to
nee would be
on murder by
if was the

'Brain Trust' Member In Conference With Secretary of Labor

WASHINGTON, Sept. 21.—
(CNS)—John P. Davis, executive secretary of the joint
committee on national recovery, was in an extended conference last week with Secretary of Labor Frances Per-
kins and Assistant Secretary
of Labor McGrady. The conference took place in the Department of Labor and had to
do with the needs of Negro
labor for protection under the
National Recovery Administration.

Mr. Davis declined to comment on the results of the
conversations, stating that he
would first have to consult
members of the joint committee on national recovery. He
could say, he declared, that
the meeting with the Secretary of Labor and Assistant
Secretary McGrady had proved
most helpful and that he
thought both administration
officials were maintaining a
sympathetic attitude toward
Negro labor.

Two stations got jumbled and
came in over the radio the other
evening. One program was a ser-
mon and the other was an account
of a baseball game. It sounded
rather funny to hear: "David fas-
tened a stone in his sling, twirled
it about his head—he's sliding! He
made it! That evens the score."

PALS S
AS SLAY
PASSES
'LAST M

By JAMES H. PAR

RALEIGH, N. C.,
—One of the mos
things about living
shadow of the elect
is seeing a friend "g
according to the ele-
ent "Death Row" tenan

Three doomed men, d
goldhbonged killers, br
and and waile with
little Johnnie Lee, Du
was marched to the cha

The undersized youth
the "last mile" long an
monish the mos hearth
three to "stop their
Lord is with m

Less than two minut
the prisoners on the
the dynamos hummin
out his life.

It was when the req
were, was loude i, that C
ton, Negro murderer,
completely. Beating his
cell floor, he shouted:
"Oh, God, Oh, God, h
Johnnic."

In the cell next to hi
Cooper, who killed, as
for hire, clenched the
cell, his face steamed
He mumbled:
"Johnnie was a goo
good boy, I tell you,"

Farther down the
Stevenson, Italian, wh
ficials think is shamm
laid on his mattress h
sobbing with emotion.

"It Eas a Pit
"It eas a pit; it re
cried.

John Lewis Edwa
scheduled to di next F
his cell reading aloi
Bible. He himself wa
to "meet my Gd"

McLam Unaff
Only Charlie Luth
white, who is also sch
next Friday, appeare
He stretched, but on
the dynamos humme
McLamb still refer
his case in det l. He
len.

To "Sister" Allen,
woman interested in r
work, Lee gave a stat
his death, in which h
"accepted Jesus Christ

LEAVES FOR WEST INDIES

FREDI WASHINGTON

Again brought into the spotlight, Fredi Washington has been selected to feature in another film production
and sails over the week-end for location iin the West
Indies. Miss Washington, who starred in the stage production of "Run Little Chillun," is also featured in Paul
Robeson's picturization of "Emperor Jones."

HER FAN SLIPPED!

QUARTETTE AT

example, borrowing from the stock of minstrelsy's grinning Negroes, at one early moment in the film Delilah is commanded by Bea to display a broad smile. On screen, Bea has suddenly hit upon the notion that Delilah's face might be a useful marketing symbol. The audience, on the other hand, is being invited to share in a putative and fittingly democratized history of how the familiar Aunt Jemima logo was invented. And like a well-trained domestic pet, Beavers/Delilah freezes into a full-screen Jemima grin, so completely uncomprehending of the purpose of the performance that she has to be ordered to end it. Stahl's use of cinematic lighting and space persistently constructs racial difference and Black subordination. In one striking scene, Bea ascends the stairs to her bedroom while Delilah descends to her subordinate space below. Both women are retreating to their lonely quarters, but Bea's destiny is bathed in light while Delilah's fate is foredoomed by the darkness around her. Delilah's loyalty to her superior mistress is played and replayed: in one moment she declares her pancake mix is a family secret to which she is sworn; in the next instant, she whispers the secret to Bea. When Bea decides to contractually bestow a small share of the profits to Delilah, the mammy hysterically rejects the gesture: "Oh, honey chile, please don't send me away. Don't do that to me. . . . I's your cook and I wants to stay your cook."[202]

Black audiences, understandably, were ambivalent towards Delilah and Beavers. Paradoxically, Peola's anti-Negro rants drew more sympathy. For many Blacks choosing between the two actresses was determined by a distinction in their skills. It was clear to many that Washington's dramatic talents were superior to Beavers's. Of course, the screenplay biased reception and interpretation. While Delilah did have some dramatic moments in the film, Beavers never achieved the seriousness or the pathos which Washington projected in her scenes. Beavers's surrender to minstrelsy contaminated those moments of Delilah's anguish, while almost every scene in which Washington appeared was awash with conflict and tinged with tragedy.[203] Even then Black audi-

202. According to Bogle, Beavers had to be taught Black movie dialect, since she had been educated in California (Pasadena High School). Bogle, *Toms, Coons, Mulattoes*, 63.

203. Harry Levette, the Associated Negro Press columnist, reported that another scene cut from the film was "a near lynching scene when Peola, pretending to be white, accused a young colored man of attempting to flirt with her. Just as they had strung him up she breaks down and screams 'don't do it, I'm a nigger too.'" Sampson,

ences might have suspected that Beavers was enjoying her collaboration with white racism.[204] Paradoxically, Fredi Washington was more sympathetic and defended Beavers, who had befriended her during the filming of *Imitation of Life*. In fact, for a time Washington stayed in Beavers's home. Having gotten this close to one of the more popular of the Hollywood Negroes, Washington temporized. For Beavers, she reminded readers of Black newspapers, the Delilah part was a step up from the maids to which she had been confined. And while Washington asserted she had "no intentions" of pursuing a film career, for Beavers, "this was her living. Pictures were the only thing she knew."[205]

As was telegraphed by his earlier exposure of the stereotypes of Blacks in American literature, Sterling Brown condemned both versions of *Imitation of Life* for the lack of realism he associated with the mammy and tragic mulatto types. Publishing his review in the National Urban League's *Opportunity*, Brown's "Once a Pancake" rebuked Hurst before a Black and liberal white audience she had previously enthralled.[206] In the following issue of the magazine, Hurst responded by characterizing Brown as "unintelligent" and "ungrateful." She defended her novel and its filmic adaptation by alluding to the codependency theme, the same theme she had so effectively muted by employing what Brown found objectionable. Jane Caputi reports that "[Hurst] finds Brown's concerns to be both 'petty' and 'carping' and chastises him for neglecting to realize 'the important social value of this picture . . . [which] practically inaugurates into the important medium of the motion-picture a consideration of the Negro as part of the social pattern of American life."[207] Brown, however, was unrepentant, and for several months letters to the journal championed Brown or Hurst. Eventually, in August

---

Blacks in Black and White, 495. Sampson is quoting from the *New York Age*, September 12, 1942.

204. Two years later, in 1937, the *New Age Dispatch* felt compelled to chastise Beavers. "Miss Louise Beavers, one of our best-known movie stars, when interviewed in Boston recently, said the 'big companies are getting tired of criticism of what they're trying to do for Negroes,' or words to that effect. We do not object to Miss Beavers' viewpoint, for we would naturally expect that it would be colored by the fact that she is directly concerned because of her livelihood." Sampson, *Blacks in Black and White*, 488.

205. Bogle, *Bright Boulevards*, 136.

206. Sterling Brown, "Imitation of Life."

207. Caputi, "'Specifying' Fannie Hurst," 701. Hurst's letter was published in *Opportunity* 13 (April 1935): 121.

1935, the editors called a halt to the debate, citing the continuing volume of correspondence.

Beavers's career flourished. For the next two decades or so, she would reprise her mammy, second only to Hattie McDaniel, who textured her subaltern roles with caustic witticisms and the flavor of insubordination. Washington's film career was virtually snuffed. She would appear in *One Mile from Heaven* (Twentieth Century–Fox, 1937) and star in the independently produced *Ouanga* (George Terwilliger, 1936), but the remainder of her acting career was on the stage. The most frequently cited rationale for the brevity of her film career was her light complexion. But the major studios may have also been wary of Washington because of her racial militancy. In 1937 she led the organizing of the Negro Actors Guild and served as its first executive secretary for the next two years (she left to star in the stage play *Mamba's Daughters*). And in 1942, she became a columnist for the *People's Voice*, a weekly published by Adam Clayton Powell Jr., her then brother-in-law.[208] In her column "Headlines/Footlights," Washington's subjects ranged over a broad spectrum, bridging politics and entertainment. In one column she might chide Roosevelt's War Department for its segregation and abuse of Black soldiers; in another, she advocated the fuller use of Black performers in the overseas tours organized by the USO, wrote celebratory profiles of such entertainers as Fats Waller and Paul Robeson, and chronicled the progress of Black performers on Broadway and in the movies. Many of the big band musicians, now big names, Washington had known in their struggling days, and she shared with her readers intimate tales of their triumphs. And on one occasion she was compelled to publicly address Peola.

Washington consistently challenged Black performers who projected Blacks as rural idiots or urban coons. And in her July 31, 1943, column, Washington had taken umbrage at elements in the stage performance of the Black comedian Tim Moore. A constant theme of her column was those entertainers who employed what she interpreted as the dated routines of Black minstrelsy and blackface minstrelsy. This time she had criticized Moore for comedic bits which abased what Washington

---

208. Powell, the *People's Voice*, and presumably Washington were under FBI surveillance: "The FBI read *The People's Voice* with great care. And the results were enough to cause the agency to question whether criminal action should not be brought against Powell and his colleagues on the paper." Hamilton, *Adam Clayton Powell, Jr.*, 177.

usually referred to as the "New Negro" and for "razor wielding, woman debasing" humor. Washington published a portion of Moore's letter to her in which he referred to Peola: "I have never seen you on the stage but once and that was *Singing the Blues* and I think they had a little dice shooting and murder. I did not see anything uplifting to the race in the part you played. I also did not see anything uplifting about the part of a colored woman you played in 'Imitation of Life,' who was ashamed of her own mother because she was dark." Washington's retort is instructive:

> I should like to point out to Tim that I do not take exception to this criticism of parts I've done in the theatre and on the screen which dates back ten or more years. But I should like to clarify for Tim and others who are confused on the issue. The fact is that ten years ago, we were a slumbering people standing still with no particular knowledge of the plight of our unfortunate brothers in far off lands or at home for that matter.
>
> ... It is hardly necessary to try to point out the terrific world-wide changes which have taken place since that time. Unprecedented attention has been given the Negro since the war began because of the fact that we are theoretically free but actually part slave under a vicious system. ...
>
> ... These and many more reasons, which certainly we must be acquainted with, are why, what was considered all right in the theatre or on the screen ten years ago, are not all right now. Today we are shedding red blood for democracy.[209]

For Washington, the struggle against fascism was a fight against racism and sexism, both at home and abroad. Moore's brand of humor and Peola's abandonment of her own racial identity amounted to identical forms of treason—a neurotic fear of blackness—and were no longer

209. Washington, "Headlines/Footlights," August 7, 1943. Washington made the same point seven months later: "It is not funny to hear a so-called joke which pokes fun at the color of one's skin. Certainly the world is full of incidents which lend themselves to comedy without resorting to perpetuating the mythical idea among most whites that Negroes are simple minded and quite unaware that even comedy has become streamlined." Washington, "Headlines/Footlights," March 4, 1944. On this occasion her target was the Black song-and-dance team Buck and Bubbles. Bubbles had performed "Shine," one of the songs Washington abhorred, in the movie *Cabin In the Sky*.

acceptable. Washington believed the war crisis had wounded racism because of the necessity of recruiting Blacks into uniform and war production. A united front for dignity and equality among Blacks was urgent. Only those too stupid or self-serving would misuse the moment. Obviously impervious to such observations, Moore would continue his minstrelsy into the next decade. In the mid-1950s he starred as Kingfish on television's *Amos 'n' Andy* and incurred the same stinging disapprobation. While the door had closed on Washington, it remained wide open for the likes of Beavers, McDaniel, and Moore.

While the reputations of *Emperor Jones* and *Imitation of Life* as critical ruptures in Black filmic representation in the 1930s rested on their construction as dramas, *The Green Pastures* was a much more ambiguous project. Assembled from narratives in the Old Testament, *The Green Pastures* purported to be a traditional rural Negro reading of Genesis and Exodus. This conceit presumably rationalized the all-Black cast, the translation of Tyndale's poesy into blackface minstrelsy dialect, and the imposition of Black vaudevillian routines onto the frames of biblical or quasi-biblical episodes.

The origins of *The Green Pastures* was *Ol' Man Adam an' His Chillum* (1928), a collection of short stories written by Roark Bradford and published in the *New York World*. Bradford, born in Tennessee, had been a journalist in New Orleans and claimed his stories were drawn from observations and interviews with Louisiana Blacks.[210] In 1930, Marc Connelly adapted Bradford's work as a musical play. The Pulitzer Prize-winning play was immensely successful (some 630 performances in New York alone) and was still touring the country when Warner Bros. decided to make their film in 1935. This was, however, Warner Bros.' second take on Connelly's play. The first was Al Jolson's *Wonder Bar* (1934), a film rarely shown on television or examined in the literature.[211] Modeled on MGM's big hit *Grand Hotel* (1932), the more modest set in the Warner version consisted of a decadent Parisian club, frequented by gigolos, sex-hungry American dowagers, adulterers, impoverished European aristocrats, and tragic assignations. Inexplicably, among its attractions was a fantastic Jolson number, a fourteen-minute minstrel

210. Loften Mitchell characterized the tales as "burlesque." Mitchell, *Black Drama*, 94.

211. The costars of the film were Kay Francis, Dolores del Rio, Ricardo Cortez (an Austrian whose original name was Jacob Krantz), and Dick Powell.

parody of "The Green Pastures" directed by Busby Berkeley which displayed Jolson and a large cast of white actors, dancers, and singers in blackface. The sequence endures as one of the most spectacular displays of blackface minstrelsy preserved on film.

For *The Green Pastures*, Warner Bros. assigned William Keighly as co-director with Connelly. This insured that the movie would be a carbon copy of the play. And due to the death of Richard B. Harrison in 1935, the studio cast Rex Ingram as de Lawd and additionally gave him the roles of Adam and Hezdrel (a nonexistent character in the Bible).[212] In addition to Ingram, the all-Black cast included Oscar Polk (Gabriel), Eddie Anderson (Noah), Frank Wilson (Moses), Edna Mae Harris (Zeba), George Reed (Reverend Dashee), Ernest Whitman (the Pharaoh), George Randol (the High Priest) and even a small part for Hattie McDaniel (as one of Noah's taunters).[213] The studio also employed the Hall Johnson Choir to render spirituals. Apropos of Bradford's initial imaginings and sources, the film opens on a rural Black Louisiana village, where children are preparing to attend Sunday school. Here is one of the film's early achievements: departing from the representations of pickaninnies, the camera loving parades close-up portraits of beautiful, intelligent young Black faces. And as the narrative journeys from the creation of Adam and Eve to the familiar tales of the Hebrews' Exodus from Egypt, both Bradford and Connelly are transcended by the "sorrow songs" arranged by Hall Johnson and performed by his choir. In one powerful moment, for instance, when Moses is refused entry into the Promised Land, the choir performs a chorus, "I want to shout glory when the world is on fire." This import of a slave-resistance spiritual transports the film far beyond the counterfeiture of its creators. Cripps was particularly impressed by the film's ending: "The new Negro, Hezdrel, Ingram's third role, is a soldier, bare-chested, fighting in a smoky battle against a nameless and presumably godless enemy who can only be racism."[214] And Bogle commented, "What transcended

212. See "R. B. Harrison, 70, 'De Lawd,' Is Dead," *New York Times*, March 15, 1935, 21.

213. According to Sampson, Ingram had earned a medical degree and a Phi Beta Kappa key at Northwestern Medical School in 1919. Sampson, *Blacks in Black and White*, 529. For a profile of Ingram, see "Emperor Ingram of 'Haiti,'" *New York Times*, July 24, 1938, 120; and for Polk, "Gangway for the Assistant Chief Big Shot," *New York Times*, June 28, 1936, X4.

214. Cripps, *Slow Fade to Black*, 260.

the shortcomings of the script . . . was the brilliance of the performances. Few film casts have ever equaled the sheer dynamics and unabashed delight that these actors showed."[215] But such instances were too few to salvage the representation of blackness from the caricatures which abounded (including the representation of Babylon as a modern Harlem nightclub with wiggling, tan beauties). In the end Bogle heaped contempt on the studio and its collaborators:

> It is now evident that *The Green Pastures* rested on a cruel assumption: that nothing could be more ludicrous than transporting the lowly language and folkways of the early-twentieth-century Negro back to the high stately world before the Flood. . . . And in this juxtaposition of low with high, there were implied Negro ignorance and inferiority. All this went under the guise of a "Negro miracle play." Nothing could have been more absurd. For Negroes of the period never pictured historical or biblical events in terms of their own experience. Indeed, the problem was that they always dreamt of a white heaven and a white heavenly host.[216]

The film was only moderately successful. And the centrality now attached to it by historians of Black filmic representation might have been missed if the movie had not been reprieved by N B C television in 1957. Angered by the laudatory reception granted the film by television critics, and anticipating Bogle, Nick Aaron Ford observed that if Connelly had done a little research, "he would have learned that of all the spirits of the other world, so far as unlettered Negroes are concerned, only the devil is black. God, the angels, and all the heavenly creatures are as white as the drifting snow."[217]

Black Improvisation and Resistance

The chroniclers of the representations of Blacks in 1930s films approached the era somewhat differently. Bogle, for instance, filtered his toms, coons, mulattoes, bucks, and mammies through the decade's movies, catching enough hits to determine which Black performers distinguished themselves or, more certainly, were most frequently victimized. Stepin Fetchit and his double, Willie Best, portrayed the comic

215. Bogle, *Toms, Coons, Mulattoes*, 69.
216. Ibid., 68.
217. Ford, "How Genuine Is the Green Pastures?"

coon. Even more frequently than anyone else, Clarence Muse played the stoic tom, Bill "Bojangles" Robinson, the dancing tom. Fredi Washington was awarded the most memorable mulatta, but the role was originally Nina Mae McKinney's. Louise Beavers and Hattie McDaniel were the dominant mammies. Paul Robeson was the physically most imposing buck; Rex Ingram, the most versatile.[218] Bogle insisted that "no one in his right mind could ever claim that the roles these performers played were anything other than flat-out deplorable. Yet no one can deny that the actors and actresses were significant talents."[219] Bogle eschewed devoting much attention to the organization of the American movie industry—studios, capital, management, and so on—because his larger concern was with how Black performers smuggled humanity into the proscriptive boundaries of the caricatures. Guerrero's approach to the Depression decade stressed the instrumental agency of movies, their propaganda function in times of social and economic crisis. The plantation genre was the dominant trope of the period, employed as an escapist experience to detract audiences from their own miserable existences and to assure white audiences that no matter how bleak their lives were, they were not black. The era began with *Dixiana* (RKO, 1930), ended with *Jezebel* (Warner Bros., 1938) and *Gone with the Wind* (Selznick, 1939), and in the middle were *Judge Priest* (Fox, 1934), *Mississippi* (Paramount, 1935), *The Littlest Rebel* (Fox, 1935), and *The Little Colonel* (Fox, 1935).[220] For Guerrero, like Bogle, the American film

218. Bogle, *Toms, Coons, Mulattoes*, chap. 3. Ironically, the interchangeability of Stepin Fetchit and Willie Best is illustrated in *A Separate Cinema*, where a still of Best in *The Kansan* (1943) is mislabeled "Stepin Fetchit." Bogle, introduction, xix.

219. Bogle, introduction, xxii, xxiv.

220. Guerrero, *Framing Blackness*, 20–25. Guerrero might have added Paramount's *So Red the Rose* (1935), a film based on Stark Young's 1934 novel which stressed the aristocratic heritage of two slave-owning families, the McGehees ("Celtic rebels") and the Bedfords ("English country gentlemen"). The nearly forty pages of Paramount's publicity package (now in the Library of Congress) feature endorsements from the United Daughters of the Confederacy, sales promotions for dresses, furniture, flowers, etc.; essay contests, old photos contests, department store contests featuring displays of six Confederate "heroes," etc. Yet Cripps wrote of the film: "A dull rehearsal of Southern agonies away from the centers of combat, it included on its periphery a strong conflict between two boldly painted slaves, the stately house servant, William Veal (Daniel Haynes), and a hard-eyed fieldhand, the rebellious Cato (Clarence Muse), who beautifully represented the poles of black response to slavery—accommodation and insurrection." Cripps, *Slow Fade to Black*, 290.

industry was one gigantic enterprise, Hollywood, which melded seamlessly into American capitalism. On the other hand, Cripps argued that the imagined significance of blackness projected by Depression-era movies required a more nuanced construction of the era.

First, Cripps maintained that the Depression itself was characterized by two movements: the initial crash and its economic, social, and cultural reverberations; and subsequently, beginning in 1933, a sort of counter-Depression which encompassed Roosevelt's New Deal initiatives, the Production Code Administration, and the literary invasion of "Eastern" liberals and radicals ("Easily the best black role appeared in a film with a heavyhanded leftist social message, Clifford Odets's *Golden Boy*").[221] And though he acknowledged that "Southern nostalgia," "Southern chauvinism," and the like were the "standard fare offered by moviemakers," he struggled mightily to resurrect the "charisma" of "the finest black roles," particularly after the "minor watershed" of 1936.[222] Because of the unprecedented frequency with which Black characters punctuated American films in the 1930s — in mysteries, musicals, prison films, romances, gangster films, comedies, etc. — Cripps has never embraced Guerrero's contention about the overwhelming significance of the plantation genre. But that same evidence has attracted Cripps to a variant of Bogle's obsession. So Cripps, too, privileges performance over ideological function. It is an understandable impulse.

Even the most hypervigilant critic or scholar ought to be sufficiently discerning to separate the ideological matrix of a caricature from the actor or actress who is impersonating it. For instance, take the extreme Black minstrel Stepin Fetchit. In *Charlie Chan in Egypt* (Fox, 1935), Fetchit lays waste to his own invention of the exaggerated lazy Negro when "Snowshoes" enjoys a bit of obvious improvisation. Having just taken a flashlight from a bed table in his tent, he walks a few steps, turns and looks at the still open drawer, considers and apparently rejects the effort, and then drawls "close yourself." In a different moment, Thelma "Butterfly" McQueen, dressed as a maid in the midst of a lavish white dinner party in *Affectionately Yours* (Warner Bros., 1941),

221. Cripps, *Slow Fade to Black*, 304. The film was released in 1939 by Columbia Pictures. Cripps is referring to Clinton Rosemond (or Rosamond). Rosemond also had important roles in Warner Bros.' *The Green Pastures* (1936) and that studio's anti-lynching film *They Won't Forget* (1937).
222. Ibid., 288–98.

reluctantly answers a phone. With deep perplexity written on her face, "Butterfly" is obviously at a loss to determine at what end of the receiver she is to speak, at what end to listen. There is a meanness here which is absent from Fetchit's bit. Both are supposedly comic turns, but the first appears more natural, a comedian toying with his own creation. McQueen's pantomime conspires with a white supremacist creed that poises Blacks on the nether side of modernity. Perhaps it is only my imagination, but I can almost hear the director, Lloyd Bacon, from behind the camera instructing McQueen to fiddle with the phone.

Lincoln Perry's self-reflexive performance as Stepin Fetchit in *Charlie Chan in Egypt* draws our attention to the persistent tension which inhabited the sites occupied by Black performers and filmmakers. Offscreen, Perry's notorious behavior was self-destructive or flagrantly compensatory. There can be little doubt that as his caricature won more fans, Perry distanced himself from the creature by countering Fetchit's passivity with his offscreen volatility, and in contrast to Fetchit's poverty, Perry made extravagant displays of wealth.[223] Other performers, more marginal than Perry simply because their stereotypes appeared less frequently in movies, were more straightforward. Among that lot was Theresa Harris, a young Black actress in the 1930s who had played supporting bits (in films starring Jean Harlow, Joan Blondell, Barbara Stanwyck, Marlene Dietrich) ranging from domestic maids, to a reformatory girl, and a nightclub singer. On rare occasions there were hints that her characters had backstories or lives of their own. Much more frequently her characters were atmospheric props, menials at worst, and at best drab, sexless creatures functioning as contrasts to alluring white bombshells. In 1937, Harris was given a romantic role opposite Ralph Cooper in the Black gangster film *Bargain with Bullets* (Million Dollar). Interviewed in the *Pittsburgh Courier* (August 27, 1937), Harris was thrilled: "The opportunity of playing the roles otherwise denied one in white pictures is a great relief to the Negro motion picture artist." And she politically challenged Black audiences to support Black filmmakers: "We have tolerated so many rotten pictures made in Hollywood by the Jews and whites, I do not see why our own people cannot be tolerant of the pioneering state of this company."[224] Vocalizing her identity as a race woman, Harris collapsed the space between herself

223. See Regester, "Stepin Fetchit," passim.
224. Sampson, *Blacks in Black and White*, 490.

and her audience, offering a collaboration of resistance in the stead of a scripted adulation. Race identity, while trumping the differences in their everyday lives, ensured that they experienced a similar disgust with what passed for blackness in the movies.

The public expression of Theresa Harris's rage at mainstream movies was enabled by two factors: the appearance of a new cluster of Black filmmakers; and, of course, the persistence of Black newspapers. Both shared Harris's acute disappointment in the sorts of Black imaging which had become all too familiar in the 1930s. Micheaux's disdain was long-standing. And his new competitors in the arena of Black audience films were even more frustrated. Unlike Micheaux, his closest competitors, filmmakers like Ralph Cooper and George Randol, had experienced "Hollywood's" racial practices up close. According to Henry Sampson, in 1936 Cooper, a popular Harlem band leader and song-and-dance man, had been brought to Los Angeles to replace an ill Bill Robinson in a Shirley Temple movie (*Captain January*, studio unknown). Probably his light complexion disqualified him. That might have also been the case when his scenes were deleted in *White Hunter* (Fox, 1936), the one film by a major studio in which he appeared. Randol, an accomplished stage actor, was slightly darker than Cooper, but he also had limited work as an actor on the big lots (*The Green Pastures*). As far as Cripps was concerned, the fault was in the industry: "Hollywood Negro roles—the butlers and the maids—demanded positive racial identity, so those with full lips, broad noses, and deep brown skins built their resumes at the expense of the Peolas. With American irony those of lightest complexion—Monte Hawley, Clarence Brooks, Frank Wilson, A. B. Comathiere, Laura Bowman, Cleo Desmond, Jesse Lee Brooks—drifted into race movies made for black folk."[225]

In 1936, Cooper and Randol teamed up to make *Dark Manhattan* (Cooper/Randol, 1937), the picture credited with launching the Black gangster films of the late 1930s and early 1940s and a revival of all-Black films. And some of the Black press, particularly the *Pittsburgh Courier*, the *New Age Dispatch*, and the *New York Amsterdam News*, published pieces encouraging this newest effort at producing "all-colored" films.

Tino Balio estimates that the number of all-Black films produced between 1937 and 1940, over fifty, more than doubled the twenty-three

225. Cripps, *Slow Fade to Black*, 329–30.

such films released between 1930 and 1936.[226] *Dark Manhattan* is associated with this surge of Black film production. Beginning in 1936 and continuing for another fourteen years, Black audiences were feted by all-Black-cast movies which ranged from gangster movies to comedies, musicals, horror films, and Westerns. And as was the case in the silent era, Black filmmakers were often in partnership with non-Blacks. Following Cooper's and Randol's collaboration on *Dark Manhattan*, for instance, in 1937 Cooper joined with Harry and Leo Popkins to form Million Dollar Productions, thus reinstating the integrated organizational form pioneered so successfully by David Starkman (Colored Players Film Corporation) and Richard Norman (Norman Film Manufacturing Company) during the presound period. According to Sampson, Million Dollar's first film was *The Duke Is Tops* (1938), which featured Duke Ellington and introduced Lena Horne as a replacement for Nina Mae McKinney, and then it monopolized the Black-gangster genre by producing such hits as *Bargain with Bullets* (1937), *Gang Smashers* (1938), *Gang War* (1939), and *Reform School* (1939).[227] Henry Sampson has described these companies as "white independents," a peculiar nomination which has the advantage of obscuring the fact that most if not all of the "whites" were Jews.[228] Jed Buell formed Association Pictures in 1937, producing *Harlem on the Prairie* (1938), written by Flournoy E. Miller and his Black vaudeville partner, Mantan Moreland; Richard C. Kahn, for example, organized Hollywood Productions in 1938 with Clarence Brooks and produced the three films which completed the Black singing cowboy series, *Bronze Buckaroo* (1938), *Harlem Rides the Range* (1939), and *Two-Gun Man from Harlem* (1938); Ted Toddy created Dixie National Pictures, which produced films featuring Mantan Moreland (*Up Jumped the Devil*, 1941; *Mr. Washington Goes to Town*, 1940; *Professor Creeps*, 1941; and *Lady Luck/Lucky Ghost*, 1941). Jack and Bert Goldberg, veteran producers of Black musicals in the 1920s, entered the Black film market in 1929, distributing Josephine Baker's *Siren of the Tropics* with synchronized sound. In 1932, Jack's company, Lincoln Productions, filmed Bojangles Robinson in *Harlem Is Heaven*, and in 1940, his new company, Jubilee Pictures, released *Paradise in Harlem*. Bert

226. Balio, *Grand Design*, 346.

227. Sampson, *Blacks in Black and White*, 224. Most filmographies (including Sampson's) document that *Bargain* preceded *Duke*.

228. This paragraph is largely based on Sampson, *Blacks in Black and White*, chap. 6. Additional data are drawn from Balio, *Grand Design*, 345–48.

Goldberg should be remembered as the producer of Clarence Muse's *Broken Strings* (1939), and Spencer Williams's *Dirty Gertie from Harlem, USA* (1946). In 1939, Bert partnered with George Randol to produce and distribute Black films.[229] Finally, Alfred and Lester Sack (Sack Amusement Enterprise) formed the most persistent distribution network for the Popkinses, the Goldbergs, and the even more ephemeral studios producing Black films in this period.

Balio asserts that by 1933 the major studios had responded to the glut of gangster movies by relegating the genre to their B-picture units: "The classic gangster cycle flourished for one year only, 1931."[230] J. E. Smyth has significantly augmented Balio's account, documenting that the ending of the gangster cycle was due more to political reasons than to Balio's implied economics. In 1935, the Hays office had imposed a moratorium on the production of gangster films (and, in addition, had refused permission for the re-release of *Little Caesar*, *The Public Enemy*, and *Scarface*). This august decree had followed several years of close monitoring of gangster films, particularly since many of them implicitly or explicitly linked the rise of the big-time gangsters to the government's mistreatment of World War I veterans. Indeed, as Smyth concludes, "The Great War, Prohibition, the criminal empires of Al Capone, Dion O'Bannion, Terry Druggan, Franky Lake, and Johnny Torrio were [Darryl] Zanuck and [Howard] Hughes's historical material; *Doorway to Hell*, *Little Caesar*, *The Public Enemy*, and *Scarface* turned the text of America's postwar history into a script."[231] The PCA and the government found that intolerable. Thus when he learned that Howard Hughes was considering a film biography of Capone (*Scarface*, 1932), Jason Joy of the PCA spoke for an industry which had "admitted the grave danger of portraying on the screen actual contemporary happenings relating

229. "George Randol Productions Merge with Bert Goldberg," *California Eagle*, October 19, 1939, B2; and Earl J. Morris, "George Randol Chosen "George Randol Chosen as Czar of New Combine; Plan Large Advertising Campaign," *California Eagle*, November 9, 1939, B2. Their first codistribution was *Double Deal* (starring Jeni LeGon and Monte Hawley). "'Double Deal' First Argus Picture," *California Eagle*, November 2, 1939, B2.

230. Balio, *Grand Design*, 284–86.

231. Smyth, "Revisioning Modern American History," 558. Capone was a World War I veteran and claimed his scars and his skills with a machine gun resulted from action on the Western Front; Samuel J. "Nails" Morton, was another gang leader and a decorated veteran. Ibid., 538.

to deficiencies in our government, political dishonesty and graft, current crimes or anti-social or criminal activities."[232] A further complication, largely ignored by film historians, is that, as Gerald Horne demonstrates, "available evidence does suggest that the mob held significant influence in Hollywood."[233] All this makes it hard to credit Cripps's contention that the wave of Black films beginning in the late 1930s were all low-budget "mirror reversals" of the mainstream movie industry.[234] More likely, with *Dark Manhattan,* Cooper and Randol gambled on the gangster genre because of its immediacy to urban Black audiences. In addition, as a Harlem nightclub celebrity before coming to Hollywood in 1936, Cooper was acutely aware of the scandal which was rocking the Harlem Black underworld.[235]

The policy, numbers, and lottery racket which serves as the setting for the picture had become highly visible in the mid-1930s. Earlier, according to the testimony of New York's special prosecutor, Thomas E. Dewey, in Harlem alone the numbers racket was pulling in $5-20 million a year.[236] And in Harlem, the most important "bankers" had been Alejandro (Alexander) Pompez, Joseph Ison, Wilfred Brunder, and

232. Joy to Hughes, May 1, 1931. Ibid., 556.

233. Horne, *Class Struggle in Hollywood,* 22. Horne notes: "Coincidentally, the thematic trend toward gangster movies began as mobsters assumed more influence in the industry. Strikingly, according to the Hollywood Left, these 'gangster pictures played' a major role 'in causing legislation against prohibition,' enabling an illicit mob-dominated business to become a legitimate mob-dominated business." Ibid., 101. For Harry Cohn (Columbia) and mobsters Johnny Roselli and Longy Zwillman, Joseph Schenck (Twentieth-Century Fox) and the mob-run International Alliance of Theatrical Stage Employees's Willie Bioff and George Brown, Bugsy Siegel and the extras' union, see ibid., passim.

234. Cripps, *Slow Fade to Black,* 330.

235. Ralph Cooper's familiarity with Alexander Pompez (Cooper spells the name *Pompeii*), Dutch Schultz—subjects of the next paragraph—and the several cliques of gangsters who invaded Harlem from the early 1920s is detailed in his autobiography (written with Steve Dougherty), *Amateur Night at the Apollo,* 51-56. About the Cotton Club, Cooper writes: "It was . . . one of the great oddities of American life—a nightclub in the heart of Harlem owned and operated by white gangsters who hired black talent to entertain whites-only audiences." Ibid., 51.

236. "Dewey Says Hines Influenced Police," *New York Times,* August 18, 1938, 12. Neil Lanctot's extensive citations from the *Philadelphia Tribune,* the *New York Amsterdam News,* and the *Baltimore Afro-American* for the years 1935-38 make it abundantly clear that the Black community and the Black press followed the investigation closely. See Lanctot, *Negro League Baseball,* 410n27.

Julius Williams.[237] Dewey's principal targets in his grand jury investigation were James Hines, the Tammany Hall leader in the Eleventh Assembly District, and Magistrate Hulon Capshaw, both recipients of protection money from Dutch Schultz.[238] As the *New York Times* had reported in 1935, "The policy game in Harlem, which once yielded profits as high as $200,000 a year to individual bankers, fell into the hands of 'the Dutchman's combination' in 1931 headed by none other than Arthur (Dutch Schultz) Flegenheimer."[239] Pompez and Ison, the most successful bankers in Harlem, were Flegenheimer's reluctant entrees into the Black underworld. And after Flegenheimer's murder in 1935, Dewey persuaded Pompez and Ison, both now fugitives, to return to New York to testify before a grand jury about the protection racket that Flegenheimer managed and about Hines's involvement. In 1938, the Dutchman's combine now in tatters, Pompez gave full vent to his contempt for the gangster as he recounted one of their meetings:

> Schultz says, "You are going to be the first nigger I am going to make an example in Harlem and I don't care, and I don't care and I don't give a damn if you make a statement from here to the Battery to the police that I am going to hurt you. It won't do you any good."
>
> I says, "I am sorry that you should talk that way. You are the first man ever [to] insult me for any reasons whatever. I was promised to come here and do business with you and you go and insult me. If you feel that way, we don't do any business."[240]

Pompez, whose banking career had raised him to prominence in the Black world, was clearly affronted by this figure whose only claim to significance was his capacity to wreak violence. Aware that the eminent circles he now habituated were entirely alien to Flegenheimer, Pompez alleged that he had quit the racket in 1934. He did venture further afield: his influence and affluence were to be critical to the establishment of the Negro National League (he owned a baseball team, the

237. "Schultz in Hiding, Ran Policy Racket," *New York Times*, February 27, 1935, 1, 6; "Testimony of Williams," *New York Times*, August 19, 1938, 1, 8.

238. Hines had financed election campaigns with gangster money as well as bribing judges, police, and other public officials. Capshaw, according to Dewey, was guilty of manipulating the trials of gangster defendants.

239. "Schultz in Hiding," 1.

240. "Capshaw Is Named," *New York Times*, August 20, 1938, 9.

New York Cubans, and one of the few home fields, the Dyckman Oval, available to the league).[241] In *Dark Manhattan*, Cooper (the "Bronze Bogart," as he was called in Black newspapers), who resembled Pompez, re-created the legend of Pompez's rise to power in the policy game. In *Gang Smasher*, written by Cooper and starring Nina Mae McKinney as an undercover policewoman, Henry Sampson described the script's villain in language which evoked a Black Dutch Schultz: "Gat Dalton, cruel, murderous gang leader forces tribute from Harlem merchants, to his 'Harlem Protective Association,' under penalty of destruction of their places and possible death at the hands of his henchmen."[242]

A second genre, the all-Black Western, though less numerous than the gangster films, also had its importance. James Kitses asserts that "for many students of the western Gene Autry and Roy Rogers have seemed an embarrassing aberration."[243] Nonetheless, it was the success of Autry's films, beginning in 1935,[244] that inspired Maceo Sheffield to pitch the idea of an all-Black singing cowboy movie two years later. The project was *Harlem on the Prairie*. This was Sheffield's (an ex-Los Angeles policeman, according to *Variety*) first venture into movies, and he was embittered by it: "Every Negro connected with the production of so-called all-Negro motion picture companies is no more than a stooge fronting for whites to whom the bulk of the profit goes."[245] There had,

241. In 1935, "Flush with cash, Pompez acquired home grounds at Dyckman Oval at 204th Street and Nagle Avenue in Harlem and invested thousands to remodel the conveniently located park, considered too small for league baseball in the past." Lanctot, *Negro League Baseball*, 43. Lanctot recounts the Dewey investigation, ibid., 59–60, 81. See also "Extradition Fight by Dewey Fugitive," *New York Times*, March 30, 1937, 2.

242. Sampson, *Blacks in Black and White*, 372.

243. Jim Kitses, "Authorship and Genre: Notes on the Western," in Kitses and Rickman, *Western Reader*, 62.

244. Autry's *Tumblin' Tumbleweeds* (Republic, 1935) was made for $18,000 and grossed $1 million. Balio, *Grand Design*, 322.

245. "Maceo Sheffield Declares that 'Fronting' for Producers Is Taboo," *California Eagle*, March 3, 1938, B2; and "Harlem on Prairie," *Variety*, February 9, 1938, 14. Quoting *New York Amsterdam News* (February 5, 1938), Sampson augments Sheffield's biography: "The heavy, Maceo B. Sheffield, spent ten years in the Los Angeles Police department . . . [and] now is part owner of several Los Angeles night clubs, the 41 Club, 833 Club, Montmartre and the Last Round." Sampson, *Blacks in Black and White*, 384. Herb Jeffries has more recently claimed that the idea was his own, inspired by observing young Black boys playing cowboys and Indians. His account

of course, been all-Black Westerns during the silent-film era, most of them produced by "white independents." In 1921, Norman Film Manufacturing had produced *The Green-Eyed Monster* and *The Crimson Skull*. The same year Bookertee Investment had released *The $10,000 Trail*; Ben Roy Productions, *The Man from Texas*; and E. S. L. Colored Feature Productions, *Saddle Daze*. In 1922, Black Western Film produced *Shoot 'Em Up, Sam,* and Micheaux had produced a "modern" Western, *The Virgin of Seminole*. In 1923, Norman Film Manufacturing reprised the genre with *The Bull-Dogger*, taking advantage of Bill Pickett's fame as a rodeo star. In 1928, Spencer Williams directed Midnight Productions' *Tenderfeet*; and Norman Film Manufacturing ended its run with *Black Gold*.[246] And now, nine years later, Jed Buell collaborated with Sheffield, Flournoy Miller, Mantan Moreland, and Herb Jeffries in a musical Western which became the first of a four-film cycle.[247]

At the time, the novelty was the appearance of all-Black Westerns. While R. E. Norman's films of nearly twenty years earlier had referenced a Black presence in the West,[248] the 1930s cycle almost entirely erased all the historical problematics of Western expansion. There were no whites, no Native Americans, no Mexicans to rupture the utopia of an all-Black society. Consequently, white racism was suspended, conquest and colonization erased along with genocide. In short, many of the elements which were encased in the classic Western's representation of white masculinity were absent. Shorn of its political, ideological, and cultural iconography, what remained was the most elemental constructs of the formula: men with guns.[249] Of course, in the all-Black cowboy movies, the white supremacist colorism of the Western (white

---

may be true, but some doubt is thrown on it by his timing (all the other principals are dead), by the quaintness of the story itself, by his erasure of Autry's achievements from his account, and by the fact that Sheffield made the claim publicly at the time of the release of *Harlem on the Prairie*.

246. See Larry Richards, *African American Films*, passim.

247. For the last three of the cycle, *Bronze Buckaroo, Harlem on the Range,* and *Two-Gun Man from Harlem*, Herb Jeffries was billed as Herbert Jeffrey.

248. Sampson records that Norman's *The Crimson Skull* employed "thirty black cowboys working on ranches in and around Boley [Oklahoma] as extras in the picture." Richards, *Blacks in Black and White*, 215.

249. Robert Warshow commented: "The two most successful creations of American movies are the gangster and the Westerner: men with guns." Warshow, "Movie Chronicle: *The Westerner*," in Kitses and Rickman, *Western Reader*, 35.

hat, white horse, etc.) merged with Black colorism (light-complexioned hero and heroines).[250] But even this explicit appropriation of racist signifiers was softened by the democratization of color in these films. Herb Jeffries's sidekicks were dark or darker; sometimes his villainous foes were as light as Jeffries (e.g., Clarence Brooks in *The Bronze Buckaroo* and *Two-Gun Man from Harlem*); and prominent screen time was allotted to dark-skinned singers (e.g., The Four Tones) and comics (Moreland and Lucius Brooks).

Cripps, being an exacting historian, made reference to the films, lamenting what he deemed their failure "to develop the West as an allegory for the black urban experience."[251] Julia Leyda, by disaggregating the films, provides a retort to Cripps.[252] Leyda maintains that the complexion of the principal hero and villains, the absence of Black dialect in the dialogue of these characters, and the sources of conflict (property in land, precious minerals, etc.) implicate a Black middle class. As such, it should be noted, one of the subtexts of the Black musical Western was a privileging of a class and the valorization of moral and ethical protocols retrieved from the Black melodramas of the silent era. The Western genre, however, had muted the class conflicts so prominent in such films as *Within Our Gates* and *Scar of Shame*. Jeffries's dark cohorts, portrayed by Black vaudevillian performers, represent a less-educated working class. They provide an active constituency for the hero's actions, a social base for his survival, and an arena for an explicit egalitarianism. For Black audiences of the late 1930s, the "Harlem" referenced in the title of three of the films signified *the* Black urban site. Harlem as a signifier smuggled into these Westerns a "home" of Black modernism, evoking urban sophistication, race pride, an elegance of style, and rich cultural achievement. In *Two-Gun*, Leyda remarks, one instance of a "strategic anachronism" is Moreland's (Mistletoe) claim that "his chili is the 'same as a swing tune from Cab Calloway's band—red hot!'"[253] Another is Artie Young's appearance as Betty Dennison in *Harlem on the Range*:

250. In the four films, Connie Harris (*Harlem on the Prairie*), Artie Young (both *Bronze Buckaroo* and *Harlem on the Range*), and Margarette Whitten (*Two-Gun Man from Harlem*), respectively, played the light-complexioned heroines.

251. Cripps, *Slow Fade to Black*, 338.

252. Leyda, "Black-Audience Westerns."

253. Ibid., 65.

When she finally appears in the flesh, Miss Dennison is the epitome of the beautiful young 1930s woman: her short hair is marcelled and she wears a string of pearls and a knee-length skirt. For an African American audience in the 1930s, the thrill of seeing a lovely black woman as a romantic lead, however abbreviated her screen time, must have been powerful. . . . This point is underscored by the complete absence of any darker-skinned women in any of the movies. Young's modern, fashionable appearance invited a 1930s audience to identify with her precisely through the anachronistic incongruities of her costume and hairstyle.[254]

And, of course, Jeffries crooned, the modulation of his rich baritone voice, his caressing of notes, resonating with the sounds audiences associated with the big bands. Finally, another matter publicized in the Black newspapers, the films were shot at N. B. Murray's Black Dude Ranch outside Victorville, California.[255]

The comedy team of Flournoy Miller and Mantan Moreland was implicated in all four films. Miller had had a long career in Black vaudeville and musicals. He first teamed with Aubrey Lyles when they both attended Fisk University in the first decade of the century. Miller, Lyles, Noble Sissle, and Eubie Blake had written *Shuffle Along*, the most successful Black musical of the 1920s.[256] And after Lyles passed away in 1932, Miller had partnered with Moreland. Moreland, apparently, greatly benefited from that relationship since, Sampson asserts, he had written *Harlem on the Prairie*.[257] But certainly both comedians lent their creativity to the Black Westerns. That might very well explain one other observation made by Leyda:

> In many ways, the coon character is the star of the movie. In *Buckaroo*, for example, Dusty [Miller] figures out how to trick the ranchhand who sold him a talking mule that will not talk. He also fires the shot that kills the villain during the climatic shootout, something that rarely happens in white westerns. . . . The real guts of the movie for some audiences may well have been the laughs Dusty generated,

254. Ibid., 63.
255. Sampson, *Blacks in Black and White*, 384.
256. Mitchell, *Black Drama*, 76–77.
257. Sampson, *Blacks in Black and White*, 544.

rather than the upstanding morality of Bob [Jeffries], compounded by Dusty's heroic behavior in the shootout.[258]

Moreland performed a similar mix of buffoonery and heroism in the later films. Thus the singing cowboy films inflected the contemporary Black world while staging a modest critique of the Westerns produced by the majors and Poverty Row. The crowning moment of Black comedic subversion, however, was still a few years away. And as Fredi Washington had intimated, it had something to do with the war which had already begun in Europe.

Mantan Moreland was a brilliant creator of inversion, angling his approach to the textual inventory of film plots in order to suggest alternative realities. Cast in a series of program mysteries in the 1940s (including several Charlie Chan pictures), Moreland consistently constructed a comedic space which paralleled, ornamented, and on occasion threatened the principal plot of the films in which he appeared. Moreland's characters always spoke in the Black dialect of minstrelsy, the imagined language of the plantation slave and the coon. This caricature constituted a contract between Moreland and the studios and between Moreland and his non-Black audiences. Costumed as a jester, Moreland resembled a trifling irrelevancy. And he appropriated for his own purposes this insistent inference of an other American, a primitive, inferior, and nearly unintelligible Black American. He imploded this alien, implying a backstory of an alternative existence into a fully realized social location and cultural field. He performed his characters as if they were presumptuous anthropologists inserted into the mundane machinations of murders and intrigues which enveloped his white counterparts. Entirely fluent and familiar with the cultural practices of this white society, Moreland (it was a rare performance when his characters displaced him) observed and continuously verbalized his field notes. And in his habit of overtly expressing displeasure, irony, and bemusement, he seemed to be fully confident that his mask of ignorance, coupled with his assigned social inferiority, would shield him. Moreland conspired with, or on occasion induced, a form of racial solipsism: he appeared to concede the premise that only the relationships of the white actors were real, meaningful, or relevant to the film's central plot. And camouflaged with the most extreme trappings of blackface min-

258. Leyda, "Black-Audience Westerns," 60.

Mr. Washington Goes to Town, *starring Mantan Moreland and F. E. Miller, 1940, Toddy Pictures.*

Come On, Cowboy, *starring Mantan Moreland, 1948, Toddy Pictures.*

strelsy ("Feet, don't fail me now!"), Moreland achieved a documented record of Black coding of filmic reality.

Much of Moreland's work appeared improvisational, or more precisely, unwritten. Sometimes, as in *The Scarlet Clue* (Monogram, 1945), he was granted the space to adapt old Black vaudeville licks like the Flournoy E. Miller–Aubrey Lyles routines.[259] Whether set pieces or adlibs, often the other actors exited the screen while Moreland remained, the director indulging one final bit of tomfoolery or *sotto voce* commentary ("I ain't moving 'til I change my mind. I changed my mind"). But perhaps the most complete example of Moreland's own inventiveness is his performance in *The King of the Zombies* (Monogram, 1941). This tabloid version of World War II centers on the conflict between the villainy of German espionage and the virtue of a still prewar America. But notwithstanding the film's politics, it showcases Moreland, yielding to him nearly half the screen time of the entire picture!

Moreland is accompanying two American government agents (Dick Purcell and John Archer) when their plane crash-lands on a Caribbean island. On the island resides a crazed German doctor-spy (Henry Victor), his wife (Patricia Stacey) and niece (Joan Woodbury), his household of domestics (Leigh Whipper, Madame Sul-te-Wan, and Marguerite Whitten), and zombies. Victor is using a combination of hypnosis and "voodoo" to extract information from a dragooned American admiral (Guy Usher). One of Moreland's first locational gestures is during the introductions of the Americans to their German host. Referring to Moreland, Purcell proprietarily claims, "This is Jeff, my valet." Moreland counters: "Jefferson Jackson is my name. You see I was named after my great grandpappy. He was the president of the Knights of the Pink Garters." Strident at the beginning, Moreland's declaration trails off as he recognizes Victor's indifference. Nevertheless, Moreland has

---

259. Cripps, *Slow Fade to Black*, 225–26. Miller and Lyles had developed a routine where one partner finishes the other's thought before the audience can imagine what the subject is. For instance, Miller might ask, "Man, have you seen . . . ?" And Lyles would respond: "I haven't seen her since . . ." Miller: "Has it been that long?" In *Scarlet Clue*, Moreland teamed up with Ben Carter. Moreland: "Boy, it's been a long time. I haven't seen you since . . ." Carter: "Longer than that. The last time I saw you, you was living over . . ." Moreland: "Oh, I moved from there . . ." Carter: "Yeah . . ." Moreland: "Sure, I moved over to . . ." Carter: "How can you live in that neighborhood?" Moreland came to his affection for vaudeville naturally. See also Mitchell, *Black Drama*, 85.

established that he is neither Jeff nor valet but comes from that other world of Black family and formal fraternal social clubs. Almost immediately, Moreland uncovers the actual subterranean workforce—the zombies—employed by the German. His superior understanding of the situation, as so often happens to him in these situations, is dismissed by Purcell and Archer. The provenance of his knowledge is that of an inferior, and what he claims to know is intolerably otherworldly. Eventually, through hypnosis, Moreland becomes a zombie, and his initial terror of the zombies is replaced by camaraderie: "Move over boys, I'm one of the gang now." Later, Whitten, the attractive mulatta kitchen maid, encounters the newest zombie marching his "boys" to the meal table. Moreland's dialogue is revealing. "Gangway for Kid Zom . . . Don't bother me woman, can't you see I'se a has-been. And don't ask me my name, 'cause I don't know. I don't know nothing."

When Whitten inquires about Archer, who has also been "zombified" (Moreland's neologism), Moreland replies, "The only ones I know about are the boys in my squad."[260] Moreland has appropriated a plot device from Edmond Kelso's script so that the metaphor for slavery, the zombies, has been brought to the surface. With Jeff, slavery no longer is justified by nature but results from the use of force and compulsion. And its demands on the slave is the erasure of his identity. Jeff, who has evidenced a sparkling intelligence, sprinkling his conversation with words like "loquacious," "kosher," and "prevaricator" and displays of social knowledge ("Don't you know Prohibition has been repealed?"), now must claim to know nothing, not even his name. The marginal distinction between servant and slave has been challenged. The implied identity between an American "boss" and German master ruptures the contest between virtue and villainy. And finally, as was often the case in his films, Moreland commands the last words the audience will hear. In this instance, comedic play decorates the denunciation of the doubled exploitation: "If there's one thing I wouldn't want to be twice, zombies is both of them."

Moreland's intervention was circumstantial. There was the war, certainly, but there was also the fact that Monogram Pictures was a small studio accustomed to working the product gaps, lapses, or remainders

260. In the script, Archer's character has been explicitly identified as Irish. Like Moreland's character, Archer's is suspicious of the German doctor from the beginning. And like Moreland's Africanness, Archer's Irishness is linked to Black magic.

of the major studios.[261] One of its staples was the mystery genre, like the Charlie Chan series.[262] The series simultaneously dignified and parodied Chinese. Coolie caricatures were rare in the series, and the younger generation of Chan's children were enrolled at UCLA, spoke standard English sprinkled with jive phrases, and effortlessly mingled with whites. In short, Charlie Chan was not a white accessory; his very appearance in a case signaled white failure and was often an explicit surrender of white conceits. And early in almost all of the films, the villains marked themselves by their inability to recognize that Chan's professional identity as a detective was more threatening to them than his racial identity. On the other hand, the old man spoke pidgin seasoned with faux Confucianisms, and no Asian actor was cast as Charlie Chan. And once Moreland joined the series as Birmingham Brown, Charlie's household was diverse, lively, daring, and comic. Just as Charlie policed the messier boundaries of American society, Monogram habituated a space between the rigid racial conventions of the big studios and an audience largely working class and with affection for mysteries, horror films, thrillers, and low comedy.

Cripps, among other film historians, asserts that an industry which had ended the decade with *Jezebel* and *Gone with the Wind* was compelled by political and consequently commercial considerations to suspend its projection of white racism.[263] Both the Office of War Information (OWI) and the NAACP had put pressure on the moguls, it is true, but the results were inconsistent. Created in June 1942, the OWI found its Bureau of Motion Pictures (BMP) monitoring agency, the Domestic Operations Branch, defunded by Congress in July 1943. Subsequently the BMP resorted to threats against export licenses reviewed by its Overseas Branch. But even with its clear mandate to remove racist stereotypes and slurs from American motion pictures, the BMP analysts were often bemused by their own immersion in a racist culture. Evaluating the script for Monogram's *Revenge of the Zombies* (1943), Lillian Bergquist observed, "The Negroes ... are presented as a strange, uncivilized and superstitious group of people living in a world quite apart from that of other Americans. They are either comic ser-

261. Balio, *Grand Design*, 321–22.

262. Monogram took over the Charlie Chan series from Twentieth-Century Fox in the early 1940s.

263. Cripps, *Slow Fade to Black*, 375–89.

vants, zombies, or in the case of Mammy Beulah, a voodoo-ist. There is not one real Negro American in this story."[264] Since Bergquist could have included almost all of the American films of the previous half century in her observation, it is not surprising that she missed the import of Mantan Moreland's performance in *Revenge of the Zombies*. Rick Worland characterized it succinctly: "stereotypical shuffling and quaking."[265]

While the war continued, it is true that to some extent the industry transferred its racial palette to the Germans and Japanese, inflecting a different kind of integration for Black Americans. But even in *Bataan* (MGM, 1943), *Sahara* (Columbia, 1943), *Lifeboat* (Twentieth Century–Fox, 1944), and the other wartime films with Black representation, some part of equality was withheld. In the all-Black films of 1943, for example, *Stormy Weather* and *Cabin in the Sky*, Black soldiers were American only within the confines of a single-race utopia which resurrected the imaginary boundaries of the Black musical Westerns. In the war genre, they were often willing sacrificial lambs, dying for a country which had made no promises and for white comrades whose most profound concession was manly affection. And when the war was concluded, and the American homeland was once again secure, the film industry relapsed. In the first gala premiere of the postwar years, Disney celebrated the release of *Song of the South* in Atlanta. The film was based on the putative Negro tales of Br'er Rabbit and Br'er Fox counterfeited by Joel Chandler Harris. Neither James Baskette (Uncle Remus) or Hattie McDaniel (mammy) were asked to Atlanta. Separate, disenfranchised, and brutally exploited, Blacks reoccupied their largely uncontested stigmatized place in American films.

In *Lifeboat*, Alfred Hitchcock had displayed how easily a racist culture could be manipulated. Like a mid-twentieth-century Shakespeare, Hitchcock had interrogated the alchemy and artifice of racism. Making his own comment on the war and a possibility of its aftermath, he deliberately transferred the racist transcript from George (Canada Lee), the Black shipmate who rescued several of the survivors, to Willy (Walter Slezak), the German U-boat captain who had torpedoed their ship. In the end, Willy was lynched. George stood apart from the small, frenzied mob, saddened by its bloodlust, comprehending that anywhere

264. Worland, "OWI Meets the Monsters," 53.
265. Ibid.

else and at any time he might have been the victim. Hitchcock's film was a minor rupture, a momentary interrogative of a cultural thread which had been subsidized for centuries. *Song of the South* figuratively set aside all such impostures. In the postwar world the usable myths of whiteness would have to be restored.

Bibliography

Adams, Alice Dana. *The Neglected Period of Anti-Slavery in America, 1808-1831*. 1908. Reprint, Williamstown: Corner House, 1973.

Adrian, Jack. *Edgar Wallace*. London: Granite Impex, 1984.

Africans in America. Part 3. Public Broadcasting System, 1998. <http://www.pbs.org/wgbh/aia/part3/3i3116.html>.

Alexander, Nigel. "Thomas Rymer and 'Othello.'" In *Shakespeare Survey* 21. Cambridge: Cambridge University Press, 1968.

Allen, Robert C., and Douglas Gomery. *Film History: Theory and Practice*. New York: McGraw-Hill, 1985.

Allen, Theodore W. *The Invention of the White Race*. Vol. 1. London: Verso, 1994.

Anderson, Addell Austin. "The Ethiopian Art Theatre." *Theatre Survey* 33 (November 1992): 132-43.

Anderson, Lisa M. "From Blackface to 'Genuine Negroes': Nineteenth-Century Minstrelsy and the Icon of the 'Negro.'" *Theatre Research International* 21.1 (Spring 1996): 17-23.

Aptheker, Herbert. *Afro-American History*. New York: Carol, 1992.

———. *American Negro Slave Revolts*. New York: International, 1969.

Archer, Jules. *The Plot to Seize the White House*. New York: Hawthorn, 1973.

Armstead-Johnson, Helen. "Themes and Values in Afro-American Librettos and Book Musicals, 1898-1930." In *Musical Theatre in America*, edited by Glenn Loney. Westport, Conn.: Greenwood, 1984.

Arnesen, Eric. "'Like Banquo's Ghost, It Will Not Down': The Race Question and the American Railroad Brotherhoods, 1880-1920." *American Historical Review* 99.5 (December 1994): 1601-33.

"Author of Fox Play Discusses Its Basic Idea." *Motion Picture News*, March 20, 1915, 51.

Ayers, Edward L. *The Promise of the New South*. New York: Oxford University Press, 1992.

Aylmer, G. E. "Slavery under Charles II: The Mediterranean and Tangier." *English Historical Review* 113.456 (April 1999): 378-88.

Babcock, Muriel. "Safari Scenes Grip Memory." *Los Angeles Times*, December 15, 1929, B13, 20.

Baker, Lee D. *From Savage to Negro*. Berkeley: University of California Press, 1998.

Balio, Tino. *Grand Design: Hollywood as a Modern Business Enterprise, 1930-1939*. Berkeley: University of California Press, 1993.

Bambara, Toni Cade. Preface to *Daughters of the Dust*, by Julie Dash. New York: New Press, 1992.

Banadio, Felice A. *A. P. Giannini*. Berkeley: University of California Press, 1994.

Barbeau, Arthur E., and Florette Henri. *The Unknown Soldiers: African-American Troops in World War I*. New York: Da Capo, 1996.

Bardaglio, Peter. "'Shamefull Matches': The Regulation of Interracial Sex and Marriage in the South before 1900." In Hodes, *Sex, Love, Race*.

Barnaby, Andrew, and Joan Wry. "Authorized Versions: *Measure for Measure* and the Politics of Biblical Translations." *Renaissance Quarterly* 51.4 (Winter 1998): 1225–54.

Barnouw, Erik. *Tube of Plenty: The Evolution of American Television*. New York: Oxford University Press, 1982.

Bartels, Emily C. "Making More of the Moor: Aaron, Othello, and Renaissance Refashionings of Race." *Shakespeare Quarterly* 41.4 (Winter 1990): 433–54.

———. "*Othello* and Africa: Postcolonialism Reconsidered." *William and Mary Quarterly*, 3d ser., 54.1 (January 1997): 45–64.

Barthelemy, Anthony Gerard. *Black Face, Maligned Race: The Representation of Blacks in English Drama from Shakespeare to Southerne*. Baton Rouge: Louisiana State University Press, 1987.

Beale, Howard K. *Theodore Roosevelt and the Rise of America to World Power*. Baltimore: Johns Hopkins University Press, 1956.

Bean, Annemarie. "Black Minstrelsy and Double Inversion, circa 1890." In *African American Performance and Theater History*, edited by Harry J. Elam Jr. and David Krasner. New York: Oxford University Press, 2001.

Beaud, Michel. *A History of Capitalism, 1500–1980*. New York: Monthly Review, 1983.

Beckwith, Jonathan R. "The Science of Racism." In Trumpbour, *How Harvard Rules*.

Behlmer, Rudy. "Tarzan and MGM: The Rest of the Story." *American Cinematographer*, February 1987, 34–44.

———. "Tarzan, Hollywood's Greatest Jungle Hero." *American Cinematographer*, January 1987, 39–48.

Benjamin, Dr. Marcus. "Memories of the Smithsonian." *Scientific Monthly*, May 1917, 461–72.

Bennett, Tony. "The Multiplication of Culture's Utility." *Critical Inquiry* 21 (Summer 1995): 861–89.

Bentley, Nancy. "White Slaves: The Mulatto Hero in Antebellum Fiction." *American Literature* 65 (September 1993): 501–22.

Berenstein, Rhona J. *Attack of the Leading Ladies*. New York: Columbia University Press, 1996.

———. "White Heroines and Hearts of Darkness: Race, Gender and Disguise in 1930s Jungle Films." *Film History* 6.3 (Autumn 1994): 314–39.

Berlin, Ira, Barbara J. Fields, Steven F. Miller, Joseph P. Reidy, and Leslie S. Rowland. "The Destruction of Slavery." In *Slaves No More: Three Essays on Emancipation and the Civil War*, by Ira Berlin et al. New York: Cambridge University Press, 1993.

Bernal, Martin. *Black Athena*. New Brunswick, N.J.: Rutgers University Press, 1987.

Bernardi, Daniel, ed. *The Birth of Whiteness: Race and the Emergence of U.S. Cinema*. New Brunswick, N.J.: Rutgers University Press, 1996.

Bernhard, Virginia, Betty Brandon, Elizabeth Fox-Genovese, and Theda Perdue, eds. *Southern Women: Histories and Identity*. Columbia: University of Missouri Press, 1992.

Bernstein, Matthew, ed. *Controlling Hollywood: Censorship and Regulation in the Studio Era*. New Brunswick, N.J.: Rutgers University Press, 1999.

Bernstein, Matthew, and Dana F. White. "'Scratching Around' in a 'Fit of Insanity': The Norman Film Manufacturing Company and the Race Film Business in the 1920s." *Griffithiana* 62–63 (May 1998): 81–127.

Birchard, Robert S. "Earliest Days of the Tom Mix Legend." *American Cinematographer*, June 1987, 36–41.

Blackburn, Robin. *The Making of New World Slavery*. London: Verso, 1998.

———. *The Overthrow of Colonial Slavery*. London: Verso, 1988.

Blockson, Charles L. *African Americans in Pennsylvania*. Baltimore: Black Classic, 1994.

Bobo, Jacqueline. *Black Women as Cultural Readers*. New York: Columbia University Press, 1995.

———. "'The Subject Is Money': Reconsidering the Black Film Audience as a Theoretical Paradigm." *Black American Literature Forum* 25.2 (Summer 1991): 421–32.

Bogle, Donald. *Bright Boulevards, Bold Dreams*. New York: Ballantine, 2005.

———. Introduction to *A Separate Cinema: Fifty Years of Black-Cast Posters*, by John Kisch and Edward Mapp. New York: Farrar, Straus and Giroux, 1992.

———. *Prime Time Blues: African Americans on Network Television*. New York: Farrar, Straus and Giroux, 2001.

———. *Toms, Coons, Mulattoes, Mammies and Bucks*. New York: Continuum, 1995.

Bond, Frederick Weldon. *The Negro and the Drama*. 1940. Reprint, Washington, D.C.: McGrath, 1969.

Bondanella, Peter. *Italian Cinema from Neorealism to the Present*. New York: Continuum, 2000.

Botkin, B. A., ed. *Folk-Say: A Regional Miscellany*. Norman: University of Oklahoma Press, 1930.

Bowersock, G. W., P. R. L. Brown, and O. Grabar, eds. *Late Antiquity: A Guide to the Postclassical World*. Cambridge, Mass.: Harvard University Press, 1999.

Bowser, Eileen. *The Transformation of Cinema, 1907–1915*. Berkeley: University of California Press, 1994.

Bowser, Pearl, Jane Gaines, and Charles Musser, eds. *Oscar Micheaux and His Circle*. Bloomington: Indiana University Press, 2001.

Bowser, Pearl, and Louise Spence. *Writing Himself into History: Oscar Micheaux, His Silent Films, and His Audiences*. New Brunswick, N.J.: Rutgers University Press, 2000.

Boyd, Robert L. "Racial Segregation and Insurance Enterprise among Black Americans in Northern Cities." *Sociological Quarterly* 39.2 (Spring 1998): 337–49.

Boyd, Valerie. *Wrapped in Rainbows: The Life of Zora Neale Hurston*. New York: Scribner's, 2003.

Bradley, A. C. *Shakespearean Tragedy*. 1904. Reprint, New York: St. Martin's, 1992.

Bradley, Edwin M. *The First Hollywood Musicals*. Jefferson, N.C.: McFarland, 1996.

Brandimarte, Cynthia Ann. "Fannie Hurst: A Missouri Girl Makes Good." *Missouri Historical Review* 81.3 (April 1987): 275–95.

Brodie, Fawn. *Thaddeus Stevens: Scourge of the South*. New York: Norton, 1959.

Brown, R. Allen. *The Normans*. New York: St. Martin's, 1984.

Brown, Sterling A. "Imitation of Life: Once a Pancake." *Opportunity* 13 (March 1935): 87–88.

———. "Negro Character as Seen by White Authors." *Journal of Negro Education* 2.2 (April 1933): 179–203.

Brownlow, Kevin. *Behind the Mask of Innocence*. Berkeley: University of California Press, 1990.

Bryant, Keith L., Jr., and Henry C. Dethloff. *A History of American Business*. Upper Saddle River, N.J.: Prentice Hall, 1990.

Bundles, A'Lelia. *On Her Own Ground: The Life and Times of Madam C. J. Walker*. New York: Washington Square, 2001.

Burroughs, Edgar Rice. *Tarzan of the Apes*. 1912. Reprint, New York: Ballantine, 1976.

Butler, F. G. "The Fair Queene Who Liked Blacks." *Shakespeare in Southern Africa* 9 (1996), <http://www.rhodes.ac.za/affiliates/isea/shake/butler.htm>.

Butters, Gerald R., Jr. *Black Manhood on the Silent Screen*. Lawrence: University Press of Kansas, 2002.

Bynum, Victoria E. *The Free State of Jones: Mississippi's Longest Civil War*. Chapel Hill: University of North Carolina Press, 2001.

———. *Unruly Women: The Politics of Social and Sexual Control in the Old South*. Chapel Hill: University of North Carolina Press, 1992.

Calverley, Bob. "Film Group Finds a Missing Star Here in Detroit." *Detroit Monitor*, March 17, 1979, 3A.

Cameron, Kenneth M. *Africa on Film*. New York: Continuum, 1994.

Cantrell, Gregg, and D. Scott Barton. "Texas Populists and the Failure of Biracial Politics." *Journal of Southern History* 55.4 (November 1989): 659–92.

Caputi, Jane. "'Specifying' Fannie Hurst: Langston Hughes's 'Limitations of Life,' Zora Neale Hurston's *Their Eyes Were Watching God*, and Toni Morrison's *The Bluest Eye* as 'Answers' to Hurst's *Imitation of Life*." *Black American Literature Forum* 24.4 (Winter 1990): 697–716.

Cardyn, Lisa. "Sexualized Racism/Gendered Violence: Outraging the Body Politics in the Reconstruction South." *Michigan Law Review* 100.4 (February 2002): 675–867.

Carr, Steven. *Hollywood and Anti-Semitism*. Cambridge: Cambridge University Press, 2001.

Carter, Dan T. *Scottsboro: A Tragedy of the American South*. Baton Rouge: Louisiana State University Press, 1969.

Catterall, Helen T., ed. *Judicial Cases concerning American Slavery and the Negro*. 5 vols. Washington, D.C.: Carnegie Institution of Washington, 1926–37.

Cell, John W. *The Highest Stage of White Supremacy*. Cambridge: Cambridge University Press, 1982.

Chalk, Frank. "The Anatomy of an Investment: Firestone's 1927 Loan to Liberia." *Canadian Journal of African Studies* 1.1 (March 1967): 12–32.

Chandler, Wayne B. "The Moor: Light of Europe's Dark Age." In *Golden Age of the Moor*, edited by Ivan Van Sertima. New Brunswick, N.J.: Transaction, 1996.

Chejne, Anwar. *Muslim Spain: Its History and Culture*. Minneapolis: University of Minnesota Press, 1974.

Cheyfitz, Eric. "Tarzan of the Apes: U.S. Foreign Policy in the Twentieth Century." *American Literary History* 1.2 (Summer 1989): 339–60.

Chilton, John. *Who's Who of Jazz*. New York: Da Capo, 1985.

Churchill, Ward. *Fantasies of the Master Race*. San Francisco: City Lights, 1998.

Clark, Thomas. Introduction to *The Clansman*, by Thomas Dixon Jr. Lexington: University Press of Kentucky, 1970.

Clarke, James W. "Without Fear or Shame: Lynching, Capital Punishment and the Subculture of Violence in the American South." *British Journal of Political Science* 28.2 (April 1998): 269–89.

Clifford, Mary Louise. *From Slavery to Freetown*. Jefferson, N.C.: McFarland, 1999.

Clinton, Catherine. *The Plantation Mistress: Woman's World in the Old South*. New York: Pantheon, 1982.

———. "'Southern Dishonor': Flesh, Blood, Race, and Bondage." In *In Joy and in Sorrow: Women, Family, and Marriage in the Victorian South, 1830–1900*, edited by Carol Bleser. New York: Oxford University Press, 1991.

Cochran, Thomas C., and Ray Ginger. "The American-Hawaiian Steamship Company, 1899–1919." *Business History Review* 28.4 (December 1954): 343–65.

Cockrell, Dale. *Demons of Disorder*. New York: Cambridge University Press, 1997.

Collins, Kris. "White-Washing the Black-a-Moor: *Othello*, Negro Minstrelsy and Parodies of Blackness." *Journal of American Culture* 19.3 (Fall 1996): 87–101.

Collins, Roger. *The Arab Conquest of Spain, 710–797*. Oxford: Blackwell, 1989.

Cook, Raymond. "The Man behind *The Birth of a Nation*." *North Carolina Historical Review* 39 (October 1962): 519–40.

Cook, Will Marion. "Clorindy, the Origin of the Cakewalk." *Theatre Arts*, September 1947, 61–65.

Cooper, Ralph, and Steve Dougherty. *Amateur Night at the Apollo: Ralph Cooper Presents Five Decades of Great Entertainment*. New York: HarperCollins, 1990.

Cope, Douglas. *The Limits of Racial Domination*. University of Wisconsin Press, 2001.

Cornish, Dudley. *The Sable Arm*. Lawrence: University Press of Kansas, 1987.

Cotterill, H. B. *Italy from Dante to Tasso*. New York: Stokes, 1919.

Couvares, Francis G. "The Good Censor: Race, Sex, and Censorship in the Early Cinema." *Yale Journal of Criticism* 7.2 (1994): 233–51.

Couzens, Tim. *Tramp Royal*. Johannesburg: Witwaterrand University Press, 1993.

Covington, Floyd. "The Negro Invades Hollywood." *Opportunity* 7.4 (April 1929): 111.

Craton, Michael. "Proto-Peasant Revolts? The Late Slave Rebellions in the British West Indies, 1816–1832." *Past and Present* 85 (1979): 99–125.

Cripps, Thomas. *Black Film as Genre*. Bloomington: Indiana University Press, 1979.

———. *Making Movies Black*. New York: Oxford University Press, 1993.

———. *Slow Fade to Black*. New York: Oxford University Press, 1977.

Crompton, Robert D. "James Thackera, Engraver of Philadelphia and Lancaster, PA." *Journal of the Lancaster County Historical Society*, April 1958, 65–95.

Cronon, William. "Revisiting the Vanishing Frontier: The Legacy of Frederick Jackson Turner." *Western Historical Quarterly* 18.2 (1987): 157–76.

Cruz, Jon. *Culture on the Margins*. Princeton, N.J.: Princeton University Press, 1999.

Curtis, Susan. *The First Black Actors on the Great White Way*. Columbia: University of Missouri Press, 1998.

Daniel, Pete. *The Shadow of Slavery: Peonage in the South, 1909–1969*. New York: Oxford University Press, 1973.

Daniell, David. Introduction to *Tyndale's New Testament*. New Haven, Conn.: Yale University Press, 1989.

Davis, Angela Y. *Blues Legacies and Black Feminism*. New York: Pantheon, 1998.

Dennett, Andrea Stulman. *Weird and Wonderful: The Dime Museum in America*. New York: New York University Press, 1997.

Dennison, Sam. *Scandalize My Name*. New York: Garland, 1982.

Diawara, Manthia, ed. *Black American Cinema*. New York: Routledge, 1993.

Dinnerstein, Leonard. "The Fate of Leo Frank." *American Heritage* 47.6 (October 1996): 98–107.

Dixon, Thomas, Jr. *The Clansman*. 1905. Reprint, Lexington: University Press of Kentucky, 1970.

Dodson, Howard, Christopher Moore, and Roberta Yancy. *The Black New Yorkers: The Schomberg Illustrated Chronology*. New York: Wiley, 2000.

Dollimore, Jonathan. *Radical Tragedy*. Durham, N.C.: Duke University Press, 1984.

Domanick, Joe. *To Protect and to Serve*. New York: Pocket Books, 1994.

Dormon, James H. "Shaping the Popular Image of Post-Reconstruction American Blacks: The 'Coon Song' Phenomenon of the Gilded Age." *American Quarterly* 40.4 (December 1988): 450–71.

Douglas, David C. *William the Conqueror*. Berkeley: University of California Press, 1964.

Douglass, Frederick. Introduction to *The Reason Why the Colored American Is Not in the World's Columbian Exposition*, by Ida B. Wells, Frederick Douglass, Irvine Garland Penn, and Ferdinand L. Barnett. 1893. Reprint, edited by Robert Rydell. Urbana: University of Illinois, 1999.

Dowd, Nancy, and David Shepard, interviewers. *King Vidor: A Directors Guild of America Oral History*. Metuchen, N.J.: Scarecrow, 1988.

Drescher, Seymour. *Capitalism and Antislavery*. New York: Oxford University Press, 1987.

Du Bois, W. E. B. "The Black North: A Social Study." *New York Times*, November 24, 1901, SM 11.

———. *Black Reconstruction*. New York: S. A. Russell, 1935.

———. *The Negro*. Philadelphia: University of Pennsylvania Press, 1915.

———. *The Philadelphia Negro*. 1899. Reprint, New York: Schocken, 1967.

———. *The World and Africa*. 1946. Reprint, New York: International, 1968.

Dugat, Simon. "Gender, Colonial 'Women's History' and the Construction of Social Distance: Middle-Class British Women in Later Nineteenth-Century South Africa." *Journal of Southern African Studies* 26.3 (September 2000): 555–72.

Dunae, Patrick A. "Boys' Literature and the Idea of Race: 1870–1900." *Wascana Review* 12.1 (Spring 1977): 84–107.

Dunn, Kevin. "Lights . . . Camera . . . Africa: Images of Africa and Africans in Western Popular Films of the 1930s." *African Studies Review* 39.1 (April 1996): 149–75.

Eisenstein, Sergei. "Dickens, Griffith, and the Film Today." In *Film Form*, translated by Jay Leda. Orlando, Fla.: Harcourt Brace, 1949.

Ely, Melvin Patrick. *The Adventures of Amos 'n' Andy*. Charlottesville: University Press of Virginia, 1991.

Erickson, Peter. "Representations of Blacks and Blackness in the Renaissance." *Criticism* 35.4 (Fall 1993): 499–527.

Ernst, Wolfgang. "Frames at Work: Museological Imagination and Historical Discourse in Neoclassical Britain." *Art Bulletin* 75.3 (September 1993): 481–98.

Evans, Daniel. "Slave Coast of Europe." *Slavery and Abolition* 6.1 (May 1985): 41–58.

Everett, Anna. *Returning the Gaze: A Genealogy of Black Film Criticism, 1909–1949*. Durham, N.C.: Duke University Press, 2001.

Farrar, Cynthia. *The Origins of Democratic Thinking*. Cambridge: Cambridge University Press, 1988.

Filler, Louis. *The Crusade against Slavery, 1830–1860*. New York: Harper & Brothers, 1960.

Fishel, Leslie H., Jr., and Benjamin Quarles. *The Black American: A Brief Documentary History*. Glenview, Ill.: Scott, Foresman, 1970.

Foner, Eric. *Reconstruction: America's Unfinished Revolution, 1863–1877*. New York: Harper & Row, 1988.

Forbes, Jack. *Black Africans and Native Americans*. Oxford: Basil Blackwell, 1988.

Ford, Nick Aaron. "How Genuine Is the Green Pastures?" *Phylon Quarterly* 20.1 (1959): 68–69.

Foucault, Michel. "Truth and Power." In *Power/Knowledge*, edited by Colin Gordon. New York: Pantheon, 1980.

———. "Two Lectures." In *Power/Knowledge*, edited by Colin Gordon. New York: Pantheon, 1980.

Franklin, V. P. *Black Self-Determination*. Wellport, Conn.: Lawrence Hill, 1984.

Frazier, E. Franklin. *The Negro Church in America*. New York: Schocken, 1966.

Freedman, Alix M., and Laurie P. Cohen. "'Gangsta' Life: In Rap Music Saga, Was Elite Accountant Victim or Perpetrator?" *Wall Street Journal*, March 20, 1997, A1.

Frey, Robert Seitz, and Nancy Thompson-Frey. *The Silent and the Damned*. Lanham, Md.: Madison, 1988.

Fryer, Peter. *Staying Power*. London: Pluto, 1984.

Fury, David. *Kings of the Jungle*. Jefferson, N.C.: McFarland, 1994.

Gabler, Neal. *An Empire of Their Own*. New York: Crown, 1988.

Gaines, Jane M. *Fire and Desire: Mixed-Race Movies in the Silent Era*. Chicago: University of Chicago Press, 2001.

———. "*The Scar of Shame*: Skin Color and Caste in Black Silent Melodrama." *Cinema Journal* 26.4 (Summer 1987): 3–21.

———, ed. *Classical Hollywood Narrative*. Durham, N.C.: Duke University Press, 1992.

Gaines, Kevin K. *Uplifting the Race*. Chapel Hill: University of North Carolina Press, 1996.

Gardner, Helen. "'Othello': A Retrospect, 1900–67." In *Shakespeare Survey* 19:1–13. Cambridge: Cambridge University Press, 1970.

Gates, Henry Louis, Jr. "The Welcoming Table." In *Lure and Loathing*, edited by Gerald Early. New York: Penguin, 1993.

Gatewood, Willard B., Jr. *Aristocrats of Color*. Bloomington: Indiana University Press, 1990.

———, ed. *"Smoked Yankees" and the Struggle for Empire*. Fayetteville: University of Arkansas Press, 1987.

Genovese, Eugene. "'Our Family, White and Black': Family and Household in the Southern Slaveholders' World View." In *In Joy and in Sorrow: Women, Family, and Marriage in the Victorian South, 1830–1900*, edited by Carol Bleser. New York: Oxford University Press, 1991.

Gerzina, Gretchen Holbrook. *Black London*. New York: Routledge, 1995.

Gevinson, Alan. *Within Our Gates: Ethnicity in American Films, 1911–1960*. Berkeley: University of California Press, 1997.

Gilman, Sander. "Black Bodies, White Bodies: Toward an Iconography of Female Sexuality in Late Nineteenth-Century Art, Medicine, and Literature." *Critical Inquiry* 12 (Autumn 1985): 204–42.

Gilmore, Al-Tony. *Bad Nigger! The National Impact of Jack Johnson*. Port Washington, N.Y.: Kennikat, 1975.

Ginsberg, David. "Ploughboys versus Prelates: Tyndale and More and the Politics of Biblical Translation." *Sixteenth Century Journal* 19.1 (Spring 1988): 45–61.

Goldfarb, Stephen. "Framed." *American Heritage* 47.6 (October 1996): 108–13.

Goldstein, Thomas. *Dawn of Modern Science*. Boston: Houghton Mifflin, 1980.

Gomery, Douglas. *The Hollywood Studio System*. New York: St. Martin's, 1986.

Gonzales, Michael J. "United States Copper Companies, the State, and Labour Conflict in Mexico, 1900–1910." *Journal of Latin American Studies* 26.3 (October 1994): 651–81.

———. "U.S. Copper Companies, the Mine Workers' Movement, and the Mexican Revolution, 1910–1920." *Hispanic American Historical Review* 76.3 (August 1996): 503–34.

Goodman, Paul. *Of One Blood: Abolitionism and the Origin of Racial Equality*. Berkeley: University of California Press, 1998.

Goodwin, James. *Eisenstein, Cinema, and History*. Urbana: University of Illinois Press, 1993.

Gould, Stephen Jay. *The Mismeasure of Man*. New York: Norton, 1981.

Graham, Lawrence Otis. *Our Kind of People*. New York: HarperPerennial, 2000.

Green, J. Ronald. *Straight Lick: The Cinema of Oscar Micheaux*. Bloomington: Indiana University Press, 2000.

———. *With a Crooked Stick: The Films of Oscar Micheaux*. Bloomington: Indiana University Press, 2004.

Greenberg, Harvey Roy. "Rescrewed: Pretty Woman's Co-opted Feminism." *Journal of Popular Film and Television* 19.1 (Spring 1991): 9–14.

Grieveson, Lee. *Policing Cinema: Movies and Censorship in Early Twentieth-Century America*. Berkeley: University of California Press, 2004.

Guerrero, Ed. *Framing Blackness: The African American Image in Film*. Philadelphia: Temple University Press, 1993.

Gunning, Tom. *D. W. Griffith and the Origins of American Narrative Film*. Urbana: University of Illinois Press, 1994.

Gura, Philip F. "America's Minstrel Daze." *New England Quarterly* 72.4 (December 1999): 602–16.

Gussow, Adam. *Seems like Murder Here: Southern Violence and the Blues Tradition*. Chicago: University of Chicago Press, 2002.

Gutman, Herbert G. "The Negro and the United Mine Workers of America." In *Work, Culture, and Society in Industrializing America*, edited by Herbert Gutman. New York: Knopf, 1976.

Habib, Imtiaz. "*Othello*, Sir Peter Negro, and the Blacks of Early Modern England." *Literature, Interpretation, Theory* 9.1 (September 1998): 15–30.

Hackett, Francis. "After the Play." *New Republic*, April 14, 1917, 325.

Hadley-Garcia, George. *Hispanic Hollywood*. New York: Citadel, 1993.

Haggard, H. Rider. *She*. 1886. Reprint, London: Penguin, 2001.

Halberstam, David. *The Powers That Be*. New York: Knopf, 1979.

Hall, Kim. "Reading What Isn't There: 'Black' Studies in Early Modern England." *Stanford Humanities Review* 3.1 (Winter 1993): 23–33.

———. *Things of Darkness: Economies of Race and Gender in Early Modern England*. Ithaca, N.Y.: Cornell University Press, 1995.

Hall, Martin. "The Legend of the Lost City; or, The Man with Golden Balls." *Journal of Southern African Studies* 21.2 (June 1995): 179–99.

Hall, Mordaunt. "Art in Negro Picture." *New York Times*, March 10, 1929, 131.

———. "The Best Ten Films." *New York Times*, January 5, 1930, X6.

———. "The Screen." *New York Times*, February 28, 1929, 22.

———. "The Screen." *New York Times*, August 21, 1929, 33.

———. "Spatting Couples of 'Private Lives' Meet with High Favor—Impressive Version of 'Mississippi.'" *New York Times*, December 19, 1931, 16.

———. "Vidor's Negro Film." *New York Times*, August 25, 1929, X4.

Haller, John S. "Civil War Anthropometry: The Making of a Racial Ideology." *Civil War History* 16 (December 1970): 309–24.

Hamilton, Charles V. *Adam Clayton Powell, Jr.* New York: Atheneum, 1991.

Hankey, Julie. *Othello*. Bristol, U.K.: Bristol Classical, 1997.

Haraway, Donna. *Primate Visions*. New York: Routledge, 1989.

Harding, Sandra. "Comment on Walby's 'Against Epistemological Chasms: The Science Question in Feminism Revisited': Can Democratic Values and Interests Ever Play a Rationally Justifiable Role in the Evaluation of Scientific Work?" *Signs* 26.2 (Winter 2001): 511–25.

"Harlem on Prairie." *Variety*, February 9, 1938, 14.

Harrold, Stanley. "John Brown's Forerunners: Slave Rescue Attempts and the Abolitionists, 1841–51." *Radical History Review* 55 (1993): 89–110.

Heehs, Peter. *Indian Religions*. New York: New York University Press, 2002.

Hegeman, Susan. "Franz Boas and Professional Anthropology: On Mapping the Borders of the 'Modern.'" *Victorian Studies* 41.3 (Spring 1998): 455–84.

Helgerson, Richard. *Forms of Nationhood*. Chicago: University of Chicago Press, 1992.

Helmbold, Lois Rita. "Beyond the Family Economy: Black and White Working-Class Women during the Great Depression." *Feminist Studies* 13.3 (Autumn 1987): 629–55.

Hennessey, Thomas J. *From Jazz to Swing*. Detroit: Wayne State University Press, 1994.

Henstell, Bruce. *Sunshine and Wealth*. San Francisco: Chronicle, 1984.

Heywood, Chester D. *Negro Combat Troops in the World War*. Worcester, Mass: Commonwealth, 1928.

Hill, Anthony D. *Pages from the Harlem Renaissance*. New York: Peter Lang, 1989.

Hillaby, Joe. "Beth Miqdash Me'at: The Synagogues of Medieval England." *Journal of Ecclesiastical History* 44.2 (April 1993): 182–97.

Hirsch, Arnold R. "On the Waterfront: Race, Class, and Politics in Post-Reconstruction New Orleans." *Journal of Urban History* 21.4 (May 1995): 511–17.

"History of Black Film." Special issue, *Black Film Review* 7.4 (1993).

The History of Racist Animation. Wavelength Video, 1988.

Hoberman, J. "Paranoia and the Pods." *Sight and Sound* 4.5 (May 1994): 28–31.

Hobsbawm, Eric. *The Age of Extremes*. New York: Vintage, 1994.

Hodes, Martha. *White Women, Black Men: Illicit Sex in the Nineteenth-Century South*. New Haven, Conn.: Yale University Press, 1997.

———, ed. *Sex, Love, Race*. New York: New York University Press, 1999.

Honour, Hugh. *The Image of the Black in Western Art*. Vol. 4, pt. 1. Cambridge, Mass.: Harvard University Press, 1989.

Horn, Alfred Aloysius. *Trader Horn*. Johannesburg: Jonathan Cape, 1927.

Horne, Gerald. *Class Struggle in Hollywood, 1930–1950*. Austin: University of Texas Press, 2001.

Howe, Irving. *The World of Our Fathers*. New York: Schocken, 1976.

Hunt, Sanford B. "The Negro as a Soldier." *Anthropological Review* 7.24 (January 1869): 40–54.

Hunter, G. K. "Elizabethans and Foreigners." In *Shakespeare in His Own Age*. *Shakespeare Survey* 17. Cambridge: Cambridge University Press, 1964.

Hunwick, J. O. "Black Africans in the Islamic World: An Understudied Dimension of the Black Diaspora." *Tarikh* 5.4 (1978): 20–40.

Hurst, Fannie. *Imitation of Life*. Cleveland: World, 1933.

Hyatt, Marshall. *The Afro-American Cinematic Experience: An Annotated Bibliography and Filmography*. Wilmington, Del.: Scholarly Resources, 1983.

Ignatiev, Noel. *How the Irish Became White*. New York: Routledge, 1995.

"In Africa with Trader Horn." *American Cinematographer*, January 1930, 9, 26.

Jackson, Donald Dale. "How Lord Elgin First Won—and Lost—His Marbles." *Smithsonian*, December 1992, 135–44.

Jackson, John G. Introduction to *The Story of Moors in Spain*, by Stanley Lane-Poole, 1886. Baltimore: Black Classic, 1990.

Jacobson, Matthew Frye. *Whiteness of a Different Color*. Cambridge, Mass.: Harvard University Press, 1998.

Jaffe, David. *The Stormy Petrel and the Whale: Some Origins of "Moby-Dick"*. Baltimore: Port City, 1976.

James, C. L. R. *The Black Jacobins*. 1938. London: Allison & Busby, 1989.

———. "On *Gone with the Wind*." In *C. L. R. James on the "Negro Question,"* edited by Scott McLemee. Jackson: University Press of Mississippi, 1996.

Jay, Gregory S. "'White Man's Book No Good': D. W. Griffith and the American Indian." *Cinema Journal* 39.4 (Summer 2000): 3–26.

Jeffrey, Julie Roy. *The Great Silent Army of Abolitionism: Women in the Antislavery Movement*. Chapel Hill: University of North Carolina Press, 1998.

Jenkyns, Richard. *The Victorians and Ancient Greece*. Cambridge, Mass.: Harvard University Press, 1980.

Johnson, James Weldon. *Black Manhattan*. New York: Knopf, 1930.

———. "Self-Determining Haiti: III. Government of, by, and for the National City Bank." *The Nation*, September 11, 1910, 295–97.

Johnson, Walter. "The Slave Trader, the White Slave, and the Politics of Racial Determination in the 1850s." *Journal of American History* 87.1 (June 2000): 13–36.

Jones, Eldred. *The Elizabethan Image of Africa*. Ithaca, N.Y.: Cornell University Press, 1995.

———. *Othello's Countrymen: The African in English Renaissance Drama*. London: Oxford University Press, 1965.

Jordan, Ervin L., Jr. "Sleeping with the Enemy: Sex, Black Women, and the Civil War." *Western Journal of Black Studies* 18.2 (1994): 55–63.

Jordan, Winthrop. *White over Black*. Chapel Hill: University of North Carolina Press, 1968.

Jowett, Garth S. "'A Capacity for Evil': The 1915 Supreme Court *Mutual* Decision." In *Controlling Hollywood: Censorship and Regulation in the Studio Era*, edited by Matthew Bernstein. New Brunswick, N.J.: Rutgers University Press, 1999.

Kaplan, Amy. "Romancing the Empire: The Embodiment of American Masculinity in the Popular Historical Novel of the 1890s." *American Literary History* 2.4 (Winter 1990): 659–90.

Katz, Friedrich. *The Life and Times of Pancho Villa*. Stanford, Calif.: Stanford University Press, 1998.

Kaufmann, Chaim D., and Robert A. Pape. "Explaining Costly International Moral Action: Britain's Sixty-Year Campaign against the Atlantic Slave Trade." *International Organization* 53.4 (Autumn 1999): 631–68.

Kawash, Samira. "*The Autobiography of an Ex-Coloured Man*: (Passing for) Black Passing for White." In *Passing the Fiction of Identity*, edited by Elaine K. Ginsberg. Durham, N.C.: Duke University Press, 1996.

Keire, Mara L. "The Vice Trust: A Reinterpretation of the White Slavery Scare in the United States, 1907–1917." *Journal of Social History* 35.1 (Fall 2001): 5–41.

Keith, Jeanette. *Rich Man's War, Poor Man's Fight: Race, Class, and Power in the Rural South during the First World War*. Chapel Hill: University of North Carolina Press, 2004.

Kilpatrick, Jacquelyn. *Celluloid Indians: Native Americans and Film*. Lincoln: University of Nebraska Press, 1999.

Kingsley, Grace. "Pathe Chooses First Talker." *Los Angeles Times*, October 19, 1928, 10.

———. "Warner Arrives Tomorrow." *Los Angeles Times*, October 30, 1928, A8.

Kirby, Jack Temple. "D. W. Griffith's Racial Portraiture." *Phylon* 39.2 (June 1978): 118–27.

———. *Media-Made Dixie*. Baton Rouge: Louisiana State University Press, 1978.

Kirby, John B. "Ralph J. Bunche and Black Radical Thought in the 1930s." *Phylon* 35.2 (Summer 1974): 129–41.

Kirihara, Donald. "The Accepted Idea Displaced: Stereotype and Sessue Hayakawa." In Bernardi, *Birth of Whiteness*.

Kisch, John, and Edward Mapp. *A Separate Cinema: Fifty Years of Black-Cast Posters*. New York: Farrar, Straus and Giroux, 1992.

Kitses, Jim, and Gregg Rickman, eds. *The Western Reader*. New York: Limelight, 1999.

Klinkner, Philip A., and Rogers M. Smith. *The Unsteady March: The Rise and Decline of Racial Equality in America*. Chicago: University of Chicago Press, 1999.

Koselleck, Reinhart. *Futures Past: On the Semantics of Historical Time*. Cambridge, Mass: MIT Press, 1995.

Koszarski, Richard. *An Evening's Entertainment: The Age of the Silent Feature Picture, 1915–1928*. Berkeley: University of California Press, 1990.

Kousser, J. Morgan. *The Shaping of Southern Politics: Suffrage Restrictions and the Establishment of the One-Party South, 1880–1910*. New Haven, Conn.: Yale University Press, 1974.

Krasner, David. "'The Mirror up to Nature': Modernist Aesthetics and Racial Authenticity in African American Theatre, 1895–1900." *Theatre History Studies* 16 (June 1996): 117–41.

———. *Resistance, Parody, and Double Consciousness in African-American Theatre, 1895–1910*. New York: St. Martin's, 1997.

Lanctot, Neil. *Negro League Baseball*. Philadelphia: University of Pennsylvania Press, 2004.

Landers, Jane. "Gracia Real de Santa Teresa de Mose: A Free Black Town in Spanish Colonial Florida." *American Historical Review* 95.1 (February 1990): 9–30.

Lang, Robert, ed. *The Birth of a Nation: D. W. Griffith, Director*. 1971. Reprint, New Brunswick, N.J.: Rutgers University Press, 1994.

Lantino, Jack. "Miles of Smiles, Years of Struggle: The Negotiation of Black Occupational Identity through Personal Experience Narrative." *Journal of American Folklore* 96.382 (October–December 1983): 393–412.

Lapsansky, Emma Jones. "'Since They Got Those Separate Churches': Afro-Americans and Racism in Jacksonian Philadelphia." *American Quarterly* 321 (1980): 54–78.

Lapsansky, Phillip. "Graphic Discord: Abolitionist and Antiabolitionist Images." In *The Abolitionist Sisterhood*, edited by Jean Fagan Yellin and John C. Van Horne, 201–30. Ithaca, N.Y.: Cornell University Press, 1982.

Lasky, Betty. *RKO*. Santa Monica, Calif.: Roundtable, 1989.

Lee, Robert G. *Orientals: Asian Americans in Popular Culture*. Philadelphia: Temple University Press, 1999.

Lee, Sir Sidney. "Caliban's Visits to England." *Cornhill Magazine*, n.s., 34 (1913): 333–45.

Levine, Lawrence. *Black Culture and Black Consciousness*. New York: Oxford University Press, 1977.

Lewalski, Barbara Kiefer. "Anne of Denmark and the Subversions of Masquing." *Criticism* 35.3 (Summer 1993): 341–56.

Lewis, David Levering. *W. E. B. Du Bois: Biography of a Race*. New York: Holt, 1993.

Lewis, Edgar. *Synopsis of "The Nigger."* LP 5235. Washington, D.C.: Library of Congress, 1915.

Lewis, Ethelreda. *The Harp*. New York: Doran, 1925.

Leyda, Julia. "Black-Audience Westerns and the Politics of Cultural Identification in the 1930s." *Cinema Journal* 42.2 (Fall 2002): 46–70.

Lhamon, W. T. *Raising Cain: Blackface Performance from Jim Crow to Hip Hop*. Cambridge, Mass.: Harvard University Press, 1998.

Lichtenstein, Alex. "Good Roads and Chain Gangs in the Progressive South: 'The Negro Convict Is a Slave.'" *Journal of Southern History* 59.1 (February 1993): 85–110.

Lindfors, Bernth. "'Mislike Me Not for My Complexion . . .': Ira Aldridge in Whiteface." *African-American Review* 33.2 (Summer 1999): 347–54.

Litwack, Leon F. "Hellhounds." In *Without Sanctuary: Lynching Photography in America*, edited by James Allen, Hilton Als, John Lewis, and Leon F. Litwack. N.p.: Twin Palms, 2000.

Logan, Rayford. "James Weldon Johnson and Haiti." *Phylon* 32.4 (1971): 396–402.

Lorini, Alessandra. *Rituals of Race: American Public Culture and the Search for Racial Democracy*. Charlottesville: University Press of Virginia, 1999.

Lott, Eric. *Love and Theft*. New York: Oxford University Press, 1993.

Lott, Tommy L. "A No-Theory Theory of Contemporary Black Cinema." In *The Invention of Race*. Oxford: Blackwell, 1999.

Lovejoy, Paul. *Haiti and the United States*. Athens: University of Georgia Press, 1992.

———. "The Volume of the Atlantic Slave Trade: A Synthesis." *Journal of African History* 23.4 (1982): 473–501.

Low, W. Augustus, and Virgil A. Clift, eds. *Encyclopedia of Black America*. New York: Da Capo, 1981.

Loyn, Henry. "Slavs." In *The Middle Ages: A Concise Encyclopaedia*, edited by H. R. Loyn. New York: Thames and Hudson, 1991.

Lubin, Alex. *Romance and Rights: The Politics of Interracial Intimacy, 1945–1954*. Jackson: University Press of Mississippi, 2005.

Lund, John M. "Boundaries of Restriction: The Dillingham Commission." *University of Vermont History Review* 6 (December 1994). <http://www.uvm.edu/~hag/histreview/vol6/lund.html>.

Lusk, Norbert. "'Hallelujah' Rings to Sky." *Los Angeles Times*, August 25, 1929, B11.

MacDonald, Robert H. "Reproducing the Middle-Class Boy: From Purity to Patriotism in the Boys' Magazines, 1892–1914." *Journal of Contemporary History* 24 (1989): 519–39.

MacLean, Nancy. *Behind the Mask of Chivalry*. New York: Oxford University Press, 1994.

———. "The Leo Frank Case Reconsidered: Gender and Sexual Politics in the Making of Reactionary Populism." *Journal of American History* 78 (December 1991): 917–48.

Madison, Otis. "Confronting Racism." Public Lecture. University of California, Santa Barbara. January 20, 1997.

Maltin, Leonard. *Of Mice and Magic: A History of American Animated Cartoons*. New York: McGraw-Hill, 1980.

Mancini, Matthew J. *One Dies, Get Another: Convict Leasing in the American South*. Columbia: University of South Carolina Press, 1996.

Manring, M. M. *Slave in a Box: The Strange Career of Aunt Jemima*. Charlottesville: University Press of Virginia, 1998.

Marchetti, Gina. *Romance and the "Yellow Peril."* Berkeley: University of California Press, 1993.

Marks, Carole. *Farewell—We're Good and Gone*. Bloomington: Indiana University Press, 1989.

Marshall, Herbert, and Mildred Stock. *Ira Aldridge: The Negro Tragedian*. London: Rockliff, 1958.

Marshall, Ray. "The Negro and Organized Labor." *Journal of Negro Education* 32.4 (Autumn 1963): 375–89.

Marx, Karl. Preface and introduction to *A Contribution to the Critique of Political Economy*. Peking: Foreign Languages, 1976.

Massood, Paula. *Black City Cinema: African American Urban Experiences in Film*. Philadelphia: Temple University Press, 2003.

McArthur, Benjamin. *Actors and American Culture, 1880–1920*. Philadelphia: Temple University Press, 1984.

McCrum, Robert, William Cran, and Robert MacNeil. *The Story of English*. New York: Penguin, 1993.

McDonnell, Janet A. *The Dispossession of the American Indian, 1887–1934*. Bloomington: Indiana University Press, 1992.

McGhee, Richard D. "'There's Something Sad about Retracing': Jane Parker in the 'Tarzan' Films of the Thirties." *Kansas Quarterly* 16.3 (1984): 101–23.

McKivigan, John R. "James Redpath, John Brown, and Abolitionist Advocacy of Slave Insurrection." *Civil War History* 37.4 (1991): 293–314.

McLaurin, Melton A. *The Knights of Labor in the South*. Westport, Conn.: Greenwood, 1978.

Mellinger, Phil. "'The Men Have Become Organizers': Labor Conflict and Unionization in the Mexican Mining Communities of Arizona, 1900–1915." *Western Historical Quarterly* 23.3 (August 1992): 323–47.

Melnick, Jeffrey. *A Right to Sing the Blues*. Cambridge, Mass.: Harvard University Press, 1999.

Mennell, James. "African-Americans and the Selective Service Act of 1917." *Journal of Negro History* 84.3 (Summer 1999): 275–87.

Merritt, Russell. "Dixon, Griffith, and the Southern Legend." *Cinema Journal* 12.1 (Autumn 1972): 26–45.

Meyer, Michael C., William L. Sherman, and Susan M. Deeds. *The Course of Mexican History*. Oxford: Oxford University Press, 1999.

Micheaux, Oscar. "The Negro and the Photo-Play." *Half-Century Magazine*, May 1919, 11.

Miller, Joseph C. "History and Africa/Africa and History." *American Historical Review* 104.1 (February 1999): 1–32.

Miller, William. "American Historians and the Business Elite." *Journal of Economic History* 9.2 (November 1949): 184–208.

Milne, R. *A Dream Caused by the Perusal of Mrs. H. Beecher Stowe's Popular Work Uncle Tom's Cabin*. Louisville, Ky., 1855.

Mitchell, Loften. *Black Drama*. New York: Hawthorn, 1967.

Mizejewski, Linda. *Ziegfeld Girl*. Durham, N.C.: Duke University Press, 1999.

Moley, Raymond. *The Hays Office*. Indianapolis: Bobbs-Merrill, 1945.

Moore, Leonard. "Historical Interpretations of the 1920's Klan: The Traditional View and the Populist Revision." *Journal of Social History* 24.2 (Winter 1990): 341–67.

Mora, Carl J. *Mexican Cinema: Reflections on a Society, 1896–1980*. Berkeley: University of California Press, 1982.

Morgan, Edmund. *American Slavery, American Freedom*. New York: Norton, 1975.

Morris, Earl J. "George Randol Chosen as Czar of New Combine; Plan Large Advertising Campaign." *California Eagle*, November 9, 1939, B2.

Moses, Wilson Jeremiah. *The Golden Age of Black Nationalism, 1850–1925*. Hamden, Conn.: Archon, 1978.

Mosse, George. *Toward the Final Solution: A History of European Racism*. London: Dent & Sons, 1978.

Most, Andrea. *Making Americans: Jews and the Broadway Musical*. Cambridge, Mass.: Harvard University Press, 2004.

Mumford, Kevin. "After Hugh: Statutory Race Segregation in Colonial America, 1650–1725." *American Journal of Legal History* 43.3 (1999): 280–305.

Murrell, William. *A History of American Graphic Humor*. New York: Whitney Museum of American Art, 1933.

Musser, Charles. "Colored Players Film Corporation: An Alternative to Micheaux." In Bowser et al., *Oscar Micheaux and His Circle*.

———. *Edison Motion Pictures, 1890–1900: An Annotated Filmography*. Washington, D.C.: Smithsonian Institution Press, 1997.

———. *The Emergence of Cinema: The American Screen to 1907*. Berkeley: University of California Press, 1990.

Nalty, Bernard C. *Strength for the Fight*. New York: Free Press, 1986.

Neill, Michael. "'Mulattos,' 'Blacks' and 'Indian Moors': *Othello* and Early Modern Constructions of Human Difference." *Shakespeare Quarterly* 49.4 (Winter 1998): 361–74.

Nelson, Scott Reynolds. *Iron Confederacies: Southern Railways, Klan Violence, and Reconstruction*. Chapel Hill: University of North Carolina Press, 2005.

Nevins, Allan, and Frank Weitenkampf. *A Century of Political Cartoons*. New York: Scribner's, 1944.

Newman, Richard. "'The Brightest Star': Aida Overton Walker in the Age of Ragtime and Cakewalk." *Prospects: An Annual of American Cultural Studies* 18 (1993): 465–82.

Nicholls, B. M. "Zululand, 1887–1889: The Court of the Special Commissioners for Zululand and the Rule of Law." *Journal of Natal and Zulu History* 15 (1994–95), <http://www.pinetreeweb.com/journal-dinizulu.htm>.

Noble, Peter. *The Negro in Films*. 1948. Reprint, Port Washington, N.Y.: Kennikat, 1969.

Oates, Stephen. *To Purge This Land with Blood*. New York: Harper Torchbook, 1972.

Ober, Josiah. *Political Dissent in Democratic Athens*. Princeton, N.J.: Princeton University Press, 1998.

O'Connor, Alice. *Poverty Knowledge: Social Science, Social Policy, and the Poor in Twentieth-Century U.S. History*. Princeton, N.J.: Princeton University Press, 2001.

Oldfield, J. R. *Popular Politics and British Anti-Slavery*. Manchester, U.K.: Manchester University Press, 1995.

Orgel, Stephen. *The Jonsonian Masque*. Cambridge, Mass.: Harvard University Press, 1965.

Oshinsky, David M. *"Worse than Slavery": Parchman Farm and the Ordeal of Jim Crow Justice*. New York: Free Press, 1996.

Outwin, Charles P. "Securing the Leg Irons: Restriction of Legal Rights for Slaves in Virginia and Maryland, 1625–1791." *Early America Review* 1.3 (Winter 1996–97): 7–24.

Paltrow, Scot. "Old Memos Lay Bare MetLife's Use of Race to Screen Customers." *Wall Street Journal*, July 24, 2001, A1.

Paludan, Phillip Shaw. *"A People's Contest": The Union Army and Civil War, 1861–1865*. New York: Harper & Row, 1988.

Pamphile, Leon D. "The NAACP and the American Occupation in Haiti." *Phylon* 47.1 (1986): 91–100.

Pares, Richard. "Merchants and Planters." *Economic History Review Supplement* 4 (1960): 1–91.

Parkhurst, Jessie W. "The Role of the Black Mammy in the Plantation Household." *Journal of Negro History* 23.3 (July 1938): 349–69.

Parlee, Lorena. "The Impact of United States Railroad Unions on Organized Labor and Government Policy in Mexico (1880–1911)." *Hispanic American Historical Review* 64.3 (August 1984): 443–75.

Patterson, Orlando. *Slavery and Social Death*. Cambridge, Mass.: Harvard University Press, 1982.

Pearson, Roberta E. "The Revenge of Rain-in-the-Face? Or, Custers and Indians on the Silent Screen." In Bernardi, *Birth of Whiteness*.

Peiss, Kathy. *Cheap Amusements: Working Women and Leisure in Turn-of-the-Century New York*. Philadelphia: Temple University Press, 1986.

Peretti, Burton W. *The Creation of Jazz*. Chicago: University of Illinois Press, 1992.

Perry, Lincoln. "Lincoln Perry's Letter." *Chicago Defender*, December 18, 1926, 7.

Petric, Vlada. "Vertov, Lenin, and Perestroika: The Cinematic Transposition of Reality." *Historical Journal of Film, Radio and Television* 15.1 (March 1995): 3–17.

Phillips, Kevin. *Wealth and Democracy*. New York: Broadway, 2002.

Pickering, Charles. *The Races of Man*. 1849. Reprint, London: Bohn, 1863.

Pierce, Joseph. *Negro Business and Business Education*. New York: Harper, 1947.

Pieterse, Jan Nederveen. *White on Black: Images of Africa and Blacks in Western Popular Culture*. New Haven, Conn.: Yale University Press, 1992.

Pimienta-Bey, José V. "Moorish Spain: Academic Source and Foundation for the Rise and Success of Western European Universities in the Middle Ages." In *Golden Age of the Moor*, edited by Ivan Van Sertima. New Brunswick, N.J.: Transaction, 1996.

Pirenne, Henri. *Mohammed and Charlemagne*. New York: Norton, 1939.

Pizzitola, Louis. *Hearst over Hollywood*. New York: Columbia University Press, 2002.

Plummer, Brenda Gayle. "The Afro-American Response to the Occupation of Haiti, 1915–1934." *Phylon* 43.2 (1982): 125–43.

———. *Haiti and the Great Powers*. Baton Rouge: Louisiana State University Press, 1988.

———. *Haiti and the United States*. Athens: University of Georgia Press, 1992.

———. "The Metropolitan Connection: Foreign and Semiforeign Elites in Haiti, 1900–1915." *Latin American Research Review* 19.2 (1984): 119–42.

Porges, Irwin. *Edgar Rice Burroughs: The Man Who Created Tarzan*. 2 vols. New York: Ballantine, 1975.

Puttnam, David. *Movies and Money*. New York: Vintage, 1997.

Quarles, Benjamin. *Black Abolitionists*. New York: Oxford, 1969.

Radano, Ronald. "New Musical Figurations." *American Music* 17.2 (Summer 1999): 213.

Raleigh, John Henry. "Eugene O'Neill." *English Journal* 56.3 (March 1967): 367–77, 475.

Ramsey, Guthrie P., Jr. "Who Matters? Review of Ingrid Monson's *Saying Something*, Burton Paretti's *Jazz in American Culture*, and Ronald Radano's *New Musical Figurations*." *American Music* 17.2 (Summer 1999): 205–15.

Reckord, Mary. "The Jamaica Slave Rebellion of 1831." *Past and Present* 40 (July 1968): 108–25.

Record, Wilson. *The Negro and the Communist Party*. New York: Atheneum, 1971.

Reddick, Lawrence. "Educational Programs for the Improvement of Race Relations: Motion Pictures, Radio, the Press, and Libraries." *Journal of Negro Education* 13.3 (Summer 1944): 367–89.

Reed, Christopher Robert. *"All the World Is Here!": The Black Presence at White City*. Bloomington: Indiana University Press, 2000.

Regester, Charlene. "African American Extras in Hollywood during the 1920s and 1930s." *Film History* 9.1 (1996): 95–119.

———. "The African-American Press and Race Movies, 1909–1929." In Bowser et al., *Oscar Micheaux and His Circle*.

———. "The Misreading and Rereading of African American Filmmaker Oscar Micheaux." *Film History* 7.4 (1995): 426–49.

———. "Oscar Micheaux the Entrepreneur: Financing *The House behind the Cedars*." *Journal of Film and Video* 49.1 (Spring–Summer 1997): 17–27.

———. "Stepin Fetchit: The Man, the Image, and the African American Press." *Film History* 6.4 (Winter 1994): 502–21.

Reichlin, Elinor. "Faces of Slavery: A Historical Find." *American Heritage*, June 1977.

Reid, Mark. *Redefining Black Film*. Berkeley: University of California Press, 1993.

Reuter, Edward Byron. *The Mulatto in the United States*. 1918. Reprint, New York: Negro Universities Press, 1969.

Richards, Larry. *African American Films through 1959*. Jefferson, N.C.: McFarland, 1998.

Richards, Leonard L. *"Gentlemen of Property and Standing": Anti-Abolition Mobs in Jacksonian America*. London: Oxford University Press, 1970.

Richings, G. F. *Evidences of Progress among Colored People*. Philadelphia: Ferguson, 1902.

Rippy, J. Fred. "The Initiation of the Customs Receivership in the Dominican Republic." *Hispanic American Historical Review* 17.4 (November 1937): 419–57.

Roach, Joseph R. "Slave Spectacles and Tragic Octoroons: A Cultural Genealogy of Antebellum Performance." *Theatre Survey* 33 (November 1992): 167–87.

Roberts, Randy. *Papa Jack: Jack Johnson and the Era of White Hopes*. New York: Free Press, 1963.

Robinson, Cedric J. *Black Marxism*. London: Zed, 1983.

———. *Black Movements in America*. New York: Routledge, 1997.

———. "Capitalism, Slavery and Bourgeois Historiography." *History Workshop* 23 (Spring 1987): 122–40.

———. "Fascism and the Intersections of Capitalism, Racialism, and Historical Consciousness." *Humanities in Society* 6.4 (Fall 1983): 325–49.

———. "Slavery and the Platonic Origins of Anti-Democracy." *National Political Science Review* 5 (1995): 18–35.

Roediger, David R. *The Wages of Whiteness*. London: Verso, 1991.

Rogers, J. A. *Sex and Race: Negro-Caucasian Mixing in All Ages and All Lands*. Vol. 1. 1940. Reprint, New York: Rogers, 1967.

Rogin, Michael. *Blackface, White Noise: Jewish Immigrants in the Hollywood Melting Pot*. Berkeley: University of California Press, 1996.

———. "'The Sword Became a Flashing Vision': D. W. Griffith's *The Birth of a Nation*." In Lang, *Birth of a Nation*.

———. "'The Sword Became a Flashing Vision': D. W. Griffith's *The Birth of a Nation*." *Representations* 9 (Winter 1985): 150–95.

Rose, Al. *Storyville, New Orleans*. Tuscaloosa: University of Alabama Press, 1974.

Rosenberg, Daniel. *New Orleans Dockworkers: Race, Labor and Unionism, 1892–1923*. Albany: State University of New York Press, 1988.

Rosenberg, Marvin. *The Masks of Othello*. Berkeley: University of California Press, 1961.

Rowse, A. L., ed. *The Annotated Shakespeare*. New York: Greenwich House, 1984.

Royster, Jacqueline Jones. Introduction to *Southern Horrors and Other Writings: The Anti-Lynching Campaign of Ida B. Wells, 1892–1900*. Boston: Bedford, 1997.

Rydell, Robert. *All the World's a Fair*. Chicago: University of Chicago Press, 1987.

Rydell, Robert, John E. Findling, and Kimberly D. Pelle, eds. *Fair America: World's Fairs in the United States*. Washington, D.C.: Smithsonian Institution Press, 2000.

Said, Edward. *The World, the Text, and the Critic*. Cambridge, Mass.: Harvard University Press, 1983.

Sampson, Henry T. *Blacks in Black and White: A Source Book on Black Films*. Metuchen, N.J.: Scarecrow, 1995.

———. *Blacks in Blackface*. Metuchen, N.J.: Scarecrow, 1980.

Sanders, Norman. Introduction to *Othello*, by William Shakespeare, edited by Norman Sanders. Cambridge: Cambridge University Press, 1984.

Santino, Jack. "Miles of Smiles, Years of Struggle: The Negotiation of Black Occupational Identity through Personal Experience Narrative." *Journal of American Folklore* 96.382 (October–December 1983): 393–412.

Saxton, Alexander. *The Rise and Fall of the White Republic*. London: Verso, 1990.

Schallert, Edwin. "Vidor Picture Unique Event." *Los Angeles Times*, October 18, 1929, A11.

Scheuer, Philip K. "Bishops to Consider Cinema 'Black List.'" *Los Angeles Times*, October 8, 1933, A1, A6.

———. "Fame Calls on Colored Chorus Girl." *Los Angeles Times*, January 20, 1929, C13.

———. "'Hold Your Man' Clicks." *Los Angeles Times*, July 21, 1933, A7.

———. "King Vidor in Fresh Venture." *Los Angeles Times*, October 13, 1929, 15.

———. "Trek Yields Jungle Film." *Los Angeles Times*, January 20, 1931, A9.

Schickel, Richard. *D. W. Griffith: An American Life*. New York: Limelight, 1996.

Schmidt, Benno, Jr. "Principle and Prejudice: The Supreme Court and Race in the Progressive Era, Part 2: The 'Peonage Cases.'" *Columbia Law Review* 82.4 (May 1982): 646–718.

Schmidt, Hans. *The United States Occupation of Haiti, 1915–1934*. New Brunswick, N.J.: Rutgers University Press, 1971.

Scott, John. "Loin Cloth, Leopard Skin, Hot Weather Film Vogue." *Los Angeles Times*, June 26, 1932, B11, B16.

"The Secret Information concerning Black American Troops." *Crisis*, May 1919, 16–17.

Segal, Harvey H. "Cycles of Canal Construction." In *Canals and American Economic Development*, edited by Carter Goodrich et al. New York: Kennikat, 1972.

Sennwald, Andre. "The Screen." *New York Times*, November 24, 1934, 19.

Shapiro, Benjamin. "Universal Truths: Cultural Myths and Generic Adaptation in 1950s Science Fiction Films." *Journal of Popular Film and Television* 18.3 (Fall 1990): 103–11.

Sheldon, Edward. *The Nigger*. New York: Macmillan, 1910.

Shepperson, George. Introduction to *The Negro*, by W. E. B. Du Bois. Oxford: Oxford University Press, 1970.

Shillington, Kevin. *History of Africa*. New York: St. Martin's, 1995.

Shipton, Alyn. *A New History of Jazz*. London: Continuum, 2001.

Simons, H. J., and R. E. Simons. *Class and Colour in South Africa*. London: Penguin, 1969.

Sklar, Robert. *Movie-Made America*. New York: Random House, 1975.

Sloan, Kay. *The Loud Silents: Origins of the Social Problem Film*. Chicago: University of Illinois Press, 1988.

Smedley, Audrey. *Race in North America*. Boulder, Colo.: Westview, 1993.

Smith, Ian. "Barbarian Errors: Performing Race in Early Modern England." *Shakespeare Quarterly* 49.2 (1998): 168–86.

Smith, Patricia A. "A Daughter's Tale: Julie Dash Finally Gets to Tell Her Story of Gullah Life." *Boston Globe*, March 15, 1992, B35.

Smyth, J. E. "Revisioning Modern American History in the Age of *Scarface* (1932)." *Historical Journal of Film, Radio and Television* 24.4 (October 2004): 535–63.

Stanley, Robert. *The Celluloid Empire*. New York: Hastings House, 1978.

Steinbrunner, Chris, and Burt Goldblatt. *Cinema of the Fantastic*. New York: Saturday Review, 1972.

Sternsher, Bernard. "Victims of the Great Depression: Self-Blame/Non-Self-Blame, Radicalism, and Pre-1929 Experiences." *Social Science History* 1.2 (Winter 1977): 137–77.

Stewart, Earl. *African American Music*. New York: Schirmer, 1998.

Stewart, Jacqueline. *Migrating to the Movies*. Berkeley: University of California Press, 2005.

Stovall, Tyler. "The Color Line behind the Lines: Racial Violence in France during the Great War." *American Historical Review* 103.3 (June 1998): 737–69.

Stowe, Harriet Beecher. *Uncle Tom's Cabin*. 1852. Reprint, New York: Pocket Books, 2004.

Streible, Dan. "Race and the Reception of Jack Johnson Fight Films." In Bernardi, *Birth of Whiteness*.

Stull, William. "In Africa with Trader Horn." *American Cinematographer*, January 1930, 9, 26.

Sundiata, I. K. "Prelude to Scandal: Liberia and Fernando Po, 1880–1930." *Journal of African History* 15.1 (1974): 97–112.

Tanner, Jo A. *Dusky Maidens*. Westport, Conn.: Greenwood, 1992.

Taylor, Clyde. "Black Silence and the Politics of Representation." In Bowser et al., *Oscar Micheaux and His Circle*.

———. "The Re-Birth of the Aesthetic in Cinema." In Bernardi, *Birth of Whiteness*.

Taylor, J. E. *The Moor of Venice: Cinthio's Tale and Shakespeare's Tragedy*. London: Chapman and Hall, 1855.

Terry, Arthur LeMont. "Genre and Divine Causality in the Religious Films of Spencer Williams, Jr." PhD diss., Regent University, 1995.

Thomas, Hugh. *The Slave Trade*. New York: Touchstone, 1997.

Thompson, Sister M. Francesca. "The Lafayette Players, 1917–1932." In *The Theater of Black Americans*, edited by Erroll Hill, vol. 2. Englewood Cliffs, N.J.: Prentice Hall, 1980.

Thurber, Cheryl. "The Development of the Mammy Image and Mythology." In

Southern Women: Histories and Identities, edited by Virginia Bernhard, Betty Brandon, Elizabeth Fox-Genovese, and Theda Perdue. Columbia: University of Missouri Press, 1992.

Tokson, Elliot. *The Popular Image of the Black Man in English Drama, 1550–1688.* Boston: Hall, 1982.

Toll, Robert. *Blacking Up: The Minstrel Show in Nineteenth-Century America.* New York: Oxford University Press, 1974.

Trevor-Roper, Hugh. "The Rise of Christian Europe, I: The Great Recovery." *Listener,* November 28, 1963, 871.

Trumpbour, John, ed. *How Harvard Rules.* Boston: South End, 1989.

———. "Introducing Harvard." In Trumpbour, *How Harvard Rules.*

Turner, Michael J. "The Limits of Abolition: Government, Saints and the 'African Question,' c. 1780–1820." *English Historical Review,* April 1997, 319–57.

U.S. Congress. *Dictionary of Races of Peoples.* Vol. 5 of *Reports of the Immigration Commission.* 61st Cong., 3rd sess. Washington, D.C.: Government Printing Office, 1911.

"U.S. Copper Companies, the Mine Workers' Movement, and the Mexican Revolution, 1910–1920." *Hispanic American Historical Review* 76.3 (August 1996): 503–35.

Vanderwood, Paul J. "The Picture Postcard as Historical Evidence: Veracruz, 1914; Invasion and Occupation by United States Forces." *Americas* 45.2 (October 1988): 201–25.

Vasey, Ruth. "Beyond Sex and Violence: 'Industry Policy' and the Regulation of Hollywood Movies, 1922–1939." In Bernstein, *Controlling Hollywood.*

———. *The World according to Hollywood, 1918–1939.* Madison: University of Wisconsin Press, 1997.

Vaughan, Alden T., and Virginia Mason Vaughan. "Before *Othello*: Elizabethan Representations of Sub-Saharan Africans." *William and Mary Quarterly* 54.1 (January 1997): 19–44.

Vaughan, Virginia Mason. *Othello: A Contextual History.* Cambridge: Cambridge University Press, 1994.

Vaz, Mark Cotta. *Living Dangerously: The Adventures of Merian C. Cooper.* New York: Villard, 2005.

Vincent, Ted. "The Blacks Who Freed Mexico." *Journal of Negro History* 79.3 (Summer 1994): 257–76.

Viola, Herman J. "The Story of the U.S. Exploring Expedition." In Viola and Margolis, *Magnificent Voyagers.*

———. "The Wilkes Expedition on the Pacific Coast." *Pacific Northwest Quarterly,* January 1989.

Viola, Herman J., and Carolyn Margolis, eds. *Magnificent Voyagers.* Washington, D.C.: Smithsonian Institution Press, 1985.

Walker, George W. "The Negro on the American Stage." *Colored American Magazine,* October 1906, 243–48.

Walker, James W. St. G. *The Black Loyalists.* London: Longman / Dalhousie University Press, 1976.

Wallace, Michele. "*Uncle Tom's Cabin* before and after the Jim Crow Era." *Drama Review* 44.1 (Spring 2000): 136–56.

Wallerstein, Immanuel. *The Modern World-System*. Vol. 1. New York: Academic, 1974.

Wallis, Brian. "Black Bodies, White Science: Louis Agassiz's Slave Daguerreotypes." *American Art* 9.2 (Summer 1995): 38–61.

Walvin, James. *Fruits of Empire: Exotic Produce and British Taste, 1660–1800*. New York: New York University Press, 1997.

Walzer, Michael. *Spheres of Justice*. New York: Basic Books, 1983.

Warnack, James. "Negro Drama Strikes Deep." *Los Angeles Times*, November 3, 1929, B13.

Washington, Fredi. "Headlines/Footlights." *People's Voice*, August 7, 1943, 24.

———. "Headlines/Footlights." *People's Voice*, March 4, 1944, 22.

Watkins, Mel. *On the Real Side*. New York: Simon & Schuster, 1994.

Way, Peter. "Evil Humors and Ardent Spirits: The Rough Culture of Canal Construction Laborers." *Journal of American History* 79.4 (March 1993): 1397–428.

Webster, Mary. *Hogarth*. London: Studio Vista/Cassell, 1979.

Weir, Alison. *The Life of Elizabeth I*. New York: Ballantine, 1998.

Weitzel, Edward. "Broken Ties." *Moving Picture World*, February 16, 1918, 1001.

Wells, Ida B. *Crusade for Justice*. Chicago: University of Chicago Press, 1970.

White, Shane. "'It Was a Proud Day': African Americans, Festivals, and Parades in the North, 1741–1834." *Journal of American History* 81.1 (June 1994): 13–51.

White, Shane, and Graham White. *Stylin'*. Ithaca, N.Y.: Cornell University Press, 1998.

Williams, Eric. *Capitalism and Slavery*. 1944. Reprint, New York: Capricorn, 1966.

Williamson, Joel. *New People: Miscegenation and the Mulattos in the U.S.* New York: Free Press, 1980.

Wilson, F. P. *The Plague in Shakespeare's London*. 1927. Reprint, London: Oxford University Press, 1963.

Wilson, Ian. *Shakespeare: The Evidence*. New York: St. Martin's, 1993.

Wilson, Joseph. *The Black Phalanx*. 1887. Reprint, New York: Da Capo, 1994.

Wilson, Robert. *Philadelphia Quakers, 1681–1981*. Philadelphia: Philadelphia Yearly Meeting, 1981.

Wilson, Woodrow. *A History of the American People*. Vol. 5. New York: Harper & Brothers, 1908.

Woll, Allen. *Black Musical Theatre*. New York: Da Capo, 1989.

Wood, Betty. "White Women, Black Slaves and the Law in Early National Georgia: The Sunbury Petition of 1791." *Historical Journal* 35.3 (September 1992): 611–22.

Wood, Forrest G. *Black Scare*. Berkeley: University of California Press, 1968.

Wood, Marcus. *Blind Memory: Visual Representations of Slavery in England and America, 1780–1865*. New York: Routledge, 2000.

Woodward, Wendy. "Metonymies of Colonialism in Four Handsome Negresses." *Tulsa Studies in Women's Literature* 11.1 (Spring 1992): 63–78.

Worland, Rick. "OWI Meets the Monsters: Hollywood Horror Films and War Propaganda, 1942 to 1945." *Cinema Journal* 37.1 (Autumn 1997): 47–65.

Yearwood, Gladstone. *Black Film as a Signifying Practice*. Trenton, N.J.: Africa World, 2000.

Yengoyan, Aram. "Universalism and Utopianism." *Comparative Study of Society and History* 39.4 (October 1997): 785–98.

Young, Joseph A. *Black Novelist as White Racist: The Myth of Black Inferiority in the Novels of Oscar Micheaux*. New York: Greenwood, 1989.

Yu, Henry. "Mixing Bodies and Cultures." In Hodes, *Sex, Love, Race*.

Zanger, Jules. "The 'Tragic Octoroon' in Pre–Civil War Fiction." *American Quarterly* 18.1 (1966): 63–70.

Zimmermann, Patricia R. "Reconstructing Vertov: Soviet Film Theory and American Radical Documentary." *Journal of Film and Video* 44.1–2 (Spring–Summer 1992): 80–90.

Zinn, Howard. *A People's History of the United States*. New York: HarperPerennial, 1995.

Index

211–12; lobbying against antimiscegenation legislation, 212; capital's conditional tolerance of, as broker stratum, 212; Jim Crow's evisceration of social contract with, 212; compromises of Booker T. Washington rescinded, 212; and championing of black male suffrage, 212; as renegades of challenge to new nationalist history and racial conceits embedded in sociology and anthropology, 212; and Du Bois as architect of renegade catechism, 212

Black migration: Great Migration period, 166, 230; to North and urban areas, 275

Blackness, 129, 132, 141, 153, 202, 316; and trope of "the plantation," 132; ambiguities of, 133; institutionalization of divide between "respectability" and, 144; appropriation of, 167n95; representation of, in *Green Pastures*, 360

Black petite bourgeoisie: militant segment of, 150; imaginings of protonation, 150

Black pioneers, 38

Black radicalism. *See* Du Bois, W. E. B.; Frazier, E. Franklin; James, C. L. R.; Wright, Richard

Black street festivals, 142, 142–43n40

Black theater, 165, 166, 167, 171; Black Little Theatre Movement, 178; Gilpin Players, 178

Blake, Eubie, 178

Blanchard, George R., 186

Blease, Cole, 110

Blondell, Joan, 363

Blues: call-and-response binary, 247–48; and slave spirituals and appropriation of exodus narrative, 248; and Nadir, 249; specific examples of, 249n187

Blyew et al. v. United States (1873), 77

Boas, Franz, 80, 81, 280, 306, 311

Bogle, Donald, 83, 86, 258n203, 354n202, 359–60; "Age of the Negro Servant," 273, 297

Bolin, Theodore Roosevelt, 173

Booth, Edwina, 328, 332, 333n145, 343; and whiteness, 333, 334, 335; relationship with Africa, 334; and spectacle of white body, 334

Bowman, Laura, 154, 177

Bradley, Arthur: on English racialism, 30n77

Brinker, John M., 185n18

Bromley and Company, 55

Brooke, Gustavus V., 57

Brotherhood of Sleeping Car Porters, 348

Broun, Heywood, 172n107

Brown, John, 44, 66, 123. *See also* Abolition

Bruce, Blanche (senator), 267

Brunder, Wilfred, 367

Bryant, Dan, 132

Bubonic plague, 17

Buell, Jed, 370

Bunche, Ralph, 339

Bureau of American Ethnology (BAE), 72

Burke, Billie, 172n107

Burlesque, 131

Burroughs, Edgar Rice, 313; fantasy jungle "romances," 314; "Under the Moons of the Stars," *All-Story*, 314; "Tarzan of the Apes," *All-Story*, 314; "The Return of Tarzan," *All-Story*, 314; and Rudyard Kipling's *Jungle Book*, 314; Promethean delusions of, 315; misconstructions of Africa, 316; army career of, 316; "The Black Man's Burden," *Pocatello Tribune*, 316; parody of Kipling's "The White Man's Burden," 316; as inspiration for Tarzan films, 322

Burt, Joseph, 172

Burton, Sir Richard, 301

Bush, Anita, 169, 170, 232, 234

Butler, John T., 173

Butters, Gerald, Jr., 129

Cabin in the Sky (MGM), 275, 379
Cabiria, 97
Cakewalk, 160–61; origins of, 160n82
California Eagle, 366n229, 369n245
Canals: Irish as dominant labor in building of, 134
Canby, Henry Seidel, 313
Cantor, Eddie, 166, 167
Capital: alignment with science and government, 67; American industrial, 92, 93; and invasion of Haiti, 117; American finance, 181; and surplus labor, gang labor, sharecropping, tenant farming, convict lease, 181; Northern sectors of, railroads, coal, and timber, 184; management and reorganization of railroad operations by finance, 187; American sectors of, and racial representations in silent films, 190; peasantry in Mexican revolution as threat to, 191; socialist, syndicalist, and anarchist currents intolerable to, 192; historical relationship with white racism, 198; apartheid as structural instrument of American, 201; Hollywood as creature of big, 204; and attacks on black middle class, 207; entry into WWI as led by American finance, 237; factions of, and the state's conflicting racial agendas, 237; and war production and new waves of Southern migrants, 237, relationship to "Hollywood," 268–69, and real estate, 269; and popular and radical politics, 270; and transfer of wealth in Gilded Age, 270; American sector of, affection for fascism, 295; critical political juncture of, 296; American-Hawaiian Steamship Company and movement of, 299–300; and National City Bank, 300, 302; subsidization of technological developments, 300; finance sector in Liberia, 302–5
— Rail capital, 73, 299; Southern Railway Security Company (SRSC), 74; and Benjamin Hill (director Georgia Central Railroad, Klan leader), 74; and Josiah Turner (president, North Carolina Railroad), 74; control of South's newspapers, 74; use of overwhelmingly black convict labor (Florida, Tennessee, North Carolina, George, Arkansas, Colorado, and Texas), 184; corporations of, 185, 186; public outcry against, 186; finance and incorporation of film industry, 187; and Mexican labor, 190; and public sphere, 270; capitalization of, by Hanover National, National Park Bank in New York, Old Colony Trust in Boston, and Bank of California in San Francisco, 300; manufacturers employed by Union Iron (San Francisco), Roach Shipyard (Chester, Pennsylvania), Maryland Steel, Sir Weetman Pearson's Tehuantepec National Railway (London), Ferrocarril (Mexico), 300. *See also* American colonialism; Fascism; Film industry; Imperialism; Racialism; Slavery
Capshaw, Hulon, 368
Captain January, 364
Caribbean Indians, 37
Carnegie Foundation, 80
Casino Theatre Roof Garden, 155
Caspar van Zenden, 10
Casablanca, 169
Census Bureau, 133, 190n28
Chan, Charlie, 373
Chattanooga Times, 110
Cheadle, Don, 84
Chejne, Anwar, 25
Cheyenne Brave, A, 120n116
Chicago, 72; audiences' militant expectations in, 242; as center of Black oppositional cinema, 242; Black working-class migration to, 244, 245; Edward E. Wilson and elite exclusion, 244; self-conscious Black

public sphere within, 244; *Chicago Defender* as indicator of impulses in, 245

—music culture, 245; Black musicians ability to earn livelihood as artists in, 245; and Black Local 208 of American Federation of Musicians, 245; evolution of blues and jazz by migrant musicians in, 246; and Louis Armstrong and Count Basie, 246; Pekin Inn, 246; Pekin Players Stock Company, 246; Robert Motts runs first black-owned theater in, 246

Chicago Star, 168

Chicago Times, 55

Chip Woman's Fortune, The (Willis Richardson), 177

Christy, E. P., 144

Christy, George, 132

Chronicles of England, Scotland, and Ireland (Holinshed), 15

Churchill, Ward, 298

Cincinnati Enquirer, 55

Cincinnati Southern Railroad Company, 184

Civil War, xiii, 54, 56, 58, 66, 69, 73, 89, 105, 115, 127, 132, 145, 181n2, 214, 278; Battle of Bull Run, 67

Clansman, The. See Dixon, Thomas

Cleveland Plain Dealer, 55

Clinton, Henry (general), 38

Clough, Inez, 154, 173

Cochrane, Robert, 97

Cockrell, Dale, 142

Cohan, George M., 176

Cole, Bob, 128, 158; *Black Patti Troubadours*, 148, 160; break with minstrelsy, 154; *A Trip to Coontown*, 154; challenge to Black Bourgeoisie, 155; "Colored Actor's Declaration of Independence of 1898," 155; whiteface performance of, 155; death of, 163

Collaborators of Christ Church (Brooklyn), 195

Collier, Constance, 172n107

Colored Farmers' Alliance, 150

Colored Farmers' National Alliance and Cooperative Union, 182n7

"Colored People's Day" (August 25), 140

Columbus Crisis, 55

Commercial, The, 59

Congress of Industrial Organizations (CIO), 339

Conley, Jim, 112

Convict labor, 13, 184, 349

Cook, Will Marion, 128, 155, 158, 165, 169; *Jes Lak White Folk*, 154, 156, 160; *Clorindy—The Origin of the Cakewalk* (and Dunbar), 154, 160; *The Cannibal King* (coauthored by James Weldon Johnson), 156; employment of dialect to masquerade criticism of racism, 156, 156n76; *In Dahomey*, 156, 158, 160, 161; *Abyssinia* (with Cook, Shipp, and Alex Rogers), 158, 159, 160

"Coon Song(s)," 140–41, 167; "Coon's Salvation Army" (Sam Lucas), 140; "All Coons Look Alike to Me" (Hogan), 140

Cooper, Merian, 344

Cooper, Opal, 172

Cooper, Ralph, 364

Cooper Union for the Advancement of Science and Art, 196

Copperhead Press (radical racist wing of nineteenth-century Democratic Party), 55, 57

Correll, Charles, 131

Coverdale, Myles, 20

Covington, Floyd, 297–98, 297n60; and jungle genre, 298

Cox, Oliver C.: *Caste, Class, and Race*, 35

Crawford, Mrs. James (vice president, California Women's Clubs), 110

Creamer, Henry, 169

Creel, George, 116

Cripps, Thomas, 83, 84, 86, 87, 88, 90, 188, 189, 198n58, 202, 204, 232n144, 242n166, 243, 251n192, 266n214, 273, 276n12, 282, 284–85n33, 297, 320,

Fetchit, Stepin (Lincoln Perry), 278, 288, 290; and Willie Best, 360, 361n218; in *Charlie Chan in Egypt* (Fox), 362, 363; extreme Black minstrelsy of, 362; surrender of white conceits, 378

Film industry, 165, 179; and rail capital, 187; honorary white identity extended to light-skinned Mexican actors in, 191; and racialization of peasantry following Mexican revolution, 191; villainization of Indian, mestizo, or black actors in casting, 192; surveillance and regulation of, 192, 193, 194, 195, 196, 197, 201; ideological designs in management and financing of, 199; studio bosses and anti-Semitism, 199; studio managers of, and racial domination, 199; opportunistic and habitual Negrophobia, 200; Hollywood studios, 203; Bank of Italy and Giannini subsidization of fledgling, 204; Felix Kahn's provision of capital for, 205; Mutual Majestic-Reliance-Epoch entanglement, 205; and relationship to capital, 269; erasure of national memory of, and concealment of capitalist agenda directed toward, poor whites, 275; advent of sound in and capital appropriation of, 290; cultural and ideological agendas of overlords of, 291; imaginary of "Golden Age" in, 291; and transformation into subsidiary of multinationals, 291; attempts to regulate content of from civic organizations, 292; new opportunities for censorship of, 292; specter of private scandals in, 292; corporations and its state adjuncts poised to envelop, 293; admirers of Mussolini in American, 295, 295nn57–58; Mussolini's control over Italian, 295–96; role of LUCE in fascist control of Italian, 296; Central Casting Corporation, 297n60; new location in Hollywood and delight in racialism of, 319; American organization (studios, capital, management) of, 361; transferal of racial palette to Germans and Japanese during WWII, 379. *See also* Motion Picture Producers and Distributors of America, Inc. (MPPDA)

Financial Chronicle, 59

First Black Actors on the Great White Way, The (Curtis), 171

First Illinois Colored Regiment, 57

Flaherty, Robert: *Moana: A Romance of the Golden Age*, 328; *Nanook of the North*, 328

Following the Flag in Mexico (Feinberg Amusement Corp.), 190n32

Forbes, Jack, 7–8; on racial significations, 8n14

Forest, Bradford, 103

Foster, Stephen, 132, 144

Foster, William, 169; *The Railroad Porter*, 169

Foucault, Michel, xi–xii

Fox, William, 97

Frank, Leo, 92, 112, 115

Franklin, Ben, 43

Franklin, V. P., 149

Frazier, E. Franklin: on importance of understanding Black church, 254n197

Freeman, Carlotta, 169, 170

Freeman, Morgan, 84

Free-Soil Party, 50

French Revolution, 42

Frohman, Charles, 166

From Caligari to Hitler (Kracauer), 85

From Sambo to Superspade (Leab), 83

Fryer, Peter, 9

Fugitive Slave Law of 1851

Fyrst Boke of the Introduction of Knowledge (Borde), 12n30

Gates, Henry Louis, Jr., 152

George, Lloyd (British prime minister), 116

East, 125; *Broken Blossoms*, 197n56;
antimiscegenation agenda, 214;
sexual economy of slavery and postbellum of, 257; adoption of Mammy
in *His Trust* and *Birth of a Nation*, 258;
obliteration of sexual exploitation of
Black women, 258; representations
of "the Mammy," 258–59; Biograph's
"faithful slave" films produced by,
224–25; trump of militant effort to
construct national discourse, 225;
coupling with "chicken thieves" of
minstrel comedies, 225; *The Zulu's
Heart*, 306–7; Negrophobic imaginary of, 307. See also *Birth of a Nation, The*

Guerrero, Ed, xvii, 90, 91; plantation
genre, 123, 273, 273n3, 340; propaganda function of films, 361

Guggenheims, 190

Gutman, Herbert: *The Black Family in
Slavery and Freedom, 1750–1925*, 60

Hackett, Francis (*New Republic*), 173

Haggard, H. Rider, 307, 313; *She*, 307,
309, 310, 310n94, 344; *Allan Quatermain*, 307, 309, 310n94; editor of
Rand Daily Mail, 307n82; *Sanders
of the River*, 307n82; "Tarzan of the
Apes," 307n82; *King Solomon's Mines*,
307n82, 309, 310n94; and production
of racial oppression in South Africa,
308; racialized imagination of, 309.
See also Jungle film genre

Haiti: Haitian Revolution (1791–1804),
39, 42, 117; U.S. invasion of, 116–17;
establishment of dictatorship in, 118;
peasant-based rebellions in, 345;
U.S. evocation of imperialist Monroe
doctrine and control of government
of, 346; counterfeiture of, in Eugene
O'Neill's work, 346

Hakluyt, Richard (*Principal Navigations,
Voyages, Traffiques and Discoveries of
the English Nation*), 12

Hallelujah (MGM), 275, 276, 282, 297,
327, 349, 350; Vidor's difficulties
in getting production started, 281,
283; filmed on location and at MGM
studios, 283–84; actresses/actors
in, 284n33, 285nn34–35; J. Ronald
Greene (assistant director), 285n34;
premiere of, in New York, 286; Mordaunt Hall (*New York Times*) review
of, 286–87; Norbert Lusk (*Los Angeles Times*) review of, 287; opening in
Los Angeles, 287; James Warnak (*Los
Angeles Times*) review of, 287–88;
Edwin Schallert on its appeal and
experience of Black sexuality generated by it, 288; Thalberg's intervention in, 289; overriding of Vidor's
casting of, 289

Hamilton, Lydia, 215

Hammerstein, Arthur, 176

Hampton Institute, 76

Hapgood, Emilie, 171, 172

Hapgood, Norman (*New York
Commercial-Advertiser*), 172

Harding, Warren, 302

Harlem (Thurman), 178

Harlow, Jean, 363

Harper's Weekly, 140

Harris, Theresa, 363; interview in *Pittsburgh Courier*, 363; identity as race
woman, 363; public expression of
rage against mainstream movies,
364

Harvard University, 81; Peabody Museum, 66n185

Haupt, Herman, 73

Hawkin, Micah: *Backside Albany*, 49;
Massa Georgee Washington, 49; *General La Fayette*, 49

Hawley, Monte, 364

Hayakawa, Sessue, 197n56

Hayman, Al, 166

Hays, Will (postmaster general for
President Hoover), 195, 366; establishment of Committee on Public

U.S. Navy, 300; and rise of social Darwinism, 301; and Roosevelt's articulation of discourse of, 301–2; and public imagination, 311; creeds of American, 313; ravages of European, 324

Independent Black Film, 130, 179

Independent Liberator, 200

Indian films: service to white supremacy doctrine, 120–22; discourse on miscegenation in, 122. *See also* Griffith, D. W.

Indian Scalping Scene, Rescue of Capt. John Smith by Pocahontas, 186n20

Indianapolis State Sentinel, 55

Indigenous peoples: modernist invention of, 4

Ingagi (Congo Pictures), 335

Ingram, Rex, 124, 361

Inside of White Slave Traffic, The (Samuel London), 187–88n24

Institutes of the Laws of England (Coke), 32

International Alliance of Theatrical Stage Employees, 367n233

International Reform Bureau, 195

Interstate Commerce Commission (ICC), 186, 187–88n24

Investigations in the Military and Anthropological Studies of American Soldiers (Benjamin A. Gould), 68. *See also* Race science

Irish American Press: objection to *Irish Hearts*, 201; objections to *The Callahans and the Murphys*, 201

Irish World, The, 200

Islam: history of, 12n30, 26n71

Ison, Joseph, 367

Jackson, Samuel L., 264–65

Jackson-Stuart, Marie, 172

James, C. L. R., 117n107; critique of *Gone with the Wind*, 227, reinvigoration of Marxist agenda, 339

James IV, 9

James VI of Scotland (James I, 1603–25), 17

Jameson, Fredric, 91

James Young Deer, 120

J. and W. Seligman, 187

Jeffries, Herb, 370

Jenkins, Francis, 82

Jessel, George, 167

Jezebel, 123–24

"Jezebels," 215

Jim Crow, 149, 165, 183, 185, 196, 207, 237, 270; and commercial exploitation of motion pictures, 180

Johnson, Anne, 57

Johnson, Eastman: *Negro Life at the South* (later titled *Old Kentucky Home*), 258; *A Ride for Liberty — The Fugitive Slaves*, 258

Johnson, George P., and Noble Johnson (Lincoln Motion Pictures), 128; Noble in *Trooper of Troop K*, 235–36; post-Johnson era of Lincoln, 236; Lincoln's privileging of rites of passage of Black middle class, 240

Johnson, Henry: awarded *Croix de Guerre*, 175n116

Johnson, Jack, 92, 115, 164, 189; white reactions to, 109–10; *Jack Johnson Is a Dandy*, 111; relationship to Belle Schreiber, 111; relationship with Etta Duryea, 110; relationship with Lucille Cameron, 110; challenge to white supremacy, 112; focus on sexuality of, 112n88; suppression of boxing film following defeat of Jim Jeffries, 194; and law prohibiting interstate sale of boxing films, 292

Johnson, James Weldon, 141, 149, 151n62, 156, 164, 170, 171, 172, 174, 178, 281, 346; *Black Manhattan*, 150, 179; "Since You Went Away," "Congo Love Song," "Lift Every Voice and Sing," (Black National Anthem), 150n60; service as U.S. consul in Venezuela (1906–9), 150n60; secretary for

Moreno, Antonio, 191

Morgan College Players, 178

Morganstern, W. W., 176n121

Morland, George: *Execrable Human Traffic*, 42; *African Hospitality*, 42

Morning Bath, A, 186

Mortgaged, 178

Morton, Samuel, 65, 66. *See also* Race science

Motion Picture News, 215, 219

Motion Pictures Patents Company (MPPC), 96, 180n1, 187, 194

Motion Picture Producers and Distributors of America, Inc. (MPPDA), 195, 261n208, 292; headed by William Hays, 292; and Colonel Jason J. Roy (second in command to Hays), 292; and Lt. Colonel Frederick L. Herron (head of International Office), 292–93; ambiguous nature of function of, 293; Colonel Edward G. Lowry as representative in Europe of, 293; interventions in production, 293–94; censoring of communist messages, 296

Moving Picture World, 197, 222

Mulatta/os, 3, 153; in U.S. census (1850), 53; transposition to Jezebel, 59; appearance in American popular culture, 86; and Blaxploitation films (1968–75), 227; and post-Blaxploitation (after 1975), 227

Murphy, Dudley, 347

Murphy, Edgar Garner, 184

Muse, Clarence, 124, 170, 361, 366

Museum Movement, 71

Museum of Modern Art, 107n72

Musicals: Black, 128, 131, 145, 151, 165, 167, 169, 272; and consumers of claims to racial privileges, 153; *The Policy Players*, 160; attention of *New York Times* to, 275, 277, 277n13, 279; *Stormy Weather*, 275, 379; narrative conventions of, 277; and naturalization of poverty, 277; spate of, 278n16.

See also *Hallelujah* (MGM); *Hearts in Dixie* (Fox); Vidor, King

Mussolini, Benito. *See* Fascism; Film industry

Mutual Film Corporation v. Ohio Industrial Commission, 194

Muybridge, Eadweard, 82

National Association for the Advancement of Colored People (NAACP), 92, 105, 119, 150n60, 211–12, 378

National Biscuit Company, 61

National Board of Censorship (renamed National Board of Review, 1916), 187n24, 194

National Congress of Mothers, 195–96

National Equal Rights League (NERL), 211–12

National Era, 50

National Museum (USNM), 72

National Pencil Factory, 112

National Research Council, 81

National Union Life and Limb (later Metropolitan Life), 67

"Negro Babes on Exhibition," 186

Negro Emanuel, 37

Negro Fellowship League, 107

Negro Intercollegiate Dramatic Association, 178

Negro John, 37

Negro Operatic and Dramatic Company (Emma Louise and Anna Mada Hyer), 148

Negrophobia, xvi, 112, 124, 224; Shakespeare's challenge to, 16–17; in American Colonization Society, 53; momentary triumph over, 55; consignment to "the South," 198; and D. W. Griffith's imaginary, 307

"Negro Problem," 185

Negro Will, 37

Neill, Michael, 22, 29

New Lincoln Theatre (New York), 169

New Orleans: as exporter of blues and ragtime to New York, Chicago, and

Pekin Brothers Stock Company, 168, 169, 170n103
Pekin Theatre (Robert Moss), 169
Peonage, 273; A. J. Hoyt's (Justice Department Investigator) observations of, 274; NAACP pressure to Herbert Hoover (Secretary of Commerce) for investigation of, 274; reportage of (*New York Times, Florida Times-Union*, and *Washington Post*), 274; U.S. Attorney in Georgia Hooper Alexander's charges white planters for, 274; crushing exploitation of, 277
People's Institute, 194
People's Voice (Adam Clayton Powell Jr.), 356
Pershing, John J. (General), 174
Peter Negro, 9, 25; knighthood of, 11
Philadelphia, 72
Philadelphia Age, 55, 57
Philadelphia Tribune, 367n236
Philanthropist, 53n145, 129
Phillips, Lionell, 301
Pickaninny Blues (Van Buren Studio), 131
Pickering, Charles, 64, 66; *Races of Man*, 64n179; *Chronological History of Plants*, 65. See also Race science
Pickford, Mary, 195
Plantation economy, 11
Plantation genre (Ed Guerrero), xvii, 275, 297, 298, 338
Plato: defense of slavery, 4, 321; *The Republic*, 104
Plessy v. Ferguson (1896), 77, 142
Poitier, Sidney, 84
Pompez, Alejandro (Alexander), 367, 368; influence in Negro National League, 368; prominence in Black world, 368; owner of New York Cubans, 369
Populism, 182; and racism, 182n7; parties of, 183; move away from anti-capitalism, 206
Porgy (DuBose and Dorothy Heyward), 178

Porter, Edwin, 83, 128, 172
Power, xi, 257; racial regimes justification for, xii; minstrelsy's conspiracy with, 127; prerequisites of, 142
Preer, Evelyn, 170, 177, 203
Prison reform pictures: *The Big House*, 276; *Hold Your Man* (MGM), 276n12; *The Last Mile*, 276n12
Proctor and Gamble, 61
Production Code, 195, 196, 197, 198n58, 199
Production Code Administration (PCA), 196, 201, 337, 366; and enforcement of Jim Crow, 198, 199; Joseph Breen's directives of, 200
Prudential Life, 67
Pudd'nhead Wilson (Lasky Features), 222
Pullman, George (Pullman Company), 185n18, 348

Quadroon; or, A Lover's Adventures in Louisiana (Captain Mayne Reid), 50
Quaker Oats, 61
Queen Elizabeth, 97
Queen Elizabeth and Her Court at Kenilworth Castle (Gheeraents), 11
Quetelet, Lambert Adolphe Jacques, 68
Quo Vadis?, 97

Race Betterment Congresses, 80
Race films: appearance, 225; *The Pullman Porter* (first of genre), 225; and "race men" and "race women," 225–26, 226n124; individual films, 226; as distinguished from "Black cinema," 226–29; and political struggles against peonage, sharecropping, lynching, segregation, inferior public education, and sexual exploitation of Black women, 227; C. L. R. James's critique of *Gone with the Wind*, 227, 227n129; Black-owned production and challenge to racism, 228; *In the Depths of Our Hearts* (Royal Garden

Company), 228; *When True Love Wins*
(Southern Motion Pictures Com-
pany), Isaac Fisher (writer), 228;
Afro-American Film Company of
New York (1913), 228n133; National
Negro Business League, 228n133;
Peter P. Jones Film Company of
Chicago (1914), 228n133; Heart of
America Film Corporation of Kansas
City (1916), 228n133; Allmon-Hudlin
Film Company of St. Louis, 228n133;
studios organized by William Foster,
Peter P. Jones, and Oscar Micheaux,
229; social geography and cultural
sophistication as influence on production of, 229, 232n144; Frederick
Douglas Film Company (New Jersey),
229; Colored Players Film Corporation (David Starkman), 229, 365; and
genre competition of Black comedies and Black melodrama, 230; and
spikes in Black silent films, 230; as
cotton industry not genre, 231; displays of bourgeois respectability in,
231; and occasion of aesthetic poetry,
231; *Scar of Shame* (Colored Players
Film Corporation), 231, 371; Anita's
Bush's authority negated by role
in *The Crimson Skull*, 233; Clarence
Muse's break with mold of, in *Toussaint L'Ouverture* (Blue Ribbon Pictures, 1921), 233; featuring Charles
Gilpin, 233; Lincoln Motion Picture's
Realization of a Negro's Ambition
claimed as standard for race film
melodrama, 233; other Lincoln films,
233, 236; melodramas and violence
directed against Blacks, 237; Black
troops as protagonists of, 240; dissolution of race by exclusion, 241;
imagined universe of whiteness in,
241; liberal conceits of, 241; projection of homogeneous society, 241–42;
Luther J. Pollard's comic productions in, 242; *Moving Picture World's*

review of *The Bully*, 243; production
of, exceed number of Soviet films,
250; self-deception of, 252; rarity of
screening to non-Black audiences,
270; and Clarence, 364; and Frank
Wilson, 364; and A. B. Comatheire,
364; and Laura Bowman, 364; and
Desmond Cleo, 364; and Jesse Lee
Brooks, 364
Race science, 3, 62, 66; popularization
of, 61; eighteenth-century emergence of, 63; first joint venture of
commerce and government in, 63,
64, 65; role of United States Sanitary
Commission in, 67, 68, 78; imaginaries of, 65; *Statistics, Medical
and Anthropological, of the Provost-
Marshal-General's Bureau* (Baxter),
68; reports of, 69; infrastructure
of, 70; and natural science, 127; and
command of resources of state and
sectors of capital, 136; and anthropological displays, 141; presentment,
repair, and actualization of, 174; and
anthropological representations, 185;
and new architecture of scientific
racism, 196; and bourgeois anthropology's construction of racial hierarchies along division of labor, 206
Racial discourses: pre-African slave
trade, 4, 6; replication and multiplication of, 80; and capital, 92
Racialism: overdetermination of, 2; and
absence of phenotypic differences,
6; intra-European, 6; in Ireland,
6; origins of American ideas of, in
England, 7; emergent seventeenth-
and eighteenth-century European
bourgeoisie role in, 14; paradigm
change in, 36; and mass culture and
new racial consensus, 50; deliberateness of American capitalists in, 58;
and cultural and social disciplines
directed against poor whites, Latinos, and Asians, 59; violent con-

inauguration of, 344; War Department of, 356

Roosevelt, Theodore "Teddy," 301; paternalism toward people of color and American policy, 302; and *Trader Horn*, 323

Rosson, Harold, 339

Russia: cinematic styles of, 250; and aftermath of Russian revolution and Hollywood stereotypes, 294; Russian Revolution, 296; and communist parties inspired by Leninism, 296

Rymer, Thomas: *Tragedies of the Last Age, Short View of Tragedy*, 29, 30

Said, Edward, xi

St. Louis Globe-Democrat, 176n121

St. Louis Post-Dispatch, 176n121

St. Louis Star Sayings, 176n121

Salome (Wilde), 177

Salvini, Tommaso, 57

Sam 'n' Henry, 131

Sampson, Henry, 163, 164

Santa Fe Trail, The, 99, 123

Schenck, Nicholas, 283

Schultz, Dutch, 368n238

Scott, Maggie, 154

Scottsboro Boys: Communist Party support of, 339

Segregation: relationship to South's strategy of capitalist development, 184

Selig, William (Selig Polyscope Company), 187; *At Piney Ridge* (1916), 222

Selika, Madame, 148

Selznick, David, 344

Shakespeare, William, xv, 7, 9n21, 15, 16, 17, 18, 93, 167n95, 177, 379; *Othello*, xv, 16, 17, 20, 22, 23, 24, 26, 27, 28, 29, 35, 36, 57, 86, 219; challenge to Negrophobia, 16–17; *Henry VI*, 15; *Richard III*, 15; *Richard II*, 15; *King John*, 15; *Henry IV*, 15; *Henry V*, 15; *Henry VIII*, 15; *Titus Andronicus*, 16–

17; *Merchant of Venice*, 17; dramatic imagination of, 17; representation of blackness, 17; *Hamlet*, 18; *Measure for Measure*, 19, 21, 22; *King Lear*, 22; Black thespians forbidden to perform, 57n158; nationalist agenda of, 70; *The Merchant of Venice*, 167n95. *See also* Negrophobia

Shipp, Jesse, 158, 159, 173

Shooting Craps, 188

Shubert, Lee, 176

Shuffle Along, 178

Shyamalan, M. Night: *The Sixth Sense*, 262, 264; *Unbreakable*, 262, 264

Simmons, Furnifold, 183

Singing the Blues, 357

Slaughter House Cases, 77

Slave (Hildreth), 50

Slave rebellions, xiii; in nineteenth century, xv, 43. *See also* Turner, Nat

Slavery, xi, 43n120, 105; pre-Atlantic, 4–7; invention of Negro, 7; appearance in England, 8; penal forms of, 8; labor power, 9; English pirates and merchants in, 11; effects of, on British economy, 11, 11n28; English colonialism and, 11, 33; English involvement in, 31; justification by whiteness, 32; nationalist rhetoric as justification for, 32; and eighteenth-century British African trade and transmigration, 35; and social power of antislavery, 36; as component of world-system, 37; end of legalized, in U.S., 54; sexual economy in era of, 153; "white slavery" hysteria, 187–88n24; and generation of white knowledge of blackness, 258; and recoding of slave trade, 337; reenactment of African, in *King Kong*, 343; zombies as metaphor for, 377. *See also* American colonialism; Capital; Negrophobia; Racialism

Slave Songs of the Unites States, 145

General Electric, AT&T, United Fruit Company), 291; financial and organizational opportunities for American capitalists during, 291

World War II, xv, 376; enlightened treatments of race after, 290; *Bataan* (MGM), 379; *Lifeboat* (Twentieth Century–Fox), 379; *Sahara* (Columbia), 379

Wright, Richard: and Marxist agenda, 339

Yerkes, Robert M., 175, 315

Yiddish popular culture, 166

Zapata, Emilio, 191. *See also* Mexican Revolution

Ziegfeld, Flo, 166; *Ziegfeld Follies*, 167

Zimmerman, J. Frederick, 166

Zinn, Howard, 108, 116, 298n62

Zukor, Adolph, 97, 166

3420